PARTHIAN BOOKS

Mama's Baby
(Papa's Maybe)
& Other Stories

The Cambrensis Initiative

New Welsh Short Fiction

Edited by Lewis Davies and Arthur Smith

PARTHIAN BOOKS

Parthian Books
53 Colum Road
Cardiff
CF10 3EF

First published in 1999.
All rights reserved.
© Parthian Books and the authors
ISBN 1-902638-03-4

This book is published through **The Cambrensis Initiative**, which is a programme of publication supported by an Arts for All grant from the Arts Council of Wales.

Parthian would like to thank the Lottery Unit and the people who make it possible for the direct support of the Cambrensis Initiative.

Typeset in Galliard by NW.

Printed and bound by Gomer Press, Llandysul.

With support from the Parthian Collective.

Cover: Young Girl by Catherine Needs.

A CIP catalogue record for this book is available from the British Library.

'If you have been born a short-story writer, one of the symptoms is that you find you have a trivial mind and a brooding heart.'

from *Duw it's hard*, in
Goodbye, What Were You? - Selected Writings of Glyn Jones

As a schoolboy at Bridgend 'County' School in the late 'thirties, I was plunged into the exciting world of the Welsh short story writers when I read Glyn Jones' story, *Wil Thomas,* in the anthology *Welsh Short Stories.* (Faber, 1937.)

The magic of his meticulous writing leapt from the page and, in the circuitous fashion of evolution, resulted – some fifty years later – in the launch in 1987 of the short-story magazine, *Cambrensis,* as a platform for today's short-story writers of Wales to carry on the tradition.

In a rather 'poetically phrased' statement of aims, the magazine called for submissions of 'stories which, by the skill and the imagination of the writer, capture a single moment of truth ... illuminate something of life ... reinforce a belief ... present a new perspective ... entertain the spirit and intellect ... open up vistas ... sing the song of life as poetically as the saetas in Seville's Holy Week ceremonies, soaring its music and poetry as arrows of sound into the sky ...'

This present volume, I hope, does all that ... and more!

Arthur Smith

The Stories

MAMA'S BABY (PAPA'S MAYBE)

Leonora Brito

2 summers ago, just after I'd turned fifteen, my mother got ill. One night in our flat on the twelfth floor, she held her face in both hands and said, "Leisha, I'm sure I got cancer!"

"Just so long as you haven't got AIDS," I said, and carried on munching my tacos and watching the telly. The tacos were chilli beef'n jalepeno. Hot. Very hot. With a glistening oily red sauce that ran down my chin as I spoke.

"AIDS?" I remember her voice sounded bewildered. "What're you talking about, AIDS? How the hell could I have AIDS?" She grabbed at my shoulder. "I'm an agoraphobic, I don't hardly go out –"

I took my eyes away from the television set and stared at her face. Then I just busted out laughing. I couldn't help myself. I was almost choking. Loretta looked at me as if she didn't know me. As if I belonged to somebody else. "J-O-K-E," I said, catching my breath and wiping my chin. "*Laugh, muvver!*" But she couldn't do that, laugh. Even when I spelt it out for her. "Like, AIDS'n agoraphobia – they're mutually exclusive, right? So you haven't got it Lol, have you?" She still didn't laugh. She couldn't laugh or be brave or anything like that, my mother Loretta.

All she could do was hit me with a slipper and call me stupid. "Orr, Mama!" I rubbed at my arm, pretending to be hurt. "You can't take a joke, you can't."

"No, it's no jokin with you." Loretta got angry as she looked at me. "You're gunna bring bad luck on people you are," she said. "With your laughin an jokin!"

Bring bad luck by laughing? Such stupidness, I thought, in my own mother. Then I noticed how her body kept shivering as she sat there, squashed into the corner of our plush red settee. And how she couldn't keep her hands still, even though they were clamped together tight. So tight, that the knuckle bones shone through. "Cancer's a bad thing, Aleisha." My mother shook her head from side to side, and started to cry. "A bad thing!"

"Orr Mama, you talks rubbish, you do." She looked at me through streaming eyes. "How do I?" she said. "How do I talk rubbish?" I shrugged. "You just do."

I remembered what she'd said about tampons. Loretta said tampons travelled twice round the body at night, then lodged in your brain. Fact. Even the nuns in school laughed at that one. They said what my mother told me was un-proven, un-scientific and an old wives tale. Chupidness!

Now Loretta was sitting there, crying and talking about cancer. I wished she'd stop. The crying made her dark eyes shine like windows, when the rain falls on them at night. There was light there, but you couldn't see in. Not really. It was like staring into the blackness of outer space. And it made me mad.

"Look, why don't you just stop crying," I said, adopting a stern voice, a mother's voice. A sensible voice. "And get to the Doctor's first thing tomorrow morning and see about yourself?"

Loretta looked at me and hiccuped. Then she started crying again. Louder than before. "Just phone Joe," she said through her sobs. "Phone that boy for me, Leish. I want that boy with me." "Okey-dokey," I took another big mouthful of taco and chewed callously. It was out of my hands now. Now Loretta had asked for Joe. Let Joe deal with it. I stood up. "Where's your twenty pence pieces then?"

I went off to the call-box with the taste of Mexican take-away still in my mouth. Joe was out with the boys, so I left a message with Donna, who was full of concern. "Is it serious?" she said. "Nah." I burped silently into the night as the tacos came back to haunt me. "It's not serious," I said. "But you know Loretta." My nostrils burned and my eyes filled up with water. "You knows my mother, once she gets an idea into her head -"

Donna laughed brightly and said not to worry. She'd tell Joe as soon as he came in. "Yeah, tell him," I said. Raising my voice as the time ran out and the pips began to bleep. "Though it's probably nothing. Something an nothing. Knowin her."

I was wrong of course. I was wrong about everything under the sun and under the moon. But what did I know? I was fifteen years old that summer, and mostly, I thought like a child.

Like when I was six, nearly seven, I found a big blue ball hidden in the cupboard of the wall-unit. I brought the ball out and placed it on the floor. Then I tried to step up and stand on it. I fell off, but I kept on trying. Again and again and again. All I wanted to do was to stand on the big blue ball that had misty swirls of white around it. Like the swirls I'd seen on satellite pictures of planet earth.

When I finally managed it – arms outstretched and my feet successfully planted, I felt like a conqueror. A six-year-old conqueror. "Orr look at this!" I yelled at Joe. "Look Joe, look!"I stayed upright for another dazzling moment. Then the ball rolled under me and I fell backwards, screaming as my head hit the floor. Loretta came out of the bathroom with a face-pack on. She silenced me with a slap. Then she took the comic Joe was reading and threw it in the bin. "Naw, Ma," said Joe. "That's my *Desperate Dan* that is."

"Too bad," said Loretta. "Maybe it'll teach you to look after this kid when I tell you!"

Joe laid his head down on the pine-top table, sulking. While I sat on the edge of our scrubby, rust red carpet and hugged my knees. I wasn't worried about Joe getting into trouble on account of me. All I was worried about was the ball. The beautiful blue ball. More than anything in the world I wanted it back.

But Loretta had snatched the ball away from me and was holding it up to the light. Palming it over and over in her hands. As if she was searching for something. But what? What magical thing could she be searching for? I watched the ball turn blue under the light-bulb. Then not so blue, then *bluer* again. And it came to me in flash – that what my mother was doing was remembering- .

But remembering what? Her creamy face was cracking into brown, spidery lines as she looked at the ball. And I got up on my knees, wanting to see more.

"*Bug-eyes!*" Joe leaned down from the corner of the table and hissed at me. "Fat-head," he said. "You boogalooga bug-eyed fat head!" Joe's words put a picture inside my head that made me cry. I opened my mouth and bawled until Loretta turned round. Her face had stopped cracking, and she looked ordinary. "Joe!" she said, "how old are you for god's sake? Tormentin that kid. She's younger than you."

"She's a *alien*," said Joe.

"Oh don't be so bloody simple!" Loretta looked across the room at me. "She's your sister." Joe shook his head. "She's *not* my sister." He kicked at the leg of the table with his big brown chukka boot. "She's my *half* sister," he said.

I remember the words were hardly out of Joe's mouth before Loretta had reached him. "Half?" she said. "Half?" She started bouncing the big blue ball upside his head. "Who taught you half? I didn't give birth to no halves!"

Loretta was mad at Joe. So mad she kept banging the ball against his head. As if she was determined to knock some sense in. Until Joe (who was twelve, and big for his age) lifted his big chubby arms in front of his face and yelled at her. "Get off've me! Fuckin get off've me. Right!"

I was scared then. I thought Joe was in for a hiding. The mother and father of a hiding. But something strange happened, Loretta suddenly upped and threw the ball away from her – just threw it, as if she was the one who was hurt. And as soon as she let the ball go, wonder of wonders, Joe burst into tears and pushed his head against her belly. Sobbing out loud like a baby, saying, "It's not fair! It's not fair!" And asking her over and over again as she cwtched him, "How come *my* father never brought *me* no presents, Ma? How come?"

Poor Joe! I sat in the middle of our scrubby red carpet happily hugging the big blue ball to myself. I realised now that I was luckier than Joe. My *half* brother Joe. And quicker than Joe and cleverer than Joe – even though I looked like a *alien*. Joe was like Loretta. I looked across the room at them, across the scrubby rust red carpet, which suddenly stretched out vast and empty as the red planet Mars.

"You takes after *my* family," Loretta was telling Joe. "You takes after *me*." I felt a pang, but it didn't matter. I had the blue ball – which was big enough to stand on, like planet earth. A special ball, bought for me specially, by a strange and wonderful person called *my dad*!

Of course, *my dad* was always more of an idea than anything else. I never saw my real dad when I was a kid. But I clung to the idea of him. In the same way that I clung to an image of my *self* at six, triumphantly balancing on a blue, rolling ball. They were secret reminders of who I really was. I held on to those reminders even more when Loretta was diagnosed as having cancer. They helped me keep my distance. And I needed to keep my distance, because once the hospital people dropped the big C on her for definite – cancer of the womb (Intermediary Stage) things got scary. And while Joe tried to pretend that nothing terrible was happening, or would happen, I knew better. And I made sure I kept my distance from the start.

Like when Loretta had to travel back and forth to the Cancer Clinic for treatment. Joe asked if I'd go with her. "Sometimes," he said, "just to keep her company?"

"I can't," I said. "I've got tests coming up in school." "Tests?" Joe looked at me gone off. "Tha' Mama's sick," he said. "She needs someone with her. I can't go myself cuz I'm in work." His jaw tightened –

"I've got a biology test coming up, I said. And maths and history –"

"Oh leave it Joe," said Loretta. "I'm alright!" She laughed, "I'll manage." Joe umm'd and ah'd a bit, then he gave in. "If you're sure, Ma," he said. Hiding a little smile, I picked up my biology text-book, *The Language of The Genes*, and began taking seriously detailed notes.

I never did go with Loretta to the Cancer Clinic. Though I could have made time, if I'd wanted. Academic work was easy for me, I enjoyed reading books and doing essays. And tests were almost a doddle. But at home I began making a big thing of it. Hiding behind the high wall of 'my schoolwork' and 'my classes' and my sacrosanct GCSE's, which I wasn't due to sit until the following year anyway.

I also let it be known that I had to go out, nights. Most nights, otherwise I'd turn into a complete mental brainiac.

So when Loretta arrived home weak and vomiting from the radium treatment, I'd already be standing in front of the mirror, tonging my hair, or putting on eye make-up. No need to ask where

I was going. I was off out, to enjoy myself. Even though enjoying myself meant drinking (alco-pops) and smoking, and hanging with the crowd. All the stuff I used to describe as 'too boring and predictable' for anyone with half a brain. Now though, it was different. Now I became best mates with a hard faced, loud mouthed girl called Cookie, who Loretta said was 'wild'.

The euphemism made me smile as I rushed around the kitchen filling the kettle and making the tea to go in the flask. I was happy and focussed on what I had to do, knowing that the sooner Loretta was settled, the sooner I'd be out through the door.

Luckily, there was no need to bother with food. Loretta couldn't swallow any food. Only *Complan*. And *Complan* made her vomit. So she stuck to tea. Weak tea, and sometimes, a couple of mouthfuls of tinned soup. Which I did think was sad, because my mother was a big woman who'd always enjoyed her food.

Now, she hardly ever went in the kitchen, and it wasn't worth bothering to try and tempt her with anything. But I brought her a cup of tea, and handed it over. And I put the flask on the little table next to the couch.

Taking a couple of sips of tea seemed to exhaust her. And she laid her head back on the cushions, tired, but not too tired to speak. "This girl Cookie —" she said.

"Yeah?" By now I'd gone back to the mirror and my mascara.

"I don't like the idea of you runnin round with her." Loretta pursed her lips. "That girl's trouble," she said. "That girl's hot!" I was watching Loretta's face in the mirror. Her face and my face, side by side. It was eerie seeing us together. Like watching night turn into day or day turn into night. There was no resemblance between us. No real likeness that I could see. And it played on my mind. Who was she, I thought? This big woman lying on a plush red couch, with a green plaid blanket pulled up to her chin? I crossed over to the couch and looked at her, coldly. "What're you talking about, hot?" I said. "You're always going on about something." Loretta sighed. "I just don't want you in no trouble," she said. "You nor Joe, come to that."

"I'm not gunna be in any trouble!"

"No?" Loretta looked up at me and smiled. "Well, god be good," she said, "let's hope it'll stay like that."

"Listen," I brought my face down close to hers and spoke slowly, deliberately. "Cookie's ways, are not my ways, right?" My voice grew colder. "Your ways, are not my ways –" Loretta stared at my face, as if she couldn't understand what I was saying. Then she took a gulp of tea and her eyes swam with tears.

"You little bitch," she said. "Anybody'd think I was a bad mother to h'yer you speak!" The sudden energy in her voice surprised me. And I tried to back away from what I'd started. But Loretta was on a roll. "Did I get rid of you?" she said. "Did I? No, I kept you. You and Joe. Even though I had no man behind me. And what's my thanks?" Her voice was angry as she spoke to me. Loud and angry. "Shit is my thanks!"

I shrugged and tried to move away, but she started off again. "'Course, it'd be different if I was posh, wouldn't it?"

"Pardon?" I said.

"They gets rid of their kids in a minute. Don't they, posh women? When they wants to go to *college* or something." Loretta looked up at the ceiling and laughed. "An no bugger ever says a word," she said, disbelievingly. "Not a bloody word!"

For some reason I found myself laughing along with her. Enjoying the unfairness of it all. Then she closed her eyes again, tired. "Look, *get* if you're going," she said. "And don't be back yer late."

When I reached the door, I turned to look at her. "D'you want this light left on?"

"No, out it." So I flicked the switch and left her there, in the dark.

It was always a big relief to me when Loretta was taken into hospital.

I was happy then, escorting her down to the waiting ambulance and handing her in. It felt as though we were celebrities, touched by a black and tragic glamour, as the neighbours rushed out of their flats and gave Loretta cards, and waved her off, like royalty.

Back inside, I always walked slowly past the lifts in the entrance hall. Then I'd whizz around the corner and start bounding up the stairs. Two at a time. All the way up to the twelfth floor.

The first few times Loretta went into hospital, I stayed with Joe and Donna in their little two bedroomed house. But I didn't

17

feel comfortable there. And when Loretta began to spend longer and longer as an in-patient, I told Joe I preferred to stay where I was, and keep an eye on the flat. Joe stuck out his jaw and said, "If that's what you want, Aleisha. I'm not gunna argue."

Which was just what I expected him to say. Though I hated him for saying it. After that, it wasn't difficult for me to ease my way out of things, bit by bit.

Whenever I made an appearance at the hospital, I was never on my own. I always came in with a crowd – usually Cookie and her sister, Cherry. Or Cookie and her new man friend, Wayne. I think they liked being with me, because I was fifteen years old and my mother was dying of cancer. It was like something off the telly that appealed to them.

Joe never came in on his own, either. He was always with Donna or one of his mates – usually Deggsie, or a caramel coloured boy called Chip-chip, whose teeth were brown and white, like pop-corn.

With so many young people around Loretta's bed, there was never any time for seriousness. All we could do was lark and joke about. Once, when they were fooling around, Joe and Chip-chip pressed down on the foot-pedals of the bed. Sending Loretta up in the air. And all she did was laugh and say, "Put me down, boys! Put me down, people can see my old blue slippers under there."

It was odd, standing under the bright hospital lights, watching Loretta laughing. And Joe laughing. All of us laughing, as if everything was right with the world. Loretta was queen of the show. She sparkled in company, which was the way she used to be, I suppose, when she was young and working in pubs as a bar- maid.

One night, Joe and Donna came in carrying a bouquet of flowers between them.

Loretta didn't care much for the white chrysanthemums, but she was chuffed with the card: "*Happy memories, luv from R. (The Rover).*" R. was Royston, Joe's father. And he'd been on friendly speaking terms ever since Joe had left school, and met up with him again.

"Now he sends me the white bouquet," said Loretta. "Maybe he wants to marry me –" While we were laughing, Donna said soppily, "Why didn't you marry him, Lol?

"Marry Royston? Prrrrf!" Loretta's voice was derisive. "He was no good, him, Royston." She looked at us. "I put his bags outside the door, didn't I? Comin his little ways. I said goodbye, tara, I'm sorry – I needs my space!"

"Orr, my poor father! I bet you gave that man a hard time," said Joe, laughing. I was in agonies in case anyone mentioned *my* father. But luckily the nurse came round, ringing the hand-bell so we had to go. Good job too, because I would have hated to hear Loretta start in on my dad.

As we were leaving, Joe leant over the bed and asked Loretta in a low voice, about her blood count. When she told him it was up a couple of points, Joe looked relieved. "Good work Ma," he said. And went off happily with Donna.

Joe never asked the doctors anything. He clung to his ignorance like a baby clinging to a bottle, and I despised him for it.

My own behaviour was more rational. Gradually, I dropped off going to the hospital on a regular basis. Telling everyone I was studying hard for my 'mocks'. Where we lived, no one understood about 'mocks' and when they were due. Instead, relatives and friends of my mother's admired my determination in carrying on with my schooling. You keep it up girl, they said. You're makin your mother proud!

No-one, not even Joe seemed to realise what I was up to. Though I saw my mother less and less, I always made sure I phoned the hospital regularly. "How is she?" I'd ask dutifully. And I'd end by saying, "Please give her my love."

But instead of studying, I spent my time lying on the old red couch where Loretta used to lay, dreaming about my life in the future. 'My dad' was somewhere out there, in the future. I knew his name (from my birth-certificate) and that he'd cared enough about me to leave me a gift – the beautiful blue ball. These days, the blue ball looked like a sunken moon, stuck on top of the wall unit. But I treasured its memory, knowing that one day in the starry future, I'd meet my dad, and we'd talk about this gift he'd given me. Of course, we'd recognise each other instantly – my dad and I, because it was obvious to me, that his genes were the dominant genes in my make-up. They were there, encoded in the double helix of my DNA. How else could I account for me?

It was strange how pleasantly the time passed when I was thinking like this. Even when I did put in an appearance at school, I didn't let go of the day-dreams. And when scary night times came around, I'd turn up the mattress on Loretta's bed, and fish out some notes. Then I'd go off with Cookie and the gang, drinking.

Not that I did much drinking, except for a couple of cans of *Hooch*. Three cans of *Hooch* and I was away. Floating. Doing stupid things. Once, I tried to walk around the side of a mirror in the pub toilets. I couldn't see that the toilet-door was a reflection – and I kept banging my head on the faecal coloured wall tiles, as I tried to go round it. The side of my head was swollen and smarting when I stopped.

"Leisha man you makes me piss!" said Cookie, laughing. "You really do!" It crossed my mind to ask her why I was so funny? And why was she Cookie, and her sister Cherry, so cool? Both of them wore shiny auburn wigs, like super-models. And they had the clothes. But Cherry was humungous in size. And Cookie wasn't much smaller. So how come they were cool?

I opened my mouth to ask – but I couldn't fit the words inside the moment. The moment just went by me. Pass. So I opened my mouth a bit wider, and started to laugh.

Coming home from a night out, I'd crash down on the old red couch and fall asleep, happy and floating. But in the morning, even before I was awake, I'd feel the weight of something miserable pressing down on me. My eyes would focus slowly, and I'd remember what it was.

Then one day, I woke up and saw a piece of blue sky through the window. I realised it was spring, and for some reason, that made me feel better. So I went and phoned Joe's house, to check up on hospital visiting times; and to see who was going in that night.

The minute she picked up the phone and heard my voice, Donna broke down in tears. "Wassamarrer?" I said, suddenly fearful. There was a long snuffly silence. Then Donna managed to tell me what had happened. She said the consultant had called Joe up to the hospital and explained there was nothing more they could do. Treatment-wise, that was it. "Oh, Leisha! I'm so sorry," said Donna sobbing all over again. "But there's no hope for her. There's no hope for Loretta!"

It sounded like the title of a book, the way she said it: "*No Hope for Loretta.*" That was my first thought. Then I began to feel empty, as though a stone had dropped inside me. And I needed to sit down, but I couldn't because I was in a call-box.

"How're we gunna tell her?" I said, helplessly.

"Oh don't you do anything," said Donna, quickly. "Leave it to Joe, Leish. Joe said he'll deal with it." So feeling especially childish and helpless, I rang off.

I didn't do any of the things I might have done, like phone the hospital. Or actually go in and see my mother. Instead, on a sudden whim, I lifted the telephone book out of the cubby-hole and began flicking through its pages, idly at first, then with more attention.It was gone ten when I arrived in school. Calmly, I sat through classes until lunch-time. Then I picked up my bag and my jacket, and left.

Once out of the school-gates I turned right, and onto the high road that ran past the school. I walked slowly, admiring the big solid houses, with their spacious lawns and double-garages. In this area where my school was, all the houses had names instead of numbers. And I said them to myself as I walked along: "*Hawthornes, Erw Lon, Primrose View, Ty Cerrig, Sovereign Chase -*" names that were as anonymous as numbers, really. But I didn't mind. It was a lovely day, warm and sunny, and I kept looking up at the blue sky, marvelling at how beautiful a day it was.

When I came to a black and white gabled house, with a big front lawn and a wrought iron-gate marked *Evergreen,* I stopped. This was the place where the man who could be my dad lived. Blyden, D H. I'd got the name out of the telephone directory that morning. It was almost the same as the one written on my birth certificate under father: "David H Blyden, O/S Student." It could be him, I reasoned. It could be my dad, living here in a mock-Tudor house with mullioned windows. Loretta had never had much to say about him, except that he was quiet. But he had his little ways, she said, like they all do. Joe had whispered to me once, that my dad was from Africa. But would an African be living around here? Maybe, I thought, if he had money.

The detached house, like all the surrounding houses, was set

well back from the road. And on one side there were no neighbours. Only a redbrick Observatory and a fenced-in tennis court. It
was all in keeping, I decided approvingly. Everything was so quiet,
and cultivated and tasteful. Then, afraid someone might be watching
from the window, I walked up onto the grassy bank, nearer the
Observatory, and sat down.

Now I could see the house from the side, facing the sun, with
the dark pine tree towering over it. The pine tree was striking. Its
dark green branches seemed to flip out like arrows, right up into the
blue sky. As though, I thought admiringly, they were aiming straight
into the heart of heaven.

I wondered about my dad, living here. I wondered if he
visited the Observatory at night, to study the billions of stars in the
universe? If he did, he'd understand just how little our lives were,
compared to the vast infinity of outer space. Surely he would? He
was the man who had given me the blue ball.

I don't know how long I sat there, dreaming and wondering
in the sun.

I imagined my African dad, climbing the steps of the
Observatory, and looking out over the mysteriously empty ball-
court. Like a priest in ancient Mexico – except that we were in
Wales. Our history class that morning had been about lost
civillisations – which was a theory connecting Africa to ancient
America and to ancient, Celtic Britain. *We were all connected*! I
suppose that fed into my mind, and kept my thoughts turning over,
magically.

It was late in the afternoon when I heard the sound of car
wheels crunching over gravel. Someone was parking a car in front of
the house. I got to my feet in a sudden panic. What if it was him, my
dad, arriving home? My heart began to pound, and I felt sick. This
could be him, I thought with wonder. This could be my dad!
Involuntarily, I looked towards the house, and my courage began to
waver. Could it be my dad, back there? It was possible, I knew it was
possible, but was it probable?

No, I decided, suddenly. No! The sun had disappeared
behind the clouds, making everything seem different. Devoid of
magic, colder. I glanced up at the Observatory, and was amazed to
see its structure in a new cold light. Now it was revealed as squat and

ugly. Shaped like a red-brick kiln against the sky. I looked again, and saw that its narrow windows or apertures were shuttered over with grey metal grilles. There was a padlock on the entrance door; and weeds were sprouting from the brick-work. The place was derelict!

And there was no mysterious ball-court. Just an ordinary tennis court marked out with yellow lines, behind the trampled wire-netting. Enough was enough. I swung my bag up over my shoulder, and started walking, fast. I didn't look behind me, not even for a last glimpse of *Evergreen*, with its lonesome pine tree standing dark and arrow like against the sky.

Of course, running away like that allowed me to keep on dreaming. And even before I was half way home, I'd begun to re-assemble my defences. After all, nothing had happened. I could always go there again, I reasoned. Not straightaway, but one day. When I was ready. The choice was mine -

By the time I stepped out of the lift on the twelfth floor, I was actually smiling. It was fun trying to picture myself living with my dad, in a big gabled house, a wrought iron gate and a plaque on the front, marked *Evergreen*.

I was still smiling as I put the key in the lock and gave the door a push. When it swung open, I almost collapsed. Loretta was framed in the door-way, wrapped in a red velvet dressing-gown, staring at me. "Ullo stranger," she said, in a croaky voice. "Wassamarrer with you, seen a ghost?"

Inside the living-room I was surprised to see how everything had been changed round. The old red couch had been pushed to one side and Loretta's bed had been brought in and placed against the wall. I didn't see Joe at first, hunkered down by the little table, fixing a plug on the lamp. When I did see him, I gave a sigh of relief. "Oh Joe!" I said, "you're here!" Joe nodded over his shoulder at me, and carried on with what he was doing.

I watched Loretta move slowly across the room. Twice she had to stop and re-tie the belt on her dressing-gown, as it came undone. Then very gingerly and carefully, she lowered herself onto the edge of the bed, and looked at me. I was terrified. "What're you doing home?" I said, in a rush. "I didn't know you were coming home –" Loretta began to laugh. "She wants to know what I'm doing home, Joe," she said, looking over her shoulder at him. "Shall we tell her?"

"Uh, Ma?" said Joe. Too busy screwing a light-bulb into the lamp it seemed, to pay much attention. But Loretta didn't need his support. Instead, turning back to me with her dark eyes shining, she leaned forward and whispered, "I'm home because I'm cured! Ain' I Joe?" she sang out loudly. "Ain' I cured, almost?"

At that moment, Joe clicked the switch on the table-lamp. Throwing a soft, glowing light over everything. Including our faces. "There!" he said, turning round at last. "Sixty watts so it won't burn." He grinned. "That's better, ain' it?"

A week later I ran away from home, and two days after that, my mother died. I suppose there was something inevitable about the way those two events were linked. But it didn't seem like that at the time.

That last week, I played along with Joe and Loretta as far as I could. What did I care? And on the Thursday night, when I'd had enough, I went out clubbing with Cookie and Cherry. It wasn't really clubbing. We ended up sitting in the Community Centre, because I was broke and Cookie announced suddenly, that she was saving up for a white wedding.

I asked how much it would cost, a white wedding? "Thousand pounds," said Cookie, proudly. "The dress alone'll set me back a couple a hundred."

"Wow."

"That's because she wants one that flows," said Cherry.

"Yeah, that dress just gorra to be fl-o-w-i-n!, man," said Cookie, snapping her fingers and laughing.

I was troubled in mind, but I laughed along with them. Just to show willing. I even asked about the car. What sort of car would they be having? And Cookie said, "One with wheels, preferably!" And while we were laughing at that, a man came over and asked if he could buy me a drink.

When I said no thanks, he walked away. All nice and polite and everything, but Cookie said I was simple.

"He had a fuckin big gold ring on his finger!"

"Yeah," said Cherry. "And that twenny pound note he was

flashing came off've a roll!"

"So?"

"So," said Cookie, "anybody'd think you won the lottery!"

For some reason, I lost my temper and started shouting. I told Cookie if I won the lottery, I'd buy *her* a friggin ticket to Mars. "And Joe," I said loudly, "I'd buy Joe a ticket to Mars, straight off!" Just then a hand tapped me on the shoulder, and I froze. Cookie and Cherry burst out laughing. They knew I thought it was Joe. But it wasn't Joe, when I turned round. Only his best mate, Chip-chip, wanting to say hello. Naturally he asked how my mother was, and I said fine. She's fine. Then Cookie and Cherry went off to the toilets, and Chip-chip pulled up a stool and sat down. He told me he was working part-time, now. In McDonald's, Mickey D's? "But really," he said, "I'm a *player*."

"A player?"

"Didn't Joe ever tell you?" he said. "I plays basket-ball."

"Oh, yeah," I said, unenthusiastically, "basket-ball!"

"Hey, don't say it like that," said Chip-chip. He pulled a face at the way I said it, making me laugh. "*Barsket-bawl!*"

"I didn't say it like that!"

"Yes you did," said Chip-chip. "Still, it's good to see you smiling, I like to see you smiling," he said. And he went off and bought us both a soft drink, to celebrate.

"Well kiss to that!" said Cookie, coming back to the table half an hour later. "Lemonade and no major money? An having to listen to all that stuff about sport is fuckin' boring!" she said. I agreed. But I still thought it was nice for him. Having an interest like basket-ball. "His little life is rounded by an O," I said, half seriously. Then I laughed and got up to dance, when the man with the gold ring on his finger came over and asked me.

While I was dancing, someone tapped me on the shoulder. I looked round with a smile on my face, thinking it was Chip-chip.

But it was Joe. I shied away from him. But he raised his arm and brought his fist crashing down on my back, again and again. "Where's your mother?" he said, as he punched me. "I'll tell you where," he said, punching me. "She's in the hospital dying," he said, punching me. "And where are you? Out!" he said, punching me. "Enjoyin yourself!"

Joe only allowed Donna to grab hold of his arm when he'd finished. Then the two of them walked out of the Centre, arm in arm.

Most of the sympathy was on my side. People said Joe was taking everything out on me when I wasn't to blame. Neither of us was to blame, they said; and I knew it was true.

But still, I felt guilty. Before going out that night, I'd brought Loretta her cup of tea and her tablets, and watched her swallow them. Eyeing my outfit, she'd asked if I was going out? "Yes, I'm going out," I said, coldly. "I can go out, can't I? *Now you're on the road to recovery –*"

Loretta didn't say anything after that. And I waited until the tablets knocked her out 'dead' as she always said, then I put on my coat and switched off the light; and left her. An hour or two later, Joe had called at the flat, and found her on the floor, haemorrhaging. I suppose our behaviour that night – mine and Joe's, was totally predictable.

A couple of days later, I left Cookie's house where I was staying, and went with her and Cherry to the hospital. Joe was sitting in the waiting-room, munching french fries and *KFC* out of a carton. Neither of us spoke. Then Joe pushed the carton of chicken across the table, and told me to take some. I did. Then we both went in and sat with Loretta until she died.

Inside the cemetery most of the stones are black marble, with fine gold lettering. I like the home-made efforts best. The rough wooden crosses that you see here and there, with 'Mam' or 'Dad' painted on them in thick white letters.

Loretta has a cross like that, though we are saving up for a stone. Right now her grave has a blanket covering of long brown pine needles over it. Fallen from the pine tree overhead. There's a row of tall pines all along this side of the cemetery – and I see them differently now, depending on the season.

It's late spring and the sky is blue and the sun is shining. Looking up at the patch of blue, through the pines, I notice the little wooden pine cones, tucked beneath the brush of feathery green branches. "Like little brown eggs," I say to Chip-chip as we walk away. Chip-chip says it takes two years for these pine cones to mature and fall, as they're doing now, all around us as we walk. Two years! I think to myself, well, that must be about right.

"Hey! Frank Sinatra's dead," says Chip-chip, as we reach the exit gate. "Is he?" I say without thinking. "Then his arse must be cold." At first, Chip-chip is shocked, then he starts to laugh. "That's your mother talkin' that is," he says. "That's Loretta!" "Yeah," I say looking at him and smiling. "I think it is!"

RUNNING OUT

Siân Preece

My mother once told me of a village that drowned.

"The people were all right," she said quickly; I was small then, and it was important to me that people be all right. "They moved away."

"Where did they go?"

"Scattered far and wide."

She looked towards the window as if they would be out there, walking down the street with their suitcases. It sounded like a story, but she said it was true.

"Did the people want to go?"

"No, they didn't want to go."

"Why did they, then?"

"They had to. The valley was needed for a reservoir. A big lake," she explained. "To keep water in, for people to use."

"The people in the village?"

"No, English people," and she frowned.

"But what happened to the houses?"

"The houses are still there, under the water."

I tried to imagine it; a house like my Nan's, with the china dogs still fierce on the mantlepiece, and seaweed curtains waving in the green water. Tea cosies like jelly fish, rugs like rays swimming over coral–bed sofas. There would be no point in closing the doors; you could just float out of the window and look down on the map of your garden, at the whole village under water like a present from the seaside. Tryweryn. Cwm Atlantis. A tap turns in Liverpool, and a church steeple breaks the surface of a Welsh lake.

I hear a chime like a church bell under water… it's the chain of the bath plug, dancing under the hot tumble at my feet. I turn off the tap and lean back, relax. At the other end of the bath, my toes bob up, white in the red water; ten little croutons in a bowl of tomato soup. I feel hot and weak. I feel as if I will be in this water forever.

At first I felt like a pervert, walking the streets of Cardiff at dusk with a Welsh costume concealed under my mac. Red skirt, checked shawl and apron. A scaled-up version of my St David's Day outfit at school; but no pungent, dusty daffodil pinned to my chest, just a flattened yellow fake. I kept my tall black hat in a carrier bag, swinging it like a bucket, until I got to work. Our boss had no shame, making us dress like that.

In the alley behind the restaurant, I told Jackie: "The Welsh costume's all made up anyway."

"Oh aye?" She picked a wad of chewing gum from her mouth and held it in her fingers while she dragged on her fag. Her face was pointed and modern over the white pussy-cat bow at her chin.

"Aye, it was all invented by this English woman. We used to wear little round bonnets like everyone else. I remember it from History."

"Well, don't tell Alwyn." Alwyn was the restaurant owner. "He've only just found one to fit your big head."

"Well, that's 'cause I've got big brains. Your hat must be titchy." I pretended to read a label at the back. "Look! 'Age five!'"

"Ha bloody ha."

In the kitchen window, froggy, pink fingers appeared and rubbed a squeaky hole in the steam. It was Fat Benny, the bald, wordless washer-up, spying on us. Fat Benny was in love with girls.

"Hiya darlin'!" Jackie tinkled piano fingers at him. "Meet you behind the bins after for a snog!"

Fat Benny's eye winked shyly in the peephole he had made. He pressed soft, round kisses on the window; wrinkled 'O's.

"Aw, Jackie, don't tease him."

"Why not? He's a creepy git."

I shushed her with my hands. "He's not creepy. He's just sad."

Fat Benny bobbed around in the kitchen window, looking quite happy to be sad.

Alwyn pounced out of the kitchen door.

"Have you laid them tables yet? Come on girls, chop chop."

We had laid the tables when we got in, but Alwyn hated to

see us doing nothing. In the kitchen he tried to arrange the two of us into a line, then stood before us with his tiny feet, in their tasselled shoes, at a perfect ten-to-two.

"Jackie, you're meeting and greeting and taking orders. Rhian, you're taking coats and showing to tables. And Rhian," he added, "Better not do any serving, is it? Not with the way you dish out soup."

He was being bitchy and I stared at him under the brim of my hat, giving him attitude, but he turned away.

It was getting that Alwyn took another job off me every night. He was right about the soup, though. If I was carrying it, there was no point putting it in a bowl; it always ended up in the serving plate, with the doily drinking it like a Kleenex. And I couldn't manage vegetables that were too round; the peas would make a break for it, and I could only keep the potatoes on the plate if they were mashed. I spent most of my time in the kitchen, scraping butter from a big plastic vat into individual china pots. The trick to getting the butter smooth on top was to breathe on it, to warm it, but I didn't let Alwyn see that.

At the end of the night, Chef would give us left-overs to take home. Fat Benny would only take bread.

"Go on, Fat Benny, there's a lonely Glamorgan sausage here without a butty. Or how about this salmon steak? Lovely bit of fish; the skin's come off is all."

But Fat Benny would shake his head and look as if he were going to cry.

"All right. Bread it is."

And we would tumble the brown, floury rolls into Fat Benny's Adidas bag.

"He do look all right on it, though," said Jackie.

"He looks like an autopsy," said Chef; and these two things meant that Jackie didn't like Benny, and Chef did.

There's a bottle of vodka on the edge of the bath, incongruous beside the two shampoos. Mine is Plus— Conditioner— for— Damaged— Hair, with a picture of, I think, a vitamin on the side. Dad's is Anti— Dandruff, with a static dribble of turquoise paste obscuring the letters. His razors are rusty and leaking, sitting in a pool of their own orange blood.

Tonight I showed Fat Benny how to make napkins into shapes.

"Want to see a crown?"

He nodded, wedged in the corner, keeping his bum warm on the oven. I flapped the napkin open, folded and pinched, folded again.

Jackie was serving in the restaurant and Alwyn was going round the tables, talking to the customers. He did it to emphasise that he was the owner; a businessman, *crachach*, not an employee like his little waitresses. When he said, "We hope you enjoy your meal," the 'we' was practically royal.

Alwyn divided the customers into two categories: the first was the Smart Regulars, who were rich, and used to eating out, and didn't bother to dress up for it. Alwyn would rub his hands and smile at them like he had greased his teeth.

His second category was the Special Occasions. These were the people who had saved up, and came dressed in their best, most uncomfortable clothes for the treat. The men had big hands with scrubbed, raw knuckles. The women wore perfume that made me sneeze. They cringed silently in their seats, spooked by the sound of their plain conversation in this chichi, unfamiliar place. When Alwyn talked to them, they stared at him like cats, and whispered when he'd gone: "That was the owner." He always sat the Special Occasions by the toilets.

Jackie's categories were Good Tippers and Bad Tippers.

My categories were Human and Inhuman, depending on how they treated us.

I was supposed to be microwaving the Welsh cakes so they'd feel fresh-from-the-oven warm. Chef had disabled the timer to stop it going 'ping' and giving the game away, so you had to watch it.

"There you go."

I gave Fat Benny the napkin crown and he perched it on his shiny head, did a little dance. His big, melon face split into a ripe smile and he made his laugh sound, a high-pitched, soprano wheeze.

"Now we've both got hats," I said, and we grinned at each other.

Chef had finished up and gone home by this time. I had

nothing to do except wait until Alwyn called for the Welsh cakes. I checked the bow on my hat so I'd be ready straight away; Alwyn was always saying, "It's not the customers' job to wait; it's our job to wait on them."

I used to complain to Jackie that, if I found the Restaurant Management book where he read that, I'd burn it. But tonight, when I looked around the kitchen at the white tiles streaked with rainbows of detergent, and the family of knives hanging from Grandpa to Baby on the wall, I thought: I wouldn't mind doing this. Creating this order, this cleanliness. I could go back to college and do Hotel and Restaurant Management. Food Hygiene. Catering.

"What do you think, Benny? Could I do Restaurant Management?"

Benny widened his eyes. He breathed in as if about to cough and, in a high, girl's whisper, said:

"The bread's not for me, it's for my Mam. She do soak it in milk. It's her teeth, see."

He put his hand to his mouth, astonished at himself, and we stared at each other. I had never heard him speak before, and now I realised with surprise that he was quite young; perhaps nineteen or twenty. I didn't know what to do. Did he want me to congratulate him, or would it just make him shy? It felt like giving someone a card when you're not sure it's their birthday.

"Benny," I said, unfolding another napkin, "Do you want to see a swan?"

Benny's Mam.

She has Benny's ham arms, encased in the sleeves of a floral dress, and the same bald head in a curly wig. She is as silent as her son; they communicate telepathically, watch sit-coms with the sound down, and laugh so only dogs can hear.

When my own mother left, I used to imagine her going back to her drowned village. Walking into the water in her dress, the skirts billowing around her as she dived and searched for her house; or crying on the shore like a mermaid, her hair streaming. But my Dad said she'd found a new boyfriend in Merthyr.

Alwyn came into the kitchen, rubbing his hands together briskly like a fly.

"Where have all the napkins gone?" he said, then, "Ah, Rhian, have you done with them Welsh cakes?"

I pressed the catch and the microwave door sprang open as if the Welsh cakes had rebelled and were kicking their way out. But they were safe, tanned and toasty under the hygienic kitchen neon. They slid wilfully on the plate, but I corralled them against my chest, sprinkled them and my daffodil with a shower of sugar, and offered them for Alwyn's inspection.

"Well, they look fine," he said. He chose one, snapped it open, and we watched as a currant gave up its last puff of moisture. The cakes were burnt, dry, as solid as shortcake.

"Oh no! Oh Alwyn, I'm sorry!"

Alwyn took the plate from me. He tipped the cakes and their greasy, sugared doily into the pedal bin, and we heard them scuttling like coal to the bottom. Without looking at Benny, Alwyn handed him the plate for washing and, when he finally spoke, flecks of spittle sparked from his mouth.

"Look, Rhian…"

"I'll do some more! It won't take a minute."

"No, no, don't bother. Just… take the dessert trolley out, will you?"

There was only one table left now, or rather two, pushed together for a party; businessmen from London, in Cardiff for a conference. We got more English customers here than Welsh. They came for the love-spoons decorating the wall, the spinning wheel in the corner, for Jackie and me sweating in our tall hats. There must have been photographs of us all over the country; two life size peg dollies with eyes scalded red by the camera flash.

"Say cheese!"

"No, say 'caws'! That's Welsh for 'cheese!'" Alwyn was taking an evening class at the university.

I had taken the businessmen's coats to the cloakroom and, alone in the dark, stroked the collars and cuffs, slotted my hands into the flat, empty pockets. Next to those tiny stitches, my own clothes felt as clumsy as a doll's.

Jackie had smelt money, and now I heard her laughing with the men, responding to their banter; giggling for tips where I would have tried for a smart answer. I wobbled the trolley towards them, the thick carpet catching in its wheels, jingling the dishes and making the trifle tremble as if it were afraid. The noise seemed vulgar. I was ashamed.

"Here's Blodwen Mark Two!", shouted a man at the head of the table.

"Hello, Blodwen!"

Jackie muttered to me through her clenched smile, "We've got a right lot here; they're calling me Blodwen too," then; "You've got cream all up your shawl."

The shawls got into everything. I wiped the cream off with my apron and parked the trolley.

"Good evening! Tonight we have sherry trifle, lemon meringue pie, apple tart and custard..."

One of the men pulled me by the strings of my apron to stand next to him.

"Never mind the meringues, Blodwen; give us a song!" He smelt of brandy and cigars, and rich–food farts. There was a splash of dried gravy on his chin.

"I can't sing!" I smiled to soften the refusal.

"Nonsense; all you Welsh can sing. Come on!" He started banging the table, waved at the others to join in:

"Song! Song! Song!"

I glanced around the table in a panic; the faces of the men ran together, became a film, a flicker picture of one man ageing. In his twenties, the shoulders still firm, the hint of a squash racquet in the back of the company car. Then the weight of seniority silting down through the years, the tailoring becoming more careful to hide the bulk. A daring, last-chance moustache at fifty, the word 'distinguished' starting to apply, then the silver hair, the golden handshake, and first-name terms with the doctor. The same man, the same men; a row of grey cloth with a shared mission statement — only the coloured ties, like a Warhol print, to tell them apart.

One of the men spoke, and the picture refracted again.

"Steady on!" he said slowly, his words chewy with alcohol. "The girlie's trying to do her job."

The first man replied as if I wasn't there: "Don't worry. I'll leave her an enormous tip."

I heard myself shout, in a furious rush,

"All right! I'll give you a song!"

They cheered, with no idea that I was angry, or even that I could be. I folded my hands across my apron like a trembling bird, and began to sing:

"There was an old farmer who sat on a rock,

"A-waving and shaking his big hairy…"

I was into the second verse when Alwyn came screaming out of the kitchen like a fire engine in tasselled shoes and dragged me away.

"What do you think you're doing!" A purple vein twitched on his red temple.

"They asked for a song."

"Good God!" He threw his arms in the air and I flinched, although he'd had no intention of hitting me. Benny cowered in the corner, frantically washing and rewashing a clean plate, as Alwyn marched up and down the kitchen, his little feet pit-patting on the tiles, repeating his mantra: "The good restaurateur remains calm at all times." Then he turned to me and took a deep breath.

"Listen," he said, "This job, well, it hasn't really been working out, has it?"

I felt sick and serious. My hands filled with sweat, dripping cold between my hot fingers.

"I'm sorry!" I said, "I'll do better in future, honest I will!"

He shook his head. "I'm sorry," he said, echoing me, "I've already spoken to another girl who worked here before. See, her husband's left her and she needs the money. We're having her back." He looked at me and added slowly, to be sure that I understood, "Instead of you." The way he said it, I knew he'd practised it. I knew it was a lie.

"*I* need the money," I said, but Alwyn had already turned his eyes down, dismissing me.

"You're young," he said, "You'll find another job, easy. I'll put a bit extra in your last wage packet. Okay? All right? All right, then. Off you go now, and bring the uniform back any time you like. By Thursday, at least. And have it cleaned, will you? There's cream all up the shawl."

I saw Benny's face like a snapshot, mournful and melting in the background. My bag was hanging on the back of the door, hidden in a row of coats on their hooks, and I pulled at it, tugged in sudden fury until the whole lot came down with a sound like snow falling from a roof. I saw my own mac sprawled under the pile of headless bodies and hauled it out. Its empty arms embraced me as I ran.

I saw a postcard once; a woman lying in a river with all her clothes on, and flowers. Now I unpin my fake daffodil, the pin resisting in the wet tweed, and hold it to my chest. The shawl is heavy with water, I feel its weight when I move my shoulders. It has become crimson where it was white before.

The water has cooled again. I let it out and run more hot, and swill my skirt around to see the dye billowing scarlet. The best, though, is the hat; the steam has broken it down, the brim is collapsing onto my face. Little flecks of black felt are breaking off and floating in the water, like the specks you see in your eye when you're tired; or like water–boatmen, who dent the smooth, wet light with their insect feet. They scatter in the breath of my laughter. Even a smile seems to move them.

I stand up in the bath and the water pours from me in a loud wave, then slows to a trickle. The clothes are heavy, but supporting their weight makes me feel strong, defiant.

I pull the plug, and the red water starts running out.

THE WONDER AT SEAL CAVE

John Sam Jones

Gethin stacked the returned books and wondered why Mr Bateman always seemed to do his marking in the middle study bay; why not the staff room, the small 'prep' room at the back of the biology lab, or even one of the other bays? Quite often, when he was putting books back in the geography section, nearest the study area, they'd smile at one another. Sometimes, if there was no one else in the library, they'd talk – but only if Mr Bateman initiated the conversation. Gethin liked these talks; he liked it that Mr Bateman seemed interested in what he was reading and what films he'd seen, or what he thought about mad cows, adulterous royals, and the war in Chechnya. Sometimes they even talked about football. When Gethin turned up for his library duty he found himself hoping that he and Mr Bateman would be alone, that there would be plenty of geography books to shelve, and that they might talk.

Mr Bateman was his favourite teacher; he was most people's favourite really. He got angry sometimes and shouted a bit, but he was never sarcastic, which seemed to be the weapon most of the male staff used to intimidate their classes into some kind of order and control. And he always made biology interesting, even if there were lots of facts that had to be memorised. He was the kind of teacher most students wanted to do well for, to please. The exam results pleased everyone; there were more A grades in biology from Ysgol yr Aber than from any other school in Wales and the school's record of success in biology was always used by the Welsh Office to challenge the cynicism of those opposed to Welsh-language science education.

Mr Bateman had learned to speak Welsh; perhaps this was what Gethin liked best about him. Very few of the English people who'd settled in the area had bothered to learn the language, but he had, and Gethin was hard put to detect an ill-formed mutation or a confused gender; Mr Bateman spoke better Welsh than many native speakers and Gethin admired him for the respect he'd shown to the language and culture of his adopted home. And there was football too; Gethin thought highly of him for that! Mr Bateman had grown up in Manchester and everyone at school knew how fanatically he still supported his home team – United, not City. Gethin supported Liverpool and went to some home games with Mel Tudor, Mel-siop-baco as everyone knew him, who had a season ticket at Anfield.

Gethin carried the Welsh novels back to their shelf wondering if he dared start a conversation with Mr Bateman. He needed to talk to somebody. The school summer holidays had been such a mixed time; although he'd been confident enough of good grades, waiting for the GCSE results had found him lurching between the certainty of staying on at school to do his A-levels and the uneasy emptiness of 'what if?'. It was then that 'the other thing' bothered him; it had been there for ages, of course, but 'doing well in your exams' and 'going to university like your brother and sister' had been a sufficient enough screen to hide behind. The kiss on *Brookside*, outing bishops and the debate about the age of consent had made the screen wobble a bit, but he really hadn't allowed himself to think very much that he might be, or what that might mean, until those moments of uneasy emptiness had folded over him. And now he knew that he was and he needed to talk about it.

He'd tried to talk to his sister. Gethin had stayed with Eilir in Liverpool at the beginning of July; he'd tried talking to her after seeing the film, but she'd seemed so taken up with her patients, her new boyfriend and the hassles she and her flat-mates were having with their landlord about the fungus growing on the kitchen wall. It was because she'd been so preoccupied that Gethin had spent his time in the city alone and had the chance to go to the cinema on a rainy afternoon. He'd read a review of *Beautiful Thing* in *The Guide* that came with Saturday's *Guardian*, and when he saw that it was showing at the ABC on Lime Street he'd loitered on the opposite pavement for almost an hour trying to muster up the courage to go in. It was the rain that eventually sent him through the glass doors into the garishly lit foyer of the cinema to face the spotty, many ear-ringed boy in the ticket booth who dispensed the ticket with a wry smile. Gethin had panicked, interpreting the boy's smile as 'I know you're queer... All the boys who come to see this film on their own are!' Only after taking his seat in the darkened auditorium did his panic subside.

It was a love story; Jamie and Ste, two boys his own age, falling in love with one another. There were no steamy love scenes and but for a fleeting glance at Ste's naked bottom there was no nudity, so Gethin got few clues as to what two boys might actually do together. When Jamie and Ste ran through the trees chasing one another and finally embracing and kissing, Gethin had become aroused; he'd wanted to be Jamie in the film – to be held and kissed by Ste... He'd wanted his own mother to be as accepting as Jamie's and he'd wanted a friend like Leah to talk to.

Outside the cinema it had stopped raining so Gethin decided to walk back to Eilir's flat near Princes Park. Wandering along Princes Avenue, he came to understand that something had changed in his life and nothing would be the same again. Behind the screen that he'd erected to keep himself from thinking about 'the other thing' he'd felt closed in silence – a silence which had left him anxious and uncertain, even fearful. But the screen had been pulled away by Jamie and Ste and their story had begun to give that unspeakable part of Gethin's life a shape. For the first time Gethin really understood what his father had so often preached to his congregation – 'that stories give shape to lives and that without stories we cannot understand ourselves'. Of course, the Reverend Llyr Jones had a certain anthology of stories in mind for giving shape to lives and Gethin knew that his father wouldn't include Jamie and Ste's story alongside those of Jacob, Jeremiah and Jesus. Llyr Jones wouldn't see the two boys' story as a 'beautiful thing'.

Gethin recalled that Sunday during the age of consent debate. His father, in a fiery sermon, had exhorted the congregation at Tabernacl (Methodistiaid Calfinaidd – 1881) to write to the local MP urging him to vote against lowering the age to sixteen. Gethin remembered the discussion over the roast beef after chapel, his father – with all the authority of an M.Th. and a dog-collar behind his words, saying that homosexuals were sinful and his mother – in her calm 'I'm the doctor, you can trust me' manner, saying that they were disturbed and needed psychiatric treatment.

Crossing Princes Park, Gethin sat by a reservoir of the city's debris that had once been a lake. He watched a used condom navigate its course on a stiffening breeze through the squalid waters between the half-submerged skeletons of an old bike and a supermarket trolley until it came to lie, stranded on the shore of an abandoned pram. He thought about his father and mother; how he loved them – but how he now didn't think he knew them at all. If he told them about the film – about Jamie and Ste and about what he now knew to be true of himself, would his father's love be acted out in some kind of exorcism and would his mother want the best medical care with visits to some psychologist? Gethin wondered if their love and trust in him were deep enough to challenge thirty years of belief in Calvinistic Biblical scholarship and 1960's medical science? A plastic baby's arm reached from the crib of slime in which it lay, grasping an empty sky; Gethin wondered if his reaching out would be as futile. Back at the flat, Eilir wanted to talk about her first AIDS patient – and about the fungus on the kitchen wall.

Mr Bateman looked up from his marking and smiled at Gethin; he smiled back and mouthed a silent greeting which Mr Bateman returned. Gethin put the dozen or so geography books back on their shelf and turned to talk to his teacher, but his head was already back in his books. With no reason to linger by the study area and insufficient courage to go up to Mr Bateman and ask if they could talk, he went to fetch the remaining pile of returns and went to the science section at the other end of the library.

For some weeks after his stay in Liverpool, Gethin had tried to prop up the screen which Jamie and Ste's story had so successfully toppled. The hikes and bike rides he and his friends had arranged made hiding from the dawning truths of his life easier, but he couldn't escape the knowledge that in all games of hide-and-seek, that which was hidden was always found. Then there had been the tense days leading up to the exam results, and those few exhilarating hours which high achievement and congratulation had brought. His course of A-level study was set, and before the trough of anti-climax swallowed him he got caught up in all the preparations for Enlli; ever since he could remember, the whole family had spent the week of August bank holiday on the remote island. Everyone had thought that this year would be different – that Seifion, Gethin's brother, wouldn't be able to come home from America; but then Seifion had phoned to say that his newspaper needed him back in London for the first week in September, so he'd be with them after all. For a whole week, Gethin packed all the provisions they'd need on the island into boxes which were then wrapped in black bin bags to keep everything dry during the trip in the open boat across the sound. At least this year they didn't have to take all their drinking water too!

Their week on Enlli was, for different reasons, special to each member of the family. His mother liked the peace and unhurried simplicity of life without electricity and phones, cars and supermarket queues – and patients! She'd sometimes come in from a walk and say things like 'Mae bywyd ar yr ynys 'ma yn gneud i rywun gwestiynnu daliadau'r oes gyfoes... – Life here makes you question so much of what we think is important on the mainland...', to anyone who happened to be in ear-shot, but such things were said in ways which beckoned only the responses of her own thoughts. Ann Jones would bake bread every day and gut the fish that Seifion caught in Bae'r Nant at the north end – things which Gethin never saw his mother do at home. His father spent hours alone reading and meditating; on his first visit to the island, more than thirty years ago, Llyr had found a sheltered cove near Pen Diben, at the south end beyond the lighthouse. It was to the cove that he retreated, drawn back by the whisperings of Beuno, Dyfrig, Padarn and other long-dead saints, to be with his thoughts and God. Seifion liked to fish for bass and pollack, and in the last years, since his work had taken him to places like Sarajevo and Grozny, he seemed to use his time on Enlli to find some peace inside himself; by the end of the week he'd be lamenting his choice of career in journalism and wishing he could stay. Eilir painted and enjoyed long talks with her mother; but mostly she painted. And for Gethin the island was where wonders unfolded. He watched grey seals and built dry stone walls; he looked, late into the night, for Manx Shearwaters in the beam of a torch and watched for the small flocks of Choughs. Over the years he'd talked with the marine biologists and the botanists, the geologists and the entomologists that stayed at the Bardsey Bird and Field Observatory and accompanied them on their field trips; for Gethin the island was a living encyclopaedia of the natural world.

On the evening before they crossed over to Enlli the whole family had lingered at the supper table. Eilir had unfolded the saga of the last days of the fungus on the kitchen wall and Seifion had told them stories about New York – the unbearable August heat, the congestion and pollution caused by too many cars, the crumbling health care system – about which he'd been doing a piece for his newspaper... Then Eilir had talked about *her* AIDS patient; Ann had wanted to know if they were using the new combination therapy in Liverpool, the one she'd read about in the *BMJ*... Seifion told the grim details of a visit to an under-funded AIDS hospice, run by a group of nuns in Queens, where people died in their own filth... Eilir couldn't speak highly enough about the loyalty and care her AIDS patient's partner had shown and how impressed she'd been with the faithfulness of her patient's gay friends. 'Gwrywgydwyr ydy'r grwp sydd mewn perygl o hyd ta... – Homosexuals are still the highest risk group then..', Ann had said. Both Eilir and Seifion tried to say something about how it was behaviours that were risky, and that the notion of risk shouldn't be pinned onto groups of people like a badge, but their words were lost as the talk shifted from health care to homosexuality... Llyr didn't believe that God was punishing homosexuals through this disease, but that the disease was a consequence of their sinfulness and the biggest lesson to humanity from the whole AIDS crisis was that if we chose to flout God's law some pretty catastrophic things would happen... Seifion talked about two gay friends, one from university days and the other a journalist; coming to know these two men had made Seifion re-think his position – the position he'd grown up with – Llyr's position. Seifion didn't think, any longer, that being gay was sinful... And wasn't all the work with the human genome project going to reveal that sexual orientation was genetically predisposed? If that was true, then gay people were an intended part of God's creation. Llyr had said that even if science did reveal the genetic basis of sexual orientation, that didn't make homosexual acts any less sinful; the Bible was clear that sexual intercourse between a man and a woman in marriage was what had been ordained; celibacy was the only acceptable lifestyle for homosexuals, as it was for all unmarried people.

Perhaps Gethin imagined that both his brother and sister had blushed on hearing this; he knew that he'd blushed as soon as they'd started talking about homosexuality. He'd thought that he might clear the table while they talked, to hide his anxiety and embarrassment, and yet, the things that Eilir and Seifion had said had been interesting and positive. Before falling asleep, he decided that he'd talk with Seifion in the morning when they drove together to Porth Meudwy at the tip of the Lleyn.

Waiting on the pebble beach for the two rowing boats to carry everyone and everything bound for the island across the bay to the larger boat in the anchorage, Gethin considered his disappointment. Who was he most disappointed in, himself or his brother? Seifion had said it was a phase that he'd pass through; he'd even shared with Gethin that he and two other boys, when they were about thirteen, had 'played' with themselves and had competitions to see who could do it quickest and shoot highest. When Gethin hadn't seemed convinced, Seifion talked about a sexual experience with a French boy during a language exchange when he was about Gethin's age; they'd shared the same room for the whole of Seifion's stay and done things in bed together; none of it had meant that he was gay. Gethin hadn't tried to explain what he knew to be true; but then – he didn't have the words to give it any shape, and alongside Seifion's experiences Gethin had nothing to share – just an intuitive knowing, without form or outline – without a voice.

Bugail Enlli rounded Pen Cristin and came into calmer water. The sound had been wilder than Gethin could remember and everyone was soaked. The two Germans left behind by the Observatory boat had sat next to him and in the first minutes of the crossing, in the relative calm of the Lleyn's lee, they'd introduced themselves. Gethin, filled with the confidence of his A*, had said 'Hallo! Mein Name ist Gethin Llyr'; he'd tried to explain that it would probably get rougher once they got into the channel and that it might be a good idea to wear the waterproofs that were tucked through the straps of their ruck-sacks. Bernd, the one Gethin supposed was about his own age, speaking in English that was better than Gethin's German, had said that it was his first time on such a small boat. When all the conversations had submitted to awe at the waves and silent prayers, Bernd wove his arm through Gethin's to stop himself being thrown around so much. Later, standing side by side on the uneven jetty in the Cafn, passing all the luggage from the boat along the line to the waiting tractor and trailer, Gethin and Bernd talked easily. The German boy was impressed that Gethin had been to the island every summer; he asked about its wonders. Did Gethin know about the Seal Cave..? He'd read all about it; was it hard to find? Gethin said that it was, but that he'd take him there if he liked.

When Bernd came to Carreg Fawr later in the day to find Gethin, Ann Jones, who'd been kneading the first batch of dough, had tried to explain that she wasn't Mrs Llyr, but Mrs Jones – but that he could call her Ann anyway. Bernd, in his confusion, had said that in Germany it was impossible for children not to carry their parents' family name. Ann had done her best to explain that her three children were named according to an old Welsh tradition whereby sons were known as 'son of' and daughters as 'daughter of' – so Eilir was Eilir Ann and Gethin was Gethin Llyr. Though Gethin had gone fishing with Seifion and Ann didn't know for sure when they'd be back, Bernd stayed with her at Carreg Fawr and she told him stories about the island; he especially liked the idea that they might be stuck there for days if the weather turned bad. When Gethin and Seifion returned with three large pollack, more than enough for supper, Bernd and Gethin went to climb all 548 feet of Mynydd Enlli; from the 'mountain-top' Gethin could point out interesting places and give Bernd his bearings.

The hour after all the supper things had been cleared away was quiet time. Gethin had never thought to question this, it was part of their life on Enlli; an hour in silence to listen for the wisdom of the twenty thousand saints and God. The last quarter of the quiet hour was evening prayer and they all came together in the small front room; sometimes this was silent too, and at other times someone would say whatever their day on the island moved them to say. Gethin thought about Bernd; when he'd put his arm through Gethin's, on the boat, he'd become aroused... He'd had an erection. The memory of it, now – before God, left him filled with shame. It would be hard to live as a homosexual in a world with God, Gethin thought, but how much harder might life be without God?

Eilir and Gethin were eating breakfast when Bernd turned up at Carreg Fawr. 'Today we explore the Seal's Cave, ja?' he'd asked. 'Wenn du willst', Gethin had said... If you like! They put some bread and cheese in Bernd's ruck-sack and set off to explore the east side of the mountain. Ann shouted after them that they needed to be careful on the sheer slopes above the sound; the last thing she wanted was to scramble on the scree to tend broken legs!

From high up on the north side of the mountain Gethin spotted Seifion, fishing from a shoulder of rock in Bae'r Nant way off below them. As they came over to the east side they saw a man sunbathing; he mumbled something about being careful on the narrow paths. Across Cardigan Bay, Cader Idris proved a worthy throne for its mythical giant and the blue of the sea was spotted with bright sail-cloth. When the path dropped away steeply, Bernd betrayed the first clue that the expedition was more dangerous than he'd anticipated; 'You're sure this is the right way, Gethin? If we fall here then – das isses..!' Gethin reassured him and suggested that they ease themselves down the steep, scree path on their bottoms. After ten minutes they reached Seal Cave.

Bernd looked disbelievingly at Gethin... 'But this hole ... It's too small ... You're sure this is the place?' Gethin remembered that he had thought the same thing that first time with Seifion. 'It's just the entrance that's small, then it opens out....' And Gethin disappeared into the blackness with 'Come right behind me. You can hold on to my leg if you're frightened...' And then he felt the German boy's hand around his ankle. Half way along the pitch black tunnel Gethin heard the wheezing and snorting of the seals echo from the underground chamber. He whispered into the darkness behind him that if they stayed as quiet as possible they wouldn't scare the seals. When they both finally pulled themselves from the tunnel onto the wide, flat rock and looked down into the cave, well-lit from a large jagged opening just below the water's surface, they saw two seals basking on the rocks just feet away and another deep in the water, an outline against the water-filtered light. They hardly dared to breathe and marvelled at the wonder of it all.

After ten, perhaps fifteen minutes, Bernd had asked, in a whisper, whether they could swim with the seals. Gethin remembered that he and Seifion had swum in the cave a few times, but that the seals were usually frightened off... 'We can try...', Gethin whispered back. Bernd stood up and as he took off his clothes Gethin saw that his body was already that of a man. 'Come... Let's swim...', he whispered, beckoning Gethin to undress. Gethin followed him into the water. The two basking seals snorted, wriggled from their rocks and dived deeply, circling them both before making for the under-water exit to the open sea. The boys were enthralled and hugged one another, each discovering the other's excitement. They swam together... Touching... Exploring one another's bodies... And they kissed... On the wide, flat rock above the water they lay in one another's arms for a long time, their bodies moving together. Bernd's sigh, when it finally erupted from somewhere deep inside him, echoed around the cave before dying away into Gethin's low moan.

During the quiet hour that evening Llyr told them the story of Saint Beuno and the curlew; he'd watched the birds for most of the afternoon, breaking off the legs of small crabs before swallowing them. According to the legend, Beuno, in the years before coming to Enlli to die, had lost his book of sermons over-board on a stormy sea crossing; in some despair, he arrived back at his cell in Clynnog Fawr to find his sermons, pulled from the sea and carried back to him by a curlew. It was a story Gethin had heard every summer on the island, but then, of Enlli's twenty thousand, Beuno was his father's favourite. Gethin's mind wandered to Bernd and to Seal Cave and now, before God, he wasn't so sure that it was the 'beautiful thing' it had been that afternoon.

Later, feeling heavy with a guilt that only Welsh Calvinism could bestow, Gethin left Carreg Fawr in search of some distraction. Near Ogof Hir he looked for Shearwaters. Beuno came to him.... And then there were two others, perhaps Dyfrig and Padarn, but their faces were hidden under their hoods.... And there were curlews; lots of curlews. Startled by the swiftness of their appearance, Gethin dropped his torch; the glass broke as it hit the rocks and the beam died. The blackness of the night wrapped itself around him and, through the curlew's melodic 'cur-lee', Beuno whispered his wisdom. Gethin didn't want to hear words of judgement and condemnation and he hit out at the three robed figures, shouting at them to leave him alone. Their robes and whisperings folded over and under him and, quiet in their embrace, he was carried back to Seal Cave. Beuno spoke through the whisperings of the other two in a babble of Latin and Welsh, Greek and Hebrew, and though it sounded odd, Gethin understood. Beuno wept for all the men down the centuries whose lives had been tortured by self-hatred because they had loved other men. 'The glory of God is the fully alive human being', he'd said, 'and as it is your providence to love men, love them well, in truth and faithfulness... Where love is true and faithful, God will dwell.... *Ubi caritas et amor, Deus ibi est...*'

The bell rang and as Gethin watched Mr Bateman pack away his books he decided that his need to talk might keep until another day. They both reached the library door together and with a broad smile, Mr Bateman asked, 'Sut wythnos ges ti ar Enlli? – What sort of week did you have on Bardsey?' Gethin said he had a lot to tell and agreed to help set up some apparatus in the lab during the lunch break. And so Gethin got to talk.

Mr Bateman listened as Gethin explained that he now realised he was gay and understood that he needed some support, but he interrupted Gethin when he started to tell him about Bernd and the Seal Cave... 'I don't want to know if you've had sex with boys, Gethin; that would put me in a difficult position...' And he explained about the school's policy on sex education and the laws which guided it; 'I'd be expected to inform the head if I knew that one of our pupils was having sex below the age of consent... And the school policy doesn't really give me much guidance on how to talk with you about gay issues.... Can't you talk about this with someone else?' After a long silence Gethin said that he didn't think there was anyone else, but that he didn't want to put Mr Bateman in a awkward position either, and he left the lab feeling let down and lonely.

That evening, when the loneliness became too deep, Gethin told his parents he was gay. Ann said she'd ring one of the psychiatrists at the hospital. Llyr knew of a healing ministry on the Wirral that had some success in saving homosexuals. They both wanted the best for him. *Ubi caritas et amor, ubi caritas, Deus ibi est.*

Later that evening Kevin Bateman talked with his brother's lover, David, about what support he might offer Gethin; 'You could suggest that he phone the gay help-line in Bangor...' He then wrote Gethin a note to say that he was sorry for letting him down and he put the phone number David had given him clearly on the bottom... *Ubi caritas et amor, ubi caritas, Deus ibi est.*

THE DAY OF THE FUNERAL

Sîan James

The small chapel was only half full, the singing uncertain. Suddenly a watery sun slanted in through the arched window and lit up the young minister's face so that for a moment or two he looked almost saintly, his closely-barbered fair hair and his skin glowing. The singing grew more confident. There was an attempt at harmony.

Glyn felt uncomfortable that the young chap – he couldn't have been more than twenty-three or four – referred to his newly-dead mother as Hester; she was Mrs Richards to everyone outside the family and wouldn't have approved his over-familiarity. Of course, the young minister didn't know her, she hadn't been to chapel for the last couple of years.

'Have you lost your Faith?' Glyn had once asked her. 'Oh no, I don't think so, love. It's just that I can't get in to my chapel shoes, that's all, and it doesn't seem worth buying any more. In my old wellingtons all day and your father's slippers about the house, my feet have got swollen, that's all.'

Glyn suddenly remembered a scene from Romeo and Juliet which he'd done for his O-level. A bit far-fetched to his way of thinking, all that killing each other's cousins for love. But Mr Montague had been real enough at that party at the beginning of the play, 'Now come on and dance,' he'd said, 'at least all of you ladies that haven't got corns.' He'd liked that. Shakespeare certainly knew a bit about elderly people's feet.

He tried to keep his mind on the minister's words, but they didn't seem to have much connection with his mother. Had his mother ever Lived in the Lord as he seemed to be suggesting? Glyn couldn't see it like that. To his way of thinking, his mother was altogether more earth-bound; had worked hard all her life – and died disappointed. And it was his fault. He was almost forty years old with no wife and no child. So that the farm was blighted, fated to fail.

As far as he was aware, his mother knew nothing of the Romeo and Juliet variety of love, but she was always stressing that love, family love, was essential on a farm to make all the hard work worthwhile. 'Get yourself a nice sweetheart,' she'd beg Glyn over and over. 'And if at first you don't succeed, try, try again.'

When he was young, Glyn had put his back into the quest. But the farm was on an unclassified mountain road, eleven miles from the nearest small town, three from the nearest village and by that time girls had decent jobs in Building Societies and Estate Agents and didn't want to be farmers' wives. Or at least no one wanted to be his wife. Even twenty years ago he was overweight and nothing of a talker. He'd persevered though, for several years, being everyone's best friend at the Young Farmers' weekly meetings, having a good laugh with all the girls, driving them here and there, buying them drinks, but never able to establish a special relationship with one of them.

'I'm giving up,' he'd announced just after Christmas one year. 'There's only so much fun a person can be doing with.' 'Don't give up,' his mother had begged. 'Please don't give up.'

He looked across at his mother's sister, his Auntie Phyllis, and her son, Hywel. Hywel was a prosperous dentist with a good practice in Newtown, a pretty wife called Jennifer and two children; a boy and a girl of course, everything falling snap into place. A good-natured chap, though, he had to admit. 'Why don't you get married, man?' he'd ask afterwards, when they were back in the lonely, isolated farmhouse. 'It's not as bad as everyone makes out and there's plenty of compensations.' 'Oh, I'm looking around,' Glyn would reply, that false, comradely note in his voice. What if he answered, 'Because no one will bloody have me, Hywel, that's why. And why should they? I'm not handsome and self-assured like you, but flabby and tongue-tied. If I was a woman, I'd run a mile sooner than have anything to do with a soft-centred bloke like me.'

He suddenly remembered that it was through Hywel that he'd first met Carol-Ann; the only woman who had really touched his heart. He'd only spoken to her a few times in all, but he'd felt close to her, perhaps because he'd dreamed of someone like her for so long. She had a lovely calm smile and eyes clear as water and she was not too thin nor too fat. Hywel had introduced her to his mother when both women had happened to be in hospital at the same time, both recovering from minor operations. 'Carol-Ann used to be my receptionist, Auntie,' he'd said, whispering afterwards, 'nice, hard-working girl. One of the best.'

His mother had found Carol-Ann good company, interested in the same television programmes, the same magazines and the same knitting patterns, and prepared to listen to all her anxieties about the sheep and the new lambs. Before she'd left, she'd invited her up to the farm for Sunday dinner, a meal usually restricted to close relatives.

'I've found you a girlfriend,' she'd announced, when Glyn had come to fetch her home. 'Well, I had to, didn't I, because you don't seem to get anywhere on your own. She's a lovely girl, too, quiet, but very hard-working and dependable according to your cousin, Hywel. She was once his receptionist, it seems, and she's very interested to meet you.'

Glyn sighed as he remembered the day Carol-Ann had come up to the farm. He'd had such hopes – it was about fifteen years ago, before he'd begun to feel so worthless. His mother had talked of her for over a week, but as soon as she arrived, she turned against her: she'd brought her three-year old son with her and had confessed to being an unmarried mother. Only it wasn't as much a confession as an assertion. 'This is my little lad, Mrs Richards. No, I'm not married. It didn't work out.' She'd sounded perfectly self-assured, but Glyn had noticed that her hands were tightly clenched together.

Glyn himself hadn't held it against her, he thought she was very brave, managing so well on her own and seeming immensely proud of little Mark. He had got on splendidly with the little lad, but had failed to make any headway with Carol-Ann. If only he'd been able to swing her up in his arms, as he did Mark, and take her out to see the lambs, they might have got somewhere, but with her he could only sweat and stammer and pull at his collar. His mother hadn't invited her back either, but kept saying they'd had a lucky escape. Glyn had thought about her for months, even years.

After that disappointment, he'd been quiet and depressed, again refusing to go out.

'How can you meet anyone stuck in the house every Saturday night?' his mother would ask. 'You know we've got money. Over a hundred thousand safe in the bank since we sold that strip of land for bungalows, and doing all right besides. Your wife would have her own car and every modern convenience, calor gas central heating, a bathroom and separate toilet. When I married your father we didn't even have an inside tap. Why don't you put a little advert in the Gazette? Everyone seems to be doing it these days.'

After a while he'd relented. 'Farmer with thriving farm w.l.t.m. middle-aged woman for pleasant evenings out and perhaps more.'

Maureen, raven-haired and big-chested, had been the only one to reply. She'd let him give her expensive Friday evening dinners for several weeks, permitting him to kiss her briefly as they parted, but refusing all his invitations to visit the farm. Then, when he'd offered to run her home one snowy evening, she'd confessed that she was married and that perhaps they shouldn't meet again.

The worst of it was that he'd grown very fond of her, admiring the way she so indomitably tackled twelve pieces of cutlery and gargantuan meals, while talking away on genteel subjects like the Antiques Road Show and growing delphiniums. Most men were scathing of women, but he really liked them; their strange affectations, their absurdly impractical shoes, the haughty faces they made at themselves in mirrors, their silky smooth skin, the smell of their make-up and perfume; and some darker smell too, like ferns on a river bank.

He joined a dating agency, but no woman had lasted the course, in fact few had accepted a second date. His mother always told him how smart he looked in his navy-blue suit and maroon tie, but though he did his best, taking the women to restaurants, concerts and films, treating them with care and deference, he failed to capture their interest. He remembered all of them with affection; Rhian was much too young for him, but he'd driven her all the way to Liverpool to some rock concert she'd set her heart on, managing to get her a ticket and waiting outside to drive her back. He remembered with pleasure how she'd thanked him so nicely and slept on his shoulder all the way home. Maxine was a hairdresser, not at all pretty, but she laughed a lot and he loved the way her lips didn't quite meet over her teeth. Lowri squinted when she was nervous, but she was tall and slender like a thoroughbred pony.

She'd agreed to meet him for the second time, but had written a polite letter telling him that a previous boy-friend had contacted her again. She said she'd enjoyed meeting him and hoped he wouldn't think badly of her. He still had the letter.

After a year with the agency, a year of these pleasant but very short-lived relationships, he'd given up and started thinking of himself as the eternal bachelor. But his mother hadn't forgiven him. 'Think of the farm,' she'd say, over and over again. 'Who's going to run the farm when you've gone?'

'Well, Glyn, it's a sad day for us all,' Hywel said as they processed to the cemetery with the other bearers.

'It is that.'

'I'm sorry,' a voice inside him wept as the coffin was lowered into the ground. 'I'm sorry. I was a failure. I let you down.'

His Auntie Phyllis noticed his tears and took his arm. She had married an auctioneer and was the lady president of the Rotary Club. She was dressed totally in black, a little hat like a black nest perched on her head. Glyn was aware that she hadn't done enough for his mother during her long, last illness, but could see that she felt guilty about it and was trying to atone. Later on she would be a Tower of Strength. She would fling open windows. She would produce mountains of sandwiches for the neighbours. She would pack away his mother's clothes to give to charity. She would ask the village women whether they knew someone who could spare an hour or so to help her poor nephew with the housework. She would make lists. He squeezed her hand.

There weren't as many people back in the house as he'd feared. He made up the fire, talked football to the young minister, nodded and smiled at everyone who sympathised with him, and carried round cups of tea. Somehow the time passed and the neighbours left.

Hywel's wife, Jennifer, was the next who wanted to leave. 'No, I'm bloody staying,' Hywel said. 'Taking Glyn out for a drink later on. Just stop moaning for once.'

'Oh please, sweetie,' she kept saying, pulling at her husband's arm and turning large moist eyes at him. 'Oh, please. You know we've got to get the kiddies back from my parents and put them to bed before we can leave them with the baby-sitter.

Oh sweetie, you said ....'

Glyn could see Hywel becoming more and more exasperated, until at last he'd thrown her arm back at her and broken away. 'Come out for a breath of air, man,' he urged Glyn who was hovering about uneasily. 'Leave the washing-up to the women.'

'She wants to go to some blessed dinner-party tonight,' he said when they were outside. 'I don't feel like socialising, but she won't take no for an answer.'

Glyn tried to change the subject. 'I was sorry not to see Jason and Melissa.'

'She wouldn't let them come, man. It would have done them good. I want them to have a sense of family and a sense of place. God, they're eleven and nine now, not babies. They can't be protected from everything for ever.' He turned fiercely towards his cousin. 'You don't know how lucky you are, man.'

'Not to have a wife?' Glyn asked, thinking the question might bring Hywel to his senses.

'Better not have a wife than the wrong one,' Hywel replied, as bitterly as before.

'Now, steady on, Hywel. You don't mean that. Don't let a little tiff get you down. Go to the bloody dinner-party tonight. It'll do you good. What's the use of staying in to brood? Think yourself lucky. Jennifer is a very good-looking young woman and anyone can see how fond she is of you.'

'Fond of what I can give her,' Hywel muttered, but with less anger than before. 'Anyway, it's you we should be talking about not me. How the hell are you going to manage up here on your own? I'm worried about you, man.'

'I'll be all right, I suppose. After all, mother hasn't been able to do much for the last couple of years, has she?'

'But she was always good company, Auntie Hester. She was genuine, a real person. Know what I mean? Not always trying to be somebody else, somebody different, somebody grand.' He kicked at a stone. 'Not like all the bloody women I know,' he said, suddenly as savage as before.

They came to a five-bar gate and leaned over it. 'You never tried to make a go of it with Carol-Ann?' Hywel asked. 'Auntie Hester seemed all for it.'

'No, she wasn't. Not once she realised about the boy. Not once she realised she was an unmarried mother.'

'What about you, though?'

'Oh, I thought she was lovely, but what chance did I have. What chance would I have with anyone, let alone someone my mother disapproved of. No guts, Hywel, that's my trouble. And no way with women either.'

'She liked you, she told me that much, thought you were very kind.'

'Yes, very kind, very nice. That's what all women think about me. I saw her again last summer, but she didn't see me. Or at least pretended not to.'

'She's lost her looks,' Hywel said, kicking another stone.

'I don't know about that. She's put on a bit of weight, but I thought it suited her. Such a lovely smile she had. Did a man good to see it.'

'Her son, Mark, do you remember him?'

'Great little chap, I thought. Duw, I can still remember how he charged after those lambs I had.'

'He's in trouble, man. A teenager now. Bit of a tearaway. Been in one of these remand centres for six months. She's worried sick about him, about what he'll do when he gets out. Nothing for him in Newtown, nothing but hanging around with the wrong crowd'. There was a short silence during which both men looked about them and then at each other. 'Look here, Glyn, I was wondering whether you could see your way to giving him a job up here. Give him some measure of independence, that would, some self-assurance. I could probably pay something towards his wages if you'd give him some sort of trial period up here with you.'

Glyn felt an icy wind clearing his head. 'Your lad, is he?' he asked gently.

A moment's pause, both men staring hard at the mountains, at the rain clouds gathering.

'Aye. My lad. Should have married her, of course, but I was engaged to Jennifer by that time and her father was taking me into the practice. And Carol-Ann not the sort to fight. Oh Glyn, I've been a right sod all my life.'

'There's plenty worse,' Glyn said. He meant it, too. He knew

Hywel was suffering. There was something decent about him at the core.

'I envy you, Glyn. You've got nothing to reproach yourself for.'

'Oh, I have. I let my mother down. Gave up too soon. Was too easily cast down. All she asked was for me to get married and have children. All she wanted was children to inherit this terrible, soul-breaking place.'

They stood together watching the clouds shifting, the colours of the distant mountains change from slate-blue to charcoal.

'You love the fuckin' place, ' Hywel said.

'Do I? I don't know. Love or hate, it's all the same at six in the morning.' Glyn suddenly straightened up. 'Anyway, I'll be pleased to have the lad if he can bear to come here. I'll do my best for him. He's my blood, after all.'

'You're a saint, man. I said to Carol-Ann the other day, "If anyone is willing to give him a helping hand, that'll be my cousin, Glyn."'

'I'll do my best, that's all I've said. And you needn't worry about his wages, man. I'm not short of money. I'll get him a little car too, so he can go to town in the evenings. I won't keep him a prisoner here, I can promise you that, and I won't work him too hard, either. But he may have different ideas of what he wants to do and I won't think any the worse of him for that.'

The two men stood looking hard at each other for a moment or two. 'And now we'll go back,' Glyn continued. 'And you must make it up with Jennifer and go to that dinner-party.'

They turned and walked slowly towards the farmhouse. 'Carol-Ann is married by this time, I suppose?' Glyn asked, with some attempt at lightness.

'Well, she is....she is....with someone,' Hywel said, refusing to meet his eyes.

'Yes, I thought as much. She's a lovely woman.'

Hywel turned towards him. 'Don't envy me, Glyn,' he said in a half-strangled voice. 'You're a free man and a good un.'

A lapwing circled above them, its harsh, desolate cry seeming to mock both of them.

ALL BOYS SEEKING ADVENTURE...

Othniel Smith

It took Kenneth quite a few weeks to realise that the recurring dreams he'd begun to experience on a regular basis weren't recurring dreams at all, at least not in the accepted sense of the term.

At first, he put it down to stress – he was going through a difficult time, and was therefore particularly vulnerable to other-worldly influences. Jobless, woman-less, and on the wrong side of twenty-five, he had just lost his two best friends. One had died following an ill-advised experiment with some pills that someone had sold him on one of their infrequent boys' nights out. The other, having, on a dare, asked a frankly rather unattractive girl to dance with him on a previous night out, had just had a child with her, and drifted out of Kenneth's orbit.

In the dreams, Kenneth was wandering through a scarred, urban landscape, sometimes in monochrome, sometimes in washed-out colour, like a faded photograph. There were buildings, but not many, not at first. Warehouses stood alone, somewhat the worse for wear, in fields of mud and broken bricks. He glimpsed distant and apparently derelict terraced streets, but as he strolled towards them, they seemed to gently recede, finally disappearing altogether, as the morning light made itself known through his unwashed curtains.

Interpretation seemed child's play. The wasteland was Kenneth's lonely bedsit, the aimless walk his life, and the faraway houses his future, simultaneously elusive and unappealing.

It wasn't until the third or fourth week of his dreaming that Kenneth realised that it wasn't quite as simple as he'd supposed. The point of a recurring dream was that it recurred, precise details remaining constant, as in the ones he used to have involving the famous German catwalk model. This dream, however, seemed to mutate subtly, almost imperceptibly as the weeks passed. People appeared, in ones and twos, walking with heads bowed, wearing once-smart suits, frocks, and coats, now frayed. Some even wore hats, and the boys were generally in short trousers. The houses began to manifest themselves more clearly, and he could make out shattered windows, absent walls, broken floorboards, and yellowing stoves and baths with their piping exposed. The ground was uneven, clearly cratered in places, and littered with broken domestic artefacts – a child's toy here, a smashed radio set there, the occasional item of clothing.

It was when Kenneth accidentally caught sight of himself in a puddle that he had his first real shock. The Kenneth looking back up at him was clear-eyed, and fresh-faced, with a disturbing rosiness of cheek. Even more striking was his hair: a floppy, greasy fringe, of the kind which he had always found distasteful, had replaced his normal, prematurely thinning, but defiantly rock'n'roll coiffure. He stood and stared for what seemed hours, until a mischievous child of indeterminate gender appeared from nowhere, jumped into the puddle, splashing his brown serge trousers, chuckled devilishly, and scampered away.

Kenneth knew that the place was London, and that the time was the late 1940's, although how he knew, he'd have been unable to explain, even if there'd been anyone to explain to. The mornings brought vague memories of crackly big band music and implausibly broad Cockney accents heard in the distance, and images of bold words on fading yellow newsprint; words like "rationing", "austerity", "nationalisation". Although whether these were the chicken or the egg to his positioning of his dream self in space and time, Kenneth was unclear, and whenever he tried to think about it in daylight, he gave himself a headache.

What did seem logical was to suppose that, sooner or later, something important was going to happen in this wasteland. While there were still times when he would find himself wandering alone, his heart sodden with the soul-crushing sadness he refused to give in to when awake, the fantasy environment grew, in general, busier and busier. On one occasion, a group of well-dressed men with clipboards and binoculars were standing in a cluster, talking amongst themselves, pointing at buildings, and trying very hard not to look as though they were trying to look important. On another, Kenneth caught sight of the first motor vehicle to invade his dream-space – an open truck, in an unflattering military green, trying to find something which might approximate to a smooth path through the urban wilds. Despite his worldliness, Kenneth could not suppress the leap of excitement within as he saw the men grappling with the large, clumsy contrivance mounted on the back of it, and realised that the machine was nothing other than a motion-picture camera.

It was at this point that, back in the real world, events conspired to disrupt Kenneth's access to his nocturnal universe. Sleeplessness inspired by the energetic personal life of the teenage couple who moved into the bedsit next door to his, and problems with plumbing and Housing Benefit led Kenneth to resort to the combination of cheap sherry and over-the-counter herbal remedies. Thus, for a good few weeks, abject insomnia alternated with a restless stupor, and his nights were dreamless, to the extent that he fancied that he was forgetting all about his post-war Metropolitan wanderings.

It was with a jolt, then, that following an unusually depressed evening, Kenneth found himself once more in his dream landscape. This time, however, it was far from deserted. This time, it was simply crawling with excitable, greasy-haired Cockney urchins, mostly male, some in their Sunday best, others rather less well turned-out. He looked down, and was pleased to note that his suit was clean and freshly ironed; however, reaching up to run his fingers through his fictional hair, he discovered it to be more disturbingly oleaginous even than before.

He had no time to worry about this, however. All too abruptly, the unruly throng was being called to order by a tall man with a megaphone, standing, with a group of other men, near the movie camera which Kenneth now remembered from before, along with various other impressively complicated-looking technical equipment. "Alright, you chaps", he shouted, the plumminess of his voice unable to mask his nervousness. "Now, all we want you to do is run... from over here... to over there – shouting and cheering as you go. Remember – you're on an adventure. You are the good guys, and you're running after the bad guys, it's jolly simple, really."

He paused as he detected a slight rumbling in the ranks. Kenneth too had registered it, and slowly realised that its source was somewhere in his vicinity. He looked around, to find a knot of grubby-faced youths glaring at him.

"'Oo are you?!'"

"Yeah! What you doin', musclin' in!"

Just as the jostling began, a speedily-despatched underling arrived in its midst. "I say, what's going on here?"

"It's 'im, sir", piped up the smallest of Kenneth's tormentors. "He ain't from round 'ere. You can't 'ave people just turnin' up, can you?"

The underling fixed the dissident with a stern eye. "It's up to us who ends up in the final edit," he pointed out, adding, with more than a hint of threat, "Alright?"

And he was gone, leaving the discontented youngsters staring at the ground. Kenneth took advantage of their discomfiture to relocate himself within the crowd, noting, incidentally, that while he must have been by some margin the oldest "boy" there, the clothing and demeanour of some of the taller youths put at least ten years onto them, making him feel somewhat less conspicuous than he otherwise might.

"And... action!", cried the director, eventually, and the boys ran their allotted fifty yards, screaming, yelping, kicking, trampling, growling and blaspheming, Kenneth amongst them, trying to remember what it was like to be eleven years old and carefree, in a time before puberty, before exams, before cool, before brown envelopes from the Department of Employment asking you to go along for informal chats.

"Alright, alright. Let's try that again, shall we? And do make an effort this time!"

And all too soon, Kenneth was awake. As he lay waiting for his eyes to open, a puzzled exhilaration mingled with the strange sense of finality in his gut – he knew, with an icy certainty, that the dream had reached its natural conclusion.

It was a week later, the whole unsettling experience almost lost to memory, that he slumped, mug of tea in hand, in front of his antique black-and white television to watch the afternoon movie. It was *Hue and Cry*, directed by Charles Crichton, and billed as "a lively Ealing comedy with exemplary use of London locations". The story concerned a gang of criminals using a boys' magazine to transmit information, and the eventual foiling of said nefarious scheme by its youthful readership. The climactic sequence came near the end, as "all boys seeking adventure", having being clued in by a cunningly planted BBC radio announcement, were making their way from all parts of the city to apprehend the evildoers.

And, as though it were the most natural thing in the world, there was Kenneth, as clear as day, at the edge of a bunch of youths running high-spiritedly over a long-since re-developed patch of urban wasteland, his grin wide to the point of instability, his too-tight suit being splattered with mud, his mop of oily hair flopping annoyingly from side to side, his gaze visibly shifting towards the camera on at least two occasions, and a small youth running behind him, obviously trying and failing to trip him up.

Kenneth failed to take in the remainder of the film. He sat for an hour or so, staring into the middle distance, wondering whether he had either lost his mind, or was about to. On a sudden inspiration, he leapt to his feet, gathered together some small change, and ran down to the pay-phone, where he spent an awkward ten minutes questioning his bemused father as to any male relatives, distant or otherwise, who might have been wasting their time in the London area around 1946. The answer was no. Kenneth decided to defer questions about any history of insanity in the family until another time.

The dreamless, sleepless night that followed was more than an inconvenience, since Kenneth had an interview for some low-grade clerical post first thing in the morning. He rose, washed, dressed, and breakfasted on automatic pilot. It was in this same mode of preoccupation that he underwent the interview, forgetting completely to be nervous, and parroting his qualifications and experience with a disinterest which, as it turned out, was mistaken for supreme confidence. Telephoning back that afternoon, Kenneth was strangely unmoved when he was informed that he had got the job, and would be starting on Monday.

Virtually the first thing Kenneth did, on receiving his first pay-slip, was to rent a VCR, and watch the copy of *Hue and Cry* that he'd already purchased, in order to verify his presence. He watched it several times over the next few months, chilling himself to the bone on every occasion. His new spending power enabled him to move into a proper flat, and also emboldened him to the extent that he started asking girls out again. There came the stage during every embryonic relationship where he would test the water by sitting down with them to watch "my favourite film". If, at the crucial moment, the young lady noticed nothing untoward, Kenneth would find himself losing interest, and the liaison tended to founder.

It was the fifth girl who perked up as the climactic scene unfolded. "Stone me", said Venetia. "That bloke looks just like you! The absolute dead spit!"

"Yes". Kenneth affected a casualness which failed to conceal the tremor in his voice. "I've always thought that, actually."

Venetia looked searchingly into his eyes. "Yes. Weird things like that happen, don't they? And you wonder if there's a meaning. And usually, there isn't. But... look... you're going to think I'm a loony or something, but... have you ever seen a film called 'Black Narcissus'? It was made in the forties, and it's about these nuns in the Himalayas, and... well, I was going through a bit of a rough time, and I was having these dreams, and...."

And Kenneth smiled his first genuine smile for many, many months.

PEACHES

Jo Hughes

I don't know why my mother told me our true family history at the particular time she chose. There seemed no reason for it. I'd suspected nothing and hadn't been asking questions. I suppose she'd been turning it around in her head for all those years, letting it grow ripe until it was full and plump and soft and close to the point of bursting.

The day she told me was hot – a real scorcher, and I was out in the back garden lying on a scratchy old tartan blanket. I had the top-twenty on the radio, so it must have been a Sunday. I'd shouted for her to came out and bring me a drink and to put some more sun oil on my back. She came, carrying a tray laden with the lemonade I'd asked for, a gin and tonic for herself and a plate of sandwiches made just how I liked them; cut into triangles with the crusts off and a little sprig of parsley crowning them. There were also some nice fresh peaches, which I reached for first. I picked the fattest, juiciest-looking one and turned it over in my hand, occasionally bringing it to my nose so that I could breathe in the sweet promise of its flesh while enjoying the tactile sensation of its furred skin. I glanced at my mother. She was watching me and grimacing. For her the surface of a peach was like the scratch of a finger nail on a blackboard. Her look, I must admit, made me caress the peach all the more.

"Ai! How can you do that!" she shuddered. In reply I bit in.

I was wearing my first bikini which was made of black shiny nylon. The garden must have been the one which belonged to the house in Ealing. The one that overlooked the common. Because I remember that after my mother unburdened her dreadful secrets, I sat unmoving in the twilight listening to the distant and joyous screams and the rattle of machinery and the hum of generators and the thumping distorted bass of the music from the fair. So it must have been August of 1978; the summer when I turned 15 and had my first boyfriend, first bra and first cigarette.

I was at that age when I'd begun to call mother by her Christian name – a thing she resented by the looks she flashed me when I said it, but as she never actually forbade it I carried on in my own sweet way. I was, I suppose, at that most difficult of ages, desperate to shed myself of childhood, to shake myself free, but yet filled with the arrogance and ennui of barely tarnished innocence.

Maybe mother could sense my transformation approaching, could smell it in the air or see it glittering darkly in my eyes. Perhaps that was why she acted when she did, catching me on the brink of change and holding me there with her secrets.

So, there I was in the garden, fifteen years old. Small breasted and skinny in a bikini built for a woman. Thinking I knew it all and about to discover that I actually knew nothing. About to learn that truth was a variable; a mere surface, like the flawless skin of a ripe fruit which hides the maggot. "Eleanor," said my mother, "there's something I have to tell you."

I sighed distractedly and undid my bikini top so that she could rub the oil on my back. I folded my arms in front of my chest in order to keep my breasts securely hidden, though there was no one to see them besides her.

"It's something you have to know. It will make you understand. It's about me and your grandmother really."

All I had said to this was, "Is this going to take a long time? Because I was going to go around Patrick's later to do some work on our project..."

"Oh, that boy," said my mother with agony in her voice and I thought she was going to give me her usual lecture about Patrick and 'nice boys' and my reputation and getting into trouble, but instead she'd said, "I'll be as brief as I can." So I resigned myself to listening, at least for a short while.

She began, "My father was..." then stopped herself. "Oh! How to tell it? Your grandfather he was... No, no, no. Now listen, you know that I was born in France in 1944? About the time of the liberation?"

"Yes," I'd said, putting all the boredom and sarcasm I could muster into my voice, but she chose to ignore this and carried on. Unstoppable like she'd sometimes be.

"The war years were very hard – it wasn't like it seems in the history books. It wasn't just soldiers and leaders. It was surviving day after day, getting by any way you could. There's nothing neat about it. War is a mess. It was not knowing what's going to happen. Imagine growing up in all that, being a young girl, wanting all those things that young girls want, wanting love."

"So?" I said archly. "You didn't live through that, you were just a baby."

In reply my mother merely gave a long drawn out sigh and took her hands from my back and tapped my shoulder twice to signal she'd done with the sun oil.

"I'm telling you how it was, just like my mother told me."

I reached around to do up my bikini again, sliding my fingers over the hot slippery surface of my back, then I turned to face her. She was rhythmically wiping the fingers of one hand on the edge of the rug and her head was bent down with her left hand clasped over her mouth as if she wanted to silence herself. I thought I'd better shut up and listen or I'd never get to Patrick's and it was important I get to Patrick's that day as his family were away for the weekend.

So I said, to placate her, "Please, tell me, Mum. Please."

My mother lifted her head and I saw that her eyes were swimming in tears. Maybe it was me calling her 'Mum' again that softened her, went straight to her heart like a knife. Maybe that's how it was with mothers, you only had to say 'Mum' or 'please' and they melted into the old clinging memories of hope.

"I wish," she began then, "I wish I didn't have to tell you, but you must know."

I nodded sympathetically.

"Your grandfather was a soldier..."

Well, this I knew. Wasn't that why we'd ended up in England? Hadn't there been the liberation and D-day and the soldiers, both American and British, swarming over France?. All of them lonely khaki heroes finding grateful love in the arms of pretty French women? Wasn't that what liberation was all about? Bottles of champagne and Pernod and dark red Claret uncovered from secret cellars to bless the lips and tongues of these laughing and hungry men? And everyone drunk on freedom and the sky an endless blue and laughter easy and language among the Babel of races reduced to signs and kisses and beckoning fingers; the gestures of pleasure in food and wine and love.

I had always thought that it was quite romantic the way my grandmother and grandfather had met, the way he'd brought her back to England like a trophy of war. Despite the big difference in their ages, the gulf between her youth and beauty and his lack of any discernible charms. Although I must admit that into certain dark shadows of untold detail I'd always painted my own bright colours. There was also the problem of dates, of birth and marriage. I suspected that my mother might be illegitimate, but what did it matter? It made everything all the more interesting. "Now," I had thought, "Now she's going to admit it."

"Your grandfather's name was Holger Herzog…"

I stared dumbly at my mother. At first only taking in the information that this was not the name of the man I always called 'Grandpa'. This was not the blunt Yorkshireman called Archibald Bratly who masqueraded in the role of grandfather to this day; sitting in his armchair by the fire, chafing his hands together and saying, "Make another brew, pet. I'm parched."

I imagined this was exactly what he was doing at that very moment. While my grandmother, accent still so thick you could cut it with a good French kitchen knife, would be scuttling off to the kitchen and obediently rattling the kettle, teapot and cups into service.

But then, the name. The name! Holger Herzog! This was no French name. This name was surely German.

The sun disappeared behind a small single cloud and no sooner had our eyes adjusted to the shadowless world than it appeared again, blinding and dazzling us. I blinked at mother and shaded my eyes. My breath came in shallow insubstantial gasps.

"Oh God," I had said, "oh *God.* "

Mother watched me. She looked ashamed, like a child caught out in a lie. "I am *so* sorry," she whispered.

I wanted to get away from her. I wanted at that instant to be transported to Patrick's house. I wanted to be in his arms in the big hammock on the patio that overlooked his parents' garden; to tell him this thing, this terrible thing and cry and be comforted. Even then I imagined it more as my mother's delusion than anything like truth.

Instead, I listened to my mother's words – what else could I do? And let her distractedly stroke the soles of my feet and ankles like she used to when I was little.

Later she called a taxi for me to go to Patrick's and stood on the pavement under the trees waving sadly as the cab drew away. I sat there watching as she shrank into the distance and the shadows, and rehearsed my first words to Patrick. I imagined myself falling into his arms, sobbing and faint as his concern and love washed over me.

I imagined many things during that short journey as I held myself hunched up in the corner of the cab, my head pressed hard against the dirty cool glass of its window. Most of them to do with Patrick.

Patrick's family seemed to me to be very rich, though Patrick, echoing his parents, said they were merely 'comfortable'. They lived in a large 1930's mock-Tudor mansion in a quiet leafy avenue near Walpole Park. His father did something for the BBC and his mother played the cello and both were, consequently, often away on business or tours. Their house was like something out of Ideal Home magazine. I couldn't imagine how anyone could live in such spotless perfection. It was as if their lives glided over the surface of everything without substance, as if their glands sent forth polish instead of sweat.

Patrick, their only child, was the sole blemish under their roof. His hair was cropped on top so that it stood up on end and reminded me of a hedgehog's back, except that when you touched it, it was soft. He wore old men's home-knitted sweaters that were always about three or four sizes too big and whose sleeves and necks ended in ragged loose ends of trailing wool. He spoke with a lazy cockney accent and his voice was husky from too many cigarettes.

When he came to the door he was wearing dark glasses with mirror lenses so that when I looked for his eyes all I saw was my face, pig-like, reflected back at me. Somehow in the taxi I'd imagined that my tears and the telling of my misery would just happen, but once there in the cool hall with him, I felt numb and dry; shrivelled somehow.

As soon as Patrick had shut the front door he put his arms around me and I, in return, wrapped my arms around his waist and put my head against his chest and shut my eyes. I could feel the plastic of his sunglasses digging into my head as he rested his head on mine. We stood like that for a long time swaying from side to side, almost, but not quite, dancing. It dawned on me as I stood there that this thing I wanted to tell him, this miserable truth that weighed on me was all wrong. I wanted his comfort and pity but I was on the wrong side. I wasn't on the side of the victims, or even the heroes, I was the aggressor. Either that or I was the daughter of a mad woman.

I kept remembering the figure of my mother under the trees outside our house – her small head and tiny body and raven-black hair which she wore in tight, Shirley Temple curls which gave her the appearance of a shrunken doll. She embarrassed me. She'd embarrassed me for as long as I could remember but until now I didn't know why. I thought it was those insignificant things like her stupid hairstyle, her continual fussing over me, the way she could never keep a man, the frown marks between her eyes, her slow and hesitant way of speaking.

I considered this as I stood rocking gently, but this other image of my mother kept clouding my resentment. Well, not an image so much as a smell and that smell was eau de Cologne on warm skin. But it wasn't just a smell either it was also a feeling; a feeling of security. And a place I'd been once. I felt tired suddenly; mesmerised by the black and white checkerboard of tiles swaying at my feet. Against my hip I could feel some hard part of Patrick pressed and his breath was hot on my neck. With some awkwardness I lifted my face towards his and pecked at his cheek leaving the imprint of my lipstick there. He responded by finding my mouth and holding me tighter.

I always shut my eyes when we kissed and I assumed that he had also removed himself to some blind place where sensation depended on touch and taste and sound and smell alone. Patrick and I were quite expert at kissing; that liquid drilling of our mouths and the tight press of our bodies. We could do it for hour after hour and frequently did. Standing up or sitting side by side with our bodies twisted at the waist towards each other or lying stretched full length. I had been waiting for the next stage which, I assumed, would be set in motion by Patrick, as he was the male and the elder and more experienced. This next stage would be the opening of my blouse, the unclasping of my bra, the coldness of his hand on the hot swell of my breast. Whenever I thought about this I would shiver deliciously and butterflies would leap and claw at the pit of my belly. But after six months all I had known of Patrick was the swirling tongue and the mysterious press of his body. I was beginning to doubt him, to not trust the looks and kisses. Yet when he put his arm around my neck it felt right, cool like water, part of me but not part of me.

I entertained myself as we stood there endlessly kissing by wondering whether kissing felt the same for everyone? Whether another boy would be completely different? How it felt for Patrick to kiss me? And, disturbingly, whether it had felt like this when my grandmother had kissed her German soldier? It was just as that last question rose in my mind that Patrick gathered all the courage and passion he'd been storing up for six months and without warning clamped his hand clumsily on my right breast.

My reaction was electric. It was as if the German, my supposed grandfather (bearer, upholder and celebrant of the ugliest episode in recent history possible) had lifted his claw in France and brought it down upon my breast over thirty years later. I leapt back gasping and opened my eyes to see poor Patrick – a look of absolute horror on his face. My own face, I reasoned, must have worn a mirror image of his expression. Or worse, exposed this terrible heritage of mine, the inherited cruelty and destruction, the love of marching and killing, the blue of my eyes, the grey of my heart.

I turned and made for the stairs, walking at first then running, taking the steps two or three at a time. Finally I plunged into the bathroom before slamming and bolting the door behind me. It was quiet up there. Quiet and cool as all sanctuaries should be. The bathroom, like the rest of the house, was immaculate, everything seemed to have been carefully arranged. From the colour-co-ordinated towels on the rail to the orderly ranks of expensive bath oil and perfume, to the trailing stems and leaves of palms and ivy and spider plants which seemed to curl or fall or stab the air in artful shapes which belied nature.

I lay down on the carpet studying the ceiling while tears ran down the sides of my face and gathered in pools around my ears, trying to stifle my louder sobs. I knew that sooner or later Patrick would come to find me.

Eventually, the door handle was gently turned. I heard a soft, hesitant tapping at the door, then Patrick's voice, "Ellie? Are you OK? I'm sorry. El? Can you hear me? I'm sorry."

Back in the garden at home my mother had told me that the man who fathered her wasn't all bad. That not all Germans had been bad. Not even all the German soldiers. She said that maybe, somehow the fact that love could still happen even in circumstances like that meant that life was worthwhile. I was disgusted by her using the word 'love' like that. I thought she used it just to soften the truth. Or even, God forbid, to romanticise this thing.

Then she told me, and by then I was trying not to listen, trying not to hear or care or remember any of it, what had happened to Holger Herzog.

Though, first she said, "Do you know how old this soldier was? He was just seventeen years old. The same age as that Patrick boy." I was surprised by that, but somehow I couldn't quite erase the dreadful image I'd created of a brutish man snarling his thick-necked guttural language into the vulnerable world and trailing destruction in his black-booted wake.

The villagers had caught him and my grandma hiding in a barn, "clinging to each other like Hansel and Gretel", mother said. They'd been wrenched apart and he had been dragged through the peach orchard by the leaders of the resistance and, helped by a small group of drunken Allied soldiers, he'd been strung from the highest tree.

As she spoke, I could not help (and perhaps this was a form of self-protection, a process by which all became a fiction as unreal as a comic strip) but imagine the rope around Patrick's throat, his neck fine and soft and delicate as a girl's, twisted and pinched by the noose. And his eyes wet with tears, fearful, tortured, knowing the end of his life was only minutes away. And beneath their feet, the wind-fallen fruits were crushed, their broken flesh giving off a sickly sweet perfume.

Then she had told me what had been done to my grandmother; the clumsy shaving of her head, the threats, the way they had marched her around the town and spat at her. But worst of all they'd made her watch him die. She felt she had killed him.

My mother and I had sat quietly after all those words, both of us exhausted. Then she'd said, "How many wrongs, do you think, it takes to make a right?"

I stood up and turned on the cold tap and splashed my face with water. I picked up one of the bottles of scent from the glass shelf and unscrewed the cap and tipped the bottle against one wrist, then rubbed my wrist against my neck. I felt better then, ready to face Patrick again.

I unlocked the bathroom door and there he was. The dark glasses were gone and his eyes looked red, as if he had been crying. He said, "I'm really sorry, El." I put my arms around him and said, "It wasn't that," and to prove it I took his hand and guided it under my t-shirt and placed it on my breast and he let out a little sigh that could have been pleasure and could have been relief. "Come on," said Patrick, taking hold of my hand, before leading me out of the bathroom and down the stairs, "let's listen to some music." We walked together towards the back of the house to a room I hadn't been in before. At the door Patrick stopped and said, "The best stereo is in here, this is the old girl's music room," before kneeling down at my feet and unfastening my sandals, "so you have to take your shoes off." He smiled up at me as I stood there barefoot, my eyes still stinging from all the crying I'd done, as he gently ran his fingers over my calves and an inch or so up my thighs. Then he stood and opened the door and ushered me in with a sweeping gesture.

I entered a room that was almost entirely white. The carpet was white, the walls were white, the fireplace a high snowy marble one whose streaks of silver and black merely emphasised the whiteness of the rest. The end of the room was dominated by a huge window hung with curtains of white muslin, in front of which was a white grand piano.

The only things which had any colour were the records – shelf after shelf – and the sheet music and the framed concert posters and photographs. A cello was propped by the grand like a squat, brown-skinned soprano waiting for the appearance of the pianist. It balanced its bulk on one impossibly slim leg.

I would have liked to touch it, to have drawn same noise from it, committing, no doubt, some violence on the untarnished air. Or better, I would have liked to have sat straddling its hourglass figure and to take up the bow and find, by same curious magic, that music, low and throbbing, swept from my sawing fingers. But I dared not. Instead, while Patrick ran upstairs to get some albums from his bedroom, I strolled around the room, studying everything. There were piles of sheet music, some of it clearly very old. I opened one at random and ran my eye along rows of an alien language; the crotchets and quavers and semi-quavers whose connection and translation into the sounds of horn or violin or cello seemed, to me, an impossible miracle. I felt like an intruder in this room – everything about it was too pure and I half understood the destruction wreaked by burglars in rooms like this. Yet I also felt a part of it all as if my relationship with Patrick gave me licence, made me valid, made me more than myself.

One wall of the room was almost entirely filled from floor to ceiling with posters, photographs, programmes and news cuttings. Each had its own frame and while these were of different shapes, styles and colours, the cacophony of their patchwork arrangement made a whole. I began to look more carefully, reading names, dates, details.

At one end, nearest the window, I found the face of the woman I knew as Patrick's mother. Her hair was a colour that played it safe, occupying the territory which existed between a young sensual platinum blond and a more staid and sensible white. It was long and she wore it drawn back, either, as on the day I met her, in a silvery ponytail, or for more formal occasions, in an upswept bun or chignon. In the most recent photograph she was accepting an award of some sort and smiling a Mona Lisa smile at a man in evening dress as he handed her some shiny metal thing on a small plinth. Above that was a brightly coloured poster which advertised 'Summer in the City; a series of lunchtime recitals in the Barbican Centre'. Patrick's mother was listed to play on Saturday the 5th of May of that year.

As I progressed down the wall the clippings from newspapers became more yellowed and the style of the posters more staid, and his mother's face shed the years; growing smoother skin and more clearly defined bones, shaking her hair loose and letting its golden highlights shine more brightly. Halfway down the wall she even shed

her name. Now, no longer did she call herself Rachel Murphy.
Instead she went by the name of Rachel Greenberg and there she
was, a tiny slip of a girl posing with a nervous smile (gone was the
knowing Mona Lisa), her hair in two long plaits, on the gangplank
of a ship with the unmistakable bulk of a cello case beside her.
Beneath, the caption read, "Child protégé flees Nazi Europe."

That afternoon in the garden with my mother seemed a long
long time ago. I sensed that from that moment on my life would
always be divided between knowing and not knowing, innocence
(intoxicating, blind sweet innocence) and knowledge. I remembered
that last glimpse of my mother under the trees and her secret seemed
like a black hole which sucked everything in upon itself. I
remembered too, her hand raised; the palm offered, in not so much
a wave of farewell, as a gesture that meant stop.

Patrick, on finding Eleanor standing quietly looking at the
picture collection, crept up behind her and gently put one arm
around her waist. He felt her stomach contract beneath his fingers
and her hands moved to rest on his. With his free hand he drew the
hair from her neck. She smelt sweet and her skin was warm; the nape
of her neck softly furred with fine pale hair. He put his mouth there
and licked, but his tongue found a bitter chemical taint and he was
disappointed. He'd imagined she'd taste like she smelled – of
peaches.

BURIED TREASURE

Don Rodgers

Hywel sat on a deserted part of the beach, his legs drawn up under him. He watched his older brother, Ifan, stooping to pick up stones to throw at the gulls.

This was the new Ifan: the Ifan that took pleasure, so it seemed, in stoning gulls.

It was with this Ifan, on another beach further up the coast, that he'd gone to watch the fishermen. They had planted their rods in the sand just out of reach of the waves, like thin trees. He and Ifan had been close to one of these when it had started shaking; the tip had quivered first, and then the whole top had trembled with sharp little jerks and spasms, and the fisherman had come running down the beach and had uprooted the rod and hauled it back high above his head and reeled in an eel. At first they had seen it just as a local disturbance in the water, a threshing just under the surface, and then there had been glimpses of silver, and then the eel twisting and turning on itself, twining itself into knots. They had watched as the fisherman extracted the hook from the mouth. It had got stuck and at last he had torn it free impatiently, tearing the eel's jaw. The eel had been covered in a slime that came off on the fisherman's hands but which he didn't seem to notice. He'd put the eel, still writhing, in a blue plastic box with holes and a strap, full of damp seaweed and buzzed round by black flies. And he'd shut the lid on all the wriggling, the frenzy, the throes. And Hywel had turned to Ifan, and Ifan had been grinning. Grinning. And he, Hywel, had wanted to cry. To find a dark hole, to burrow down into the sand, into a dark hole, and to be left alone.

Hywel was startled out of his recollections by the cries of the gulls as they rose in alarm off the beach.

"Stupid buggers!" Ifan shouted at them as they flew out of reach of his stones.

Hywel realised then that, without being aware of it, he had

been digging sand out from beside him with his hand, digging a little tunnel back into the slope where the sand was firmer. His fingers had stopped their work because they'd come up against something hard. A stone? Probably. Or maybe treasure. Buried treasure. A little gold casket full of pieces of eight, doubloons and... and things. Diamonds maybe.

Hywel looked up. Ifan was walking up the beach towards him but not looking his way as yet. Hywel pulled his arm out of the tunnel and quickly moved his towel to cover the hole. It was his treasure.

Ifan came and stood over him. Hywel felt, not for the first time recently, a twinge of fear.

"Come on. Race you down to the sea!" Ifan said. "Ready, steady -"

Hywel was up and off before "go", he knew that trick all right, he was up and running barefoot over the warm sand down to the sea.

But of course Ifan got there first. He always won. He was twelve and a foot taller than Hywel, who was nine.

"Slowcoach!"

"I'm not a slowcoach. I trod on a pebble, that's all."

The wet sand that the tide had been lapping over was cold under their feet. It was September and though the sun was still warm there was a chilly breeze.

"Let's play ducks and drakes" Ifan said. "Bet I beat you."

And before Hywel could say anything, Ifan was already picking up all the best stones.

How many times had they played this game? On rivers, lakes, ponds? Countless times already. And how many times had one of Hywel's stones outskipped those of his brother? That was easier to count: nought, nil, zero, zilch. It was a stupid game. And anyway, could you play it on the sea?

"Get a move on" Ifan's voice rang out imperiously. As always, and as usual almost to his surprise, Hywel found himself obeying.

At the beginning Hywel picked up stones randomly, half-heartedly; but he soon found his blood warming to the challenge. After all, this time he might win. Why not? If he could only find that perfect stone...

Five minutes later Hywel was still on all fours, scrabbling about along the line of pebbles and shells washed up by the sea.

"Do get a move on, Hywel boy. A tortoise is like the road runner next to you."

Hywel boy. Ifan had started calling him that not so long ago, after their mother died. He didn't like it, although he didn't quite know why. Then one day, shortly after that, when he'd called him "Ianto" as usual, his brother had rounded on him, almost viciously.

"Ifan to you, Hywel boy" he'd said. And from then on he was Ifan.

They had five throws each, that was the rule. He only had four stones.

"Look, do you want one of mine?"

Hywel looked up. To see Ifan standing over him, tendering him a smooth flat pebble, a real beauty. He couldn't believe it. He was right. For when he looked up to Ifan's face he saw a sneer. His grey eyes in their mask of freckles were glinting. Perhaps it was just the sun – the sun that made his red hair burn. His, Hywel's, hair was brown, boring old brown.

Hywel snatched the pebble from the outstretched hand, catching Ifan by surprise.

"Give it me back!"

Hywel scuttled sideways on his hams like a crab, out of reach of the swiping hand.

"You said I could have it."

"Give it me back or I'll break your neck." Ifan was always threatening to break his neck these days. But he hadn't done it yet. Just punched him on the arm. On the soft upper arm just below the shoulder. Always the same spot. It hurt.

Ifan advanced on him.

"Give it me." His voice was icy.

As usual now, a desire to stand up to his brother fought with a tide of panic, of fear. As usual, fear and panic won.

"I don't want to play anyway." Hywel threw all the stones – Ifan's and his own four carefully chosen pebbles – out into the sea. They scattered and made five different plops.

Hywel stomped back up the beach, trying not to cry. What

had happened to the Ifan of before? The one he'd gone to see The Jungle Book with at the cinema that time? Afterwards, in the sitting-room, they'd danced round the furniture swinging their arms and singing "Scooby-doo, I want to be like you-oo-oo." They'd laughed so much they'd hugged each other for support. The warmth and closeness then, Hywel would never forget it. But now – where had that Ifan gone?

Hywel sniffed. But no, he wasn't going to cry again. Ifan hadn't cried. Ifan had called him a cry baby. Dad had cried though, when he came back from the hospital without Mam. But Ifan hadn't cried, so he wasn't going to either – not any more.

Hywel looked round. Dad was round the corner out of view, on a more sheltered part of the beach. There was nobody here. Just him and Ifan.

Then Hywel remembered his treasure. In the heat of the moment he'd forgotten all about it.

He sat down on the towel nonchalantly – not quite whistling, but almost – and after checking that Ifan was busy trying to skip stones over the waves and failing – reached his hand back down his tunnel. Yes. It was still there.

Hywel's fingers scratched at the surface of the buried treasure. It was hard all right. And knobbly. It definitely felt knobbly. A knobbly casket? Well it didn't feel like a stone anyway. He scraped away some more of the sand round the object, until he could get his whole hand round it. Perhaps it wasn't a casket after all; but treasure, oh yes, it was definitely treasure of some sort.

"What are you doing?"

Hywel jumped. Ifan's voice had come from right by his ear. He had crept up without him noticing.

"Nothing." Hywel could feel his ears warm up like an electric fire and his whole face go red. Stupid, stupid face.

"What's in there?"

"Nothing."

"Let me see then."

"No."

"I thought you said there was nothing."

"There isn't."

"Then let me see."

"You can't."

"Why not?"

"It's mine."

"You said there was nothing there."

"There isn't."

"But it's yours."

"Yes."

Ifan made a lunge for the hole, Hywel grabbed his arm, and the two of them wrestled for a moment, rolling over and over in the sand. The outcome was a foregone conclusion: Hywel sprawled on his back on the sand, Ifan sitting on his chest, his knees pinning down Hywel's arms.

"Let's have a look at this nothing then, shall we? I've never seen nothing before" Ifan said, his voice all sarcasticky. He leant over without shifting his weight off Hywel, who was getting more and more squashed, and reached down inside the hole.

"A funny sort of nothing," Ifan said.

"It's mine," Hywel protested.

"Shut up," Ifan replied calmly, "or I'll sit on your face."

Hywel shut up at once. It was no idle threat that on Ifan's part. He'd done it before. It had smelt awful.

Hywel watched helpless as Ifan used a bit of broken shell as a digger. At last, with a grunt of effort, Ifan brought out the treasure.

It was a toy hand-grenade. At least, it had to be a toy one, didn't it? Hywel was reasonably sure it was plastic. He thought he'd seen some like it in a shop in the town, near the buckets and spades. Some boy must have lost it. Or buried it for a game.

Ifan was turning it over and over in his hands, gazing at it in admiration. He stood up, holding it cupped in the palms of his hands, looking for all the world as if it were precious water from an oasis and he was going to drink. Hywel was able to wriggle out backwards from between his legs.

"It's got a gold pin, an arm and everything" Ifan said.

"It's only plastic. It's a toy," Hywel said, on his feet now, a few yards from Ifan; wary.

Ifan looked at him.

"What makes you think that, Hywel boy? Oh no. It's a real one. A real live hand-grenade. From the second World War, I should think. A soldier's."

Hywel wasn't sure how to react. He couldn't always tell when his brother was serious and when he was joking. Especially not these days.

"What you do," Ifan said in a voice like a teacher, "is to pull the pin out with your teeth, while holding the lever down against the body of the grenade. Like so."

Hywel didn't want his brother to see he was getting scared. He knew it wasn't a real one, it was only a toy one like in that shop. But there again, what if it wasn't really?

"If I let go of it now, it will explode in three seconds, scattering deadly shrapnel all over the place. Blowing you to bits. To millions of smithereens, Hywel boy."

Ifan's eyes were glinting again. Hywel suddenly felt like running away. But that would be silly. It was only a game, wasn't it?

"I'm going to blow you up," Ifan went on calmly, coldly, "because you're a cry baby. You and dad are both cry babies. You both cry about nothing."

Hywel felt his chin quiver. For the first time he felt that his brother really disliked him, hated him even.

Ifan grinned a sickly grin.

"Run rabbit, run."

Hywel didn't understand.

"Go on Hywel boy, run, run. I'm going to blow all cry babies to smithereens. You'd better run rabbit run. Run, run, run!" Ifan's voice rose up wild and angry.

Before Hywel could run, before he could properly understand what was happening, Ifan had thrown the grenade at him. It hit him on the leg and fell onto the sand by his foot.

"One, two..." Ifan started counting in a shouting, laughing voice.

In complete terror, Hywel scooped the grenade off the sand and sent it flying back at Ifan. It hit him full on the chest.

"Three!" Ifan shouted, laughing and laughing till the tears ran down his face. "Boom!" went Ifan and jumped in the air and fell flat on his back, arms and legs apart, still laughing. "Boom! I'm dead. You've killed me. I'm dead."

Ifan lay on his back on the sand, laughing so much his body

flapped about – flapped about like a fish caught on the end of a line.

Hywel stood still, staring wide-eyed at his brother, who was lying on the sand, still shaking, but not with laughter now. He had turned onto his front and was burrowing with his hands down into the sand, until both arms were buried up to the elbows. The sand would hold his arms and be cold and clammy on them.

"I'm dead," Ifan repeated, but in a softer, tireder voice, a voice that reminded Hywel of the old Ifan. "We're both dead," he said. And at last Ifan lay still, his face, wet with tears, turned away from Hywel towards the sea.

Hywel stood for a moment, undecided; then went and lay down beside his brother on the warm sand.

"I'm dead too," he said.

DEAD BLOKE

Jacinta Bell

Fifty quid, cash-in-hand. That's what Phil promised Lloyd if he did the job. He'd said it wouldn't take more than a couple of hours, just cleaning up the mess and putting the dead bloke's stuff into plastic bags. Someone else would pick up the rubbish later so the flat would be clear for the new tenant tomorrow. Couldn't afford to have flats standing empty any longer than that these days, not with the waiting list being so long; like with hospitals – admitting new patients before the beds were cold.

The door was ajar when Lloyd got there. He was glad, since both his hands were full, carrying buckets, mops, cleaning sprays and bleach, but the smell hit him as soon as he nudged the door open with his toe – rotten meat. He heaved as he breathed in the stale, putrescent air. Propping the door wide open with one of the buckets, he pulled his scarf up over his mouth and nose and lunged over to the window, unlocking the catch and letting it fall open. The air was colder than inside the flat and heavily-laden with carbon monoxide, but Lloyd didn't care. He stuck his head out and sucked in mouthfuls of it before clamping his scarf back over his mouth and surveying the room.

The bed was unmade, its sheets wrinkled and grey with a single matted brown blanket showing through as the dead bloke's only means of warmth, in the days when he was alive. A small upholstered chair sat to one side of the electric bar heater, a short square table next to it. On a small chest sat the dead bloke's telly – little portable black and white job. The wardrobe doors gaped open and Lloyd could see a solitary jacket hanging from the rail like the victim of a hangman's noose. A threadbare carpet covered the floorboards, dirty but unstained. That was a shame. Lloyd hoped the dead bloke had fallen on a carpet, then he'd just have to roll it up and throw it out, but there was no sign of any blood in here.

Lloyd opened the door next to him, behind which lay a tiny,

dark bathroom. The bath and basin were stained where the taps had dripped constantly down the years and the toilet seat was raised in readiness for the next user. The bowl was brown and marked with the detritus of living, the water sitting in the bowl still and old. Lloyd flicked down the seat. It landed on the porcelain with a crash, then he flushed the water away with equally old water that had been sitting in the cistern since the last time the dead bloke had taken a piss. He hadn't collapsed in the bathroom either.

Lloyd went out and put his head round the door to the kitchen. He wasn't surprised by what he saw. There was no lino on the floor, just bare floorboards where the dead bloke's blood had collected and settled, some of it seeping into the gaps between boards. It wasn't as bad as Lloyd had been expecting. Where once it had been fresh, deep liquid before turning tacky, it was now hard and brown, powdery at the edges. Age had taken its horror away.

"Alcoholic," Phil had told him, when he'd asked Lloyd to do the job. "He haemorrhaged. Must have been dead about three weeks, the doctor reckoned. We only found him because we'd gone to serve him with a notice to quit. Hadn't paid any rent for five months. We should've looked into it earlier but we're so bloody overstretched here."

Lloyd nodded.

"I feel a bit bad about it really. He'd been with us nearly four years. No trouble, rent on time, no complaints about the flat. It was only when we were audited last month that we realised he'd stopped paying rent. I was the one who interviewed him when he first applied to us. He'd been a musician – played the sax. Quite famous in his day, or so he said. Poke around his stuff, see if you find anything of interest – the police have already gone through it. What's left will only go to the dump. No next of kin. Sad really."

Sad really. The words echoed in Lloyd's mind as he looked at the place where the dead bloke had fallen, his last stand marked out by the bloody stain. He walked around it, as if the body still lay there, and opened the window.

He filled one of the buckets with cold water and wished he'd had the foresight to bring rubber gloves. Then he poured half a bottle of floor cleaner into the bucket and dropped the papery cloth into it, where it floated, criss-crossed pink and white, on the surface.

He pushed it down with the tips of his fingers, inhaling sharply as the chill stung his hands.

He slopped the cloth onto the edge of the stain, easing himself in gently to the idea of washing the blood away. As he rubbed at the marked floorboards he cursed himself for forgetting his Walkman. The silence was too loud.

He glanced around but couldn't see a radio or anything – you would have thought with the dead bloke being a musician and everything... Lloyd dismissed the criticism and thought about his own sound system that he'd bought last month. Well, not actually bought. He was still paying for it, and would be this time next year, but couldn't have survived without it. He needed music more than food. When he'd finished paying for that he'd seriously concentrate on getting himself that bass guitar. It cost so much more than the music system, though, and credit was impossible to get when you were on the dole. Especially for single men. Fly-by-nights, with no sense of responsibility.

He dropped the cloth onto the blood again. It was moistening but not shifting – rather it was the cloth dissolving with all his scrubbing. Jesus! They wouldn't give a job like this to someone doing Community Service, however bad their crime. He focused on the fifty quid, which he needed for the gig tonight. He'd persuaded that bloke from Virgin to come and listen to them play. He'd said on the 'phone how impressed he'd been with their demo tape and Lloyd knew it would be up to him to organise the drinks for him and everything. The band looked to Lloyd as their leader, relying on him for all things practical and artistic. He was the only one with drive and tonight, at last, was his big chance.

He sat back on his haunches and looked at the stain. He was getting nowhere. He leaned over and pulled open the cupboard door under the sink. It was empty but for an old scrubbing brush, its bristles chewed, and a bottle of cider lying on its side, the top pointing at Lloyd. He reached for the brush and soaked it in the bucket, then attacked the floorboards again with it. The effect was immediate, the bristles cutting right through the blood.

Lloyd felt better now that he was making progress. He glanced up at the cider bottle, the top, like an eye, watched him, and he wondered about the dead bloke. Maybe he'd been coming in here for that bottle when he'd collapsed and died. The last drink he'd never had. Lloyd felt a chill run down his spine, afraid of the depths that the dead bloke had sunk into. When had his music stopped?

The circular movement of Lloyd's brush lifted and liberated the blood as well as some coins which must have fallen from the dead bloke's pocket when he collapsed. Gingerly, he picked them up – three one pound coins and twenty-four pence in change. He looked at them, brown and soiled, in the palm of his hand and wondered what he should do with them. Blood money – he didn't want it, then caught sight of the cider bottle still pointing at him like the Lottery finger. Seemed a shame to leave them here. He threw them into the sink so he could clean them later.

Lloyd filled his bucket for the last time. One more rinse to wash away what little was left of the dead bloke. One musician wiping away another. He liked the idea of that – a thought without malice, raising the status of his job from the practical to the ethereal.

Having finished in the kitchen Lloyd started to fill bin bags with the dead bloke's rubbish. There were empty bottles rolling about in drawers as well as loose socks, a couple of pairs of baggy underpants, some used and clean handkerchiefs and one shirt rolled round an empty bottle of vodka. As he tore the sheets off the bed, three bottles jumped up into the air, one of them smashing as it hit the floor. He unhooked the dead bloke's jacket and squashed it on top of the other rubbish then tied the corners of the bag into a knot.

Three plastic bin liners were all the dead bloke left, mostly filled with empty bottles. There was no evidence of his life before the fall.

Lloyd washed the coins and put them in his jeans pocket. He didn't like the feel of them wet against his thigh, still unclean, and planned to drop them into a glass of Coke when he got home to really clean them up.

He dropped into the office on his way home to pick up the money.

"How was it?" Phil asked, handing over the notes.

"Okay. I left the windows open to try and get rid of the smell."

"I'll go round and close them later. Don't want squatters

getting in. Sorry I didn't make it to down there to help, but you can see how busy it is here."

Lloyd couldn't, but nodded anyway, then stuffed the notes into his back pocket. Fifty quid from Phil and three pounds twenty-four from the dead bloke. A whole week's money for an afternoon's work.

Walking home he was distracted by the bookie's office, its door wide open welcoming the spring. Lloyd could hear the drone of a race commentator from inside and followed the sound of the voice. He'd never been in before. Smoke hung in the air like smog and weary men lined the walls. Cigarette butts and balls of white paper peppered the floor, Lloyd inadvertently kicking them as he walked across to pick up a betting slip. He looked up at the names pinned to the boards and saw his horse at once. *Charlie Mingus*, running in the four-thirty at Cheltenham, with odds standing at twenty to one.

Lloyd passed his slip under the glass to a woman who started tapping the information into her till.

"Paying the tax now?"

"Yes." Lloyd pushed the notes towards her then pulled the sticky coins from his pocket and slid those through as well. The woman sneered before dropping them one by one into her till.

It didn't matter, Lloyd kept telling himself as he walked over to a seat. It didn't matter if he lost it all – it was fifty-three pounds and twenty-four pence that he hadn't had that morning. Easy come, easy go – he was losing nothing. He lifted his head to watch the television screen and wondered which was his horse.

Out on the street Lloyd trembled with cold, then heat, then thought he was going to be sick. The manager of the betting shop had just handed over nearly eleven hundred pounds, the notes were rolled and squashed tight in his hand. On jellied legs he walked down to the high street, through the passage and across the road to the shop where the Music Man Stingray bass guitar sat in the window tantalising passers-by. It was on special offer, *This Week Only* – £1069.99. With sweaty fingers Lloyd swapped his wad of notes for the instrument and carried it home like a new-born infant.

As he put the key in the lock of his front door he thought he heard the kid next door practising his clarinet, but when he stopped to listen the music was gone. He shivered, then very, very faintly, deep in the core of his being, he felt a nudge.

Good luck, boy.

WELSH LAMBS

Fiona Owen

Caryl is telling me the story of her life, and she's almost up-to-date. It has been a long hour, although I'm trying not to think about time, about the essay we should be discussing, about the fact that I've got a story too, with an as-yet unwritten ending. I am trying to give her my full attention, because I know that attention is what's needed in the world. I learnt this from Jan, but maybe I learned it too late. Now, I am practising what she always preached. I am leaning forward and holding this young woman's hand, supporting her, because the tension is building: she is coming to her climax.

"It's just that I thought we had something … special." Her voice breaks, and here come the tears; it's as though a thin membrane in her eyes swells to capacity then ruptures, spilling the contents. Tears/tears, I think, detached enough – how appalling – to consider the words side by side. I squeeze her hand, and we sit, then, in silence, because she is making no sound. Amazing, the way she abandons herself to the steady flow of pain down her face – just sits there, eyes downcast, with so much fluid running unstopped that I stare, rudely it feels. I jump up and fetch the Kleenex from the coffee table, pull one out, push it into her hand, sit back down.

"Thanks," she says, blowing her nose with a goose-like honk, which sounds outrageous in the tick-tocking hush of my parents' front room. I swallow hard on an inappropriate urge to laugh; fortunately, my gulp merely makes me sound moved.

Anxious to make amends, I lean more forward and say, "I think you should just take your time. No rush."

"Thanks," she says again, sniffing. "You're very kind."

I murmur a "Not at all." I in no way want to be thought of as any kind of hero figure. I have already, on three occasions, been on the brink of 'stealing the attention' – Jan's terminology – by telling her about my own experiences of broken love affairs at her age. And how easily I could go on, stealing. I could tell her all about

86

how I'm hurting more than she is, guaranteed, because doesn't she know that older hearts hurt more when they break than younger ones, and take twice as long to heal?

We sit in silence, across the table. Part of me feels fatherly, tender, honoured, almost, by this girl's ability to share her feelings with me, a virtual stranger. The other part is feeling out of his depth, embarrassed and unclear about how best to next proceed. At twenty something, this girl is just starting out on the road. There'll be plenty more knocks along the way, and this thought tires me, so that I sigh. Caryl raises her tragic eyes, all the waters running.

I search for something wise to say.

"I'm sure he didn't mean to hurt you. He just needed a change."

"But he *loved* me," she says. "I believe he really did. And you don't hurt what you love, do you?"

"No," I mumble, thinking of Jan and me, and some of the things I'd say in the heat of the moment. That was always my excuse. "I didn't mean it," I'd say. "It was the *heat of the moment*."

She'd be lying on the bed, maybe, crying and hurt, and I would see what I had done in my heat and, seeing it, coming to and seeing the scene for what it was, I would go to her and be sorrier than I'd ever been.

"Words wound, Alun," she'd whisper, stroking my hair, forgiving me. "They scar. You can't just hurl them at me like that, like pieces of flint. Imagine what real sticks and stones would do to my body if you threw them at me."

"But it's not quite the same," I'd say, resisting even then.

"It's *exactly* the same. Sticks and stones for the physical, words for the mental and emotional."

Jan's interested in Buddhist things, like right action, right speech. I am, too, but I'm all theory and spout, opting, I suppose, for the easier option of papering over the cracks.

"Would you like a cup of tea, Caryl? Shall I put the kettle on?" I instigate action by peeling my hand out of hers and pushing back my chair.

You're absconding. It's what you always do. These are Jan's words, her voice. We may be physically separated, but her mental presence is uncanny.

"Okay. Thanks." Caryl dabs at her eyes with her ruined tissue: left eye, then right. Left, then right. She wipes under her nose, and says: "I'm being such a nuisance," and I am about to utter a breezy "Nonsense," when her face darkens and deepens like storm sky, and, with an explosion like a thunder clap, she showers the desk, the open copy of Blake's *Songs of Innocence and Experience*, her hands and myself with torrential tears.

I sit back down and reach for her hand, but she withdraws it. She needs it, and the other one, to cover her face. "The bastard," she's sobbing now. "The utter bastard."

Feeling helpless, I find myself gazing over her shoulder, out at the garden through the picture window. It's April. The juices are running, and all the spring clichés are in sight: daffodils and tulips, busy birds, lambs gambolling in the field beyond.

"Bastard, bastard, bastard," Caryl sobs, rocking in her seat.

I'm a bastard, too. Jan's called me one on a few occasions, when I've driven her to it. "Why won't you talk to me? Why won't you listen, you *bastard*?" And I've known how much it has hurt her to say it, how she's regretted it immediately, said "Oh, Alun. I'm sorry. You didn't deserve that." Thing is, I probably did.

"He said we were forever, you know? He said that only …" Caryl is panting now, and digging her left palm with the nail of her right thumb. " … that only … death would separate us."

"Caryl, calm down. You might hyperventilate."

She's looking a bit weird, too, staring into space like that. I can't help wishing my parents hadn't gone to Chester for the day.

"Well, maybe it will."

Oh, God.

"Caryl," I say, but I falter, not up to it.

She leans across the table, head in her folded arms, and the raw sound she makes shakes me. Beyond, the window beams soft light into the room. This is the first Welsh spring I've been home for in – how long? Must be five years. Christ, where has the time gone? Being here, in spring, here in my parents house, the home I grew up in, has been making me feel poignant. It's taken me back to childhood days, when summers were long, you know, that kind of romantic retro stuff. I used to climb in and out of the picture window as a boy, especially in the summer. It was my short cut to the garden. All this week, I've been helping my father make a new flower-bed in the middle of the lawn. I trace its kidney shape with my eyes, glance at Caryl, the top of her head, her dishevelled hair, and return to the kidney bed. It's hard witnessing someone else's suffering at the best of times, but now, in my own vulnerable state … The truth is, I'm suffering, and Jan's suffering, and my parents are suffering because we're suffering. But then, thinking about it, the whole damned world is suffering. Suffering is The Way Things Are. Part of living in *samsara*. We always expect life to go all our way, all of the time. Why do we do that?

Some flicker of movement catches at the corner of my eye, but I ignore it, because Caryl is sitting up again, and I know I must do right by her.

"I'm through with men."

"Yes. I don't blame you." Another flicker, like a white hanky being waved.

"He's wrecked my life." Her devastation troubles me and I want to tell her the one about time and healing, and about being young – what the hell, bring on all the dancing clichés. Trouble is, I'm staring over her shoulder, through the window and into the garden. Two sturdy lambs have scrambled, spring-playfully, onto the dry-stone wall from field-side, and pinging themselves upwards and outwards, they land four square on the lawn, garden-side. A third lamb appears on the wall, preparing to follow its cousins.

"I'll never be the same again. He's changed me forever."

I try to focus on Caryl's face, but my eyes keep sliding left. The third lamb's landed now, and is loving the adventure, apparently, by the way it careers across the lawn, kicking up its heels. Squinting slightly, I think I can make out a dip in the dry-stone wall, a growing weakness. There used to be wire along it, to stop the sheep escaping; it must have come down.

"I mean, you don't lie like that, do you? Not in a true relationship."

And oh, oh, here come the distressed mums: one, two, three. They've pulled some more of the wall down with them.

"And he didn't have to sleep with Angharad, did he? I mean, she's my best friend – or was."

Two more lambs trickle over the wall, followed, presumably,

by *their* mothers, who join the others by way of the kidney bed.

"No, he didn't," I say, but then I hurriedly push back my chair and stride over to the window. "I'm very sorry, Caryl," I say, over my shoulder. "But there are sheep, you see."

" Sheep?" Her chair scrapes back.

"Sheep in the garden, wrecking the kidney bed. £100 worth of shrubs in there."

Caryl arrives beside me, wiping her face, and I say, "I think I'm going to need a hand."

The garden flock has grown again and more woolly faces are appearing at the deepening gap in the wall. I undo the window and slide it open. There's hardly a breeze, and the air smells green and growing. I breathe in yellow light and antiphonal birdsong, a long deep draft of it. I'm out of the window before I've thought about it.

"Come on, Caryl."

She hesitates, looks doubtful, then climbs out, somewhat awkwardly; then we both turn to where the sheep have clustered on my father's veg patch.

"We'll head them off, back up the garden," I whisper, and we edge towards them with our arms spread out. Something about our almost Tom & Jerry stealth, our body-shapes, the camaraderie of two, triggers boyhood memory again: Roger Duffy and me, the Lone Ranger and Tonto.

Twelve pairs of eyes consider our approach, and I'm just thinking, Yes, we'll get round them and it'll be a cinch, when one of the lambs panics and bounces off in the wrong direction; needless to say, the others turn tail and follow.

"Oh, no!" The greenhouse is down there, and the fruit garden and the pond. I have visions of my parents coming back to smashed glass, broken raspberry canes and bleeding sheep, their precious garden like a war zone.

Caryl sniffs and murmurs "Sheep will be sheep," in defeated tones. But I'm already after them.

"You take the left side, I'll take the right." And I grin back at her, big and broadly. The corners of her mouth twitch and she shrugs her sloping shoulders.

"Okay," she says, and takes up her position.

But it's not easy, not at all. The sheep bunch and scatter,

bunch and scatter. We circle them and just when we think we've got a chance to manoeuvre them back up the garden, one of them makes a dash for it and the ball of baaing wool unravels. Yet, ridiculously, I'm enjoying it – the ludicrous chase, the skidding onto my knees, Caryl's long flapping arms, and the dear silly sheep who bump and crowd into each other and generally go the wrong way. I glimpse an image of us on film, the whole thing sped up to madcap pace, with the theme from *The Beverley Hillbillies* twanging away.

It takes us the best part of half an hour to herd the sheep back up the garden, safely past the kidney bed and back over the wall, where their fellow flock members are waiting to welcome them back into the fold like state dignitaries greeting VIP's. By the time we've built the wall back enough to curb further invasions, and checked the garden over for damage – of which, surprisingly little, considering – another three quarter hour has gone, and it's getting dark. I've got grass stains on the knees of my jeans, my hands feel like sandpaper, and Caryl looks like a wild woman. But she's chatting away about university, her favourite lecturers, how she once wanted to be a vet, that sort of thing, and I'm chipping in the odd anecdote of my own, making her laugh.

We go back into the house the proper way, through the kitchen door, and, as we do so, an awkward formality returns. Caryl's expression changes, her face remembering what it was doing before the sheep came.

We each wash our hands at the kitchen sink, drying them on my mother's tea towel.

"We'd never get away with this if she were here," I jolly. "She's fussy about her tea towels."

Caryl breathes a small smile.

Then: "That cup of tea."

"Oh, no thanks. I'd better be getting back."

"Are you sure?"

"Yes. Honestly."

We go back to the front room, where the books are laid out on the table, alongside the pile of used tissues.

"How do you think you'll do?" I am meaning about the exam, but she says:

"I'm over him. Thanks very much for everything."

I smile and shrug. "I think it was the sheep that did it, in the end."

I reach for the Blake, flick through the pages, open it on 'Auguries of Innocence' and scan down:

"*Man was made for joy and woe, and when this we rightly know, thro' the world we safely go ...*" I look up, note her nodding, solemn expression. "And that's as much for me as it is for you."

She begins to tidy away her belongings. Sliding the Blake into her bag, she says:

"You should go back to your wife."

I didn't know she knew, and my mouth dries instantly.

Caryl snaps shut her bag, looks up, and smiles seriously. "She'll be missing you."

"Yes," I say, clear at last. "She will."

HAST'AL FIN

Robert M. Smith

The first thing he saw when he opened his eyes was the sun rising peacefully over the hill, far beyond the window.

He had dreamed that the pain in his kidney was a shrapnel wound, and, though the wound was his imagining, the pain was real enough. He knew about shrapnel wounds, from the Catalan hospital in Lerida where they took him after a fascist grenade had shattered his right leg on the Barcelona front.

But that hospital had not been like this one. This modern, clean, antiseptic-smelling infirmary. Could you still call them hospitals or were they 'trusts' now?

Trust.

Faith. Confidence. Loyalty.

All those things he'd gone to Spain for.

Of course he had faith and confidence in the doctors here.

Beyond the grimy window, morning mist still clung to the lower slopes of the rounded hill while the top was bathed in Spring warmth.

His mind was dusted free of its dreamy half-thoughts as Doctor Blair the consultant swept in with a trail of students and spoke too loudly at him, as if he were a child. And a stupid child at that.

"The old ticker playing you up, eh Herbert?"

Nobody calls me Herbert. It's Bert. And you already know of my various cardiovascular problems, he thought.

"Not too bad, Doctor."

"Not to worry! We'll have you charging about like a two-year-old in no time," the consultant shouted.

You're a bloody doctor, why do you assume my bad heart affects my hearing?

"Not with my leg, you won't," Bert disputed.

"Leg giving you trouble, Herbert?" The consultant rifled his notes.

"Did it in Spain," he started to explain.

One of the students, a slavering, expectant puppy living only to please its master, nuzzled his way in.

"On a little holiday, were we, Mister Davies ?"

I hate that fucking 'indulge the doddery old git' voice.

Bert thought about explaining the intricacies of the Spanish Civil War, but felt too tired. He looked at the young trainee and allowed himself an internal smirk, saying, "Yes. A little holiday."

"I think it's wonderful that you still do that," the student cooed, looking at the doctor not the patient.

If he pats my hand I'll deck him, condescending little bastard.

"Very good then !" the consultant said, to nobody. He smiled at Bert, then seemed to evaporate. Students vortexed out of the ward in his invisible slipstream.

Nobody wanted to hear about Spain any more. His son, who had once sat spellbound by tales of red flags and black flags in Barcelona where the workers walked with dignity and waiters refused tips, lived far away and was more concerned with his job, his wife, his golf. His great niece didn't mind listening to the stories of beliefs and bloodshed, comradeship and ideals. She was the only one, though.

A good girl, our Carol, he thought as he drifted into a deep sleep.

"No visitors this evening, Bert ?" asked Sue, his Named Nurse.

In the bed opposite, Les started croaking 'A Nurse named Sue', to the old Johnny Cash tune, as he did every time she came on duty. His voice was a wheezing, cracked tenor.

"You ought to do something with that voice," she teased over her shoulder, as she picked up Bert's thermometer, flicked it briskly and slipped it between his dry lips. "You could be on the stage, couldn't he, Bert ?"

"I only sing for you, my love," Les told her, thinking of another girl he'd sung for, long gone.

"Aaaah ! You old charmer," she said.

She looked at Bert's eyes; pale, blue, watery eyes which she'd only ever seen in old men. Eyes which looked as though tears weren't far away, but couldn't come.

"Silver-tongued old charmer, isn't he, Bert?" she said, nodding her head towards Les. "Charm the birds off the trees, he could."

"Charm the knickers off a nun," Les said.

"Leslie !" she shrieked, mock-horrified.

Les chuckled, which made him cough, which made him breathless and he reached for his oxygen mask.

She took the thermometer from Bert's mouth and studied it.

"Thirty-eight point five," she said, placing it carefully back in its antiseptic-filled holder on the wall above the bed.

"What's that in old money?" Bert asked.

"About a hundred and one."

"Oh."

"We'll be frying eggs on your arse if you get much hotter, Bert !" Les gasped over his mask.

"Is your son coming up this weekend ?" the nurse asked Bert, hoping he hadn't sensed urgency in her question. She knew he was fighting an infection in his kidneys.

"Yes."

"I've been looking forward to meeting him. You've been here a fortnight."

"A fortnight ? Tempus don't half fugit."

"Busy is he ? Your son I mean."

She was writing on the chart at the foot of the bed.

He recalled a nurse in Lerida with hair the colour of a crow's back: so black it shimmered deep green and purple when the Spanish sun caught it, like wet slates, shining when the shower's past.

"Yes. Our Michael is a very busy man."

"What did you say he does ?"

"Teaches English at a Grammar School in Hampshire. Head of the department."

Her silent response seemed like an invitation to go on.

"Busy time of year, this is, for him. A Levels, O Levels, I don't know what levels altogether."

"Well, it'll be nice for you to see him," she said.

People came every day to see Les: his daughter, one of his sons, the grandchildren, an old workmate, one of the boys from the allotments. They always smiled, "Goodnight," at Bert, who heard so much of their conversation that he almost felt they were his visitors too.

The view was good, you had to be fair. Out across the car park and the gardens, the trees feathered with may and cherry blossom, the early evening sunlight cast gentle warm tones on the distant hillside.

At least my eyes are still good. As good as the day I picked off that fascist machine-gunner across the low scrub.

He watched a tractor following the contours of the hill made of the rich red soil which gave the countryside its emerald prosperity. The surrounding landscape was a quilt of greens, yellows and browns like the colours of the dress Gwen had worn the first night they went to the Plaza together to see *Angels with Dirty Faces*. Cagney and Bogart. What a load of old rubbish ! Still, she'd let him kiss her afterwards.

Michael drove up from Hampshire late on Friday evening, depositing his wife, Amanda, at his father's house, because she was too tired to face a hospital visit. He was so late that he only had twenty minutes with his father. "I'll be along tomorrow, Dad," he promised as he was going.

He returned to his father's terraced house, tucked in a row of others identical yet unique, and found Amanda searching the pantry for ingredients for a meal. It was ten years since she had been to the house, but the look of disdain on her face was as fresh as ever.

"You look as though you've discovered dog shit in the biscuit barrel," Michael said.

"There's hardly any food here," she said. "Corned beef, spaghetti hoops, tinned potatoes. I found a sponge sandwich with the sell-by date in Roman numerals."

"I'll get a take-away," he decided.

"Mmm," she agreed. "Cantonese would be nice. Or Thai."

"Up here ?" he asked, a note of incredulity in his voice. "Cod and sixty penn'orth if you're lucky !"

"I was forgetting," she admonished herself. "Welsh culinary excitement: a choice of red or brown sauce on your chips."

"Now now," he reproached. "This is my home."

"Lucky escape," she said.

Her neatly ordered prejudices were slightly ruffled when he returned with vegetable balti, naan and pilau rice.

"Can't stand their food, but I like to see the people," Bert responded when Michael told him about their meal, the next day.

Amanda couldn't resist.

"I'm surprised the local fascists haven't fire-bombed them by now," she said.

"What local fascists is that ?" Bert asked, a spark leaping in his eyes.

"Well, the Valleys are hardly the most cosmopolitan of areas."

With gentle determination, Bert threw back the bedding, bent uneasily forward and tugged at the leg of his pyjama trousers.

"See that, girl ?" he asked, calmly pointing at the scarred, pale limb.

Its colour and suggested texture made her think of the poultry counter at Sainsburys.

"I got that fighting fascists. I watched men from these valleys spill their guts and their life-blood fighting fascists."

"Dad," Michael started to say but Bert was in no mood to be thwarted. Or patronised. He felt powerful; weak, yet calm and powerful.

"Half the doctors in here are Indian. The shop on the end of our street is run by Pakistanis. My oldest friend is Italian. My heroes are Paul Robeson and Doctor King, even though I could never be a pacifist like him."

Michael raised his eyes to the ceiling then shot Amanda a warning glance. She read it quickly and reacted.

"Oh, Bert," she said. "I wasn't suggesting that *you* are prejudiced."

"One thing Spain taught me: race, religion, colour, they're only skin deep."

Michael was making furious eyes at her.

"I'm sorry," she said in a voice nurtured to charm vicars and public school mistresses. "Oh dear, I always put my foot in it."

Michael was gesturing with his eyes, towards the door.

"I know," she said. "I'll pop down to the shop and get some sweets."

Touching Bert's arm, she asked, "What would you like?"

I'd like you not to be such a toffee-nosed bitch.

I'd like you not to treat me like a piece of shit.

I'd like you not to have stolen my son from me.

He said nothing. She rose and left the ward, convinced that a bar of Dairy Milk would smooth things over. Either that, or a packet of jelly babies. She had the wicked idea of removing all the black ones, wondering if he'd notice.

He thought of the dying convulsions of a fascist machine-gunner.

"You're looking pretty good, Dad," said Michael, totally misunderstanding the smile which had danced on his father's lips. He was aware that the other occupants of the ward, patients and visitors, seemed very interested in them; when their conversations lulled, he looked quickly around and caught their gazes just before they looked away.

"I'm all right, boy," Bert answered.

"Reckon you'll make it into the Welsh pack next season, eh?"

Their weekly phone conversation usually contained rugby references, one of the few remaining points of shared interest between them.

"I think they'll have to manage without me," Bert answered, the smile on his lips now weak and forced.

"Have to manage without you !" Michael echoed, laughing loudly for public consumption.

"How's school ?" asked Bert.

"Oh, don't ask !" moaned Michael. "The exams start in a few weeks so it's all of a panic at the moment with extra revision classes and dozens of past papers to mark. And we have an inspection in October, so we're trying to get everything organised ready for that. And did I mention that Phil Menzies is retiring?"

"The deputy head ?"

"Yes !" Michael was surprised and rather pleased that his father remembered.

He went on, "I have an interview for the post on Wednesday."

"You never said."

"I was told only this week."

"Well congratulations and good luck. Not that luck should come into it."

"Thanks."

Conversation never had been easy between them but time, distance and ageing had made it even harder. Bert looked out of the window at the treetops and the hill a few miles away while Michael read the five 'Get Well' cards on the bedside locker. There was the one he and Amanda had sent; one from someone called Sandra who he vaguely recalled as his father's home help; one from his cousin's daughter, Carol; one from the Senior Citizen's Club and one from a Mrs. Khan. Michael didn't know her. She kept the shop at the end of his father's street. Long ago it had been *his* street, too.

Both were relieved when Amanda returned with a large bar of Dairy Milk and a bottle of Lucozade. Smiling benevolently, waiting for a *Thank you* which wasn't going to arrive, she handed the chocolate to Bert who put it on top of his locker.

"I'll have it after tea," he said.

Across the ward, Les' three visitors had stood up and were saying their farewells. Amanda looked at her thin, gold watch and Michael slapped his hands onto his thighs and said, "Yes, well, I think we'd better be making tracks too, Dad. Long drive ahead… and I've got to do some preparation for the interview."

"Of course you must," Bert said. "I'm very proud of you, Mikey, you know that, don't you ?"

It was that name, *Mikey*, the name which only his dad had ever called him and which he hadn't heard for many years, which caused a lump to rise in Michael's throat. The calm sea of his neat life swelled massive and lifted him, bathing him with warmth and comfort, almost drowning him in lost memories: the brylcreem smell in his father's cap; a bat and ball duet against a blood orange sunset; seeing the world from strong, sure shoulders as they walked among gorse and heather on the mountains. He felt achingly close to his dying father, and had to tell him he loved him.

"Dad, I lo…," he started to say. But the wave had gone, broken on the shore of his cool, efficient, semi-detached reality. He adjusted his words. "I'll, er, see you in a few weeks."

But I shan't see you.

They shook hands, Michael feeling not the bone-crunching grip of the former wagon-maker but the desperate, weary clinging of a frightened old man.

After they had gone, Bert turned over to look out of the window. A fog had descended and he couldn't see the hill.

AN END

Barrie Llewelyn

Last night I dreamt again. It happens often now. The same thing night after night and sometimes dream after dream. When it wakes me, I am demented for a moment or two. And then the strangest thing happens – my groggy mind tries to imagine an end. An end.

I hold the gun first in one hand, then using my other to keep it steady – point and pull hard with my index finger. And BANG, PRESTO, my problem is gone.

But I cannot see who I am aiming at. Is it him or her? Sometimes I think (and I am always horrified by this) it is their child or their dog that is my target.

And that is it.

Then fantasy. What happens next? What is the outcome of my murder? I would not go off into the proverbial sunset with him. Not now, not after. Nor would I give her the satisfaction of widowhood. Although it would suit her: marital status without the despised sex. Possibly she has already achieved that; I have no way of knowing since. No, it is only a simple dream. Hold the gun and aim. An easy, smooth power. That's probably all. There are no answers to the rest.

I went to work this morning and Jan, who manages the Lo Cost, told me that one of the customers wants to sell his gun. He confided in her about his reasons. They all do. His, she says, are political; there is an election coming and both parties are about to submit to popular demand for tighter gun control. This guy wants to dump his pistol before it becomes a white elephant. Jan told me because she thinks I might appreciate the story. She thinks that I am quiet because I am deep and arty. She doesn't know that, mostly, I am not interested. Jan thinks I must be cool or something. She is married. Settled with two or three kids. Grey hairs sprinkled over. I go home alone to my drawings (always black and white) and the cats.

Jan laughs often and when things aren't funny, high and thin and too sure. She was laughing now as she taped up the notice the guy had prepared for the board, 'Who does he think could possibly be interested in buying a gun around here?'

When she went out back to the storeroom, I wrote the phone number on my palm.

At lunch time, I walked. Thinking about the gun. How to approach. Imagine the conversation: Hello Mr Green. I read your ad. How much for the gun? Will you show me how to use it? Or: Hello, Mr Green. How much for the gun? Will you tell anyone if I use it?

The prosecution will argue that I was hoping to see Brian. Hoping that he'd drive by in his clapped-out Escort, and thinking that I was stranded, offer to pick me up and...what? I don't know. For one thing, there was no car. He was on foot. And I so busy thinking, did not even see him coming until he was there. In the middle of the High Street. Smiling. He was smiling.

'Coffee,' Brian said, as if this was normal. And it was a statement. Thank you, God – I am irritated. Still, to him, a statement of intention: Let's go to bed. Let's go to your place and go to bed. But my irritation did not show or turned to something else, because I must have smiled or changed my expression, and he said, 'No, I really mean coffee.'

Was the same expression stuck on my face like fly paper when we slid into either side of a booth at The Castell? Was I cool and in control? No, Your Honour, I was hot and agitated. It has been six weeks. And since then, I have wondered every day. I have wanted you every day. I have regretted. And I need to know what happened after. Have you been miserable and wretched? Has your life been filled with the sound of your wife's hysteria? Do I sit with you at every meal, sleep between you in your bed? Should I tell him that I fantasise about shooting one of them, or myself, or even their dog? My crime needs structure.

Brian tried to make eye contact. And never stopped talking. Finally he got up again to get our drinks. If I'd been calm, I would have walked out, leaving him standing alone with a cup of cappuccino in each hand. But I didn't. I hadn't recovered from the last time I left him standing.

He returned and continued speaking. All gibberish. Case notes really; a brain-damaged boy showing signs that he might regain some of his speech. A matter of therapy – new methods. Searching for something that would excite the child so much that the desire to express would change a few limited sounds into words. I could feel the excitement of the project, but couldn't enter. Surely he knew that. I sat feeling dull and stupid. Unable to contribute. Picking at my fingernails in my lap. Then I saw his hands fiddling with the cup and saucer and tearing at an empty sugar packet.

He was nervous. Good. Let him be the nervous one. Let him talk and I can concentrate on memorising his voice and his eyes. Two months ago, there seemed no reason to ask for a photo, or take one myself, and in the interim one of the hardest things to bear had been not really remembering. If you draw someone, you will never forget what they look like. I have sometimes called myself an artist and yet I never took the time to sketch his face. I saw that his eyes were green – not ordinary hazel, more like a never-changing willow. Now and again, they flashed in a certain remembered way. I did not dare let myself look at his mouth, but his voice was clear and strong. Once he told me that he would have liked to be a preacher. He was articulate and interesting; sometimes he could be funny. We'd laughed and fought. Discussed politics and modern art and television. Our friendship began and ended with debate, but it was the way he listened to me, weighed my importance. That was how he'd seduced me.

He did not look at his watch or at the other customers in the pub as he talked on and on, filling up the space for my unasked questions.

Finally, he paused and looked at me closely, 'Another?'

The time, I thought. What the hell. 'No thanks. You go ahead.'

He came back with a real drink. A short. Maybe scotch.

But I was sober, Your Honour. Whose honour? I have none left.

He drank. I said, 'So?'

'Let's go,' he said. I always liked command, actually. And this time I was not irritated.

Lo Cost lost out. We did the usual thing. I walked to my flat.

He followed me five minutes later. The flat is over Boots. Very convenient. I have lived here a long time. Brian fits in as if he has lived here too. He throws the cat from the bed and turns down the duvet. He strips off quickly. He seems chunkier than I remembered. His legs are short, his body long and mostly hairless. Heads for the shower. He knows that will please me. Wash her off you first.

It doesn't take long. It never did. Why did I think? And after, he talks some more; finally, some of the questions are answered. He went straight back to her, of course. I knew that. Straight back. Then the blame.

'It was you who didn't want me, you told me to go. What did you expect?'

Suddenly tired of him, I turn away and remember again the detached frenzy of the day he'd told his wife.

The phone was ringing. It was a Thursday. Just in from work. I thought, it will be Brian. He always phoned on time.

'Hello,' I purred (Yes, purred) into the phone. The other voice was shrill and loud. It hurt my ears at first until I realised who it was and began to listen. First to hysterical accusations.

Then:

Did I realise there was a child? They had a daughter, what about her? Did I know that there were others? Did I know that he said he believed in God?

Later, he arrived with a case. She phoned again and sitting in my chair curled into a ball with a cat, I could hear her from across the room.

'She has ruined my life,' she screamed. I could hear him too, telling her that he was going to stay with me. He told her that he did not love her, cruelly and without apology.

Then he brought the phone to me. I couldn't think. I felt sick to hear her pleading. And when I took the phone she was quieter.

'Hello –I'm sorry,' I said. It sounded hopeless.

Then, very calmly, she offered him to me.

'He is not worth it,' she said.

I put the phone down and told him to go. I sent him away. I thought I could see the reflection of my weakness in his eyes. Her voice has been with me since: *he's not worth it.*

'I'm too old to live with my parents, you know,' he was saying. His breath smelled – or something. It could have been his body.

In a movie, we would have made love endlessly. The big reconciliation scene. But no.

Instead he took my hand, 'Have you had a tattoo?' He was looking at the number on my palm.

'Whose number?'

Can he be worried? He thinks that I have already found a new man whose phone I can ring.

I laughed, not like Jan. Haughty, in control.

His confidence is pretty low already. It's all a show. His wife says he smells, he's not good in bed. She's right. It's probably his fault that she hates it. He should not have told me so many of their secrets.

I took my hand away from him and got up from the bed. Do I give him something for his breath? I've got some gum here, somewhere. Really, I just want him to go again.

Naked, I look through my bag. It seems to arouse him. He comes up from behind me. His hands heavy on my waist, I continue to search in my bag.

'I probably can't manage it again, not just yet,' He whispers.

'Here, take this.'

And he just takes the gum from my fingers and pops it into his mouth without a question.

Much later. He has gone. Back to her again, as he always will. There is no point, I'd finally said. Don't phone. Or.

I think he was relieved, actually. I know that I am..

Waking later, from cats swimming in the black and white bath and happy shoppers dressed as mad cows, I see Mr Green's phone number on my hand. In the shower, I scrub it until it disappears.

BREAK UP

Elizabeth Griffiths

When they were young Maggie and her twin sisters sat halfway up the tall vicarage stairs, not knowing what else to do with their evenings. There they stayed in the quiet of the house while the gloom gathered in the high ceiling space of the hallway, and fell over them like a fine grey mist until they could no longer see each other clearly.

Miriam sat highest up, resting her chin on her hand, Stella tucked herself sideways into the wall and Maggie, the eldest, crouched below them both.

They developed this habit during the time when their mother was ill upstairs and hardly moved from her bed for three months. They were told she was having a nervous breakdown, but they couldn't imagine what that was, or why she wouldn't respond to them or even recognise them when they went into the bedroom.

"Why doesn't she look at us when we say goodbye before school?" Miriam asked aloud one evening, expressing the confusion of them all, yet making the other two squirm the way she came straight out with it. Miriam had small, piercing eyes which glinted down on them, demanding an answer.

"Everything'll be alright, won't it?" Stella wondered, throwing a nervous glance up the looming staircase, her soft small mouth half-open. Surely nothing really bad could happen to them.

"Everything will be fine," Maggie told them, not for the first time. She was the one responsible for the answers and was surprised at how carefree and certain she managed to sound even though her throat had practically seized up.

"You'll see, it'll be alright," she kept telling them, to stop them from saying or thinking otherwise. But in her heart she was afraid that everything would fall apart and that it wouldn't be long before their world was smashed to smithereens. Like the dusky light massing in the corners of the ceiling, a threatening feeling was growing and growing in the house – a feeling that it was full of secrets, full of abnormality.

Even before her mother's illness, at least from the age of eight, Maggie had nursed a strong secret dread that her family might fall apart. Where did this dread come from? Her parents never argued or quarrelled in front of her, and when they did speak to each other it was only about ordinary things. True, her father had his moods and tempers, and the rest of the family had got used to listening out for the agitated flip-flap of his cassock around the vicarage.

"Where are those papers I had a minute ago? I need them right now!" he would say, bursting into the kitchen as if he was announcing disaster, his sensitive handsome face, with its slender, bony jaw, quivering like an antelope's. And their mother would look at him then, just for a second, as though he were a speck far off on the other side of a desert, before turning away quietly, without a word, to begin the search.

Maggie, witnessing such an everyday episode, was filled with a sense of danger for her family, the same feeling of insecurity that from time to time forced her to order and tidy up all the messy drawers and cupboards in the house which were stuffed with odds and ends that had no proper home; or convinced her that a household mishap – such as the time Stella twirled around the living room and knocked the precious new television set off the sideboard – was a catastrophe they would never recover from.

Maggie had always known that because her family was a Church family, they were expected to set an example, a standard, to the rest of the parish. The houses they lived in were huge and situated on their own or on high, surrounded by rambling grounds and reached along long driveways, and here they were at anyone's beck and call, even the fearsome tramps' who begged for a bit of food and money. Yet at the same time they were set apart from everybody else.

None of their relatives had ever been in the Church before. Her father had been a poor miner's son and her mother's family ran a business making butter. They were only there because of what her father had become, and there was no money or background to support them. Each time they moved, they were installed in grand poverty over the other families in the neighbourhood, and after two or three years they were gone, posted by the bishop to a new parish.

People in the small Pembrokeshire villages they arrived in made a great fuss of them. The women, especially the old ladies and well-meaning farmers' wives, looked down on Maggie and her sisters with great interest as if they were an unusual species of child, and deferred to their parents as if they were little gods. Maggie understood from this that if her family did anything odd or unexpected, it was bound to lead to everyone's disapproval and disappointment.

And she wasn't at all sure that her father was capable of carrying them through without disaster. Whenever he was worked up about something, they had to creep around the house, being very very careful not to disturb him doing whatever he did for hours on end in his study.

"I don't want to hear a single sound!" he warned them in a strangulated voice, even if they were being as quiet as mice.

The best time was when they moved to a new parish. Their father was happy then and his most attractive, charming self, full of plans and dashing off excitedly to this or that meeting. At meals he said what a wonderful place it was, what a lovely house and garden they had, how lucky they were!

But before long he seemed troubled again – the parish was full of problems after all, people could be very difficult and he had far too much to do. More and more he kept to his study and they had to be quieter than ever. They watched him flying through the house in his black cassock looking very het-up and annoyed, as if somebody was to blame for something. It wasn't until Maggie was in her teens that she discovered he drank in secret.

So she and her sisters tended to look to their mother to hold the household together, rather than their father. The enormous vicarages needed endless cleaning and when she wasn't toiling away at housework, their mother was rushing around preparing for parish functions – Mothers' Union, Young Wives, fetes, bring and buys, trips, teas......

She was preoccupied with so many tasks that she hardly ever just sat down and did nothing or played games. Although her temper was much less changeable than their father's, her nice pale face often had a strain in it as if she was constantly thinking ahead to the next job she had to do.

Maggie and her sisters were used to keeping each other company in their self-contained unit of three, knowing that their mother was busy on their behalf in the background, that they could rely on her and that she would always do what was right and good. So it was an extreme shock to them when one Good Friday, just before Maggie's tenth birthday, she started to cry uncontrollably after returning from church and hurried off to bed. It was the first sign they had of the nervous collapse she was already suffering.

During those days of her illness, the normal routines of the vicarage stopped and in the absence of the order they were used to, Maggie and her sisters found the atmosphere in the house very strange.

They did as they liked when not in school and their father went about in a peculiar, absent-minded way, drifting haphazardly through the house as he had never done before and checking up on them at odd hours. Maggie couldn't fathom why she felt uneasy about him when he passed them by on the stairs looking so unusually relaxed, as if he wasn't quite all there and not really connected to them any more.

Parishioners, friends, relatives must have stepped in to help keep the household running, though later on Maggie couldn't remember how they had managed, how they had eaten or had clean clothes. She herself was convinced that her family was about to be smashed to pieces and all their secret weaknesses laid open to the world.

From time to time her mother's parents, Grandma and Grandad Mitchell, came over at weekends from their butter factory in the Amman Valley. Whenever they announced they were visiting, Maggie felt her whole family brace itself as if for a test or inspection. Before they arrived, her mother had the cooker and Hoover going all morning, and she and her sisters kept out of the way, playing subdued games upstairs. Her father disappeared altogether.

Maggie had always been aware that for some reason her grandparents strongly disapproved of her father. It was one of those mysterious, yet apparently fixed and deeply rooted circumstances of her childhood. And their chilly and suspicious manner towards him seemed to spread like a dreary cloud over them all, casting a shadow on her mother, her sisters and herself, whose fault it was to be connected to him.

Their grandmother, solid and self-contained as always, took up a position with her knitting in the high-backed chair near the Rayburn, while their grandfather, short, very rotund and wheezy from smoking, spread out his butter invoices on the kitchen table and totted up the amounts out loud all through the afternoon (not a minute was wasted even on weekends). He brought the family a box of provisions for which he wrote out a bill charging the wholesale price, since he didn't believe in giving things for free, or so he always said.

Maggie and her sisters loitered around the kitchen during these long afternoons, trying to answer their grandmother's stern-sounding queries and to avoid their grandfather's harsh teasing. Maggie had nothing against her grandparents except that they were hardly ever cheerful or approving. Their presence alone – weighty, purposeful, immoveable – seemed to undermine her family's effort at existence and to accuse it of falling short of expectations.

They were always asking questions and saying what should be done, as if only they knew the proper way to go about things. And they brought with them an atmosphere that was alien to the vicarage – an atmosphere of trade and town, of business and briskness, that made Maggie's heart ache strangely for her family, as though they were innocent and defenceless in the world. It never occurred to her in those days that her grandparents were worried about her family. She only felt they disapproved of it.

"Where is he then?" or "No sign of him then?" her grandfather would say, after everyone's bits of news had been aired and examined, and he would nod his bald head derogatorily in the direction of the closed study door off the hallway.

The expression on her mother's face would suddenly become more anxious, as if she didn't know how to answer the question, whether she should apologise for him or defend him. "Oh, he's out," she would say uncertainly, or "He's working on his sermon."

If Maggie's father had no choice but to pass through the kitchen while the visitors were still there, he could hardly bring himself to look at them, but shied away from them as if they were about to stick needles into him, like porcupines. He would stare over their heads, fix his eyes desperately on her mother as if she was his last ally in the world, and mutter that he was "going to a meeting."

Maggie thought it satisfied her grandparents to know that her father deliberately made himself scarce during these visits, as if this proved them right in their low opinion of him. There were certain things which gave Maggie clues about why they objected to her father – for one thing, they spoke slightingly of "his people", her father's family, who also came from the Amman Valley but a poor part of it.

And for another, they were always asking her mother about money, and how was she going to manage. Once or twice she had seen her grandfather hand over a few notes to her mother in a meaningful way. But even with these clues, Maggie could not have answered the question: what was so wrong with her father?

After their mother had been in bed for about three months, Grandma and Grandad Mitchell took her away and soon afterwards returned her to the vicarage, apparently recovered. She was up on her feet again and carried on her functions as before. Maggie was the first to go off to boarding school on a scholarship, and there were days on end when she never thought of her family at all. At a distance she could imagine that they were just like any other family and there was no need to worry.

But if the housecaptain said there was no letter for her on the day she was expecting one from her mother, a cold rush of fear would surge through her like a dam breaking, and she couldn't rest for thinking there had been a terrible catastrophe at home. And all the exams she passed and the tests she came top of, all the academic honours she accumulated, she half perceived as an insurance against family disaster: nothing could really go wrong so long as she succeeded.

One summer when she and her sisters came home for the school holidays, their father made an elated announcement – the family was moving to Carmarthenshire to make "a fresh start." She noticed he looked different, as if he had found a new, more youthful self, and later on he drew her close to his side, explaining in a low fervent voice that he had been into hospital to dry out and now he was better.

This unusual close contact with her father made Maggie feel peculiar and inclined to shrink away from him. She felt as if she had known all along what had been happening in the house, without putting it into thought, but now she was strongly averse to being told the details and wanted to shut her ears.

Her mother seemed to acquiesce in the move to Carmarthenshire, though without any of the excitement or optimism of her father. Maggie sensed that her mind was elsewhere and from time to time glanced secretly at her pale mask-like face to see what she could read in it, and in her unanimated grey eyes.

A few years later, when they were settled in Carmarthenshire, the family did break up after all. For Maggie and her sisters the end of the life they had known came very suddenly and quietly, without their being aware of any outcry or ruction. Maggie was in her first term at university by then, and Miriam and Stella were still at boarding school. Their mother wrote to explain that she had moved out of the vicarage to a town in the Black Mountains, where she had managed to find a nursing post in a psychiatric hospital.

Maggie's immediate reaction to the news was calm, almost dispassionate, as if this was something she had been expecting for a long time, and now she could put it behind her and get on with her life at college.

She still made her way across the wide open spaces of the university campus feeling as light as air and almost heady with a sense of freedom and independence. She was relieved that she had somewhere of her own to base herself – new studies, new friends, new surroundings! When she remembered what had happened to her family, she was only uneasy that it didn't bother her more. Now and again, the thought of her father living on his own in the vicarage flashed into her head, but she let it fly out again immediately.

Halfway through term, she visited her mother at the hospital and together they walked along the lengthy grey antiseptic-smelling corridors to the nurses' quarters. In the room her mother was sharing with one or two other nurses, they sat side by side on the firm institutional bed and Maggie was reminded of the times when she used to sit on her bed at boarding school saying goodbye to her parents at the beginning of term.

"I'm sorry I haven't anywhere else to take you, Maggie."

"Oh.....that's alright, Mum." Maggie looked away and turned her head around the room as if she was inspecting it. Her mother's face was pale and looked sad and vulnerable, almost close to tears. That same peculiar shrinking reaction to a show of emotion, such as she had felt when her father confessed his drinking problem years ago, came over Maggie now.

"I don't know if your father's been in touch lately, has he?"

"No....."

"Well, you might as well know. He's met someone else, from a well-off family he knows near Carmarthen. They own newspapers, I think. He'll probably be leaving the Church to go and work for them." She explained all this emptily, as if she was past caring, but a moment later Maggie noticed that tears were trembling on the rims of her eyes.

"I keep thinking of you and the twins," she went on falteringly, biting her lips to stop crying, "I keep thinking of you when you were small. I can see the three of you again wrapped up in your cots, your little faces peeping out. It keeps coming back to me in my dreams....."

Maggie stayed silent, feeling too uncomfortable to say or do anything other than scrape the sides of her shoes on the shiny hospital floor. She wondered if her mother was going to cope, and what would become of them if she had another nervous breakdown. At that moment, a large, tall, grey-haired man came hurrying into the room and apologised for being late. Maggie's mother immediately covered up her distress and greeted him in a pleasant tone of voice.

"This is Hugo, one of the nursing officers in charge," she told Maggie. "He interviewed me when I applied for a job and now he's trying to get a hospital house for us before Christmas. Isn't that kind?"

"Good God, it's nothing!" huffed Hugo in his deep booming voice. "She has to have somewhere to live, hasn't she?"

His blustering tone only showed how self-conscious he was feeling, a strange state for a man so big, so paternal-seeming, so used to being in charge. Maggie felt sorry for him, and at the same time suspected that his kindly and hearty manner towards them both, the impression he gave of having great funds of cosiness and security to endow them with, were at that moment being directed purely and simply at one person – her mother.

Just before Christmas, Maggie went back to the vicarage for the last time. As she loitered outside in the familiar driveway, scanning the rose beds on one side and a screen of conifers on the other, she thought how strange it was that the old place, with its tall confident Victorian gables and solid stone walls, should still turn such a benign and reassuring face on the world. Surely nothing untoward could happen in a house like that!

But a removal van had not long rattled down the drive with most of the vicarage's contents, and her father was inside juggling frantically with the skeletal furniture that was left. Nearly all the best pieces – those that had come down from her mother's side of the family – had been taken away, leaving only a jumble of jointly purchased odds and ends, mainly unimpressive functional items, and a small collection of impractical antiques her father had acquired himself.

"Don't just stand there Maggie! Give me a hand, will you?" he implored her, the sweat standing out – pitifully, Maggie thought – on his forehead.

He was in a desperate hurry to get the house straight for his new fiancé and to disguise the inadequacy of the furniture. Maggie could tell that he was irritated by her blank reaction to what was happening, the way she tacitly set herself in opposition to his frenzy by doing nothing.

"Christina will be here soon," he panted, "and we're not nearly ready!"

Christina stepped into the house just as the first snow began to drift with soft light beauty from the sky. Maggie had avoided asking her father for details about this new relationship of his – how they had met and so on – and that was the way she preferred it.

Christina was beautifully wrapped in the warmest, downiest of fur coats, her shining blonde hair swinging like a bell above the collar. She was shy coming forward to meet Maggie – there were only five years between them, so they could have been sisters – and

Maggie felt her trembling inside her lovely shimmering coat as they embraced. Christina was obviously nervous about her reception, but what really overcame her was the huge irrepressible happiness of being in love.

"Hello! Oh, thank you! Thank you for having me!" she whispered into Maggie's ear, her voice fervent and husky. Not knowing how to respond and clasped against the small fine bones and soft scented skin of the other woman, Maggie had never felt such a dumb oaf, or so scruffy in her college clothes.

She left them to it, and went upstairs to wander aimlessly through the empty rooms. In all the upheaval of the day, she had felt flat and uninvolved, and now the bare disorder of the house depressed her. The atmosphere of the dusty, dismantled rooms was suffocatingly dreary, like her mood, and there was no getting away from the truth that here something had failed and was finished.

In her old bedroom the only thing left was a light-coloured wool carpet which her father, in a flush of hopefulness, had extravagantly bought for her when they moved in. Maggie was sorry to see that carpet still looking so new and beautiful through lack of wear. Her room had two tall arched windows, pointing up to the ceiling like a pair of enquiring eyes, and from these she looked out over the driveway, now covered in snow, and at the screen of conifers opposite, which shut out all sight of the silent village beyond.

"Everyone knows, everyone knows....." she repeated to herself a few times, because it was no use imagining that there was anyone beyond the trees who hadn't heard what was happening at the vicarage.

But she was surprised at how calmly she could think about it now – all those unseen eyes and mouths judging her father and mother, the old people gossiping in their cottages, the farmers chuntering at the field gate, the mothers chatting outside the village school. And with a sudden, defiant lift of her heart, as if she had at that moment managed to raise a heavy weight and bear it, she saw that after a certain point, when you were fully enmeshed in events you had dreaded – events which went against everyone's expectations – what other people thought or said ceased to have a hold over you. It was the least of your worries.

She moved next door into her sisters' den, where the vibrant salmon-pink colour of the walls was a strong reminder of their intense and secretive occupation of the room, even though every last bit of their clutter had gone.

Dawdling by the window again, she looked across at the churchyard opposite while her fingers made random restless marks in the grime on the sill. She was in that unconnected state, that condition of suspension, which made a nothingness of thought or feeling. And the scene outside, snowbound now, was mesmerising in its stillness, a perfect tableau: the small ancient church struggling to reveal itself through the hoary branches of the graveside trees, its squat Norman tower only just rising above the topmost twigs. The soft fur of snow that lay over everything, on the low church roof, over the tall protective yews, between the rows of nestling gravestones, looked so perfect that it was almost impossible to imagine it would soon melt and disappear.

"Maggie? Maggie! Come down a minute. There's something I want to show you," her father called up the staircase in a high urgent voice, the same voice he used to project litanical responses into the back of the church.

From the landing she saw him standing out in the gloom of the hall below, wearing a new jersey of robin-breast red. His uplifted face was hectic, boyish, and his eyes, catching all the light from the landing window, were two fluid spots of brightness.

Slowly she came down the stairs on heavy legs. She hadn't the energy to join in her father's elation, or to resist it either. On balance, it was easiest to go along with it.

He threw an arm around her shoulder and holding her against him more tightly than she wished, he guided her purposefully towards the dining room. The strong after-shave he was wearing accentuated his male, almost acrid smell and he was losing weight – a sure sign that he was cutting down on his drinks. Instead of eating breakfast in the morning, he had started gobbling down a handful of pills, vitamins and Brewer's Yeast.

"Well – what do you think?" He opened the door with a grand gesture, and there was Christina, standing expectantly in a corner of the room, behind a table she had laid with a new cloth and all the glass and cutlery she could find.

It was still early in the afternoon, yet Christina had lit a row of glittering candles which threw an unreal glow over the whole arrangement. The handsome brass candlesticks were the ones Maggie remembered her father bringing home from an auction a long time ago – he had come in brandishing them in both hands, like booty, and at once anxiety about money had frozen over her mother's face.

"We wanted you to have a special Christmas meal with us before you go," her father said, and his bony hand squeezed her shoulder excitably.

He led her to the table where Christina was waiting, smiling and flushing hugely. Neither of them could contain their pleasure in springing this surprise on Maggie. They were both brimming over with generous feelings.

"Hasn't she done a wonderful job, the clever girl!" her father said, switching his arm from Maggie's shoulder to Christina's.

He gazed down intently on his fiancé, like a youth, while she coyly twisted her head into his torso, into the thick wool of the jersey she had bought for him. Maggie looked down at the ground as they canoodled – it made her feel peculiar to watch them.

She was quiet during the meal, subdued by the strange formality of it, the brilliant table, the elegant food, the champagne. She felt no resentment towards Christina and her father, only it was odd to be treated like a guest, waited on and attended to, in the room where she was used to eating everyday meals. She had a feeling that her role here was to be a witness to the occasion, a recipient rather than a participant, and she smiled to herself, imagining that she was like one of those spinster chaperones who, in days gone by, watched young people enjoying themselves at balls.

"I know the house must seem rather strange to you without all the old furniture, Maggie," her father said benevolently, leaning back in his chair. "But you mustn't mind too much. What we've all got to do now is look to the future and see this as a new beginning...."

He was, after the champagne, his most expansive self – relaxed, gay, attractive – and he wanted to draw her into his happiness. It would have spoilt things for him to feel that she was not joining in.

"I can't tell you how grateful I am to you, Maggie.......how nice you've been," Christina said, stretching one of her slim arms, decorated with pretty jewellery, across the table. "Anyone else might have – well, made difficulties......my coming here and taking the place of.......you know....."

Both of them were suddenly embarrassed at this near mention of Maggie's mother.

"It's alright," Maggie muttered, fixing her eyes on her plate. "It's nothing....really...."

She said this not out of modesty, but out of an awkward feeling that Christina's gratitude was misplaced. The truth was, she was able to accept this temporary ménage more effortlessly, more fatalistically, than the other woman imagined – in fact, Maggie rather despised Christina's notion that she might have 'made difficulties.' All her life she had dreaded the break-up of her family, sensed its imminence almost as long as she could remember, and now that it had happened, she was surprised at how detached and reasonable she was capable of being. She could even manage a wry inward smile, remembering the comforting illusion she had nursed all through school – that her spectacular academic success would act as a sort of glue.

"Oh but I shall have to keep myself hidden away while I'm staying here," Christina giggled. "After all, we don't want the parishioners making difficulties."

"You're not to worry about a thing, darling!" said Maggie's father catching hold of Christina's hand in a protective, fatherly gesture, a gesture which reminded Maggie of the times he had caught her hand crossing the road when she was small.

"Anyway, we shall only be here until the New Year and then we'll be off to make a new life."

For a moment her father sounded as if he was quite prepared to leave his ministry without any regrets, and Maggie wondered how in his own mind he managed to square his circumstances with the Church's teachings. His future plans were still vague, but it seemed that Christina's father was going to help him start a second career in newspapers.

"I want us all to drink to a fresh start," he said, raising his glass so that it glinted in the candlelight. "Come on – a fresh start!"

Maggie and Christina raised their glasses self-consciously, and all three glasses met in the middle of the table and clinked together. "A fresh start," they intoned, the toast fading away portentously, as toasts do.

Looking over the rim of her glass as the bubbles of champagne burst against her nose and mouth, Maggie saw that her father, wrapped up in his present happiness and full of future dreams, was, for the time being, completely free of thoughts about the past. It was as if this new love of his had made him over again, rolled back twenty years and entirely erased the period in between with all its difficulties and sorrows.

At that moment she sensed in him something touchingly innocent, something so childlike and innocent that it fell outside the bounds of moral judgment.

By the next day, the snow had already started to thaw. Maggie's father and Christina went off to do their Christmas shopping, so that Maggie would be on her own when her mother came to collect her. They said their goodbyes merrily enough, but at the last moment, her father touched her on the shoulder and looked at her with a queer intensity, as if he was trying to convince himself that she really was his daughter, his child.

Left to herself, Maggie wandered through the front rooms of the house, keeping watch for her mother's car. As usual before a journey, she was all keyed up and had got ready to leave too early. She tensed her muscles inside her coat and wrapped her college scarf more tightly around her head, to ward off the frosty air hovering in the high ceiling space. The musty-smelling rooms were stripped of furniture except for an old unstable table nobody wanted, discarded in a corner.

Pressing her forehead to one of the cold windows, Maggie saw that fragments of snow left on the fir trees were melting steadily now, and in the silence of the house, she could hear watery leaves of sound falling softly, insistently, all over the ground.

Suddenly a car horn shrieked outside, and a small new car pulled up at the end of the drive, outside the gates. Maggie could just make out the permed silhouette of her mother's head through the reflection-darkened glass of the car window, and she waited a moment to see if she would get out and come to the house, already knowing she would not. The head stayed quite fixed and still, and in its rigidity Maggie read all her mother's reluctance to set one foot in her former home.

"Why won't she come in?" she thought irritably, knowing full well it was pure emotion, not reason, that kept her mother in the car.

Still the little vehicle waited at the bottom of the driveway. Maggie could hardly bear the sight of it, and for a moment a spasm of revulsion took hold of her against that unmoving head – the sort of unexpected revulsion that arises out of too much pity.

She hurried to gather a few belongings together, and as she moved, she began to feel better, lighter. It was a relief to act, to do something definite at last after the limbo of yesterday. She was glad to be getting away from the empty spaces of house, the incessant dripping of the trees and her own echoing footsteps. She took one final look around – at the bare floorboards, the pictureless walls and that old table that had always tipped off its pedestal whenever anybody leaned on it – and left.

As soon as she got into the car, Maggie noticed a blanched, remote look about her mother's face. It was not a look of weariness exactly, but her skin had a drawn, transparent, fragile quality as if all the trauma of recent months had cleaned her out, left her washed up on some distant shore. She wasn't in a state of tension, more beyond it.

All the same, her mother's presence at the wheel immediately made Maggie feel more secure and ready to hand over responsibility for herself. She was just relieved, pure and simple, that she was being taken away. She leaned back in her seat, letting the familiar artificial smell of her mother's hair lacquer overpower her. In the end Maggie never doubted the safety of those hands on the wheel – hands which, she now noticed, were steering the car with a verve and control she hadn't seen before.

"Everything alright, was it?" her mother said in a light tight voice, as they zipped out of the village in a matter of seconds, without one glance back.

The car veered straight up a steep slushy mountain road, rising high above the Carmarthenshire farmsteads settled in the fields around. Looking down on the distant farm buildings, on their neat rectangular shapes, Maggie had a memory of turkeys hanging upside down in barns, and the kitchen larders of well-meaning farmers' wives, packed with meat and cakes for Christmas. How far away those things seemed now.

"Oh everything was fine," she said, and the vacuity of her response, the difficulty of elaborating on it, stymied and depressed her, so that she concentrated instead on the murky view outside.

By now they had entered the forest at Brechfa and were imprisoned on each side by a misty wall of dark conifers, by rows of pencil-straight trunks and dense foliage weeping with disintegrating snow.

"Good," her mother said. "I'm glad."

And in those few simple words, in the doubting, mournful edge to her voice, Maggie heard all her mother's disenchantment with her father, all her distrust that anything could be 'alright' as far as he was concerned. But she also sensed that her mother was straining, almost against her will, to hear something about him, and trying to form a idea of what was happening in her old home. The connection was still there in spite of everything.

Maggie felt it was impossible to speak freely. In fact, she was afraid that any mention of her father might easily pierce the shell of her mother's calm exterior. So she stayed silent, fixing her eyes gloomily on the claustrophobic forest. The tall packed pine trees and the sweet stuffy atmosphere in the enclosed space of the car oppressed her, and every particle of air seemed infected by a great false silence.

"This car goes well," she said eventually, still staring out of the side window at the heaps of dirty snow shrivelling at the roadside. There was no hope of a white Christmas now.

"When I left your father I didn't have a penny," her mother suddenly explained, in a voice bleak with disillusionment, but not exactly bitter because she was the kind of woman who, to her last breath, and out of an ingrained moral instinct, would keep unbridled bitterness at bay. "That's why Grandad bought this car for me – I had to have something to get around."

Maggie would have liked to shut her ears to this, but her mother continued to talk in her new reflection-hardened voice, and with a new openness which arose from a conscious effort to distance herself from her old situation.

"I should have left years ago, but I just couldn't. I had to think of you and the twins – and I had nowhere to go. You know, when I finally did leave, your father wouldn't let me out of the gate. He tried to stop me – physically. He tried to force me back into the house and I had to run down the road to a neighbours' house and ask them to get me a taxi."

Maggie visualised the episode with shocking vividness, though she had never in her life witnessed such a scene between her parents – had never seen any show of strong feeling between them. Her instinct was to reject it, but her mother's voice went on, a flat, calm voice which made Maggie feel that she was speaking from a great distance away.

"I was never happy with him after we got married. No, never – there was no pleasure or enjoyment in all those years. It was always one thing after another....."

Maggie had never heard her mother talk like this before, and even though it confirmed what she had always known, she wished she didn't have to listen. All the time her mother was speaking, she hardly took a breath and held herself tighter and tighter, until she felt a terrible pressure building inside her, bursting to get out. She knew that eventually she would have to let go and breathe, just as she realised that whether she liked it or not, she had to register what her mother was saying, and bear it.

"I hope all this won't have too much effect on you and the twins," her mother said finally, a more obvious vulnerability returning to her face and voice. "At least you're all much older now."

They had for some time been driving in less familiar country, having passed through miles and miles of forestry and emerged among the foggy yellow fields and hills towards Brecon. Before long the small town they were heading for came into sight at the foot of the Black Mountains, and on its highest point, overlooking the narrow streets, stood the tall grey Victorian hospital. In the shadow of the hospital crouched a terrace of red-brick houses, neat and small, and here they pulled up. They were home.

"Look – Grandad has fetched the twins back from school

already. There's his car," her mother said. "I'm afraid there aren't any Christmas decorations. I just haven't had the time."

The compact hospital house was jam-packed with large heavy pieces of furniture that had easily found their niche in the vicarage, but here looked absurd and useless. The house was also full of people – Miriam, Stella, her grandparents, and Hugo – and the suffocatingly intimate smell of food.

"Hello Maggie, how's coll?" her grandmother asked, briskly wiping her hands with a tea towel as she emerged from the kitchen.

Grandma Mitchell gave Maggie a quick efficient peck on the cheek, not expecting an answer. But her tone of voice hinted at a certain respect for her eldest granddaughter who had proved to be such a clever student. With each phase of academic triumph, Maggie had sensed her stature growing in her grandparents' eyes, and now, with one successful term at college behind her, she suddenly felt rather confident and grown-up.

In the small box-like living room, her grandfather and Hugo were sitting in cahoots at a table. Both were smoking, and the air was choking with cigarette fumes. Behind them Miriam and Stella were each lounging in an armchair with their legs up. Maggie, seeing them there in their unflattering school uniforms, with bored, trapped expressions on their faces, felt sorry for them.

"How's he then?" shouted her grandfather in his gruff voice as her mother flitted past the doorway towards the kitchen. Not getting an answer, he looked conspiratorially at Hugo, and puffing at the cigarette stuck in the side of his mouth, remarked, "They keep some funny people on in the Church these days."

Hugo, the prospective son-in-law, gave a grunt of agreement, a rather obsequious one, Maggie thought. She and her sisters looked at each other, feeling implicated, as usual, in the insult to their father.

"Why don't we go for a walk?" she said to Miriam and Stella.

"Butter!" bellowed Grandad, jabbing a short fat finger down onto a page of his invoice book. "Cheese! I make that......two pounds and forty-one pence......well, we'll call that forty." He was counting up what their mother owed for provisions he had brought from the factory. They still got them for wholesale price, not for free.

"And don't I owe you something for evaporated milk?" their mother said, hurrying into the room with her purse, keen to show promptness of payment.

"Put that away now, I'll get these," Hugo growled self-consciously, and roughly he threw a five-pound note onto the table. Their mother sank onto a chair beside him for a moment, and Maggie thought she looked relieved that at last she didn't have to apologise for lack of money, or her man.

"We're going for a walk – to explore," Maggie told her.

In the narrow hallway, Stella and Miriam shrugged themselves awkwardly into their heavy school coats, while their mother went to join Grandma in the kitchen.

"There was no need for you to get all this for us," they heard their grandmother say reprovingly, referring to all the prepared food. "We could have made do with a cup of tea." This is what she always said, but a family gathering without a proper meal was unheard of. Their mother bustled around the kitchen, her eyes wide with the strain of getting everything right.

Out of the coop at last, Maggie, Miriam and Stella walked quickly out of the town, falling into a line – one, two, three – across the width of the road. There was no need for them to say anything, or even think anything. It was enough to breathe the free and easy air of their old unit.

"Hugo's just like Grandad," Miriam said finally, coming straight out with what they all thought.

"But it's good they're both happy again, isn't it?" Stella said pacifyingly. "They've both got someone else now."

For some reason this fact lay on Maggie like a dead weight. "Yes....." she said. "But it's all rather quick, don't you think?"

"I can't imagine Dad on his own though, can you?" Miriam blurted out. And Maggie and Stella had to agree, although it was hard to say why.

"But Mum," said Maggie. "What about her, I wonder?" A stifling, oppressive feeling gathered in her chest when she thought of her mother's new 'situation,' as if she longed to break free of it on her behalf. "I suppose it means security though," she added unenthusiastically.

They hadn't really noticed where they were going, and now

found themselves emerging onto flat wild heathland which stretched up to the foot of the mountains. The mountain tops were completely hidden in mist.

They cut across the common, following a rough narrow track between dripping tall grasses and reeds, and here and there, low clumps of stunted trees and short solitary conifers. The snow was quite gone, but they were hemmed in all round by a heavy grey wall of fog. Eventually they stood together beneath a small circle of trees, stamping their feet on the ground and trying to decide whether to go back.

"I expect they'll both soon be married again," Miriam said, summing up the mood of dreary uncertainty.

"Where will that leave us, do you think?" Stella wondered, creasing her eyes up at the mist, as though she might see through it if she tried hard enough.

"We'll be alright!" Maggie said with automatic brightness, out of old habit. But then, in an uncharacteristically demonstrative gesture, she put one of her arms around Stella's forlorn shoulders. "It'll be alright, you'll see. Come on Miriam, there's no need to be fed up."

She put her other arm around Miriam, who resisted at first, then gave in to this threefold embrace beneath the umbrella of the trees.

"It'll be alright," Maggie repeated, realising that for the first time she herself believed what she was saying. The worst had happened – yet they had come through and here they were. The future, though unknown, no longer seemed frightening, and something to be dreaded. She felt an unfamiliar strength growing and growing in her body, as if she were a tree putting roots down into the earth and her arms were enveloping branches. And there, beyond the mist – she was sure of it – was a burgeoning luminosity as if the sun was trying to break through at last.

"Come on, let's go a bit further," she said, and led the way forward into the mist.

THE PARIS CONNECTION

Robert Nisbet

In the red corner, Billie, auburn, amiable, freckled. Her mission: "les maisons", the shopping spree of all time. In the fair corner: Lynne, blonde, statuesque, culture vulture. Her mission: paintings, the Louvre, Musée d'Orsay, every single painting that Paris had to offer, be it on the wall or on the pavement. In their wake, struggling more and more as the holiday went on: the poet and Rhydian. Their onetime dream: a café culture, the leisured indolence of Paris in the spring, endless cups of coffee and pavement chatter.

The first morning of their stay went very much the boys' way: a long, lazy, coffee-swilling sprawl the length of the Champs Elysées. And then, later that day, a lovely, languorous afternoon, a saunter along the banks of the Seine, with its second-hand bookstalls and arty postcards, with all their attendant Bohemian savour.

Then the pace really hotted and, through the second day, Billie carted them all on the most monumental maison-crawl, through the lower reaches of the Champs Elysées and through the length of the Rue de Rivoli. Coffee and pavement chat were in altogether shorter supply. The poet, however, was bolstered by a day's observations of Les Parisiens and their females and was able to regale Rhydian with his findings.

"Have you noticed," he mused, in about the fourteenth maison, "that the Parisian male is immensely courteous to the female? Notice, at lunch, in that restaurant. Two quite elderly gentlemen, talking so nicely to that young waitress. Did you notice? Absolutely no funny business. Quite, quite charming."

"Had something else struck you?" asked Rhydian. "Parisian males absolutely don't come into couturiers and fashion shops with their females. In every shop we've been in today we've been the only blokes in there. Interesting."

"My God," said the poet. "It's more than interesting. It means the females are bound to drop their guard, doesn't it?" At which point, they both seemed to notice a rather leggy young woman in the next aisle casually slipping off her skirt, preparatory to trying something on.

The boys were suffused with embarrassment. And then Lynne re-appeared, accompanied by an assistant, to show off a blouse. The boys were now utterly and irrevocably aware that the assistant herself must regard their presence in the shop as, at best a joke, at worst, the harbinger of a major assault on Parisian womanhood. All they could manage by way of reply was Rhydian's comment, in loud, accent-ridden French: "C'est trés chic, n'est-ce pas?" And then they fled.

No one was precisely clear as to whose idea it had been to visit the Moulin Rouge, but all the signs were, as they filed in there at midnight, that Billie and Lynne might have been responsible. Rhydian and the poet were dubious from the start. As they entered, Rhydian grew resentful of being accosted by smooth, oily Parisians in evening dress, wishing them "Bonsoir", and clearly intent on peddling them cheap champagne, in part repayment for their exorbitant entry fee. The poet took it even harder: he was sombre, severe and socialistic, muttering to himself about chandeliers and gilt and pseudo-opulence and the opium of the people. Perhaps it was the cheap champagne, perhaps it actually was the boys' discomfiture, but Lynne and Billie rapidly became hilarious.

When breasts came to be bared (some four dozen of them) the boys sat anaesthetised and gobsmacked.

"Difficult to know quite what to say about that," said Rhydian.

"I shall just quote 'Eskimo Nell'," said the poet. "It may be rare in Berkeley Square, but not in the Rio Grande."

"Cheer up, boys," said the uproarious Billie. "It's Knockers Night."

Knockers Night it may have been, but even that didn't really prepare the boys for the naked buttocks (again, some four dozen in number).

"You boys have gone very quiet," said Lynne.

It was then that it became clear that the cheap champagne had had a befuddling effect on Rhydian also, for only a drunken man would have glared around the table and declaimed, "You must remember that what stimulates is not excess. It is not acres of naked flesh, it is your discreet and delicate revelation. Just that touch of detail, which promises much and delivers little."

Lynne mused: "Mmm. I'll remember that."

For many days the boys had done little by way of Bohemian stuffing. On the return journey the poet was constantly at pains to reassure Rhydian that, just as Paris had a café culture, so there was the quite exotic phenomenon of a British Rail buffet culture. On the crossing, they ate little, preferring to cosset their delicate stomachs (while Lynne and Billie rampaged from bar to deck and back again, knocking back schooners of red wine). But Britain would be different. They'd get to Paddington, the poet said, and the train down West, and they'd feast off beakers of steaming tea, crisps and pork pies. They laid their plans.

Their tube across London was delayed, so they had to rush from Paddington and bypass the buffet. Strangely, there was no buffet on the train.

"It's to do with the strike on Tuesday," said the guard. "Can't help you." So, growing now genuinely hungry, they waited on a feast of tea and pies at Swansea, as Billy Bunter might have awaited a midnight feast in the dorm. Train delayed by signal failure at Cardiff. Into Swansea, but straight out again on waiting connection. No buffet on branch line trains, that they knew, but the poet had pinned his hopes on Carmarthen.

"Sorry, boy," said the guard when they asked him. "The buffet in Carmarthen closes at six." Their train pulled into Carmarthen at quarter to seven and the boys contemplated a future without tea and comestibles.

Maybe Billie and Lynne had been overcome with remorse. Whatever. They'd had a wonderful holiday and felt now they'd like to spread some of their joy into their partners' lives. "Hang on there," said Lynne. "Billie and I will have a look around."

Arthur and Gareth were railwaymen who'd worked on Carmarthen station for decades, and had retreated in their spare time, to Pontyates and St. Clears respectively, there to live lives of unblemished respectability. Nothing in their previous existence had prepared them for the events of that evening.

It was April, getting on for seven, light enough for them to perceive clearly what was shortly to be perceived, but growing gloomy enough for the mysterious quality of that sight to be hidden away from other passengers on the platform.

Arthur and Gareth were in the guards' office, drinking tea, smoking, and none too harassed by the 6.10 Swansea to Milford Haven, which was in the background waiting to pull out. Then there walked, unsteadily it seemed, past their window, two women. Fine women, lovely women. One was tall, blonde and statuesque. (One says "statuesque" – Arthur and Gareth would probably have said "stonking"). The other was auburn, pretty, funny. (Arthur and Gareth might have said she was "a piece of all right" – but remember, their previous lives had been blameless).

It seemed that the blonde one (called "Lynne", they overheard) wasn't well. Her friend had an arm round her waist and seemed to be comforting her. Eventually, she steered her friend over to a spot right by the two railwaymen's window. They were well clear of the few other passengers and the friend seemed to want to screen Lynne from view – perhaps, so the railwaymen suddenly realised, as a prelude to some intimate adjustment.

"Just try loosening your tights for a second," said the auburn one, in a voice that was clearly audible to the railwaymen on the other side of the window. (It seemed the women were unaware of Arthur's and Gareth's presence just a few feet away). Fighting off a growing sense of unreality (and mounting erections), Gareth and Arthur watched as Lynne, hemmed in by her friend, raised her skirt a little way and lowered her tights just a shade. Their lives, before so blameless, were visited now by a wondrous vision: just a glimpse, a moment's flash (a suggestion, the idea, no more) of lush, white, naked thigh. It seemed as if Fate had intended it for them alone.

When the knock came on their door, just seconds later, the railwaymen gave voice simultaneously, but huskily. "Come in." The auburn one led in her friend.

"I'm terribly sorry to bother you," she said, "but my friend isn't too well. May she sit down?"

"Course she can," said Arthur, hoarsely still. Then, rallying: "Can we get you anything?"

As the blonde smiled gently but wanly around the little office, the auburn one said, "Well, this is an awful thing to say, but we had to rush on at Swansea after a delay and I was hoping I could get Lynne a cup of tea at Carmarthen. And of course we're late and the buffet's closed."

"She'll have a cup of tea with us," said Arthur, reaching for the pot steaming beside him.

Lynne sighed tremulously. "That's really so kind," she said, "but I don't think I could take a cup for a little while ... Have you any . . beakers or anything to take it back on to the train?"

"Gareth, get out those buffet beakers. Sugar?"

Lynne and her auburn friend smiled gently, sadly, wistfully, á la Mona Lisa. The auburn one said, "I'm sure this is the most awful cheek, but .. well .. when my friend's blood level goes down too far, she has to eat. I don't suppose ..."

"Now don't you worry, love. The boys have got plenty of grub here. How would your friend fancy a pork pie?"

Buffet culture. The boys contemplated Billie's parcel. Two beakers of hot sweet tea. Four pork pies, two chocolate éclairs, six ham sandwiches, an Eccles cake, four packets of cheese and onion crisps and a small sachet of Worcester sauce. They contemplated also the warm, outward-opening April evening, the spring, the summer to come – and the real, deep joys of middle-aged marital love. That most particularly: a curious tenderness in the gut.

THE VANISHING LAKE

Boyd Clack

Mike was broke. It was frustrating. He was seventeen. He was in the Lower Sixth. Most of his friends had left school and were working, or not working, as the case may be. Either way they were having fun. They were alive while he was dead.

It was 1968, what was to become known as 'The Summer of Love'. Mike saw hippies on the TV news: a beautiful girl at a rock festival writhed in primitive ecstasy, her naked breasts adorned with psychedelic paint; a tall thin American with long black hair slipped a daffodil into the barrel of an automatic rifle. People were making love, expanding their consciousness, exploring their potential while he, Mike Evans, 'Poet Laureate of Despair' was forced to traipse Eloi-like each day to Cefn Glyn Grammar School to be force-fed the useless junk-food of bourgeois education.

It nauseated him and he was broke.

Terry was broke too. Terry was Mike's hero. He was grown up. He was nineteen, nearly twenty. He lived alone in a one-bedroomed flat behind the vegetable shop.

Terry didn't work; he lived on his wits, and the dole. He was tall, good looking. People either liked him or loathed him. He played guitar and sang like Bob Dylan in a Welsh accent – a sort of Bob Dylan Thomas: 'It's all right ma ..I'm only dreaming.' Terry was Mike's friend.

Mike's parents were disappointed. There were lots of decent boys he could have as friends. Terry was 'no good'. It was rumoured he had got a girl into trouble. He got into fights. He once went into a fish shop to buy a bag of chips with his white shirt soaked in blood from a punched nose and a split lip. The blood fell onto the chips like tomato sauce. He was *known* to the local police; they used to stop him in the streets. Mike once heard him tell a copper his name was Jumping Jack Flash. He even spelt it out for him as he wrote it down in his little book. Yes, Terry was a bad lot and Mike thought he was great.

Mike sat on the wall outside his house. It was Friday evening. The summer was coming to an end. It was still light though. There was nothing to do.

The previous night he had been drunk. He and Terry had run singing and shouting along the street behind the school. They had cursed the narrow-minded little town. They had been warriors in the war between the old and the new. The mystical forces had been with them. Tonight though, minus the adrenalin of youthful defiance and the liberating alcohol, Mike made a forlorn figure, perched there in front of the battleship-grey railings.

A car pulled up. It was Royston Parks' father's car. A posh, fast car. Royston Parks' father was a bookie; his mother had a mink coat. He had problems stemming from his parents' stormy relationship. Royston took Valium. The car doors opened and Terry and Royston got out.

"We're going to Porthcawl. You comin'?" Terry asked.

"I can't, mun. I'm broke," Mike replied with measured pathos.

"I got some money, don't worry about it," Terry said, as Mike hoped he would.

"Aye, I got a couple of bob an' all," Royston Parks added.

Terry laughed. "I broke into the electric meter. Got fourteen quid all in two-bob bits." He jangled his pockets in confirmation.

"Won't you get into trouble?" Mike asked, instantly shocked at his own naiveté.

"Bugger that!" Terry replied. "You comin' or what?"

Mike climbed into the back seat of Royston Parks' father's car and off they roared, listening to Sgt. Pepper's on the radio as they sped through the twilight. Royston Parks drove fast. His eyes, manic from the medication, darting from point to point; his fingers tapping out the beat of the music on the steering wheel. Terry smoked Woodbines and sang along. Mike just stared out the window, fascinated by the strange, speeded-up world that shot by, wondering whether he was, in fact, intelligent, like he'd been told, or not. By the time they arrived in Porthcawl he had come to no concrete conclusion.

Their first port of call was 'The Buccaneer', a large pub on the sea front. It was the haunt of degenerates, home of free love and cheap drugs. They ordered three pints of Snakebite and three packets of smoky bacon crisps and sat at a table near the door. It was almost dark outside and 'The Buccaneer' was full.

Mike studied the people around him as Royston Parks beat out some internal rhythm on a beer mat. The females flitted from table to table like exotic butterflies. One of them settled on Terry. She seemed to know him. She knelt adoringly at his feet, dressed in a skimpy shirt. Mike studied her face, her short blond hair. She was laughing and telling Terry about some wild adventure she'd had with the members of a local rock band. Mike couldn't make out the details but there was obviously a very pronounced sexual aspect to it.

He stared at her teeth as she spoke. Her beautiful damp lips ... He longed to kiss them; to run his tongue along her perfect white teeth; to taste the rum-and-blackcurrant of her breath. She took no notice of him. It was as if he didn't exist. For a moment he felt perplexed, and hurt. Couldn't she see that he was a poet? A romantic figure? Could she possibly be so shallow as to be put off by his glasses? Who could tell? His emotion turned from pain to distaste as, with a snorting laugh she completed her anecdote and kissed Terry on the lips. He watched as she sauntered, with unseemly gyrations, back to the unsavoury coterie from which she had emerged.

"What a slag," was Terry's sole comment. Mike could only nod his head in solemn agreement. After five pints at the Buck, the boys left and went into another pub, and then another. The night passed in a haze of cigarette smoke, pint glasses and flashing jukeboxes. Conversation ranged from the trivially humorous to the philosophically inept. By chucking-out time they were semi-paralytic. Royston Parks insisted on stopping at a hotel where his father knew the manager and getting a dozen cans of Tartan Export to take away with them. He drove at a demented pace along the winding coast road, guzzling triumphantly from one of the cans, before screeching to a halt just above a dark and secluded beach.

They left the car and stumbled down a grassy bank to the unseen sand below. They laughed, threw sand into the air and kicked water at each other with their feet, aware that the salt was permanently damaging the leather of their shoes. Terry sang at the top of his lungs; "Come gather round people and heed ye the call!", his rich, husky voice echoing through the darkness. A small pool glistened.

"I'm going for a swim," Terry declared. He ran towards the pool and flung himself forward full length into it, and landed with a smack. He groaned and rolled over. The knee of his trouser was almost torn in half. The 'pool' was a slab of wet stone illuminated by the moonlight. Mike and Royston Parks were paralysed with laughter and Terry, anaesthetised by the alcohol, soon joined in. He tore off the bottom half of the trouser leg and flung it into the sea. Then they clambered back up the sandy bank to the grass, which took some time as each of them found himself slipping back as soon as he had reached the top, and this gave rise to further bouts of hysterical laughter. Eventually, though, they made it and, sitting on the grass, gasping, exhausted, catching their breath, they looked out at the waves and the starlight that was glinting on the sea. Royston Parks opened more cans of Tartan Export to replace the ones they had spilled on their descent to the beach.

The sky sparkled. The sea sparkled. The night glittered. The world was magical and fresh. Disneyland. The future and past stood side by side, in stillness. Life wasn't such a terrible thing after all.

"What d'you reckon about stars then?" Royston Parks broke the silence.

"What about them?" Terry responded.

"D'you reckon people live on 'em or what?"

"I dunno."

"Aye, but what do you *think* ?"

"I don't know, mun! What's the point of thinkin' if you don't know?"

"Surely," Mike interjected, "Surely that negates any discussion of things like philosophy and religion altogether, don't it?"

There was no further discussion on the subject of extra-terrestrial life. Mike's incongruous remark had given birth to an unquestioning silence.

On the drive back a weariness overtook them. They were hypnotised by the whizzing blackness, by the headlights on the road. As they got to the outskirts of home, the Glyn Mountain loomed – a more intense blackness than that of the night that surrounded it.

Mike gaped at it, gaped at the starlit sky above it.

There was a legend attached to the mountain – a lake that moved. Children would find it from time to time; play beside it, dip their feet in it, even swim in it. When they went back to find it again, it was always gone. It would turn up at some other spot later on. The Vanishing Lake it was called, not surprisingly. Mike had never seen it, but he'd spoken to those who had. He wondered where it was now. Was it, at that very moment, involved in the process of appearing, or disappearing? Did it ever appear without human eyes to look on it? He strained his own eyes to see, but the darkness was too comprehensive.

That night Mike slept on a speeding roller-coaster. The ceiling spun. He was semi-conscious inside a kaleidoscope of colour. When he woke his bed was soiled with confetti-textured sick.

He took the quilt to the bathroom and washed it under the hot tap, telling his mother he had spilt a cup of tea. She didn't believe him; she put it down to unnatural practices. Mike's mother was big on unnatural practices.

Saturday passed in anti-climax. The wonder of the night before night faded as grey reality re-established itself. Mike thought about San Francisco, Haight Street, Scot McKenzie, pot and LSD. He did his homework and drank tea. There was a film on TV but it wasn't much good. He went to bed, falling asleep with T.S.Eliot clutched in his hand.

Sunday afternoon, Terry called at the house.

"Can I see Mike, Mrs Evans, please?" he asked. Mike came to the door in his slippers.

"Orright, Terry?" Mike's mother shuffled off in disapproval.

"Aye." There was a brief silence. "You heard about Parksey?" Terry continued in conversational tones.

"No."

"He's dead. Crashed his father's car. Into the wall it was, down by the factory." Terry seemed embarrassed by the information that was his to impart

"Jesus Christ." What else could you say?

"They reckon he did it on purpose. Had a row with his mother." Terry shrugged; it wasn't up to him to adjudicate on such matters.

"Good God."

"Aye." Terry brightened up. "Comin' for a pint?"

"I can't..." Mike began. He thought for a moment. Why couldn't he? "Yeah, right. Hang on an' I'll get my jacket."

Royston Parks was buried on a cold grey day. Mike and Terry didn't go to the service. They didn't go to the reception either; but they did stand among the small band of people at the graveside. Parksey's mother was there, in her mink coat, crying. His father stood at her side, motionless in his black overcoat. It was clear that they didn't love each other any more, but for the moment they were united in grief.

Eventually the others wandered off and Mike and Terry were left alone, with Royston. Mike found himself thinking about the stars, about the Vanishing Lake, about the Summer of Love that had ended so tragically.

"It's all right ma...I'm only dying..."

It began to rain, so they left.

DOCUMENTS

Stevie Davies

She does not whimper. Her voicebox constricts, her mind freezes. Even a tiny, ignorant child does not have the luxury of exclamation in such extremity. Powerless bewilderment is total. She stands like a statue to be shaven. Metal clippers cold on her neck mow over the crown of her head; clusters of pale curls drift down at either side. Her bald head under the bathroom light when she climbs up to the mirror shines like stone.

Later the skull of stone becomes a stubble-field, sprouting black hairs like a man's chin.

You've bottle-blonded her, the man snarls. *What do you take me for, woman, a cretin? Palming me off with some Slav's bastard.*

Later a medley of trains; the Channel-crossing; Swansea and the safety of a Jenkins stepfather, Jenkins aunties; growing up, teacher-training; the hairdressing man never seen or heard again.

"I'm going out to work in Germany," she told her stepfather in the Oystercatcher at Mumbles, their local, where she sipped at lager and lime while he drank his lunchtime pint.

"Oh aye?" he queried in his steady way.

"Yes, there are opportunities, you see, in the Forces schools ... my German's fluent, and ... I need a change, I suppose."

"Well, you'll write to us." He pretended to take it phlegmatically, ruffled her rebellious dark curls. "Those little blue airmail-jobs: mind and write small, there's not that much room."

"I'll see you *lots*," she tried to josh him. "The world's so small. We have aeroplanes nowadays, Owen, it's the 1950s, in case you haven't noticed."

"It will be ... difficult for your mother. To see you go back there."

"But it's not the same now, is it? It's a new world. They're our allies now. You can't hold the new generation responsible for what the old ones did."

Owen took a drink of his beer and restored the glass carefully to the beermat, as if great matters depended on accurate placement.

"She was much ... hurt," he stated.

Isolde's dander came up. Were they to live under the constant tyranny of Renate's unspecified misfortunes, two decades done with, for the rest of their lives?

"Well, I know that," she said with some impatience. "Well, I don't know, actually, do I, because she won't talk about it."

Always this fearful tiptoeing round her mother's susceptibilities. What evicted them from Germany in that time before Isolde's memory was properly rooted? What tacitly forbade her to enquire into her own history? Renate exuded martyrdom. But Isolde could not see her mother as a victim: this lush, commanding, flaxen woman who towered above all the Welsh aunties, with the sole exception of Lennie, and all but two uncles. Only with Owen did her mother drop the guard; the domineering manner seldom asserted itself and she submitted to his reign of stoical gentleness with every appearance of contentment.

Yet even here lay an element of prohibition. Renate's high, intelligent forehead spoke of burdensome secret wisdom, won far too late and at too high a cost, knowledge tinged with dark apprehension. She flapped and fussed around Owen's health, as if he were sure to be wrenched from her by whatever malign spirits controlled the world. And she would fight them every step of the way, prevent ambush by coddling and feeding him, weighing him on the bathroom scales, for God's sake, the poor chap was weighed every week like a baby and begged to plump himself up. Owen was naturally gaunt and wiry but he must be fattened.

There were lulls of inert detachment. Renate would sink down at the dressing table, her pale hair down her back, crinkling from the net that bagged it overnight, her head propped on one hand, staring not at her sidelong face but into the space beside it, the three-quarters of the mirror which reflected back the wall behind her, the door with its shadowy dressing gowns hanging from twin hooks.

Isolde could not construe her mother's gaze, the abyss in her eyes. That limitless withdrawal had used to scare her; with the years it repelled her, as Renate's arrogance did the rest of Owen's family.

And then the peculiar because passionate ambivalence of her mother towards herself, alternating ironic tolerance of the little creature and its foibles, with feints at rigid discipline and phases of desperate possessiveness, holding Isolde's wide face up to the light with too hard a grip, yearning toward it with more hunger than Isolde could possibly fulfil. Not as if she looked for Isolde there but tracked someone who came before Isolde, and was the message Isolde was supposed to be delivering, but had scrambled in the transmission.

Oh Liebling ... Schatz ... and a host of endearments in German, which had, Isolde felt in adult life, an operatic quality. Other people's mothers just took them grumblingly for what they were – whereas a sense of an elusive someone else, somewhere else, had haunted her. A clandestine other, hidden within herself or lurking behind her. Isolde in her twenties was sick of secrecy. Why couldn't Mum spit it out? It couldn't be that bad.

The trouble was, it could. She had read about the death-camps and so on. So it could be that bad. But Isolde was Welsh, not German. Isolde was the new generation, free of all that. Her own speech bore no vestige of an accent, though her mother's could still be thick, marking her out as a foreigner in an area where even the English were foreigners, and whereas tribal intimacy could encompass family feuds of fabulous longevity as an aspect of bonding, it winced away from strangers. Especially a busty Kraut who knew her own mind, flaunted sunburnt skin in skimpy floral sundresses and made no secret of regarding her husband's family as the bottom of the barrel.

"If you could just be a little more ... tender of my sisters' feelings," suggested Owen.

"Bear with their prejudice and provincialism and small-mindedness? That's what you mean, *ne*? Yes, all right, for you, Owen, I'll try to *shrink*."

Shrink she couldn't. Issie watched her explosively keeping her trap shut while the aunties wittered. Issie liked the aunties and could see nothing demeaning in their unlettered, cosy conversation. She sat on a pouffe at Auntie Margiad's coal-fire and let herself be blessed by the continuum of ordinariness, summed up in choirs of knitting needles accompanying gossip which seemed at one with coalsmoke in shabby Morriston rooms tinged with the tang of damp. Renate acted hoity-toity in this air that suffocated her; that was the only way her self-respect could articulate itself in an alien world.

"Displaced persons," she once told Isolde. "That's what we are."

"*I'm* not." Meaning: you be if you want to be but leave me out of it.

"You don't understand," Renate said vaguely. The Mumbles train chuntered round the arc of the bay. Isolde, looking out at the glistening crescent of mudflats and the incoming tide, felt totally at home.

"I'm Welsh," she affirmed, loudly, so that the other passengers travelling to the pier and lighthouse could hear. As if offering them all a sight of her passport.

"Are you? Well, that's good. Yes, that's very good." Her mother reached for her hand and squeezed it. Now, realised Isolde, her mother had to be displaced on her own. The sun sparkled on the waves in mean mockery; the pane interposed a screen between them and the outside and Isolde felt her vitality ebb. "My little Welsh *cariad*," said Renate, tacitly agreeing to be displaced on her own.

The trained stopped at Oystermouth and folk got off and folk got on.

"I'm the same as what you are," stated Isolde with bleak loyalty.

"Shall we have fish and chips at the pier? Ice-cream?" asked Renate with new gaiety. It was as though Isolde had released her own energies for Renate to rise upon.

"What shall we have? We can have whatever we like." She still childishly marvelled at the lifting of rationing; a penance of stint completed .

"I'm not bothered," sulked Isolde.

"What's up, little love?"

"Nothing." The train pooped and resumed its leisurely chuff round the bay. Isolde pouted and looked down at her knobbly knees poking out of her cotton skirt. There was a pause and then the brainwave hit her. Before she could think to put the brakes on, she blurted,

"Are we Jewish?"

"Jewish?" Renate swivelled, in astonishment that moved rapidly to affront. "No, of course not. What's got into your head now?"

"I thought we might be Jews, that's all. How do I know?"

"No, thank God. You may absolutely and categorically assure yourself that we are pure-blooded Aryans. Good God, do I look like a Jew?" she hissed.

"I don't know. I don't know what one looks like."

"No, well, let's change the subject to something, something" – she groped for an English word and finding none, hissed, "*sympathisch*."

Now it was Renate's turn to be sullen and withdrawn. She breathed heavily and falteringly as Isolde devoured ice-cream in the seafront restaurant at Mumbles Pier, squinting out at the tide foaming and boiling as it powered its way in, until they seemed to be floating on an Ark above the waters. The sea rushed in upon the rocks on which the flimsy restaurant sat and pounded them satisfyingly. Spume flew up in jets. As Renate's spirits fell, Isolde's convulsed, and she became loud and raucous. She clamoured to have a go on the roundabout and slide, and whined for a swim, though they had brought neither costume nor towel. She ignored two tears that bled from her mother's eyes, to be wiped away by Renate's thumb in a gesture of self-contempt.

And how could one tell the difference between the unspeakable guilt of the perpetrator and the unspoken suffering of the victim? They both dived for the same cover: numb, exilic silence.

"I can't tell you, see, if she won't," said Owen, shifting from haunch to haunch on his stool. "It would be a breaking of her confidence. Let's talk about something else now, lovely." Isolde bent her head and said nothing. The nothing that she said was a silent condemnation, a reply in its own terms to the barrage of silence with which her innocent questions had been met by both parties. Beyond that silence lay something threatening, yes, but a wounding knowledge that was due to her.

"I've brought you up as my own, Issie, my one ewe lamb. As far as I'm concerned, you are my own. I've never had the gift of the gab. Not my style, see. But can't that be enough for you? It is for me."

It was unprecedented for the shy and undemonstrative Owen to come out with such a speech. It was less than manly, he assumed, to express emotions. You should just know, without having to be told. But now his pale eyes, so striking in that unremarkable, rather weasly face, held hers with level candour. He had been her rock. She returned the gaze like a mutual grip. In his own person, he comprehended all she needed of a history. Her restless inquisition stopped there, at his habits and routines, his liking for roast lamb and mint sauce, his propped socked feet on the fender to doze after tea. What more did one need? She was replete suddenly with the generosity of her portion in life, and, looking over at him, suffered a qualm at knowing him mortal.

"You've meant everything to us," she murmured.

The foggy hubbub of the pub, with its beery gales of laughter and babble of eternal anecdote, embraced them in its tepid fug. It was not clear that Owen had caught what she said, turning round to squint over his shoulder at the clock. At any rate, he said nothing in reply. Yet she did think he had heard, for as he turned back, his eye snagged in hers, and she saw, with a squeeze of the heart, that he was moved. They both looked away in different directions.

"Walk it off on the beach?" he suggested after downing his half.

"Get some good sea-air in our lungs."

They stumbled across the pebbly wilderness beneath the shelving parapet, bending to glean razor-shell or driftwood. Salt-laden gusts threw back the gulls breasting the current. Isolde stood in the flow of wind, looking out, the mudflats a gleaming crescent of sudden desolation, for she looked by the light of smell, and that was rank, mortal, telling of evisceration and decay. The exquisite mother-of-pearl, pink-lipped shell in her hand was the husk of a life only, a life digested into other lives, themselves devoured. The rank, marine odour combined with the moody mobility of the cloudscape, light dissolving into a looming grey bank. The smell told now of rot, now of vitality, as if indeterminate between womb and gut.

"Try to break it to your mother gently," counselled Owen as they toiled up the steep hill into Mumbles.

*

"Why?" Renate could not see why any rational person should choose to quit Wales for Germany. She held that truth to be self-evident.

"It's an opportunity," said Isolde.

"For what? An opportunity for what?"

"Well, for seeing something of the world."

"I particularly do not wish that you go there. I wish you do not."

"But I particularly do want to go."

"Yes, yes, and don't we all know why? To spite me, your mother. That's why. Because I went to all that trouble to get you out, your perversity insists on going back. Despite having such wonderful qualifications – we scrimped for you, did you not notice? We went short ourselves to put you through Froebel. But despite the grief you knew it would cause me – or *because* of it? – you go. You go. Of course."

Chip off the old block, Isolde's chin came up. "Of course not. That's nonsense."

"Oh, so I talk nonsense, do I?"

"Yes."

"You are punishing me – for something that was – not – my – fault!"

"I am *not* – punishing – you! What would you need to be punished for?"

Renate went white. "Look at your hair!" she screamed, preposterously. "*Deine Haare*, Isolde! It's a disgrace. It's like a ... bird's nest."

"What the hell has my hair got to do with it?"

"It's greasy, that's what." She choked. "Look at you!"

They were shouting, one at either end of the dinner table. Emotion dishevelled Renate's English accent and grammar, revealing what she most wished to abandon, her roots. When her mother raged in this berserk way, Isolde had generally knuckled under.

"If you don't like how I look," retorted Isolde, "that's up to you."

"You are a cold, ungrateful girl!"

"*Me* cold!"

"Yes. You. After all what I've done for you!"

"What? What have you done?"

"Owen, she asks what I've done for her! Where are you going? Owen, where do you think you're going? Oh, that's right, run away – go on, skedaddle when the going gets tough. Didn't even fight in the war like a man, him, no, he was in a Reserved Occupation. Real men don't turn tail and run away, they stand by their women, real men fight," she raged, following him out into the corridor where he was lifting his jacket from the peg. "Where are you going?" and she actually made as if to collar him, her lunge accompanied by a look of pleading fright.

"Out for a drink," he mumbled. "Out for a bit of peace."

"But you've just come in from a drink!" she wailed.

Off he trotted out of the front door, which he gently latched.

"Oh, leave the poor bloke alone," said Isolde. She hated it when her mother, roused, seemed to revert to some primitive code that held it offensive for a man to be so inoffensive. You could see any day what 'real men', tanked up on booze and brotherly bondings, did to their hangdog wives.

"He's a lovely man."

"Yes," said Renate, pausing. "He is. A lovely man. What for do you want to leave him then, *Liebling*?"

The storm abruptly abated; the wind went out of Isolde's sails with a banal deflation. She plumped down in the chair.

"I don't want to. There's been a bit of trouble at school. Man-trouble." She bet her mother wouldn't press her to any shameful disclosures. Renate stared. Her eyes bulged slightly. Then she too subsided.

"So – you are going to Germany against my explicit advice. And you will want a passport, *ne*? And to acquire a passport, you will need your birth certificate."

Isolde said nothing. They seemed to be reaching through to some core which she had not conceived. Her mind flashed back to the possible cause of her mother's distress, which she now clearly recognised as her first father.

"*Mutti*," she said, recurring to the baby-language of their earliest relationship, "I don't care about my Dahl father – if that's what you're worrying about." She reached across the table-cloth, with its field of pallid cream flowers and the ghosts of long-ago stains lingering semi-legibly. "Really, I don't. I couldn't give a bean. Owen is my father, I'm a Jenkins, really, I feel like a Jenkins. I wish Owen had adopted me." Her surname had never felt organically related to her Christian name. It was an arbitrary code you came with, like a number, and among the crop of schoolmates, from Roberts to Williams, 'Dahl' had seemed no more alien than the Scottish Farquhar or the Italian Bianchi.

"I'm not going to Germany for my roots," she assured her mother. "I've got roots. Too many roots. I'm all root. I'm leguminous. Aunties, uncles, cousins. Honest. I'm not that daft."

Renate visibly relaxed. Having calmed her mother, Isolde did not want the monster that lurked in her roused by further probing, though there were things she yearned to know: why had Owen never formally adopted her? What about her German father?

The birth certificate was extracted from a locked tin in Renate's room and placed silently, like a sacrificial offering, on the table in front of Isolde: "There you are."

"Right. Thanks." She did not wish to betray the avid curiosity she felt, and allowed the document to lie unread on the table, with its Gothic script in ink that had once been black on white and now was sepia on grey.

"Don't you want to inspect it?"

Isolde looked down as bidden, and opened it with affected nonchalance.

Father: Paul Heinrich Dahl. Occupation: Official of Race Board. Age: 23.

"He did not accept that you were his." Renate reached a glass from the rack and began to dry it, with meticulous scrupulosity, holding it up to the light so as to be sure she had purified and polished it. "After the divorce, you and I became non-persons."

"But, *Mutti,* why?"

"Your dusky skin he didn't like apparently, 'slanty eyes, wide face, high cheekbones, square build'," Renate mimicked, as if she had only heard some fool uttering the offensive phrases yesterday, round the corner. "We were both fair so you could not possibly be his, oh no, 'Asiatic *Mischling*', according to Mighty Mind," said Renate. She was quivering with indignation that had been festering for twenty years. Suddenly she thought better of it. Stood and, quivering, swerved her sights to aim at Dahl's daughter. "He was only worth forgetting. I can tell you no more. I beg you should not pester for information that cannot now concern you. You have assured me," she stated, her voice rising in a threatening checkmate, "that you don't look for antecedents. You feel you have plenty of family already. Excess of roots. You are a Welsh girl. A Jenkins. Good. Let that stand. When I am dead, you are free to poke about in my private past, Isolde, and until then you must just be patient. End of discussion."

"But, *Mutti*," whispered Isolde, her voice husky. "Was I his?" Her insides churned and tumbled. "Was I?"

"How dare you ask?" Renate blazed.

The door closed in Isolde's face. It made little difference whether it was latched gently in her stepfather's way, or furiously slammed in her mother's, whose pain reverberated through the house. Isolde could sometimes distinguish the violence of the pain from the impotence of the person. She did so now.

"OK," she acquiesced. "OK."

"OK is American slang, not correct Queen's English."

"OK, I'll stop it then."

"Isolde, I tell you one more thing. You are an average person, *ne*? Average for Swansea, average for today. Had you been raised where and when I was born, also an average but very correct and patriotic person, imagine, you might have believed wrong things. You might have married an up-and-coming fellow at seventeen and had black swastikas on your wedding cake. Later you began to see some flaws in the system – and you have to live with that, every day of your life, you have to live with being you. I go down to the fishmonger now and fetch some cod."

Isolde sat on her bed, spelling over the name *Paul Heinrich Dahl* with faltering breaths. She might be getting flu, her skin was all aquiver, her stomach felt nasty. Mrs James from next-door clopped past the window, lingering in case a Jenkins should emerge to share a morsel of choice Queen's Road gossip. *Born in Munich. Swastikas on your wedding cake. Race board. Average person.* In Isolde's genes, the filth of Paul Heinrich? She looked down at the sunburnt arm and hand he had disowned, the document in her lap. *Asiatic Mischling?* Beserk, dirty-minded language. Don't let him be my father. But Renate is her mother, oh yes, no getting away from that. Breeder of this mistake, this tawny hybrid: no escape. She wished she were Lennie's child, or Margiad's.Documents ... *Dokumente...* The word drifted up from years ago, when documents were precious, mythical to her ignorant mind, longed-for by adults who spent days and weeks aching and agonising over them; and, when procured, the documents were held in both hands tenderly like holy wafers. Documents were keys to unlock one gate that let you out, another that would gain you entrance.

A man's hidden voice behind a tall counter with formal politeness requests *Dokumente.*

Panic stations. Hearts pounding. She can feel *Mutti*'s hammering. Now or never. Isolde on tiptoe dressed in a dark green velvet coat, her nose just above the counter-top, peeps over to the bespectacled official who lets them through. *Quite correct. Please pass along.* She can feel her mother's faintness .

They are on their own. The train-rhythm urges: *Dokumente, Dokumente, bitte.* Snuggling up to *Mutti* on the train, hanging on tight, sitting as close as one can without entering the other person, thumb hooked through one of the button-loops of Renate's coat, cheek against the comforting fur of the animal that had been killed and stripped to make the coat.

Silver fox. I got it dirt-cheap from Mrs Levi ... but she didn't need it where she was going.

Mrs Levi, who was she? Isolde imagines a woman culled and stripped to make the coat in which Renate Dahl luxuriates – the coat into whose depths she pushes her face as the train flees through polders of an eerie sameness, rushing from one flatland to its mirror-image, on and on. *Dokumente, Dokumente.*

If you must be seasick, darling, for God's sake don't be sick over my coat. My daughter is bilious, she requires a bucket.

A long night over the bucking channel. Disembarkation into a foreign land, with a language of estrangement.

Have your documents to hand, please.

She grasps the silver fox hem with both hands while Renate fishes out papers, hand thrust forth shakily while they are examined, entreating immediate return. In her imperious black hat with a silver pin and a pheasant-feather.

Off down a labyrinth of corridors, through waiting rooms, antechambers, pausing for a cup of thick syrupy tea dispensed from a kiosk, more mazes, the child dragging in sullen exhaustion at her mother's gloved hand: *Want to go home now.*

This is home, Liebling.

A later panic. In Swansea or Cardiff, because the accent is musical and home-like, but depersonalised, through a tannoy: *Bring your personal luggage and have your documents ready for inspection.* They shuffle along in a queue, sweating in heavy coats, the day being mild. She and *Mutti* tightly clutch one another, interned as Enemy Aliens. Whiff of Renate's sweat cloaked in talc, stalking along, head high, magnificent chest puffed out in indignation, for in what way are refugees aliens? Have they not suffered enough? To be pelted with coals. To be transported to an island and shut up behind wire fences sharing quarters with *Ostjuden:* "East European Jews," whispers Renate. "Dregs of the dregs. Look at their parrot-noses." Isolde remembers that phrase especially, for after the parrot accusation her mother adds to the catalogue of Eastern Jewry's sins: "Their oily dark skins. Such black, greasy hair."

Then her eyes slew to her daughter's dark hair as if it bears witness and condemns her in a court of law. She quails, tucks in her chin and purses her lipsticked mouth, rocking herself slightly. A whimper escapes and her throat works. She twists a swathe of Isolde's rich, thick hair round one hand and kisses it, her face contorted, as if it suicidally fought itself.

Then Renate turns to the woman next to her, a dignified person just spurned as 'parrot-nosed' and tremblingly offers a cigarette, which is quietly declined.

I had blond hair once, is the thought that now, as she muses on her document, pops up in Isolde's mind. *Honey-blond but it was a lie.*

Isolde sees it all in her mind's eye, too keenly, so that a fist seems to grasp her heart and screw it round in her breast. Tears film her eyes. For in the sudden snapshot of memory, she is a little girl, being roughly hoisted out of Renate's lap; can hear herself roar in protest.

She is set down at the centre of a room, beneath a standard lamp. The strange cold tool is applied to her nape. It trawls from nape to forehead.

"Keep still."

She does. She stands in mute terror, swags of pale hair falling away to either side. She shuts her eyes, so as not to see the man with the clippers. She feels his breath on the bald track across her skull. Now he shears the sides, which drop softly away. She holds her breath, tight-closes lips, eyes, mind, but her ears she cannot close.

A fundamental cleansing, she hears him say. *We'll see what's underneath this filthy bleach, bitch.*

Around red-sandaled feet tendrils of fair hair scatter in a benign circle of yellow light. The waves, like the mess on a hairdresser's shop floor, appear alien, impersonal. They could be anyone's.

Why doesn't her mother intervene? Why just sit there, pale and haggard? Is she ill? Does she also see Isolde as somehow infested, infected?

Isolde looks in the mirror and weeps for pity of the bald child staring back. A deathshead. A moonman. Chilly, shameful sight. Some woman (not her mother – a maid? do they have maids? are they rich?) has wrapped the bald head in a blue silk scarf. Cool and fluid, it keeps slipping so as to expose the hairless scalp beneath.

It was stupid of me, Renate was confiding to Owen in one of their midnight conversations, as Isolde prowled the stairs like a ghost barefoot after bad dreams: *But you see we were all blondes those days – blonde was the in colour – and a good three quarters out of a bottle. There was actually a black market in hair dye, believe it or not. What is one to do? He wants a boy. He wants a pure Saxon boy. Instead he gets her, a dark little Arab. And when I see this and the marriage on the skids, what do I do? I take action. Namely I bleach the child's hair, for her own good. The mother hen protects her chick. Nature, ne? You could not fault me there. But he spots the roots, you see, he spots the roots. She is his throwback, some Slav ancestor on the mother's side, but he blames it on me! me! My pedigree pure Aryan back to 1711 so I must have been playing about, mustn't I? Can you imagine me throwing my eye at another man, no, have you ever, Owen? Of course not. Would I lower myself, would I stoop? What does he think I am, some kind of ... trollop ?*

No reply from Owen. Isolde would see his lips sucking at one another, like an old man's. He kept masticating on nothing, swallowing draughts of his own saliva. He digested obscene absurdity into the stuff of his own normality. Was that capitulation or difficult mercy? Did he lie down as a human bridge between ethical worlds, and offer his body for Renate Dahl to stagger belligerently across? Or just kowtow; anything for the quiet life?

The silver fur coat, thinks Isolde, *it's still here somewhere, isn't it, and I'm going to Germany anyway, what's the odds?* She pokes about in the wardrobe among the violet mothballs, dangling on strings and smelling of stale mints. Out it comes, many long-dead pelts sewn seamlessly together. *Where is the ash that once wore you?*

FLAMINGOS

Gail Hughes

Ellie was five when she saw the flamingos. It was the spring her mom cut her hair off short like a boy's all over. She saw them one evening in the time of cottonwoods – fluff was floating all over town, getting up people's noses, making everybody sneeze.

"Flamingos live in Africa," her dad said later. "There's no way any flamingo could ever come to feed in the Nancy creek." But she knew they were flamingos because they were just like the ones she had once seen in the Calgary zoo, stepping delicately through a concrete lake on toothpick legs, dipping their pink necks into the water – dipping and arching, in search of edibles.

Ellie's dad was returning empty milk churns to the depot by the grain elevators on the edge of town and Ellie went with him to get out of the house. The churns belonged to Sam Hercules. "I don't know why I should take them," her dad grumbled. It was part of the big changes after they left the duplex by the park in the city for this sprawled out prairie town. All the towns hereabouts had girls' names – Dorothy, Irma, Elsie, Caroline: "The pioneers called the towns after their sweethearts left at home," Ellie's mom told her.

Her dad came to teach in the four-room school in the centre of Nancy, the only brick building in town except for the firehall. In the school were girls with pageboys who whispered in clumps on Main Street and tittered when Ellie's dad passed by, boys who are too big for their age. There was a wood frame church in Nancy with a recording of chimes that played on Sundays. A bar on the boardwalk by the service station. A curling rink. Rows of clapboard bungalows and, on the outskirts, the dusty road leading to Sam Hercules' farm. "I've seen a lot of frouzy towns," Ellie's dad said, "but this one takes the cake."

This particular evening Ellie's dad has parked beside one of the grain elevators. While he unloads the milk churns from the back seat, Ellie wanders off. At first she stays in the shadow of the towering wooden structure but when she looks up, her head spins and the elevator tips over as though it is about to crush her. So she skips into the strip of sunshine along the railway tracks. As far as she can see there is nothing but low bush scrub and grass, young wheat and the rails glinting in the sun. In the other direction is a twisting shadow along the horizon. That, Ellie's dad says, is the deep valley of the badlands, "You can dig dinosaur bones after a good rainstorm." But Ellie hasn't seen any dinosaurs, only small birds and hares racing across the plain.

On the far side of the tracks a grassy bank plunges to the creek and that's where Ellie wants to go. Her dad is deep in conversation with Mr. McGinty, the Wheat Pool man:

"There's a lot of ducks over on the slough by Caroline," says Mr. McGinty.

"Is that so?" says Ellie's dad who keeps a shotgun in the back of the closet in their tiny bedroom.

Ellie holds her breath and, with a dangerous thrill, she takes two frog jumps – the first into the track bed and the second to the far side. She tucks her yellow skirt between her legs and scrambles down the bank, smelling the fresh damp grass and the musty odour of mud. Brown with spring runoff, the creek slides past, almost reaching the toes of her black oxfords. She decides to pick some Queen Anne's Lace to give to her mom.

Ellie's mother is not happy. She hasn't been happy since they came to Sam Hercules' farm. The house is too small. Also, no matter how early Ellie's mom gets up in the morning, Sam Hercules is there before her, leaning against the stove, watching with a cup of coffee in his hand. From his fleshy lips he blows smoke rings which drift across the room getting wider and wispier until only the smell of Virginia tobacco remains.

"Guess you'll be wanting your breakfast now, Mizz Mayhew," he says, and bows to Ellie's mom and takes a big step to one side. Ellie's mom shrinks away as though there was a river of snakes between them. Every morning Ellie's mom shakes the porridge into a saucepan trying to ignore Sam Hercules who just stands there, humming under his breath.

The Queen Anne's Lace is just starting to bloom and Ellie feels very happy. She starts along the bank of the creek, the wild bright green of new grass underfoot, gathering white clusters. A meadowlark warbles with joy and from the willows overhanging the creek a bird with a voice like a rusty gatespring answers back. She pictures her mom's face when she sees the bouquet, "What a wonderful surprise, darling!" She imagines her mom's big hug and he dad standing nearby, looking embarrassed as he always does at public displays of affection but pleased just the same to see her mom wreathed in smiles.

On Sunday mornings, when the electric chimes fill the air and Ellie and her mom are usually just leaving for church, Sam Hercules kills chickens: "For you, Mizz Mayhew, so you got somethin' decent to cook." Ellie's mom always begs him not to do it for her sake but, "There ought 'a be one good meal in a week," he says. "Jeez, you're payin' me enough rent for this room here," and he strides out to the farmyard in his big boots with his fat belly pouring out of the red shirt. He always wears a felt hat on the Sabbath, pulled down to his ears. "You'd think he could at least shave on Sunday," Ellie's mom says that night in the bedroom.

"Which one we havin' today, Mizz Mayhew?" Without waiting for an answer Sam Hercules sets off after the hens who scatter, squawking, when they see him. They run and hide under the old Dodge behind the barn but he always catches them up. He jack-knifes his enormous legs and reaches one arm under the sill. When the arm comes back there's a hen's neck clenched in his fist. Very slowly he straightens up while the hen gasps and gabbles, and then Sam Hercules saunters over to the tree stump near the ashcan with the hatchet sticking out of it and he slaps the cackling frenzy of feathers down onto the stump, like a poker hand. And he takes the hatchet and he chops off its head. And rocks back on the heels of his big boots and watches the headless chicken skitter crazily in the dust with a fountain of blood spurting from its neck. When the blood-soaked feathers are finally still, Sam Hercules picks up the chicken and disappears into the barn.

Ellie doesn't know how many chickens Sam Hercules has killed since they came to Nancy. She doesn't know how long they'll have to go on living here with the uncomfortable smell of fear in the barnyard. But there are things she does like: the arched bridges of rainbow light that stretch from one edge of the prairie to the other, the shadow of the wind rippling across wheat.

Most of the things that Ellie likes are not connected with people because they don't know anybody. Nobody visits Sam Hercules. Ellie plays alone on the rusty machinery in the yard. She plays with cardboard boxes in the barns. The small barn is best – it's full of grain and she buries herself up to the neck and listens to the mice running along the beams.

After lunch on Sunday, Sam Hercules drinks whisky out of a tumbler stencilled with rosebuds and then he tries to get Ellie's dad to play poker with him. "Come on, Jack," he wheedles, "we'll play for matches if you don't wanna put your hard-earned cash on the table!" Ellie's dad usually refuses although once or twice he's let Sam Hercules push him into it. Sam Hercules always licks the pants off Ellie's dad, and "Not again, Jack," her mom sighs. So he's started going to the schoolhouse on Sunday afternoon to prepare work for the kids, leaving Ellie and her mom to fend for themselves in the house.

On the Sunday after Easter, they are on their own in the kitchen – Ellie's mom, folding a pile of freshly ironed shirts to take upstairs; Ellie, sitting on the red lino cutting out paper dolls with her mom's small pointed thread snippers – when Sam Hercules comes in and without a word crosses to the cupboard above the sink and gets out the rosebud tumbler and the bottle of whisky. There isn't left much in the bottle. Ellie's mom looks at the trail of mud across the floor but she doesn't say anything. Ellie sits, quiet as dust, cutting very carefully around the flowers on the hats and the high heeled shoes because once you snip off a heel or a stem you can't glue it back.

Sam Hercules fills the glass and takes a gulp. "Well, Alice," he says, "what's about a game of poker?" Ellie's mom just ignores him and keeps on folding. "You don't mean to say you can't play poker?" His voice is dry and the words crunch like the shale on the barn path, "Well, if you can't, then it's high time you learned!" He drinks some more.

Ellie is watching out of the corner of her eye. She can see her mom, still wearing her church dress with the brown basket buttons, holding a pile of laundry. She can see Sam Hercules, leaning against the towel rail of the stove, glass in hand. "Whassa matter, Mizz Mayhew," he croaks, "doncha like it here? Whassa nice young lady like you doin' in a place like this?" and he steps unsteadily toward Ellie's mom.

"Don't you dare come near me!" Ellie can hear the panic on her mom's voice now as she backs away from him. But it seems that once Sam Hercules is in motion, nothing can waylay him. Swaying like a poplar he takes another step, and then another.

"I'll show ya how to play poker, Mizz Mayhew!" With every step Sam Hercules takes forward, Ellie's mom takes one back. Until she is standing in the open cellar door.

Suddenly Sam Hercules shoots out his hand. "Whoa, Alice!" he cries. And just at that moment Ellie sees her mom disappear out of the doorway. She hears the muffled thumping of her mom's body sliding down into the dark hole under the stairs. Where there is no light at all.

"I had a helluva time carrying her up them stairs," says Sam Hercules to the doctor later. When he lays her out on the sofa, Ellie is sure she is dead. But slowly she comes round, "Ellie? Can you get my handkerchief? The one Grandma made with the flowers on?" Ellie races upstairs. It's in the top drawer, ironed into a neat square. The border of mauve and yellow pansies glistens. It smells of gardenia from the crown shaped bottle tucked between the piles of clothes.

When Ellie gives the hankie to her mom, she unfolds it with pale hands and begins to cry.

By now Ellie's hands are full of flowers. She glances back at the massive grain elevator. It stands proud and comforting, like a lighthouse in a vast rippling sea. From here she can see the giant solitary head of wheat beside the letters that say Alberta Wheat Pool. Her dad and Mr. McGinty are hidden by the curve of the bank. She rounds the bend in the creek and finds herself at an open marshy place where the emerald crown of young wheat comes almost to the edge of the rushes.

The creek is still, with dizzying reflections of clouds which you could fall into if you weren't careful. Ellie forces her eyes back to the red sun just dipping below the distant fields. And then she sees the flamingos.

Three of them are standing at the water's edge, dipping their beautiful crescent beaks to the water, arching their long pink necks into S shapes that ripple in the bronze mirror. Holding her breath, Ellie stands still as a pebble. She can not believe her eyes. The flamingos become aware of her presence and incline their necks in her direction, regarding her with beady golden eyes. For a moment Ellie and the flamingos are joined in a perfect hush, broken only by birdsong. Then the flamingos, ever so slowly, move off upstream.

At the very moment they are settling back to feed again, Ellie's dad begins to holler after her. Ellie is paralysed. She doesn't dare startle the birds by shouting back but then her dad yells again, closer now, and the spell is broken. The flamingos rise on their great pink wings. The air is filled with beating. Very soon they are lost in the sunset and she can no longer separate wing from cloud

Clutching the bouquet of Queen Anne's Lace, Ellie heads toward home.

HAVE A NICE DAY

Phil Carradice

"God, I'm fed up with this," snarled Mike. "I think I'll get the hell out of it!"

It was a cold, wet January morning. Outside, beyond the streaked and melting windows of the staff room, rain beat down onto deserted playing fields and empty quadrangles. We were tired and depressed, fed up with the start of a new term and the after effects of a Christmas with just enough anti-climax to ruin the memory of the whole holiday.

"Get out of what?" I asked, looking up from a pile of dog-eared exercise books I was pretending to mark.

"This!"

Mike gestured wildly around the staff room, his dismissive sweep taking in the worn carpet, the cluttered notice board and the dirty coffee cups which lay like carbuncles on the table.

"Just think, Paul," he continued. "Away from all this crap. Away from this bloody awful place. Away from 4C, away from ..."

"Michael!" cut in Dewi, his Welsh accent high and prominent in the oppressive room. "Michael, Michael. There will always be a 4C. Wherever you go."

Mike sneered, annoyed with having his flow of invective broken.

"Alright. Maybe there will. But just to get away. Anywhere's got to be better than this."

I sighed.

"OK, pal, but where exactly are you supposed to be going?"

"The Bahamas!"

Mike grinned. He had an infectious smile which split his lop-sided face from ear to ear and vividly displayed his crooked teeth. I could never work out what women found so attractive about Mike but the fact remained that they did. He was never short of female company. Even Dewi noticed it.

"Mike seems to change his women like other men change their underpants!" he once remarked.

Now, I watched Mike's animated face and smiled.

"The Bahamas? Where the hell did you get that idea?"

"Aha!"

Mike raised his finger, an admonishing professor or preaching pastor. He rummaged amongst the pile of educational periodicals and old exam papers we had irreligiously thrown into a corner of the room and pulled out a three week old copy of *The Times Educational Supplement*. He flung it at me.

"Page 68. Read!"

"'Teachers Urgently Required'," I read. "'Experienced and qualified teachers of'" – here a long list of relevant subjects – "'are needed to take up appointment at schools in the Commonwealth of the Bahamas. Mr J. T. Robinson will be at St David's Hotel, Oxford Street, on Saturday 26th January. Ring for an appointment'."

Mike snorted and snatched the paper from me.

"I doubt if you'll ever make the Old Vic," he said, "but you've managed to convey the general idea."

I shook my head in disbelief and went back to my marking. Yet Mike hadn't quite finished.

"Come with me, Paul. You've got no ties, no family to think about. Let's both go. Just think of it man – fishing, sailing, golfing. All that sun. All those ... ."

"Bloody great sharks!" said Dewi viciously.

With that the bell rang for the end of the period. I went off to do battle with 4C and promptly forgot our conversation.

All teachers quickly learn to appreciate the weekends. To me, at that time, those two days were like a cup of water held out to a dying man in the Sahara. They were all that kept me sane in a week when I tried, each day, to cram Shakespeare and Dylan Thomas down the throats of bored kids. Their only aim in life was to get through the purgatory period of school with as little effort as possible. What did they care about Wordsworth or Shaw? John Eynon's Visual Biology Lessons behind the boys' toilets or gyrating to the latest reggae hit in the local disco were their sole concessions to culture. Looking back on it now, they probably had a point.

It was the Saturday after my discussion with Mike. As usual, it was raining and, as usual, I was in bed. I reasoned, with the casual air of a man who is used to living alone, that I would stay in bed until 12.30, grab some lunch at the corner café and still be at the rugby ground half an hour before kick-off. Smugly, I turned over and went back to sleep.

When a sudden earthquake erupted from the landing outside the door, my first thought was that there had been a gas explosion. Opening my left eye I quickly realised that my body and the room were still intact and that the noise was, in fact, being caused by somebody hammering on the door in an effort to gain admittance.

"Go away!" I called.

The hammering continued. I ducked under the bed clothes and decided that I would stay there until the caller lost interest.

"Get up, you lazy sod!"

There was no mistaking that voice. Mike – Mike in one of his demonic, megalomaniac moods. I sighed.

"It's open," I called and turn onto my side.

The next thing I knew was that Mike had deposited himself on my chest and was furiously trying to pull my pyjama jacket over my head.

"For God's sake, give over!" I yelled.

Mike ignored me.

"Come on! We're going to be late! It's 10.30 already."

Eventually, I managed to push him away and sat up, yawning.

"Late for what?! I said, suddenly noticing his suit and highly polished shoes.

"Are you going for an interview or a funeral?" I asked.

Mike threw me a withering glance.

"Funeral? Don't be a bloody fool. And no, I haven't got an interview – we both have. At the St David's Hotel, 11-o-clock. Don't you remember? I told you yesterday. For the Bahamas."

Something deep inside my head began to register itself. Mike had yelled at me as I had rushed out of school at the end of the previous afternoon. Something about packing my swimming shorts.

"Half past four on a Friday is a bloody fine time to tell me anything! Anyway, I don't want to go to the Bahamas. I'm quite happy here."

Mike perched himself on the edge of my coffee table and casually lit a cigarette.

"What? Happy here? Then you must be bloody barmy, mate! Do you really mean you want to spend the rest of your life cooped up in that red-brick monstrosity down the road? Scraping to the Head for a few extra quid a year? Begging books and equipment from a Local Authority which doesn't give a damn about you or the kids? Teaching yobs like John Bloody Eynon who don't want to learn, who only want to cause as much trouble as they can before they bugger off and produce more little Eynons for stupid half-wits like you to worry yourself to death over? Is that what you really want?"

He paused, out of breath but not enthusiasm. He gazed around my sparsely furnished room and slowly shook his head.

"Well, not me, laddie. It's not worth it, not when you can get out. OK, so Dewi is right. Kids will always be the same, wherever you go. I know there'll be Bahamian versions of John Eynon just waiting for me to walk into the classroom. But it won't be the same. Because whatever the little so and so's are like, there'll be compensations out there! Just think what you can do when school finishes – swimming, sailing, surfing, holidays in America. The sea so hot you can swim in it all year round. Sun on your back, rum dakari in your hand. Hell, boy, there's so much you can do out there. But here? Well, just look at the bloody weather. Now get your clothes on and let's get going!"

Trying to argue with Mike in that mood was like trying to stop a runaway steam roller with a match-stick. Consequently, in five minutes flat, I had dressed in my best suit, washed, shaved and cut myself three times. A further two minutes elapsed and I found myself in a carriage on the underground, holding a handkerchief to my bleeding face with one hand and trying to rub out the beer stains on my trousers with the other.

"Stop worrying," said Mike. "Just be yourself. These guys can see through pretence in a minute."

I said nothing but thought, bitterly, of my warm bed. If anybody was worrying it certainly wasn't me.

When we reached the St David's Hotel we were interviewed

separately, Mike going in first while I sat and brooded in the foyer. Suddenly London seemed very dear to me now that I was about to leave it behind. Even the weather seemed natural, almost invigorating.

Eventually, Mike came swaggering down the wide and elegant staircase, a look of supreme satisfaction on his face.

"Piece of cake," he crowed. "They couldn't wait to offer me a job. I'll sit and write out my resignation while you're in with this Robinson bloke."

I went upstairs, apprehension beginning to gather like a fist in my windpipe. Robinson was tall and detached and his first question took me by surprise.

"Mr Davies, why do you want to teach in the Bahamas?"

What could I say? I don't? Mike just dragged me along.?

"I ... er ... the fishing."

"What?"

"No. Sorry. No, I mean .. er .. I'd like to see the world and I think I've got something to offer."

Robinson stared at me, coldly.

"Just what do you have to offer, Mr Davies?"

It was a valid question. What the hell did I have to offer any prospective employer? Three years experience in a broken down South London comprehensive, a season for Richmond RFC 3rd XV and that was about it. The utter futility and waste of my life had never seemed as clear as it did just then.

In the end I waffled my way through the interview and was glad to get out to Mike who was pacing impatiently up and down the pavement in front of the hotel.

"Well?"

"They turned me down."

Mike didn't seem too upset. He was far too excited by his own success and talked about the relative merits of shark fishing and scuba diving all the way home. Curiously enough, I didn't mind either. Of course it hurt the pride to be rejected but, then, I hadn't really wanted to go in the first place. My heart simply hadn't been in it. I concluded that I was not the roving sort and that a cosy log fire in the centre of London would suit me just as well as basking in the sun on a golden Bahamian beach.

We had the usual staff party to send Mike off. He went in grand style, carried out, dead drunk, at 10.30. For the rest of us the party was boring enough, simply an excuse for the Head and other senior staff to patronise the junior teachers. It was mainly memorable for two things. One was a long and graphic piece of Welsh pornography, vividly told by Dewi, and the other was a remark Mike made to me just before he passed out.

"You know, Paul," he slurred. "I shall miss you, old mate, I really shall. Will you miss me?"

I did miss Mike. We had been quite close, had got drunk together, played rugby together and, occasionally, when Mike had fixed me up with a date, had shared the same parked car in the same deserted lane. So when he was suddenly not there any longer, it was as if somebody had cut off one of my legs.

To begin with I received regular letters. He talked of beach parties and skin diving, of the two cars he owned, of the beautiful girls – everything to make me squirm with envy. I wished, with every ounce of my being, that I had had the gumption to try harder at the time of the fateful interview. It was an idle exercise. I'd had my chance and I'd blown it.

"That lucky sod," muttered Dewi one particularly foul winter morning when I showed him Mike's most recent postcard.

It was quite a card – a blood-red sky with the sun sinking effortlessly below the horizon. The caption read 'Sunset at Harry's Bar, Deadman's Reef' and Mike had scrawled a simple message on the back – 'Say No More!'.

"Do you know?" said Dewi, "I think I'd sacrifice the Black Mountains and all the hiraeth ever thought of to get out there with him. The lucky sod."

That seemed to sum up all of our feelings. We had laughed at Mike when he first told us of his idea but he had certainly had the last laugh. Above all we envied him and wished that we'd had the courage to get up off our fat, middle-class backsides and, like him, grab what we wanted out of life. I think, in many ways, we held him up as a symbol, an image of what we could all achieve – if we wanted.

Gradually, however, I heard less and less of Mike. Friends go away promising to keep in touch for ever. Yet it never works out like that. People who have been close sometimes grow more distant after a time – being apart only quickens the process. Soon I was hearing from him only at Christmas, with the occasional additional postcard whenever he was on holiday in California or Jamaica or some other exotic location. It was only to be expected.

One other change occurred in my life at about this time. I got married.

Anna had always been there. She had joined the staff at the same time as Mike and I. She taught Science in the junior school and was regarded as a pretty little thing but without that undefined sparkle which makes a really attractive girl. Perhaps that was why Mike had never really noticed her.

After he left I found myself seeing more and more of Anna. We were thrown into each other's company and soon it came as natural for us to have our lunch together in the pub across the road from the school. Eventually, we just drifted into marriage, as if by coincidence, and somehow it seemed a far safer bet for a good future together.

Mike, of course, sent us a wedding present, something suitably avant garde, and we settled down to married life in a small terraced house not far from the school. Within two years Anna was pregnant. She gave birth to a baby boy on a rainy January day and, somehow, that seemed rather appropriate.

Then came the news that Mike was coming home. His contract had expired and despite the pleading of the entire Bahamian Government – or so he told us in a suitably expansive letter – he had decided to call it a day.

One night, as Anna battled with the baby, as the rain beat against the windows and I tried to brighten up the old house with its fortieth or, perhaps, fiftieth coat of paint there came a knock at the door.

"See who it is," called Anna.

I put down my brush and opened the door. There stood Mike, a healthier, browner Mike with a tiny black moustache below his long, straight nose, but it was undeniably Mike.

"Hello, Paul," he said. "Long time no see."

He made suitably interested sounds over the screaming baby and sat down next to Anna on our lumpy, sagging settee. He glanced at the partly painted walls and nodded his head, half critical but, somehow, half approving as well.

"Working hard, I see. As usual. You were always a worker, Paul, always have been, always will be. Christ, I remember you slogging away trying to teach English to those bloody kids. What was that boy's name? The one who used to drive us all up the wall?"

"Eynon," I said. "John Eynon."

"That's it. Little bastard!"

He smiled across at Anna and, again, I was left with the impression that his words did not quite match his emotions. I opened the bottle of wine he had brought and handed him a glass. He smiled, winked at Anna and squeezed her knee. Then he inclined his head in my direction.

"He should have come with me, you know. No more John Eynons for him then. No more John Eynons for me either. Not any more."

"You made that much money?" Anna asked, gently easing his hand off her leg.

Mike laughed. It was a harsh sound, brittle and unexpected, and did not fit with the man we both knew.

"No. Like hell I did. Oh. I made money but I spent it just as quickly. I think you can say that the lifestyle out there is a trifle expensive. No. I married a fairy tale, a real live American heiress."

Anna and I were amazed and exchanged swift glances. Mike pretended not to notice.

"Stinking rich," he continued. "Rolls her hair in dollar bills. Know the sort? Daddy owns half of Texas and most of the oil options in the Gulf of Mexico, I should say. And she's beautiful as well."

I widened my eyes in mock horror.

"She couldn't be anything else, could she, Mike? Is she here with you? Where is she?"

He quickly looked away.

"She's in the States. She can't stand the weather over here – too damned cold and wet for her. So she's gone home for a few weeks. I'm flying to Houston next Friday to start work in the family business."

He stretched. Like a cat, he was preening and self-satisfied but he also had the animal's instinctive apprehension, as if constantly watching for an unexpected assault.

"Yes, got myself a nice little slice of Daddy's business. No more teaching for me. Executive work from here on in."

He did not stay long. Somehow it wasn't the same. He seemed caged and ill at ease, almost as if the tiny house was too small to contain his restless energy. He had clearly changed, not just physically but something internal, something to do with his attitudes. I said as much to Anna.

"Yes," she said. "Americanised, I suppose."

"That's one way of putting it. Mike was always boasting about his possessions – his cars and his women – it was a part of him, part of his make-up, I guess. But he cared. Underneath it all, he cared. That's what made him acceptable. Now he just seems to own things – his wife included. He's sharper, not so real."

Anna came across the room and perched herself alongside me.

"Do you know something? I think he envies you."

"What? Envies me? With all he's got?"

"Yes. Because he's lonely. Oh, he's got his rich cronies and his money and his beautiful wife. But he hasn't got this."

She gestured at the half-stripped walls of our living room.

"He envies you this. The anonymity, the comfort, the way you're always there – in the background. Not out in front like he is. When you're out in front you've got to keep moving. A moving target is less easy to hit. He called you a worker and that's exactly what you are. It gives you a kind of security , a security he'll never have. The one thing you've got which he never will – because he's the type of man he is – is happiness. I don't think Mike will ever be content."

We see Mike quite often these days, whenever he flies into Britain on business. I've never met his wife. I've got no evidence to prove it but I have a distinct feeling that things are not quite right there.

And seeing Mike each time, it makes me bless that shabby old suit with the beer stains and the way I messed up that interview so many years ago. Anna was right. I am content, I am happy, and

Mike clearly isn't. Only sometimes, when the rain beats against my classroom window, I wonder – if I had the chance again, just Mike and I for that interview at St David's Hotel, how would I play it? What would I do? It's a question I never answer, not even to myself.

NOMAD

Nigel Jarrett

My father should have seen me at first, feeling sorry for myself when I ought to have been a bit more imaginative. Take a grip of the situation, he would have told me, his knuckles blanching as he illustrated his point. But I was upset. The start of that whole business with Mick made me physically ill, and not just because of a sense of loss or failure. It's hard to explain how I've just about got over it late in the day. Maybe I caught a glimpse of a hidden self.

Molly and I used to look forward to the time when we would finally be on our own. The whole place to ourselves. No dependants under the same roof, a feeling of paid-for freedom. Even the cat was part of the scheme, its death the end of a relationship that nothing could replace. We saw this sequence: everything would go as planned, leaving only the two of us. We all need time to look at life, to examine our lives, and decide what's in and what should be out, done with. And others may have to make sacrifices to ensure we can do so.

Perhaps it was a mistake to move into this house, the one Molly's great-grandfather built. There are four of them, identical but discreetly separated, on the road out of town, and in their way they still look quite modern. Molly's Uncle Max lived here before us but he had to be moved to a nursing-home – he's still there, hanging on – so we bought it from him, partly to provide him with funds. Error or not, I have come to love our house. The architect, a friend of Molly's great-grandfather, went mad, threw himself out of a high window, his long moustaches swept back like the wings of a swift. I think there must be a lot of him in the design, a lot of the superfluous stuff, off the point, enclosing a solid core. I once read a piece about Bell, the inventor of the telephone: it appears that, in his dotage, he thought a massive block of ice might be raised by the condensation coming off it, like a hovercraft. I suppose it was a case of genius run to seed – bitter, split, impotent. Anyway, in this house there is a long landing with recesses and gargoyles, and at the end a circular window of stained glass.

At the time, I was selling insurance and Molly had been working for three years as a nursery assistant. Pensions were the coming thing; I was being trained to go out and tell people how flawed their pension arrangements were – that was if they had made any at all. It was true: people never think of the future. For once I felt I was being paid for doing something worthwhile. Molly seemed happy, though Mick, our teenage son, was becoming a handful. One night he arrived home skewingly drunk, bundled out of a taxi on to the drive. We ignored it, put it down to an overstretched adolescence. Then, one afternoon when she was with her kids on a trip to a nearby town, Molly saw Mick, who should have been at school, walking in the park with an old man – older than me, at any rate. The man had his arm around Mick's shoulders. I smiled inwardly when Molly told me she'd had to divert her crocodile of little charges. She was certain it had been Mick – well, almost.

Strange as it may seem, we couldn't bring ourselves to tackle Mick about it, not even the truancy part. He'd never gone absent from school before. In fact, he was bright and attentive in class. But things got worse. One weekend, he ran away, leaving a note. We received a picture postcard from London. It showed a woman smothered by pigeons at the foot of Nelson's Column. She was feeding the birds, this woman, yet seemed to be consumed by some kind of private torment while all around her laughed or strolled idly by.

Neither of our other two had ever been difficult. John, the oldest, is a teacher in London, which raised our hopes for Mick when the boy began to give us grief. Settled down – that's the expression we all use to describe the time after we've taken hold of our lives. John was settled. Maria, too, our middle one: she was married to Jed, a trainee supermarket manager, and they were about to make us grandparents. You could say we'd been model guardians. Not that we'd tried; we had just done what we'd thought was best by our children and had hoped things would turn out well.

On the Saturday Mick left, we went over to the house Maria and Jed had bought. Jed was fitting kitchen units and decorating. Unlike me, he's very practical. I remember his cheek was smudged with paint, like a lipstick heart, when he came into the living-room.

"That boy needs a kick in the trousers," Jed said of Mick. (We'd sorted out straight talking as well, though its unguarded expression often gives me a jolt.)

"You must feel terrible," Maria said. She'd already referred to her younger brother as a tearaway. She was wearing one of those dungaree outfits specially shaped for mothers-to-be. She was carrying all before her.

Molly was exasperated.

"It's not us!" she stammered. "It's him we are worried about."

But Jed was unmoved. He shook his head at the pair of us, Molly and me, and just for a moment I understood why so many people spurn the pity of others. It must make them feel small. A sense of injury developed in oneself is not the same as seeing oneself portrayed by others as a victim. We didn't need moralising from Jed; we wanted him as someone not much older than Mick to offer an explanation for his behaviour.

Back home later the same evening, we phoned John. He had been out in the day and now he was halfway through marking. I could hear a jazz record playing and other voices in the background. I didn't ask if he had company and he didn't mention it. I quite like that. It's evidence of another life going on independently of your own, with small private happenings that have nothing to do with you even though you are conscious of them.

"Well, he hasn't contacted me," John said, a bit matter-of-factly. "What's the postmark?"

I told him 'N15' and there was a pause as we both must have admitted to ourselves that this represented the proverbial haystack. I formed a vision of endless streets, and a vast swarm of the desperate and dislocated.

"He can look after himself," John said, cheeringly. "He's not dull. Perhaps he'll contact me. Perhaps there are things he needs to sort out."

I think John silently acknowledged my equally tacit recognition of the hint of exclusion in this last remark. Molly was hovering at my shoulder. As if catching it too, she signalled me to hand her the receiver.

"Why couldn't he have discussed it with us?" she asked. "There's nothing wrong – nothing."

She stared at the wall, then handed John back to me, her fellow conspirator.

"There was a bit of bother a while ago," I explained. "Or so we think."

He listened without interrupting as I told him about the incident, or possible incident, in the park. I think it was knowing that he was not alone in ignorance of the facts that he remained calm – a case of parents still exercising their right to privilege of information, no matter how old their children.

"I'll do what I can," he said. "The police up here might be able to help. But don't forget that he's gone of his own accord. They usually aren't interested."

I somehow felt that he was speaking from a kind of wearisome experience. He tells us horrendous tales of schoolmastering in the slums. Inner-city deprivation is what they call slum-dwelling now. I suppose it sounds more hopeful.

When we sat down, Molly and I, it was obvious that she had expected more from John, such as an immediate tour of north London with his jazz-loving friends. I couldn't see it myself. I thought of John gazing briefly out of the window, telling his pals about a rebellious brother, then palming another exercise book from the unmarked pile. I don't know why I thought this. With independence, some things have to be taken for granted. A certain coolness prevails, encouraged by distance, other worlds, the very stuff of striking out on your own from where those who have nurtured you come to terms with the difference between love and the memory of love. I couldn't help considering that snipping the apron-strings, as one must, leaves one totally lacking control, that studiously avoiding overbearance in life turns loved ones into, albeit favourable, strangers.

Molly and I saw to it that Jed, Maria and John would be there when Mick arrived home for the first time. We all managed to mask our different feelings about what had happened. It wasn't exactly the best arrangement for discovering why Mick had run off. He seemed, outwardly at least, well-adjusted, if a little downcast at the anxiety he had caused. I got the impression that, in some odd way, Mick had done the right thing. Chastising is almost foreign to me and Molly; it's just the way we are.

"If there's anything we can do, just say," Molly told him when she cornered him alone in the house on that half-celebratory weekend. But little any of us said actually sounded as if it connected with what he must have been feeling inside. Then he left again, without ceremony and almost without warning, before we had embarked on a long discussion. Maybe the threat of an ensnaring adult superiority was what made him go.

I wouldn't say Molly lost interest in Mick's wanderings from then on, because the rest of the family also grew resigned to his peculiarity, if that's the word. We kept the postcards. Within Molly and Jed there developed an unspoken indignation which I think they found supportive. I have always been uncomfortable about taking unwarranted offence, so I had nothing to erect between myself and Mick when it came to adopting an attitude towards him. Of course, I pitied Molly beyond that barrier, in the place where she was exposed and uncomprehending. Just before events took their surprising turn, I began trying to make sense of what was happening. The first thing I understood was how difficult it is for us to communicate the predicament of a third party to others except through the mechanism of our own pained alembic, when what emerges is necessarily one-sided. The problem is, if the intelligence we transmit appears sympathetic, we are less likely to be taken to task for presumed sins of omission; if it is critical, we might as well start cowering before the tirades of those who side with our subject, for they will surely come. I mention this now, only to introduce the fact that I took up writing just after Mick left – or, rather, after it became clear that his leaving seemed to have no provenance in domestic hostility, apparent or real. I simply became curious where the others, as far as I could tell, hid behind affront, even humiliation, particularly when Mick indicated by default that he was surviving. I am not a very good writer but in recognising my limitations I am able to imagine what it might take to be a better one. I can't explain why I began to write; I do know how much it might mean to me, how it is that we might at any time be turned in unexpected directions by unseen forces. In this confessional, I do want to set things down, to recognise, even, the thresholds of confesssing; not things deliberately suppressed but things impossible to recover or detect, or hinted at. Others will have to speak for themselves. At the end of the day (no cliché this: it's the trawling time, when we attempt to gather everything in, however disappointing the catch), all we have are bits and pieces floating tantalisingly in the ether. When I recall Molly's story of seeing Mick in the park with his mysterious comforter, it is the image which persists, inviting surmise, and there are moments when I would prefer this evocation to be all there is, like the picture I retain from my father's testimony of my uncle (a boy then, later to die young of rheumatic fever) sprinting bare-chested like a lunatic around my unemployed grandfather's allotment, his shirt billowing behind him, as dusk and dampness infiltrate their sustaining half-acre; it is in the Depression, this dewy pretension to joy and innocence.

I was at home nursing a cold the day Mick's letter from Marrakesh arrived. I saw it float towards the doormat as I was going downstairs to make myself breakfast. It was addressed to me. Its thin air-mail paper belied the visual gravity of its contents, which, on being unfolded, seemed to demand to be read aloud. 'Dear dad', it began, 'As I write this, the imam is calling the faithful to prayer...' The rest was nothing less than a story, a fascinating story. I imagined Mick in a white, loose-fitting garment, exuding the confidence of one totally assimilated by place. He shares a home with others, by the sea. The tall palms bend a little before the on-shore winds. There is trouble with Allal, the gardener. Allal is trying to get his boyfriend moved into the house, which is owned by a Frenchman with a pointed beard. But the Frenchman won't allow it on the grounds that Allal will want to live in, too, and thus neglect his duties, which involve keeping the grounds tidy for prospective buyers – the house is always up for sale but the Frenchman is a laconic vendor. It is Mick's problem because the Frenchman has appointed him unofficial custodian in his absence. One of Mick's jobs is to see that Allal turns up on time and completes his allotted hours. Mick has clearly risen in some loose hierachy, some distant confederation of the languid. Instead of wondering what Mick was thinking of in sending such a disarming, guilt-free missive, I tasted brine on my tongue and began to worry about overgrown funerary urns. When Molly arrived home from the nursery, I betrayed what might have been an expected confidence by telling her about the letter. She shook her head while reading it.

When I told Jed and Maria, I merely indicated that we had received a message from Morocco to say that Mick was well. This seemed to satisfy them, though perhaps I interpreted satisfaction as lack of curiosity. John's greater inquisitiveness never exactly pinions you, but I knew that holding nothing back would pre-empt further questioning. Then a second letter arrived, and a third, each addressed to me. Molly took no offence at this partiality; she was glad I had pocketed the problem. Just when we were getting used to Mick's odd lifestyle in the same evasive way we diminish madness by calling it eccentricity, his story grew darker. Allal moves in with his boyfriend, and the Frenchman is murdered. This was not the sequence, but inverting it helps me remove a connection. Though Mick made none either – the killing is remote in all senses of the word – I felt ill at ease, especially as the Frenchman's prophecy had been fulfilled, his garden now an imminent wilderness accommodating the shadows of two men at play and a third trembling at the fringes. I began to fear for Mick as I never had before. I saw a storyteller about to be engulfed by the events he was witnessing. There followed an appeal for money, and the first hints of friction between Mick and Allal over the state of the garden, the future of the house. With the Frenchman gone, anarchy is displacing a nominal, exotic order. There is talk of occupying the building. A lawyer's emissary is seen off by Allal and his companion amid much laughter. Others move in. Mick sends a letter of disturbing incoherence. Then a postcard from Algiers. Then nothing. Some of this I share with Molly and the rest, and I suppose that what I don't share is the magnitude of the difference between us. There is little we can do. Little I can do.

Molly and I often stand on the landing as evening closes in, gazing through the stained glass window for Mick's next unannounced homecoming. That dotty architect designed things so that the declining sun, summer and winter, strikes the glass, filling the top of the house with diffuse, kaleidoscopic colour. At other times, and these depend on one's momentary feeling or point of view, it is the effect of the glass on our external surroundings – the garden, the road, the meadow, the tree-fringed mountain, the silvered estuary nicked into faraway cliffs – which appeals to us as we hold fast to our anchorage.

John, with his metropolitan unconcern and his deepening imperviousness to shock and surprise, tells us not to worry. Jed and Maria, now parents themselves, are absorbed totally with child-rearing and have neither the time nor the desire to ponder the bothersome forms of its end result. (In any case, Jed has been promoted, and it seems to me that if one is involved in betterment and its spiralling elevations, the plight of those who have free-fallen into life cannot inspire by their example or move by their weaknesses and shortcomings.)

It's almost a year now since any of us heard from Mick. Molly and I keep the postcards in an album, slotting them into polythene cases so that we can view the scene and read the message, itself never expressing more than a holidaymaker's transient pleasure. I don't blame Molly for continuing to remain perplexed, a state in which indignity and anguish keep colliding. Yet, when I re-read the letters and scan the postcards, particularly the first one of Trafalgar Square, I can't help thinking that each is an affirmation of intent like nothing we will ever know. It searches us out. When we glimpse it, the effect is unnerving, and we step back, secure in our foothold. As I say, there are only three other houses like ours, but it is enough. They go on and on in our imagination, these refuges, with their hints of waywardness, their ghosts, and their transoms opening on to peril and adventure under open skies.

DANCING IN THE BOOKSHOP

Ray Jenkin

Pugh owned the last independent bookshop in our town. His shop was an anachronism in the eighties when Jennifer arrived and so were we, his staff, dusty museum pieces who had been there for years and knew no other way of life. He was known locally as a 'character' although his eccentricity and sheer energy and drive had burned out years ago leaving a placid husk of a man who was concerned that what remained of his old age should be as comfortable as possible.

There were not enough customers to justify a staff of five at that time and when our Miss Price retired I don't believe Pugh intended to replace her but he did. Jennifer was aged seventeen, the daughter of John Phillips, an old friend of Pugh, who had died at the tragically early age of forty-three. On meeting Mrs. Phillips one day and learning that Jennifer was unemployed and lacking motivation since the death of her father two years previously, Pugh offered the girl a job as assistant without even the formality of an interview. It was a touch of the old Pugh coming out in him, I suppose.

Lacking motivation. I wondered when I heard that phrase whether it was ever used about me behind my back. My Connie had died two years ago and although I hadn't been 'in love' with my wife for a long time I didn't realise how much I depended on her. Not for food and laundry. I can manage matters of basic housekeeping very well but when she was alive I had reasons for doing things – for working, for planning a holiday, for booking a seat at a theatre or a concert. Now none of that seemed important.

On that April morning of Jennifer's arrival I was rearranging some shelves before the shop opened when there was a tap on the glass and I looked around to see a slender dark-haired young woman with candid blue eyes, waving to me.

"Hi," she said, when I unlocked the door. "I'm Jen Phillips. I start today."

I introduced her to the other staff at the back of the shop. "This is Jennifer. Jennifer, Mr. Pugh you know. Mrs. Dunnock deals with accounts. Ralph, Naomi."

"And who are you?" asked Jennifer, addressing her question to me. Who was I? I was nominally the manager although Pugh managed everything that mattered. Aged sixty-two, post-balding and a widower. That complete autobiography ran through my mind and it didn't seem to amount to very much.

"I'm Mr. Edwards," I told her. There was something gently coaxing in her expression that compelled me to add, "Jack."

I had never used my first name in the shop before. Come to that, no-one in work or away from it had addressed me by it since Connie died. Certainly not Ralph or Naomi. They were, until today, our youngest members of staff but they hid it well carrying with them a weight of extra years like spare clothing.

"Jack," she repeated. "That's a nice name. Like Nicholson."

Her comment startled me into laughter and the sound of my own laughter startled me again. "That's right," I replied. "I think that's all we have in common."

"Just as well," she answered and although there was not even the slightest peceptible flicker of her eyelid I could have sworn she was winking at me. I realised suddenly that I was the only one in the group who was laughing.

"Naomi," said Pugh, with great dignity. "Show Jennifer where to hang her coat."

Her coat was a bright pink jacket which matched her shoulder bag. As the two women went up the back stairs I could hear her talking and Naomi giggling.

"Sounds like a bit of a bimbo," said Ralph, smirking.

"Could be a discipline problem there," Mrs. Dunnock observed, looking hard at me. "Don't give her too much rope." This was quite a speech coming from Mrs. Dunnock who was small, timid and seldom ventured an opinion.

"She seems very pleasant," I answered, irritably.

"Don't forget," said Pugh, "that this so-called bimbo is the daughter of one of my closest friends. Let's have a bit of respect."

It fell to Ralph to instruct Jennifer in her work. He did so during the first hour of the morning when things were always quiet, explaining the system to her in his usual severe tone of voice. He would never have deliberately hurt anyone's feelings but he was a terribly repressed young man. His features seemed all sharp angles and edges like frost-shattered rock and his awful spectacles didn't help – bottle-glass lenses that made his eyes huge and staring like the eyes of some alien temporarily inhabiting his thin face.

At ten-thirty Ralph had to attend to Dr. Massey, a retired man who never bought anything but who visited us regularly because, perhaps, he was lonely. Naomi was taking a coffee break so Jennifer, the only other assistant, had to deal with her first customer, an elderly lady who was studying the poetry shelves with a worried expression on her face.

"I don't think you can help me, dear," the lady said. "I'm looking for a poem about a blackbird."

"Is it enough for it to be about a blackbird or does it have to be a specific poem?"

"It might as well be 'any "poem for what I can remember of it. All I know is that it has a line about 'celestial chimney pots'."

"I know it! I know it!" Jennifer exclaimed, causing Dr. Massey to break off in mid-sentence and look around for the source of the disturbance. "'Above our dingy garden plots those are celestial chimney pots.' Something like that anyway."

"Yes, yes," said the customer, catching her excitement. "I haven't heard it for years but there was a blackbird singing outside my window yesterday evening and I just had to read it again."

"I've got that one in an old collection of bird poetry at home. Published by Pelican, would you believe? The collection must be out of print but I'll write it out for you tonight if you like."

"Could you?"

"Ye-es. No problem, as long as you can read my writing that is, which might be the biggest hurdle. I'll have it waiting for you tomorrow."

"Thank you so much. I feel I should buy something now I'm here and you've been so very kind. What would you recommend?"

"Me? That's tough. How do you rate Alexander Pope?"

"Mm. I think I'd prefer something a little lighter. What about an anthology?"

Jennifer surveyed the titles. "This?"

Favourite Poetry of Wendy Craig.

"Ah! That's more like it."

After glancing at the contents the lady decided she would buy the book. Jennifer stood in the doorway waving to her as she left the shop. When she came back inside Ralph was waiting for her.

"Jennifer, a word of advice. We don't go in for the hard sell at Pugh's"

"Well, that's right. Glad to hear it. I agree."

"What I'm saying is that we don't put pressure on customers. As you were doing just now."

"Me?"

"Trying to get that old dear to buy Pope. She looked as though she'd never even heard of him. It's the wrong approach. It puts people off."

"Old dear. That's a bit condescending. How do you know she'd never heard of Pope? She just didn't want a book of his poems, that's all. Anyway she bought a book. Four pounds in the till. My first sale. How much did your customer spend?"

I saw the back of Ralph's neck turning red. "That was Dr. Massey. He's a very difficult customer. You can deal with him next time he comes in. It'll be good training for you."

Dr. Massey called again the following morning just after the elderly lady had collected her copy of *The Blackbird* printed in block letters because of what Jennifer called 'my awful scrawl'. The lady also bought a second copy of the anthology for a friend, putting it ahead of Stephen King and Virginia Andrews in terms of sales so far that week. As the doctor was walking through the shop towards Ralph, Jennifer brought him to a halt by asking, "Dr. Massey, can I help you?"

"Well, yes, perhaps you can."

Although we all knew Dr. Massey none of us addressed him by name save for Pugh and myself. Ralph, suspecting that she was blotting her copy book, turned away with a barely concealed smirk on his face. It appeared, though, that Dr. Massey was flattered by her attention. A long conversation ensued, culminating in his placing an order for a complete set of *A La Recherche* in translation. It was a good sale. Pugh thought I was joking when I told him. Jennifer seemed not to realise the significance of what she had done.

"It's only one book, isn't it?" she said, as though she was being accused of something.

Ralph and Mrs. Dunnock were both suspicious of her extrovert nature. I think they resented the fact that rules they had rigidly applied to their own conduct within the shop had been broken in less than a minute by a girl of seventeen.

She often shared lunch-breaks with Naomi and there appeared to be an immediate rapport between them. They sat at the table in the dark little room we called our canteen. The one small window overlooked an alleyway.

"Are you a Ritzy person, Naomi?" Jennifer asked one day over a cup of coffee.

"Don't think so, Jen." Naomi exhaled a cloud of cigarette smoke. "What's a Ritzy person? Doesn't sound like me."

Jennifer passed her a card. "They were giving these out in the High Street. The Ritzy's a new club opening next week. See? It says that if you're a Ritzy person you get free admission on the opening night. A female 'Ritzy person', that is."

"Oh!"

"Coming?"

"What do I have to do?"

"Just put on your glad rags and show the card at the door. I went past twice so I picked up two cards."

"Jen, I'm not a Ritzy person. I'm too old. The way I feel today I'm more of an EXIT person."

"Oh? What's wrong?"

"M-E-N. Mine's just accepted a job in Dundee of all places. He didn't even tell me he was going for the interview. The bastard. Are you courting, Jen?"

"Mm-mm. I was going out with this boy but... you know."

"Don't I just? Don't get involved, Jen. It always ends in tears."

There was only five years between them but it looked like a lifetime. Naomi was fair-haired and pretty, but her face wore the expression of someone who has seen all that life has to offer her and has not been impressed. Jennifer's ideal boys occupied some celestial daydream at which she would gaze with her chin resting on her hand.

Things had become livelier at Pugh's and this only served to emphasise the coldness and emptiness at home. At work I now felt myself to be a different person but in the house I was as I had been for two years, only gloomier. I was sitting on the bus one morning musing on the awfulness of life, staring through the window at my disappointing past and my uneventful future. Suddenly I realised that somewhere between my eyes and the infinity on which they were focussed someone was trying to attract my attention. Another bus had pulled alongside and Jennifer was waving madly to me from her seat. She was wearing a black-and-white jumper with horizontal stripes and carrying, as always, her pink shoulder bag. I waved back with the same extravagent enthusiasm. How strange I must have looked – a bald solemn old man in a funeral suit waving like a long-lost friend to this lovely young woman, waving until the other bus pulled ahead and she was out of sight. Looking around at the other passengers I realised that most of them were as I had been a few moments earlier – far away, their faces indicative of boredom, weariness, perhaps pain. Even the younger ones looked as though they were wearing blinkers – unable to see beyond the narrow tunnel of the dull day that awaited them. What right had I, in the circumstances, to be miserable? The day that lay ahead of me promised laughter and surprise.

By the end of June, when she took a fortnight's holiday, Jennifer had made a deep impression on both staff and customers. On learning that she was absent Dr. Massey said that he would call again in two weeks. This was bitterly resented by Ralph.

"He was my customer," he said, his eyes looming large and almost tearful behind the spectacles. "She poached him from me."

"Ralph, you gave him to her as a penance," I argued.

"Well, why didn't you stop me?" he snapped back.

Naomi was subdued until the holiday was over. She and Jennifer often went out in the evenings, sometimes walking home together in the small hours either to Naomi's flat or to Jennifer's house. I had never seen her as full of life as she was in her new friend's company.

At the beginning of September Jennifer told us it would soon be her eighteenth birthday. The actual date fell on a Sunday and she was planning a quiet evening with her mother and a few friends including Naomi. The two girls were going out on the town on Saturday. She also wanted to celebrate with her friends from Pugh's and she asked if we would mind if she brought in a cake and some other food on Friday so that we could have a small party after work. Pugh, who was the only one whose decision counted, had no objection and so she went ahead with her preparations.

Naomi organised a collection and we bought between us a Wedgwood trinket box with a pattern of pink roses. On the Friday afternoon, the two girls disappeared upstairs at about 4.30 and when the shop had closed the rest of us went up to the canteen. Two lighted candles imparted an air of snugness to the gloom. On the red formica tables were laid out crisps, pickles, salads and French bread as well as an iced birthday cake. I suddenly felt very mean. I hadn't envisaged anything like this and we should have been doing it for her, not she for us, on her birthday. There were two bottles of wine, one red, one white.

"Don't know anything about wine," Jennifer explained, "but these were the biggest in the shop."

She had changed out of her working clothes into a long filmy pink dress and white shoes. Did she realise how beautiful she looked? Could she realise?

There was a small radio recorder on one of the tables and a collection of tapes. "These are Mum's," she explained, indicating titles by Jim Reeves, Frank Chacksfield and Mantovani. "I promised I'd take care of them. I don't think everyone would like Wham."

So we sat in that awful room, munching cakes, drinking wine and listening to Country and Western music. When we had eaten, the tables had been cleared and pushed to the wall, Jennifer put on the Mantovani tape. It was a lush tune in waltz-time, 'Around The World' or something like that. She turned to me and said, "Mr. Edwards, may I have this dance?" I couldn't believe she was asking me. Connie and I had won prizes for ballroom dancing but that was many years ago. As I rose to my feet I said, "Jack."

"Jack," she repeated, looking into my eyes and giving me that invisible wink I remembered from her first minutes in the shop. Turning to the others she called, "Come on, everybody. Grab your partners. It's my birthday."

I didn't want the music to end. As we waltzed around that

little room I felt I was a young man again and that all of my life so far had been a prologue to this moment. She had probably never danced a waltz before but she was as light as a feather. When the tune finished we all seemed to understand that the dancing, too, was over. I saw in the flickering candlelight that Ralph had been dancing with Naomi, and Pugh with Mrs. Dunnock. There was a moment as though we were all suspended in some magical bubble and then, as the next track began, Jennifer herself broke the spell with a laugh and a windmilling wave of her arms. Somehow I felt that although that dance had been mine she had been dancing with all of us. I know it happened but looking around that room from a seat at one of the tables, as I have on many occasions since, I find it hard to believe that three couples danced there on that evening as though it was a candlelit ballroom in a dream.

Only a few weeks later we learned that she would be leaving us. Her mother was moving to Bradford to live near relatives. Naomi was devastated. So, too, was I but I hid my feelings until I went home in the evening. To do otherwise wouldn't have been the right thing.

Jennifer knew I would miss her. "Everything has to change, Jack," she said to me on the last morning when I was trying in my faltering way to say goodbye. "That's life. I'll pop in and say 'hello' when I'm in town."

We both knew that she wouldn't but the pretence was a poultice on that wounding day.

Although she kept in touch with Naomi by letter and once by telephone, as far as we knew she never came back. Naomi told me about the phone call. "It was girl talk," she explained. "She's met a bloke and... love has happened to her. She doesn't know where she's at. She wanted my advice. Me. Her older friend. Like asking Nero for lessons in fire prevention."

"I hope things work out for her," I said. "She made us all so very happy. She changed us all and we did nothing for her."

"She loves us all very much. Her dear friends she called us in one of her letters. That's going some for Jen. She was having a rough time when she came here. She needed us to help her through. The support wasn't all one way. There was an exchange going on although we didn't know it."

Last month I retired. Ralph is the new manager. He's good. He has big plans for the shop. It took a long time for him to accept Jennifer but he has changed more than any of us. He's in touch with his feelings now – he's married to an extrovert young woman who has helped him to come to terms with what ever pain he had in his past. There's a warmth between him and Naomi and Mrs. Dunnock that wasn't there before although Mrs. Dunnock will be Mrs. Dunnock till her dying day, not Jenny which I happen to know is her first name.

I miss my friends. Poor old Pugh seldom leaves his house these days. I think it's Parkinson's Disease. I visit him in the evenings, we talk and often I'll read aloud. He enjoys that. He's always very grateful, unaware that there is an 'exchange going on'.

Naomi heard nothing from Jennifer for a long time after that phone call but there was one last message, a card at Christmas a year later. Inside was a note which Naomi showed to me. It read, 'I'm still living with Mum but I have a little baby boy now. His name is John. Love to everyone from Jen.'

I hope that wherever she is and what ever she is doing she has not lost that quality, that radiance, which made her so very special. Before we met her we were not particularly wicked or unkind people but our world was no bigger than the bookshop. We had no dreams although in a sense we were asleep. Now I look forward to every hour of the time I have left to me. I still believe that even on my darkest days I might suddenly see, through a window or around a corner, a hand waving and a face smiling, telling me, "Don't worry. It's okay. We're alive."

NUMBER TWO

Claire Lincoln

There are two points where this situation could have been avoided. Number one was back in mid-1973. I'm not sure about the biological details, but it involves chromosomes and was when Kathy egg decided to remain Kathy egg and not become Kevin egg. Number two was about two months ago, when Kathy late teenager, fully aware of the lack of prophylactics, whispered into Matt's ear "Please, just once." and became Kathy late-teenager plus fertilised egg. I now face two similar choices; fulfil the biological role that was chosen for me nineteen years ago or continue with the callous irresponsibility of more recent years. Maybe I'm being too harsh on myself. Millions of people get pregnant every minute. It happened to me, it happened to Jo's sister, it happened to at least thirty per cent of my class, it even happened to Madonna (both of them).

I don't much like choices, especially when I'm being forced to make the wrong one, but then again I am sitting in the back office of Save the Foetus, so I don't know what I really expected. Well, I certainly didn't expect to be with child for a start. I'd just wanted to make sure that I wasn't and this was one of the free options. If I'd gone to the doctors Mother was sure to find out.

I presume that the back office is where they take you to "come to terms". The prim ashen-haired receptionist whose nails had clicked hold of my urine sample to take to the lab, had been replaced by the resident calmer and persuader. Mrs Hampshire sat opposite me now, leaning over her name stand, her brow scrunched and lifted as if the weight of her voluminous auburn hair was too much for her.

"Katherine, or is it Kathy?"

"Kathy."

"I know how difficult this time must seem, dear." She fingered the ends of ties that gathered the drab floral fabric of her brown dress around the folds in her neck. "I too was in your position many moons ago. Hard for a young lady like you to believe I'm sure, but it's true."

I was looking at the thin gold links of her watch disappearing into her bloated wrists, like an elastic band round a marshmallow.

"You're confused. Obviously you are. I know I was. Shocked too, I'd imagine. Yes, I remember that feeling all too well." She was trying to get eye contact.

"But looking back, I know that there was no need to be confused or frightened or even ashamed. (I lifted my eyebrows at her – damn she'd got me!) Yes child, I know how you may feel like that." She smiled and shifted her weight even closer to me, creaking and banging the wooden chair top back into its pre-scored hollow in the wall behind her. "All that we want to do is help you, show you that this is a natural way for you to be, that these feelings of uncertainty are equally natural and to help you through what should be, at your age, a relatively easy pre-labour period. One of our representatives can even be there to hold your hand at the birth if you like!" She smirked and made a grab for my hand.

"Thanks but....."

I scraped back my chair, lifting myself off it as if I were already fit to pop. "Believe me, child, it'll all turn out for the best, I remember when...." I didn't hang around for any more reminiscing. It was a relief to shut the door on the smell of parma violets. I felt sorry for her saved foetus. Probably about thirty now, I can imagine him. He works in the Post office but still lives with Mrs Hampshire in a bungalow. And he's into model trains and Star Wars.

Jo was on her lunch break. She's worked in the same travel agents on Queen Street since we were sixteen and she's now Assistant Manager. She hates it. We normally meet in Jaspers for lunch on Wednesdays to break up the week, plus Jo is hoping that she'll meet some rich guy in there some day. Yeah right, have you seen the clientele lately? The only person she's likely to meet is the same person she normally buys her sexy little going out tops off in some snoot shop. She should recognise them by the uniform sunglasses on head and aversion to any non -calculated acts of friendliness. Someone needs to remind them that they're just shop assistants. I need another coffee but Jo's got other things on her mind.

"The things that she comes out with, I can't believe it sometimes. She's sooo annoying. Do you know what she said today? Well, you know like she only started say, how long? Two, three months ago? I don't know, but anyway, she says to me, well no, first I asked Tina if the new discounted price lists had come through from the Intercontinental Flights promotion. I wasn't even talking to her, and she says, the cheek of it, like she's been there forever and I'm stupid or something: 'Jo, have you checked in the new promotions file or on the back of the discount flight screen?'. Can you believe it? As if that wasn't the first place I'd checked."

"Did you tell her that?"

"Well, I don't want to upset her, do I? I mean, she hasn't been there very long, but I gave her such a look, saying like "as if I haven't looked there already!". She soon shut up, I can tell you."

I didn't get a chance to tell Jo that lunchtime.

Now I think about it, Mark's the only bloke that I've ever really loved. I've been out with lots of guys, of course, but none of them have made me go stupid like Mark, even with what happened at Suzanne's.

I met Mark in Greece. Quite romantic really. Bobbing along in the not-quite-as-blue-as-the-travel-brochure-but-not-far-off sea, I was imagining my weightless body in a profile horizon, clamped between the yin and yang of burning sky and lapping blue, wiggling water between my toes and flicking the surface to make that smacky kissing sound. What noise there was from the beach was melting into the white noise of salt water in my ears and I had closed my eyes against the sun. There were no clouds in the sky over Zathinos. The next thing I realise is a splash near my head, which was a bit of shock in my relaxed state. Treading water now I saw that there were four lads laughing and pointing, not the most comfortable thing when it took two shots of last night's ouzo to get you into your bikini. I plucked a pair of sopping shorts from the water beside me and started waving them in the air. And that's how I met Mark, Paul, Dave and the unfortunate Neil, all from Barnsley, Yorkshire.

I spent the afternoon talking to them on the beach and mucking about in the water. That night they picked me up from my apartment and we did the bars – cocktails at Grasshoppers, Ouzo at Kinky's and dancing on the tables to "Walking on Sunshine" in the

Kiss Bar, which is where, coincidentally, we first kissed. He'd leant over his flaming zambooka, risking a severe singeing of his Cast T-shirt, and asked "Do you know why it's called The Kiss Bar?" I shook my head. " I'll show you," he said, what a smoothie. From then on we did everything together, literally. My parents were glad that I'd found some young people my own age to have fun with.

I've got his picture beside the bed now, next to my copy of *Cosmo* and *Bridget Jones's Diary* (I haven't started it yet). Everyone agrees that he's gorgeous when I show them the photo of him on the beach; sun-bleached hair, blue-green eyes, and a better tan than I could ever get. I cried so much on the plane home that I made myself ill. Mom thought that I was being a bit of a baby over air-sickness. But Mark was right, Barnsley is such a long way from Cardiff, it wasn't practical, it wouldn't work. "What's wrong with the train?" Jo had asked.

I did go to visit him once, I couldn't have beared not to. Things didn't go too well. He seemed much too casual about it all and I made a fool of myself on the last night, I begged. We've only spoken a couple of times since. I was so upset when I got off the train in Cardiff that I got straight in a taxi to Suzanne's in Canton and in true mate fashion she immediately opened a bottle of red wine and off we went.

Much later, I sat up in the darkness of the lounge to the sound of footsteps in the hall. The lounge door opened releasing the light in from the hall and Suzanne's brother Matthew came in, flicking the light on as he did so. He jumped back into the doorway when he saw me on the sofa, a mess of black hair and swollen eyes.

"Oh sorry, sorry, I didn't realise."

"It's OK, Matt, I wasn't asleep. Come in if you want. Where've you been?"

"Town. Shall I put the lamp on instead, it's a bit bright isn't it?"

He wasn't too steady on his feet as he walked over and I could smell the smoke on his clothes as he sat down. Luckily, he wasn't at the slurring stage yet.

"What's up?"

"Oh nothing, I just had a really shitty weekend, that's all."

"What happened? Oh I'm sorry, you don't have to say. Don't

cry. Come here."

I sobbed my way through the story of my infatuation and disappointment feeling like a silly little girl and making a big wet patch on his shirt into the bargain. I've known Matt for so long that it seemed natural speaking to him. As I spoke he kissed the top of my head and stroked my hair.

"So I came back here and I feel like such an idiot. I thought that it was really special. He told me that he'd never felt like this about anyone else when we were in Greece. Why did he lie? Do you think that he's just trying to be cool about it so that I won't get hurt? I mean, I'm sure he's right about the distance thing."

"It wouldn't stop me."

"Have you had a long distance relationship before then?"

"Yes, once, but I'm not talking about that. I mean you. I think he's mad. I think that you're beautiful and it wouldn't put me out to come up and see you any weekend."

"That's really sweet, Matt, thanks."

"No, I mean it."

"What?"

"I mean it. About you. I mean it."

I was shocked and I must have looked it, but with Dutch courage spurring him on there was no going back. "Can I kiss you?" He took no answer for yes and I must admit that I put up no resistance at any point during that night. When I woke up in the morning, I was calm and happy and smiled as I snuggled down into his arms, until sense took over and I realised this wasn't Mark and I panicked. I could hardly imagine what Suzanne would have said if she'd walked in, or even worse, her Mom! I didn't wake Matt as I extracted myself from the sofa, alcohol and exertion, not mentioning the obvious, having plunged him into the depths of major unconsciousness. He looked cute all cuddled up, but I felt terrible; I had betrayed Mark.

For the next five days Matt called me but I was always out, until my parents got sick of lying for me. When I finally got up the courage to speak to him (the second time that I accidentally answered a phone call), I told him that I couldn't see him because I loved Mark. He didn't understand, but stopped phoning me anyway.

There are two others in the ward room with me. A mousey-haired girl opposite, who's been working her way through a heap of magazines and a dark-haired lump in the bed next to me. She hasn't moved for hours. I've told Mom and Dad that I'm away with Jo for the weekend. She's coming down later. Jo wanted to be here now but had work commitments. The clock above the doorway says ten thirty-five. That's a.m. It seems much later than that. I miss Mark. It seems weird to be lying in bed when I'm not ill. I'm resting my head back on the regulation stamped pillowcase and staring at where the paint has flaked off the ceiling onto the floor. This doesn't feel right. I haven't eaten yet, Dr. Marshall said that I wasn't allowed, I didn't feel like it this morning anyway. The blonde nurse will be back in a minute with my pre-op, I can't remember her name. I can't think properly. This is such a serious thing, such an important thing and all I can do is lie here and stare. I need to think. I think I can feel her sometimes, when it's really quiet and I'm on my own. I imagine her all curled up inside, not very big yet but smiling and warm and perfect. But it's not reality, is it? It's not the being up all night, the feeling that I'm wasting my youth, the stretch marks, the fact that I'm doing it on my own and who'll want to be with me when I've got a kid, the money, the crying, the pain. How can I make this choice? How can I not make this choice? It's the only sensible option. There's nothing else I can do, it's not fair to bring up a child in doubt but is it fairer to kill it? I wish that I had someone to talk to. Jo's great but she finds it easier to talk than to listen. I need someone now. I can't do this on my own. I need to think logically.

I'm leaving. I want to go before the nurse sees me, I don't want to explain. It probably happens a lot, but I'm not changing my mind, it's just not made up properly yet. The magazine girl doesn't even look up as I leave and I manage to get past all the nurses without a problem. It's easier to escape from a clinic when your injuries are internal. I need to get to a phone. I know that there's one in the lobby but I'm still scared of confronting a nurse. I don't need to be persuaded any more, just listened to. I can see a phone box just down the road outside the petrol station and I'm heading for it. This is a busy road but the phone is free. I'm going to do what I should have done in the first place, I know that this is the right decision. I lift the receiver and dial.

A TRICK OF THE LIGHT

Herbert Williams

The first time she had the dream, Sonya thought little of it. It was just one dream among many, vaguely remembered in the blurred moments between sleeping and waking. An archway, set in open countryside. Night-time. A vague sense of unease. Then she was awake with Merrick beside her, full-lipped mouth slightly open, bulbous eyes closed, curly hair tangled, broad brow with strange, questioning look. What could he be asking? She nudged him, his eyes opening wide. "Seven o'clock," she said gently. He stared, uncomprehending. She waited for a groan, a curse, but none came. She slipped out of bed, went to shower. Another day had begun.

She was painting landscapes now, as detailed as photographs yet startlingly three-dimensional. The clouds swirling around the mountain tops leapt out of the frame. They were of actual places but had the strangeness of the legendary. They seemed to come from a parallel world in which everything was more intense and exalted.

His interest in her work was barely polite these days. At first he had been enthusiastic, praising it in terms which suggested keen understanding. She had long realised that this was mere trickery. He had absorbed the language of the connoisseur as he had absorbed so much else, even the power to display emotions he did not really feel. She thought of him now as a sponge, soaking up whatever was around him and allowing anyone to squeeze out what was necessary.

"Where are you off to today?" she asked, over their muesli and wholemeal bread breakfast.

"Bangor Uni," he replied briefly.

He looked, now, like an exhausted Dylan Thomas might have looked if he had lived to be fifty, with slats of grey in his hair and crow's feet puckering his eyes. When they had first met, fifteen years ago, there had still been something of the angelic Dylan in him, springy hair like ripened corn, eyes bright with the knowledge that the unexpected might always happen.

She had learned long ago that looks can be deceptive, and that Dylan Thomas was an accident that could not be repeated.

"Will you be late home?"

"Can't say. Might have to go to Manchester after." He wiped his mouth with a pink tissue from the box on the table, pushed his chair back. "Expect me when you see me."

Ten minutes later she was alone, and he was on the road to Bangor in the blue-and-white van that was his trademark. It still surprised her that he dealt not in words but in computer technology. A small, credulous part of her was convinced that one day he might still produce a Poem on His Birthday or a new paean to Fern Hill.

The second time she had the dream, it was more precise. The arch was made of dark grey stones of different sizes, judiciously placed and rough-mortared like those of the castles flung up by medieval English kings against the turbulent Welsh. There were fields on either side, dimly lit by a crescent moon. A hedgeless road, innocent of white lines or cat's eyes, ran through the archway. There might or might not have been figures on the far side. Again, the sense of unease and mystery.

He had a tendency to sleep late these days and often she had to rouse him. He woke up grudgingly, even resentfully, his eyes asking her a question she could not define. She wondered if he too had dreams he could not explain; wondered, in fact, if he had any dreams at all. It puzzled her that the longer she knew him, the less she knew of him. The memory of their first days together seemed like early chapters in a book she had long set aside.

Alone in the house, she washed up their breakfast things and then sat down, listening to the silence. She could do this for hours, if the will to paint was not there. The house had long been sunk in sleep before they had taken it over. Silence and sleep had permeated the walls. Merrick had done his best to expel them, banging and scraping as he performed radical surgery upon this old fabric. Yet, when he ceased, the house seemed much as it had been before, absorbing the changes as it had absorbed so much else.

It was the perfect atmosphere for Sonya. She worked best amid stillness. Her studio, once a bedroom, looked out the back of the house, over the scrubby, unused garden to fields of wiry grass with the mountains beyond. The most constant movement was that of the clouds, their shadows subtly changing the texture of the landscape like the deft touches of an artist.

She had an exhibition soon at a gallery in Liverpool. She had enough to send there as it was, but wanted to complete one more canvas. It was of a cleft in the mountains near Capel Curig, where the rocks had strange shapes and appeared, in certain lights, oddly fluid. Legends about them had come down through the centuries, carrying greater weight in the past than today. They seemed, to Sonya, like abandoned gods, in whom the loss of faith in others had induced lack of belief in themselves.

She stirred herself, shaking the plump cat from her lap. It stared at her, yawned, and stalked away, tail held high in derision. She went back to her canvas. She was not sure whether she had caught the curious quality in the rocks that had first attracted her, the sense of movement within their apparent solidity. She set to work, not on the rocks themselves but on the heather growing on the overhanging cliff above. She left such touches till late and was uneasy about this today, feeling that if the main theme failed there was little point in perfecting minor details.

Thoughts of Merrick became increasingly obtrusive, a sure sign that she was not in tune with her craft that morning. He was becoming tired of her; that was obvious. Did he have another woman? That was always a possibility. He was the kind of man who attracted women without trying. "I can't bloody help it," he had told her once, crossly. "I don't know why they bother." She knew why. It was the things about him that attracted her, the sense that here was a vibrant, sensual man who had it in him to please women in all kinds of ways. She had fallen for it, and she did not blame others. But she had to protect herself; at least, she had thought so. Now she did not try, knowing all effort was counter-productive. If he strayed, he strayed. She had no wish to hear his lies, or his explanations.

But that questioning look was something new. It troubled her. What was he questioning? Herself? His own reality? Perplexed, she put her brushes aside and went downstairs. The cat was nowhere to be seen.

She sat again in the green mock-leather chair they had bought at an auction in Cricieth. It was not especially old but looked in place in this farmhouse, which had once rung with the sounds of rough boots on flagstones. There was a time when she had tried to picture the generations who had lived there, but their ghosts had withdrawn long since, perhaps offended by the sight of this couple living in sin together, city dwellers casting their shame upon everything.

The cat, returning from its saunter in the garden, looked at her speculatively and then jumped back on to her lap. It settled there, her long fingers coaxing out a purr which became steadily deeper and more sustained, so that it throbbed like a small generator. Soothed by the sound and the cat's warmth, she began to feel sleepy. She knew she ought to shake herself awake but could not. The sleep of many centuries seeped out again from the walls, claiming her. Again she saw the archway set in open countryside, with a road running through it and fields on either side. The moon was fuller now, the light brighter. For the first time she noticed a thin line of grass running along the centre of the road. There were shapes of hills in the distance, which the weak light of the crescent moon had not revealed before. The archway was thrown into bolder relief, and she felt that if she reached out she could touch those craggy stones of different sizes, so cleverly bonded together. Two figures slowly emerged from the darkness. She could not see them distinctly. They were on the far side of the archway, standing at the roadside. She peered at them, straining to make out their faces. The harder she stared, the more vague they became. And then she was awake, bristling with impatience. The cat leapt down and, annoyed with herself, she went straight back upstairs to her unfinished painting.

He arrived home unexpectedly at lunchtime. Marvelling at herself even as she did so, she flung her arms around him and kissed him warmly on the mouth. He laughed, his red lips curling voluptuously. They kissed again, shuddering. "God!" he cried. "What's all this?" "All what?" she said, wickedly. They made love hungrily, as if after a long absence. "Jesus," he said afterwards. "Jesus."

Alone again, she went walking. The brittle brown leaves snapped under her feet. To one side of the lane was a conifer forest, to the other a small lake where anglers hunched silently in the summer. She walked briskly, bareheaded, a red scarf round her throat like a gaping wound. She knew that their lovemaking had solved nothing. The unasked question was still there.

When she heard his van return that evening, with a small, familiar squeak of brakes, she half knew what to expect. He clumped into the house and spoke more loudly than usual, as if hoping to keep her at bay with busy-ness and noise. She felt amused, by the sheer emptiness of men. She responded as she knew he wished, with idle talk about nothing and an evening in front of the telly. They had been together a long time. That lunchtime might never have happened.

She finished the painting of the mountains in time for the exhibition. It still fell short of her expectations, but she decided to display it just the same. He was all attentiveness, even offering to go to the opening with her, something he hadn't done for years. When she set off in the hired van, he stood in their doorway, waving.

She thought the dream of the archway had disappeared into limbo but that night, in Liverpool, it came to her again. The moon was full this time, flooding the scene with an eerie glow. The grass down the centre of the road was more clearly defined, and so keen was her perception that she felt she could see each individual blade. She marvelled again at the craftsmanship of the masons who had created such symmetry, and for what purpose? Then she realised something was missing. The two figures were no longer there.

The exhibition was launched as usual with barely drinkable wine, a great deal of condescension and a flurry of luvvie-type enthusiasm. She was asked a few intelligent questions and many stupid ones. A half-cut art critic promised to come down to her studio to give her a write-up. She had heard it all before, and barely kept her patience.

Home again, she went for long walks for a day or two to shake off the nonsense, then began the painting she now regarded as predestined. She could see it all so clearly that she scarcely thought of it as an act of creation. She painted what she saw with her inward eye, as if it existed already.

The pure light of dawn, ethereal on the canvas, came as a surprise. She had imagined it would still be night, as it had been when she dreamt it. The moss on some of the stones, only dimly perceived before, stood out with startling clarity. The thin line of grass stiffened into emerald green tufts. A river mist shrouded the trees in the distance.

What startled her most of all was that her whole perspective was altered. It puzzled her until she realised she was now the other side of the archway. She, the artist-onlooker, was gazing at the place where she had been standing in her dream. But she did not see herself there; she saw somebody else.

She was wearing the kind of loose, gossamer clothing of pre-Raphaelite women. Her richly auburn hair streamed down her back. She was walking away, not hurriedly but without hesitation. She half-turned to look at someone she had left behind, and this is how Sonya caught her.

Unexpectedly, the art critic rang. He had a commission to write her up for one of the Sunday-paper supplements. She did not tell Merrick, fearing his jealousy. It had become clear to her that he thought himself a failure, and she damned herself for her obtuseness.

The critic arrived late, with severe indigestion. He refused coffee, drank tea, swallowed a pill from a packet he kept in his pocket. He asked her a lot of questions, not all of them silly. He made her talk into a little tape recorder she hated.

In the studio he stopped by the still incomplete picture. "That's amazing," he cried. "Who is she?" He asked her more questions and was irritated by her answers. He thought she was holding something back but she wasn't.

When the painting was finished, she asked Merrick if he would like to see it. He gave her an odd look, as if suspecting something. She led the way to the studio, with Merrick close behind her. She found herself thinking he could quite easily kill her.

He stared at the picture, unmoving. Then: "How on earth...?" he began, bewildered. The incomplete sentence hung between them, suspended between his reality and hers.

She shook her head.

"It's finished," he said brokenly. "God dammit, it's all over." For a moment Sonya thought he was about to fling himself at the canvas. Then, very softly, he began weeping. She reached out a hand and touched him. The woman's face seemed to harden with contempt, but it must have been – surely – just a trick of the light.

WAITING FOR PERESTROIKA

Gee Williams

It's a war out there.

They attacked early that morning. Five past ten we drew up at The Bay Horse car park, opened the door and they were on us, half a dozen at least – one grossly fat – all trying to climb aboard. The van laboured on its suspension and the books shifted.

"You got us anything really nice, today, Sally?" said the first. "Anything new?"

"Well, there's the latest Catherine Cookson," I said. I don't approve of blood sports and this was like tossing somebody's tabby to hounds.

"You got that? Where? Where is it? I thought we 'ad to go on the list!"

Nothing could be said without excessive body-movement. The very frail old creature that had that moment heaved itself up the step was instantly lost at sea.

"Just joking," I said. "You might get a look at it ... oh, two thousand and two, or some time after."

Dot and her sister Megan cackled. "Oh, you madam. She's a mean little cow, that one! Isn't she a mean little cow, Meg?"

"Language, ladies," I said. "Any more of that and I'll put you on a course of Antonia Fraser, all terribly genteel."

"Oh no, we don't want none of that – we don't want nothing too stuck up!"

"But," I couldn't help pointing out as I reclaimed the eight assorted romances, "most of this stuff is about ... about," I picked one at random, "'Merial, the beautiful, estranged, daughter of a mining engineer that inherits her father's diamond mine in Australia and comes into conflict with Nick Van Owen, the ruggedly handsome geologist who nevertheless...' I flicked through its dog-eared pages, "She ran a thin white finger along the proud bones of his tortured face. "Oh, God, Merial," he breathed, "Oh, God, Oh

God, oh God! You're just too beautiful to touch!" The girl's hand dropped onto the fine silk of her dress just as his- oh for goodness sake! I mean not exactly gritty realism, is it?"

"It was good, that one was," Megan said, "'is mam 'ad bin widowed when 'is dad's wagon went off the road late one night nobody knew 'ow."

"Hit a kangaroo, I suppose."

"an he'd paid 'is own way through school an' that was what made 'im a bit on the pushy side, you know."

"Don't tell me," I said, "he was a rough diamond."

Dot let out a shriek that set off the pub's Rottweiler. "Take no notice of 'er, Meg. She's just windin' you up. In your face, she is today."

"Where do you two pick up this jive-talk? Thank God for Mills and Boon. They keep you inside and off the streets... otherwise you'd be out goosing old men and selling glue to poor teenagers."

"No," said Megan, "that's where you're wrong, Miss Clever Knickers. We'd be out goosing young men and selling our favours."

"Bloody 'ell," said her sister, "We'd be bankrupt then."

And all this was the day Dan came in and said something I never expected to hear in the back of the travelling library.

"What have you got by Solzhenitsyn, please? I'll need them all but *Cancer Ward* would do for a start."

It was just so right: his skin as pale as a chronic invalid's, his eyes glittering in the gloom as Alexander Pushkin's were said to glitter when he gave a reading.

"Well, the short answer is, I've got none ... not here. I can get them for you. If you'd like to order them I can -"

"Don't you bother, boy," Dot interposed, clasping his arm, making it clear they were all acquainted, "I say, Megan, tell Dan 'ere not to bother orderin' stuff off this one. Tell 'im, Meg."

"Oh, that's right! Don't be doin' it. Twenty-two weeks she 'ad me waiting for *Passion in Paradise*. Twenty-two weeks! I bet it didn't take the girl that long to write the bloody thing."

"I bet it's not a girl, " I said, stamping the new batch she had chosen with unnecessary force. "All this stuff's churned out by a bloke called Brian, living in Basingstoke ... a great big scruffy ex-policeman with ginger hair coming out of his nose." Meg and Dot glared. "Brian," I said, "he's Sonia Logan, Marianne Clark and," I banged Meg's final selection on top of the heap "and this, er, Ginetta Gale. All Brian from Basingstoke, every one."

"Twenty-two weeks," said Meg, "an' then when I got it some kid 'ad scribbled all over the back page."

"There you go, then," said her sister. "See you next week, Sally love."

"Do you know those two?"

"Yes." When he smiled he looked less unusual, less intense. "I'm the new tarecaker – caretaker! At their flats, you know?"

"Oh yes, I know. Your lot are my best customers. In fact, mostly they're my only customers. It's funny, when I get back to Mold, with the van, and I've done all these villages and I've issued all these romances and whodunnits – Winnie, the er, the fattish lady, very into murders, she is, gorier the better – and I think, something must have happened out there. What it is, they've slapped this enormous tax on reading. You know, five pounds per book or whatever, and nobody told me ... oh, yes, but they've exempted pensioners ... that's why Grey Girl Power there are the only ones can afford it."

"To order the books...?" he prompted.

"No problem, I'll get you *Cancer Ward* and *The First Circle* for next week. I have this hunch they'll be available. You'll have to join the library. Just fill this in."

Daniel Jenkyn, I watched him write, The Annex, Ffrith House. He laid the card down very carefully and then lined up his Council identity badge so that they just touched.

"Great, that's great. I'll get you a ticket made. See you next week, Daniel."

"Dan," he said, "It's just Dan. Thank-you... um."

Bad sign. Three chances, at least, and he hadn't picked up my name.

A week later I had the collected works of Solzhenitsyn under the counter. It doesn't do to look too keen. There was Dan, helping old Miss Roberts back down onto terra firma while she clutched Jacqueline Suzanne's *Valley of the Dolls* – again. I suspect she just couldn't believe some of the things described the first time around.

Megan and Dot – and I – watched him depart with with

every word Alexander Isayevich Solzhenitsyn had committed to print.

"Studying," said Dot. "Open University."

"Oh yes," said the other one, "up early and the telly on all hours at night."

"How do you know?"

"Oh, she can see in from 'er flat, isn't that right, Meg? Specially if she leans out the bathroom window with 'er feet tucked under the wash-basin an' 'as 'er distance glasses on."

"You're a disgrace," I told them and, "keep off – he's mine."

For the first time ever Dot turned serious on me. "Stray dogs, Sally."

"Mm?"

"It's what our mam said – when I was a girl. Watch out for stray dogs, they always snap."

I didn't see him for a while. My employers in their lack of wisdom sent me to a series of 'Violence at Work' seminars (which did not equip me to eject smelly old men off the van with a single, neat flick of the wrist). Whoever renewed Dreamy Dan's set texts when they were due, it wasn't me ... and then, one morning, there he was: his face paler if anything, his hair longer, his fingers tapping an irritable Morse message while he waited his turn.

"Hello," I said, "how are things in the former Soviet Union?"

"Very interesting."

"You'll want all of these, again?"

"Yes, if that's O.K. I'm still working on Marxism, Character and Culture," he said self-importantly ... and he did something horrible: he grinned ... no, he smirked. The young Martin Amis – the one with all his own teeth – had just vanished before my eyes.

Folding my arms across a broken heart, "Why don't I get you *Dr Zhivago*?" I said.

"It's a film."

"Yes, a film of a book. Just because it's a film doesn't mean to say it can't be a great book as well. I mean he got the Nobel Prize-"

"Solzhenitsyn did."

"Yes, but so did Boris Pasternak."

"Who?"

"Pasternak ... a revolutionary writer – except that he wasn't, I don't think. Loads of Character and Culture and not much Marxism but then it was probably safer that way ... I mean, who are we to judge? Stalin, Beria, the Gulags –"

"But Solz-synetshin –" now Dan was struggling over a name he'd pronounced perfectly every other go – "Solz-hen-itsyn ... he's the master, right? That's what it said – in the notes – *the* master Russian novelist."

"Well he is ... a master, anyway. I'm just saying that there are others – Dostoevsky, Tolstoy –"

"No-o! I don't want to ... in here there's everything ... look ... look."

He grabbed *August 1914* off the very inadequate counter that separated us. (Employers, I recalled from my violence course, have a duty to ensure the safety of staff by the manipulation of the physical environment. Where was my panic button and my armourplated security glass? ... where was my Group Four mace-wielding personal minder? Didn't the Council understand it was the front line out here in the travelling library van?)

"Look," Dan shouted, his pale-but-interesting face now the colour of *The Writers' and Artists' Year Book* – well the red bits, anyway.

I did look – in horror at the passage he was pointing to. The little swine had magic-markered it and there was a great big asterisk at the top of the page. Completely unselfconsciously he began to read:

" 'This was an emergency worse than a fire or a flood; at moments like this officers were useless – a sergeant-major with two brawny arms was what was needed. For all their generations of book-learning, officers could only cough apologetically when there was man's work to be done.' See? There it is. The whole of the class-struggle summed up in those few words."

Did I mention he had this wonderful voice? Anthony Hopkins with a bit of rough? All the same, we're still waiting for perestroika to break out in the travelling library service.

"You've defaced it," I said.

"Oh, that, I just ... just noted it for my essay. But you see what I mean? You don't have to know everything to get to the heart of it. I can't read all these others you're going on about. I've left it too late. But it doesn't matter ... I can see what –"

"I'm sorry," I said, "but mutilating books is a very serious matter."

I thought of Joe Orton and his war against publicly owned volumes everywhere but I kept my expression bland. Never, they had stressed on the course, allow these things to become personalised. "The library service may require payment to cover the cost of the damage and ... or may cancel the borrower's ticket."

Dan snatched up his Solzhenitsyns. "Excellent," he said, "outstanding. When I bring these back ... when I've finished my essay, well you can just chop off my hands ... or, or gouge my eyes out. How about that? Or you could just stick your library stamp up where the sun don't shine."

He jumped down the steps and ran off as though he expected someone to give chase and wrestle him to the ground over a few grubby hardbacks and one Penguin Modern Classic. When he'd gone I couldn't really tell if it was the van that kept on shaking or if it was me.

And I never saw Dan – or the Solzhenitsyns – again. He did return to the travelling library but it was a couple of months later and I was off with the 'flu. The new spotty kid that they'd just taken on was doing the rounds and of course Dot and Meg were there to see it all.

"Oh, yes," said Dot, her thin lips saying 'shame' while her wicked old eyes rolled with remembered pleasure and excitement. "Terrible it was ... jumped up 'ere 'e did, never a word to that poor lad you'd sent, Sally."

"I didn't send him," I protested.

"Jumped on the van," said Meg, "an' just starts throwing the books off. All of them. Hated reading, now, 'e said. Great armfuls of books ... sweeps them up and chucks them onto the carpark. Wet it was too, wasn't it?"

"Oh wet – we'd had nothing but rain ... all those lovely books lying in puddles and then, Dan, he goes an' he sits down with 'em and starts tearing out the pages and cryin' like a child. Sobbin'...it did upset us," she finished with relish.

"Back in hospital, they say," said her sister. "Best place, really.

All that studying, it must've turned 'is brain."

I stamped eight assorted tales of sexual repression and big moustaches in Edwardian England. I handed them over in silence.

"The police came, you know?" Dot persisted, "a man and woman. Swearin' he was, by then. Twice over he used the f-word."

"What, fines?" I said. "I don't think I'll be seeing any of them."

WHITEY'S BIRD

Caryl Ward

She took her place with the other teachers at morning assembly the first day of the Autumn term. She was the only new teacher, so there was no mistaking her. Mrs Gittson Games and English, who came from Bontddu in the next valley. Girls sucked in their cheeks and looked at whoever they happened to be standing next to, and boys nudged each other, muttered and grinned.

All eyes were on her as she sat between Ma Mathews History, a spinster with a grey crop, yellow teeth, and elephantine legs, and Ma Humphries Biol, who dyed her hair by rinsing it with her own pee.

She wore a plain white T-shirt under a skimpy black pinafore dress, the skirt of which ended well above her bare knees, where her brown legs were crossed. A black strappy sandal swung from the toe of her right foot, which she moved rhythmically in small circles, as if she were listening to the slow beat of music, rather than old Pricey's droning voice.

Her arms were as brown as her legs, the fingers of her left hand with a gold wedding ring rested on her thighs at the point where her skirt ended, and her right hand rested on the wrist of her left and was circled by a narrow silver bangle.

Straight blond hair framed her face, which bore no trace of make-up, and hung to below her small-boned shoulders, and when she bent her head for the Lord's Prayer it splayed out like spun gold. When they filed from the stage and out of the hall, she was like a ray of sunshine amongst the other foggy, bored faces, her right sandal flapping as she walked.

Whitey sat with the rest of 5B, watching, as if mesmerized, Gitty's left foot moving in small circles as she talked about Keats' 'Ode on a Grecian Urn', her black shoe dangling from her toes.

She'd been at Nantdre two terms now, and was affectionately referred to as Gitty. She'd run the gauntlet of the boys' coarse remarks and jokes and the girls' crushes, and come out admired and liked by everyone.

Everyone that is, apart from Whitey. Whitey was in love.

He tried not to show it, and denied it – even to himself. He listed her faults, and added to them as often as he could.

1. She must be a lot older than she looked.

2. She was careless about her appearance. She never wore make-up and her hair often looked uncombed.

3. She could never keep her shoes on, and her habit of perching on the edge of her desk and swinging her foot in circles and running her hand through her hair when she was talking to the class was distracting.

4. She treated everyone the same.

5.Why? Oh why? didn't she notice him.

"*Bold lover never never canst thou kiss*
Though winning near the goal – yet do not grieve;
She cannot fade though thou hast not thy bliss,
For ever wilt thou love, and she be fair."

She quoted Keats' *Ode on a Grecian Urn*, looked up from the book and began to talk about the figures being in a state of suspended animation caught forever on the urn, her foot moving in small circles, the black shoe dangling.

"But the moment of intensity will last," she said. "In the next two stanzas we see that it has become art." Her shoe dropped to the floor revealing five pink-painted toenails. She ran her fingers through her hair and her eyes fixed on Whitey's face.

"Would you read the next two stanzas, Clive?"

"*... More happy love! more happy, happy love.*
For ever warm and still to be enjoyed
For ever panting and forever young..."

Noso sniggered in the desk next to him and Whitey's voice wavered. He could feel his face was red, and his mouth was as if it was full of pebbles.

"*A burning forehead and a parching tongue.*"

"Thank you, Clive." She smiled at him, making eye contact. The bell rang. "Well, you've all got the essay titles for Keats' Odes. Don't forget I want them in by next Tuesday." She slid down from the desk, slipped her foot into her shoe and walked out of the classroom. "Have a nice weekend all of you."

Whitey shoved his books into his bag and made for the door, ignoring the others, who were talking about the Friday night disco at the King's Head.

"Clive, Clive, wait," Shirley Griffiths called after him. He carried on walking fast down the corridor, and she ran to catch up with him.

"Are you coming tonight, Clive?"

"No."

"Oh why don't you come, Clive? You didn't come last week. I'm going." She blushed. "Everyone's going."

"I can't afford it," he muttered.

"It's only a pound. And I'll buy you a drink. Try and come."

"I'll see," he said, walking even faster. Shirley was all right, quite pretty, even if she was a bit thick. He'd walked her home from the disco two months ago and kissed her goodnight. She'd made a big deal out of it, and started calling him Clive. She was the only person in the school who used his proper name, apart from the teachers.

Lying on his bed that night, Whitey hated everyone. He hated his parents for being so boring, sitting like zombies in front of the television every evening, gardening and washing the car at weekends. He hated Shirley Griffiths for having frizzy hair and making it so obvious that she liked him. He hated his nickname, which had been given him when he first started school on account of his blond-white hair. He hadn't liked the name then, and his mother had said that his hair would get darker as he grew older. But it never did. The name followed him to the Comp and it had stuck. It was better than Noso. Noso was called Noso because he had a big nose, and Whitey called Noso Noso without thinking about it. He rarely thought about the name Whitey now, he was used to it. But the way that Gitty had said, "Thank you, Clive," that afternoon had made him feel like a different person.

He imagined himself in an expensive restaurant with her, him pouring out red wine. "Thank you Clive," she'd say, lifting the glass to her lips and smiling at him. When they'd finished their meal, he'd say "Your place or mine?" and she'd drive him to her house, and there'd be a white shag-pile carpet and pink light bulbs, and a brilliant stereo. She'd put on Oasis, and say, "Fix yourself a drink, darling, I'll have a Tequila Sunrise." And there'd be crystal glasses and a silver cocktail shaker, and plenty of ice in a big silver bucket. He'd fix himself a Harvey Wallbanger, and carry the drinks over to the huge sofa where Gitty would be reclining. She'd have kicked off her shoes, her dress would have ridden up her thighs revealing her black suspenders.

Whitey had never actually seen a woman wearing suspenders, but he thought about them a lot. In the magazines on the top shelf of the newsagents, which the boys passed around in school, it wasn't the air-brushed crotches and various sizes and shapes of breasts that fascinated him, it was the thin narrow lengths of elastic resting against white skin, between scanty black lace panties and black stocking-tops. He'd studied the pictures carefully, wondering how the little button things on them worked, worrying that if he ever had the opportunity he wouldn't be able to undo them. He knew he'd have no problem with a bra. It would just be like unhooking fish off a line, and they'd slither into his hands – child's play.

A few months ago, when he'd been in Cardiff, he'd gone into the ladies' underwear department in Marks & Spencers to suss out the mechanism of suspenders. He'd waited until there was no-one around the corner where they hung on little hangers, with the elastics dangling. He went up close to a row of black ones, feeling as if he was standing on eggs, and gingerly tried to fasten one, with the fingers of one hand. He was trembling all over, and it was as tricky as he'd thought it would be. He was surreptitiously trying to manage it two-handed, when he saw a young woman two feet away from him, by the hangers of panties, grinning at him. Whitey had fled to the food department, where he'd bought a corned beef pasty. He'd eaten it sitting on a bench in Queen Street, where he'd been bothered by pigeons pecking for crumbs.

But on Gitty the suspenders would be no problem. Then he'd roll her stockings down her legs and over her pretty feet and pink toenails, until they were scrunched up and looked like those round plastic scouring pads that his mother used, and he'd toss them over the back of the sofa.

"How does it feel undressing your teacher?" she'd say, undoing his shirt buttons.

"How does it feel undressing your student?" he'd say, as she unzipped his fly.

"Oh, Clive, darling," she'd say. "I've wanted this for so long. You know that don't you? You're not like the others. You're special."

"You're not bad yourself," he'd say casually, peeling off her panties and tossing them in the same direction as her stockings.

And then she'd stand up, wearing only the suspenders.

"Let's take a shower together, darling," she'd say.

The bathroom would be huge, with a jacuzzi, and gold taps and a thick carpet. And there'd be two shower heads, and a real good spray, not the miserable dribble that there was at home. And she'd leave the suspenders on in the shower, and they'd look as if they were painted on her white skin, and...

But he hated Gitty. She'd made him look a fool asking him to read that Ode about the way he felt about her. He hated Keats. He hated English. He hated school. He hated Nantdre and the stupid King's Head discos. He hated Bontddu too, because that was where Gitty lived with him, and he hated him, although he didn't even know what he looked like – Gitty's husband.

Instead of going to the disco he wrote his essay on Keats' Odes. He finished it in the early hours of the morning and couldn't sleep.

When dawn began to break, he went downstairs and made himself toast and coffee. It was a breezy April morning, and he decided to go for a walk. Soon he was on the narrow road up the mountain. A weak sun shone, taking the chill off the wind. From the top he could see Nantdre to one side and Bontddu to the other. Life was stirring in both valleys, smoke was rising from chimneys of the terraced houses. An early bus passed along Bontddu's main street.

Whitey sat in the shelter of a large rock and stared at the slagheaps and the disused colliery at the top end of Bontddu. His mind was still teeming with Keats.

> *But when the melancholy fit shall fall...*
> *And hides the green hill in an April shroud;*
> *Then glut thy sorrow on a morning rose...*

Someone with a dog was walking along the road up from

Bontddu. The dog ran ahead, and obviously its owner called to it every so often because it ran back, and then ran ahead again. When the person got further up the road Whitey could see that it was a woman with blond hair wearing blue jeans and a green anorak. He'd been thinking that he'd better move. The grass was damp and the rock was cold against his back, but he didn't feel like meeting anyone. He decided to stay where he was until the woman and dog had passed and then walk down into Bontddu and get a cup of coffee in the Italian cafe.

The road was to the left of where Whitey sat, and when the woman got nearer the dog was way ahead, and sensing him, bounded towards him wagging its tail.

"Hello, boy," he stroked the dog, and it nuzzled against him.

"Toddy ,Toddy," he could hear the woman calling.

"Go on, Toddy. Off you go," he said. The dog lay down beside him, its head on its paws.

"Go on, you're wanted," he said. "Go home."

The dog refused to move. Whitey stood up, and his heart leapt.

"He's over here," he shouted.

She walked towards him, her hair streaming, her cheeks pink in the wind. "Oh it's you, Clive." The dog ran towards her wagging its tail and then ran back to Whitey. "He's rather too friendly really." She laughed as the dog ran back and fore between them.

"You're up here early. I usually don't meet anyone in the mornings," Gitty said.

"Do you often walk up here then?"

"When it's fine at the weekends, and during the holidays," she said. "I'm an early bird, and so is Toddy. It's a lovely view from here, isn't it?"

"Yes," he said, looking into her eyes.

"You look tired, Clive," she said.

"I haven't been to bed."

"A wild night at the King's Head, was it?"

"I didn't go. I don't like the King's Head."

She smiled sympathetically. "There's not much for young people to do around here, is there? But you'll be going off to university in a couple of years. You are going to apply for university, aren't you ?"

"I don't know yet," he said.

"Oh I think you should. You're very bright. You should do well. Are you going to take English for one of your A Levels?"

"I don't know yet. I expect so."

"I hope you do."

"Do you really?"

She smiled. "Yes, really. Well, I'd better be getting back. Which way are you going, Clive?"

Whitey stared towards Bontddu and saw a bird flying against the wind. "I'm going back to Nantdre," he said.

"I'll see you in class then. Don't forget your essay for Tuesday."

"I've already done it," he said.

"You seem to be really into Keats, Clive."

She walked away and the dog followed. He got to his feet and walked in the opposite direction, cursing himself every step of the way. He'd been going to go to Bontddu anyway. He could have asked her to have a coffee with him in the café, got to know her better. Who knows what might have happened, perhaps she would have invited him to her house. She'd said she wanted him to do English A Level. Perhaps she really did like him.

Walking up the main street, Whitey saw Shirley Griffiths coming out of the Co-op with a carrier bag.

"Oh, Clive, you didn't come last night after," she said. "I was hoping you'd come."

"I was busy," he said.

She fell into step beside him. She was wearing a biker's jacket, a short red flared skirt, and Doc Martens. She didn't look bad really, Whitey thought. Still, she irritated him. He'd only kissed her goodnight after all. She was a stupid fool who'd made a mountain out of a molehill.

He clenched his jaw, and quickly crossed the road in front of a line of traffic. He glanced back, and she was halfway across the street waiting for a gap. She darted across in front of a van, and the contents of her carrier bag spilled into the gutter. Whitey bent down and helped her pick up the groceries. Thick ribbed tights under white cotton pants with blue dots, he noted, handing her a pound of sausages and a packet of frozen peas.

"Thank you, Clive. The handle's snapped." She beamed at him, her cheeks like red apples.

They walked along in silence. In front of the chip shop last night's fish and chip papers and coke cans were blowing across the pavement. He stopped at the corner of Victoria Terrace.

"I'm going this way," he said. "See you Monday."

"Are you coming out tonight, Clive?" She had blue eyes.

"I don't know yet," he mumbled, hurrying away.

A few yards down Victoria Terrace he noticed an early rose bush blooming in one of the gardens. He turned and ran back to the corner.

"Shirley. Shirley." Whitey's voice carried on the wind.

SOMEONE OUT THERE

Alun Richards

The cry was at the back of the throat, like an animal's, hardly human. It couldn't shape a word. There was not a recognisable syllable, but it came from within; despair, terror, and exhaustion too. An awful sound. Truly awful. And then half- choked sobs, like footsteps between one abyss and another. It was the sobs that made it human, that told you: *"There's someone out there... A Person... There... Somewhere... But where?"*

First the dawn, one of those early mornings you could hardly see because of the mist rolling in, the siren on the lighthouse moaning at intervals – one sharp, one long – and all along the sea front every noise was somehow enclosed by the mist as if everything was happening inside a paper bag. Drop a key and the clang was hollow, muffled, and across the road a high spring tide sucked against the sea wall, its lapping also muted like someone slapping a child a long way off. Everything was close, yet everything seemed distant and even the battery hum of Maxie Keefer's milk float might have been out in the Bay, not just around the corner. You could hear it but you couldn't see it, and you didn't know where it was coming from. (Later, the woman's first cry was like that, lost, disembodied, enclosed; somewhere out there...)

From my bedroom window I could see the masts and halliards of the sailing dinghies chained to the Hard opposite but the wall obscured their foredecks and that too was eerie because the masts looked as if they were hanging down, not standing up. This is what mist does when it's that thick, but it wasn't cold or really damp like a winter mist, and, I suppose, from a visitor's point of view, in the few yards you could see, in front of you, everything looked normal. You were in your own little world, just you and nobody else; cut off, enclosed.

At least, that's what I suppose the woman felt. I hadn't seen her then and I never saw the child. There was a boarding house next door but one, but it was going down, 'no class at all', and although they did a few bookings, it was mostly casuals. But the woman was a booking because of the child, we later learned. She had been there before. Only she couldn't tell anybody. She was one of those unfortunates who have no roof to their mouths, my mother said. But this was later, all later. At the time nobody knew in which boarding house she was staying. There were nineteen dotted along the front.

So . . . at six o'clock there was just me hanging out of the window, the sea lapping across the road and the hum of Maxie Keefer's milk float. I knew Maxie was chancing it because he wasn't sixteen and didn't have a licence. Sid Fairfax, the real driver, got himself dropped off at a widow's he knew, Maxie'd do half the round, then pick Sid up again, Sid giving himself a spell most mornings. There was a lot of gossip about that, but Maxie handled it in a very diplomatic way.

"Where's Sid?" people said in that knowing way.

"Suh-Suh-Suh-Sid likes his greens," Maxie'd say with his cheery stammer, that half-melon grin creasing up his pinched face, the basin-cut hair style falling over his ears, his fingers checking the list to remember his orange juices and creams where the bonus was. That, and no more. He was always on the move and he was willing. He wasn't very bright, not three ha'pence short of a shilling, just not very quick on the uptake. In school, the woodwork master had a nail cabinet, three drawers, all different sizes of nails, tacks, bolts. If they got mixed up, he'd empty the lot on the floor, then send for Maxie to sort them out.

"Job for you, Maxie!"

"I'll huh-huh-huh-have a go!" Maxie said. Happy as a sandboy doing that, sitting cross-legged on the floor. He spelt no trouble for anyone. They didn't seem to notice the sores on his legs, his thinness, the years he went without proper meals. You notice people who complain. Maxie just had a go. He wasn't from the village: outside. But he came every day.

That morning I heard the hum of the milk float, then it stopped. I couldn't hear any footsteps at all, then the cry came, the first one. You won't believe it, but there'd been a fox on the mudflats that summer. We'd had bracken fires everywhere and they said the fox was short of prey and had come right down the cliffs, patrolled the beach, then went out on the mud, waited, sprung, and caught a seagull. You've got to be fast to do that. The fox was fast. It had never happened before, not in living memory. But it happened. There were feathers everywhere, and pad marks on the beach, and the scrape of his brush. And it had been seen, a dog fox, long legs. And so, hearing the sound, I mixed it up in my mind. I didn't know if a fox howled like wolves did. I wasn't a country person. And the sound was so unnatural, I mean.

So I paid no attention. I dismissed it. I heard it first and I dismissed it! There was no sign of the mist lifting so I pushed up the window and went back into my bedroom. Everyone was asleep so I got back into bed. Just lay there. Oh, the times I've thought about that! I heard it and I did nothing. Nothing! I just went back to bed. And I could've been a hero! But I went back to bed.

The next thing I heard was Maxie running, his daps flapping – he always had a loose sole and the laces were too long – then voices, the splash and the shout, and the woman again.

I went to the window. But you still couldn't see. It was further along from us. And the mist was getting thicker. I thought I'd dress. Might as well. I put on a matloe's jumper, crewe neck, the wool hard. You could brush mackerel scales off it, but it itched. So I took it off, found something else, then shoes, down the stairs, unlocked the front door, put the clip back. They wouldn't let me have a key of my own. I had to ask always. That hurt. Then I went out.

I still couldn't see anything happening. The mist was thickening. I crossed the road, climbed over the wall on to the Hard. The tide was high, up to the top of the sea wall, and in the water below me you could see a mess of flotsam, a semi-circle of it, weed, timber wedges, a twisted bundle of lobster twine and netting. The tide was beginning to run now but the rime was still there, close by the steps, enough to put you off swimming because it looked so dirty. But further down...

I heard the woman again, moaning now, a deep moaning in the chest, but it seemed a long way off. So I began to walk. I was curious, but half-scared. I thought, sometimes people on holidays fight. Couples, I mean. They get in the pub and have real up-and-downers. The women were worse than the men, my mother said. The thing to do was keep away. For a second, I thought it might be one of those.

I went on, still peering in the mist. Then I saw her with her back to me, thin, round-shouldered, an old black overcoat down to her ankles, her hair in a turban like the factory girls. She was reaching down over the sea wall to receive something, breathing now in short convulsive gulps as if she'd had a fit. Then there was Maxie, coming up the wall like a seal, soaking, his hair plastered, his clothes clinging to him. You could see the line of his underpants through his sopping trousers.

It looked like he was handing her a bundle. The woman seized it, turned and ran away, her back to me. Maxie was half-kneeling, laying across the top of the sea wall like a bent sack. He had no breath. He was panting – great sobs, looking at the stones, his eyes frantic, staring, as if he'd thought he'd never see them again. I could hear the woman hurrying away, scolding, but never finishing the words.

"Yaw. . yaw. . yaw. . yaw. . ." all in the back of her throat.

And then she was gone and I could hear the fog siren and Maxie's gulping.

I remember going up to him and keeping away because he was so wet. There was stuff coming out of his mouth too. He didn't see me. I thought: "Look at the state of him – he'll cop it!' I bent over him.

"Maxie. . . "

He looked up. He still couldn't get his breath back. You could practically see his ribs through his shirt, all moving. He looked for her. She was gone. Then he said:

"She was talkin' to me."

"What?"

"She was talkin' to me, the little girl. Under the water. She was sittin' on the sand talkin' to me. Under the water. Down there..."

The bundle was a little girl.

"Did she fall in?"

He didn't know. He'd heard the woman, saw this shape in the mist, went over. The woman kept pointing to the sea but he

213

couldn't see anything. It was flat calm, nothing to see. But the woman caught hold of him, tugging, groaning. She was so fierce she tore his shirt.

"Down there, Missus?"

She kept nodding, dribbling.

"She couldn't speak proper," Maxie said.

So he went in. Dived. At first, he couldn't see anything. The tide moved the child down. It was no more than a few yards from the wall, but it was a big tide, seven foot of water and the child sitting down there, talking to him, a little girl, her hair swirling around as if in the wind. But it was under the water.

He couldn't understand that.

"She must've been nearly drownded," he said.

It didn't seem possible. It didn't seem to have happened. We went back over the road to the milk float. We didn't know what to do.

"Nearly drownded. Definite," Maxie said.

There was nobody about. Nobody you could ask. We just stood there. You couldn't see a soul. Then we heard a motorbike. It was Bunty, one of the lifeboat boys, coming off shift in the docks. Maxie wandered into the middle of the road, stopped him. He could see by the state of Maxie something was wrong. We explained. The woman had just picked up the child and run off. There was something wrong with her. "Mental, like. Definite. She couldn't talk. Just, like – gruntin'," Maxie said. The child wasn't talking either. "Nearly drownded." What to do?

Anything like this happens, you're glad when someone takes over, and Bunty was the boy for taking over. In minutes, he had them all there, police, coastguard, and just about everybody else out on the street. And very soon that picture was in everybody's mind, the little girl sitting on the sea bed, talking under the water.

What they did, they turned out the boarding houses. Was there a woman with a child? I don't know when they realised – who put it together, I mean – that the woman wasn't quite right in the head. It was her own child, but she'd stolen it from foster-parents, come down for the weekend to where she'd been before. Somebody told us this later – come down to where she was happy once.

They found the woman and the child, cuddling up in bed.

She was pretending nothing had happened. The curtains were pulled. It was warm in there in the dark. It hadn't happened. It was all right.

But it wasn't. They did artificial respiration in the bedroom. No good. Then the ambulance, hospital. No good.

And that was the end of it. There was a lot of talk after, bits and pieces of information, what people thought they knew.

"Wasn't it awful? A little child like that? And the intelligence of the woman? I mean, I ask you . . ."

First, Maxie was in big trouble. And Sid Fairfax. Maxie'd left the switch on in the milk float. The battery went flat. By the time Sid had left his widow and come looking for Maxie, the Boss had come down from the depot in another float, saying that both of them were going to get the bullet. The rumours had got back to him, he said. And look at the state on Maxie! "Was that any way to make deliveries of a pasteurized product?"

It was Bunty who spoke up. And the Police; and, in the end, Maxie got a medal. *"Although not a good swimmer, acting on his own initiative, he did not hesitate the moment he realised a life was in danger."* And that was that.

But when the mist is thick, I hear the woman's voice still. It is as if all the world's pain is echoed in it.

"There's someone out there. A Person . . . There . . . Somewhere . . . But where?"

And Maxie: "I'll huh-huh-huh-have a go!"

THE CUTTING

Tim Lebbon

When I was thirteen years old, I discovered the value of life.

I was curled up into a ball on the settee. A much-thumbed book of ghost stories stood propped open on my knees. The monsters and ghouls barely held me entranced any more, now that I knew they were not real. But their tortured souls and pathetic wails possessed a pleasing nostalgia, which I was still too young to identify or appreciate.

The knock at the door stirred me from some eldritch basement. I dropped the book with a start, jumped up and leapt into the hallway, almost colliding with my Granddad.

"Great lout!" he exclaimed, but his lips twitched into a smile as I beat him to the front door. The frame had swollen in the damp. It squealed as I hauled on the handle. A shadow fell in, sprawling across the hall carpet like a drunk. Outside, darkening our step with his immense bulk, stood a man. He had a head the size of a pumpkin, arms like bags of cricket balls and a paunch that already seemed to be trespassing.

"Jack Jenkins, I'm after," he roared. I cringed and took several hasty steps back, bumping against my Granddad where he stood behind me.

A strange silence settled over the scene; stranger still, because I had been expecting a loud exchange. Granddad had a booming voice, but Mum said it was there to drown out bad memories. I'd never really understood that. I couldn't come to terms with how shouting could cover your thoughts, though I was often berated for trying it myself.

The stillness was almost complete, intensified by the lonely intrusion of everyday sounds. The click of the hall clock. The steady *drip, drip* of rainwater falling from the broken porch gutter.

There was silence, true, but above me a whole conversation was held in one glance.

"Henry," Granddad said, his voice unreadable.

"Jack." The man reached over my shoulder, and I sensed my Grandfather clasping the hand in his own. Then came the frantic rustle of clothing as they shook. Weirdness vanished, and smiles lit up the scene.

"Davey, this is Henry Jones, my old Sergeant Major." Granddad beamed down at me as I moved aside. I'd only ever seen this look on his face when he uncovered a series of books he'd read as a boy, or when he reminisced about building dens in the hayloft or chasing geese around his Mother's garden. It was an appreciation of past times, which I could never really share with him. It made me want to leave him alone with his old Sergeant.

"From the war?" I asked.

"Well, yes, son," Henry laughed, "from the war." His face was made of clay, changing expression from grim to hearty without passing any intervening stage. "Your Grandfather not talked about me, then?"

Another awkward silence. Granddad never spoke about the war. Mum said that was why he was so excited when other memories came to him, because it meant he'd found something else other than his time in the camp to talk about. I'd always wondered whether these other things would ever run out, and force my Grandfather into an eternal muteness.

"Don't really mention it, much," Granddad said. Henry nodded, shrugged, still looking at me, as though he had been expecting as much.

"Davey, run into the kitchen and rustle us up a pot of tea, won't you, son? I'm sure Henry fancies some tea. Tea, Henry?"

Henry nodded and smiled, clapping his hand on Granddad's shoulder, exuding a natural sense of authority. Granddad led him through the door into the front room. He switched off the television mid-way through a football match, an act virtually unheard of. As the huge mass of Henry Jones lumbered into the room the door swung shut behind him, as if repulsed by his bulk.

I stood there for a moment, suddenly feeling excluded, cold, frozen in time. Grumbling fragments of conversation drifted through the door, losing their meaning in the wood but still holding their tone. It was one that I could not identify. Words and phrases

217

sprang at me from the story I had been reading – *surreptitious...insubstantial footfalls on the wet floor...the painful memories of times long since fled* – but none of them really seemed to suit the occasion. Or maybe I just didn't want them to.

I was sorely tempted to press my ear to the door, but my parents had brought me up to respect my elders and their privacy, so I went straight into the kitchen. Still, the disturbing sounds reverberated in my mind, refusing to lose themselves, conjuring terrible images.

I put the kettle on the stove and went about preparing what I thought would be a suitable afternoon tea. My Mother was usually here to do it, but today she had gone into town to buy some beef for our upcoming celebration. My Dad was forty in three days' time. I put tea in the pot. One spoonful each, one for the pot, which I thought invariably went to make a horrible brew, but adults seemed to live by the rule. I found some cakes in the cupboard, only fairy cakes from the local school fayre the previous weekend, but still fresh and attractively decorated.

The kettle mumbled away on the stove. I sat on the kitchen stool, flicking my fingers together, rocking slowly as I tried desperately to remember the big man's name. Much as I took pride in an above average intelligence for my age, my powers of observation and short-term memory left much to be desired. Always had my head stuck in a book, so Mum said. Mind elsewhere. Wandering.

Granddad had seemed strange. Animated, more so than his usual plastic, stern self. And there was something else, a reaction that I could identify from my reading that afternoon. He had been in awe. As though the man he was looking at on our doorstep – the man whose name I was still struggling to recall – was a ghost.

Images from my ghost book haunted me. Strangers on the doorstep. Old men with wizened heads. Cruel ghosts with no form, but plenty of anger.

The kettle began to whistle and I almost fell from the stool. I waited until the water was bubbling, then poured it into the pot, blowing steam away so that I could see the leaves stirring and tumbling in the water. I could read no future in their frantic motion.

The door burst open. For the second time that minute I

jumped, scalding myself with splashes of spilled water. I yelped and rubbed at my arm, fighting back tears.

"Sorry, son," Granddad said. He ruffled my hair again as he passed by. Unbelievable! I loved receiving affection from him, but the occasions were rare. Today, twice in a row!

"Is your Sergeant Major comfortable? I found him some cake."

"Good lad. Yes, he's fine. He won't be staying long, though. Just come for something." My Granddad stood in the pantry doorway, staring in, as though vaguely uncertain of what he was looking for. From behind, standing like he was, he looked years younger.

"What?" I asked. A tin lid clattered to the floor and rolled from behind the door. I poured milk into two mugs, the tea soon after. The sugar was in a bowl in the living room. Granddad cursed quietly under his breath.

"Son?" he said.

I turned around. He had opened the holiday savings tin. We were going to Cornwall for a week in the summer, all of us, to travel around the coast and visit the old fishing villages. Most of the time we were going to camp, but for the first and last nights, my parents were saving to put us up in posh hotels. It didn't really bother me, camping was great fun as far as I was concerned, and hotels were an unnecessary luxury.

And now, Granddad had the money from the tin rolled into a clump in his hand, like a dead origami bird.

"Son," he said again, "I have to ask you a favour." He shrugged. He seemed bashful. He smiled uncertainly and trod from foot to foot, like a child in front of their headmaster. "Well, two actually. The first is that you don't tell your Mum or Dad about this. Not about Sergeant Major Jones, nor this." He waved the wad of money at me. "It'll be replaced, and they never need to know about Henry. We'll not see him again, I reckon."

"The tea's ready," I said. "You all right, Granddad?" He nodded, and he was telling the truth. He was fine. I could see it in his stance, a sort of tension preceding the realisation of an old ambition. As though he'd been waiting for this day his whole life.

"The other favour...could I borrow your savings? I need

another twenty pounds, and I just don't have it on me." There was something different in his voice, something alien. I realise now that this was the moment when he spoke to me as an adult for the first time.

My Granddad, asking to borrow some money from me! I almost couldn't answer, such was the shock, but then something nasty wormed its way into my thoughts. Nasty, and worrying. Like why did he suddenly need this money? What were he and Sergeant Major Jones after?

"Why, Granddad?"

He jerked back slightly, as though he had not expected me to ask. For a moment so brief that I may even have been mistaken, he looked as if he were going to tell me off. Then, a rueful smile pressed his lips together and he nodded his head.

"I'll tell you this once, son," he said. "But it's like...a secret. And a wound; it hurts! And it may be strange to you. Difficult to understand. And I'll probably never mention it again." He suddenly looked pale, but it was a greyness beyond terror. It was more like a memory of death.

I sat down slowly on the stool, forgetting the tea, forgetting the big stranger, who may or may not be a ghost, sitting patiently in our living room. He was waiting for his refreshments and the bundle of notes in my Grandad's hand, but for a while it was as if he had never arrived. It was just my Granddad and me. I realised quickly that I didn't want to hear what Granddad had to say. I imagined that it would cloud the way I looked at him for the rest of my life.

I was right. It did. But at the time, when I was a scared boy with ghost stories still reverberating in my head, I could never guess in what way.

Granddad leant against the kitchen units and stared at the bundle of money in his hand.

"When the Japanese had me," he said, "on the railway of death, I was in a labour camp with Henry Jones. We were cutting the railway into a mountain. Literally moving the mountain by hand. There were over a thousand of us when we started." He did not look at me, just kept his eyes on the money. He did not tell me how many of them were left by the time liberation came.

"The camp guards were a mixture of Korean and Japanese.

They were cruel, sometimes for fun, sometimes because there was hardly enough food and water for them, let alone us. They did terrible things, son. I hope you never have to see anything like that, or live through it. And you don't have to know. But they were terrible things." His voice cracked, but his expression held no tears. It displayed a mixture of anger and what I could only identify as pride. I sometimes saw the same expression when he watched me playing rugby for the school. I was painfully bad, and usually did more damage than good to the team effort. But Granddad told me that trying was the most important thing.

"One time," he continued, "we'd been at the cutting for ten hours, non-stop. They'd only given us one drink. We were passing out, dehydrated. The heat there. Awful.

"But there wasn't enough water. So I asked Henry if I could have some of his. I said I'd pay him one hundred pounds when we got back to Wales, if he'd only give me half a cup full. He smiled at me. I remember that, because I think it was the only smile I saw that day. But he agreed, and he took me up on the offer, and he gave me the water."

I could barely speak. The tea was growing cold, and my Granddad's knuckles were white bones around the money.

"Now, he's here to collect the IOU I gave him," he said, smiling at last.

"One hundred pounds?" I said, aghast. "For a cup of water?"

Granddad shook his head. "It isn't for the water, son," he said. "It never was. Henry was as certain as any of us that we were never coming home." He went back to the living room.

I never did take the tea in to them. The stale cakes ended up in the bin. When Henry Jones left soon after, he glanced down the corridor at me. I saw something on his face which looked almost impossible on such a huge, rugged man – the diamond glint of tears. He smiled briefly, and I thought he was embarrassed at crying. It showed how much I had to learn about being grown up.

Granddad never mentioned that afternoon again. For a while after Sergeant Major Jones had paid us a visit, I wanted to talk about it. I wanted to ask him whether he thought a ghost had visited him from the past. Now, years later, I think he would have smiled and said nothing. But even at the time I knew it was something to do with honour, and I kept my word.

As a man proud of the promises he himself had made, I think Granddad appreciated that immensely.

THE END OF SUMMER

George Brinley Evans

It was half past six in the morning, only six and a half hours into the new year and bitterly cold. His mother pulled the collar of his overcoat tight about his neck, her lips brushed his cheek, "Be a good boy now." He caught the clean scent of her. His father and brother waited in the back yard. "You got your water and your grub box?", his father shouted. "Yes."

"Come on then, let your mother go in out of the cold!" He followed his father and brother out of the yard. Two weeks earlier he had left Maesmarchog Elementary School, December 1939, with three of his friends. Will 'Jammy' Owens, Glyndwr Hill, and Talwyn Gimblet; Talwyn was the eldest, fourteen years and ten weeks old. This was to be their first day as collier boys at Maesmarchog Colliery. Twelve hundred men worked at Maesmarchog, Wales's biggest anthracite mine. The road to the colliery was packed with men and boys, all huddled against the biting cold, no one spoke, except for a brief, "Shwmae!" or a "Duw duw! It's a bloody cold 'un!" Their hobnailed boots struck out a staccato rhythm on the frost hard surface of the Sarn Helen. A rhythm he felt that made him as one with generations of boys who had strode to manhood over the ancient Roman way. The manager's office was full of overmen, firemen, gaffer-hauliers, reporting on, or off shift. The comfortable never-to-be-forgotten smell of Davey lamps burning, the urgent ringing of wall telephones being wound up. Men he had known as neighbours, looked different, more authoritative. Mr. Bob Jones, sidesman at St. David's church, not wearing his Lloyd-George collar, but the blue flannel shirt and dark crocheted tie, the badge of the South West Wales colliery official. 8186 "Shwmae, Rees?" the overman greeted his father. "Bob!"

Mr. Bob Jones looked down at him, his gaze steady. "Take him in to John. He'll give him his number and sign him on. And you, young man. You pay attention to what's going on around you.

Right!" "Right," he gulped, his mouth dry. His father guided him by the shoulder into the chief-clerk's office. "Your number is twelve twenty seven, Hywel bach. Remember it now! Sign here where I've marked with a blacklead," John Lewis instructed. He dipped the pen into the ink, then carefully tapped the nib against the rim of the inkwell and signed his name neatly, under W. J. Owens. The colliery yard was crowded with horses being led by their hauliers. Powerful animals, standing between fifteen and sixteen hands and weighing anything from fourteen to eighteen or nineteen hundredweight. Bred in Ireland especially for the drift mines of South West Wales, out of breeds such as the Suffolk Punch, Percheron and the heavy Cob. No place here for the proverbial pit pony. Each horse had a feed bag tied about its neck and wore a collar and bridle, the bridle being a sturdy leather mask covering the whole face, except for the eyes, nostrils and ears. They were stabled in the best of conditions, a stall measuring twelve feet by eight, fresh, clean bedding, a full manger of oilcake and new cut chaff every day. After a shift of hauling trams weighing two tons and more, up from deeps. Or shafting trams down from heading, with gradients so steep the overwhelming weight would often bring them to their knees. Brought out to the surface to be brushed, curry combed and hosed down with warm water, piped from the boiler house, they shivered with pleasure as the anodyne water poured over their tired, aching limbs. Unled they homed into their spotlessly clean stalls, each stall with a nameplate, Ajax, Caesar, Hector, each and every one a suitably brave name. Little wonder they pranced, arched their necks, held their heads in haughty arrogance and snorted steam into the cold morning air. His brother had collected his own lamp and their father's powder tin and was standing near the lamproom hatch. "Here's your powder tin. I'm off with Edgar," he handed the tin of gelignite to their father. "See you after," he winked and grinned at his brother and hurried away to find Edgar. "Let's get you a lamp then," his father dropped his lamp tally on to a pile of shining brass tallies. Everything about the lamproom shone. Rows of Davey lamps, their yellow flames burning evenly behind polished, sparkling glasses, that reflected in metal burnished bright by work-hardened hands. Behind them, row upon row of electric hand lamps, with fully charged accumulators feeding their flat white lights. Some boys were still given oil lamps when they started work. From what he'd been told, he hoped he wouldn't be given one. The light would go out at the slightest bump. Then you'd have to walk back in the dark to the locking station, to get it relit. Or if you carried it on your belt, they got very hot, and the buttons of your flies became undone, "It'll make your eyes water for sure!" his brother had mocked. "How's it going, Rees?" Wil Jones, lampman, handed his father his lamp, "Now then, we got to find one for you, Hywel boy." Wil reached to the side and lifted an electric lamp off the shelf, "Let's have a look what we got by here," he twisted the top, to test the lock then twisted the bottom to test the switch. "Here you are then, number four hundred and seven. Pick that tally up at the end of the shift. Right, Hywel!"

A crowd of men stood around the mouth of the Drift, waiting for the horses to clear. The collier boys stood to one side, away from the men, one or two called out to him, his brother was there. "You stay by here, for today! Give us your cigarettes," his father said quietly. He handed the Oxo tin with two Woodbines in it to his father, who put it with his own cigarette tin into a hole in the retaining wall. The lamp was heavy, much heavier than an oil lamp, no wonder they called them bombies, and there was more than two miles to walk. They were searched and had their lamps tested. For the first five hundred yards it was level going and dry underfoot. Then the roof disappeared into a nothingness; the ground, wet and slippery, fell away to an incline so steep he'd had to put his hand on the sides to steady himself. It was a fearsome place. Three hundred million years before the earth's crust had been ripped apart by massive earthquakes. Nowhere more than in the anthracite coalfield, causing great faults that sometimes threw the coal seams hundreds of feet down: this was such a one. The rock beds stood vertical and water poured down everywhere, water that stank of rotten eggs. The huge timbers reached up into the darkness, reminded him of the arcading he had seen in the great cathedral on his last school outing. They turned into a tunnel going off to the left. There were lights in front of them, bobbing about, caplamps, only hauliers wore caplamps. The air became warm with the smell of horses. This was the double-parting, the marshalling yard, where the journeys, trains of trams were made up. He heard a sound like no other sound he had ever heard in his life before, an awful gulping. A horse pulling a loaded tram into the parting, its breath coming in strangulated gasps, as it plunged against the massive weight pulling on its collar. Head low, swinging from side to side, mouth dripping, body fully distended, belly almost touching the ground, expanding and contracting like a bellows.

The horse swerved to pull at an angle, to shunt the tram up to the journey, and cracked its fetlock against the rail. The tram banged into the journey, the horse strained with all its might to hold, nostrils flared, gasping for breath. "Good boy!", the haulier encouraged, stuck a wooden sprag into one of the wheels and pushed himself between the trams, to unhitch the horse and shackle the tram to the journey. "Back a'bit good boy! Back a'bit!" Out on to the main deep of the four feet seam, a tunnel, lined with steel and timber, almost a mile long. Armoured power cable draped from one steel arch to another, supplying transformers that buzzed softly. The first level to the left was blocked off by an air-door, the braddice cloth nailed to the bottom of the door flapped nosily in the current of air that whistled under the door, short circuiting into the fandrift. The steel arches gave way to timber, French timber, pine with thick, red bark. Resin oozed from the notches cut into the crossbeams, forced out by the constant downward pressure from the roof, and brought with it the fragrance of the forest. His father turned to the right, through a braddice curtain, into their level and hooked his finger on a roadnail that had been driven into an upright. "Hang your things by here." A rat froze at his foot, then scurried away. He hung his top coat, then his small coat, his school blazer; now with the customary two large pockets sewn on the inside, one to hold his bottle of water, the other his tommy-box, on the nail. "What's the curtain for?"

"To keep the air going down the main. Here, take hold of this." His father unlocked the toolbar and handed him a sledge-hammer and took a mandrel for himself. "Right, let's take a look at it, then." He had tried to imagine what a coalface would look like, the amount of colour surprised him. The shining grey, marble-like roof, the absolute blackness of the void from which the coal had been taken, the gob, contrasted with the pale hue of the barkless Norwegian spruce faceposts. Held fast between floor and roof by white, fresh cut wooden wedges. The coal, glass-hard, reflected their lamplights, like a wall of tiny mirrors. "We'll bore a top-hole, that's going to be our first job." His father tapped the roof with the head of the mandrel, it rang hard like a bell. They carried the boring machine on to the face, his father opened out the heavy, square telescopic stand to its full height and stood it upright. Flipped the handle of the threaded spindle, on the top of the stand, which spun and tightened against the roof, keeping the stand in its place. "Pass me the worm. That threaded bar!" The worm in place, ratchet handle fitted to one end, drill chuck to the other, they were ready to bore. His father hung his shirt on the side, the blue flannel cummmberbund he wore next to his skin accentuating the power of his strong, lean body. The cummmberbund was a habit many men his age had picked up, serving as infantrymen in the Great War. His father took sight from the worm to the rockface with the mandrel, and began to hack a notch for the drill to bite. The force of the blows sent stones flying everywhere and impelled air, through his father's clenched teeth. He was seeing this quiet, soft-spoken man in a new light, and it frightened him a bit. "Pass me the short drill, there's a good boy." The old easy tone in the voice chased away the fright. The drill was fitted into the chuck and turned until it was tight against the rock. "You stand top side, put your hands between mine. When I pull, you push." His fourteen year old schoolboy hands were small, like a girl's, between his father's large fists.

His father set his feet. "Right!" and pulled the handle towards him. The drill squealed and screeched its way into the rock. He pushed with all his might, the soft skin on the palms of his hands folded and pinched against the iron handle. The ratchet played a small tune as the handle freewheeled back. Slowly, half a turn at a time, the drill screamed its way into the rock. Once or twice he lost the stroke and got pulled back but his father didn't seem to notice, he had the swing of an oarsman. First drill out, four foot drill in, a swig of water, another half hour of pulling and pushing, and the bore-hole was complete. "You alright, Hywel?" his father was drenched in sweat. "Yes," he puffed. "But my hands are burning." "When you want to pee, pee on 'em. It'll sting a bit mind! But then it'll be ok!"

They dismantled the drill-stand and carried it back to the

tool-bar. His father unlocked the powder tin, took out six sticks of gelignite and the place filled with the smell of pineapple. "Don't you ever rub your hands in your face, if you handle this stuff, mind! Bring on some of that clay and roll it into plugs for ramming."

"How many?"

"Bout half a dozen." Danny Shot pushed through the braddice curtain. He was loaded with the tools of his trade, copper ram rod, leather detonator bags, safety lamp, roll of yellow cable and a battery firing box. "Ready for me, Rees? Hello, Hywel!" he laughed. "Top hole first day, hey! Never mind, better luck tomorrow."

"We'll give it six, Dan. That should do it." His father handed the shot-firer a stick of gelignite. Danny thrust a brass marlin spike into the gelignite, took a shining detonator from a leather bag, unwound its long fuse wires and pushed the detonator into the hole he had made in the explosive. Placed the stick of explosive into the mouth of the bore-hole detonator end in first. Pushed it to the back of the hole with the copper ramrod, allowing the long fuse wires to trail through his fingers. His father fed in the reminder, Danny ramrodded them home, then the clay plugs, letting just six inches of the detonator fuse wire hang from the mouth of the bore-hole. Danny lifted his Davey lamp to the roof and tested for gas, it was clear. He started off back to the outby, paying out cable as he went, through the braddice curtains, came back and started preparing the hitch to the borehole. His father put his shirt back on. "You go back with Danny, I'll go up through the face and stop anyone coming down!", he ducked into the face and was gone. "Right, let's get back then!" Danny led the way through the tarred curtains, "Get in by here!" He turned into a tumbling place. "You face the side now!" Suddenly his voice was stern. He picked up his battery box, hitched the cables, fitted the brass firing handle, yelled at the top of his voice, "Fire!" and turned the handle. The sudden violent crash of the explosion engulfed him, his ears popped and his mouth was forced open, and for a moment he was stunned. The braddice curtains flapped loudly, clouds of thick, white, bitter-tasting smoke billowed around them. His father came around from the top level. "Alright, Dan?"

"Sounded good, Rees," he laughed. "Made old Hywel by

here jump a bit." Danny put a hand on his shoulder and patted him affectionately, "Never mind, first day's a bit of a shock for everybody, Hywel bach. Know what they told my old father on the day he started work? And that was more than sixty years ago! "Mae yr haf, bachgen, di wedi pasio – Your summer, boy, is over. Danny Shot laughed as he translated. He looked towards his father, who he knew was watching him, through the thick, swirling, white smoke.

ONE DAY

Catherine Merriman

William stood at the centre of the small empty beach, staring out to sea, the yellow-stone hotel facade behind him. The early-morning August air was not yet hot; even so, he unbuttoned his shirt, slipped it off, and tied the arms loosely around his hips. He felt his naked skin tighten and prickle in the breeze. He walked, slowly, the short length of the cove, and then back again. A few years ago, when his hotel duties had been less onerous, he would have swum now. As a teenager, every day in the season, weather permitting. These days the short walk on the beach, the exposure of his skin to the sea air, was more ritual than true relaxation. Just something he did every day at quarter to eight, before the guests were up, shaking off the previous intense hour of office work.

The exercise was nonetheless invigorating. At the top of the beach he left the sand and bounded up the wide steps to the hotel terrace. And there was immediately dragged back to duty by the untidiness of the flower displays in the concrete urns along the frontage. None of the annuals deadheaded, the packed compost inside each doormat dry. Getting competent staff and keeping them, such a distance from town, was a permanent problem. Guests came to the hotel for the quiet solitude, the inaccessibility, of the place. Staff were reluctant to stay, or even travel in daily, for the same reasons. He unrolled a length of hose from its wheel, turned the outside tap on, and started to gush water into the urns.

As he was flooding the last a voice behind him said, 'William?' The tall, aproned shape of his mother leant from the open staff door, her hands pressed against the jambs either side.

'It's me,' William said. 'Just watering the tubs. D'you need something?'

The sun on the thick lenses of his mother's spectacles made them look opaque. Usually, in morning light, and before her eyes grew tired, she could see well enough to recognize him. But perhaps she was dazzled.

'Grapefruit juice,' his mother said. 'Sorry, dear. Two guests have just come down. They'd prefer it.'

'Right,' said William. 'Be along now.'

His mother withdrew. William frowned. Why couldn't his mother find the grapefruit juice? As always, any indication that her sight might be deteriorating further caused a flicker of alarm, along with a flicker of something deeper: a kind of alertness, almost an excitement. Accompanied by a tiny shameful voice that whispered: *one day, one day*. He turned off the tap and rerolled the hose – guests could fall over anything – and went inside. His mother never usually involved him in breakfast. She laid it out in hot dishes on the dining room sideboard, from which guests helped themselves. The regime worked well; there was more waste than with waitress service, but much less work involved. His mother could still cook, magnificently – her food, as much as the idyllic location, was the hotel's main asset – but could no longer serve at table.

He opened one of the larder fridges. The juice cartons were in the door, obvious, surely, even to his mother; what she had been unable to work out, he realized, was the difference between grapefruit and orange, when the undecorated packs were unopened and she couldn't use her nose.

Relieved, he broke open a carton of grapefruit and poured it into a jug. Then discarded the crumpled shirt from his hips and put on a clean white chef's shirt from the pile beside the cooking range.

'Which guests?' he asked. He didn't say, 'Shall I take it through for you?' because his mother disliked reminders of what she couldn't do.

'Mrs Jennings and her sister.' His mother was good at voices. She was preparing picnic boxes on the stainless steel work table behind him. Her movements at this sort of job were so deft and competent that no stranger entering the room would have guessed at her disability.

He carried the jug through to the dining room. Mrs Jennings – Katherine Jennings, she had entered herself in the register, with a defiant flourish – had been here earlier in the season with her husband and two young children, and had returned yesterday with her sister Geraldine. Geraldine was a darker, more compact, quicker-eyed version of Katherine. The only other occupants of the dining room were the Clayton family over by the window: mother, father, and sixth-form age daughter.

'Oh, wonderful!' Katherine Jennings cried, as William approached their table. 'Personal service. We are honoured.' Her sister gave a snort of amusement.

'No trouble at all,' he said, smiling at both of them. 'I'll make sure there's some out for you tomorrow.'

'Great. And William – it is William, isn't it?' She glanced across at her sister.

'It is.'

'Have you got any sunbeds for the terrace? We fancied a lazy morning.'

'Of course,' said William. 'I'll put some out for you.'

He moved on to check the Claytons were happy. While standing over their table – of course they were happy, everything was quite marvellous – he avoided their daughter's gaze. William tended to ignore very young women. Young women were uncomfortable reminders that in another, less responsible, less dutiful life, they would have been his companions, friends, lovers. This girl was, what, seventeen, eighteen? He was twenty-four. The same generation; but it was a generation from which he felt irrevocably excluded.

He was aware, as he took leave of the family, that the two older women at the other table were silent and motionless. Eyes on each other, waiting for him to leave the room. As he did, he caught their upper bodies moving toward each other, heard the first hiss and giggle. He wondered briefly about them. Flirts could operate in pairs; serious adventurers, probably not. William did, just occasionally, run across serious adventurers. Holidaying women off the leash, off the beaten track, determined to enjoy themselves. Usually women in their late twenties, thirties – the sisters were both well into their thirties – past the age of shyness, or romantic notions. Of course he never pursued them; but he did, just occasionally, find himself pursued. He was perceived, he guessed, as a safe, discreet, uncomplicated target. Rightly perceived. Over the years, with diminishing guilt, he had slept with several such women. There was no real crime in it. He was a young man. With the hours he worked, opportunities were few enough.

He returned outside to unchain a nest of sun loungers from the lean-to at the far end of the terrace and laid several out across the stone flags. Then went back to his office behind the reception desk to finish off the paperwork he had started before his stroll. He kept the door open, so he could be seen by passing guests. After twenty minutes or so he was interrupted by a tentative, 'Hello?' It was Mr and Mrs Clayton. He went out to greet them.

'We're off for the day,' said Mrs Clayton. They were carrying two of his mother's picnic boxes. 'I hope you don't mind, but Fiona would prefer to stay here.' She laughed, adult to adult, as if he were nearer their age than their daughter's. 'The beach, sunbathing, you know...'

'That's perfectly all right,' William said. The Claytons, he guessed, were not regular hotel-goers. Used to bed and breakfast stays. 'She must do as she pleases.'

The Claytons looked relieved and grateful. He saw them off, tidied up the last of his paperwork, and returned to the staff quarters to check the two cleaners had arrived – by taxi, at the hotel's expense – and then consulted with his mother about the evening menu and the fruit and vegetables required. When he emerged with a list he found the Claytons' daughter – Fiona, her parents had called her – in shorts and skimpy halterneck top, hesitating outside the kitchen door.

'Can I help you?' He could hardly ignore her here. She had a smooth, un-madeup face, her hair scraped back into a neat French plait.

'Ah, well, yes.' Her expression was friendly, undaunted. 'A cup of coffee would be nice.'

'Of course,' he said. 'Where would you like it? There are sunbeds on the terrace.'

'Oh, terrific.' She smiled gratefully at him as he directed her through the lounge.

When he took the coffee out she was lying on her back on one of the sunbeds, alone – no sign yet of Katherine or Geraldine. Her limbs were straight and slender. He felt a familiar ache, standing over her.

She sat up. In a small rush, as if she had been rehearsing the words, she said, 'Do you mind if I ask you something?'

'Fire away.' The colloquialism just slipped out. As if she wasn't a guest at all.

'Are you the manager of this hotel?'

'I am indeed. And owner.'

Her eyes became circles. 'Owner? Wow!'

He smiled. 'Along with my mother, and, of course, the bank.'

'Your mother – have I seen her?'

'The cook.'

'Oh, the amazing food. Sorry... I know this sounds nosy, but I'm starting a course next month, in hotel management. I was going to ask you how you got into it, but... '

'I was born into it,' William said. 'I've never known anything else.'

'God.' Fiona looked at him with wonder. 'You could tell me lots...'

He had errands to do. The fruit and vegetable list. And young women, he always told himself, were painful company. All the same.

'I'd love to. But right now I have to go out. Unless...' He hesitated. He denied himself pleasure, to avoid the pain. The promise of pleasure was suddenly overriding. He didn't want to suggest anything of which her parents would disapprove, but they saw him as a responsible adult, didn't they? And he was a responsible adult. 'You can come with me, if you like. See what I get up to.'

'Shadow you? Wow!' Her expression, as she swung her legs off the sunbed, gulping at the coffee, was astonished, delighted. She was genuinely interested. She was not flirting. He was not flirting. He would, quite simply, show her what he did.

In the white hotel van he told her to call him William. She asked where his father was, if he worked here too, and he told her that his father had died a few years ago, and that was why he was now the manager. She didn't say, 'Oh, I'm sorry,' just nodded, as if a few years was a lifetime ago, and said she was eighteen, nearly nineteen, and couldn't wait to leave home and start college.

'We're going to an organic farm,' he explained, as he drove the van inland. 'Meat and fish are delivered, but vegetables we buy in daily. At the farm we can choose exactly what we want. This isn't really a manager's job,' he stressed. 'My mother used to do it, but she had to give up driving because her sight's so poor, and there's no one else.'

At the farm Fiona made herself useful, loading earthy boxes of produce into the back of the van. She sniffed at a tub of basil and sighed, 'Oh, bliss,' and he said, 'The scent of the sun, don't you think?' He made her smell the dill too, which, he said, was the scent of the sea. She looked so excited and eager; it re-awakened some of the same enthusiasm in himself.

Driving back she asked him what hours he worked, how much holiday he got.

'I start about six-thirty,' he told her. 'Office work, while the place is quiet. And I finish about nine, ten in the evening. When dinner's over. There are slack moments during the day, obviously, but I have to be in the hotel. Around.'

'Every day?'

'In the season, yes. We're quieter other times. We close down altogether for a month after New Year.'

'It doesn't sound as if you have much time for a social life.'

'A manager for a chain hotel would have more free time.'

'You don't mind?'

'I have the guests. It's a sociable job. You have to like meeting people.'

'Even so. What about friends?'

'I count some of the guests as friends.'

'But they go away.'

'And come back. Some of them. You make what you can of things.' He smiled apologetically at her. 'I haven't put you off?'

'No, no.' She shook her head vehemently. 'I just, well, you must really love your job.'

He said, 'Yes, of course,' and thought: I did, once. He had just told her what he rarely told himself: that he had no time to himself, no real friendships. His job was his life. But he loved life, didn't he? So perhaps he still loved his job. He said, 'Yes,' again, more emphatically, but couldn't stop adding, because it was true too, 'My mother couldn't manage without me, in any case.'

Back at the hotel they unloaded the van at the kitchen entrance, where the boxes were received by Mrs Naughton, the daily help, who was an elderly, slow worker, but experienced and versatile, and without whose presence William would have felt unable to leave his mother.

'I've opened the bar,' Mrs Naughton announced. 'Two ladies wanted a bottle of wine. They're on the terrace.'

William nodded. He could guess which ladies.

'And,' Mrs Naughton went on, 'there's another guest, an older lady, looking for you. Says she's lost something. Sorry, didn't catch her name.'

'Right.' William showed Fiona the staff washbasin and while she was cleaning earth from her hands he poked his head into the snug bar, the lounge and the dining room. All were deserted. Perhaps whatever had been lost was now found.

Next he took Fiona up to the first floor and together they inspected three empty rooms allocated to two bookings due to arrive that afternoon. He ran his hands over surfaces, checked bathrooms, opened windows behind vases of fresh honeysuckle.

'In a big hotel there'd be a floor manager,' he told her. 'Responsible for all the rooms on a particular floor. Here, well, we're small. Most guests come for several nights. The cleaners pop in daily but I wouldn't until they left. Make sure they haven't forgotten anything. And then again before new guests arrive.'

Downstairs a telephone rang and, a second later, the reception bell clanged.

'Which first?' he asked Fiona, leading her quickly downstairs.

'The telephone?' Fiona suggested.

'Both at the same time, if I can manage it.' He swept into reception, said, 'Excuse me a moment,' to Katherine Jennings, who was dressed only in bikini and sarong and leaning against the counter. He picked up the telephone, listened to someone hesitantly making a dinner reservation for five for the weekend, and at the same time raised his eyebrows at Katherine. She mimed swigging from a glass. He smiled and, covering the telephone mouthpiece, murmured, 'Be with you right away.' Katherine raised a thumb, gave Fiona a broad grin, and marched back to the snug.

William finished on the telephone, wrote the booking down, and said, 'My mother or Mrs Naughton would have taken it eventually. There's an extension outside the kitchen.'

He led Fiona through to the snug where Katherine was perched on one of the bar stools, tapping a beer mat against the beaten copper bar.

'Ah,' she said, dropping the mat. 'Could we have another bottle of wine? Dry. White. Cold.' She smiled. 'Please.'

'I'll bring it out.' William turned to the chill cabinet.

'Great.' Katherine grinned again at Fiona, slipped off the stool, and left the room.

William took the bottle out alone. The women were sprawled on loungers, a low table between them, the previous empty bottle on the ground nearby. He placed two fresh glasses on the table and poured a measure of wine into each. Then stood the bottle between them.

'So,' said the woman Geraldine, who was lying on her front, wearing shorts and a loose, sleeveless, low-necked top. Her lifted face was little more than a teasing grin and huge dark glasses. 'What's she got that we haven't?'

William smiled back at her. They were both tipsy, of course. 'Fiona Clayton is studying hotel management. She's shadowing me.'

'Ah,' said Geraldine. 'That's what they call it now, is it?' Both women laughed.

William picked up the dead glasses and empty bottle and turned to go.

'No.' Geraldine's lips puckered to a pout. 'Stay and chat for a while. You're always rushing off.'

'Of course,' said William. 'I'll be glad to. Just let me take these inside.'

Back in the snug he suggested Fiona have her lunch and, if she wanted to continue their arrangement, to come and find him again about three, in the office, when he'd show her the accounts computer and introduce her to hotel paperwork. He poured himself a mineral water and went back out.

The women had placed a garden chair between them, the far side of the low table. Geraldine was still on her stomach, her head nearest him, while Katherine had lifted her backrest and discarded her sarong to sun her front. Her legs were crossed at the ankle, her painted toenails almost touching his chair cushion. He pulled the chair away to sit down, lifted his glass, and said, 'Cheers, ladies.'

Both women echoed his toast. Katherine pressed her head back against the fabric of the chair and sighed, 'This place is magical. Beautiful building. Beautiful food.'

'Beautiful views,' murmured Geraldine, as if it was another echo, but fixing William with her dark glasses and lifting her front on to her elbows. The thin material of her top fell in a loose arc below her body, revealing a hanging pair of small white breasts. The nipples just brushed the inside of the material. Since William guessed he had been placed here intentionally, precisely to receive this view, he didn't remove his eyes. The curve of Geraldine's mouth approved his lack of embarrassment.

Katherine said, 'Geraldine doesn't believe you're the manager. Won't listen to me.'

Geraldine grinned at him. 'She's joking, isn't she?'

'Certainly not,' said William.

'William and his mother run the hotel together. I told you.'

'Your mother?' Geraldine looked baffled. 'Have I seen her?'

'The cook,' said Katherine, smug with knowledge. 'With the glasses. She's rather short-sighted, isn't she?'

'Something like that,' William agreed.

'God.' Geraldine regarded him with affront. 'The boss, already...'

'And she wants to know if there are any more like you hidden around here. I told her no, and that you're on the go from dawn till dusk. She's a deeply disappointed woman.'

'I'm sorry to hear that.'

Geraldine sighed. 'So no chance of your company this afternoon?'

'I'm afraid not. Perhaps this evening, after dinner...?'

'Well, perhaps.' The breasts jiggled with amusement. William's senses hovered between arousal and irritation. If this was still just flirting, it was faintly cruel. His role as manager gave him privileged access to the guests, but could also trap him, place him at their mercy. Katherine's presence suggested that this was still just a game, and he didn't enjoy the sensation of being played with.

A slim middle-aged woman in a safari-style cream dress and canvas lace-ups stepped out of the building on to the terrace, not four yards away. As her eyes fell on them she became immediately confused. Even took a step backwards, as if she had changed her mind about coming outside.

William rose instantly to greet her. 'Miss Henshaw. Can I get you anything? A lounger...?'

'No no.' Miss Henshaw overcame her confusion to smile at him. He smiled back and waited. Miss Henshaw had been coming to the hotel for years; he knew he had to be patient. As usual he was rewarded with a calm, much more organized response. 'I seem to have lost my binoculars. Stupid of me. I have a horrid feeling I left them downstairs last night. Possibly in the lounge. Perhaps someone has found them... one of the cleaners?'

'I'll check now.' This must be the loss Mrs Naughton had mentioned. William turned back to Katherine and Geraldine and said, 'If you'll excuse me...' Geraldine sighed extravagantly. Katherine rolled her eyes. He steered Miss Henshaw back into the building. 'Do you remember exactly...?'

'I was sitting near the window,' said Miss Henshaw. 'I lent them to a little boy to look at a sailing boat. I remember him giving them back, definitely. But...' She shrugged. 'After that... I can't remember.'

'We'll find them,' said William. 'Don't worry.'

Together they searched the lounge, but without success. William sent Miss Henshaw off to have her lunch and questioned the two cleaners, who were adamant that they had seen nothing. He checked with Mrs Naughton, and even his mother. He tactfully asked the few guests he came across if they had noticed the glasses, but no one had. This was bad news. Miss Henshaw was a keen birdwatcher – the fulmars and peregrines along the coast were what drew her here – and the binoculars essential to her hobby. They were also extremely expensive, quality glasses. And large, too. Not something that could be accidentally dropped into the wrong bag without the recipient noticing. The tediousness and disruption of lost valuables bore down on him. As a last resort the hotel would refund Miss Henshaw their cost and claim it on their own insurance, but this would not help Miss Henshaw now, and nor was a reputation for lax security good for business. Miss Henshaw's modest refusal to make a fuss about it, when, at two thirty, he found her and apologized for his lack of progress, only made him more frustrated. He lent her a pair of his own binoculars from the office but knew that they were inferior to her own, and an inadequate substitute. And, as if he didn't have enough to put up with, the women on the terrace were being exasperating. They had requested lunch outside and every time he passed within earshot – which was quite often – they made loud, patronizing remarks to each other. 'Still busy, poor boy.' 'A manager's job is never done.' 'Legalized slavery, I'd call it.' There was a lack of respect in their voices that was quite insufferable; though suffer it he had to, since sharpness to a guest was unthinkable.

At three he realized that he had overlooked his own lunch and made himself a sandwich in the kitchen. He was interrupted twice by phone calls and, while taking the second call at reception, spotted Fiona in the office behind. He had quite forgotten about their arrangement. He apologized profusely, blaming the distraction of Miss Henshaw's loss, and suggested they try another session tomorrow, as he was now quite behind in his duties. Fiona agreed with such alacrity and understanding that he regretted her absence the moment she was gone. She's what I need, he thought. A girl like her. An assistant. Even a boy. Company. Help. For days like this. Except the hotel couldn't possibly afford it. His father, of course, had had himself.

At four the first of the new arrivals turned up, followed within half an hour by the second. These were a couple with a disabled child, for whom various special arrangements had to be made. Soon afterwards guests who had been out for the day trickled back; when he could, between other duties, he caught them and mentioned the missing binoculars, but nobody remembered seeing them. Tomorrow, he knew, he would have to report the loss to the police. Not that they would send anyone out – and he certainly wouldn't encourage a visit – but simply to obtain a crime number for the insurance company. Miss Henshaw had had a wasted day, and would indeed have a wasted holiday, if they remained unfound.

The barman, Joe, turned up at six with his sister-in-law, who was the evening waitress. Both had been working the previous night but both also claimed not to have seen the glasses. William believed them, as he had the cleaners earlier. All had worked at the hotel for at least six weeks, during which time nothing of value had inexplicably disappeared. Employee thieves never waited long before they struck. He went up to his own room to shower and change and under the water spray indulged himself in two common fantasies: first, that some cataclysm would happen that would force his mother to give up work, or at least bring home to her the impossibility of their situation, prompting her to gracefully retire; and second, because the first caused him such pain – his mother was passionate about her work, she would be bereft – that he would meet and marry a woman as entranced with hotel life as he had once been, a woman with inexhaustible energy and patience, who would love and protect his mother as fiercely as he did, and whose beautiful, willing body would await him, nightly, in this very room. It occurred to him, drying himself, and knowing that his mother's failing eyesight would one day force the issue, that only the second was a true fantasy.

There were nine tables occupied for dinner – almost a full house. William deliberately allocated Katherine and Geraldine's side of the room to the waitress so he wouldn't have to serve them. On another occasion he might have been entertained by their banter, but not tonight. The hotel served dinner only between seven and eight – no non-resident meals on weekdays – so by nine he could leave the waitress to cope and went into the kitchen to have his own dinner with his mother. The steel surfaces were already spotless and the dishwashers loaded, though because the machines were old and noisy they wouldn't be turned on until the dining room was empty. After dinner he washed up their plates by hand and then accompanied his mother to her room. He stayed chatting for twenty minutes, during which time he checked that she had everything she needed to hand and read her details of radio programmes from the listings magazine. He left her with a pot of jasmine tea and the radio on.

In the dining room the waitress was busy laying tables for breakfast and in the snug Joe was serving drinks and coffee. William sought out Miss Henshaw, who was reading in the lounge, sat down beside her, and confessed that he hadn't found her binoculars.

'Well,' said Miss Henshaw, 'that'll teach me to be more careful, won't it.' She smiled at him bravely. 'Silly me.'

'No,' said William. He tried to explain that losses in the

building were the hotel's responsibility, not the residents', but she just shook her head. He recommended they report the loss to the police, for insurance purposes, but she insisted no fuss or action was taken at all. He was sure she was being kind to him personally, because she had known him since he was a boy, and somehow this kindness was difficult to bear.

'Claiming for them is simple,' he pressed. 'Just a few forms. Please let me do it.'

'No,' she said. 'You have enough on your plate already. I don't want to add to it.' If she had been a less inhibited person, William thought, she would have patted him on the hand. He felt depressed. A good hotelier made the work seem light, easy, nothing at all. A good hotelier didn't have concessions – ridiculous, expensive concessions – made for them by sympathetic guests. He said, 'You're too kind, Miss Henshaw,' and sighed goodnight to her.

In the corridor outside he was caught by Mr and Mrs Clayton.

'Fiona's told us all about this morning,' Mrs Clayton said warmly. 'We would have thanked you at dinner, but you were so busy...'

William wondered where Fiona was. He would have welcomed a chat, an injection of her enthusiasm.

'She's upstairs already,' Mrs Clayton went on, 'or she'd have thanked you herself. Some television programme she never misses.' She chuckled indulgently.

'Do tell her my offer for tomorrow stands,' said William, hoping he sounded sincere, not just formally polite. Sometimes even he found it hard to tell the difference. 'As early as she likes. I enjoyed her company.'

'Oh, we will,' Mrs Clayton trilled. 'Of course we will.'

In the bar he helped himself to an ice lager, the first alcoholic drink of the day. 'Take your weight off,' Joe murmured, and William nodded at him – he was a good barman, Joe, never asked for help – and said, 'I intend to.'

As he settled himself on a stool the customer side of the bar someone tapped him on the shoulder.

'Free now?' It was Geraldine suddenly beside him, looking very black-eyed and sultry.

'Absolutely.' He swivelled to face her. She drew up another bar stool and sat down.

'My sister's gone to bed.' She chuckled. 'Crashing headache. Out of practice, these married women. No stamina.'

Geraldine, William thought, looked as if she had plenty of stamina. Fit like an athlete. He guessed, wearily, that he would probably spend the rest of the evening with her. And if she suggested more? He didn't know. Maybe. It would be a kind of recompense. And self-denial took energy.

Joe closed the bar at eleven, and by then William and Geraldine were the only customers left. Geraldine had become increasingly friendly. She had touched him several times in the last hour, light brushes on the arm, the shoulder, most recently on the thigh. The waitress helped her brother-in-law clean up and restock the bottles for the next day, and when they'd finished William followed them to the staff entrance door and locked it behind them. Geraldine was waiting for him in the hallway behind. He turned to see her laughing silently into the back of her strong tanned wrist.

'What's so funny?' He had had three lagers himself now; he felt relaxed, loosened up. Whatever the joke, he was prepared to share it.

'How about some room service?' She could hardly contain her mirth. 'Sorry. Just struck me as funny...'

He laughed. It wasn't an original invitation, but at least it was clear. He felt himself slide easily over the guest/management divide, and, coming to stand close to her, murmured, 'It'd be a pleasure.'

Following her upstairs he reminded himself that liking these women wasn't necessary. That the liaisons actually worked better with the emotions unengaged. He would be following with much more ambivalence, much more intimation of loss, if the body in front of his was, say, Fiona's. This woman was like himself, concerned only with physical pleasure. And she was physically pleasing. Indeed her bottom, swaying tautly in front of him, a just-discernible pantie-line bisecting each buttock, was quite mesmerizing.

Inside her room she closed the door behind them. As the catch clicked in its socket William felt the last weight of the day drop from him. He was now off duty. In here, shut away from the rest of the hotel, they were just man and woman. About to do what men and women did.

He caught her hips, drew her close, and kissed her. Like drinking a rare, robust, fierce-flavoured wine. Even her lips were muscular.

She pulled back, licked at the corners of her mouth, and started to unbutton his shirt. 'So, Mr Manager. Do you do this often?'

'Certainly not. Do you?'

She laughed throatily. 'Depends what you mean by often.' When his shirt was fully undone she crossed her arms at her waist and pulled off her silky top. A lace-trimmed quarter-bra pushed her breasts upwards into impossibly firm half-spheres. Adventurers, in William's experience, always wore exotic underwear, or none at all. She undid a clip at the front and discarded the bra. Her eyes mocked his expression. She whispered, 'What would your mother say?'

'That she trusted my discretion. She's not a prude.' Necessary lies. His mother would be shocked, probably. But then blame herself, feeling her demands, or those of the job, had driven him to it.

Geraldine pushed the flats of her hands under his shirt, across his chest. She regarded his flesh meditatively. 'Mmm. Just as nice close up.'

He didn't understand. Her lips twitched. 'Were you aware of being watched? This morning. On the beach?'

He grasped what she meant, and automatically glanced across to the window. 'No,' he said, astonished. 'I wasn't.'

She was still stroking him. On the window sill was a pair of binoculars. He found her wrists and stilled her hands. Large, expensive-looking binoculars.

'Hey,' she said, pulling against his grip.

'Are those yours?'

She looked across the room, saw what he was looking at. 'Whoops.' She bit her lip, her eyelashes batting. 'Caught red handed.'

He could think of nothing adequate to say. Here he was, in the room of a half-naked, willing woman, actually holding her, and there were the binoculars. He had been looking for them for hours.

She knew he had. She thought the discovery funny. He pushed her aside and walked over to the window.

'These are Miss Henshaw's,' he said.

Geraldine came up behind him. Carelessly she said, 'She left them in the lounge last night. Kathy told me about your morning strolls. I was going to take them down tomorrow.'

'Why didn't you return them today?'

She laughed. 'What? Admit I'd taken them? And why. Ha!'

'You could have said you'd found them. Or left them somewhere obvious.'

'Well I didn't.' She pulled at him impatiently. 'Come on. You should feel flattered. They're only a stupid pair of binoculars.'

He resisted. 'Miss Henshaw uses them for birdwatching. They are very important to her.'

'For goodness sake.' Geraldine was scornful. 'Silly old bat. Do her good to do something different.'

William could feel rage rising in him. 'You have stolen from one of my guests.'

'Borrowed, not stolen. Your guests.' She said the words with a sneer. 'Don't be so pompous. Honestly.'

He felt like striking her. Slapping her naked flesh. Her body was beautiful, callous, totally self-centred. He had been about to have sex with her. His own body still wanted to but to do it, now, would be an act of utter betrayal. He started to rebutton his shirt.

'What the hell d'you think you're doing?' Geraldine tried to push his hands away.

Firmly he persisted. 'I'm taking these downstairs, now.'

'I thought,' she said acidly, 'that the guest was always right.'

'Not always.' His shirt was done up. He picked up the binoculars.

She looked at him with hard eyes. 'You are a pompous little prig.' She tried to touch his genitals but he turned his body away. 'Well, fuck you.'

'Cover yourself up,' he said.

'Oh.' She put her hands on her hips and swung her breasts at him. 'So now I offend you, do I? God, you hypocrite, Mr Holier than Thou. Panting for it a moment ago.'

'You have stolen from and insulted another guest. It's

245

unforgivable.' He knew he did sound pompous. He couldn't help it. He was saying what he felt.

She was suddenly savage. 'What a sad little life you must lead,' she hissed. 'Sad little boy, playing the sad little manager in your sad little hotel, getting your sad little screws where you can. You and your fucking mother. What a life. Pathetic.'

'I would like you to leave in the morning.' William kept his voice steady. 'With or without your sister.' He had never before asked a guest to leave, though he remembered his father doing so once, also for blatant theft. He was perfectly within his rights. He had even thought of saying it before she said, 'fucking mother'.

'You've got a nerve.' Her mouth was twisted with outrage. 'And what if I tell everybody –'

'Say what you like.' He lifted the binoculars to where she could see them clearly. 'But you'll only look a fool.' It was the closest he had ever come to insulting a guest, and it made him feel hot. He moved to the door. 'I will say nothing to anyone about where I found these or why you are leaving, but I would like you to go straight after breakfast. Certainly before ten.'

He didn't wait to receive more abuse; he could see she was boiling with it. He closed the door and walked quickly down the dim-lit stairs to the office, where he locked the binoculars in the safe. His hands, turning the dial, were shaking.

Up in his own room he lay back on his bed and waited for his mind to stop racing. He was experiencing a powerful sense of alarm. But it wasn't rational. Geraldine wouldn't say anything to anyone, except perhaps her sister; she had too much to lose herself. Even the fact that he had been in her room, if his motive were exposed, would reflect more odium on her than him. It was obvious to everyone what sort of woman she was. She had to be ten years his senior. She, not he, would be seen as the exploiter. Besides which, practically nothing of a sexual nature, in the end, had happened.

He resolved, however, to give her a wide berth in the morning. A woman like her might be impulsive, spiteful. Irrational. She might accept damage to herself as a worthwhile price for damaging him. His very presence might be provocative. As long as she did as she was told, and left before ten, he would take pains to leave her alone. That would be the humane thing to do, in any case.

He slept eventually, and woke as usual just before six. After taking his mother a cup of tea, and having one himself, he went to the office and made out a bill for both Geraldine and Katherine, though keeping the accounts separate, in case Katherine decided to stay on alone. He thought this unlikely, however, since they had arrived in the same car. He put the bill in an envelope, wrote their names on the outside, and placed the envelope on their table in the dining room. Then returned to the office and concentrated on paperwork.

At the back of his mind, as the hour passed, he heard the hotel slowly come alive. Noises above, doors opening and closing. Pipes hissing. A faint, just detectable smell of grilled bacon, coffee. A domestic clatter somewhere closer. At quarter to eight he rose. Breakfast would now be on the sideboard, or in the process of being carried there. Time for his walk.

Outside the office he hesitated. Further down the corridor, almost outside the dining room, one of the walk-in cupboard doors was ajar. The cleaners' cupboard. Odd. He walked quickly up to it – no human sounds from the dining room yet – and glanced inside. One of the vacuum cleaners was open and empty, presumably awaiting a new dirt bag, but otherwise everything looked as it should. He closed the door firmly and, avoiding the open dining room door, left the building.

But the walk along the beach, usually reviving, was an effort today. The sense of being alone, separate from the hotel, had been spoilt for him. Geraldine had spoilt it. Today he felt no inclination to remove his shirt; it would be a self-conscious, embarrassing, not liberating act. He was tired. Tired of the hotel. Tired of the guests. Tired of the responsibility. He wished his father hadn't died. He wished he hadn't said yes, with such naïve, unthinking eagerness, at the age of twenty, when his mother suggested he take his father's place. He wished his mother's sight was perfect, so she could employ anyone, or that she was helplessly blind, so that, even if he still had to care for her, it need not be here. Either way, he would regain an element of choice. He was a young man, but he felt middle-aged. He wanted his youth back.

Somewhere behind him, up at the hotel, a car engine started up. Early for someone to be leaving. He hoped it was Geraldine and her sister. Whoever it was, they were driving fast, racing through the gears. He listened to the sound rise and fade, heading towards town. He bet it was them, roaring away from trouble. He hoped they hadn't stripped their rooms of towels, ashtrays, vases. Petty acts of revenge. He hoped they had left a cheque somewhere for him. But the hopes were mere thoughts, no emotion behind them. As long as they were gone.

And now there was someone on the terrace. Someone waving at him. Running towards him. A small, young, flying figure. Fiona. Something was wrong. He strode towards her, thinking immediately, heartstoppingly, of his mother.

'William,' she gasped, running up to him. She turned and tugged at his arm, urging him back to the hotel. 'Come quickly. Quickly!' She was close to tears. In her free hand she was flapping something, an envelope. She thrust it distractedly at him. 'It's from those women. I'd come down early, because you told my parents I could, and they met me just as I was going in to breakfast. They said to give it to you. William, I think they've done something terrible.'

William tore open the envelope as he jogged up the steps to the terrace. Inside was a cheque, and a folded paper napkin. On the napkin was written: 'Hope everyone enjoys breakfast!!!' He slowed, staring at it.

'Come on!' moaned Fiona. 'Other people will be down soon. I put oven cloths over them, but...'

He followed her through the French windows of the lounge, along the corridor to the dining room.

'Thank God, thank God,' Fiona said. 'No one here yet. Look. Look.' She whipped cloths off the three dishes on the sideboard, and lifted one of the lids. William knew what he was going to see. Under a mass of filth – dust, grit, hairs, fluff, all the detritus a vacuum cleaner bag contained – were what had once been grilled plum tomatoes, the black gills of field mushrooms.

'It's in all three.' Fiona was anguished. She picked up another lid. Somewhere under the filth should be scrambled eggs. There was actually an alive, maimed moth, fluttering amongst the mess. 'Horrible, horrible.'

William said quietly. 'Does my mother know?'

Fiona shook her head quickly, as if it was a straw to cling to.

'I don't think so. Really, I don't think so. She actually came in with toast, while the lids were off... but I don't think she could see them...'

'No,' said William. A leaden weight had settled in his guts. This was the cataclysm. It had to be. He could stop other guests seeing the revolting messes, but new breakfasts would have to be cooked. An explanation given to his mother. Even if he did the cooking himself, he couldn't do it secretly. She was there, in the kitchen. She would have to be told. She would know that only extraordinary luck had prevented a disaster. She would be devastated.

Fiona was peering at him, reading him. 'Tell her there's been an accident,' she urged. 'Tell her... tell her...' She lifted up the lid of the china coffee jug and said, 'Ugh,' clamping it down again. Then glanced around to the side table, with its boxes of cereal and jugs of juice. 'They're all right,' she said. 'It's just over here. Tell her...' She lifted all three lids from the dishes and feverishly started to pour what had once been coffee, now thick with dirt and hairs, over the contents. When it was empty she folded the jug into one of the cloths, and banged the bundle violently against the wall. There was a dull clatter of breaking china. She opened the cloth and scattered the shards over the swimming mess in the dishes. 'Tell her I did it. That I'm terribly, terribly sorry. That I was just holding the jug, and I dropped it, and there's mess everywhere. Oh God. Oh God.' She put a hand to her mouth and, as if she really had done it, and was indeed most terribly, terribly sorry, burst into tears.

He put a gentle hand on her back. Patted her. Acknowledged to himself that it would work. He would simply take the dishes and jugs back to the kitchen, slide all the messes into the bin, tell his mother that there had been a ridiculous accident and how upset Fiona was, and his mother would rush out to comfort and reassure the girl, believe her tears – who wouldn't, when they were genuine? – while he washed the dishes; and in ten minutes or so new breakfasts would be on the side. The leaden weight had gone. But so had the window above. The window he had dreamed of. The moment when his mother might have asked *can we go on*? And when he might have found the courage to confess *I'm not sure I want to*. What Geraldine's wickedness had handed him, had been snatched

away again by Fiona's generosity. And because the option had been
given him, and because the cataclysm was, to some degree, his own
fault, he would have to take it.

He patted her again on the back, and then, with his hands
wrapped in the oven cloths, picked up the first two dishes.

One day, he thought. But not this day.

SACRIFICE

Nia Williams

Typical of her to come on Friday. My free day. Even though she isn't due for another hour, even though she'll be later than that, I am unable to enjoy this silence. I am waiting. Waiting for her to crash into the day.

I am fending it off – her arrival. Breathing steadily, doing my tasks. I lean against the kitchen sink, grasp the cold edge and look out at the rosemary and hyacinths: a traveller, braced against a ship's rail, swaying to the beat of sea and sky. But there is a more insistent pulse in the side of my head. She will be here in 45 minutes.

She has never known how to do this: to store the silence. When we were at school, both studying for exams, I would be enclosed in a corner, in Father's old armchair – the only chair large enough for comfort – absorbing a book. And there was Millie, perched on the window seat, papers drifting, one leg primed under her, ready to spring up: 'This is terrible! How can they expect –'. And then the final, desperate, concentrated night-hours that always fired her into a day of brilliance or spectacular failure. I was consistent: I did well enough.

She could have come in the morning, before the day settled, or in the evening, when I could count the hours until bedtime. ('Early to bed again, Mo! I reckon you've had a man tucked away up there all these years.') Instead, she tears my best day in half. There's a different sound to weekdays: a muted, privileged sound of preoccupation, of others at work. I can stand in my house, safe, calm against the suburban chink of birds, watching the stony afternoon light circling into the sink or sprawling over the arm of my reading chair. There's a faded slab there, where the sun has left its bleached reflection. I rather like it. It suggests the passage of days, the private patterns of a solitary life.

Screech of the doorbell. My stomach muscles clench, my mouth tightens. I am battening down the hatches. Beyond the frosted panel a small, slim girl fidgets with energy. She moves in against me as soon as I open the door, brushing my chest with the side of her face in a rushed imitation of embrace. Scissor-strides down the hall, into the kitchen, all hair, tight jeans and shoulder bag. I follow, slowly. She will have to face me, eventually. She will have to pause and turn towards me, and then the blur of youth and movement will settle into reality.

'Jesus, I thought I'd never make it, the buffet car was shut, not even a bloody trolley...'

Mean lines twitch around her mouth; two angry grooves pinch her forehead. Millie is beginning to look shrivelled. My large frame, my broad, smooth face, once so cumbersome as she chirruped around me, now bear their own strength and density, while Millie crackles into nothing. Time is vengeance. That's what Mother used to say.

'Good old Mo, I knew you'd cook up something scrummy'. *Scrummy*. A child's word. No – a word from a children's book: imagined by an adult. A false note. Millie is cutting a fat wedge of Victoria sponge, although it hasn't cooled yet. She is lunging at it, thumbing it in to her mouth, dropping moist blobs of sponge where she stands. She hasn't even put down her bag.

'I love your cake,' she says, with her mouth full. 'I wish I could do all that stuff.'

('Mo has a Baking Day' she once announced to her friends, while I balanced my bulk on the edge of the only recognisable chair in her flat. 'Oh, that's so organised,' they sang, 'You put me to shame,' 'I can hardly find time to make toast these days.' Assuming that I could not hear the accusation in their voices: dinosaur, blackleg, all those years struggling out of the kitchen, rejecting the domestic ethic, and you have a Baking Day.)

Millie swallows the sponge, fluttering her hands: 'Take it away, or I'll finish it in one.' She lets her bag fall and shrugs off her flying jacket. She is wearing a skintight, long-sleeved top. She has the figure of a girl and she cannot possibly be wearing anything to help underneath. She wanders from kitchen to living room, and I follow. I wonder whether to tell her about the phone call. She smooths her jeaned buttocks, and those ridged hands seem alien, predatory, on her neat rear.

'You could do with lightening up this room a bit' she says, with her back to me. I say nothing. I know what will come next.

'How long to go now?'

'Two years' I say. She shakes her head. I almost expect to see dust float from that swaying hair – though that is unjust. She is always clean.

'Oh *God*, Mo.' She stares at the floor. 'How can you *bear* it? What will you *do* with yourself? Well, of course, you've always been able to occupy yourself, you're good like that. But still…Jesus. Two years! You'll miss the kids.'

I smile. The children, as a matter of fact, will miss me. I am a good teacher. Ordered. Predictable. My absence will be the crumbling of a wall. Pupils who have barely noticed me in eight years of schooling will suddenly recall me in their dotage, and summon up everything that was reliable in their youth.

Millie moves to the mantelpiece, fingers the photograph of Mother, then the chiming clock. I can hear her thoughts. She is wondering whether she could ever bear to live here, in Mother's old house, should the need arise.

'You'll miss the staff, too.' She gives me a coquettish, sideways look. I have Barbara Lewis to thank for this: calling round without warning, that last time. Came at 10 in the morning, sniffing for gossip, I dare say, when Millie was still shuffling around in her kaftan. Only the fresh coffee lured Millie in to join us and she drooped over her cup, detached from the conversation, until Barbara made some puerile comment. 'Of course you'll know all that from *Geoffrey*' – something of the kind – with a slide in the voice that Millie snapped up like a bird.

'Geoffrey Mallett,' I explained, wearily, after Barbara Lewis had gone. 'He teaches Physics, he's 37 years old and he has a wife and two very charming daughters'. She ignored the rebuke and gazed at the flush of colour climbing my neck and cheeks. I understood that look: poor Mo, it said. At her age. Pathetic. Absurd. What Millie doesn't understand is that I am well aware of my limits.

'Freedom is knowing your limits,' as Mother used to say. I know precisely how much pleasure to glean from Geoffrey's entrance into the staff room; from a smile; from his recollection of something I once said. And I know how little to say, how much distance to keep between us. I do not expect Geoffrey Mallett to relish the company of a spinster in late middle age. I experience neither hope nor disappointment.

Millie has always known peaks and troughs. She loves when she is loved. I remember the expression in their faces – her boyfriends, lovers – reading her. Searching. Pleading. I would sit watching as they set off for town, leaving the house to me and Mother. I would hear them, too, clear as a bell on summer evenings, when the front room window had been raised a crack to let in their chatter with the air:

'Are you *sure* she's your sister?'
'Oh, don't be mean.'
'She *must* have been adopted.'

The only one who stood out of the crowd was Edward. Naturally, he didn't last two minutes. It set my teeth on edge every time she called him Eddie, and it was quite apparent that he wasn't easy with it – but Millie never could leave a name alone. Millicent was quite wrong for her: it had to be Millie and always was. Nobody else has ever called me anything other than Maureen, but she snips it down to Mo – a desperate bid, I imagine, to lend me some frivolity.

She would call down the stairs in her underwear – 'Mo will look after you' – and Edward and I would sit quite content, in the front room, until she was ready. I would tell him about my early encounters as a trainee at the secondary modern. Edward was studying for a postgraduate degree. Social hierarchy in the 16th-century rural community: a case study. He brought me draft chapters from time to time. When he talked about his work, his thin, ascetic face would flicker and glow like a flame. One evening, as he was describing a new direction in his research, he paused and said:

'Have I told you this before? Sometimes I think I've told you, because I've been telling you in my head.'

Poor Millie. All her years of frenzied loving and leaving and she has never known that depth of joy.

Millie props herself across the angle of the kitchen chair, legs stretched full-length, crossed at the ankles. She balances her third cup of coffee on her flat stomach.

'I'm not saying you should slog on for another ten years. You know what you want, after all. It's just that word. *Retirement.* Sounds so...*final.*'

'Not to me,' I say, refilling my own cup. 'It sounds like a release.'

'A release! Oh *God*, Mo. You're only 53, for Christ's sake.'

'That's exactly the point. I'll have plenty of time to myself. I'll be able to plan my own timetable, for a change'.

Millie moves her legs and lets the exasperation clear from her face before saying: 'You are *funny.*' She usually says this before sneering at some habitual phrase or gesture of mine. Mother used to throw the same words at her – 'you are *funny*, Millie' – but with no edge of disgust. I believe Millie must have been a lot like Father. I could see Mother's mood lift, despite everything, whenever she came breezing in.

'You and your routines,' says Millie. 'You're so organised.'

I consider telling Millie how I plan to spend my days in retirement, but decide against it. She would be horrified by the banality of a daily walk to town for lunch and groceries, followed by a stomp back across Memorial Gardens and the common. A routine designed to be adjusted and adapted over the years. When the walk becomes too rigorous for my weakening knees I can cut back by the tennis courts and turn home, and no one will have the opportunity to say How sad for dear old Maureen, how her life has telescoped, how little she can do, these days. Besides, I suspect that I'll still be up to the entire route at 90, riveted into good health by my solid bones, coasting along with the momentum of my own weight. While Millie will be mincing around in wrinkled jeans, stooping a little nearer the ground each year.

Time is vengeance. Mother's saying crows in my head again as I look at Millie across the kitchen table. Age is drawing her pixie-face into a perpetual scowl. I wonder whether this is a good time to mention the phone call. I suppose we must have filled out a form of some kind. That must be how the woman traced this number. She had a curling, intimate voice, and was treading carefully. 'It's for you to decide,' she said. 'I'll leave it with you.' The daughter, she assured me, is ready. She has reached a stage. She wants to know.

Millie puts her cup down and stretches, lifting her nest of hair behind her head.

'I'll have a bath before supper,' she says, 'if that's OK.'

'By all means. There's plenty of hot water.'

I have re-set the boiler ready for Millie's visit. She always takes a bath in the evening, and makes it a long, languid occasion, filling the room for hours afterwards with a sweet, lazy fog. What does she think about, lying there for an hour at a time, up to her chin in froth? Nothing, I dare say. She has that gift of emptying her mind. I did see her once, many years ago, when she was in there with the door half open. (She has hated closed doors since childhood.) She was lying in the bath, hair looped and knotted, holding her hands out of the water, turning them this way and that. Examining. And she was chanting softly to herself – 'Oh, God. Oh, God'. Maybe she does think, up there. Maybe she dwells on things. But the chances are that she was simply fretting about her age.

I am in the kitchen, chopping onions, when Millie returns, wrapped in the kaftan, still shimmering from her bath. As she appears in the doorway I am saying 'quite remarkable'. I say it aloud because I have forgotten that I am not alone and must contain my thoughts.

'What?' she says. She takes a piece of raw onion delicately between finger and thumb, pops it into her mouth, sits and crunches, looking at me, waiting for a reply.

'Oh, I was just thinking. I saw a documentary the other day. About Incas.'

She raises her eyebrows to indicate both interest and indifference.

'They used to march their children to the mountain peaks and give them to the gods. And now they've found some of them, frozen. Perfectly preserved. Remarkable.'

Millie winces. This is one of the words that annoy her. One of Mother's words.

'When are we eating?' she asks, eyeing the rest of the onion, which I stack and deal into the pan.

She used to eat the most extraordinary things when she was expecting. Raw leek. Stealing the little white disks as Mother cooked. Raw cabbage. Once she ate a raw brussels sprout.

Mother was sharper with her at that time than ever before or since. Cross, I suppose, at the carelessness of it. And, of course, Mother and I had to deal with it all. The boyfriend, whoever it was, had long gone by the time Millie was showing: I doubt whether he even knew. Actually, it was all rather straightforward, in the event. The child was simply wrapped up and taken away. Best not to form a bond, they said. Mother and I waited in a kind of ante-room, while Millie was in labour. She didn't roar, as they do in films; at any rate, we didn't hear anything. We waited, and at one point Mother put her hand on mine and said 'Life doesn't come in fair rations.' She said it with a heavy pity that made me want to slap her face.

'Beef stew!' Millie watches as I pinch the spongey, purple meat and then cut it into deft slices. 'Comfort food.' And then, 'You get more like Mother every day.'

People came back to the house after Mother's funeral. Millie insisted on inviting them to 'the wake', which rather startled the elderly relatives. I took them into the front room and passed sandwiches and brave words. Millie was busy in the garden with the friends who'd come for her sake, pouring wine, offering party food. Olives. Dips.

Dips? I had said. Are you quite sure?

She had stared. Millie can convey a shift of mood without rearranging her features. '*You'll* be doing the ham and sherry, I suppose.'

After they had all gone she was a little drunk and tearful and she clung to my arm and said 'I'm not stoic. I can't help the way I am.' Then she gave my arm a shake and said 'You *never* let her down.'

Theresa. That's the girl's name. I say 'girl' – she must be 30 by now. I take a sly look at Millie as I nudge the sizzling meat in the pan.

Her hair is fringed with damp. She is worrying a piece of loose skin by her fingernail. Maybe Theresa would come here for their first meeting. They would sit there, at the table, facing each other. More relaxing than Millie's flat, with its jangling metal things drooping like insects from the ceiling. I imagine their conversation, Millie seducing the girl with her unembarrassed interest and her anecdotes. I see myself preparing the food and Millie laughing about my Old-lady Cakes and Hard-Crust Pies, and Theresa passing me a thankful look. Millie is calling her Terry. My fantasy, following its own course, delivers a brief spasm of pain. Poor Millie – missing the point again. She doesn't understand that the young can talk in that bright, receptive tone while a private joke glitters in their eyes. Perhaps she would have suffered as a mother, felt shut out. But then, Theresa is no longer cruelly young. She is mature, balanced, a woman with a life of her own. Millie has nothing to worry about. She need only accept.

'That smells amazing,' says Millie. 'You must *make* me wash up afterwards. Do my share.'

'You can start laying the table if you like,' I say, but she doesn't move. The meat spits and whispers. In the garden, a blackbird sings out the last of the daylight. Millie stretches her arms high above her head, throws her head back and yawns, long and luxuriously, like a contented child.

I decide not to mention the phone call. For the time being.

INSUFFICIENT EVIDENCE

Adam Thomas Jones

Time passes slowly when you're sitting in a parked car with a broken radio. Nothing to listen to except the dull, insistent drumming of rain on the roof. First you get edgy, then you get bored. You start to stare at the clock on the dashboard, willing the minutes to pass more quickly. And that, of course, is the most futile exercise of them all.

That's what I remember most clearly when I think about that night in February. The boredom. Which is strange when you consider what happened afterwards.

"What if he really didn't do it?" I asked. In truth we had gone over the matter countless times during the previous week. I only asked the question to break the silence. I knew there was no going back now.

My brother Cal sighed. He twisted the cap off the half-pint bottle of vodka, raised it to his lips, sucked greedily. "He did it," he said. "We both know that."

I glanced across at him, trying to judge how drunk he was. With Cal, it's always hard to tell. "They found him not guilty," I said.

Cal shrugged, lighting a cigarette. "They said they couldn't prove he did it. It's not the same thing." He took a drag on the cigarette, blew smoke at the roof. "Anyway," he said, "this has got nothing to do with them. It's between us and him."

I nodded, knowing that what he said was the truth. Still, I couldn't bring myself to leave it alone. I was starting to get a really bad feeling, as if we were travelling on a speeding train, watching the scenery flashing past outside, powerless to get off.

"But what if something goes wrong? Like he has a heart attack or something?" I was sickened by the wheedling tone of my own voice.

Cal was silent. I knew that, as far he was concerned, the subject was closed. He took another tug at the bottle of vodka and when he exhaled, his breath made a soft whistling sound. He offered the bottle to me but I shook my head.

Two weeks earlier, Cal had come home from work and found our sister, Jess, huddled in a corner of the shower, her arms wrapped about her head as if she was trying to ward off some invisible airborne attacker. There was blood in the bottom of the cubicle, flowing steadily, mixing with the water, swirling down the plughole. Cal had put his hand on her shoulder and she had turned to face him. She had not screamed or wept. She had looked at her older brother as if she did not recognise him. The previous day, Jess had turned seventeen.

Cal had hauled her out of the shower, dried her, dressed her in his pyjamas. He sat her at the kitchen table and asked her over and over again who had done this to her. She had not wanted to talk to him, but by the time I got home that evening he had a name.

Now Cal was leaning forward in his seat, his mouth set in a tight grimace. I followed the line of his gaze with my own.

He was coming out of the pub across the road, weaving slightly, his hands held out in front of him as if he suspected that at any moment he might lose his balance. He paused for a moment, his head lolling to one side. I was sure then that he was looking through the windshield at us.

I glanced across at Cal and saw that he was smiling. The orange light of the street lamps seemed to glint against the edges of his crooked front teeth.

"Are you ready?" he asked softly and I nodded.

We got out of the car and walked over to where he was standing, Cal staring straight ahead, me checking up and down the wet street for observers. Everything seemed perfectly still then, perfectly quiet but for the sounds of the falling rain and our feet upon the pavement. I knew then that I would go through with it and the realisation made me suddenly calm.

At the last moment he seemed to recognise us, because I remember him taking an unsteady step backward, his mouth falling slack. Perhaps he meant to speak, to offer some apology. If so, he never got the chance. Cal's fist looped out in a wide arc, all flashing white knuckle, catching him squarely over the temple.

He staggered back awkwardly, arms reeling. He would have

gone to his knees if his back hadn't connected with the wall of the pub. I stepped forward, wrapped a hand in his hair. He turned to face me. I looked into his eyes and saw nothing but dumb terror. I wanted recognition, understanding. His slack expression made me furious. I drew back my fist. I caught him a good one in the mouth, felt the skin over my knuckles split as his front teeth snapped.

He did not struggle as we dragged him over to the car. His body was limp and amazingly heavy, seemingly filled with some slow, viscous fluid. It was like carrying a drowned man. He was muttering something over and over, his speech slurred from the alcohol and the beating.

I grabbed him around the chest, supporting him while Cal got the boot open. I had thought he would resist but when I nudged him forward he sprawled right inside, like a man who has not slept for two days finally reaching his bed. Then he just lay there, grunting, his legs hanging down over the bumper. Cal grabbed his ankles and swung them into the boot and I slammed the lid down.

"Give us a fag," I said, panting. I watched as Cal lit two, handed one to me. I stood there for a short while, inhaling smoke. I realised that I did not care if somebody saw us and the knowledge made me feel untouchable, invincible.

I drove fast, paying no attention to the speed limits. I was laughing out loud, swinging the car through sharp bends, making the tyres squeal. I could hear him grunting weakly back there, the thumping sounds as he was tumbled around in the confined space. I was thinking about the expression on his face when we pulled the trick on him. The expectation made my blood sing.

Cal's hand was on my arm. "Calm down," he said. "You're freaking out."

I was annoyed at Cal for spoiling the moment, but I nodded. "I'm alright. Just having a laugh."

The hand was heavy on my arm, pinching, kneading the muscle there. I tried to shake it off but his grip was too firm. "Don't laugh," he said, almost dreamily. "Don't do anything except what I told you."

The field lay five miles outside the village and it was very quiet there. The darkness seemed to intensify, pressing in on the car, sucking the light from the headlamps. The ground was uneven when we left the road and the old car's suspension groaned as it steered slowly forward. No sound came from the boot now. I could almost taste his terror, thick and salty, like blood in the back of my throat.

Cal was tapping his fingers on the dashboard. "This will do," he said and I stopped the car, switched off the engine.

"Leave the lights on," Cal said. "I'll get him out. You get the petrol can."

We had hatched the plan a week earlier, during a long night at the pub. Usually, I did not drink, but Cal had coaxed me out, telling me there was something he wanted to discuss with me. When he had mentioned the petrol can I had looked at him as if he was insane. I had waved my hands in front of my face. I had told him that I was not a murderer. Cal had only laughed quietly, as if to himself.

I know that I am giving the impression that everything was Cal's idea, that I was some hapless sidekick dragged along by the force of his will. That is far from the truth. Thinking back, I believe the idea was already there in my mind, unformed but still present, like a statue in a block of granite, not yet carved.

When Cal had explained that the petrol can would be filled with water, I was relieved. Relieved and a little bit disappointed.

I waited in the car while Cal dragged him out of the boot. It seemed he was offering some resistance now. I could hear Cal grunting, cursing quietly as he tried to manhandle the bastard. The car began to rock violently on its suspension.

I got out of the car, walked around to the back. Cal almost had him out, but he was gripping onto the lip of the boot, both hands pale against the dark metal. I stood there for a moment, watching him struggle. I could hear him sobbing quietly.

Cal turned toward me, frowning. "Give me a hand," he said. "He's stronger than he looks."

I walked over to the back of the car, put a hand against the rear wing to steady myself. I brought one foot up, drove my heel down onto his knuckles. He let go with a low whine. Cal had him by the legs and he fell face down into the grass.

"Get him round the front into the lights," I said. I went around the car, leaned inside to grab the petrol can off the back seat.

If he was drunk now, he showed no sign of it. He squatted

in the harsh glare of the headlamps, his legs tucked up against his chest. He was staring down at the ground, eyes half shut. He had stopped crying.

I walked over to Cal's side, the petrol can swinging heavily in my hand. "Look at us," I said. When he did not, I swung the can against the side of his head. It connected with a hollow sploshing sound, driving him over onto his side. Still the bastard wouldn't look at us. I stepped forward to put another one on him but Cal raised a hand to my chest.

"No," he said calmly. "He has to know what's happening to him."

Something in the tone of my brother's voice made me turn to look at him but the glare of the headlamps prevented me from making out the expression on his face.

Cal walked over to him, went slowly down on one knee. "Listen to me," he said, almost tenderly. "My brother is holding a can of petrol." He patted the front of his jeans. "I've got a box of matches in my pocket."

That made him look up, alright. His head spun around sharply and his eyes were very wide. He opened his mouth but Cal shook his head slowly.

"You'll have your chance," he said. He got up, took a step away. He stood for a long moment, seemingly lost in thought.

"We know what you did," he said, "and you deserve to die for it. The thing is, you can still walk away. All you have to do is admit it."

In that moment I felt an overwhelming surge of respect for my brother. Ever since we were kids he had always known how to carry himself, how to say exactly the right thing, just like he was doing now. Right then I knew that, as long as I did what he told me, nothing bad could happen to us. I knew it with a deep, deep certainty and I loved him for it.

Cal reached into his jeans pocket, pulled out the box of matches. He held the box up to the light, rattled it playfully. "Speak up," he said. "We haven't got all night."

He lay there in the long grass, staring up at us. I could tell from looking at him that he believed we'd actually go through with it. I knew he was just trying to work out whether it would do him any good to confess. He was extremely afraid and it amused me to see him like that.

He was silent for a very long time. I could hear the soft clicking sound his throat made when he swallowed. I held the can out in front of me and started to unscrew the metal cap. That seemed to clinch it for him.

"Okay, okay," he blurted and his hands flew out in front of him in a gesture of surrender. I realised then that I had never heard him speak before, that his voice was somehow different to how I'd imagined it. It was a voice I'd heard countless times before on the streets, in the pubs, on the factory floor. It was the same voice that came from my own throat when I asked for a pint of milk or a packet of fags.

"It was me, okay? I did it. Just don't burn me. Please don't fucking burn me, okay?"

Cal listened to this, nodding slowly. When he turned to me, he was smiling. "That's good," he said. He started to fumble with the box of matches. "Now wet the bastard down."

He started to scream as I walked slowly toward him, unscrewing the cap of the petrol can. His heels kicked frantically at the earth and his head rocked violently from side to side. His splayed fingers raked the air, as if he believed he might actually find purchase there and drag himself up out of the reality of the situation. Still, I don't think he would have been capable of running, even if there was somewhere for him to run to. He was that far gone.

I knew there was something wrong, even as I up-ended the heavy can above his head. Pale liquid showered down over him, drenching him, soaking his hair, saturating the thin fabric of his shirt. The falling beads drew the light from the headlamps, caught it for an instant before casting it outward once more in tiny orange shards.

I threw the empty can away from me, stared down into his upturned face. The liquid was running from his nose, from his mouth, dripping steadily from the tip of his chin. He was still crying, but silently now.

I turned to Cal, suddenly aware that I was completely numb. "Cal?" I said weakly. "What?"

And then I knew. The smell.

Cal shrugged. He raised the box in front of him and struck a match.

We still live together, me and Jess. She's getting better these days. Still, sometimes she comes into my room late at night and climbs into bed beside me. I let her stay. Is that sick? I'm not sure. I don't think there are any rules when it comes to getting over something like that. We hardly ever talk about it, at least not directly.

We used to go and visit Cal every week. Jess still does, but lately I've been making up excuses to get out of it. To tell the truth, I've always been a coward. I hope that Jess understands. I know that Cal does.

He took the blame for both of us. I think they know I had a part in it but they could never prove it. Cal said in court that he did the whole thing on his own. There were no witnesses and Jess said I was there in the house with her the night it happened. Insufficient evidence, they call it. All things considered, I suppose that's pretty funny.

The last time I visited him, Cal said something to me. It's been going round my head ever since and I suppose it's one of the main reasons I don't go to see him any more.

We'd been talking about stupid stuff, local gossip, empty, irrelevant crap. The only stuff that two brothers can talk about while sitting face to face with a prison table between them. The talk eventually dried up and there was this awful, heavy silence. I was staring down at the surface of the table because I couldn't bring myself to hold his gaze.

Cal leaned close to me, so that the guards started to move casually but purposefully toward us. "Don't be sorry," he said. "I couldn't have done it without you."

The worst thing is, I know that's true.

AN ADVENTURE

Richard Griffiths

In the summer his mother rises early and drinks coffee on the patio in her dressing gown and slippers. He is often nudged into consciousness by her absent-minded humming, the wistful clack of saucer and cup. Sounds which inform his waking mind, as much as the chimes of the grandfather clock or the early hour thunking of pipes, that he is at home in his own bed, that everything is as it should be. He watches her through a crack in the curtains. In her pyjamas at the edge of the dewy grass she looks like a figure from a dream: her sad mouth set, head to one side, lost in thought as the cat rubs the question mark of his tail against her calves.

Huw is home for the summer vacation. Last night he met up with school friends in the local pub and this morning his tongue is crusted and dry and his temples throb insistently. This morning the sound of his mother whispering to the cat as though the cat understands her implicitly irritates him. He flops onto the bed and sticks his fingers in his ears. His parents have done nothing but get on his nerves since they picked him up from the station yesterday afternoon – the sight of his mother in the passenger seat, her eyes lit up, eager, *in broad daylight*, to kiss his forehead and ruffle his hair, angered him inexplicably. Then, after he had barely lugged his boxes into the house from the car:

"You've lost weight."

He went upstairs. She followed him.

"Would you like me to make you some salmon sandwiches? A glass of squash? Or a cup of tea?"

He took a bath just so that he could lock the door and afterwards, when he discovered that his mother had sorted through his underwear bag, he became so speechless with indignation that he left the house without saying anything, not even where he was going.

She is standing at the kitchen sink gazing out over the

garden, puzzled, as though there is something to decipher in the branches of the birch tree. When Huw says 'good morning' she blinks out of her trance and begins to dry the plate she is holding in her hands. He recognises something in her face and when she says, almost to herself, "You know, sometimes, I still miss my mother terribly," it feels inevitable, like a premonition. His body tautens. *What are you supposed to say to something like that?* He pretends to read the back of the paper while she dries the rest of the washing up and makes a pot of tea. Besides the loose change of children's laughter some gardens away the kitchen is silent and his mother's sentence hangs over them until she whispers excitedly for him to come to the window. The cat is chasing his tail on the lawn in a whirl of ginger and white. "He hasn't touched his breakfast," his mother says. "He's ruined, absolutely *ruined*." She carries a saucer of milk outside and clicks her tongue at the cat which dances sideways away from her, his ears pinned back, and claws his way up the trunk of the tree. As she traipses back to the house in mock-exasperation Huw notices how, in the early light, the skin over her cheekbones blushes with broken blood vessels. How her pullover seems half a size too large.

"Your father wants you to do that favour for him this morning," she says, laying the table. "He's in the garage filling the water tank."

He had forgotten. *Damn.* His father appears around the side of the house and wipes his feet on the kitchen mat. He is wearing his decorating trousers; grey flannels he used to wear to work, streaked now with white emulsion. "I've told him about the favour," his mother says, gesticulating to Huw with her eyes. Huw puffs out the paper in front of him and rattles through its pages. "Do you mind?" asks his father, his voice almost apologetic. "No," Huw says from behind the paper, and he leaves his coffee untouched and goes to get dressed.

The sky is flawless and still, apart from an aeroplane trail which stretches out like frayed cotton wool over the hill beyond the farmhouse. Huw drives slowly through the narrow country lanes, beeping the horn at the blind bends. He cannot think of anything to say to lighten the weight of silence that sits upon them and he grips the wheel tightly. He has remembered a story his mother used to tell him, of when she and his father were first married and had kept a dying wasp alive for a whole day by feeding him marmalade on the end of a lollipop stick. "He didn't once try to sting us," she would say with a sigh that sounded like the tide going out. "He knew we were trying to take care of him. He *knew*." Huw had always enjoyed the confusion of sadness and love that the story induced in him, although now, in recollection, it seems such a stupid, futile thing to do. *All that effort for a wasp – what's the point?*

By the time they reach Evans's farm his back is covered with a thin film of perspiration. They pass the fortress wall at the edge of the forecourt. How astonished he'd been as a boy when his father told him that the wall, six feet thick, had been built by the Romans over a thousand years ago. *A thousand years.* He shut his eyes and tried to imagine it. "Dad," he asked after a long pause, "do you know everything?"

"Here it is," his father says and they pull over at the side of the road and Huw reverses the car up a dirt track which leads to one of the farmer's fields. A small flock of sheep regard them indolently through the bars of the gate. Huw would never have noticed the ditch had he walked past it; he is blind to country things. His father spotted it on one of his long walks up to the top of the Garth.

"Look at the poor devils," his father says in a dry voice, leaning over the ditch with his hands on his knees. "They'll be dead by tomorrow. It hasn't rained in weeks."

The ditch water has evaporated, leaving behind a high-mark of scum. Tiny black bulbous-headed tadpoles with long tails swirl in a current around the edges of the remaining shrinking pools of water, separated by clumps of dried mud.

"I mean – if we only save half..."

Huw opens the boot of the car and struggles to lever the tank of water over the side. His arms plunge with it towards the ground, throwing up a cloud of dust. He wipes the sweat from his eyebrows with the back of his wrist and begins to drag the tank along the track. "It's okay," his father says, and he yanks the tank off the floor with a grunt and carries it at his side, leaning his body in the opposite direction. He drops it next to the ditch and takes a handkerchief from his pocket to wipe his face which has turned a deep shade of red. He unscrews the top of the tank and his lips tighten with concentration as he tilts it so that the water begins to trickle slowly onto the grass.

"We don't want to throw up any mud."

The tadpoles scatter and shoot about in confused surges. Some of the dead ones wash up onto the banks. Beads of sweat hang from his father's nose as he empties the last drops of water from the tank. His translucent shirt clings to his shoulders and he exhales through his teeth as he straightens himself. Huw fetches the jam-jar and the bucket from the car. His father bends down low over the ditch, scoops a jar-full of water and holds it up to the sky. Three or four tadpoles are swimming groggily in its cloudy water. He shakes his head.

"This is no good. We'll be lucky to save a hundred."

He empties the water back into the ditch and tries again. This time he captures a few more. "Try near the edge," Huw says. "They're more dense there." His father dips the jar slowly at an angle into the water and dozens of tadpoles are drawn into it. He holds it up to the sky; it is black with whirling tadpoles and his face breaks into a smile. "*That's* more like it."

He catches his breath and pours the tadpoles into the bucket where they dart crazily about its circumference, then he squats down again until the heels of his shoes dig into the soft mud, and scoops up another jar-full, and another, until the water is up to the rim.

"I daren't fill it any more in case the water swills over the edges in the car."

He wipes his face as his chest rises and falls heavily, and frowns at the tadpoles they have to leave behind. The sweat has matted his thin grey hair to his forehead.

The midday sun is directly above them. A trail of dandelion seeds and the sharp scent of cow dung are carried above the tall hedges along the lanes in the breeze. Over the brow of the hill appears a shaven-headed man wearing a green army shirt and heavy army-surplus boots, followed by a forlorn spaniel on the end of a rope. The dog sniffs the bucket and Huw's father's sweat-soaked trousers, then nuzzles his open hand. The man regards them quizzically before tugging on the rope and Huw feels his cheeks flood with embarrassment. *Mind your own bloody business!*

His father carries the bucket gingerly back to the car and lowers himself into the passenger seat. As the car rocks slowly along the dirt track onto the road he holds the bucket in front of him to prevent the water from spilling over the rim. Huw drives in second gear along the lanes towards the pond where they will release the tadpoles. The swirl of perspiration, acrid and sweet, fills the car, and, once more, a silence settles upon them. His father opens the window and looks out over the sloping fields which tumble down to the railway line. There was a time when Huw would open the front door for him when he came home from work, would wake him up at seven o'clock on Saturday mornings. What adventures they had shared in the countryside behind their house! Up and out while the rest of the street slept, with packed lunches in their duffle bags and sticks to whip the air. Once, they tiptoed through a field of grazing bulls. Once, they climbed to the top of the Garth and looked out across the vale to where the sea, a coruscating sheet of foil, stretched out beyond Cardiff bay. Returning home at dusk through fields purring with crickets, tired and ravenous with thirst, the last of the lukewarm squash long gone.

Huw grips the wheel tightly again and watches the bucket in his father's lap.

"If you pull in here on the left, then I can cut straight across to the pond."

He slows the car to a standstill in front of the gate and switches the ignition off. His father clears his throat.

"They come back to the same spot every year, you see, to lay their eggs," he says. "None of the poor devils would have survived."

Huw nods his head and pulls on his ear lobe.

"Are you doing anything tomorrow morning?"

"No."

"Would you mind doing another run?"

"No. Fine."

"Thanks," his father says, opening the car door. "Don't wait for me, I'll see you back home." He lifts the bucket over the gate and climbs its bars deliberately as though his limbs have stiffened. Before hoisting the bucket to his side he catches his breath and waves goodbye. Huw raises an arm distractedly. There is something he wants to say but he can't quite think what it is, he can't think where to begin again, and then his father is too far away and it's too late, and he watches him struggle with the bucket through the tall grass, until his lopsided body disappears over the horizon of the field into the morning.

STRANGERS

Meic Stephens

'Run, boys, it's Jerry!'

The aeroplane was much too high for them to know whether it was a Spitfire or a Messerschmitt as it slowly, silently crossed the narrow strip of blue above the valley, but the word of Dilwyn Harvey, the biggest of the boys, was not to be doubted, and they stopped playing immediately. Picking up their coats that had served as goalposts, they scarpered from the Bute Field in all directions.

Glyn Pardoe, the youngest, didn't even look up. Without a word, he jumped on his tricycle and, pedalling furiously, rode down the rough track that led past the foundry and into Greenleaf Terrace. He'd heard about this Jerry. He was the one who'd tried to drop a bomb on the power-station where his father worked, but had missed, and the huge crater up on the Garth was proof of that. Some nights the boy had spent hours huddled in the cwtsh under the stairs, listening to the wail of the sirens.

He raced up the gritted lane and skidded to a halt at the backyard-door of his house. Dismounting, he carefully wheeled his bike inside and put it under the lean-to where the family's tin bath was kept. Nothing grew in their yard except some sooty rhubarb and a few dog-daisies, but it felt safe and he was glad to be home. Nevertheless, he took the precaution of bolting the door and removing the pump from his bike, just in case. If Jerry was around, it was best not to leave things where he might find them.

In the small scullery he dashed some cold water over his face from the tap above the bosh, and then dried it with a tea-towel. As he did so, he heard voices in the living-room — his mother's, his grandmother's, and two others that he didn't recognize..

'Glyn, is that you, love?'

'Yes, Nan.'

The boy stood awkwardly in the doorway between the scullery and living-room. His mother and grandmother were chatting to two men in khaki shirts who were sprawled in the armchairs on either side of the hearth, their ties undone and their boots off. There was a coal-fire in the grate, burning low in this warm weather, a spotless white cloth on the table and the best crockery had been brought out from the wall-cupboard.

'Don't be shy, my lovely. Come and say hello to Frank and Gerald.'

The two strangers were grinning at him.

'Watcha, me old china plate.'

One winked and everyone started laughing.

'Cor-blimey, missus, is this one of yer nippers? Come on, me old currant bun. Take a butcher's at this.'

The soldier had removed his bayonet from its sheath and was holding it out to him. The steel gleamed coldly as he twisted the weapon by its heavy black handle.

'Well, come on then, the cat ain't got yer tongue, 'as 'e?'

Failing to get a response, the man quickly lost interest in the boy and turned to his mother. 'Thanks for the nosh, love. 'E don't say much, do 'e?'

'Oh, he can be a real little chatter-box when he wants to. He's a bit bashful, that's all — isn't it, Glyn? You know what kids are like at this age.'

The boy's wide eyes were on the table, taking in what was left of a meal. On each man's plate lay the broken shells of two eggs and, near the big brown teapot, half a basinful of homemade brawn and a dish of chickling. He'd never seen anyone polish off two whole eggs before. You had to save coupons for things like that.

'Nan, I'm hungry,' he said at last.

His grandmother bustled at the table and then handed him a long crust which she had sliced off the corner of a loaf and dipped in condensed milk. Well, it was better than junket or tapioca.

'That's it, spoiling him again,' said his mother with mock disapproval.

With a sidelong glance at the two men, the boy went out through the front-door into the street. It was quiet this evening, with only a few people about. Mrs Shettin, their houseproud neighbour, was vigorously scrubbing the pavement in front of her house, as she did twice a day. It was all very much as usual and the boy liked it that way. He settled himself against the brass rod of the threshold, chewing his sticky crust and trying to work out who the strangers could be. He would have to ask his father. This week he was working nights. Sometimes he came home from work so tired after a double shift that he fell asleep in the armchair before he could have his food. Tomorrow afternoon, when Glyn took his father's shredded wheat up to him in the blue dish, he'd ask him who these men were.

Just then Dilwyn Harvey came by on his paper-round.

'Ow be, Dil?'

'Heard the news, Glyn boy?'

'What about?'

'Jerry's landed!'

The younger boy didn't know what to say.

'Never!'

'Gospel! It says by here.'

Dilwyn held up an *Echo* and read out the headline: 'Enemy Lands on British Soil. Channel Islands Occupied.'

It must be true if it said so in the paper, and Dilwyn Harvey always knew what he was talking about.

'Ow long before he gets here, then?'

'Matter of days, mun. He've got tanks, see — Shermans. Some could be here already on the quiet.'

'Come up from Cardiff, will he?'

'Aye, unless the road's blocked at Tongwynlais.'

'Ow will we know it's Jerry?'

'Talks funny, like, and he've got a bayonet.'

'What'll we do if he comes down Greenleaf Terrace?'

'Talk to him in his own language, mun. Say Gootan morgan mine hair and salute like this —'

Dilwyn raised his arm in the air with the palm of his hand turned down, and clicked his heels.

'What's that mean?'

'Don't shoot! Ow's trix?'

'What if he don't understand?'

'He will.'

'What if he don't?'

'Run like buggeree!'

With that Dilwyn Harvey carried on with his paper-round. The street fell quiet again, but the boy could hear his heart pounding as he rehearsed the magic words: Gootan morgan mine hair. They'd be easy enough to remember. But when he raised his arm he wasn't sure whether his hand should be turned up or down.

Later, lying in bed, he found it hard to sleep. The summer night wafting in through the box-room window brought with it the many smells and sounds of Greenleaf Terrace. The scent of honeysuckle from next door's garden. On someone's wireless the ten o'clock news and Arthur Liddell reading it. The strong whiff of hot metals from the foundry. Traffic on the Cardiff Road, and a train coming up the valley ... In the siding that morning he'd seen a big loco, its trucks camouflaged and jeeps being loaded onto them ...

At last he fell asleep but was woken around midnight by a commotion at the front door. Someone was crooning at the top of his voice: 'Underneaf the lantern baoy the barruck gyate ...'

'Eisht! You'll wake the boy, Gerry.'

'Deyarlin', I raymember the woay yer used to woayt ...'

He could hear stifled giggling.

'Twas theyar that yer whisper'd tayanderlay, that yer loved me, yer'd always be –'

They seemed to be scuffling in the porch.

'Maoy Lillai of the lyamplight, maoy aown Lillai Marlaeyn...'

'Oi, behave, will you? And enough of that, it's one of Jerry's songs.'

She was putting the key in the door.

'Is that you, love?'

'Yes, Mam, it's me.'

'Remember to draw the blinds, won't you? We don't want the warden knocking us up in the small hours. Could be in for it tonight. That old Lord Haw-Haw's been on the wireless again — Long Row, John Street, Llantwit Road, the Mining School, and Greenleaf Terrace, he said.'

The door slammed and the voices became muffled. But he couldn't sleep. Jerry talked funny and had a bayonet and now one of his songs was being sung in the living-room. Perhaps Dilwyn Harvey was right. The Enemy had Landed on British Soil. Some could be here already on the quiet. Gootan morgan mine hair, he whispered to himself, raising his arm with his hand turned down and then up, to be on the safe side. He wasn't sure how to click his heels but tomorrow he would practise.

It was very close in the box-room and he wanted a drink of water. He got out of bed and, clad only in his summer vest, made his way across the unlit landing and down the narrow stairs, pausing as he reached the bottom, listening intently. Someone had put a record on the gramophone and it was playing, very quietly,

'Bless 'em all! Bless 'em all! The long and the short and the...'

'What'll you have then, Gerry?'

'Wherever yer got, love.'

'Glass of stout?'

'That'll dao.'

'Last bottle — left over from Christmas.'

'Not one for the pig's ears then, yer old pot and pan?'

'Come again?'

'Don't like 'is beer, yer hubbie?'

'Never touches the stuff — we're chapel.'

'Well, I do. Life's short enough, ain't it?'

The boy didn't know what to do. If his father had been home, she wouldn't be up this late talking to Jerry. His father would have been angry because Jerry had tried to bomb the power-station. But he was very thirsty.

'So cheer up, my lads, bless 'em all!'

He decided to go in and ask for a drink of water.

The man was holding his mother's hand in the air and his arm was around her waist; she had hers around his neck. He had seen men and women lying in the ferns of the Bute Wood but this man and his mother were standing up and swaying gently to the music. She looked very pretty and he'd never seen her so flushed, except on wash-days. Her lips were redder than usual and she was wearing shiny stockings.

'Mam, can I have a drink of water?'

His mother, flustered, quickly turned the gramophone off. The man flopped into an armchair with a groan.

'Of course you can, my darling.'

She went into the scullery and filled a glass from the tap.

'Here you are, love.'

The water was cold but the glass was shaking in his hand and he took only one sip of it. The man was studying him closely.

'Watcha, mate! Ow's trix? Wanna see my bayonet naow?'

The boy was mesmerized by the gleaming steel.

'Gootan morgan mine hair!'

His hand shot up, but dropped limply to his side when the man, startled, made no response. They stared at each other for a long moment. Then, wanting to humour the boy, the man too raised his arm, just like Dilwyn Harvey had done, and said, 'Seeg hiley, and Doitshland oober allies to'yaow, mate!' Then he sprang to his feet and clicked his heels.

Now the boy knew it was true. The Enemy had Landed on British Soil. Some could be here already on the quiet. Tomorrow he would have to tell Dilwyn Harvey that Jerry was staying in his house. It was too late to block the road at Tongwynlais. Jerry must have come up the valley by train after all.

Suddenly he found himself being bundled into his mother's arms and carried back upstairs. There was scent in her hair and he could feel the warmth of her familiar body through the silky stuff of her dress.

'Mam, can I sleep in your bed tonight?'

'But you're a big boy now, Glyn. You're not bad, are you? Oh, alright then — just this once. You won't tell your father, though, will you? I was only having a bit of fun, see.'

'With Jerry?'

'Yes, with Gerry.'

'No, course not. If he asks, I'll fib and say I wet my bed and had to sleep in yours — alright?'

Smiling, she plumped up the pillow, tucked him under the cool sheets, tousled his hair, kissed him on the cheek, and put out the bedside lamp.

Early next morning there was a great stir in Greenleaf Terrace, like when the Sunday Schools were going on their annual excursion to Barry Island. A lorry with a tarpaulin hood was parked at the top of the street and soldiers were clambering aboard. The trucks of the big loco in the siding were full of men and machines getting ready to leave for an unknown destination.. There was talk of an Emergency and troop movements somewhere down England way. It was all very hush-hush. Mrs Shettin was out early, too, giving the pavement its first scouring of the day.

The people of Greenleaf Terrace were seeing the billeted men off. On the front step of the boy's house Gerald and Frank were saying goodbye to their hosts. None had noticed the boy peeping from behind the curtain of the upstairs window.

'Well, Abyssinia, love — and thanks for everything.'

A peck on her cheek.

'Look after yourself, Gerry. And don't forget — you'll get no promotion this side of the ocean.'

The soldier gave her a broad grin and a wink.

'You too, Frank, lad.'

'Thanks, Mr Pardoe.'

'So long, pal.'

Bleary-eyed, the shift worker smiled and stuffed two packets of Woodbines into their battle-dress. He also served, though on another front.

The military policemen were now blowing their whistles and the stragglers ran up the street lumbered with their kitbags, helmets and rifles.

'Ah well, pack up yer troubles, eh? All aboard the Lusitaynya!'

Then the soldiers were gone.

'Oi, where's our Glyn? He's missed the show.'

'Not up yet.'

'Alright, is he?'

'Not sure. Don't think he liked that Gerry much. He was shouting his name in his sleep all last night, and talking funny. Delirious, like. Didn't take to the fella myself either. Bit of a Tom Pepper, if you ask me. Ah well, don't suppose we'll be seeing him again.'

The troop-carrier, turning into John Street, had disappeared from view, and the people of Greenleaf Terrace, their day of excitement drawing to a close, were going back into their houses.

Suddenly she remembered the boy was still in their bed and her husband, who had to sleep during the day, would soon be going up.

'There's some warm milk on the hob,' she called over her

shoulder as she made her way upstairs, 'and your shredded wheat's in the blue dish.'

Hearing his mother's voice, the boy came away from the window, ran across the landing to the box-room and jumped into his own bed, pretending to be asleep.

'I'm just going to see how the kid is. Don't know what's got into him. He could be sickening for something.'

THE BEAST OF BONT

Niall Griffiths

20 past nine, misty mountain morning and Chris woke up, reached down over the side of his bed and scratched the head of his dog thus waking him up too and opened the curtains on the single window of his ramshackle caravan (lets in the rain, shudders as if in terror in anything stronger than a breeze) and saw four men standing outside carrying guns. Big guns, shotguns. The men wore woolly hats and waterproof coats and wellies and had the facial complexions of strawberry jam common among those who farmed these hard hills. One of them noticed Chris staring at him through the smeared glass and crooked his knuckly index finger at him. The others turned their heads to look, indifference shading into contempt. Chris put on some clammy jeans and a shirt and stepped over his back-asleep dog (big and strong, offspring of boxer father and alsatian mother) and opened the door. The cold morning air slapped him in the face.

- What d'you want? he said. Trying to sound firm.
- Just this.

One of the men, the biggest and oldest-looking, stepped up close and held his face two inches from Chris'. Chris could smell tobacco and bacon on this man's breath and could see the wind-ripped capillaries under his skin and was reminded of a satellite photograph of a coastline: all the little deltas and estuaries.

- That your fucking hound's been at my sheep again. Tore another's throat out last night he did. That's three in the past month. Things are bad enough as it is without your fucking hound making it worse.

Chris protested: – It can't've been my dog, I made sure he was in all night, I kept him in 'cos –

- I'm sick up to here with the fucking thing I am. And I'll tell you something else, I'm, we all are sick to death of you as well, with your drugs and your parties. Don't fucking want you here we don't. Tell you, I'm going to be waiting and –

He broke the breech of his shotgun to prove to Chris that it was loaded – the two brassy discs of the cartridge bottoms like the exposed bums of burrowing grubs.

- And your mutt'll have it, both barrels. And accidents can happen, out here in the mist like; a man seen from a tidy distance can at times resemble a large dog if the light's poor like, d'you get me? Especially if that man's scratting about in the long grass by the old mineshaft looking for his marijuana crop, d'you understand what I'm saying to you?

He snapped the gun back together and jabbed a finger as fat as a raw sausage in Chris's face.

- Now you've had fair warning. You and your dog – fuck off. Now. No, in fact don't disappear just yet and deprive me of the pleasure of blowing your fucking hound to bits for what it's done to my bleeding lambs and you can carry its bastard carcass away with you. If you're not out by this time tomorrow we're going to burn your van. Twenty-four hours. Fair warning. I mean what I say.

He walked off, followed by the other three, one of whom ignored Chris completely, one of whom levelled his shotgun at Chris's face and squinted along the barrel (the two black holes like crow-plucked eye sockets) and the last of whom squirted through his teeth a bolt of frothy spittle onto the sheet of slate used as a doormat at the single step into the caravan, a faded 'WELCOME' on it in chalk. Chris watched them go for a moment then stared out at the crest of the mountain rising leviathanly out of the mist and then closed the caravan door. Hands in pockets he stood for a minute staring down at his bare feet, the long hairs on his long toes like scribbles of black ink against the bright white of his goosepimpled skin and the blue traceries of veins and the icy red of the bony knuckles and ankles. He stood like that for a while, flexing his toes against the slimy lino of the caravan's floor, then he put the kettle on the camping stove for tea and wormed his numb feet into thick hiking socks. He made tea for himself and used the leftover hot water to add heat to a bowl of bread and old boiled vegetables which he placed by the dog's head.

- Come on, Loki. Breakfast time. It's morning. Time to wake up.

He scratched the dog behind the ear and it opened its droopy eyes to stare once at him then once at the food bowl and then sighed and closed them again. Its tail slapped the floor three times and it made a noise in its throat, a kind of comfortable groan.

- No? Not hungry? Ok, I'll just leave it there for you then. You eat it when you're good and ready, no rush.

He sat back on his bed to sip his steaming tea and smoke a mild spliff. The weed hadn't been dried out sufficiently and was still fairly damp so he had to draw hard, sucking his already thin cheeks and jaw into skeletal dimensions. The dog rose slowly, yawned and stretched, scratched behind its ear with a back leg and then began almost begrudgingly it seemed to eat. Chris watched it, admiring the dynamism of its posture, the thick neck bulging the worn leather collar, the well-defined muscles of its shoulders and flanks and the ridges of the pronounced spine underneath the short and reddish fur. Big, powerful animal. Good dog. Constant companion on Chris's exilic journey through the wilder places of this land, the howling moors of Yorkshire, the deserted bays of Cornwall, here, the fog-gulped mountains and lakes of Wales, sometimes the choked and concrete wilderness of the great cities. Chris and the dog moving on and being moved on, living on petty theft and the dole and the decreasing biscuit-tin savings amassed over two years working in a yoghurt-packing factory in Shropshire. Moving on and being moved on. Banishing the boredom, just moving on. Motion. Always away from stasis and suffocation and towards water and hills.

The dog finished the food then sat back and began to lick its paws. It barked and stood upright when the door thudded suddenly and Chris stubbed his spliff out in the saucer ashtray and opened the door to Simon, twitching and wired, at ten o' clock in the morning it was Simon from the town, twitching and wired and grinding his jaws.

- Morning, Chris. It's me.

Chris let him in and closed the door. Simon sat on the sagging bed and began immediately to roll a spliff the size of a pool cue on a road atlas balanced on his knees while the dog sniffed his feet and shins. His eyes were wide and his pupils small and he chewed his cheeks like a cow would cud.

- How's yourself, then? Still living I see. Surviving, is it. See the Beast was at it again last night. Another lamb all torn up like aye, throat out, guts out, same old story. Kids at the primary school saying they saw a large black cat like a panther scooping fish out of the park lake. Others saying they saw a UFO hovering over Cader Idris. Aliens wanting samples like. Vampires, werewolves. Fucking crazy. But the lamb, like, this last one, its arse had been all cored out and its innards sucked out as if by a hoover. What kind of animal does that, eh? Specially in this country. You tell me.

He shrugged and the atlas tilted and threatened to spill but he caught it before it could slip off his knees. The dog watched him with interest.

- Well, Loki seems to be a prime suspect, Chris said. – Had the fucking farmer boys up here this morning again with their guns. Said they were going to burn me out like. Shoot Loki and burn me out. Bastards. Same old bloody stuff.

- Ah, no, not Loki.

Simon stroked the dog's head and the dog whapped the floor with its tail.

- Wouldn't hurt a fly, you, would you, eh boy? Big softie. What did you say to them?

– What could I say? Nowt. They had guns, all four of them. Near shit meself I did.

- What are you going to do?

Chris shrugged. – Don't know. They might just be bluffing like, trying it on, like before, but they didn't seem to be this time. Seemed more serious this time somehow like. I don't want to move on, I like it here, for the time being at least, but. . . . He shrugged again. – I don't want to be burned out either. Nor for Loki to get shot.

At the sound of his name the dog turned his head to look at Chris. Chris tickled him behind the ear.

- I haven't got anything else in the world.

Simon twizzled the end of the spliff and lit it with a Bic and took a deep pull, holding it in his lungs for several seconds and blowing hardly any smoke out.

- So that's it then? You're moving on?

- Suppose. Don't see that I have any other choice. I mean, I don't want to risk it like, Loki getting shot. Or me van being destroyed. I'd have nothing then, would I?

Simon took three rapid sips on the spliff then handed it to Chris. After he'd exhaled he said: – Nah, listen, here's what we do. I don't like those fucking farmer boys and I know several lads, big lads like, who feel the same way, especially after that party in Devil's Bridge, d'you remember that, when the farmers smashed the place up? So tomorrow morning like they come up here with their petrol and their matches and their shooters and there's a crew up here just as tooled up, waiting for them like. I know those farmer boys, know what they're like, they'll shit themselves and scarper and leave you well alone. They can only survive on local support like, and if they see a group of townies, familiar faces like, up here protecting you they'll turn tail and leave you well alone. Easy.

Chris liked the sound of that: 'protecting you'. He sucked on the spliff. – Will it work? I mean. . .

- Course it will, aye. Worked for Jayne, didn't it? Out Bontgoch way? Blonde girl with the kids? Same thing happened; vigilantes turn up like with a jerrycan of petrol and there's me and Ikey and Griff and Roger Price and Llyr all waiting for them, axes, basies, the lot. Turned tail and ran they did. About nine months ago this was and where's Jayne now? I'll tell you; still fucking there, boy. Only went to see her yesterday to score some billy.

Chris took another toke and handed the spliff back. Simon went on: – I mean, we don't want to see the best weed dealer in Ceredigion disappear, now, do we? No way. We've got a vested interest in you staying put, boy. Too bloody right we have. Don't you worry about a thing. It's sorted.

He grinned through smoke at Chris who grinned back through the same small blue cloud and the dog lay slowly down between them and rested its chin on its paws, droopy eyes slowly closing. They finished the spliff and then Simon clicked his fingers as if suddenly remembering something and reached into the pocket of his overcoat and brought something bright out and handed it over the dozing dog to Chris who took it and looked at it: a toadstool, bright red with white spots, caricatured funny fungus like something out of an illustration for a fairy-tale that tells of a young girl who gets lost in the wild wood where organisms like this sprout big at the dark and mossy bottoms of trees.

- What's this?

- Agaric mushroom.

- It's poisonous.

Chris went to hand it back but Simon shook his head and held his palms out in front of his chest and waved them side-to-side. – No no, it's not, only if you use it wrong. It's only poisonous if you don't do it right. People have been using these things for thousands of years man, it's perfectly safe if you know what to do with it. Honest. And I'll tell you something else – it's the best hit I've ever had in my life. I mean that: In. My. Life.

Chris hefted the fungus in his hand, admired its vivid and obvious colours. Its very appearance brought a small smile to his face, but he had no idea why. It just did. It was somehow pleasing to his eye and his mood.

- The Celts used to eat that before they went into battle for the warp spasm like or if they wanted to communicate with the gods or the dead or whatever. The berserkers ate it before fighting bears for their skins and wearing them into war. Telling you, Chris, it's part of a great tradition boy. Loaded with history, that is. These mountains once trembled under the boots of rampaging hairy-arsed tribes all fired up on that stuff. It's the best drug I've ever had.

Chris gently stroked its smooth head, cool and velvety yielding yet resilient, almost rubbery. Like he imagined the skin of a dolphin to feel.

-So what do I do with it then, to make it safe like?

- Ah now, there's the thing. It is poisonous raw, like, I mean if you ate it now just as it is you'd be dead before I could make it back into town. You need a middle-man, see, a go-between like, something to filter it through. Like the Laplanders use it, right, but what they do is, is they feed it to the reindeers who go off their heads for a while and then when they've calmed down they follow them round with a bucket and as soon as the reindeer starts to piss they're under there with the bucket and they collect the piss and then they drink it. Just sips of it like, reindeer piss. Sends them into a trance. Sounds horrible I know, but all the poison's been filtered out see. Reindeers can handle it.

Chris pulled a face and looked puzzled. – So I have to. . .

- No, you don't have to drink reindeer piss, no. Not many reindeers round here is there eh! Nah, just a sheep'll do like.

- What!

Simon laughed. – Nah, just joking. But the point is, see, is that you need to filter the badness, the poison. An, erm, a sluice like, a purifier, that's it, a purifier. What I did was, and I read how to do this in a book somewhere, some stupid hippy rubbish like, what I did was I boiled it up with a load of vegetables and meat for about an hour and then strained the liquid three or four times and drank it. And I tell you, it was the most amazing hit. . . aw, pure bliss, honest. . . mix E and acid, the best bits of the acid like, and I suppose you're somewhere near it. Within a million miles at least. And I'll tell you another thing. . .

He leaned forwards, conspiratorial, secretive, his voice dropping to a whisper.

- What?

- It's, erm, it's, it sounds daft I know but it's like. . . sort of magical. Telepathic.

He sat back, almost smug.

– What are you talking about? How can it be telepathic?

- Well, when I took it, you know my cat? Yeah, well she was there right, and I was lying back on the floor like just chilling and feeling fucking wonderful and I began to, like, I could understand what she was thinking. No messing. It was like all of a sudden I could see through her eyes. I could. I could see myself lying a few feet away looking at myself looking at myself. One of the most incredible experiences of my life. Truly amazing. Really spiritual, y'know? Like they always go on about spiritual experiences on mushies and acid but I tell you they're fucking nothing compared to this stuff, boy, nothing. I'll never forget it as long as I live. Just for a minute I knew what it was like to be a cat. Can't put it into words like, but it was like a dream, a lovely dream in which I was awake. Totally fucking amazing. Unreal.

Chris stared down at the mushroom, a slight ringing in his ears. It seemed to throb, now, like a heart; pulsate like a membrane. It seemed more alive than an ordinary toadstool, more animated; it seemed possessed of a burning and an agility quite apart from the unwavering patience of other vegetables. It attracted him and terrified him at the same time.

Simon stood up to go. – New experiences, eh? Can't beat

'em. And you'll have a dream of a one with that, I'll tell you that for nothing. Boil it for at least an hour with a load of other organic stuff like and you'll be fine. I envy you, your first time. Like losing your virginity. Alright?

Chris nodded. – Yeh yeh. Just excited.

Simon smiled. – So you should be. Let me know tomorrow how you get on, I'll be up here with the boys first thing. You're not going anywhere, man, you're staying put with us. Don't worry about a thing.

He ruffled the dog's head and went out. Chris put the toadstool in a pan with water and carrots and grass from outside plucked out of the mountain and potato peelings and boiled it for an hour and a half watching it all the time then he sieved it several times and when the liquid was cool enough to drink he drank it and it tasted like dust, slightly salty dust. Then he lay back on his bed with his arms behind his head and his legs crossed and stared at the ceiling. He watched the dog stir and stand up and look at him for a moment and then pad across its claws click-clicking on the linoleum to the pan of vegetables and grass and fungus boiled to a mush and he was powerless to stop the dog from licking it once and then licking it again because he couldn't move and anyway even if he could he didn't see anything untoward about his pet dog Loki licking and eating a lump of vegetables and grass and fungus boiled to a mush. Nothing at all wrong with that. Just doing what dogs do. He watched the dog walk in circles by the side of his bed and then settle down to sleep again and he watched its eyelids slowly close as his began to slowly close also and their breathing deepened simultaneously until they were both asleep.

It is smell that awakes him, strong pungent smell, or, rather, not smell simply or one single strong scent but a riot, a carnival in his face, a gorgeous orchestra of odour in which he can distinguish the distinctive tang of many things, the warm and sweet-meaty whiff of the sleeping man on the bed and the host of lingering food smells hanging in the air or trodden into the lino along with country-mud and city-dirt and the rich and dark memories of shit not his own. The smells hit him like bright colours twinkling in his eyes to compensate for the monochromatic night-time world he has woken up in, all the diverse shadings of grey. He lifts his large head up off the floor and looks along his reclining body, the muscles swelling the fur, the curved claws sharply tipping the large and mucky-white paws. He thinks: I am inside the dog. My God, I am looking out through the dog's eyes. He can hear his own heart booming and can hear behind that the whistle-click and flicker of bat's wings outside the caravan, the swooping gust of an owl prey-plunging and the hot and ready breathing of sleeping sheep on the hillsides. The low groaning of the mountains as the world turns. He stands and it is like being in control of a large and powerful machine, tree-thick pistons ready to plunge and judder and propel him unstoppably not across or over but through the earth which he can feel unfolding before him, parting, showing itself, becoming accessible and wide and wild and stuffed full of promise and possibility, turning the fury that has always been in his heart into something not unlike rapture. His claws click across the lino, a little sound entirely out of keeping with the coiled and oily cable-springs that he feels his legs to be. Easy to rise then on those hind legs and forepaw-pull the door handle down and be out in the massive night, stars sprinkling cold salt frost down to spike the grass and bejewel the mud-ruts, mountains colossal and continents entire in themselves darkening the night sky with a blackness even deeper, great holes of starlessness. He runs and bounds and leaps up the mountainside through a copse of leafless trees moonblue highlighted and halts on the very crest of the mountain from where he can see absolutely everything ever all-crawling all-soaring and all in between and knows it all to be one and one only and never designed to be forced apart or asunder or separate. Awed and hidden eyes are on him as he cranes his head upwards on the twin-muscled column of his neck and the high moon draws from his guts a long howl, at first low then rising into a strident roar of accepted mourning for everything caught in mist or mud, for every blood turned to dung and for every breath become smoke, for the rabbit transfixed in the eye-rays of the plummeting raptor, for the eel forever twisting and turning back on itself never escaping the pike's teeth. Terror and wonder, terror and wonder.

He runs. White shapes sprint panicked from the thunder of his coming and an old taste burns in his throat and an old memory blooms in his brain. The planet spins beneath the balls of his feet.

288

His speed is incredible, star-blurring, and he bears down on his prey and in this action he is forever caught, long teeth bared, streamers of saliva scapula-swinging over his rising and falling shoulders, eyes drilling darts through the darkness onto the back of the terror-stricken and hopeless quarry. He leaps roaring and leaves the earth and then his teeth are tearing at wool; there is screaming and roaring and he bites, rips and spits wool, bites, rips and spits wool and there is screaming and roaring and then at last there is meat in his teeth, hot and yielding, and he snatches and bites and rips and there is more screaming and his neck bulges and his shoulders strain and then there is release and an explosion of taste throughout his entire body, a squirt and sizzle onto the frosted grass and a hissing puddle quickly mirroring the moon. He leaps again and straddles the sheep and takes the tossing head in his jaws; crunch and snap and burst and slobber and then no tossing or screaming only the grunting and wet rending of his quiet frenzy below the twinkling stars until blood-muzzled and entrail-necklaced he sings again to the moon.

In a calm and impossible joy he returns heavy-bellied to the caravan. The man still lies on the bed, breathing deeply, the eyes open but with little movement in them. He wants to go to the man and sniff and taste and explore but exhaustion breaks upon him like a wave and he crawls contented under the bed and with a sense of having returned from somewhere beautiful and very far away falls deeply into sleep.

They stand in a shallow semi-circle watching the mad flames like men of mist as the heat draws the moisture from their clothes and turns it into wraiths rising upwards towards the lightening sky. The eldest and biggest of the four regards the blaze almost affably, a grandfather sitting before the hearth and silently reminiscing. The youngest, red of cheek, pale blue of eye, blinks rapidly and swallows and shuffles his boots in the liquefying mud.

- Was he not in there, then?

- No.

- You're sure?

- Course I'm bloody sure. You saw me check it, didn't you? He wasn't there. What the bloody hell d'you think I am, a murderer?

The caravan's rear window explodes like a bomb and a

burning shape springs out, a howling fireball streaking across the mountainside towards the red stain of dawn as if seeking the protection of a parent. Smell of overcooked pork hanging on the morning air.

- Ah. There goes the dog.

- And good bastard riddance to it. Sheepkiller.

The youngest one watches it go. – Should we not follow it? Shoot it, like? I mean, it might be in agony. . .

- Nah.

The oldest one shakes his head. – Bastard deserves to burn for what it's done to my lambs. I gave'm fair warning.

They watch it bolt over the hillside into the darkness which yet dwells there, growing smaller, smaller, blowtorch candle matchstick spark, snuffed. And in a few hours time a party of hikers will find it at the bottom of a cairn, charred and smoking, a bone-bared and twisted dead thing, impossible to put a name to what manner of beast it is, or was.

THE LATE CALLER

Ron Unsworth

"Caller on line one please" the kindly voice urged. There was silence for a brief moment, then, "Er...Yes sir," a voice croaked over the telephone.

"And what's your name, m'dear?" the man's voice asked.

"My name's Lynne, sir!" The girl sounded very young and obviously nervous, "What can I do for you, Lynne?" the voice crackled from the radio, again there was a pause for several seconds. "I...I'd like you to tell me anything you can about me and my future, sir," she stuttered.

The radio presenter politely coughed, then in a sympathetic Lancashire accent, asked, "Forgive me, dear, but you sound rather young, how old are you, lass?"

"I'm fifteen, sir!" she stammered nervously, her Welsh accent evident, "Ah I see," the sound echoed from the radio, "Now, I can see that you're troubled over something, am I right?" "Yes, sir!" she replied.

"Would it be something to do with a parent?........you see, I can only see one adult around you."

The line went quiet, Lynne paused, wondering whether to carry on.

It had only been three weeks earlier since she'd waved goodbye to her mother when she'd left for school in the morning.

One hour later, Sheila, her mother, had died from a massive heart attack.

Lynne had been devastated, she had been very close to her mother. Her father had spent more and more time out in the evenings, since he'd been made redundant from his job.

Her eyes widened in amazement as she tried to contain her emotions, "Er....yes sir, but I don't know how....." she was interrupted by the presenter of the North Wales radio station's Psychic show.

"Tell me, love, have you by any chance lost one of your parents?" She sat bolt upright, her mouth agape, "Yes," she gasped, "I have......my mother!"

"And," the Psychic added in his broad Lancashire accent, "would that have been very recently?" the phone line went quiet as Lynne was awestruck, "Y..Yes, sir, three weeks ago!" she uttered wistfully.

"I'm sorry to hear that, my love," answered the Psychic, as he fought back his obvious sorrow at the young girl's loss. "And was your mother very ill for a long time my love?" The young girl's voice faltered as she replied, "No, sir, she had a heart attack........while I was in school."

"Stay on the line, m'dear," the man's voice echoed, "We'll just have a break, and this is Elton John with Don't go breaking my heart!"

The music blared from the radio while Lynne wondered what to do next; the record was nearing the end when she glanced at the bedside clock. Ray, her father, was due home at any time, she put down the telephone receiver.

Ray had gone very quiet since Sheila's death, Lynne had screamed at him in her grief, shouting that he should have spent more time at home. It had hurt Ray badly that she should accuse him, he had tried so hard to make a living since losing his job.

In the weeks following their loss, the father and daughter had drifted into silence, the words said in the heat of the moment appeared to echo in each other's minds. Ray found it hard to forgive his daughter for her accusations, and Lynne still felt that her mother would still be alive if Ray had known she'd been so ill.

It was an hour later when Ray unlocked the door and checked on Lynne to see she was safely tucked in. He did as he had done for the past three weeks, sat weeping for hours until he drifted off to sleep in his armchair.

"Are you alright?" Ray asked, his softly spoken Welsh tones echoing across the breakfast table, Lynne's eyes settled on him for a second, "Yes!" she abruptly answered, leaving to clean her dishes.

"Do you want me to pick you up from school?" he asked, "No!" she shook her head, closing the door behind her. Ray sat looking down at his breakfast, he'd felt hunger pangs, but had suddenly lost his appetite. Inside, he knew Lynne was hurting at losing her mother, and that her sudden attitude was not her usual bubbly character. His anguish was how to make her realise that him being at home wouldn't have made any difference, and that he'd had no idea that Sheila had been feeling unwell.

The days passed by, each much the same. Ray tried unsuccesfully to start a conversation, by asking if she'd had a good day. When Lynne didn't seem to be too preoccupied, he brought up the subject of her mother. "Look, Lynne, she died instantly, it was a mass....." "No dad!" she screamed, "You don't know....you wasn't here!" He dropped his head in grief, not knowing what else to say or what to do.

Lynne was waiting for the weekend show on the radio. She pondered whether to give it another try, and whether the Psychic would be annoyed at her for hanging up on him, the previous week.

Alone in the house, she settled down with her radio blaring away, the music stopped and the station announcer read out, "Here is Mr Mystic, we are waiting for your calls!"

She listened to an elderly lady talking to the Psychic. The lady was amazed at Mr Mystic's insight, he told her that she'd had a few major operations and that the worst was now over. "Am I going to be alright?" she begged him, "Yes, m'dear, you're going to get stronger and stronger, and may even be taking a holiday abroad soon too!" "YES!" she shrieked, "I am, I'm going to Florida with my son and his wife, I was wondering if I would be fit enough!"

Lynne was convinced, she reached for the telephone and rang the radio station's number. "Hello," answered the man's voice, "Who do we have on line one?" She paused, and took a deep breath. "I'm Lynne," she stammered, "I...I'm sorry about last week," she continued. "Oh yes, I remember," the friendly voice said sapiently, "You're the young lass who rang about your mother, aren't you?"

"Yes, sir, I'd like you to tell me if you could... if.."

"Yes dear, your mother's alright, she tells me that she left you so quickly she didn't have time to tell you a lot of things." The line went quiet for a few seconds. Lynne's mind was in a turmoil, she glared into the mouthpiece of the phone. "Can you speak to her?" she implored, "Can she talk to you?"

The Psychic soothed Lynne's barrage of questioning, by

asking her not to hang up. "We'll be back in a few moments after The Carpenters and Yesterday once more." "

The young girl glanced at the clock anxiously, then heard the record come to an end. "You still there, miss?" asked Mr Mystic, "Yes, sir.......please?" she sobbed, "Can I talk to my mum?" There was a brief pause until the voice replied, "She's on the other side, dear, but she tells me she loves you dearly, and that you are a wonderful, caring daughter."

His words fell on deaf ears, she sobbed wistfully, and repeated her question beggingly, "Please can I speak to her?"

"She says she doesn't want you to cry over her, m'dear, she's sorry she left you and your father, but she's alright and in no pain....." Lynne heard no more of his words, she replaced the receiver and cried herself to sleep."

"Why don't you go out this weekend with your friends," Ray urged her over breakfast. "It's been a while since you had a good night out!"

"No!" she snapped, "I've got loads of homework to do for my exams."

Throughout the week Ray reflected on the good times he and Sheila had had with Lynne, days out to Rhyl and Blackpool, the times they would take their little girl to gigs when Ray had played in a comedy showgroup some ten years earlier. Lynne had giggled constantly at his efforts to do impressions of famous stars, then wondered why everyone cheered and clapped his antics on stage.

He tried to make himself available for Lynne, waiting outside the school with her coat when it was raining, offering to run her in the mornings, but Lynne retained her silence.

When her father left the house on the Friday evening, Lynne settled down on her bed once again, the radio on at her side. She stared at herself in the mirror of her dressing table. She was the image of her mother, with long black hair and deep blue eyes.

"Oh mum!" she whispered sadly, "I wish I could tell you how much I love you!" At that moment, Mr Mystic's signature tune blared out of the radio. "We're taking calls for Mr Mystic now!" the announcer prompted.

"Hello!" she croaked down the phone. "It's me, Lynne, again, I'm sorry to bother you!" "That's alright, m'dear," the reassuring voice soothed, "What can I do for you ?"

Lynne hesitated as she thought of how to put her questions forward. The radio airwaves were quiet momentarilly, the Psychic waiting for the young girl to speak, "Umm," she stuttered, "Please can you tell me what's going to happen in the future........to me I mean, sir?"

Again, there was a short pause before Mr Mystic answered the girl's question, "Have you any siblings m'dear?" he asked, "Siblings?" she sounded puzzled, "Yes, dear........brothers or sisters?" he explained.

"Oh! no, sir, only my dad, but......." she trailed off in mid answer, "But what love?" asked the voice from the radio, "Is there a problem there?"

After a pause, Lynne gave out a huge sigh, "Well," she gasped, "he's hardly ever here......and we don't get on since what happened to mum.."

"Look, love," the friendly voice echoed, "He could be hurting in the same way that you are, we all take personal loss in different ways, m'dear." A sob was heard over the airwaves, "Don't cry, love, try to tell me how you feel, and I'll see if I can help, but you haven't any other family around you except for your father?"

Lynne wiped away a tear, "No, sir....I haven't, only my dad."

"So I'm right on that then?" "Yes, sir!" replied Lynne. "Mum died some weeks ago." "Yes dear, it's been playing on your mind, hasn't it?"

Lynne glanced across her bed into the dressing table mirror; her eyes welling up with tears, she mumbled, "I'd like to talk to mum, sir!"

"Your mother's alright, m'dear, she tells me that you're very much like her, and that you're going to do well for yourself." Her face lit up at the thought that her mum was in contact with Mr Mystic. "Please?" she begged as she heard the mild-mannered Psychic urge, "Now who's on line two?" Taken aback, she exploded angrily, "But....But..." The line was dead, the next caller was already talking on the radio.

As the days passed, Lynne got more and more angry, to the point that she couldn't concentrate on her homework. The only thing that was on her mind was contacting her mum through Mr Mystic.

When Ray left the house in the evenings, she rang the Welsh radio station, but on each occasion was told that Mr Mystic wasn't there and anyway, he only took calls while on the air.

"Mum wouldn't want you to grieve like this!" Ray sighed to her one morning, "She would want us to get on together, you know!"

"She wouldn't!" Lynne replied bluntly. "If I could, I'd prove it to you!"

Ray dropped the subject, the tension between them still evident. He was getting very worried about Lynne's health. Her already slender frame appeared to be getting even more slim, he'd noticed that she spent more and more time in her room, and she wasn't eating the meals he'd set before her.

"Who is Jimmy or James, my love?" the voice asked, "Oh, that's my brother Jim!" crackled the reply on the radio. "And is Jim your only brother, m'dear?" "Yes but..." Mr Mystic interrupted the lady, "and it's a few years since Jim went over to the other side isn't it m'dear?"

"Oh my goodness, how did you know that?" the lady chirped. "Jim wants you to know that he's better now, his head doesn't hurt any more, and he's with Cerys again....who's Cerys, love?" Lynne stared at the radio in dismay as she heard the ecstatic lady chortle. "She was Jim's wife, she died six years ago, then Jim died of a brain tumor three months ago!"

"Oh, I think you're amazing, Mr Mystic!" she gasped as the announcer called for more listeners to ring in to the station.

"I'm Lynne again, sir!" the young girl declared, "I hope it's alright."

The telephone line went quiet. Lynne gazed at the phone wondering if she was going to be rebuked for her persistence. Suddenly, the man's voice boomed via the radio and telephone, "Yes dear, it's about your mother isn't it?" "Yes, sir, I'd like to......."

"It's alright, my love, I've spoken to her and she will speak to you through me," he announced nervously. Lynne's youthful pretty face lit up in excitement. She suddenly found her head spinning searching for words as she heard some strange fumbling noises coming from the radio.

"Stay on the line!" Mr Mystic's voice demanded in a stern

manner, then music blared out. "That's strange!" Lynne whispered as she realised he hadn't done his usual announcement to introduce the record.

Minutes passed before the end of the record, Mr Mystic's voice sounded flustered as he told his audience, "I won't be taking any more calls tonight after this one.....are you still there, m'dear?"

Lynne's hands shook as she croaked, "Yes sir, I'm still here."

"Your mother's here, dear, what would you like to say to her?" Lynne fought back tears, she mumbled, "Mum....I love you.....why did you go?"

After a pause, Mr Mystic, his voice faultering, replied ,"Your mum says she was ill for some time.......she says she and Ray, is that your father, love?" Lynne mumbled her reply. "They were very happy together, love, and she says they both think the world of you.....they love you very much."

"But......but my dad......" Lynne croaked, "Your mother says he didn't know, dear, she didn't want him or you to worry about her."

"Mum" Lynne pleaded, "Mum......what was wrong?"

The muffled sounds on the radio appeared to be coming from inside the studio, "We'll break for a record and come back, please stay on the line, miss." Mr Mystic boomed.

The young girl sat on the edge of her bed waiting for the record to end. "Are you there?" came the voice on the phone. "Yes, sir."

"Your mother tells me she had a heart complaint, and was waiting for a bypass operation." Lynne paused, taking in what she had heard, "But Mum, you should've......." Mr Mystic interrupted her, "She didn't want to worry you or Dad, she says, You've got to do well in your exams, and Dad was depressed at losing his job...........she would have told you both when she had a letter to go in for the operation."

The teenager slumped her body on the bed, holding the phone closely to her ear. "Mum," she declared wistfully, "I've been rotten to Dad......I thought he didn't care.........." Quietness filled the room as she searched for words.

Listeners to the radio heard raised voices echoing around the studio, then suddenly, just as Lynne was about to speak, a voice reverberated from the radio. "This is Dan Davies with your favourite music from now until 2 am."

Lynne frowned as she glared at her transistor radio, the silent telephone still in her hand. She glanced up at the clock to see that it was near midnight, she lay thinking over everything that had been said, until she fell asleep.

Ray sat at the breakfast table with two places set out, he glanced up to see Lynne walk quietly into the room. "You alright?" he asked.

Lynne seemed to look brighter, she smiled back at him, "Yes, Dad, I'm fine!" She sat down and toyed with her corn flakes, her head bowed. "How are you, Dad?.......are you feeling ok?" she looked up to see Ray's eyes fill with tears as he smiled back, "Yes love, I'm fine."

Word is that Mr Mystic was fired from his weekend spot on the radio; his bosses weren't too happy with the advice he was giving his audience.

Things between Lynne and her Dad are great now. Ray stays home at nights while Lynne finishes her homework then shouts, "See you later, Dad, won't be late!........ Love you!"

He waits for the sound of the door closing, then in a curiously familiar Lancashire accent, whispers, "OK lass..... take care, m'dear...... love you!"

THE BUS TO MALPAS

Alex Keegan

I was on a No 3 double-decker bus going back to Malpas when the guy sitting the other side of Dennis Potter said, "Hey, that play, *Pennies from Heaven,* Dennis, I really liked that play. What are you doing now?"

My heart ached for Dennis. He was so polite, he couldn't just say to this guy, "Hey, dummy, I'm dead, remember?" I leaned over, excused myself for butting in and said, "This is a recording, pal, you know? You remember the interview with Melvyn Bragg? Dennis had to stop every few minutes to take morphine, his cancer was hurting him that much."

Dennis smiled at me and I said to the guy, "See, it's a recording, Dennis isn't really here."

I put out my hand and Dennis held it. He was warmer than I expected.

"Well, what's he doing on the bus to Malpas then?" this guy said. I didn't answer. Sometimes there is no answer. Dennis really did feel warm.

At the front of the bus, well two or three seats in front of me, my first wife was sitting. She was staring at the back of the driver's head. Kathy wasn't dead, at least, I didn't think she was, just forever gone, with a piece of me, and me a little dead. Her long fair hair was perfect. I was too scared to get up and go forward. The bus was going very fast and lurching from left to right.

I wanted Kathy to turn round. I wanted to look at her face. Just after the divorce I had gone to see her at her parents. She had come to the door in long black flared trousers and a white blouse. She had lost weight and her eyes were bright. She'd told me she'd got a job behind a bar to get herself out more and things were OK. She couldn't let me in, she said, her father would kill me, but she did walk down to the pub with me. Everybody there knew her and she smiled a lot and her eyes were wide. She told me that a guy who fixed washing machines had asked her out. What did I think?

"Go for it," I said. I had wanted to say, "Let's go home and try again," but I told Kathy it was great she was getting out more. She had touched my thigh for a moment, taken a slow breath and looked away for about ten seconds.

At the front of the bus, on the dashboard, next to the driver, there was a small silver casket. I knew it contained my daughter's eye, the one she lost in Birmingham. I saw it, then I looked away like Kathy had done, for a few seconds. When I looked back the casket was gold; either that or the sun was making it look like gold. My gut ached and Dennis Potter squeezed my hand.

We were passing along a quiet, smooth black road. One side was the sea, a bright, light-blue, full of promise. The other side, soldiers stood slowly to watch us go by. They were all dirty, they looked tired, but every now and then one would half raise his hand as if to say hello as the bus roared on. Then the bus was going the other way and now the sea was on the right instead of the left and the soldiers just stared. Then I heard the Mindbenders singing "Groovy Kind of Love" and Kathy got up to come back and say a quick hello.

"Our song," she said. "How are you, Jim?"

I was cold. "OK," I said. "And you?"

"I had a kid," she said. "A girl, Melanie. Me and the guy from Leeds, we split up."

"What guy from Leeds?" I didn't know any guy from Leeds.

"The one who fixed washing-machines. I told you in that last letter, when I said we had to stop writing."

"Oh," I said. That was when I'd stopped loving Kathy because she wasn't clever. I was about to marry Jenny. My insides had been black as Hell. I had burned the letter. I must have missed the thing about the guy from Leeds.

"I'd really like it, if you could sit next to me," I said.

"Maybe later," Kathy said, "but I'm with someone."

She put her hand on my thigh for a moment. Then she took a breath and looked away. Then she went back to her seat. Outside there were trees, tall thin trees, pines, evergreens of some kind, row upon row, and in between the dark trunks, in the dark forest, shining yellow eyes.

After Kathy went back up north, after the split-up, but before the divorce, there was a time when women seemed to think there was something about me. I was empty and dark but they saw me as charged and driven and they wanted to screw me. One was called Tina, she had a retarded son, and there was her friend – Carol, I think, whose husband wasn't very tall, and once they set me up with some woman I took home for the worst sex of my life, with Otis Redding's *My Girl* playing on repeat. I don't think she wanted to. She was dry and she only felt vaguely amorous when Otis was singing *My Girl*. That was the time when I was trying to do the poetry. She was sad and the night was dark. I still think the Otis Redding version of *My Girl* was way better than the Temptations, though the Temptations version was good.

I can't remember her name. She lived in a cottage in Caerleon and was sort of living with a caretaker from St Cadoc's. She was the ugliest woman I ever slept with. At work, when I laughed about her, I called her a good-looking monkey. Now I wish I could buy two dozen roses and send them Interflora "From an admirer." I never set out to be a bastard. It just happened.

Jenny was clever, learned almost, and she was large and safe and solid. She wanted me to study, to write more, and I liked talking to her. Somehow we had sex, but I was never, you know, really into her that way. Maybe that was why we got married and why, three weeks later, I rang Carol and we went up the mountain and screwed the once for old time's sake.

Then Jenny was pregnant and we bought a house, a stereo, some nice glasses and some cutlery in Howells of Cardiff. Toby was born. I was still playing football then, still fixing televisions, studying. I used to take Toby to training and put his carry-cot on the touch-line. I couldn't believe this, this thing, was possible. Having a kid wasn't that real. It was only when Clare came along that it began to be real. Two kids, I couldn't pretend any more. I think Jenny, Toby and Clare are upstairs on the bus. Sometimes I think I can hear them talking. But Clare's eye is in the casket on the dash, by the driver.

I'm thinking all of this and I know that Dennis Potter will understand me. I think Dennis knows I didn't set out to be a bastard, it just happened. At least he hasn't let go of my hand.

I don't know if falling in love with Ruth counts as being a bastard. I really did fall in love, probably the only time. With Kathy, getting married, it was the idea, the thing that came next in life; with Jenny I thought it was the right time to do something solid, and with Sally it was obsession, pure and simple. Over that I *was* a bastard, but I thought at the time that it wasn't my fault.

But Ruth was what I was, deep, deep inside – tiny, timid, frightened, but with scarlet dreams twice as big as the world and a desperate, desperate need to share them with someone. She read my poems in her room while I cracked jokes in the bar and the next day, our last, we walked through manicured gardens by the side of water, and she gave me a letter, told me to read it and put a finger to her lips when I asked her why.

She had written about what love is and that she was leaving then, me, blind and raucous, letting this little bird fly away, to agonise and re-read the letter, re-read the letter, re-read the letter. But she let me take her to the train and we sat together, holding hands in the station buffet, and it was so joyful, and so very, very dark. And pain and love I knew then were indistinguishable and the one needed the other. But what was different was that for the first time the pain was mine and not someone else's, and now for this first time I wished I was a better person.

Yes, we eventually found a way to commit adultery – I was persistent, even then – in some hotel near Potters Bar which backed onto the fume-smeared Great North Road, and overlooked a light-blue swimming-pool, a gleaming, flashing pool, a white bridge, sunshine.

And I kissed Ruth's tiny, nut-brown body. She had a Caesarean scar just like Jack Kerouac's tiny lover, Terry, her hips so narrow she couldn't bear a child without being gashed open. But for us it was no weary morning and our shelf was next to the A1, but it was delicious yes, and tearful, and there was no time to fall asleep.

For we were wretched, damned, bloody. We were damned, for there were other things present, beside our bodies, souls. There were commandments, commitments, children, consequences. And Ruth, so tiny, was so strong, and she left us. And though for a while we telephoned across seas, we never met again and on my thirtieth birthday she said, "Let us stop. The pain, the pain is far too great."

And I told Jenny and I destroyed her. I needed to be allowed to cry so I told my wife. I did this for me, to explain my tears, and it destroyed her.

With Ruth I might have learned what being human was. Without her, I was just a man and a cruel, poor man to boot. A good man would have suffered alone, become a drunk, a workaholic – perhaps run dizzy distances on the moors; but I had drifted into being a bastard, a simple, selfish, bastard and I poured my needs, my dreams, into a closed world, a paper world. I had once been a mechanic, a technician, then an academic, now I was a writer – but first and foremost I had perfected a fine selfishness and I had brandished it, roared it, let anger and bitterness be some flag, some hypocritical badge of honour, as if failing was a sign of strength and cheating was the mark of greatness.

And now, I think fittingly, I am on the bus to Malpas.

Jenny and I did not split up, not then. No, we were adults, academics, sensible. Toby was, I think, four, Clare less than two, and we stayed together, citing the children as our excuse for not admitting we came from different worlds, were different colours, had incompatible dreams. Instead, we built things, we strove, we worked hard. Jenny turned back to study, gained a masters, a PhD, a professorship, I graduated, sold things, made money, then switched to writing full time and learned to smile for my book-jackets.

And I learned to loathe, to be disgusted, to see nothing but falseness in those around me. I even learned how to make the magic in my children fade to black. Until one day I ripped out my daughter's eye and I was complete.

I was practised. Jenny was practised. I did my duties and this one, this day, was a picnic in a park, somewhere just far enough a drive to stop me doing anything else. It may have been a nice day, but that's immaterial.

We had eaten. We were going to walk. Jenny had asked, "We should go for a walk now." I did not want to walk. We both knew this, but the game was now perfected. "Do we have to?" I said even as I rose and walked away from the unlocked car, my neck prickling.

And she shouted after me, *"The car!"* and I thought, *"Fuck you!"* and she shouted again, *"The keys!"* and I turned, and I saw her, really saw her, this woman made ugly by the ugliness in me, and she shouted *"Keys!"* again, and I threw them, tossed them like a grenade at her, and I almost turned my back.

The people upstairs on this bus might understand this, the driver might understand. I don't quite understand, but I *knew*, right then, I knew the instant I had thrown the keys, what was going to happen. The keys contained every foul moment of my then life, every dark frustrated second of our hypocritical contract, all the red anger, all the nightcold beds, all the pathetic technical screwing, the smiles at candlelit dinner-parties, and me no longer being able to see the light dimming in my children.

It was sunny. The sky was bright blue. And the keys, my coward's dagger, sailed in a mathematically perfect arc towards Jenny's hands and then, just, just, over them. And Clare, my little baby, barely walking, still open, still untouched, still sweet enough and innocent enough, looked up and smiled and guided all my anger straight into her, into her eyeball.

Of course we tried. We rushed to a hospital, a police escort wailing and flashing blue, but my baby had lost her eye. She had lost it long before, on my thirtieth birthday but the wickedness had taken a long time landing.

Then, in the December, Clare finally got her glass eye, an amazing technical achievement. They gave it to her on Christmas Eve and Clare ran into my arms as if she didn't care, as if she didn't know, what I had done.

And Dennis still holds my hand. Dennis isn't really here, this is just a recording but he still holds my hand. He holds my hand, even though this is a recording and the guy sitting by the window, next to him, can't get it through his thick skull.

Oh, I loved *Pennies from Heaven*, I loved *Lipstick on Your Collar*. And *The Singing Detective*, that was his masterpiece but I think I identified with *Pennies From Heaven*, with Bob Hoskins, with being executed.

After Clare's eye – we called it an accident – I tried a little harder, and we looked almost normal for a while, but then I gave up on the writing and went back to making money. I hadn't been happy before, but a part of me had thought itself satisfied, but now I felt I didn't have the right not to earn money any more and going back into the real world made me more weary. It was a little easier to sleep.

Sally was next, Sally was my secretary. I don't really feel like talking about her but that seems to be the thing on the bus and I'd hate it if Dennis Potter let go of my hand. My secretary. It happened slowly. When I realised, I avoided it, avoided her, but it happened and I thought it was love again, Ruth again, and one night I just didn't go home. I had started writing again, sitting in the dark again, drinking more than was wise, and Sally, well she just seemed to want me and didn't think I was a bastard, and I thought I could see a faint, distant light. I didn't go home.

Yes, Dennis, I was a bastard. Toby was hurt. Clare, my little Nelson, was hurt. And they put on weight, they became difficult, they fell away at school. Oh, I ached when I thought of them, Dennis, cried when I could, but I was a man, Dennis, and screwing myself silly, walking into the bathroom just to see Sally in the bath, her flat belly, round, still-firm breasts, the sad, perfect triangle of her sex, the deep darkness of her, the place where I died, night after night after night after bloody dark night. You know this, Dennis? How through all this pain I can still feel hard thinking of her?

But that is finished, as it had to be, and I am on the bus.

I think there are more people on the bus I will have known. Kathy is up the front, though she seems to be OK, and upstairs, there's Jenny and the kids. Ruth's husband, I wonder if he's up there? I never did meet him, just smelled his pain. The others are sat behind me.

The bus is slowing, one side the sea, the other side, the forest, no soldiers. I have to let go of Dennis Potter's warm hand. He smiles. Dennis has such gentle, intelligent eyes. As I get up, incredible pain in my joints, and my skin itches. I see the driver's eyes in his mirror but they smile too because he knows my decision. Now the bus is going the other way again and we pass the soldiers and we really are headed for Malpas now. The soldiers look disappointed.

The bus comes to a halt at the last stop before the terminus, near the house where my parents lived. They've been dead a while. This is really Malpas, and the bus is real, yellow and green, smelling of diesel, and with the town's crest on its side, two fish, a shield, gold and silver and red.

I don't know why I decided to come back here right now,

except it seemed fitting. The specialist explained. Months, years, even decades, he said. They could treat the pain, make it not too bad, but the side effects would mean less time. He thought, on balance, that to take the analgesia was best. He said that nobody deserved this kind of pain, but I wasn't sure he was right. I said I would think about it, take a train to my home town, think about it for a weekend.

I am not a brave man so saying no to the doctor wasn't easy. But then I got on the bus to Malpas. I could have stayed on the bus, gone the quick easy way, but I got off one stop before the terminus, things to do, still.

There are times when I wonder where I found the courage, but then I don't think it's courage, just the need to find a balance. And I had help; if you discount the pain, the last couple of years haven't been too bad and I think Clare and I have come to an understanding. Toby has made it into university already, and with a little help from me, Clare's heading the same way. I think Kathy is all right, it may even be I did the right thing there. I try not to remember Ruth, and Sally, well she's one of those people who always comes out on top.

Jenny's hair has gone prematurely grey, but she says it was the long nights studying, not us. I have a little flat and I'm writing again. At Christmas, my second one already, Toby and Clare bought me Dennis Potter's biography. He suffered so long, so very long, but he finished what he had to finish and he ended a fine, warm and intelligent man.

As for sending those flowers, red roses, I think not. I am trying to be wise. The gesture would be for me, not for a small, sad and less than pretty lady. The brief false light they might mean would only make the next darkness darker for her. I think, on balance, best she waits for the next bus.

A DRUG STORY

Rae Trezise

Candida was violently sick. Sick nothing though. A whole lot of coughing and retching, all for a string of phlegm and a few spots of blood. She lifted herself from the toilet bowl, glancing at her broken fingernails and wondering what exactly the powder had been cut with. Of course, there was nothing virginal about what she had done, it was just that Rusty always used glucose which he said was cheap and didn't make it too awful to swallow. They'd bought some, which was blue, on the way to the Hippo Club, under the Cardiff bridge, one flush giro day and then spent the rest of the night staring and dancing with their mouths burning, and in between Rusty was continually shouting, "Thez no need fuh tha shit man, fuckin' Ajax!"

'Yellow,' she thought. 'It was yellow, wasn't it?' Candida could remember when her brother still lived at their mother's and the old terrier had the mange. 'Eczema' they called it. The dog was balding and scabby so Tristan and her plastered it with sulphur powder and muzzled it to stop it washing itself. Then Candida tried to forget it because she knew that sulphur could not be taken internally. She concentrated instead on the Paul Weller move-alike snorting the mystery substance from her milk, tattooed midriff the evening before, with Oasis' 'Defintely Maybe' crackling somewhere in the background.

'Crackling' was the perfect word. It couldn't have been any better and yet it was much less than Candida expected. A travel lodge in a hidden corner of Pencoed with three Sky channels. She'd wanted to watch Sheryl Crow on the Lottery draw but by then Trent was well into business and she thought asking to put the TV on was a little ignorant seeing as he'd paid and all. She was confused about the money. It just so happened that she could have paid that week, but she didn't know what to say because it wasn't at all like buying a round for your mates. When Trent slapped her thigh and said, "I'll be spending a lot of money then?", she just looked down and eventually said, "Yes."

While she waited in the window for his car to pull up the previous day, she thought him easy. But then, it had taken him a year to notice her and a further two months to phone, and then she decided being easy is no clamour for disrespect anyway, because all men and most of her girlfriends were. The fact that he was cheating on his wife could have moved her if she hadn't asked him to do it. She needed something to base her arrogance on. She needed to be arrogant to take the nervousness away. She could hardly get her eyeliner on, which could have been an omen for the next day when she woke up next to Trent with mascara down her cheeks and half of the skin from her chin missing because Trent hadn't shaved.

One night to solidify God knows how much lust. How do you make twelve hours last twelve hours longer? Trent got it all wrong buying twelve cans, a bottle of vodka, a bottle of wine, two grams of cocaine and a packet of condoms. Candida always did prefer men's minds to their dicks, she just didn't know it yet. 'We could have talked first or something,' she thought. Once it started there was only a mean moment of consciousness when in spoons, Candida caught herself in the mirror, her hand knotted into the back of Trent's short, thick, dark hair. She smiled at her little victory and tightened her grip, then Trent pulled her over, out of view, into piety.

The same mirror that made that night memorable showed Candida to be just a blur of red skin and peroxide curls the morning after and she hardly knew her name, save her realising she had missed Glastonbury 97 for sex she couldn't remember and one might painful coke comedown. Despite a few claw marks in Trent's back and some semen sticking the insides of Candida's thighs together, it seemed like it had never ever happened, when it should have been an adventure for them both. He has that band of gold which snagged the buttocks of her trousers the first night they talked properly at the Wine Bar, and she has a boyfriend in college far away. She hardly remembered where because she hadn't seen a postmark for such a long time, and then she'd fancied Trent far too long to enjoy something so planned out. Or maybe she talked about it far too much because her friends left 'Get Well Soon' cards with smutty comments about Trent inside them, as though the event of her actually sleeping with him meant nothing compared to Glastonbury. She felt insulted, initially.

Perhaps that's how Candida's friends wanted her to feel because none of them ever liked Trent, although they all said that the two of them would make a good couple because they were both complete narcissists.

"'E don' know the difference between real wurld an' dream wurld," Leanne had said.

"Whaddya mean?" Candida asked offendedly.

"Well isnor like SPFB ara signed band'r anythin' isi', bur 'e walks round like 'e's God, like 'e's a millionaire or summink. This is the Rhondda ini'?"

"Bu' you gorra make the most like, treat this place like London, people might start to act liki'. Otherwise I'd be shaggin' the class B wankas you do."

"'E's married anyway inne?" Peggy adds.

"Tha's the problem ini'?" Leanne says. "Alwis revolves around yer men in suits shite."

"Least I don' revolve around a pulse," Candida mutters.

Candida's social life is based inside a flat above a butcher's shop. Everyone who lives there becomes a vegetarian after moving in, out of frustration more than morals. The saw goes through the bone each morning and the shrill sound it makes vibrates up the walls and wakes them up. The bedrooms were once used for storage and the markings of the freezers are still visible, but hidden by Prodigy posters. Penny wakes up in the nights sometimes and relocates to Ian's room, reckoning she can hear bleating and mooing coming from the wardrobe.

Leanne: unemployed, with blunt speech and sharp fists. Ian: unemployed. Ian is a father. He fell in love with a well-known lesbian who fell pregnant. When the baby was born she went back to her girlfriend and sent him a solicitor's letter stating his flat was no place for a baby to be. He never saw them again. Penny: unemployed. The betting shop next door to the butcher's is rumoured to have once run a book on whether Penny would first contract HIV or give birth. Rusty: drug dealer. Rusty has children all over Wales. Candida: student. Candida shares her six GCSEs with her flatmates, two for her and one for each of the others. When she passes her A-levels she's going to Egypt to study Archaeology, apparently.

It was coming on stronger and stronger. Ian was sitting cross-legged right at the edge of the blue-grassed verge. His head was lowering slowly, slowly but surely, his chin thirsting to touch the surface of the translucent water. The river, surrounded by tedious Rhondda valley shrubbery, was visible from the kitchen window in the flat. The dirtiest brown available to the iris, but the smoky, condensated window was not visible from the river. Out there though, in the night, all together, yet far away on your own, the water was clean as a dentist's surgery and smelt like it too. Candida could see Ian falling but couldn't do anything which required voluntary movement or speech. She could be dead, so still and silent, on her side the way she wanted to be buried, just like Madonna. Penny was smiling at something above, laid out flat, her arms smoothly circling the ground around her. Candida closed an eyelid, from camera one Penny looked like the Michaelangelo sketch on at the beginning of *Panorama*. From camera two she looked young and beautiful and it became easy to ignore her shoplifting, compulsive lying, and sex which is way beyond casual habit, just for a moment.

Rusty jumped from the wall he had been balancing on and landed in the centre of the gathering. "Hold on," he shouts. "You can do it, no sleeping now." He claps his hands loudly. "Sit it out boys and girls, we can do it, only 30 ml."

"I'm only lulling," Ian says. It sounds so far away, yet so close. 'Like in Tony's house with his Nicam stereo sound,' Candida thinks, 'the voices of old, dead actors, alive and kicking in his father's living room.' "I love Tony," she says out loud. Faces turn to her, tortoise slow. The members of the flat had an understanding, which Candida never quite understood. They treated each other like sexless human beings, like there was no such thing as a lady or a gentleman. That's not to say they never had sex, they did, but viewed it more as taking and giving what is needed. In fact they treated most outsiders that way too. 'Love' was not a mentionable word. "I mean like one o' you," Candida says, trying to rectify the situation.

"No' one ov us as long as 'e's workin' for Midland Bank on a

Saturday, Cand," Rusty answers. It could have sounded like a serious argument put to Candida on behalf of the flat if Rusty hadn't been saving all his energy to fight the undesirable first effects of valium in order to get the best bits which came after.

Leanne stands up and immediately falls over Penny's protruding leg. "Set iss line up 'en Rust, I'm goin' for i'," Candida says, kneeling and brushing away soil and the odd grass blade.

"Why d'you bother with this fishin' crap, the water's only two inches deep," Penny says before lifting herself up to look for her cigarettes. "Iss cruel anyway."

"Naw, no feelin', issa Nirvana song inni'?" Rusty says. "The last one on *Nevermind.*"

"Nevermind. Nevermind. Nevermind," Ian's voice echoes around the field.

"The bollocks," Leanne screams, having always been more of a punk than a garage fan.

Time for more. Everyone has left their fishing rods and gathered around Rusty to make sure they get their share of the little helpers. Candida doesn't mind though, she's watching the water. She misses Glastonbury this year. It's where they should be now, in a dance tent doing real drugs except ... She feels a pull on her line. It's stuck. Something is caught down there. While she is investigating she becomes adamant it is a man. Something told her so, something spiritual. (Which could just as well be something artificial.) She stands. He stands. She holds her cigarette up still, so does he, waiting for something. She walks to the ledge, he comes closer. His tie has floated to the surface. A burgundy white polka dots affair. She wants to pull him out with it. He's looking at her but however long he looks it's not long enough for her. If she turned away she would forget he had brown eyes. He has car keys. They're shining. He is trying to jingle them but the water is drowning the noise. "Oi, there's someone in the water." Candida is trying to keep the line in place while moving as close to the water as possible.

"Who's in the water, Cand?" someone asks mockingly.

"Trent!" she yelps. "SPFB, Trent fuckin' Morgan." There is a roar of laughter from the other side of the field, but it is too far away to make Candida want to join in. She's putting her hands in the river and before anyone notices water has risen to her elbows.

"Candy!" Leanne screams and they all rush to the edge in a surge of sober energy.

Candida is all in, tangled with the line, kicking and splashing. Everyone is worried and everyone is wet. Candida pokes out her head, smiling, revealing her ugly teeth, water escaping from their gaps. "Trent!" she gasps excitedly and then disappears back down. Splashing and scraping pebbles from beneath. The line is twisting and twisting around her. There are rocks in the way and Candida is kicking them with her water-filled boots. All she can see is Trent and all she can feel is water and mud. Her excitement turns to anger and she returns to the surface to say, "Ger this fuckin' line sorted".

Rusty tries to unravel it but it's difficult when Candida is still kicking. The girls walk into the water, it reaches their mid calves when they're standing. They're pulling Candida out. Leanne has her feet. Penny has her arms. They're all on the verge again. Rusty is still tugging desperately at the line. Does he believe there's a man there now? "Between these bricks," he says, getting into the water and pulling them apart. "Pull e." Ian pulls the line with such force it springs back and whatever is attached to the hook stings Penny's posterior, which is bent over Candida. Candida's eyes search for the end of the line. Everyone catches it simultaneously as its pendulum swings down.

"A clothes peg?" Leanne squeals, matter-of-factly, sounding more disappointed than Candida looks. The boys thought Candida had said it but she was on her side again, panting as though her respiratory system had just failed.

"We'd better go to Glastonbury next year," she whispers. "The grass'll be grown by then won't it?"

Summer 96 inevitably opens up to a cool Autumn and Candida has not mentioned Trent Morgan since she tried to catch breakfast all whacked up on scooby snacks. She has, however, moaned constantly about old Eavis cancelling the festival and spoken frequently about saving pennies in the form of a swear box, for the 1997 event.

Nevertheless, she is there when SPFB platform, late October in the Kit Kat Club because the landlady is short on afternoon profits. She's dressed for Sunday, hangoverish, like a maid of rags who was Cinderella the night before. Ian and Penny followed her to the club, so whilst she welcomed them in with aching muscles she missed Trent arriving in paisley neck tie, Rachtman guitar in hand, amp carried by unknown sycophant. And when she caught him, Ian and Penny were too busy downing no.1 drink of the day to notice Candida's eyes fill up with dirty, unwanted water.

Candida felt queasy but she wasn't sure whether the onslaught of last night's 'bad for your health' concoctions were actually the symptoms of it. Between Candida's resented sightings of the ladies' loo and her shrinking violet glimpses of Trent Morgan's pupils, Penny begins to feel an unnatural energy around her friend, stopping her from being able to touch Candida. It is a familiar feeling but Penny tries her best to ignore it. Nobody really wants to know what it is because haves and haven'ts burn with jealousy and pride in equal phenomenal amounts among Candida's friends. It is hushed up and shrugged away with polite sarcasm each time it rears its unwanted head.

"Shoes," Penny injects into Candida's nervously divided attention. "Look at those fuckin' Gucci shoes." She is looking at Trent's feet, her eye level five foot lower that Candida's. "Supersonic Pop Fat Bastards. That's what SPFB stands for, Cand."

Ian had left by the time SPFB were cleaning up and I had drunk enough lager not to notice that Candida had said, "C'mon Pen, let's go down the front". We had moved closer and closer to the stage and suddenly it was too late. We were leaning against the egotistical cunt's amp when Candida revealed her lack of being able to hold alcohol by shouting, "Le's 'ave a fag 'en Trent" at the Morgan bastard. Instead of telling Candy to fuck off and smoke her own like I thought he would, the wanker squeezed between us and held out his mint packet of Embassy, then waited for Candida to strike up a bit more conversation. She came out with the 'good gig' crap that she says to most musos and for a moment I thought that she was seriously trying to chat the insurance, accountant, whatever he is... up. But then she ran out of stuff to say and crinkled up like she wanted him to go away again. He went. Safe again, except Candy kept on shouting for more cigarettes, even though she had plenty. He left his packet on the amp and counted them now and again when passing. Then she got all tetchy and wanted to go home. I told her that she should just ask him for it if she wanted him that bad, like I used to when me and Rusty were half an item, not that I wanted that shirt-and-tie arsehole shagging one of mine, but he wouldn't so it didn't matter what Candida said. In fact she did the right thing, walking out, not saying anything, with the dickhead's fags in her combat trousers pocket.

Candida found it difficult to turn the taps. She needed a bath to wash the chemicals away, the chemical laden depression, the chemical degrained skin, the chemical laden muscles which would not work, the chemical feeling of Trent's chemical body all over her chemical body. She rubs the soap from her navel into the centre of her breasts in a make do straight line, the way he had snorted. "Make love," he called it. Changing words and phrases to different phrases and words to make yourself sound different. A bit like changing 'whizz' to 'amphetamine' so that it becomes acceptable for a fully grown adult to take it. It doesn't work, and he changes 'fuck' to 'make love' so that it doesn't sound as dirty as it actually is. She takes a mouthful of her tepid bath water in an attempt to rid herself of the taste of stale tobacco and vomit.

Trent reminded Candida of herself too much. That was probably the reason they ended up in that hotel room last night. She had thought for a month or two of coffee dates and floral gifts that she and Trent had been on the same wavelength, a higher one than the usual eat, sleep, shit existences which make up ninety per cent of the Rhondda Valley. And then twelve inseparable hours had come along and shown her how naive they both were.

She misses her flat mates for a moment. They'll be on the train home, cold and muddy, queuing for a bath in less than two hours with their Glastonbury 97 programmes, and there Candida is, using the last of the water.

Once the inhabitants of the flat above the butcher's had grown bored of teasing Candida about meeting John Peel in the Green Field and their ridiculous hats, life as they knew it resumed. Saturday came round again and they dressed themselves for their usual nightclub in their usual Tonypandy location.

Rusty has been out since dawn, 'working'. When Penny,

Candida and Leanne arrive at the club the first girl converses with him at the bar in a series of nods, grins, smiles and thumbs-ups.

"Drizabone for powda tonight, Cand," he says on her return to her seat. She waits for a sore reaction but Candida's attention is with a jigsaw of cigarette papers under the table. "Looks like it's a lager and marijuana night then, girls," Candida eventually shrugs her shoulders tightly so as not to disturb the carefully-placed loose tobacco.

"Old days," Leanne smirks, banging her empty pint glass on the next table before making for a refill.

Ian and Rusty are piggy banking around the dance floor to Rage Against the Machine when Trent enters with his wife, but all eyes are dreamily fixed on the acrobatics. Leanne produces a bottle of poppas. Candida goes first, both nostrils. The music gets louder and the faces get smaller. She doesn't recognise Ian and Rusty returning, exhausted. Beautiful Amyl Nitrate black. She wakes to Penny squealing, "The Charlatans suck," to the change of song.

"You ever notice 'ow 'Country Boy' sounds like ar gypsies song Cher done?" Candida asks, as though it is a serious subject she has been considering for some time. They see each other laughing but can only hear themselves. "Le's get some decent stuff on," Candida pushes out of the wooden tables and makes her way to the DJ. "Gor any decent music on ewe then?"

"Like wha'?" he asks, pupils dilated.

"How bow Catatonia?"

"No Catatonia beaut, they're Man U."

"So wha'?" she says. "Wales' finest an yew won' play 'em cos they're Man U. If I was Liverpudlian askin' fuh Catatonia, you'd tell me to fuck off cos I'se English."

"Fuckin' right," he says, with the corners of his mouth facing upwards.

"Fuckin' ipocrit," Candida laughs.

On her way back to the table she is tapped on the shoulder by Richard I Love You. "Candeedar."

'Fuck off,' she thinks, looking back at the DJ in SOS mode while a cigarette is lit for her. Richard I Love You places a glass in her hand. "I'm nor shorts tonight, Rich." She tries to move but he's pinned her into a recess. She's tense for a moment, then she bolts the vodka, hands him back the glass and loosens to her Catatonia tune. She's not listening to Richard I Love You but he is speaking. She nods and shakes her head in what she thinks are the right places.

She has noticed Trent but only vaguely. He is standing directly in front of her, his head over the back of his wife's shoulder, winking and smiling at her, but Candida is looking through his eyes. They're not brown any more, they're not even there. Candida is stoned-serene and at the fading of a song she hears one of Richard I Love You's anecdotes come to an end ... "It's funny how things turn out isn't it, Candeedar?"

"Yes it is, Rich," she says, staring down the pillar behind and visible through Trent. "It's funny how things turn out, how a year ago the only thing we had in common was cigarettes, now we're both sad valley people trying to make out we're not. Funny how I'm proud suddenly to be smoking my own fags." She could have been speaking, or perhaps only thinking, in either case it wasn't directed at Richard I Love You.

A hand pokes through the crowd and suddenly Candida is arm in arm in arm with Ian and Penny, being dragged to the dance floor.

"My friends," she smiles, "'ave alwis been the same."

THE ISLAND

Sharon V. Rowe

Swathed in a golden light, the island breaks through the ocean and stands as an illusion. I'm almost a mother and still my childish mind creates this perfection, complete in its utter enchantment. She is clothed in a green cape, an empress crowned by the stars lifting her head in majestic magnificence, and I am left in awe of what I can never become. Imperfect in my bloodied mind.

The Faraway Tree became my first escape. Blyton never mentioned me in the text, but I was there, climbing the tree with Bessie, Fanny and Jo. Together we went to the lands of *do-as-you-please* and *take-what-you-want*; I ate the *pop biscuits* and slid the *slippery slip* to the bottom of the tree. But by the age of ten the magic island had captivated me, and Enid Blyton was placed on the shelf to become grey with dust and time.

Rhys and I would sit together in the big field opposite my home. In front of us, the infinite sea; behind us, the endless road. He would point into the distance, 'Look look, can you see?'

'See what?' I would answer impatiently. 'What, what?' I knew he was looking at something alluring, and desperately I would scan the horizon. It didn't matter how long I would yell at him 'show me,' 'it's not fair,' or 'why can't I see too?' because *I* could never see the rugged cliffs and the green meadows of the island. And so the fairy folk became exclusive to Rhys, and I would sit with my head bowed and eyes closed imagining the blue water glittering in the sunlight where dolphins leapt high to turn and twist with elation.

'It's like heaven,' I once said, my mind full of the dreamy and seductive magic.

'I'm lucky. I know the secret. Wish I could tell you, but can't.' I heard some satisfaction in his voice, but on reflection it was probably my own paranoia.

Time had motioned her hand and was passing me by. My mind was slowly closing; becoming dry and brittle as adulthood progressed.

Dave was scruffy and unshaven. Not my type at all. But he was intelligent, and more importantly, successful. That attracted me. Lynne, our mutual agent, suggested we meet. She wanted him to see my illustrations. 'If you don't take the plunge now,' she said, 'You never will.'

I told him he might find them dull, flat and somewhat lifeless; incomparable to his writer's mind. He took them from me offering a slight wink of encouragement, or maybe it was just flirtation. Then silence as he sat with the pictures in his hands and his eyes turned downwards. Expressionlessly, he sipped slowly at his coffee; my own large mug was beginning to grow cold. The sound of my breathing was irregular, my hand shook; and then, after about 15 minutes of torture, Dave looked at me. His eyes held a seriousness I found intimidating. But then unexpectedly he broke into a huge grin.

'Dull, flat! But these are tremendous. Just look at the richness of these colours. You have the eye for it, you really do.' He looked at me slyly, 'enchantress,' he quietly whispered; and flattered, I reddened.

'I already have the story in my mind. It came to me as I looked at your drawings. Leave them with me,' he begged; and not being able to resist his sultry but somewhat manipulative eyes, I agreed wholeheartedly.

'Fantastic. Look Sarah, we've got something big here. I know it. Oh god, these little people, they're just perfect.'

'Fairies not people,' I interjected. Correcting him, but not too assertively.

'They're just like flowers, and the wind has become not just visible, but almost tangible.' Intently, he looked me in the eye, almost seeing too much. I became embarrassed. From which direction this feeling arose, I was not sure, and why he thought the illustrations so beautiful, I really could not fathom. I had every belief he could write an exquisite story. He did have a great reputation. But an audience! I could not imagine it. Not for this.. Rhys had never needed to share, so why should I? Yet something still stopped me from ruining Dave's enthusiasm. Or more importantly, the attention he was paying me. His invasion frightened me, but I could not deny that I found him, and it, exciting.

'Let's have another drink,' he suggested, 'Something a little stronger. Cold coffee is not at all sexy.'

Business was turning into leisure and another drink would surely steady my nerves. 'Yes... Yes, let's,' I sounded a lot more confident than I felt. 'But somewhere else. This place is a little stuffy.' We needed intimacy. Intimacy stirred with the confusion of alcohol and lust. Only one avenue lay open to us, and we found ourselves in the corner of a quiet and dimly lit pub. The city dived into night. Drink fuddled my mind and the heart of London dreamt and reminisced of childhood. As we fell asleep shortly before night broke into a dawn of orange haze, it felt perfectly natural to reach out and push my fingers through his hair. In darkness I was human again, but I was all too aware that daylight would soon be upon us.

Sleep becomes confused with wakefulness. A child enters someone else's dream and sees the life of another. I lose myself in tangled sargasso's, the webs of dusty nights.

He is alive in my dreams while I am slumbering. No longer dead. Momentarily, the pain disappears. Not like reality; too good, too perfect. Dreamt that he took me there. We sat in a rowing boat, the sea like a millpond, and all around me the straight line of the horizon with no break of land. Silence filled the air, raucous in its noiselessness. Rhys, in a trance, watched the island. 'We're not far away now,' I was quietly told.

Out of the clear crystalline water appeared dolphins. Ten, twenty of them circling the boat, swimming and breaching as if in sheer joy, over our heads and inches from our noses. Creatures of precision, twice our size with immeasureable power. I laughed loudly as they encouraged me and pure excitement filled the air. This was the gift the dolphins bought to me on that wide empty sea. They moved in front, almost as if guiding and protecting us from treacherous waters.

'Close your eyes tight,' Rhys instructed me. No longer seeing the dolphins, I listened for their splashes and breathed quietly with them as water shot from their blowholes. It began to rain with heavy spots. I felt them fall on my face; and I pictured the island as Rhys began to describe it to me. He put his arms around me and held me tight.

'The land of the fairies is in front of us now.' The colours formed in my mind and shapes began to emerge. The raindrops fell so hard they almost hurt. 'It's a small island,' he continued. 'Only about a mile by half a mile but the cliffs are steep. At some points they fall almost vertically into the sea.'

I was dying to open my eyes but it was out of the question. The raindrops fell down my neck and my damp back ached. On the island were many valleys and some of them could be seen from the boat. Rhys told me of all the colours strewn across the rolling hills; I tried to guess what flowers they were. 'You can't,' Rhys said. 'These flowers only grow on *their* island.' Rare pine trees were also dotted on the hillsides, there was not a cloud in the sky and the sun was shining brightly up above. A world on its own; precious and haunting.

'I can see the fairies,' he said. 'They are dressed in bright colours and are waving to me.'

I pictured them standing on the cliff tops, waving across the sea, looking like flowers dancing in the wind.

The cat jumped on the bed meowing very loudly, deciding unfairly, I felt, it was time I awoke.

'At last,' I sighed, folding the newspaper and placing it back on the table in front of me. Taking a sip from my mug of coffee I reached out for the paper, obsessively re-opening it to the page that contained a large coloured picture of the island. It sat amidst a Caribbean blue sea. The sun, again, was shining; and the flowers were painted in bright colours. At the bottom right hand corner, in small, but very black letters were the words, 'illustrated by Sarah Sealey.'

'Chandler's rich storytelling,' I read, 'and Sealey's dreamlike vision marry to create a poetically vibrant and ingenious tale of an imaginary place that has the ability to be alive in us all, whatever our age.'

The sickness rose from my stomach to my throat. Fear gripped me. I'd never aspired to achievements; or more worrying, its obligations.

'Have you read it?' Lynne queried on the other end of the telephone wire. This was her achievement too, and she thrived on it. 'Dave's ecstatic. You're both gonna get that award you know. Damn right too. I've been fishing around the judges. They don't give much away, but I did get a couple of hints and they like it y'know. Now you've got a month or so to suss out what you're going to say in your acceptance speech and don't forget to say "thank you" to me; remember, I bought you two together. Right, what I rang for; drinks tonight to celebrate your first great review. May there be many more. My place, be there.' With that she hung up, and I was left aghast.

My isolation, my cocoon, was to be invaded. Apart from the night with Dave, I had lived the past year since Rhys's death with only his ghost and my cat. This was the beginning. The start of something big, and all the while Rhys lay silent and dead, arms tight round *her*. At night-time, in dreams I watch them like a shameless voyeur.

Three hours later, I sat silently with a glass of red wine, hoping not to be noticed. I spoke blindly to people, not aware of their words. I drank glass after glass and watched Dave as he mingled, and I left quietly before he reached my corner of the room.

I'm afraid they'll see it glistening in my hand, beautiful yet deadly. I'll watch them blame me for my guilt as horror colours faces and hate forms in mouths.

'That'll blow the cobwebs away,' I could almost hear Rhys's voice whispering in the wind that swirled and swept, rummaging through my body and my head. It was Saturday afternoon and behind me the tall grass blew backwards and forwards like long lithe yellow and green bodies dancing the salsa. In contours they stretched their way across the landscape rustling like paper tearing through a shredder. This is the sound of the wind. All around me seagulls cry as they search for carrion. In the distance a gannet balanced and poised, not moving against the powerful wind, tail arched and wings spread prepared himself to dive in pursuit of an unfortunate fish below. Watching its descent, and its powerful impact; I held onto the cliff, so the wind would not blow me away. Regretfully, I knew that the gannet would go blind one day and then die, no longer able to plummet into the sea after food. 'It happens to them all,' Rhys once told me.

I listened and heard the sound of the wind moving with haste through the green and blue sparkling sea. White peaks formed, raging with the elements and smashing the jutting rocks on the horizon. I almost mistake this sight for a giant whale breaching. The sun splatters a path on the water like a road paved with gold. It ends on the jagged cliff-face of Ramsey. Along this path a single boat heads towards the island. 'The farmer,' I thought. Only one farmer lived on Ramsey and I had seen him earlier loading up his boat with slabs of lager and crates of wine. Now he's heading back to the solitude with his supplies of enjoyment. Dotted around Ramsey are smaller islands, silhouetted against the horizon. All are jagged and some have steep, dangerous cliffs and headlands. But none have the bewitching beauty of the green valleys, coloured flowers or the pine trees of Rhys's island.

I looked out to sea scanning and trying to see just as I had done many times as a child, and I returned to reality with the bells of the cathedral. I could not find the island but I did see a small neat dorsal fin slice the water. It seemed right to see a dolphin. Just like my dream.

The next day was Sunday, a year to the day my lover died, and I sat in the pouring rain surrounded by dense fog and strangers at 7.00am in a matchbox boat on the uninviting sea. I stretched my hands in front and was barely even able to see my fingertips. How would I spot the dolphins? Little did I know how easily they would find me. The dreariness contrasted Rhys's sun-drenched magical island. The day before had been gusty and bright, but the weather had changed drastically. It did not affect the skipper who seemed jolly, so I tried my best to scan the blemished seas, or what I could see of them. We were placed strategically north, south, east and west on the deck. Most of us had our anoraks over our eyes and our heads buried between our legs to prevent not only the rain but also the seawater from pouring over the side of the boat and drenching our faces. The dolphins found us and when I heard lots of screaming and excited feet running across the deck I knew that like my dream, the dolphins were leaping, twisting and bow riding inches from the speeding boat. The smallest mishap could prove fatal, but they were much too precise for that. I ran to the bow and leant over the side almost touching the sleek mammal below. Turning on its side, the eye was visible. Time stood still. I felt warmth and security. My mind faced the pain and I remembered the crimson arm, knuckles clenched white.

Lithe limbs stretched upon my bed. Cold eyes wandered in my direction. Moist lips freshly kissed, vaguely upturned and slightly ajar mocked my presence, my home and my life. I left as silently as I had entered, then nosily cried.

Washed through and cleansed, I returned an hour later to listen as he told me of his day. *She* had obviously kept quiet because he never found out we'd met. After that I conceived that every event was possibly the last. The end inevitable; the pain determined. I never envisaged the macabre outcome that followed.

I reached over the side of the boat and continued to meet the dolphins' gaze. I was left with a mindful of confused words and illusive meanings.

'St David's,' he murmured. 'Go home, Sarah, stand on the mossy grass, down by St Justinian's. You will see it.'

'At last,' I breathed. He wanted to appease me or maybe he just knew I could do it. Then just days later he was gone. All I needed to do was take one step out the door and face life alone.

As we headed back towards land, I noticed that the mists were clearing and the sun was desperately clambering through the clouds. After climbing off the boat I said 'goodbye' to my fellow dolphin watchers and headed back to my hotel. I needed to make a phone call.

'Hi, Lynne, it's me.'

'Sarah, where are you? I've been trying to get hold of you for days,' Lynne scolded.

'I'm in West Wales. I've come home for a while. Needed to get away, think about...'

'Oh a little holiday,' she mocked, cutting me off. 'How nice. But listen, you've got to come back. Firstly because the prize- giving is on Thursday and you have to be there; and secondly, we need another book A.S.A.P! Dave's working on a story right now. It's about dolphins or something. We need you, *Please*.'

Why did they need me so badly? There are other illustrators. But *dolphins*; it was meant to be. I'd do it.

'Is he really holding out for me?' I asked slyly.

'Of course he is. He won't work with anyone else now, darling.'

'Okay. Look tell him, tell him, I'll be home tonight......'

I had only a few days to prepare. Lynne thought we were going to win. For the first time I hoped she was right. We deserved it. We'd worked damn hard. Dave and I had listened to one another, felt and drunk the sadness from each other's skin. Now we would stand next to each other, as a team. Dave would speak first and I would follow:

'I had an image in my mind,' I would explain. 'A place of solitude, somewhere to escape, to run away from the world. Because of Lynne Edwards, my agent; and Dave Chandler, my partner in crime, this island has become real for many children, whose minds crave those timeless, flawless places.

I am indebted to you all, for your support and encouragement. Dave and I are both thankful for the honour of this prize and hope that in our next story we can continue to keep the magic alive.'

I would turn to Dave, as the audience applauds; and maybe, just maybe he'd wink, so I'd know he understands and forgives. But maybe I'm wrong and he will not.

I leave my hotel and drive through Newgale Sands and St David's, back at St Justinian's. Things are slightly different and have changed. The cliffs hang rugged and still beside the road and the beaches and alcoves fall away into the distance like tropical lands. I stand on the mossy grass among the cliff tops. An innately spiritual building sits in the distance behind me. I look out to sea and feel the child move inside me. I'm pregnant with life and success. There in the distance I see an island with rolling hills and green valleys.

It's time to face my part in his death, the salvation and my loneliness. I see my island of escape, of peace and of freedom. As I look harder I can see pine trees and even tiny brightly adorned flowers, and when I squint I swear they are waving to me; and they really are, just like flowers dancing in the wind.

KING OF WALES

Brian Smith

You may have seen my butty, Leon, King of Wales. That is if you've ever been in the centre of Cardiff on a weekday, round by the Capitol or in The Hayes. If you have seen him, and he's pretty memorable, you'll have heard him too. After all, a tall, skinny, black bloke wearing a crown and spouting from an upturned beer crate isn't something you're likely to forget now, is it? One thing's for certain, you won't have seen me in the vicinity, not these days. No, I'm waiting for the big one, the event that's going to make my mate famous and put Wales on the front pages world-wide.

Leon was always a bit different, right from when I first got to know him in Canton Infants. He was black for one thing and although there's plenty of black Cardiffians over in Butetown, what they've now started calling the Bay area, he was a bit of a novelty in Canton. He lived with his mother who was white and rather refined; not the type of mam the rest of us were used to. She was a North Walian, a Gog, and she spoke Welsh. I found out by accident one day when I was round there and she was speaking to someone on the phone.

"She foreign then, your Mam?" I asked him later, out their back.

"That was Welsh, Christopher," he'd said, "our native tongue. My mother's from Gwynedd, descended from princes."

We were only about eight but Leon always spoke like a grown-up. Dead posh too.

Me, I'm as Kaairdiff as a pint of Brains or faggots and peas in the market and all this malarkey goes over my head at the time. Looking back now I suppose that Leon must have grown up with this "man of destiny" thing in his background, taken it in with his mother's milk like.

"Cor, do you speak it too?" was all I could think to ask at the time.

"Of course, it's my birthright," he'd answered.

When I got home I remember asking my mother why it was that we lived in the capital of Wales and didn't speak Welsh.

"'Cos your father's lot are from somewhere over in the west of England and my family came here from County Clare." All this in Mam's lovely Cardiff tones.

Leon's mother was Miss Llywelyn but Leon was Leon King on the register at school. Yeah, I know .... seems a bit of a coincidence, doesn't it? They didn't have anything to do with his dad but my mate had taken his father's surname and his old man had chosen Leon too. He was Jamaican apparently. "No royal connections as far as we can determine," Leon had explained to me when I'd expressed an interest. "Although we do know that his family were taken to the West Indies from The Gambia and that chieftains were highly prized by the slavers so he may well have come from a sort of African *uchelwyr* originally."

Bloody hell! I knew enough from being around Leon that *"uchelwyr"* meant sort of lords and ladies. Made me feel dead common that did. Bog Irish on one side and Mummerset yokels on the other.

We laughed and scrapped our way through primary school, me and Leon, and we remained friends at the comprehensive. It was a bit more difficult there, what with Leon being black, opinionated, clever .... and let's face it, as far as most of the other kids were concerned, a real oddball. Luckily for him he was a good sportsman and in Wales you can get away with being intelligent if you can hack it physically. Leon was tall, sort of gangly looking but incredibly well co-ordinated. Basketball was his main game in school and after his mam bought him a table one Christmas, he developed into a pretty mean pool player too.

We were in the Sixth Form when *The Lion King* came out. He approached me in the Common Room, waving the film page of the local paper under my nose.

"We have to see it, Chris. This weekend if you can make it."

Leon is one of those people who speak loudly and confidently at all times and seem unaware or unconcerned that others may be listening in. I tried to shush him but it was already too late.

"Leon King ....the lion king. I feel it may be a sign. My destiny beckons, Christopher."

Disney films are very definitely uncool when you're seventeen. I was as embarrassed as Mr. Pink in *Reservoir Dogs* but Leon took the jeers and catcalls in his stride, as proud as Caradog paraded through the streets of Rome.

My two sisters had an unexpected treat that Saturday afternoon. It wasn't often big brother took them to the pictures so they made the most of it ………. popcorn, drinks, icecream, hot dogs. Cost me a fortune. Still, they provided my excuse if anyone saw us and Leon insisted on sharing the expense so it wasn't too bad. I'll admit to enjoying the film as well. Sentimental old tosh but quite moving somehow, the way the fatherless cub overcomes all obstacles and succeeds to his kingdom.

I could hardly believe Leon's reaction. For the first time ever I saw him speechless. He hardly said a word on the bus home and he was still in a state of subdued excitement the next day when I went round for a game of pool and some help with my history essay. They say that books have the power to change people's lives, but a Disney movie, a product of the Hollywood dream factory? He told me he was going to see the film again that night, this time with is mother in tow. And before I left he read me part of a poem by Iolo Goch. It was in Welsh and concerned Owain Glyn Dwr, one of Leon's many heroes from the past. He translated it for me but the only bit that made much sense was *un Pen ar Gymru*…… the sole head of Wales.

"That's what's needed you see, Chris, one person, a figurehead the whole country can unite under."

I think I probably smiled and nodded. Leon was into politics in a pretty big way for a Sixth Former, leastways a Sixth Former in our old school, it may have been different in the Welsh-medium Comps. Most of us were vaguely left-wing but mostly apathetic. I suppose the only political action I took at that time was to buy a copy of *The Big Issue* every now and then. Leon devoured newspapers, watched current affairs programmes, knew about policies in the same way the rest of us kept up to date with Oasis and The Manic Street Preachers. He'd flirted with Welsh Nationalism and was dead keen on the establishment of a Welsh Assembly. Once, he'd even shown me some bomb-making instructions he'd downloaded from the Internet. "Dangerous things, computers," he'd said, " I think, on the whole, I'm in favour of a ban." The Plaid Cymru thing hadn't lasted. "Too socialist and too exclusive and I can't come to terms with the contradiction," had been his verdict. Myself, I reckon it had more to do with him being rebuffed by this student member he fancied. He never had much luck that way.

Midway through that week he came to me with part one of his masterplan and asked if I'd be willing to help. It was time, he said, to convince the people of Wales that what they needed was a monarch and with *his* ancestry *he* was the prime candidate. He was descended in direct line from the princes of Gwynedd and there was indirect connections to those of Powys and Deheubarth. It was his destiny.

"We've already got a prince of Wales," I told him.

"Yes, part German, part Greek and wholly English," he said. "At least I was born in Wales of Welsh stock, and I'm talking about a king rather than a mere prince."

The whole idea was crazy but curiously exciting and in the end I let him talk me round. Referendums, devolution . . . they were the first step . . . . . what Wales really needed was a Monarchist party and a royal personage who would provide the unity and stability to guide the country into the unknown territory of the twenty-first century!

"And look at this!" he demanded, taking out a crown from the M & S bag he had in his hand. "Pretty cool, don't you think?"

'Cool' was not one of Leon's words and I soon twigged he was being ironic. It was crown-shaped all right and had some purple velvet behind the gold-painted stiff card but basically it looked like what it was . . . . . a prop from the Drama room.

"It will do nicely as an initial symbol and it should help to attract attention. What do you think?"

"Great," I said, "when do we start?" Inside I was trembling. This was going to be far worse than queueing outside the Odeon with a couple of little girls.

"Saturday, by the tea-stall in The Hayes."

"Bad idea," I said. "It's where John Lennon's vanished."

"What are you talking about, Christopher?"

"His independence," I replied, "it seemed to vanish in the

haze." I laughed, inviting him to join me. Normally he would have but this time he just looked hurt.

"Sorry," I said. "You'll need something to stand on. We've got this old plastic beer crate in our glory-hole. I'll dust it down."

So it was that The King of Wales first got up on his soapbox in the year of our Lord 1995 in the centre of Cardiff. He addressed the populace first in English, then in fluent Welsh, appealing to their latent sense of national identity and proclaiming his royal ancestry. He alone was the future of Wales, and, as soon as he had the funds, he would commission the creation of the Welsh crown jewels, crafted from the red gold of Dolau Cothi. It was heady stuff.

Me, I was skulking in the entrance to Waterstone's, pretending I wasn't with him yet hanging on his every word. Charismatic is what he was, part preacher part Nye Bevan. At first people ignored him, sailed past as if he were just another loony. Then a crowd gathered, kids at first, attracted by the crown; older people joined them and as they listened they seemed to fall under his spell. He spoke about "The Matter of Britain" . . . . . King Arthur, and all that. Then he went on to Rhodri Mawr, Llywelyn and Glyn Dwr . . . . . . and this was the killer, the Welsh prophetic poetry that spoke about a saviour, a *Mab Dorogan* who would end foreign rule and restore Welsh sovereignty. It seemed to strike a chord but, at more or less the same time, disaster struck.

A group of boys, teenage and twenties, began barracking Leon, heckling him and generally taking the piss. He held his own for a while, giving as good as he got until one of them called: "How can you be king of Wales? You're bloody black as the ace of spades?"

I held my breath. This is what I had been dreading.

Leon was truly majestic. He threw back his head and declared that if anyone wished to challenge his claim he must beat him at fencing, shooting, one on one basketball and pool, starting with pool.

The pool table in The Old Arcade was free and my 50p released the balls for the game. I was holding the beer crate and the M & S carrier so I had no part in the side bets. All I can remember is this boy with bad acne making the break and declaring that a tenner was at stake.

The game was over in about ten minutes. I think the fight lasted about two before the bar staff jumped in and threw us all outside. We tussled on the pavement for a while until our attackers seemed content that we'd both had a good tuning and were no longer a threat to the status quo. I glanced over at Leon's bloody face and threw him the carrier bag. "Here," I said, "you're still monarch of all you survey, but don't expect me to fight for the crown next fucking weekend." My nose was beginning to swell, my ribs hurt and I was pretty pissed off.

Leon's puffy face contorted into a smile. "Pity," he said, "I was considering making you my Minister of Defence."

We clung to each other then, giggling like maniacs, and didn't stop until we parted company outside his house back in Canton.

Things had altered though. They always do. At least for us mere mortals. I came face to face with the fact that I was ordinary. That I didn't have enough commitment for politics, not even when it was my best friend who was involved. Passing my 'A' levels, having a good time, finding a girlfriend, not getting beaten up . . . . . these things began to look more desirable . . . . . and easier. We didn't quarrel, just sort of drifted apart. Leon even listened to my advice and only took his soapbox into town on weekdays. No chilling out in the Common Room for him, every free period he was up in town pumping out his monarchist message, gaining perhaps one or two converts, making a handful of people reconsider what it was they really believed. Occasionally I'd go down and listen in. Always in the background, mind, and feeling a strange mixture of excitement and embarrassment.

We both passed our exams. I went up North to Gog-land . . . . . Bangor to be precise . . . and Leon stayed at home, studying Economics in Cardiff. He still went out on the stump, drumming up support for his dream of a nation united under his rule. He formed The Welsh Monarchist Society at college and attracted a small crew of romantics . . . . . sort of Welsh medievalist revolutionaries I suppose . . . . who churned out leaflets and acted as a sort of royal court cum bodyguard when he addressed the populace.

There's Mali who seems to worship him and is like a royal consort and queen in waiting. And Geraint, a wild ginger-haired bard from West Wales who deals with publicity and is handy with his fists. There are others too, drawn by Leon's personality and unerring vision, the belief that he generates in the future of Wales and his own part in that future. I sat in pubs with them during my weekends at home and after a drink or two I could almost share their passion. Leon was a good man. He was more a Welsh patriot than a nationalist and his vision of Wales was one that reached out to people. It was inclusive, a positive ideal rather than some sort of last-ditch linguistic defence against perfidious Albion. He seemed to care about the whole of Wales and he made monarchy sound respectable . . . . . even radical. But in the sober light of day I'd find myself wondering how I could be so naïve. If Wales had a separate future it was as an independent republic in a federal Europe, not some crazy Ruritanian kingdom of happy peasants and workers!

I was back at home for the last International at the Arms Park and for the first time since our initial outing Leon had decided to try a weekend rally. He was there in his usual pitch by the Hayes and, never one to duck an issue, he addressed the crowd on race and nationality: "Can a man be black and Welsh?" He answered the question to his own satisfaction. If Nigel Walker can play rugby for Wales and Colin Jackson can win Olympic medals for Wales then of course a man can be black and Welsh. Thus it must follow that a man with an impeccable Welsh pedigree, who just happens to be black, must be a legitimate Welshman.

His rhetoric was superb but even to me, an observer on the edge of things, it was obvious that those who considered themselves Welsh saw his blackness first and those who were black thought he was too Welsh!

Later that day he put the same question to me. "Can a blackman be truly Welsh, Chris? Welsh enough to rule?"

"Don't ask me," I said, "I'm a bloody mongrel, part English, part Irish. *You've* more claim to Welshness than I have. I'm Kaairdiff but I really dunno if I qualify as Welsh." I was already a bit tired and emotional.

Leon's reply has remained with me, a sort of talisman against doubt. "Anyone born within the boundaries of Wales, no matter what his or her ancestry, Welsh speaking or monoglot English, can claim to be *Cymraeg*." He went on to speak about a Welsh patriotism that was universal, based on social justice and a view of Wales that was free, independent and royalist. Despite the fact we'd just lost to the old enemy . . . . or maybe because of it, Leon's words once again managed to stir my soul. Bugger democracy . . . . to hell with the media élitists who seem to hold all the power in this benighted country of ours. What Wales really needed was a benevolent despot with royal blood in his veins. I had a hell of a hangover the following morning.

Times change. The UK elected a new government in May, promises have been made and decentralisation seems to be on the agenda. A referendum will be held and Wales looks as if it might have its own Assembly at last. I went back to Cardiff over the summer and was pleased to see that Leon had retained his sense of humour. He's got a transit van he uses for student removals...... Cathays to Roath, Newport Road to Penarth, that sort of thing. I suppose it earns him a few bob and pays for printing his leaflets. On the side in Celtic lettering, it reads: *King Of Wales.*

I tackled him about the future and that's when he revealed his secret weapon.

"What's going to happen," I said, "when we vote for a separate Assembly and with a bit of luck we take the first steps towards a Welsh Parliament?"

"That, Christopher, is when I intend to come into my own. That's when I'm going to need the support of friends like you, when Leon, King of Wales, can no longer be dismissed as a fantasist or a buffoon but becomes a threat to the present ruling class."

I looked for the sly smile, the raised eyebrow, anything that would indicate irony. There was nothing. He meant every word. He was just like he'd been the time we'd taken my sisters to the cinema. Intense, purposeful, yet calm.

"What've you got planned, some sort of monarchist coup?" I tried to raise a laugh.

"I hope it won't come to that," he said. And then, thankfully, he did smile. "You're one of my oldest friends, Chris. I know you've doubted in the past but I know in my heart you'll be true and my heart grows tender towards you. Come and look what I've got in the shed."

I remembered those computer printouts he'd shown me years ago and I went cold. Not bombs, God, don't let it be bombs. I followed him down the path to the end of his mother's garden and there, in amongst the plant-pots and garden implements and the smell of oil and compost, I witnessed a revelation, a marvel.

Reverently, and in a sort of cathedral hush, he plucked away an old, stained sheet. There, in a huge and weathered block of granite was Arthur's sword, Excalibur. I knew at once it wasn't a fake. It was too real, too massive, too fucking magnificent.

Leon smiled again. "*Caledwlch*," he said, his voice caressing the word. "It's been in the family for generations but until now the time has never been right. Try to pull it, Chris."

The air about me seemed charged with enchantment and this garden shed in Canton could have been Camelot or Avalon. With a mystical sense of awe I grasped the hilt and heaved. It would not stir.

Leon stepped forward then and with one hand, lightly and fiercely, he pulled the sword from the stone. He held it for a moment as if weighing its power and majesty before thrusting it back into its sheath of rock.

So, you can see what I mean about waiting for the big one, the event that's going to change the history of Wales forever. Just imagine the scene. Outside that new assembly building and with the entire nation watching, Leon will unfurl the banner of *y Draig Goch* and draw the sword of Arthur from its magical stone. The world's press in attendance, TV cameras rolling . . . . I intend to be there on that momentous day, and not skulking in the background either.

PAYDAY

Nigel Duke

"Go on, chum", said the first voice, cockney.

RAT - TAT - A - RAT - TAT ... TAT - TAT!

"Yeah mate, you'll feel better," said the second, Australian.

The boy released the heavy brass knocker having hammered out his customary greeting. He waited, his ear pressed tight to the door of the tiny, Valleys terraced house. No answer.

"Aye, we'll help ye, don't worry", added the third, Scots.

"Try again son, he's probably got the telly on too loud or he's out the back or something."

"Sir! We cannot allow this! I protest! I protest most strongly!", said the fourth, English Public School, young.

"Ok, Dad.." The boy once more stretched up on tiptoe, grasped the lion's head that gleamed in the bright summer sun and repeated his staccato message. RAT - TAT -A - RAT - TAT ... TAT - TAT! Again he waited. Still no answer. Concern made the young face look suddenly old.

"We cannot allow what, Lieutenant? I don't see anything ... and neither do you. Clear? Dismissed!", concluded the fifth voice, the same open, rounded tones but older, much older.

"Hold on a minute, Davey, let's have a look-see." The young man went to the window and, using his hands to shade his eyes, peered into the cluttered little room. The room was filled to overflowing with Japanese artefacts, a curious mixture of the old and the new, the past and the future. The walls were decked with exquisite silks depicting the isolated splendour of mountaintop pagodas too beautiful to be real, where long-limbed herons gracefully dipped spearpointed beaks into gently rippling water and cherry blossoms allowed their ethereal blooms to float endlessly to a soil happy to receive them. Glass-fronted cabinets contained blue and white teapots and sake bowls and tiny white-faced No dancers that threatened to shatter their porcelain if you looked at them too hard or for too long. In stark contrast to these frail colourful reminders of the past splendours of the old Japanese Empire were the stark, robust matt black and chrome indicators of the glory of the new. Jockeying for space in the little room were a Sony colour television and video cassette recorder, a stacked hi-fi system bearing the name and logo of the Hitachi Corporation and perched on the little table next to the worn armchair where the old man was seated was a huge Panasonic combined radio-cassette.

"Come on you bastards, out here! Now! Chop, bloody chop! Bastards! Move!", the sixth and final voice, a hard Ulster brogue, spat out the words.

"Well, he's there alright, son, he's sitting in his chair by the fire, listening to the radio by the looks of it."

Metal meshed with metal.

"Is he alright, Dad, not bad is he, is he? Why didn't he answer the door? Dad? Dad?"

The firing and the screaming began.

"Alright, Davey, alright," the young man replied, his words fogging the pane. "He's probably got the radio on too loud and can't hear you knocking the do...."

The words died in the young man's throat as he wiped the glass with the sleeve of his jacket. The old man's hands? Why were they curled up like that? Like he was holding something in them, gripping something. But they were empty, weren't they? He pressed his face closer to the pane. The old man seemed to be shaking in his chair, his whole body jerking as if seized by some unseen but irresistible force. What the hell ......?

"Stay here, Davey, stay here a minute, son." Reaching into his trouser pocket, the young man walked quickly back to the front door.

The firing and the screaming continued, on and on, getting louder and louder, rising to an obscene crescendo. On and on, louder and loud –

"Dad? Dad? You alright? You ok, Dad?" The young man stooped in front of the chair and put his hand on the old man's shoulders. "Dad? You alright, Dad?"

The screaming and the firing abruptly stopped.

The old man stopped shaking and a moment or two later he slowly looked up.
"Eh? ....Whaa? ....Uh ....oh, oh it's you Jack. I ....I ...."
He gazed uncertainly around the room for a moment and then looked at his son-in-law once again. "I ...."
"You alright, Dad? You want the doctor? Let me get the doctor for you."
"No, no, son," he waved his hand, dismissing the idea, "I'm ....I'm alright now, son."
"You sure? It looked like you were having a fit or something. I'll run you up the hospital, if you like. The car's outside, won't take a minute, come on."
"Look, look, I'm alright. I'm alright." The old man replied, impatience creeping into his voice. "Honest, boy, honest. I'm alright. Now, now where's that Davey then, eh?" The old man said, rapidly changing the subject. "Where's the birthday boy?"
"He's outside, Dad. I told him to wait a minute, in case there was something wrong. You're sure you-"

"Alright, Davey boy, come in now son, come in!" The old man called over his shoulder, ignoring the young man.

The boy came hesitantly into the room and stood beside the chair staring anxiously at the old man. This was his beloved Grampa, the gentlest, kindest, sweetest, wisest, strongest man in the whole wide world. The man who had never lost his temper with the boy, not once. Not even that time when, just for the fun of it, the boy had pulled the chair away just as the old man was about to sit and he had ended up in a dazed, undignified heap on the hard kitchen floor.

"How's my boy then, eh? How's my favourite grandson?", the old man smiled. The boy instantly forgot his anxiety and chuckled, reminding the old man that he was, in fact, his only grandson.

They had done this a thousand times before, neither seeming to tire of the ritual, the joke somehow always fresh.

"We been knocking for ages, Grampa, then Dad used his key, sleeping were you?"

"Aye, nodded off in front of the fire I did."

"Come on then, Grampa, are you ready to go?", the boy asked, with barely contained eagerness.

"Go? Go where?", the old man queried in a suddenly confused voice.

"To Ralph's for fish and chips and then to the cinema of course come on Grampa come on.", the boy explained in one long breathless rush, as he pulled ineffectually at the old man's shirt sleeve.

"To the caffi for fish and chips and then to the pictures? Duw, Duw, Duw ....Queen's birthday, is it?", he asked, bewildered.

"No, it's *my* birthday, Grampa ....you didn't forget, did you?"

The boy answered, suddenly crestfallen. For a second or two he stood there staring at the floor, defeated and deflated. Then, looking deep into the old man's eyes, he saw the twinkle, that familiar, tiny twinkle.

"Ohhh, Granpa, you're having me on again, aren't you? Teasing me again, like you did last Christm-?"

Before the boy could finish his protest the old man had grabbed him with a strength and speed that always took people by surprise and then, holding the boy in a vice-like neckhold, proceeded to tickle him until he begged for mercy.

337

"Pleeeeesse ....Graaampa ....pleeesse!"

"Give in? Give in?"

"Yeeeess, yeeeess, I ....I ....giiive innnn!"

The old man finally released the boy, allowing him to slump, breathless, to the floor.

"Go and look under the stairs," he winked at the red-faced boy lying panting on the the hearth rug, "you never know, you might be lucky."

As the lad raced through the door and careered down the narrow hallway, bouncing off the various pieces of ancient furniture, the old man turned to his son-in-law.

"Alright now, Jack, don't look at me like that. I know I spoil him, but he's a good kid and anyway that's what grandparents are supposed to do, aren't they? And another thing, I don't recall your missus going without on her thirteenth birthday either, eh?"

"I know, Dad, I know, but stil –"

The crash of falling objects echoed from the passageway.

"David, be careful."

"Right, Dad," came the muffled response from the depths of the cupboard under the stairs that contained the Hoover, the clothes horse, assorted pairs of wellingtons and shoes and God alone knew what else.

"But nothing. Anyway, it's done now, so there's an end to it. Now pass me my boots and let's go and see this bloody film of his," the old man tut-tutted and shook his head as he bent to tie his bootlaces. "What ....what's it called again?"

The young man sighed. "It's called 'Indiana Jones and the Temple of Doom.' Dad, as you damm well know and you've been wanting to see it as much as our Davey has. You're not fooling anyone, you know."

The sound of wrapping paper being frantically torn to shreds drifted into the room.

"Ah ....well ....yes. Anyway, I hope it's better than that rubbish I watched on the telly last night. Well, well, well." The old man tut-tutted and shook his head some more. "Burt Lancaster ....now there's an actor, why don't they put more of his films on, eh? And that other one, what's his name now?"

"Robert Mitchum, Dad," the young man replied with exaggerated patience, knowing full well how this particular conversation always went.

"Aye, that's the feller, mun. Robert Mitch -"

"OHHH BBOOYYY!", the cry of unashamed delight coming from the hall interrupted the old man's train of thought and so he continued lacing his boots in silence, a mischievous smile dancing on his wrinkled face. For a moment the young man stood there watching him swiftly and expertly lace up the boots whose leather reflected every gleam and sparkle from the open fire in the hearth. Finally, he spoke.

"About this Japanese business, Dad. What's going on? I mean it's getting a bit out of hand now. This, this is one thing," he took in the contents of the room with a sweep of his hand.

"But the business with the factory and the Japanese lessons. Why are you doing all this, what's it all about? You know that Edwards bloke from the Legion?"

"Wanker," the old man growled, without looking up from his laces.

"Yeah, well, he had a go at our Maggie yester –"

The old man's head snapped upright, his face twisted in anger.

"Margaret!? What did he say to her? The little git! He upset her?"

"No, Dad, no. You know what she's like – take more than a prat like him to upset her. No, she told him where to get off, in no uncertain terms. No, it's not that, it's just that she ....we ....we want to know what's going on. What's it all about Dad? Eh?"

"Never you mind, nothing to do with you, son. Don't worry about it."

"I'm not worried about it Dad, I just don't understand, that's all. I-"

The old man got quickly up from the chair and, stamping his boots on the floor, called out.

"Action Stations! Thunderbirds are go! Look out Ralph, here we come!"

"HOOORRAAYYY !", came the cry from the hall.

The old man crossed nimbly to the door and, cupping his mouth in the palms of his hands, shouted down the hallway.

"Last one in the car buys the choc-iceeees !"

Then, head down, like some ageing, demented prop-forward, he clattered off down the passage. "Charge !"

He intercepted the boy long before he reached the front door, and grabbing him around the waist, resumed the delightful torture.

"No, stop it, Grampa ! Nooo, nooo, that's not fair ! Tell him, Dad! Dad !", the boy protested in between giggles.

"Ooohhhh, jingle bells, your bum smells !", sang the old man in reply.

And meanwhile, his voice drowned by the laughing and the scuffling and the cries of delight and the shouts of pretend anger that echoed throughout the house, the young man stood slowly shaking his head.

"Oh, I give up, I bloody give up."

It was November and as usual the windows of the café were misted slick with condensation. Every so often the young girl who "helped out" on Saturdays would wipe a clear circular patch on the plate glass and stare disconsolately out through her pearl-studded porthole. The old man was sitting at the little table with the handwritten "Staff Only" sign sellotaped to it. He sat tucked away in the shadow of the water boiler, an ornate silver monstrosity that stood ominously hissing and steaming on the formica-topped counter. Ralph, as usual, was busy dashing back and forth buttering doorstep-sized slices of golden brown toast and pouring cups of mahogany tea from the oversized metal teapot. Ralph was, by now, well overdue for retirement, but he and the Malay wife he had brought back to the valleys in 1947 had run the café for nearly forty years and old habits die hard. The old man, cigarette burning unheeded between his fingers, was staring at the pictures suspended from the rail high above the counter. Pictures of Singapore. Some were recent photographs, lush with colour, taken by Ralph on the last visit to his wife's family. The others were older, black and white photos, the monchrome images bleak in comparisoon. These had been taken in the late 'thiries, shortly before the Imperial Japanese Army had used its bicycles to render the mighty shore batteries impotent. Shortly before that day when, bulging kit bag on shoulder, he had said goodbye to the troop ship that had been his home for so many weeks. The black and white photos were enough for him, all the old man needed - his memory would do the rest. It would set the brightly coloured "bumboats" and the ramshackle junks in the harbour bobbing on the morning tide, it would send the crowds in their dazzling shirts and sarongs swarming along to the marketplace, it would also send the rickshaws with their skinny cursing owners zooming and weaving down the thronged streets. So too would his memory supply the clamour of the streetvendors, the tinkling giggles of the young girls, as they covered laughing mouths with tiny hands, so too would it summon the temple bells and the rhythmic chants of the faithful. It would go on to call up up the sirens and the hooters of the ships, large and small, as they came and went, from and to who knew where. Eyes closed, he inhaled slowly, carefully through his nostrils. Yes, there they were. He savoured the insinuating aroma of Chinese cuisine and the relentless assault of its Indian counterpart as they competed for palates and stomachs, in the same way that their respective religions competed for souls in that magically confused and confusing place. And the saltwater tang of the wind coming in off the South China Sea. And then there was the ... His senses were inundated, overwhelmed, getting near to overload. Perspiration broke out on his brow and his upper lip as he felt the humidity once more descend upon him. The same humidity that, in those first days, had felt just like a heated, lead-lined overcoat that he was obliged to put on each morning. He was nineteen again, an excited boy from the Valleys walking down a creaking gangplank into an uncertain future. He could feel the gangplank swaying beneath his fee-

"Helllooo."

The old man opened his eyes and looked up to see Ralph standing beside him, a steaming cup in each hand.

"Anybody home ?", Ralph smiled at his old friend, "you were miles away then mate, miles away. Looks like you're too near the boiler there too. Here you go, this'll cool you down." He put one of the cups in front of the old man. "Or do you prefer it stonecold, eh?"

The old man looked at the skin that had formed on the surface of the cup of tea that lay untouched in front of him.

"At least I won't burn my mouth on it, now will I ?, he smiled back. Ralph slid into the seat opposite his friend and sipped from his coffee cup.

"Christ, I've been poisoned !", he theatrically grabbed his throat with both hands. "Bloody girl, doesn't listen to a word you say. Boyfriend trouble ... again." He rolled his eyes and reached for the sugar bowl, the whiteness dotted with brown lumps of congealed tea and coffee. As he methodically stirred a third spoonful of sugar into his milky coffee he looked across the table at his lifelong friend.

"I've had that Edwards bloke from the Legion in here today going on about you not going to the Remembrance Day service again and not wearing your medals. You still keeping them in that bloody Oxo tin ?" He shook his head slowly. "I don't know, mate, but sometimes I just can't make you out. You're the most decorated man in this town. Bloody hero you are, boy."

"We're all heroes, Ralph, all the boys who went over there - especially the ones who didn't come back. And anyway, you can remember them just as well in your front room as you can in a church and a two minute silence standing on the Brecon Beacons is just as quiet as one at the Cenotaph. And as for medals..." He snorted. "I'd give all the bloody medals in the world to bring back one of them lads, just one. "Shorty" Jenkins, "Woodbine" Harris, Tommy Price, any of 'em. And another thing -" Ralph stopped stirring his coffee and stared his friend straight in the face, locking eyes with him. He leaned across the little table.

"Now you listen to me, pal," he hissed. "Don't you bloody lecture me about fallen comrades and all the rest of it ! Where do you think I was in 'forty-two - Barry fuckin' Island ? Eh ? Now we've been friends a long time Ken and I'd like to keep it that way, ok ?"

"Yeah, yeah you're right, Ralph, I'm sorry. I'm sorry, mate. It just sounded like you were on their side for a minute there."

"It's not a matter of taking sides Ken, all I'm saying is that I can see what they mean. I can see why they're so upset, it wouldn't kill you to go to the service, now would it ? And all that Japanese stuff in your house, all them holidays in Japan and the evening classes. I mean -"

"That's my business, Ralph."

"Fair enough, Ken, fair enough. Look, I know you've helped a lot of people in this town, getting the Japs to build that factory here and everything but watch your step with Edwards."

"Spent the whole war in the bloody Pay Corps polishing a chair in Delhi with his fat arse. What does he know about it ? Eh ? Jesus."

"Just calm down, mate, alright ? I know he's an arsehole but he's got a lot of pull in this town, that's all I'm saying. Right ?"

"Aye, you're right Ralph, as usual. What would I do without you, eh? Are you sure you haven't got your collar on back to front again?" He chuckled and turned to the young girl at the window.

"Bring us one of them custard slices, will you, love ?" The boss here's buying," he called, indicating Ralph with a nicotine-stained thumb.

The girl turned languidly from her vigil at the window and looked at her employer for approval, before commencing the arduous trek all the way to the cake stand. Ralph nodded at the girl and turned back to his friend.

"You should get it sometime in the next day or two," he said with a helpless smile and a slow shake of the head. "And if I'm buying the cakes," he continued, "then the fags are on you, you tightarse."

While Ralph helped himself to the packet of Embassy Regal on the table between them, the old man flicked the wheel on the engraved brass Zippo.

"How about Mickey Evans then ?" asked Ralph, his cigarette bobbing in and out of the big yellow and blue flame.

"Eh ? "

"Mickey Evans. Would you bring him back, if you could ?"

"Yes." The old man sighed. "Even Mickey bloody Evans."

And they were still smiling at a shared memory when the custard slice finally arrived.

"Here we are, Mr. Davies, the tapes you ordered. 'Japanese for Business and Commerce'," the girl behind the library counter read the label aloud. "Well, rather you than me," she laughed, "and I think the book has come too, let me see now, where ...?" She dived cormorant-like beneath the huge oak counter.

The old man smiled good-naturedly at the comments that seemed to come from nowhere as the young librarian fought her way through the organised chaos that reigned supreme beneath the counter. The rummaging continued for a moment or two until finally the girl resurfaced, proclaiming triumphantly, "Got it! Right, here we are, Mr. Davies." She pushed her glasses back up onto the bridge of her nose and appraised the title. "'Japanese Grammar and Syntax. Upper Intermediate to Advanced Level', a little light reading at bedtime, is it, Mr. Davies?" She smiled. "Well, you won't need sleeping tablets with this now will y –"

"Let me see that!" Suddenly, a man in an immaculate blue Burberry, Burma Star Association tie in a Windsor Knot at his throat and with a tightly furled umbrella on his arm sprang forward to snatch the slim volume from the young woman's grasp. He didn't quite make it. A hand that seemed to have come from nowhere flashed out and locked onto the intruder's wrist.

"When the young lady is talking to you, then the young lady will be looking at you. Alright?" The old man hissed into the interloper's ear, savagely twisting his wrist at the same time. "Do we understand each other?" He increased the pressure. "Hmmm?"

"Let me go! Take your hands off me! What, what do you think you're doing? Do ... do you know who I am!?". The man protested as he was led away out of earshot of the girl at the desk.

"I know exactly who you are, Mr. Edwards," came the calm, measured reply, "You're someone who interferes in things that don't concern him. Now why don't you just go about your business like a good little boy and allow me to get on with mine, hmm? And one more thing, lovely boy. If you have something to say to me, then say it to me and not my daughter. You bother my family again and I'll rip this fucking arm off and beat you to death with it. Alright? Now, off you go and mind the traffic when you cross the road, there's a good boy."

The raincoated man keeled over when his arm was finally released and collided with a display stand, sending a pile of shiny leaflets fluttering and his umbrella skittering across the polished wooden floor.

"You ... you haven't heard the last of this, you mark my words, oh no. Yes ... yes, I can assure you of that! That's assault that is. I'll have the law on you! I ... I ..." he blustered, propelling himself out through the revolving doors with all the dignity he could muster. "Oh yes, you mark my words, you haven't heard the las ..." His words faded into the distance as he made his way down the steps and onto the rain-slick street.

"Sorry about that, love," the old man said as he knelt to help the young librarian clear up the mess.

It was about a week after work had begun on construction of the giant Tagaki plant that the old man finally went to see Dr. Honeyman about the pain that had been becoming more and more difficult to ignore. And it was then that he had to ask the question that all patients dread having to ask and all doctors dread having to answer.

"How long have I got?"

The tanned, uniformed young man with the heavy kit bag held firmly in one strong hand strode purposefully in through the hospital entrance. He had celebrated his nineteenth birthday on his way back from the Gulf and his head still hadn't quite cleared by the time he got off the train at Merthyr Tydfil. It hit him as soon as he pushed open the heavy glass door, that unique aroma that only hospitals somehow seem able to generate. The smell of institutional cooking and the odours associated with bodily functions wafting out from the wards combined with the bouquet of stale cigarette smoke and machine coffee from the waiting room – all partially masked by the tang of disinfectant. He asked a young nurse where he could find his grandfather and she pointed him towards a solitary figure seated at the far end of the green, lino-paved corridor. He walked as softly as his boots would allow and came to a stop beside the hunched form in the grey plastic chair.

"Mam?"

The head tilted slowly upwards and he was shocked to see how old his mother had become.

"Davey? Oh, Davey, is it you?", she asked, her eyes still not quite registering.

"Yes, Mam, it's me. I came straight from the station." He said, carefully lowering the kit bag to the floor. His mother's red-rimmed eyes ran over the name, rank and serial number stencilled in big white characters on the side. "Grampa? How is he? Is he –?"

"Oh, Davey, Davey, Davey. You're here, you're here!"

She jumped up from the chair and, putting her arms around her son's neck, seemed to lose ten years from her face.

"Oh, Davey, Davey. Come here, love, come here!"

Finally, after a great deal of hugging, kissing and crying, she allowed the young man to go to the darkened cubicle. He quietly opened the door and poked his head inside.

"Grampa?" He whispered.

No answer, just the sound of quiet, ragged breathing.

"Grampa?" A little louder. "Grampa? It's me, Davey."

"Eh ... what ... uh? Oh ... oh ... Davey ... Davey, my boy. Is that you?"

"Sleeping were you?"

"Aye, nodded off I did."

The young man stepped inside and gently pulled a chair up to the bedside. He looked deep into the eyes of the man in the bed, searching. Was it still ...? Yes! Yes, there it was. The twinkle was still there – just.

"How's ... how's my favourite grandson then?" They both chuckled at the old, old joke. "Help me up a bit, son. Help me sit up a bit, so I can have a proper look at you."

He bent over the form in the bed and, slipping his arms into the old man's armpits, heaved him upwards. He nearly threw him through the ceiling. In the semi-darkness of the cubicle he hadn't been able to see him clearly, but as his eyes became accustomed to the gloom he saw why his grandfather had been so easy to lift. Where had he gone, his Grampa? Where was the rest of him? He had lost so much weight, so much flesh, that he seemed to be nothing more than a collection of bones. He stood there in shock for a second or two, feeling his embarrassment fill the tiny room until the old man finally put them both out of their misery with a playful reprimand.

"Duw, Duw, boy. Take it easy, take it easy. What ... what they been feeding you on, eh? Don't know your own strength, you don't."

Giving a little confused sort of laugh he pulled the old man upright in the bed – gently this time – and rearranged his pillows.

"Better, Grampa?"

"Aye, that's it, son. Tidy, tidy. ... Desert Rats, eh?", he said, motioning towards the young man's shoulder flashes.

"Aye, Grampa. That's us." He replied, his voice swelling with pride.

The old man nodded smiling and gave a short dry chuckle that suddenly turned into a rattle, and then into a coughing fit that wracked his wasted body for one very long minute. Gradually the coughing subsided and finally he got his breath back.

"Alright now, Grampa?"

"Aye, son, alright. Must have swallowed a bus or something ... double-decker too by the feel of it," he smiled. The young man smiled back and they shared a moment or two of silence before the old man spoke. "Rough over there was it, son?", he asked looking the young man straight in the eyes.

"Yeah, Grampa. No bloody picnic."

"Changes you, son, you may not feel it but you're different now, take it from me. I know, son, I know all about it. Listen, son, I know I haven't got long and –"

"No, no, that's not true Grampa. You'll be alright, you'll be up and –"

"Come on now, son, don't talk daft, we both know the score, don't we, eh? So let's not waste time, eh? That's why I'm going to tell you now what everyone else has been dying to know all these years."

"What? About this Japanese business, you mean?"

"Aye, son, I reckon you're about the only one in the family who'd understand. Keep this to yourself, son, alright? This is just between me and you, ok?"

"Yes, Grampa, right, whatever you say."

The old man sipped from the thick plastic beaker of lukewarm water at his bedside and began ...

"It was back in 'forty-five after I had been liberated from that POW camp in Burma. I was angry, Davey, bloody angry, I hated the Japanese like I had never hated anyone or anything before in my whole life. After what they had done to me and the other lads at that camp I felt that any nation capable of producing people like that deserved to perish – every man, woman and child of them. When I heard about the atom bombs dropped on Hiroshima and Nagasaki I laughed, I laughed until I thought I was going to be sick. I was just sorry that they had only destroyed two cities, I wanted the Americans to drop a bomb on every city, on every town, on every village and to keep on dropping them until the whole of that country and everyone in it was wiped from the face of the earth – forever. I wanted revenge, son. Revenge. You plan it and plan it. You think about it all day and dream about it all night. You eat, sleep and bloody drink it. It takes you over. I, I wanted to make those bastards suffer the way I had suffered all them years in that bloody camp. And anyone would do, son, anyone as long as they were Japanese. That was all I could think about, it was eating me up from inside just like this ... this ..." He pointed to his stomach. " Just like this bloody thing is now, only worse, much worse. I would gladly have sold my soul to the devil to make them suffer, even if it was only for a minute." He sipped again from the beaker before continuing. "Then one day I got my chance. Oh, aye, I got my chance alright. I can see it now, son, after all these years I can still see it, clear as day. These soldiers – an Aussie, a Cockney, a Scotch boy and this Irish lad, never forget 'em. And there were these two officers there too, a young one, the lieutenant, he was angry at first but the older one, the colonel, told him to shut up and in the end they both just watched. They didn't do a thing to stop it, they just watched."

"Watched? Watched what, Grampa?"

"The soldiers sat me down on a couple of old ammunition crates behind this machine gun and I remember that three of 'em had to hold me up from behind. I was too weak to sit up straight on my own, see? Just like I am now. The Aussie, he fed a belt of ammunition into the gun from the right, cocked it and then held the belt taut so that it would feed straight into the breech without jamming. Very professional he was, did it just the way it said in the manual. All I had to do was hang on to the grips and press the trigger inbetween with my thumbs. Just as well, because that was about all I could manage, even with three of them holding me up from behind. To turn a gun like that you don't swing it back and for, like you see them do in the films – you hit the grips with the heel of your palm and jolt it a degree or so in the direction you want. Hit the left grip with your left hand to traverse left and the same thing with your right." The old man demonstrated, pyjama sleeves flapping around wasted arms, as the young soldier nodded his understanding. "I didn't even have the strength to do that, Davey, but they said they'd take care of that for me too, very helpful they were, very helpful. I sat there for a minute with the sun so bright in my eyes that I couldn't see too good, wondering what the hell was going on. But, I soon found out. Oh, aye, I found out alright, because it was then that they brought 'em out – Japanese soldiers. They marched 'em out, ten of 'em, and tied 'em to these stakes in the ground, telegraph poles by the looks of it. I couldn't believe it. There they were, the enemy, the bastards who had tortured me and all them others in them camps for so long. Evil little fuckers, yellow slant-eyed little bastards they were standing there in front of me – in front of the machine gun. Suddenly, I understood. At last, after all that time waiting I was going to get what I wanted. I was so happy. No, not happy ... ecstatic! I'd waited so long to pay them back for what they had done to me and all them others like me and now the day had finally come. Payday. I was like a kid on Christmas morning with a treeful of presents. I pressed the trigger with my thumbs and the gun started firing. And firing and firing and firing. The gun hammered away, giving me what I had wanted all that time, what I had dreamed about for so long. I remember it all clear as day. The hammering of the gun, the cordite stinging my nose and the way my whole body shook with the recoil and me laughing out loud all the time. It was a Vickers machine-gun, one of them big old ones with a tripod and a pipe attached to a tin of water to keep the barrel cool. It fired three-oh-three ammunition, lethal at a mile."

The old man paused a moment staring into space and into time. "At that range the bullets went through those bodies like a hot knife through butter, carried on through the telegraph poles and out the other side." He closed his eyes a moment or two before continuing. "They were ripped to pieces, Davey, there was blood and flesh and bits of bone everywhere. White they were, them bits of bone – just like the splinters of wood from the telegraph poles. It got so you couldn't tell which was which, all mixed up like that with the blood and the chunks of flesh flying through the air. It seemed to go on forever, like it was all happening in slow motion, on and on and on. One by one the bodies were torn apart and one by one they slid down the poles to the ground. Some of them telegraph poles had been sliced in two by the bullets. In two! Can you imagine that, son? But this one body stayed where it was, like he was nailed to the pole. The force of the bullets had trapped his flesh in the wood and that's what was holding him up, I suppose. And the blood, it was just pouring out of him. Oh, God, it was like ... like he was being crucified. And the way he screamed as I cut him in half with that damned gun. Screamed and screamed and screamed."

He stopped speaking and turned his head away from the young soldier for a moment to wipe his eyes with the sleeves of his pyjama jacket. "Jesus ... kids they were son, bloody kids, younger than you are now, just frightened bloody kids. That's all they were. They had nothing to do with hurting me or any of them others in them camps. They didn't want to kill anybody, they'd probably given themselves up the first chance they got. If it hadn't been for that fucking war and the bloody politicians they would have been at home with their families, still in school probably. Christ. I ... I tried ... I tried to stop, but the gun wouldn't stop firing ... it was like the gun was in charge of me and not the other way around. I ... I remember asking them to help me stop it but they couldn't hear me I suppose, I was too weak to shout and that bastard gun was making so much noise. Christ, I can see them now, their faces. The one feeding the gun was looking at me and laughing like we were enjoying ourselves you know, like we were out on the town and having a bloody good time. And the three holding me up and helping me work the gun, they were leaning over my shoulders smiling, thought they were doing me a favour, I suppose. But to me they were just like evil spirits, demons sitting on my shoulders digging their claws into my flesh and grinning at me. Then I couldn't see a thing because I was crying so much but I could feel the tears, hot they were, scalding hot as they ran down my face and I could taste them in my mouth – all salty like. I ... I must have passed out or something because the next thing I knew there I was tucked up in bed, just like I am now, nice clean white sheets, clean pyjamas – tidy like. Then I saw the MO standing over me with a needle in his hand telling me not to worry, I was going to be alright and to get some rest because I was going home soon. I felt the needle go in and I told myself it was all a dream, just a bad dream. I hadn't really killed ... murdered those young boys like that, but I could smell the cordite on my hands and my fingers were still curled up like they'd been when I had hold of the gun. D'you know, son, I can still hear their voices sometimes, those blokes on the Vickers and the officers turning a blind eye. And sometimes, sometimes I can even feel their hands on my back holding me up and the shaking of the gun in my hands and the noise of the firing getting louder and louder and louder, until in the end it's all I can hear, that and the screaming, those young lads screaming and screaming. Oh, Oh God ..." The old man let out a series of long, deep sobs that made the young soldier look away. Finally, after the old man had regained his composure, he looked at his grandson. "Do you understand, son? Do you understand what I'm trying to say?"

"But they had it coming, Grampa. Those bastards had it coming after what they did to you. Just like the bloody Iraqis and that Sadd –"

"No, son, no! You're wrong, Davey, Christ, you're so bloody wrong! Don't make the same mistake I did, son. Don't you see, son, don't you see? By doing that I was no better than them bastards in the camps that had made my life hell for all them years, I was just as guilty as them when I murdered them scared young lads. I was just like them, the bastards that I had hated for so long. But I'm not just like them, I'm better than them, better than that scum. I won't let them drag me down to their level, to make me like them. I'm not an animal like them and I won't let them make me one. I won't! I won't! I won't!"

Once more the skeletal frame was subjected to a merciless coughing fit. It took the old man longer, much longer to recover from this one. He took another sip of water from the beaker the young man held to his lips and continued. "I had to try and make amends, d'you see? I owed it to myself and I owed it to those boys. We have to talk to each other in this world and not just through the barrel of a gun." The young soldier was nodding his understanding as the old man's hand flashed out across the sheets and clamped onto his own.. The old strength and speed were back and the soldier's heart leapt. He was going to be alright! His Grampa was going to be alright again! Thank you, God, thank you! He could have shouted the walls down as he gripped the skinny hand as tightly as he could. He smiled at the man in the bed, his face feeling like it was going to split wide open with joy. The old man smiled back, slowly closed his eyes and suddenly there was only one still squeezing.

I stood at the graveside in civilian clothes, as my grandfather had requested. "No bands, no bugles, no medals – none of that three shots over the grave nonsense, promise me, son, promise me." I reached into my pocket and took out my grandfather's medals hanging from their brightly coloured ribbons and looked at them for a moment, running my thumb over the raised lettering and the heads of dead kings. As well as campaign medals from the European and Far East theatres, there was the Distinguished Conduct Medal and next to it the Military Medal. I looked at the unpolished metal glinting dully in the watery Autumn sun and I thought of the story Ralph had told me the night before. Over several glasses of his favourite single malt he had told me about how my grandfather had saved his life and those of maybe a dozen more men during a short but bloody confrontation while acting as part of the rearguard covering the British Expeditionary Force evacuation from Dunkirk. He had told me of my grandfather's selfless heroism and how he would surely have got the VC if there had been an officer left alive to witness the incident. "But so what?", Ralph had sighed, pouring himself another generous measure, "The old bastard would only have stuck it in that bloody tin with the rest of 'em. If I had your grandad's medals I'd sleep with the buggers on my pyjamas. Jesus." The vicar started speaking and I came back to the here and now. I looked across the graveside and studied the resolutely immobile features of the Tagaki Corporation executives arranged opposite me. It was then that I suddenly realised there were ten of them, and I don't know if it was the sun in my eyes, or maybe I had just been staring at them too hard for too long, but gradually they appeared to change, to somehow transform themselves. Now they were no longer middle-aged businessmen in dark suits and tightly knotted black ties, but young, very young men in the brown leggings and peaked caps of the Imperial Japanese Army. I watched as their eyes followed my grandfather's coffin lowered into the dark Valleys soil and I saw the briefest of smiles flitting across their smooth, hairless faces. Not smiles of pleasure at seeing an enemy finally vanquished but rather, smiles of compassion and understanding. This time there were no vengeful soldiers' words of incitement to murder, no officers' complicity, no reek of spiteful cordite, no bullets hungry for human flesh and bone speeding from an eagerly fed machine-gun. No, not this time, Grampa. But something else was just the way you described it, Grampa, that night in that dark, stuffy little room ... the slow, hot trails on my cheeks and the salty taste in my mouth.

> "Revenge, at first though sweet,
> Bitter ere long back on itself recoils."
> *John Milton (1608 – 1674)*

SOMETHING SPECIAL FOR THE WEEKEND

Kate Terrell

Claire never really saw herself as a workaholic. She just enjoyed her job and, if she was honest, she had not really minded all the extra hours it had been necessary to put in to complete her last assignment. However, now that the project was finished and deadlines had been reached, she was satisfied that she had done a good job. But she was exhausted. Feeling the relief of a Friday afternoon, Claire relished the prospect of the relaxing weekend before her. What she deserved was a real treat. Something really special.

After the last frenetic weeks, the most attractive option was definitely a couple of days of peace at home, curled up in bed with something inspiring from the library. That would sort her out – spiritually and physically. With all the extra work, Claire had not had time to visit the library for ages, so, once she had quitted her office and had made the usual Friday evening excursion to the supermarket, she made her way towards the centre of town.

It was an imposing building, to be sure. Dating from the days when the local worthies had been all too eager to display their commitment to education and book learning, it had been constructed in the grand style, with an impressive flight of steps leading to up to a mock classical facade of Corinthian pillars and a huge brass embossed door. Claire looked up admiringly. How she loved everything about this building, from its pretentious statuary to its wonderful smell of old leather bindings. She was really glad that it had been preserved, despite the fact that there were no books any more.

No one was sure who had had the original idea, but it had truly been an innovation. After the great Genetic Plague, society had changed so radically that many of the old edifices had been swept away and replaced with superior new technology.

Without any men left in the world, the rebuilding of their lives had proved much easier than anticipated. Still, some women had missed the company of men. So once the clone banks were fully stocked and the men were ready for public loan, it had seemed enormously sensible to utilise the old public library service. After all, they had all the structures in place, the appropriate buildings, the software and microfilm facilities, and a network of staff expert in cataloguing, filing and helping customers make selections.

These changes had all taken place a long time ago, but Claire's grandmother could just about remember her visits to the very same library as a child and she always said that it had hardly altered at all; only in those days she had selected videos, CDs, and occasionally a storybook (as her father had been the old-fashioned sort). Nowadays the usual loan period was much shorter – often just for the weekend, although it was possible to arrange for a longer loan, if you asked the Librarian. In fact her grandmother had only just recently returned one man, after a period of four months, because he had proved himself a reasonable card player.

Claire made her way through the ornate vestibule and into the lending area, catching the eye of Miriam, the Deputy Chief Librarian, with whom she had struck up a sort of friendship. Miriam was deep in discussion with a stem-faced and unblinking middle-aged woman and appeared more than a little cross. Her brief glance to Claire had indicated that she would be with her in a minute, so Claire decided to have a browse.

Naturally, the men themselves were not kept in the library, just their record cards and an introductory CD ROM. They were much more appropriately housed in large pubs on the outskirts of the town. Here, they had everything they required – companionship, a large screen television in each room permanently tuned to the sports channel, pub grub and unlimited beer. Their very own tabloid newspaper was also provided, usually a reissue of an archive edition with the date changed. As long as they liked the headlines and the pictures, they rarely ever noticed that the news bore no relation to the real world. Most of the men were very happy in their environment and even regretted their brief forays outside. However, there were a few that found this life distasteful, but by a kind twist of fate, the men who felt like that were curiously the ones who were most often selected for loan, so it all worked out very well.

Claire wasn't really sure where to start. The shelves were, for the most part, categorised according to their former book library days, but Claire rarely just picked something off the shelves at random. Normally, she would study the reviews to ensure that she got something interesting – even educational. She never bothered with the visual presentations; after all, how could you possibly judge the content by its mere appearance. Her friendship with Miriam had meant that sometimes she would be given a personal recommendation. As a member of staff, Miriam got to handle all the new releases and Claire had to admit that there was something agreeable about being the first person to take home a new issue. But it could be risky. Just because something was new did not guarantee its quality, and frequently she had been disappointed. They were okay for passing the time, but were, in the main, not very satisfying.

Much more interesting was the shelf of recent returns. By looking at the number of times the item had been taken out, it was possible to deduce which were the most popular, especially if there was also evidence of long loans. Claire perused a few of the record cards, but did not find anything to her fancy. As usual, most of the really popular items were from the gardening department and Claire had already had as many herbaceous borders as she could cope with.

"There you are," said Miriam, coming up behind her. "I'm sorry about that."

"No problem," said Claire, "I could see you were busy."

"Busy? Stupid cow! Honestly, you wouldn't believe the condition in which some people return the goods. That poor man. He was wrecked. She didn't even give him any breakfast."

Claire was shocked. "She didn't look the type to go in for abuse."

"Don't you believe it," snorted Marion. "That sort are often the worst. Poor old chap. I'll just have to see what he looks like after fumigation. If he's too dog-eared, I'm afraid he'll have to be taken out of circulation."

"Incinerated?" Claire had not expected things to be quite as serious as that. Miriam was sometimes prone to exaggeration.

"No, probably not," Miriam relented. "I don't suppose he'll

look too bad once he's cleaned up. We might put him into one of our used copy sales. I'm glad you take better care of the men in your care."

"Well, it's public property and should be treated with due respect," Claire replied as they watched an assistant help the bedraggled little man to his feet and out to the van waiting to collect him.

"No wonder most of the books had to be destroyed, if people took as little care of them as she did with him."

Miriam nodded agreement. "Now, what are you looking for?"

Claire outlined her plans for the weekend and for a moment Miriam narrowed her eyes in thought.

"How about a romance. Something a bit steamy?"

"No good," said Claire decidedly. "I can't be doing with silver-tongued bimbos. And besides, their egos are too fragile. It's too much like hard work. I want to relax."

"Poetry, then?" she suggested.

Claire paused and considered. "Poets are okay, but you don't always know what you're getting. Having a way with words can be very attractive, but the last few I've had have just wanted a good rant. I want something a bit more gentle and house trained. Besides, all the best poetry is written by women."

Miriam lowered her voice. "And I take it that you still aren't interested in joining our Female Pursuits section? The Librarian in charge tells me it's awfully exciting."

Claire smiled. "Call me old fashioned. .. no, I spend all my life with women and very pleasant though it is, I need a break."

"Me too," said Miriam. "But no doubt if I was transferred to that section, I could be persuaded to appreciate the benefits. Well, don't bother looking in the New Releases – they're all dire."

"That's what I thought," said Claire. "I suppose you've flicked through them all already?"

"Librarian's perks," smirked Miriam. "Although with this month's offerings, it's hardly that. Come on, down to business. You enjoy dipping into the foreign section. How about something from there. What about Irish History?"

·She looked archly at Claire who blushed to the roots. Yes, it had been a glorious few months – a long loan, even. Liam's soft brogue and dark curls had been something special alright. And he could recite poetry. Maybe it had all been blarney but it had certainly been intoxicating. It was very very tempting but...

"I haven't time," she groaned. "You know what I'm like about Irishmen..."

"Sure do," said Miriam. "The fine you paid kept us Librarians in chocolate digestive biscuits for weeks. I had to send you four reminders before you gave him back."

"And thank goodness you did," said Claire with conviction. "Otherwise I might still be there daydreaming. I've got a life to live and a job to do."

"Definitely a bit distracting." Miriam paused and looked around her. "Actually, we were all as jealous as hell when we realised you'd discovered something like him without us having any idea that anything that good was on the shelves. We sent the reminders so we could all have a go. That's how I got the promotion. The Principal Librarian still hasn't come back."

They both laughed at the thought of Joan Trimble succumbing to the delectable Liam. How dog-eared would he be when he was returned? Would she ever come back?

"Okay," said Claire. "So what can you recommend?"

"Well," pondered Miriam, "as usual the DIY section is almost completely empty. If you want any shelves put up this weekend, you'll just have to get here much earlier than Friday evening. It doesn't matter how many copies we have, demand always seems to outstrip supply. Men still have their uses, it appears. However, as it's you, I have got one put by. A special order, but it's nearly closing time and she hasn't turned up yet. I hear he's really good with his hands. An expert."

"Thanks but no thanks," Claire replied quickly. "I told you. I want to relax. Anyway, I can put up my own shelves now. Angus showed me."

"Now there's a popular little number." You could hear the admiration in Miriam's voice. "Always in and out. Not only handy, but one of the few who doesn't show a cleavage when he bends down. Tasty."

"I know," said Claire, weakly. "I've booked him for the

autumn to build me a patio."

"I thought you'd already got one?" Miriam gave her one of those looks.

"Three actually," admitted Claire. "But he's such a lovely worker."

Miriam went through some of the other possibilities. She rather favoured the Classics, but Claire, like many women, had been rather put off by being forced to study them as a schoolgirl, and considered them somewhat dull and unadventurous. "Easy Listening" was okay for some, and although unimaginative, she admitted that they could be good company. At least the "Middle of the Road" style had proved more durable than rock stars.

Miriam had once told her that some bright spark from Libraries HQ had come up with the idea of cloning some of the rock icons of the 1990's. It had turned out to be disastrous. She had assumed that, as so many women had raved about them at the time, they might be worth acquiring. DNA samples had been procured and the clones developed, but the venture had not been a success. The legends and their inaccessibility had been their best features. 'In the flesh', so to speak, they had turned out to be rude and untalented, barely able to string a few words together and, even worse, enormously vain. They were immediately withdrawn from general circulation, apart from a few copies retained in the reference section, for supervised use in the library only. But, like most of the things in the reference library, they were rarely requested.

"It's no good," said Claire eventually, "I feel totally uninspired."

Miriam looked furtively around her, registering that they were alone and volunteered, "Well, we do have something else... I'm not really allowed to show you. Strictly Library staff only. . . but I know you are reliable and you won't let on."

"More perks?" ventured Claire.

"You could say so," replied Miriam, signing for Claire to follow her.

Discreetly and quietly, they passed through the small door behind the counter marked "private", along a corridor past the tea room and offices, then down a short flight of stairs to the basement.

"You'll like this," said Miriam as she switched on the light.

And so she did. "Now this is what I call really special," gasped Claire, as she beheld the wall to wall, floor to ceiling shelves of books. Row upon row, inviting her to reach out and caress their spines. Now she was reassured. This was going to be a spectacularly good weekend.

BACILLUS

Kaite O'Reilly

They knew it was nearing by the presence of militia on the streets. She counted sixty-eight vehicles move out through the town one night. They used no headlights. It was then she knew it was going to happen.

"Are you okay?"
"Yes."
"Safe?"
"Uh-huh."
"Be careful."
The phone went dead.

When it was over those who could began to go home. Their passports carried the name of a country other than the one on their birth certificates. Others stayed where they were, becoming numbers on official lists. Banks reopened. The Government encouraged spending for the economy's health. The national anthem played on the hour every hour on radio stations. She tried to whistle it doing the housework but strayed. She kept going back to the old one.

On New Year's Eve she went walking through the snow up to the frozen river. She stood and looked at the place where they had gone swimming in the summer before the shells. She crossed the bridge they had sat on, smoking cigarettes to keep the gnats away in the dusk. In the snow the village opposite was still smouldering. Earlier the army had blown it up with a left-over incendiary, to celebrate. She didn't go any further.

Outside the baker's she pauses by what seems to be a life-size gingerbread man cutter. She reads it is a hand-gun target practice, memorial to the dead. She shivers, the wind picking up, and draws her coat together at the collar. Her fingers pinch white. She walks the square rather than go back too soon. With the door shut, the silence becomes demanding.

She has developed the habit of collecting stones. Her pockets bulge and gape, wrecking the line she once tailored to accentuate her slimness. Her thin body has been transformed. No longer desirable, she disguises it under jumpers. It is a sickness. She walks back to the flat, a suit of loose skin covering dry bones.

She will go out tonight because it is expected. There will be a party, a disco, people dancing. She will go out tonight because otherwise she will be tormented. "I'm not going if you're not." "I won't be able to enjoy myself thinking of you in here all alone."

She will go with her friends who will tell her she is pretty. They will compliment her figure and pretend to be jealous of her weightlessness. She knows they will be undressing her with their eyes, horrified at the jag of bone visible through thin material. Privately they will say she is haggard. One may even suggest she sees a doctor. For a week they will watch her eating habits and then forget, focusing their attention on someone else's problems. Always someone else's problems. That is the way they survive.

Getting ready she puts on the radio which plays marching tunes. Instinctively she gathers her rations, for before it was a sign of an alert. No news would be given, just stirring marching tunes on every channel. It finishes as she is putting a toothbrush into her bag. She unpacks to a romantic ballad.

Her finery have hung at the back of the wardrobe for so long they smell of disuse. Taking them out she finds moth holes in the fabric. She looks at the colours and is pained by their naiveté. The woman who chose them did so with much care, believing such things to be important. She tries to remember that woman but finds it is beyond her. The spoiled clothes hang on her like rags. She no longer resembles herself.

"Jivali!"

362

"Jivali!"

"Life!"

Their glasses clink.

The school hall is throbbing. Teenagers dance wildly to a mediocre record. It is the first public event since it all began. She is aware some young people here have never been to a disco, dance or live concert. They stand bewildered to the side unsure of what to do.

Her friends are jovial, trying hard. They drink and smoke too many cigarettes. "Oh well, you have to die of something." They attempt an air of recklessness but she can see in their eyes they are still using peripheral vision. Widen your scope, develop sight in the back of your head. They have spent years watching life out of the corners. Without looking they move in unison as a drunk stumbles past, narrowly missing their shoulders. The radar is still working.

Her friends think they ought to dance. They sway to the music, motioning her to join them with their fingers. One mouths entreaties, her enunciation unnecessarily large. She smiles weakly and waves, indicating "later". They will not accept that and drag her up, pushing and pulling her hands as if they are rowing. She endures it, stiffly rocking from one leg to another. They cheer and clap. "You were always a good dancer."

In the past her body flowed like a forest fire spreading. She was fluid, joints oiled, the crackle of sparks beneath her feet. Now she feels ancient, bones calcifying into one structure. No longer with vertebrae, she has gone back in the evolutionary chain. She does not think she can move her pelvis. She has been steel-plated together, shuffling as a casualty.

Someone throws a firework and there is silence for a minute. The gunpowder flours the air as taut faces grow relaxed. A man laughs then rails, is led outside softly weeping. "Too much booze!" his brother yells. "He is not used to so much plenty!" Her friends show their teeth and nod. "Yes! It is good! So much of everything – the drink flows as a river!" He thanks them with his eyes, arms shielding as he ushers. His brother was janitor at the local school until needed for the last effort. "I loved work," he tells everyone, "but now, every little bang, every sound..." He shrugs. "But children are still noisy," he brightens. "Children will not stop being children. Despite all, that is good."

Generosity and bonhomie overspills, sickening her with its buoyancy. She wants to resist it and remind them where they have been. She wants to tell them she is not deceived, although she realises it is not deception. Her friend frowns slightly, pre-empting her. "Hush." She stalls the words with a hand on her arm. "Do not think badly of us. We are only trying to be alive."

With Branca there was no need to work at existing. Every moment was a small miracle, thanksgiving for each inhalation of breath. She thought of her lungs, fine roots in spongy soil, and gave up smoking. She wanted to be clean, pink healthy tissue unclogged by black tar. She wanted to expand her capacity, oxygenated blood hurrying in her veins. Branca was a specialist in respiratory disease. There were many problems with the men at the front; there was talk of illegal chemicals. Branca was going there to be of use. On their last night they lay on the bed breathing shallowly, slow hands finding quiet openings.

A man invites her to dance and she agrees, lurching passively against him. His fingers rest on her waistband but neither recoil at the brittle touch. He too has the sickness. Their skeletons rasp against each other on the dance-floor as she imagines they will, later, in his lodgings. She presumes they will couple emptily, exchange a joyless fuck. Afterwards they will embrace because that is expected, a perfunctory nod to tenderness, what the textbooks call trust. They will not have connected except biologically, wearily going through the motions. The instinct, they will think, is still strong. They are organisms and this is what organisms do.

Later, she will dress, slipping out into the young year, so new it has not yet felt its first dawn. They will both be relieved. There would not be room for all, his bed being peopled with ghosts.

She stands by the frozen river, a pillow-slip heavy with her collection of stones in her hand. Some are brick, others rubble. There is the forefinger of a stone angel, an inch of slate from someone's back step. They are her souvenirs, her ghoulish mementoes. A piece of stone for every six killed.

Once, she intended to fill her pockets and go skittish and

sliding along the ice to her death. Her clean lungs would fill with water, like Branca's taproots congeal and swell.

She stands by the frozen river and knows she will not step out upon its waters. Convalescing, she feels she has lost a lung, but the other organ still works its bellows.

There are many kinds of Tuberculosis, Branca had told her. A form of meningitis in children, a cannibal virus in adult limbs. It could eat the ends off long bones, whole vertebrae crumbling. As consumption it attacked the soft lungs of English romantic poets. One Sunday afternoon in bed they had watched a sentimental film, velvet-clad victim coughing genteelly into lace cornered handkerchiefs. Branca had laughed unpleasantly, bucking the duvet with kicking legs. "It is a basin you would want. It is a stream of blood, up to a pint, frothing."

Her mother had died from it. Nursing her, Branca had changed her ambition from being an ice skating champion to a TB specialist. She had succeeded, winning first class honours and a strong reputation for one so young. She had headed a small research team into the re-emergence of TB in developed and Third World countries. She believed, combined with HIV, it could reach global epidemic proportions. A sinister alliance. With TB present, HIV mutated quickly into full blown AIDS. She was about to publish a paper on her findings when the whole thing began. Her data was lost somewhere in a shelled-out laboratory and there was no official report on how she was killed.

The year becomes less new, greying at the edges like the stubborn snow. The Government claims total regeneration and recovery is attainable, but there must be a strict regime and sacrifice.

"Yes, we have given much, but our health relies on exercise and diet." She listens to the news as she cooks her evening meal. "We are battered, we are sore, but we all need to take strong medicine." She swallows a spoonful of cod liver oil, washing it down with a liquid food supplement. "For our nation's body to be well we may have to do things we do not choose, but what is good for us." She switches off the radio and stares at the ceiling instead. It sounded like the fascists, it sounded like the communists. She is

365

disappointed the socialist republic has found nothing new to say.

"Whoever you voted for, the government got in," Branca used to say, neglecting her duty to vote. She black x-ed instead the rising numbers of infected patients, calculating TB potentially existed in two billion carriers world-wide.

She found virulent strains and resistant mutants, bacteria immune to antibiotics and treatments. She campaigned for compulsory BCG inoculation, tried to publicise it was no longer a poverty disease. When a TV weatherman contracted it, he was misreported as having leukaemia. He preferred that to the truth, to what he saw as a nineteenth-century disease, existing in ghettos and workhouses.

Branca had tried fashion propaganda, getting a young designer to make sloganed t-shirts. TB KNOWS NO CLASS DISTINCTION. TB OR NOT TB: GET INOCULATED NOW.

There was a counter-movement from campaigners keen to stall what they saw an unnecessary jabs. NORTH SOUTH EAST WEST NO TO SCIENCE MOTHER NATURE KNOWS BEST.

Branca had despaired, watching children waste away to nothing, but when the greater child killer began her preoccupations seemed indecent. What was the sense of preventative measures where death fell daily and without judiciousness from the sky. Her national screening maps were obsolete as borders shifted and the population were relocated in cattle trucks. She put away her specialism and widened to practise generally. Then the call from the first line came.

In her kitchen in a pool of oily sunlight she hears the boundaries are finally internationally recognised. An American envoy comes to talk business and minor royalty begin a string of state visits.

New shops open; the tourist industry relaunched. The currency seems less brittle, passed with rumpled edges across post office counters. Unfamiliar coins no longer rattle awkwardly in her pocket. She stops noticing the faces on banknotes and spends them confidently without pausing to check their denomination.

Her friends talk of getting married – all they need is the spouse. One wants blue eyes, the other a sense of humour. They agree with the newspaper analysis: the country has been dysfunctional for too long. It is time for stability, family life and morals. It is their duty: the population needs boosting. Contraceptives become less readily available.

She argues with her friends, saying they are being treated as chattel and brood mares. No, she did not want a child. No, she did not want to increase the new community. Her biological clock was not ticking; it got smashed with many other things just after the whole thing began. She threatened to end the friendship by calling them lewd names she immediately regretted. They looked at her, soft-eyed. It is loneliness, they said. We are lonely. They wept soundlessly behind closed eyes and she never broached the subject again.

She wakes in the night, sleep-blind rushing to a mirror. Her eyes crease against a spotlamp, she touches nostrils, lips, chin. In her dream they were eaten away, her own system turning cannibal. "Biting off your nose to spite your face", Branca's phrase.

Her skin had been distorted, features chewed away, deleted. In the morning from Branca's notebooks she read it was Lupus Vulgaris, the common wolf. A virulent form of TB, it reduced the face to something canine and inhuman. A self-mutilating carnage, physiognomy reduced to a living skull.

It did not say if there was any cure.

She begins to paint their bedroom and fill the cracks caused by explosions. One night the roof had rumbled as a jet carrier dropped its cargo on the town. She had rejected the shelter and lay stiff in bed, willing the house to be struck. Branca's base had been hit the week before. All colour had seeped from her eyes.

She polyfills the holes as in Geneva the Government deny the charges of mass murder and genocide. Fresh earth graves have been found in a football stadium. The Government claim it was not them but the others, keen to tarnish their reputation. She smoothes the walls with her scraper. The radio blares. As she throws it through the skylight the glass tinkles and breaks, shards of solid water falling in upon her. Distorted, the radio still speaks. It has got caught in the guttering.

She sits on the edge of a chair, pointed elbow on knee, waiting. She lights a cigarette, disliking its familiar furring of her palate. Moss grows inside her cheeks. She puts on music, sits listening to it on the edge of a chair, pensive. There is nothing to do. Chores demand completion but she is unable to contemplate their simple complexities. She changes the music, fast forwards to a favourite track. Sits. She lights another cigarette, feeling the coat thicken on her tongue. She looks out the window to the house bricks across. No windows. No life. Merely mortar. She lights another cigarette, forgetting she already has one smouldering in a saucer. She watches the column of ash increase, the slow burn from solid white to shiver grey. Her elbow presses into the pinched flesh of her thigh. She rises, walks through her three rooms, looking vaguely. The music ends. She returns, sits. She does not know what she is waiting for, only that it will pass. She puts on more music but decides she prefers silence. She sits and smokes a cigarette whilst she waits for it to pass.

The Spring arrives hesitantly, a tincture of yellow in the afternoon light. She unhooks her curtains to wash them and leaves them beating from the window-sill to dry. The cost of living goes up. The Government asks for voluntary reductions in wages, to which the workforce voluntarily comply.

Her friends come to visit, wearing one another's clothes. By sharing they double their wardrobe; they laugh girlishly at one another's dress. She offers her own which they fall upon with cries like little birds. On rounded flesh the fabric falls correctly. They spin and twirl in her cartwheel skirts. She kneels on the bed, watching their dip and caw over the remnants of her wardrobe, seeing their curious fingers withdraw from Branca's side of the chest. Faces avert but eyes dart into that side of the closet. They look bashful and with distaste, as though it were flesh, not material, silent on the rails.

She has taken to sleeping with Branca's clothing on the nights when unconsciousness will not come. She imagines she can still smell the trace of a warm body cooling in the threads.

Woollen fibres are the best. A scent of perfume, laboratory antiseptic and clean skin fresh from the shower. She pads the sweaters with old t-shirts, the better to hold and to intensify the smell. She knows in truth it is her imagination. Branca had washed everything, in preparation for the front.

After it happened, one bag was returned. An army regulation sack, soiled and anonymous on the kitchen table. She put it away into a cupboard; another time to deal with that. It smelt of death.

Branca's last belongings lie under telephone directories in the closet as she sleeps with her laundered clothes in the too-big bed.

With some forms of Tuberculosis, the treatment is so intense symptoms are relieved almost immediately. Owing to the complexities of strains, many tablets need to be taken, often with unpleasant side-effects.

What Branca had asked of her infected patients was absolute commitment to its cure. A full course could take three-quarters of a calendar, the gestation period of a human foetus.

Unless carried full-term, the treatment became ineffectual. Although externally well, the patient could be a highly contagious walking incubator, nurturing mutant strains. When passed on to another, it might be months before a reliable treatment was devised. A cocktail of toxins to counter the lethal infection. If that patient failed to complete the course of antibiotics, mutations of mutations would cell divide, each bearing the idiosyncracies of the individual's make-up.

It had given Branca nightmares. She would sit over calculations, reworking the alternatives of a mutant collision into a web graph. The possibilities covered the bedroom floor, crawling up onto the bed. She sweated, woke thrashing in the night, fingers working invisible microscopes. Her colleagues said she was strained, she was driving herself too hard. Take a holiday, have a break ... She out-stared them and walked away.

It was the silent flexibility of the disease which gripped her. Its cunning. She looked at human bodies in the street, the outward sign of affluence and health, inside which the poison might be secreted. People standing together at a tram stop, rubbing shoulders in a packed lunchtime cafe. Any age any race any class any sex. The disease could be harboured safely beneath that tent of skin, not yet ticking but waiting for detonation. One slip, a biological hiccup and the bacterium could be activated, its manifestation in many guises. She cursed its cleverness, its consuming promiscuity. Her private name for it was hate.

As the summer comes people shyly begin to go down to the river. They undress slowly in the trees' shade. She sits on a towel, cautiously unbuttoning. Like the others, she is meditative, exposing an inch at a time.

The Government claim they have found the extreme factions and will punish them severely after a public trial. The accused affirm their innocence, their defence argue that they are scapegoats. Opinion becomes heated, there are demonstrations and comments in other countries. To avoid civic unrest, the Government says the trial will be in camera. Three days later the accused are found guilty and privately executed for war crimes.

A peace activist dies in a freak household accident. On page twelve of the newspaper, her post-mortem is recorded as Death by Misadventure. Students rally in the streets, peace centres work for tolerance and multiculturalism. She had been from a former enemy state and had received racist threats. Allegedly. The Government claims it is merely coincidental. The country has been purged of such things. They are a nation, they are united. The future beckons. It looks bright. It is with regret the right to demonstrate is temporarily revoked. They are confident the citizens will understand. It is for the country's stability and health.

She swims in the river, a t-shirt protecting her skin from sun burn and stares. Wet, the cotton clings to her. She watches her exposed skin change colour, from milk white to tea stain. Her freckles make a bridge across her nose. Lying on her towel, a child practises counting on her ribs. His mother calls him away sharply, a sarong wrapped loosely about her shoulders. Their eyes meet briefly. They recognise they both have the sickness. The mother's eyes drop. She speaks harshly to the child and puts on more clothing. Ants crawl in the grass. She lets them clamber over her fingers.

It was debatable whether TB would develop or not in a carrier. Data was insubstantial, the bacteria only visible when animated. It was covert, in stilled suspension, held napping under so many skins. The person beside you at work, Branca said. Your favourite film star, the baby in the buggy you cooed over politely. Traces were in the air, sucked into lungs to claw there, pocking.

Research grants had been few for it was considered to be obsolete. There were many kinds of Tuberculosis, all of them shocking. It was an ancient malaise that was denied, not suitable for the twenty-first century. It was a condition which did not exist. The human race had developed. It was a disease which had been beaten, like so many other things, after the Second World War.

Branca had smiled bitterly. On occasion she would weep.

She walks up through bronzing bodies to the place she had stood on New Year's Eve. She remembers the ice and her pillow-slip of stones. She smokes a cigarette on the bridge where they had both stood, the summer she gave up smoking. The village across is being renovated for problem families. Earlier, the bulldozers had been in to clear away all trace of the original inhabitants. Dust still spirals the air. She inhales it, breathes deeply, holds it in her capillaries and lungs.

All air is poisoned, Branca had said. Everything is contaminated, there is nothing that is pure. It is sheer luck or genetic design which determined whether the bacterium developed or not. She did not know. She would never know. Perhaps it was inevitable.

She stands. She holds her breath.

A PLOT OF LAND

Babs Walters

There are fourteen steps leading to number Fifty Pit Street's front door. From there you can look over the river wall and across to the railway line, and that's what Abel is doing now; sitting on the doorstep, in his working clothes, having a smoke, and counting how many trucks the engine is shunting towards the pit. There must be plenty of empties, when he comes into the back kitchen he's rubbing his hands together, and saying, "Well there's hopes!"

His sister Lily May and I know – there must be plenty of empty trucks – empty trucks mean Abel has hopes for a full week's work.

I'm handy for my Auntie Lily, when I'm not in school. I've scrubbed the steps from top to bottom, she has rewarded me by buying a Film Fun, it's my favourite comic, I love to draw, you don't need to go to school to learn to draw, I've drawn Oliver and Stan's bowler hats, and I've perched them on their heads just like they wear them in the pictures; and I can draw Joe E. Brown's big mouth.

"Absent again I see," Abel looks at me, his black face has red rimmed eyes. He begins to preach to his sister. "I have told you often enough, if she doesn't go to school regular, when she leaves school, she won't go to work regular." I place my hand under my chin screwing my face into what I think is a look of pain.

"See, it's still swollen."

"Aye, I must admit she does look a bit lopsided,"– he turns to Lily May and says – "take her back down the surgery; have him to take another look at her."

I hide my comic under my jumper, and make to leave the kitchen.

"You stay there," she said. She is frying him an egg, she's an expert with eggs, she spoons the hot bacon fat over the yolk until there's an almost transparent blue veil covering it, carefully she transfers it from the frying pan to his plate, he has washed his hands;

they are white to the wrists. Because he still wears working clothes, he puts a sheet of newspaper on one of the kitchen chairs, he pours his tea into his saucer and dips the crust of bread into the egg's yolk, and Lily May's work of art disappears.

"I'll take her back down to the surgery," she says, "but he's the Doctor and he should know."

"It won't kill him to take another look; I don't think it's Mumps, that swelling have been there a long time, I see by my docket he's had another pay rise, more stoppages before I get my pay again, I see he has a car, I think it's brand new, and there's me working all the hours I can and I can't afford to buy a plot of land to keep a pig!"

I seen the doctor's car – it went whizzing around the corner by Sidoli's yesterday.

"The doctor needs a car," my Auntie said. "We don't need a pig!"

Abel already has a plot of land; he rents it from the farmer, two shillings and sixpence a year, on one half is his allotment, on the other half my Auntie keeps chickens. My Auntie hates pigs – but she loves chickens, her newly hatched chicks, tweet tweet, and mess the flagstones on the kitchen floor, but she doesn't mind not one bit, she has an old cardboard box, she puts one of her old cardies in the bottom and pokes holes in the lid of the box.

"So that they can breathe properly," she says, she lifts them gently one by one and they sleep quietly all night near the hearth. I used to clean her chicken's cot – until her red rooster flew on my shoulder and pecked at my head – Abel heard my screams, he came full pelt from the allotment and flung her rooster against the wire fence. I ran into the house screaming to Lily May that her brother had killed it. The next morning she took me by the hand, to the hen house, and there it was strutting amongst the hens.

"As large as life," she said, "and as cocky as ever!"

Abel crumples the paper he has been sitting on into a ball and throws it into the fire, the iron boiler is on the hob, he tests the water with a finger.

"Hot enough for a bath – but I don't think I'll bother to shave."

"We wouldn't expect you to," she says, "the only decent shave you have is on weekends – then you get all togged up to visit the barmaid in the Jenkins Arms, and when you have wet your whistle enough, you come home singing that old Irish song Cockles and Mussels," she puts his Dai cap on and imitates him and I must admit she does good job of it too. I join in with the "Alive – Alive Oh!"

When I first came to live with them I wouldn't have dared to laugh, that dark stubble of my Uncle's makes him look fearsome, and I was scared of those bony fingers of my Auntie's. But I needn't have been, those fingers of hers are clever, she makes my dresses and petticoats on her treadle machine in the middle room, she can treadle at a terrific speed and her fingers guide the material under the foot, nimbly turning the cloth this way and that and then abruptly stopping, she draws out the thread and bites at the cotton – I hope I'll be able to sew like that one day.

And there is no need to be scared of Abel, his bark is worse than his bite – that's what most people say. Tommy Jones, he's in my class in school, reckons his father is stronger than Abel but he's not, when the fair came to the village, Abel rose the hammer and rang the bell every time – since that day Tommy Jones doesn't brag.

Abel lifts the iron boiler off the hob as if it was a feather, his hands are like shovels, they are peppered with blue scars. Attached to the belt that holds up his working trews is a piece of leather, when I first seen it I asked him "What's it for?" "That's to protect my arse," he said, "When I'm lifting the trams."

"That's not the kind of language to use in front of a little girl," Lily May had scolded – "It's called 'Pisyn-Tyn', bach, it's to protect your Uncle's bottom. He pushes hundreds of trams, at pit bottom, in and out of a pit-cage every day, it's always wet and cold at pit bottom, and the men doing that work are always the first to start and the last to finish. That's why your Uncle always looks so sour when he comes home from work."

Abel kneels besides the tin bath plunging his face into the steaming water soaping his short cropped hair vigorously. Lily hands me the soap and flannel to wash his back, the water runs down his neck and over his shoulders creating patterns. Lily inspects my handiwork.

"Splendid – as clean as a baby's bottom."

When he's washing his bottom half, we leave the kitchen and go into the middle room, from there we will know when he has finished, we'll see him through the middle room's window emptying the bath water down the sink in the backyard. Now that Abel's out of earshot I ask Lily , "Are you going to have babies?"

"NO, never! I don't like men."

"Will Abel marry?"

"Him – he'd run a mile if a woman as good as looked at him, anyway I'm the only woman who would put up with those sour looks."

It turned out that Abel was right about the swellings not being Mumps – they were Tubercular glands.

"Consumption – that's what they mean, Dear God, that's what her mother had, my dear sister bless her soul – Nora, you will have to go to hospital."

"Hush, woman, can't you see you're frightening her?"

"I'd rather go to school," I said. Abel was right, she was frightening me, my mother went to hospital and never came back, and I don't want my Auntie to bless my soul, she goes to the spirit meetings, and she talks to her mother's and father's souls. "When you're older I'll take you," she said. "But you must promise never to tell Abel."

I know – because Abel says we should all let the dead rest in peace.

It was an Easter time when my mother brought me to Pit Street, my father had bought me an Easter egg wrapped in silver paper tied with wide blue ribbon.

"As blue as the colour of your eyes," he had said. He had called the red hat my mother wore, "a wicked looking thing!" The egg had been moulded into the shape of a tubby policeman, complete with truncheon helmet and tunic – I ate the buttons on the tunic on the train. We travelled through Welsh tunnels under mountains, the carriage we were in swayed like a ship in a storm. I clung to my mother like grim death and when the lights went out I began to cry.

"Don't worry my lovely," she had said, "I know the train driver!"

My mother's lipstick had been the colour of her hat, when she left, Lily May had wiped the kisses away with Abel's rough flannel. I had been afraid of her bony fingers then, but as I have said, I'm not now, she earns a few bob on the sewing machine, she buys fags but Abel doesn't know. I sleep with Lily May in her double bed, she's like a block of ice in bed. I arch my back and draw my knees into a lap, her bottom sits snugly there.

"Anaemic – that's what the doctor said I am – that's why I'm so cold. What's Anaemic?"

"Pink blood," she says.

I pretend I'm asleep when she comes to bed, she doesn't disturb me. I dream my father has made a fortune, and he comes to visit, driving a car the same colour as my mother's hat and even posher than the Doctor's. He takes us to Aberavon seaside and we eat ice cream and fish and chips.

It's Abel's voice shouting up the stairs that wakes me. "You don't have to go to hospital, it says so in this letter, you just have to attend a Clinic three times a week for treatment."

"They don't die in Clinics – do they, Abel?"

"Of course not – don't be bloody silly!"

We go by bus to the Clinic – Abel is worried about the bus fare, and Lily May is very bus sick. Her spirit friends advised her to put brown paper under her corset, she sits on a bench in the waiting room and every time she moves the paper rustles, she doesn't know where to hide her face.

"Bright blue eyes, pink cheeks – but two stone under weight." That's what the doctor said, I told Abel.

"Did you tell him you eat like a horse?"

I nod my head to Abel's question but the Doctor makes me

feel shy and I don't say anything.

"This one is tongue tied," he tells the nurse.

"What do they do to you behind those closed doors – that's what I want to know?" Lily May said . I take a deep breath and I tell her.

"My treatment is called violet ray – there's a huge lamp in the middle of a huge room – they put a screen around us and we sit on chairs and get sunburnt all over, but when we have finished, we go under a shower, it's always cold and I'm glad to put my clothes on. We only wear our knickers and a pair of dark glasses, and there we are sitting behind the screens with only knickers on." I have never seen Lily May only in knickers.

"That's why they give you dark glasses to wear," she said. I didn't say but the glasses didn't prevent me from leaning that when you grow up breasts will come in all sizes!

The lump wouldn't go away with the treatment, so they said it had to be cut out. I wasn't very brave before the operation, but I was very brave when it was all over.

"It didn't hurt," I told Lily in the bus going home, the nurse told me to keep very still and that I wouldn't feel anything. I didn't believe her but I didn't feel nothing honest, the Doctor said he had been able to do a neat job!

"Is it bleeding?" Lily May was a green colour. I lifted a wad of bandages. "Take a look," I said.

But she wouldn't look; when we got home she went straight to bed.

"I'm starving," I told Abel, "she wouldn't even take a look." He cut me a thick slice of bread and plastered it with butter and strawberry jam.

"Lily had to go straight to bed because the bus made her sick again but she promised next week when I go back to get the stitches out, she'll take me into Neath Market for faggots and peas. I heard the doctor say I was his last operation in this country and that he was going to America, fancy going to live in America – where all the cowboys are – when I grow up I'm going to be a Doctor and learn how to do neat jobs and go to A -"

"OH! shutup about America – what did they say about you?"

"ME, I'm going to be all right Abel – all I need now, they said, was plenty of mountain air."

"That's a bloody relief – mountains we have plenty, and fresh air costs bugger all."

I tell you it was a good job my Auntie was in bed – she wouldn't have approved of all that cursing.

That summer the Pit was on slack time. Lily moaned at having to stretch the pennies. Abel borrowed the farmer's mare, we travelled the mountains, me on the saddle and him walking beside the horse holding the reins, when we got to the top of the highest mountain I thought I would be able to touch the clouds, and I told him so and he laughed and then confessed that he had thought the same when he was ten years old. It was funny to think of Abel being ten. We rested on the top of the mountain, he pointed down into another valley , and told me that my father's sister lived there. I remember my father's sister, she came for a visit and left some material that my father had sent her to give to Lily May, she made a matching skirt and bolero. We eat Lily May's hard boiled eggs on a rock that jutted out on to the valley below, we eat the boiled potatoes that Abel had from his allotment, Bess the mare pulled at the grass and the wind blew the long grass, it looked like the waves of the sea. I did what I liked doing best – draw; I drew Abel sitting on the rock waving his arms as if to fly, or I watched him cleverly pleating rushes into a baby's rattle, he told me his mother had taught him to do that. I made a whip out of the rushes – it tapers , and it will make Bess trot on the way home, on the way home we see the smoke leaving the chimney pots in a straight line – Abel says that's a sign of a fine day tomorrow. I draw Lily May standing on the front doorstep anxious-eyed waiting, arms folded.

"Is my father dead, Abel?" Before he answered, he knotted his muffler neatly, there's a hazy film over his eyes.

"Of course not – we would know if he was dead – he'll come back, the man would be a fool not to – knowing there's a little girl of his very own waiting for him."

"Oh! Abel if he won't, let me be your own, I will sell all my drawings – and we'll buy a plot of land and you can keep a pig and I can keep a horse!"

"You tell that to your Auntie when we get home!" My Uncle smiles and my Auntie reckons when Abel smiles it's like the moon coming over the mountain.

THE PRIEST AND THE WIND

Anthony James

Their eyes watched him almost unblinking, neither friendly nor hostile and he knew that they silently noticed the awkward way he was holding his head. He was impressed by the strangely dignified stillness of their manner and by their shrewdness, acute yet neutral.

"I just called to say how sorry I am that this has happened. I feel ashamed to live in this community. I would like you to believe that not everyone here is alike. Many of us are ... sickened by what was done to you."

"It is good of you to call, Father," the man said. Eugene was surprised by the cultured, perfect English which the man spoke and then was immediately ashamed of his surprise. There were fine, soft lines around the man's eyes which, together with his greying hair, gave an impression of weariness and sophistication. Below the eye there was a deep raised cut in the dark brown skin with four stitches in it. The woman smiled, but painfully; the left side of her face was swollen to twice its normal size and its colour, Eugene guessed, was as bright as the colours of the sari she wore, though the lividness was muted by make up. He knew that she was watching the rather twisted posture of his neck and head.

There was a sudden, swirling knot of movement behind him at the door of the shop. A boy of seven came to the counter, levered himself half up on it with his elbows and pointed to some chocolate bars. The woman passed the bar and took the money in a single soft movement, while looking at Eugene.

"It is kind of you to come. We will remember," she said in English, not quite as perfect as her husband's. The little boy's mother shouted coarsely at him and coming into Eugene's line of vision, she made an obscurely frightening impression on him. She wore jeans which were very faded and her hair was short, but her fair hair, pale face and eyes all seemed to be the same, almost colourless, shade as her jeans.

A man with a thick short neck and a dungaree jacket with no buttons walked purposefully to the counter with a tabloid newspaper, on the front of which was a coloured photograph of a young woman taken from behind, naked except for a tiny pair of white pants which were around her knees, beneath the photograph was a headline : VIRGIN'S FIVE HOUR ORDEAL WITH SEX FIEND.

"If there is anything I can do – anything at all, please let me know," he said.

"Thank you," they both said with the same absence of any warmth or any abruptness.

Eugene left the shop and walked a little way down the hill. The wind seemed not so much cruel as impatient, streaming out of the west, up from the sea and over the mountains, a restless March wind full of the mingled elements of Winter and Spring, tearing on, changing the world, transforming sky and land.

This area was pitched on the highest ground for many miles and the whole industrial landscape, muted, half healed, oddly tranquil in this age in which the heavy industry had gone, could be seen for mile after mile and so could the city itself, right to its centre.

A disconcerting city, Eugene had thought, five years ago when he had first come here. The rolling slopes of pine, with their secretive clearings, their burnt-out cars and their stray horses, reached almost into the centre of the city. The wind was dragging the loose grey hems of clouds over the forested slopes, but in the west the weather was clearer and the clouds were coloured crimson, pink and apricot by the setting sun.

A policeman stood by the smoking remains of a large building. The concrete had been cracked by the heat and the metal was twisted, the shattered glass was blackened. The officer was unusually tall and powerful and his face was strong and well shaped, but the eyes were surprisingly small and vague, barely sketched in.

"Good evening, Father."

Eugene smiled and looked at the remains. "This community could have done without those shopkeepers being beaten up, and this within twenty-four hours," the priest said

"I expect the guy and his wife could have done without it at any time," the policeman said and laughed.

"I don't find it funny, Alec. I've just been to see them. Have you seen their faces?"

"Yeah. Seen them. Seen worse too."

Eugene noticed the unpleasant thinness of his voice and was irritated by it.

"I don't find it amusing."

"Don't you, Father? Well, last Saturday night we had one car, two officers and a sergeant on the control desk to cover the entire East side. So don't take our laughter away, Father, or we might go mad and be taken away to a rest home and then everyone can get on with killing each other in peace."

"I'm sorry."

"Well, they got their brand new community centre built which you and all the other good people have campaigned for all these years. And in three months they've burnt it down. Well, what can we give them next?"

"They've been neglected and forgotten for years enough, and their older brothers and sisters and their parents before them. Perhaps they find gratitude a little hard to deliver, particularly as they are fed on films which tell them that violence and destruction are right. You have your frustrations, they have theirs."

"Naturally, naturally, Father. I was brought up a good Catholic. Doesn't the wife come along to Mass every Sunday? Can't make it very often myself. She says that it's not much like Mass, more like one of her father's union meetings. And of course, I've read about your views in the papers. Well, when we get the ones that burnt it and the ones that done the Asians up the road, I'm sure you'll be on hand to tell them they're forgiven. And I'm sure the courts will take a very enlightened view. Well, I'd better be going."

Eugene said nothing as the officer walked to his car. After watching the car drive off, he crossed himself and without being able to invest the words with any meaning or emotion, he prayed that understanding and communication between races, between generations, between individuals would not entirely break down. But the words sounded too bland, and too much like the platitudes uttered on the five-minute religious spot on a morning radio programme, and he had to force himself to finish the prayer.

On the way home he suddenly felt wildly happy. For a time that restlessness, which had haunted his waking moments since the age of twelve, left him. Always he had the sense that he had not done enough, had not accomplished enough, that time was running through his fingers; always he feared chaos because he could not keep up with all that he was supposed to complete. Eugene was not in the habit of praying for anything for himself but if he had done so he would have prayed to be relieved of this feeling. Yet he knew also that this was theengine which drove an unusually productive and active life.

The sunset made him think of his childhood and of his mother. Great showers of rooks and crows pitched across the sky there, as they did here, where the hills and the marsh and the streets of the council estate touched each other. He had been a frail child, and when he was ill he remembered his mother giving him potatoes left over from the supper she had cooked for his father the evening before. He remembered the intense happiness of sitting up in bed, eating the potatoes and watching the crows and rooks passing across the evening sky in a cloud. He used to say that he had always loved God, and always wanted to be a priest as long as he could remember; the words, images, sights, sounds, smells and stories of the Church had drawn him in. Yet lately he wondered if that was quite true. There was a very early memory of sitting in sunlight and in wind, on the fresh grass near the house with the strong sense that there was some ....element, some presence benign and powerful, somewhere beyond the trees and clouds and wind, beyond the air itself which he knew intimately. And this, he was sure, was before he had ever heard the name of Jesus. Then, he had no words to describe what he felt and he could hardly find them now as he relived that moment.

He was working late, sitting at the word processor when Marilyn called, indeed he rather expected her to call, and felt a mixture of fear at what might bring her here, and pleasure. He opened the door and looked with narrowed eyes into the darkness and wind and listened to the rustling of the bushes by the path. She hesitated, well back in the shadows; her visits always began with this uncertainty and diffidence. "Come in," he said as soon as he saw her.

Inside she sat down immediately, breathing rapidly. Her face was flushed and the eyes glazed.

"Just let me be quiet for a while," she whispered. He sat facing her silently.

"Marilyn..." he said after some minutes.

"He got into the house again."

"Isn't there any way –"

"Come on, he was a marine commando for years. In one of the special units. He doesn't find it difficult to get into a council house."

"What happened?"

"He banged my head against the wall a bit. I've got some bruises on my ribs. Do you want to see?" she asked, suddenly smiling with that sharp, almost feverish, brightness which made men turn away. Eugene did not turn away but smiled back and said, "That wouldn't do any good. I'll call a doctor if you want me to."

She shook her head, relaxed now, and he noticed again how she always looked like a young girl though she must be nearing forty. Whatever had happened earlier, her clothes were immaculately turned out and she wore the same short skirt as ever, from under which she carelessly showed glimpses of stocking and suspender. On her second visit to him she had crossed her legs a little higher and said, "Isn't it lonely being a priest?" Then came the smile, a smile on fire and relentless which always returned to her and was never gone for long. The smile which said : I can see straight into your soul. Now laugh, for God's sake, laugh at life – and then we'll go to bed.

Eugene had smiled straight back into those glistening green eyes with their amused expression, turned down slightly at the inner corners. He had lived a celibate life and not having to think about his appearance in usual terms, as most people did, he was coolly objective about it. He knew that he did not look like anyone's idea of a priest. He looked like a tall Irish sailor or truck driver; or perhaps more like some male film idol playing a sailor or a truck driver. At times, his looks had been useful to him because of the impression they created.

"Marilyn," he had said, "You are a very beautiful woman. If

talking to me does any good, I'm happy. I certainly like your company. I know that some priests find the vow of celibacy difficult to keep. But of all my vows I have not found that one difficult to keep."

"How's that?" she asked, amused as ever.

"I don't know. For some priests it is the right life, the only life."

She looked over at the mantelpiece where there was a framed photograph of Eugene and another young man, almost equally handsome, both about twenty years old.

"Bernard. A friend. A lifelong friend. I don't lust after men either," he said laughing.

"Are you sure I can't get you a doctor this evening?" he asked now.

"No."

"But just to record the injuries. You did say he beat you up."

"Yes. And did the other thing which gives him pleasure."

"But if he raped you -"

"I should go to the police? But my eldest boy adores him. So do I have his father sent to prison? And then what's rape exactly? It depends what you mean by rape."

"Only you can answer that. But no woman should have to ask herself that question. If there was any room for doubt, it was his fault and not yours."

"I know. I know. You're a nice man. It's just that we were married for ten years, some of them happy."

"Where are your children?"

"With my sister. They were with my sister when he got into the house. I was on my own – this time."

"Shall I go and see him, Marilyn?"

"No. Not yet, anyway. I'll let you know."

"Tea? Coffee?"

"Do you have any whisky?"

"Yes," he said smiling, "I get a lot of colds in the Winter."

"What's wrong with your neck? You look as if you are in pain."

"Oh, just a stiff neck. Age."

They sat for some time in silence. Marilyn drank a whisky quickly and then a second more slowly and Eugene drank coffee. The light from the lamp on the table at which he had been working lit up her long, thick red hair.

"They taught him these skills so that he could fight for his God, his Queen and his Country, now he's using them on me. He does what he likes. Comes and goes when he wants to."

"There are skills you can call on. Mine for instance. I'll go and see him. You must do something before –"

"I'll think about it," she said, apparently quite recovered now. "The trouble is I can never say no. I never could as a young woman and I don't find it any easier now. Let's see, I was brought up a good Catholic, went to a convent school. You'd tell me that the temptation to –"

"I would tell you – I am telling you – that I wish sex made you happy instead of so unhappy. You may find it difficult to say no, but if you do say it, no man has the right to ignore that. I wish you had a happy sex life, if that's what you want."

"But I've lost my faith. I got divorced. I've ditched the Church."

"You can return when you want to. The Church is waiting, if that's what you want."

He knew that she saw the sadness, the desperation, as well as the physical pain in him though he tried to hide his emotions by pouring more coffee from the tall insulated pot with the ornate handle shaped like a snake.

"I don't want to return. It doesn't mean anything to me."

"I'm sorry."

"I've had four children. Three surviving. And two abortions. What do you think of that, Father? Isn't that a sin?"

"I think it is terrible that circumstances make people reject children, make people feel they have to reject life."

"And my little boy? The one who died? I suppose I should tell myself that he's waiting for me and we'll both be resurrected into eternal life together. Well, that means sod all to me. He's gone. Why can't I touch him now? Hold him now? Why did he die?" She put the whisky glass down on the floor without seeming to notice that she had done it. The smile had left her now, she looked as she had when she had arrived – worse.

"I believe in forgiveness and I believe that death is not the end. I believe there will be an end to grief and separation and loss and that we shall be reunited. That's my faith. I wish you could accept it too."

He knew he sounded bewildered as he said it – not unbelieving, but surprised, mystified.

"That's not fair," she said, the smile was back now, but heavier, tinged with something colder. "The Catholic faith says that some things are true and others aren't. Christianity says that some things are true and others aren't. You're a bit evasive for a priest – or a Christian."

"Sorry."

"When I was in London I knew some people who got into black magic in a big way and ended up terrified out of their wits. I also knew some people who got into witchcraft, I mean belief in the old pagan gods, which seemed a lot healthier than Christianity. Now the faith says : 'Thou shalt not suffer a witch to live.' What do you think? Should those people be killed off or not?"

"I think that society is corrupt and cruel, and offers people very little, and that the Church has too often failed them. I'm sorry that some people turn to evil in their confusion. There are many religions, of course, some with a lot of truth and beauty in them, it is to be expected that other people will turn to those."

"But what does that mean? About killing witches?"

"I'm not Christ. I'm a priest – and not a very good one." He felt immense relief at adding these words. "If you want to ask what our Lord meant, cross the road, go into the Church and ask Him. Perhaps He will answer, though probably not immediately and not in the way you expect."

"You're a sly bastard, Father."

"Part of the job."

For several minutes he had been wondering if she was deliberately tormenting him, deliberately mocking him. But there was no cruelty in her face and no appetite for cruelty. He realised that she had seen that he and his faith were travelling down the road which she had already travelled. Beneath the words was a tenderness and a wish to share that experience with him, a sense of fellowship, comradeship. He also knew that if it had been anyone else who had called on him – as they frequently did – he would have put up with it and given the best answers and the best advice and comfort he could, while all the time feeling nothing but weariness and distaste. "Bernard is coming to see me tomorrow," Eugene said thoughtfully, nodding at the mantelpiece and the framed photograph.

"Good looking."

"Not any more. He's got very fat and lost his hair."

"Is he another one like you?"

"What does that mean?"

"You're not exactly a usual or conventional kind of priest are you? If you were, I wouldn't be here. Anyway, everyone in this city has heard about those sermons and then that stuff in the papers and on TV I just wondered if he was like you."

"No, he's not much like me. I suppose he's unique enough in his way."

Eugene had celebrated Mass without feeling on the following morning which was a Wednesday. He was depressed by the feeling that the church itself was a flimsy, insubstantial building, floating irrelevantly, like a forgotten inflatable toy from a carnival, through these gouged and graffiti-slashed streets. His lifelong sense that the church during Mass was a vessel of eternity in a sinful world, that here for a time men and women could be together in another realm, in the presence of God, had left him. Whatever his tiny congregation felt, Eugene had no sense of sanctity or the presence of God, nothing shielded him as he went through this mechanical set of words and actions from the squalor and anxiety of daily life, and he felt that Mass was one of the more absurd activities of ordinary living. His face hurt with the effort of restraining his tears and while he spoke other words he inwardly offered a prayer that all that he had lost, his sense of wonder and joy might be restored to him.

That afternoon he attended a long meeting with some local councillors on what should be done now that the new community centre had been burnt down. Afterwards, a reporter from the local paper was waiting for him. A well-known right-wing councillor, who had recently lost his seat, had made a speech blaming the recent racial attacks in the area on Eugene personally. Radical statements such as Eugene's, the man had said, undermined respect for the law, undermined the position of the police and shifted the blame for violence, from the thugs who committed it, to society. Eugene said that he had no comment to make on blatant absurdity and that he was sorry the man had chosen to make himself so ridiculous in public.

The wind was still surging up out of the west as he walked home, sending the clouds spinning before it. Everywhere was a flickering dance of yellow and pale green. Somehow daffodils and fresh buds and leaves seemed to be growing everywhere. He remembered his early childhood again and the thick bed of daffodils near the house, and for a little while he felt happy.

Some youths were standing in the doorway to a block of flats drinking from cans and pressed up close against each other, hiding from the wind, and from their own lack of confidence, and their own fear.

"You pissing queer! Go and iron your dress for Sunday! Queer! Tell your God to kill me now if He can! I don't give a shit for God! Get back to your church, arsehole!" Their shouts were curiously eager.

Eugene turned and walked towards them slowly and deliberately. Once he had always been able to deal with this kind of situation, he had gained acceptance, respect and trust from the local youth, many of whom actually liked him. He always began by meeting their hostility by talking to them, he even carried a packet of cigarettes, though he had never smoked himself, in order to offer them to the young people he spoke with – to the outrage of some parents and teachers. He had spoken to them like equals, calmly, asking them about their attitudes, refusing to mention his faith or to admonish them. Now everything had changed. The youths ran off a few yards, stopped and began to shout the same abuse; he kept on coming but they ran a little further. Their shouts were so relentless that he could not even make himself heard, particularly at that distance. One of them threw an empty can at him. Again he walked steadily towards them, again they ran away, and again.

Finally, he turned away feeling tired, cold and above all bored, also, he wanted to get home because Bernard was coming to see him.

When Father Bernard Dignam arrived, Eugene decided that he looked physically more of a mess than the last time he had seen him. He hugged Eugene in a moment of pure delight. They had known each other all their lives. Bernard's head, which was bald, and his face were shapeless. But there were the eyes. They were eyes of the lightest grey, their expression almost abstract and their gaze still, straight, two lenses set in a mass of putty. The odd pucker of Bernard's lower lip revealed his essential kindliness and prevented him from seeming inhuman and intimidating. "I've just come from the bishop," Bernard said, lowering his equally shapeless body onto the sofa on which Marilyn had sat the night before.

"Really? Tea?"

"Please. Lots of it. No one makes tea like yours." Bernard rubbed his hands together. "The wind! Whenever I come here it reminds me of that trip to Greenland, the wind never stops blowing in Narssarssuaq either, just like this place."

"High ground. Would you like the Darjeeling ?"

"I would... The bishop is rather concerned about all the publicity. Your sermons and media pronouncements."

"I preach the faith and I attack sin and evil where I see it. Excuse me, I just need to bring the kettle, everything else is ready on the table here."

Eugene left the room with a trace of irritation.

"I'm not criticising," Bernard said when he came back. "I just mentioned that the bishop is concerned. You don't just say that there is evil in society, you say in print and on television as well as in church that certain political leaders and certain policies are chiefly responsible. You called those leaders the enemies of Christ and the Christian faith."

"And so they are."

"Yes, well, the bishop is concerned, that's all. – Ah, you know me, don't you dare spoil that beautiful drink by putting milk in it.

Thank you. – he's a little concerned, he would be in his position."

"He wants me to shut up."

"I didn't say that. He'll be writing to you today, though."

"I shall preach the faith to the best of my ability. Anyway, no one cares what a local priest says."

A change came over Bernard, a sudden chill of tension and sadness; he looked for some moments at the surface of his tea, at the beautiful amber liquid which caught the light from the lamp on the table. He was adjusting his mind, putting aside any possibility of a happy visit to his friend. His finely tuned intuition and the powerful clarity of his mind had perceived something terrible in this house, something almost tangible like a vast solid bulk.

"What's the matter with your neck, Eugene?"

"Probably a bit of rheumatism. My mother suffered with it in the neck. It's nothing to get concerned about."

"Have you seen a doctor?"

"No, but you forget that I did a year's medical training."

"See a doctor. I don't like the way you are holding your head."

"Don't fuss."

"What's wrong, Eugene? What has happened? And I don't mean your physical state." Bernard spoke abruptly, almost savagely.

Eugene stared at the carpet. He did not particularly like tea and was only drinking it to share in the almost festive pleasure which Bernard took in the ritual. He looked up at Bernard and asked, "Some lads shouted insults and abuse at me on the way home. Nothing uncommon. But I couldn't even get near enough to speak to them, they kept running away... What would you say to a woman, a Catholic who has lost her faith, the victim of a violent ex-husband, who has had two abortions and lost one child while still a baby? What would you say in answer to her doubts, her questions, her grief? Quote the Holy Father's latest encyclical?"

"I'm sure you gave your own answers. Why ask for mine?"

"I just wondered."

"Get out of here, Eugene."

"Where to?"

"Somewhere where people are dying, starving, where they need you, need the comfort you can give. It will take time and effort, but see the bishop as a first step."

"Things get worse, more rotten every day, and this is the time you tell the shepherd to leave the flock?"

"Things are not rotten in the way that you can help them – not you, not here. Your energies are no longer engaged. Go. You need to be on the front line. This society which you attack is poisoning you and your faith."

"Well, that should suit the bishop very well. The cause of his concern would be removed," Eugene said and finally put the cup away from him half drunk.

"That is as may be. Can you really believe it to be the reason why I am giving you that advice?"

"No," Eugene said after a long pause.

"Then go. Or at least begin to plan to go. It isn't easy to follow the faith in Christ. It wasn't two thousand years ago and it isn't now. It's even harder to be a priest. But faith doesn't exist in a vacuum, it exists in a certain context, within a certain way of life. You have to look at what is staring you in the face. You have to choose the best way in which you can serve God, use your clear wits. If you choose the wrong way, your faith will wither. If it does, blame yourself, not your faith."

"Will you hear my confession?"

Bernard stood up. "Don't ask me. Don't ask me again. When you have seen the bishop, when you have taken the first step, then I will hear it gladly."

Night. It was three days since Bernard had visited him and Eugene was sitting at his desk. There were three unfinished pieces of work in front of him, a sermon, an article for a Catholic magazine published in English and based in Paris, and a letter to a man whom Eugene had known since he was a young student. The man was a scholar, the author of several books on ancient Greece and Rome and a poet in his own right. He was not exactly a lifelong atheist, but rather someone who believed that the gods are cruel, life is tragic and can only be lived courageously – existence is like that and always will be. He did not so much disbelieve the Christian message as detest the

Christian God personally. Now that he was dying slowly and painfully his beliefs seemed stronger than ever.

When he tried to work, Eugene's mind was either blank, or when he found words, they seemed as disconnected and useless as a set of chess pieces would have seemed to him if he had never heard of chess. Anger began to rise in him like a stream of overheated and thickened liquid being driven with force from one end of his body to the other. He stood up and drove his fist into the crucifix which hung on the wall over his desk. It broke in half, snapped through the wood and the little ivory figurine of the body of Christ. Eugene sat down and began to cry, he reached out and put the pieces of the crucifix on his desk. His hand was bleeding and the blood dripped on his papers and on the two halves of the crucifix. If Eugene could have believed that some divine fire would strike him, it would have been easier, but he felt only a dull, nauseating ache. A friend on whom he had relied had disappeared from his life without explanation or any word of comfort, and all that was left were two broken bits of wood and ivory.

It was three weeks later and once again Eugene was celebrating Mass. Communion was about to begin and he stepped forward to the rail. He had been away for the last few days, attending a national conference on racism, which was being filmed and shown on television. By the morning of the second day, Eugene realised how the local M.P. for the area in which Eugene lived was playing an elaborate game with him. That game was part of the larger game being played in parliament by the M.P's party, based on what was seen as strategically correct to oppose the government over and what, on the other hand, the party should keep silent about. From that moment on, Eugene refused to talk to the press, refused to say more than hello to the M.P. or share a platform with him, and spoke only during the sessions of the conference.

He bought a paper several stations before the train arrived in the station that was only a mile from his church, directly below it in the valley. When he read that Marilyn's body had been found battered and strangled in her home and that the police were seeking her ex-husband, he was surprised that his grief was not as strong as his disgust that he should learn of her death from a newspaper on a train because of something so ineffectual and corrupted as the conference on racism. He knelt in the railway carriage, despite the giggles of some passengers, and offered a prayer for her soul. The rest of the prayer seemed remote from him, empty and absurd, but when he referred to Marilyn as 'our sister', the words suddenly moved him to tears and he found them comforting.

Today he intended to offer prayers for Marilyn in church and to devote his sermon on Sunday to her and her death. The first of the congregation, a woman and her son, who suffered with Down's Syndrome, began to make their way forward to take communion. Eugene extended one hand and arm in a gesture he had made since he had celebrated his first Mass; it was a gesture that was informal, almost casual, yet welcoming and at the same time it contained a faint shrug of helplessness and submission: Here I stand, just as much as all of you in the presence of this mystery, we cannot understand, we can only love and participate....

He took another step towards the rail and began to feel the bile rising in his throat, an odd roaring seemed to come from beneath the church. He had the hideous sensation that someone was behind him and was about to strike him on the head, a hateful, intolerable sensation like having his arm bent too far behind him. He tried to turn, but everything had gone blurred and looked far away. Then the bile stung his throat and he was in darkness. From a great distance he felt and heard the impact of his body on the floor.

There was certainly darkness, oceans of it, a vast silence in which he was suspended as a still point, a passionless, sensation-free existence for some enormous length of time. Then he began to be aware of himself, to think and to remember and slowly, faintly he was aware of sounds and fleetingly, sights from the world around him. Unhurriedly and with greater and greater clarity he began to think. He knew he was in a hospital and his hearing was at times abnormally sharp. There were discreet murmurs from just beyond doors, instructions, names of drugs. His own memory seemed clear, his own medical knowledge intact. Now he considered and analysed what he had refused, had not wanted to consider before. Did he, then, want this? Bernard had known, or guessed. A tumour pressing, pressing at the base of the brain near the spinal cord... and then the haemorrhage and the paralysis. If he could think clearly now, why not before? But his concentration was softening, ebbing away.

He could see the room fairly clearly, Bernard was there, but he looked very small and distant as if seen through the wrong end of a telescope. He could see that Bernard was preparing to give him the last rites. That might mean he was going to die but he had no sense of death being near. Bernard took his hand and Eugene found that his hearing, so sharp a little while ago, had left him at that moment. In any case he knew the words Bernard was saying off by heart and he knew the questions which Bernard, who could see that he was conscious, was trying to get him to respond to, questions about which of two eternities Eugene would go to if he died here at this moment. But Eugene felt comfortable and content and at peace for the first time in years and suddenly the words Bernard was saying didn't seem important. Instead he was thinking of sitting on the grass in the wind and sunlight as a tiny child and of the benign presence somewhere beyond the trees, the clouds and the wind. Suddenly he found he could move the forefingers on his right and his left hand and he could feel Bernard's hand with one finger. He could have pressed on the hand to respond to Bernard's questions but instead he stroked the hand once. If he lived, paralysed or not, he knew that everything would be different after this. And if he died, everything would be different and there was no need to do anything. It was enough to stroke Bernard's hand once, in recognition of a friendship which had lasted since childhood.

holes in the beach

Anna Hinds

today

as the fat rain started the holes filled up with water like piles of glass; a pretty array of fishponds, or the blue puddles on the duvet.

was enough to make me forget the ugliness of the beach, the ugly crude taste and sight and feel and sound of the beach, and to make me want to wade into the waves once more. Replaced were the ugly, vulgar memories that had torn at my insides for a decade – they were replaced by these new beautiful, singing memories that we had made. It was as though what we had done had wiped the slate clean, washed away the bad memories, the memories of what happened there, by the sea, what had happened to me.

when I was small

remembered what my uncle Ed said: "I would love to drown in the Welsh sea", was what he said, once, privately and conspiratorially to me as he sucked a long yellow cigarette in the kitchen before breakfast. He was reckless with words, throwing them about like dirty water or paper planes and I liked to listen. He said peculiar things, un-self-conscious about his words, and made people laugh, even people who loved him anyway. He said he wanted to drown but I couldn't think of dying in the Welsh sea. In my mind's eye I saw the sea around me, like a big brother, not a killer or a murderer. I thought Ed was wrong. I thought he was stupid but I didn't say so, not then.

before I was that old,

Ed said, "the sea has many secrets," exhaling loudly onto the cold window, "it knows the secrets of everyone." I never told the sea anything after that. It might tell other people. Cautiously I kept my voice low even in the house, in case the sea was straining its ears to hear. I wondered what secrets had the sea of its own?

one day in 1984,
it was a Friday, and I was 12 and old enough to walk there on my own, I found myself beginning to understand. As the sea tickled my toes and shouted noisily, I thought I was understanding a little bit more. As it screamed and scratched my eardrums like crows, and the waves yelled and called as they collided, I put my hands over my ears. And ran away from the noise, back home, thinking all the way that perhaps Ed was right after all and the sea was a secret killer.

the year after 1984
the sea was black for a month and seagulls circled restlessly, like litter caught in a windstorm, and some fell into the sea. In my bedroom I watched through the window and cried as the seagulls' noise penetrated the glass.

and then the sea became the killer. I saw the sea as a killer. It was not easy to look at the sea anew after those years, but I had to accept that Ed was right. I agreed with my head.

I fell asleep

in my dreams
the sea reeling and laughing, cawing and rocking, rearing up over the beach, screeching hysterically, and blackly seizing victims, dispassionately: babies with ice-cream mouths, snoring grandpas in deckchairs, cockle-picking toddlers. It reared up like a bear on its hind legs, and scooped them up laughingly.

once upon a time
continued Ed, "and when the sea drowns me, I will be taken fearlessly, and won't scream." Smiling as he reached for the jug on the table, and staring not at me. I was not supposed to listen to his stories, to the words that flew out of his mouth when his face was white. He said he had dreams too, and his dreams told him secrets… the secrets that he would tell me. My mother said not to listen. She said I mustn't take any notice because Ed "wasn't all there". But I think she was afraid of him because he told the truth.

when I was five

reached out and handed me one from his pack of twenty, grinning preposterously, and then laughed as I stuck it into my pocket. Like a stick of rock it poked into my leg, largely, and I walked down to the beach, because I thought the sea would enjoy it. (Before I hated the sea I would give it presents – pictures I drew, and leftover boiled sweets from my hot grimy pocket.) Later on when I went back to the house, after I threw it into the waves, Ed said: "that'll be our secret," and cackled just like the sea. I thought then, for the first time, that perhaps Ed was the sea. I also thought that Ed wasn't all that great, after all.

1988
like refuse he tipped his unwanted love over me and it burned my skin, but he tipped until I protested: and then he carried on. And the sand was no protection, it was no brother to me, and the sea watched, mocking my innocence. The sea watched and was my killer. It was my killer for not rescuing me.

Mocking my innocence like a tuneless song. It watched the invasion he inflicted upon me, as I struggled in the sand. Before my eyes rushed an absence of colour: a blackout.

today
like clean freshwater, he tipped his love over me, gushing and trickling softly. I wanted it to last forever. We went to the beach for it, to the private place that was mine in childhood, and as we made love the sand exploded beneath us. All the sounds at once, and all the feelings I had ever known happened at once, in a huge moment.

The moment crashed briefly around our ears, sand flying from underneath us, as we laughed and shared eyes like children do. I tasted his clean breath and watched his clear eyes.

1988
and regretting the impulse to visit the sea was I. Lying in the sand was I; helpless like a five-year-old was I.

Hating the sea and its memories was I.

What was he?

He was "not all there".

today

the moment stopped as the sand cleared and we saw the holes we had made. Tasting his unsmoky breath and looking into his clear, capable eyes that made sense, I could hear the sea.

laughing with us and enjoying our moment, uninhibitedly. Kissing my toes were the waves, sorrowfully. The sea was sorry it hadn't rescued me.

memories were new and fresh. I remembered that my mother told me that to move on you must create new memories of old places, and absolve parts of your life.

was forgiveness part of it? I forgave the sea on the spot as our lips met and the waves sang in time.

today

and as the fat rain started the holes filled up with water like piles of glass; a pretty array of fishponds, or the blue puddles on the duvet.

was enough to make me forget the ugliness of the beach, the ugly crude taste and sight and feel and sound of the beach, and to make me want to wade into the waves once more. Replaced were the ugly, vulgar memories that had torn at my insides for a decade – they were replaced by these new beautiful, singing memories that we had made. It was as though what we had done had wiped the slate clean, washed away the bad memories, the memories of what happened there, by the sea, what had happened to me.

BUNKERED

Liz Hinds

Today's modern supermarket offers its customers their choice from a huge range of tinned goods, from the family's favourite baked beans to the more unusual delicacies such as stuffed artichoke hearts. Tins, as well as being a safe convenient way to feed your family, make excellent building bricks.

I shouldn't really be here. I feel I'm wasting your time. Am I wasting your time?

What have I got to grumble about anyway? I've got a good life, a good husband, healthy children, a comfortable home. I shouldn't really be here. I shouldn't really be her, the woman in Sainsbury's. But I am the woman in Sainsbury's, I've always been her, as long as I can remember, I've been the woman in Sainsbury's.

But I wasn't always, was I?

Bunker. Bunker. Bunker. If I keep saying it, I'll remember it. Won't I?

You see, I wasn't always like this.

'Do you work?'

'No, I'm just a mum.'

The woman smiles apologetically. Her dinner party neighbour is appalled. How can he be expected to maintain a lively conversation with a 'justamum'? His reputation for witty intelligent talk is under threat from this justamum. She is about to speak. He cannot face hearing what baby did with his dinner tonight, and turns to the red-nailed career woman on his right, fondling her knee while sharing office gossip. Justamum looks from right to left at the wall of manly shoulders wedging her in and turns her attention to her plate. Her plate of chicken in kiwi and chocolate sauce, straight from last week's colour supplement, outstares her and she wishes she had eaten less, or more, of William's leftover fish finger and beans. She is beginning to identify her place in life.

Excuse me, Madam, do you want those tins? Shall I put them in the trolley for you? Madam?

Mother-in-law is visiting. She takes the opportunity to extol her daughters. 'Helen is flying back from America on Monday. It looks as if she will have to spend more time there the way her business is taking off. And Katherine's boss wants her to take charge of the office he's setting up in Bournemouth. Well, she practically runs the office at the moment, standing in for him as she does.' Mother-in-law looks at Justamum. 'Have you thought about getting a little job, dear?' Justamum shakes her head. 'Now the children are older, wouldn't you like a little part time job? It would get you out of the house.' Mother-in-law looks around. 'You could get someone in to clean for you.' Justamum reads her mind and sees the cobwebs and the finger marks and the dog hair. 'I'm happy as I am.'

I used to know who I am. Someone's wife, someone's mother. It was easy then. I had a role. I knew what to do. Suddenly I have to ask the question: what am I doing here? What reason is there for my continued existence? What justification is there for me being? If my purpose in life is gone why do I remain? I have played my role; I have borne babies; I have fed and clothed them. If they no longer need me, what am I? A drain. No longer giving, only taking. Society frowns on takers. The sun no longer shines on me.

SUPERMUM Amanda Blackwell, 34, as well as being a director of Hughes, Morgan & Price, current leaders in the world of marketing, is also mother of four children — and, as if this wasn't enough, this petite powerhouse insists on designing and making her own Christmas cards.
(*Good Housekeeping*, December.)

Justamum is looking for a job. She scans the evening paper. She considers her qualifications. She looks again. Twenty years of motherhood have prepared her for nothing. They haven't even prepared her for the empty nest. Husband sets standards. 'You don't want to work in a shop. You're too smart for that. You want to find something that's more suitable.' 'Such as?' Husband returns to Top Gear, and glamorous lady who understands cars. A man's dream.

The doctor says it's hormone discontent. And my age. And my circumstances. Children leaving home, empty nest. Very common in women of my age. That's why she sent me to you. Thought you could help. Can you help? Can anyone help? It's the not understanding, the unknowing of it that is so frightening.

Family holiday time doing family holiday things. Together. (For the last time?) Children insist on crazy golf. Justamum has fun in the sun, hitting little white balls down little black holes. Justamum wonders if this is a metaphor for life but is unsure what metaphor is so keeps mum. Instead asks question that has been worrying her. 'What do you call those piles of sand on a golf course?'

'Bunkers!' shout children and husband spontaneously, simultaneously.

'Ah, yes,' Justamum smiles, able to put niggle to bed for now but later same day is plagued again. She doesn't know why she wants to know only knows she doesn't know. Immediately imminent insanity is suspected. 'What do you call those piles of sand on a golf course?'

'Bunkers!' shout children and husband this time accompanying it with much head-shaking and hand-patting. 'There, there, Mum.'

Justamum makes a joke of it but knows deep down that imminent insanity is confirmed.

There's a line in the film where Crocodile Dundee hears about people having therapists. He says, 'What's the matter, don't they have any friends?' Of course I have friends. Don't I? But they're all out at work, or busy, at least in control of their lives. What would they think of someone who's lost the plot. The trouble is, I didn't realise this was part of the plot. I wouldn't have started the book if I'd known.

It's mid-morning and Justamum is alone in the house. Justamum walks into bathroom, looks around, and steps behind door. She is hiding, she doesn't know why. She breathes deeply. This is safe. She wants to understand but is willing just to hide for now. That'll do for now. That'll keep the fear from the door. Until later.

Can I help you, Madam? If we could just move these tins, only they're blocking the aisle. People can't get past to do their shopping. Would you like me to put them in your trolley, Madam?'

Justamum has always considered herself to have one redeeming feature: she is a good cook, a vital ingredient for the wife of a Welsh man who nurtures memories of his mam's apple pie. Tonight she ceased to be a good cook. Tonight her cawl was judged to be below its usual standard, the latest in a long line of not-as-nice-as-usuals. Justamum is puzzled. She did what she always does yet the end result is lacking. Another example of life mirroring reality. Is it possible, she wonders, to put this down to her hormones? Somehow she doubts it, and behind her smile lies the growing conviction that she has outlived her usefulness, passed her sell-by date. She will soon be found with the other damaged slightly shop-soiled goods, in the going-cheap basket.

I love the sea. Do you like it? Have you ever dived? No, nor me. They say that the further down you get, the blacker it gets. Light can't penetrate. Imagine diving down there. Nothing but black ahead of you. You can't see the dangers lurking. Or the beauties. It's just black but you keep going down. And all your mind sees is shipwrecks and poisonous fish. But you keep going because you can't stop. Even when you want to stop, when you want to turn round and head for the light again, and you struggle and gasp and fight, even then you're reined in by the black tentacles of the deep. And no one can hear you scream.

Justamum is in the bedroom. She walks to the window, then back to the edge of the bed. She hears the noise of the lawnmower outside. She rocks back and fore, hugging herself. She is afraid to let go. She realises her breathing has stopped and grasps hungrily at the air. She wants to cry but doesn't know why. She tells herself to calm down, not to be stupid, she has nothing to cry about, her life is good, it's the life she wants, she thinks. She thinks, then stops, thinking is too confusing. She doesn't understand. Justamum wonders if screaming would help. She doesn't know how to scream, has never had cause to scream. She does know you have to breathe to scream. Breathing is important for most things. She must remember to do it.

Come on now, dear. Come along with me please. We don't want to make a fuss, do we? Just come along to the office. Don't worry about those tins, this lady will put them all back on the shelves for you.

The cupboard is bare. The children have noticed. 'Mum, when are you going to Sainsbury's? We haven't got any.'

'Crisps.'

'Corn Flakes.'

'Apple juice.'

'Mum, what's for dinner? I'm starving. Dad's home. Mum, what's for dinner?'

Justamum views fridge. Empty shelves stare back. A failure even at her chosen profession. Takeaway again.

'Chip shop chips tonight. I'll go to Sainsbury's tomorrow.'

I feel really guilty wasting your time like this. I'm sure you have far more serious cases to deal with. With which to deal. Sorry, bad grammar there. Not that it matters anyway. A little thing like that in the grand scale of things. But as I was saying, you must tell me if I'm wasting your time. I would hate to do that. I feel enough of a fraud as it is. I mean what have I got to complain about. I've lived my life just as I wanted. I've been spoiled really.

Except now I always seem to be scared, scared of falling into nothingness. Never getting out. Discarded, as unnecessary. Can't cook, won't clean. Served her purpose. No, I'm being silly, I know. I'm lucky. I've got it all. So why am I here talking to you? Why am I here, full stop? I don't know. That's the real problem. Not knowing, not understanding. I'm not stupid but I'm losing control. While life was run to a routine I could manage. But routine's changing and I'm not ready. I liked it when I knew the words, could sing along to the songs, didn't have to think what they meant, just enjoyed them. Now I can't remember the words. And I don't know why.

The tooting of a car's horn makes Justamum jump. 'Sorry, sorry.'

She hadn't realised she had stopped. She can't stop here. This won't get the family fed. She makes it to fruit and veg. She grips the trolley handle. She reasons with herself. She is an intelligent woman. She has been here hundreds of times before. She has chosen carrots thousands of times. She has selected sausages millions of times. She can do this. Switch to autopilot. The red light is on for autopilot. There's no one at home. You're on your own. You can do this. Breathe deeply. Breathe slowly, remember what you were taught. There is nothing to fear.

I can't come, not yet. Don't you see? I've almost finished. A few more and I'll be safe. Wrapped in a tower of tins. Safe and snug forever in my own little bunker. Until I'm ready to break out. If I want to break out.

THE VENDOR

T.J. Davies

He was watching her. She was sure of it. "Big Issue... get your Big Issue... Big Issue... get your Big Issue..."

Sheryl stopped her slow, rhythmic chant for a moment and looked at the man on the other side of the street. He was standing side-on to her, and seemed to be examining the window display of the bank on the corner. But there wasn't much to see. A few notices about mortgage offers and interest rates, that was all. Not enough to hold you there for minutes on end. She could feel his gaze on her when she was looking elsewhere.

"Big Issue ... get your Big Issue..."

She'd seen his type before. All ages, all shapes and sizes, but always with that particular look about them, a kind of speculation. Usually they left it at that, eyeing her up and down as they cruised slowly past or lingered nearby. But occasionally they'd try their luck, come up to her and say what they wanted.

When they did that, she told them to fuck off.

And, usually, they did. Walking rapidly away, gob-smacked how wrong they'd been in their assumptions. They thought they could get away with it because she was young, and blonde, not bad-looking, and homeless

She soon put them right.

"Big Issue, get your Big Issue ..."

This one, she reckoned, must have been fairly young, in his thirties; maybe, though at that distance it was hard to tell. She looked across again to where he had been standing.

He was gone.

She shrugged to herself, and carried on.

"Big Issue, get your Big Issue ..."

She had positioned herself carefully, at the Cardiff Castle end of Queen Street, where the unending stream of people passing down the pedestrianised street slowed down, to either turn left and go down towards The Hayes, or cross the road and carry on to the shops and pubs of St Mary Street. As they slowed, manoeuvring among each other for position, they were more likely to notice her than if she was farther back up the street, where they could flit by at full speed, as if she were invisible. And, sure enough, a young woman, about her own age but much better dressed, loitered to a halt in front of her, avoiding her eye as she held out a pound coin in exchange for the paper.

"Oh, great, thanks, I'll just find you some change," said Sheryl, dropping the coin into her pouch and ferreting about for the right coins.

"That's all right," murmured the young woman, hurrying off.

"Brilliant ... thanks very much," called Sheryl after her as she vanished into the crowd. She turned back, and found the man standing right in front of her. He smiled.

"How d'you do?" he said, his voice jaunty and unnatural.

"Hello," replied Sheryl, carefully. He had dark eyes under heavy eyebrows, was clean-shaven and had thick black hair, swept back with a touch of gel. She thought her first estimate was about right, mid-to-late thirties, though she was still a teenager and found it hard to judge the age of anyone over about twenty-five. But he obviously wasn't short of a bit of cash, from the look of him. Brushed woollen coat, silk scarf. Tailored suit. Brogues.

Too well-dressed for a DSS snooper.

"Bit cold for this sort of thing, isn't it?" he asked.

"It's OK," she replied. It was a late autumn day, with a clear blue sky and the first hint of a chill in the air. Sometimes her breath clouded in front of her. She was very well wrapped up, and she knew she'd be glad of the rug at her feet when she came to sit down for a break. He obviously felt the need to wrap up well, but Sheryl didn't think it was that cold. Not yet.

"Ah well... I'd better take one of those," he said, nodding at her sheaf of magazines. She whipped one out and thrust it towards him, hoping that now he would clear off. She held out her hand for payment, and he dropped the coins into it. Exactly the right amount. The coins were warm. He must have been holding onto then while he sized her up. She dropped the coins into her pouch.

"Thanks," she said, with a small remote smile.

He folded the magazine and tucked it under his arm, but showed no sign of moving.

"Been doing this for long?" he asked.

"Not long," she replied.

"I'll bet it doesn't bring in much," he said, searching her face for information.

"I manage," she said, giving nothing away. She started to look beyond him, scanning the faces in case she was missing any customers.

"How much do you make on a good day?" he asked.

"Don't know, haven't counted," she replied, deadpan.

"Not that much, I bet," he said. Sheryl said nothing, but drew a deep, audible breath.

"Look," he said. dropping his gaze, "I'm in a position to offer you a substantial amount of money..." Sheryl looked sharply at him as he trailed off and looked up at her again with the wantingness she had come to know so well.

"What do you mean?" she demanded.

He went red as he muttered a response.

"You know what I mean," he said, shifting about.

"Yes, I know what you mean all right. What do you think I am, a prostitute?" she demanded angrily.

"Of course not," he hissed urgently, glancing around to see if anyone was listening, "I wouldn't be asking you if I thought you were."

"Then what are you asking me for? Thought you'd be the first to get your leg over before I turn professional, did you? Here, take your money back," she said, scrabbling about in her pouch for the right amount, "go on, take it," she shouted, holding the money out to him as he began to back away.

"You've got it all wrong," he said.

"Like fuck I have," she replied. Abruptly he turned to go, then just as suddenly turned back and moved towards her.

Automatically she flinched, thinking he was going to hit her. But he just stood there, looking at her in a funny way.

"I'll come and see you again when it gets colder," he said, turning and going before she could say a word.

She waited until he had gone, then took a couple of deep breaths, staring without focus at a spot a few metres in front of her until her heartbeat came back down to normal. After a minute or so she took a final, deep breath and started to scan again the faces that surged endlessly by.

"Big Issue, get your Big Issue, help the homeless..."

Presently one of her regulars, a middle-aged woman who bought a copy off her every week, filtered herself out of the crowd and came up to her.

"Hello dear, how are you?" she asked solicitously as she delved into her purse.

"Oh, not so bad, thanks, how are you?" replied Sheryl, sliding a copy out ready. "Well, you know, getting along. Still in the Shelter?" asked the woman as they made the exchange.

"Er, no, not really... I'm sort of between places at the moment," said Sheryl, hoping the woman wouldn't ask why. The woman frowned as she slid the magazine into her bag.

"That's a shame ... I hope you find somewhere soon ... they say it's going to get a lot colder before long," said the woman as she prepared to move off.

"Yes, so I've heard. I'm on the look-out, don't worry."

"Good, good ... Well, see you next week, if not before," said the woman, moving off.

"Yeah, cheers, thanks a lot," called Sheryl after her as she disappeared.

"Big Issue, get your Big Issue ..."

Sheryl fell silent. Her voice was getting tired, and so was her whole body. She sat down cross-legged on the rug. Relief spread through her muscles like the warmth of the sun. She propped the magazines in her lap and let her gaze wander through the forest of legs. She listened to the traffic as it roared past the castle, in and out of town, and let her mind wander where it could. Then she realised her bum was getting cold.

She tried to ignore it for an uneasy minute, and when that didn't work she tried to avoid it by jiggling her buttocks around and shifting the weight. But there was no escape. Her bum was cold from the stones of the pavement, even only after a couple of minutes, and even through the warmth of her soft, thick rug.

Pretty soon it would go numb, and then it would start to hurt.

She climbed effortfully back to her feet, cork-screwing clumsily up as she tried to keep her balance, her knees popping quietly as she straightened out. She rubbed her bottom vigorously and stamped her feet to get the circulation going again.

"Big Issue, get your Big Issue, help the homeless, get your Big Issue..." she began again, in a tired and sandy voice. It was cold all right. A lot worse than she had realised, seeping up through the ground from where she hadn't expected it, at least not for a while yet. And this was just the start. It was going to get a lot colder yet.

Much colder.

Bastard.

CHANGING THE SCRIPT

Mike Jenkins

The director Bryn took her to one side afterwards. His eyes were wide with sympathy, but she still felt inadequate.

"Look, Rhian, I'm really sorry. I know it's a small part, but it's right for you ... there'll be another chance next year, I'm sure."

Always next year. It was what she'd been told since attending these workshops and at school as well, where doing GCSE drama hadn't even improved things.

"I aven' got the right figure, ave I?"

"Don't be silly. That's nothing to do with it."

She peered, searching lies. It wasn't only that, but other things she couldn't mention. Stephanie given the main role and her father working in the Beeb. Her accent too, that Valleys scar which couldn't be erased. She wanted to confront Bryn and watch him squirm, then she remembered her mother's words, "I's like tha love ... oo yew know." She walked away from him without her cheery, "S'long!".

Meeting her mam to go shopping in Cardiff, her anger came gushing ... "I'm bloody sick of it, mam. Think I'll pack it in, onest. A chicken in *Animal Farm*, a bloody tart in *Oliver* and now this ... a fat friend oo's practiclee a chocoholic! Why do I bother?"

"I know, love. An I bet yewer better than tha Stephanie. Look at-a Stereoglyphics, ey done it."

"Phonics mam."

"Yeah, they might elp an all!"

Her mam was like a friend, but she couldn't get it right. She could give Rhian a cwtsh and was always there for her, though the encouragement never convinced her. Boys who fancied her only wanted one thing and that wasn't help with their homework, unless it was Personal & Social Ed. Her mam tried not to favour Rhian's brother Chris, but it was obvious that she did and this made Rhian very jealous.

As ever, she tried on all the wrong clothes. In River Island, a skimpy dress her mam could've fitted when pregnant made her legs stand out like tree trunks. She tried in vain to cheer her up.

"I know, le's get some marzipan in Thornton's ... whoops!" She gulped back the gaff seeing Rhian's expression. Her mother's handbag drew Rhian's attention and thoughts away from her own problems.

"Come on, mam. Le's go an look f'r an andbag f'yew. I think tha one belongs in St Fagans.."

The tattered brown bag hung from her like a mouldy coconut. She laughed and her mam reluctantly agreed, always wary of spending money on herself. So they searched in the handbag department of every store for one not too expensive, not too plasticky, big or small, with a short thin strap and definitely not smelling of leather, till they ended up roughly where they'd begun, in the precinct. They went into the Handbag Shop, an obvious choice they'd neglected.

Her mam proceeded to pull the padding out of numerous bags to try them for size, with her purse, brush and other essentials. Rhian kept her distance, especially when Stephanie Marshall entered, complete with tanned, open-shirted boyfriend.

"This seems orright, Rhi. What d'yew think?" Her mam hailed her in a embarrassingly loud voice. Padding was strewn everywhere. Stephanie was browsing, sniffling, her hunk in tow. She spotted Rhian and smiled, nodding, "Hi!" Her boyfriend caught round her as if to steer her away.

"Le's go, mam!"

She stomped off before her mam could protest, out into the precinct.

"Rhian! Rhian!" Her mam followed, calling like she was an escaped toddler. The shop alarm was triggered, and her mam stood shock-still, a stolen handbag full of her belongings in her hand. Rhian took pity on her and turned back into the shop just as Steph and her Romeo appeared smirking. She wished she was an infant again, so she could dart into the crowd and be lost. Luckily, she explained the situation to an understanding manager, and they had no choice but to buy that bag. Stephanie had seen her. She could never return to drama now.

In the car later, Mrs Griffiths was furious. "I don' care oo yew seen. Sort yewerself out! ... I jest wish yew ad a dad around t'back me up."

"A father, but not im, mam?"

"I tol yew. 'Ee wuz a slob."

She clammed up, brooding. Her mam had never really explained. He'd walked out because he was such a kid, chasing other women, out with the lads. That was it. The rest she had to imagine.

That night she even dreamt of Stephanie. It was becoming an obsession. In the studio together, she and Steph were dressed for Judo, opposite each other, bowing. She let out the Banshee yell and broke all the rules, flattening her. It was more like Sumo wrestling as she thought, 'At least my flab's good f'summin!', while two security guards (like the ones from the precinct) dragged her off her adversary, who lay on the floor whimpering. As she was marched off, Bryn ran up to her screaming, "You're finished! That was a trust game!"

She felt exhilarated when she woke, until Chris's annoying whistling brought her down to earth. He was so wiry and could scoff as much junk as he liked. She didn't want to play stodgy Gloria, longed to take Steph's part: weird and wild, yet funny at the same time. There was a small photo of herself on a shelf dressed as a Red Indian, chubby and ruddy but totally content. She vaguely recalled her dad playing with her, hiding behind the sofa pursued by soldiers as their buffalo grazed in the hall.

Her dad warning, "They're goin t' slaughter ower buffalo love!"

"No, dad, we carn let em win!"

Later, she had a real barney with Chris and he called her "fat bitch". Her mam took his side because she'd kicked him. She went on hunger strike all day, forcing her mam into pangs of guilt. She couldn't be anorexic though, she loved her food, especially the spicey stuff. Her mam once went on about this artist Rodin and his nude sculptures. Maybe fashions would change.

School brought her out of herself. Her friend Trish was even more buxom and didn't seem to care whatever. Rhian drew strength from her determination. Trish was a match for any snotty boy's comments.

"Oi! Ippo bum!!"

"Wha d'yew wan', welly-merchant? Wool on yewr flies, or wha?"

Trish could get a PhD in Insultology. She was the expert and Rhian her apprentice. Coping was one thing, motivation another and by next Saturday's drama workshop she hardly knew her lines and told her mam she was too shattered to go.

"I think yew'll find thin's ave improved," Mrs Griffiths insisted. She sounded as if she knew something. Rhian didn't pursue it, but went along with her as always.

Stranger than strange, Bryn actually greeted her and Steph wasn't to be seen. She was dying to ask Beth (who went to Steph's school) but she didn't want to appear concerned. After warm-up exercises, Bryn got them together, explained that Stephanie had had an accident and he'd like "Rhian Griffiths" to take the main rôle. For a moment she assumed there must be another Rhian Griffiths, till she noticed the bemused facers focussed on her.

Amazingly, there were no protrests and she nodded modestly. The dream: did she possess extraordinary powers? Was she some kind of witch maybe?

They read the first part of the script. She couldn't concentrate, but tried to put every emotion into the part. Jo was highly strung, brilliant, yet loathed both her parents. Her father was having an affair, her mother lived for work, not realising she was being cheated. Jo found out, relishing the combat she created between her parents. A great part, though she still felt on trial, or worse, a substitute.

When Bryn spoke to her afterwards, she expected him to be hypercritical.

"Rhian! You did fine ... you know, your mother's a great lady!"

"Eh? Wha?"

"I talked to her on the phone the other night ... didn't she tell you?"

"No!"

"She said you were out. She explained how ambitious you are, when I told her Steph had broken her leg. She's very persuasive, you know."

They were in the corridor outside the studio. She stopped dead.

"Bryn! Yew didn give me the part coz of er, did yew?"

"No way, Rhian. I was considering you anyway ... but, given your background, I thought you'd be ideal."

"Ow d'yew mean? Wha's she said?"

But he avoided the answer and busied himself with a swift "Bye!"

In the car home she confronted her mam.

"Why aren' yew more pleased, love?"

"What did yew tell im, mam? Bout me, bout ower famlee?"

"I seen a script when I woz tidyin yewer room. Couldn elp it ... well, it woz a bit like yewer dad, that sod avin a bit-on-a-side."

"Thanks a lot, mam."

"I on'y done it f'yew."

"An ow am I goin t'lose two stone f' the performance, eh? Chop off a couple o'limbs?"

Mrs Griffiths nearly veered off the road, they laughed so much. The first time together for weeks.

She was riled by her mother, but knew she could do it: put on Jo's accent and manipulate people as she did. As rehearsals progressed though, certain lines didn't fit. The dumpy friend Gloria was now played by a less dumpy girl than her and Jo's boyfriend - played by an arrogant boy called Paul - was uncomfortable complimenting her on her loveliness. Bryn even suggested changing "radiance" to "attraction" and he wasn't joking.

He reassured Rhian they'd pad up Gloria and make-up would perform wonders on her face. She enquired if they could manage a facelift!

She did feel that she was becoming Jo, however. So much so that Chris began to moan about her "snobby voice". She slipped into character without realising.

"Mother! You're always working. Why can't you relax?"

"Workin? Part-time down-a Spar?"

Except that there was no father to practise on. He'd gone, jumped the script. She spoke to him in her head: "I know all about you. I saw you with her, so don't deny it! Of course I won't tell Mother, but you must agree to help me a little bit more."

Two nights before the dress rehearsal she had another clear dream. Her dad appeared, a cross between Bryn and Sion (who played Jo's dad). They wer walking down a railway track. She was little and dressed only in her knickers. She felt so ashamed. Rhian pulled free and he strode on into the dark, never looking back. She could hear a train coming. When she shouted, "Daddy!" he'd disappeared. She rolled off the track and woke up, glad to have her nightie on.

She puzzled over this. After the dream about Steph, she wondered if there was an important secret about her dad. The dream still plagued her. The make-up did allay some fears: not a butterfly, but a colourful moth. She was confident of every scene except the one where she had to talk dirty to Ross, Jo's boyfriend. The lines sounded perfect coming from Jo: "Ross, I want you to do it like I saw my father doing it. Do you think you can manage that?" It wasn't shyness, because they were disturbed at the crucial moment. During dress rehearsal, when Paul froze, she knew it was her fault. He didn't say his line. Bryn was furious.

"What the hell's going on?"

"She can't relax! It was different with Steph!"

"Both of you, loosen up and grow up! Take it from Jo's line about you managing. The bloody writer must've known."

They forced themselves along and Rhian even bit Paul on the ear. This made Paul's energy and childishness come alive in his character and Bryn even complimented them on their improvisation after.

She was enjoying being Jo. For once, in control of her destiny and with a boy to lick her feet.

She was less afraid on the night. All the others were wound up backstage, bantering like a group of DJs. Rhian felt strangely calm and as the drama progressed it took her over completely. Even the aborted sex scene was acted with gusto. Nearing the finale things began to fall apart, because of her over-confidence. She started to alter the lines. She had a sense of someone partlicular watching from the audience. Her changes threatened the play's logic.

"Ross, my father ... he hasn't gone away ... he's dead, you know ..." She strove to correct herself. "I mean, it's as if he's dead ..."

Paul was thrown. He continued, more mechanically.

It was as though someone spoke through her and the play had become one of her dreams. When she transformed the last lines to, "I'll not let him haunt me. I don't need parents anyway!" it was heresy, yet the applause was resounding. As she took a bow, there in the second row she saw Steph sitting next to a middle-aged man. Rhian stared at him, aghast. It couldn't be...it was impossible !

Backstage, Bryn cwtshed her at the same time whispering "Why the hell did you change those lines, Rhian ? You nearly blew the whole show !"

Jo was finished. She'd never play her again. She rubbed the make-up off slowly and carefully. How could Jo reject her family ? There was a knock on the door.

"Come in !"

Steph hobbled in on crutches, followed by the man. If only he....

"My dad !...You were utterly brill, Rhian ! And I loved the improvising. It made Jo seem more humane. Did Bryn suggest that ?"She kissed her on the cheek. Her dad handed Rhian the bouquet. She was delighted and feeling generous.

"I didn even look like er. Yew'd ave bin much better Steph.."

"The way things are going, I can see futures for both you girls," her dad said and he sounded sincere.

"Rhian, you were great, honestly. I'll see you at the workshop when I get rid of these props."

As they turned to leave, Steph added, "By the way, was that your mother in the Handbag Shop ? She looked a real character and a laugh. I can see who you take after."

In the car home, her mam was full of praise. She kept repeating how glad she was that Rhian wasn't "like tha silly bitch Jo".

"I cocked up up the endin, mam !"

I know, love. Bryn tol me arfta. Ee woz quite 'pecific mind."

Mrs Griffiths eyed Chris to check he was asleep in the back. She fell quiet, sighing occasionally.

"Rhi, love ?"

"Wha mam ?"

"It worries me !"

"What does ?"

"Y'know, why yew never tol me before, tha yew knew bout him."

"Mam! Yew never tol me the truth did yew?"

"I did, Rhi. Well, as much as I could."

Rhian gazed into the distance, up valley towards her town. The confusion over what she dreamed and what was real met when the road followed the railway line. At that point there was a tunnel through the mountain. She'd never noticed it before.

THE DEATH OF A FRIEND

Sarah Cornelius

Mr Richards has started his idea about the swimming pool again. I heard him and Mrs Richards talking about it today. I was sitting in an apple tree and I could hear them, even though they couldn't see me. And I was chewing the apples real slow so as they didn't make much noise crunching and Mr Richards wouldn't look up. It was a real hot day and Mr and Mrs Richards was saying they wished they'd made the swimming pool last year like they said. Then they wouldn't be having to sit in the hot sun now. That nearly made me laugh. I saw Mrs Richards trying to drink a glass of orange juice but the fruit flies wouldn't leave her alone and she was brushing them off and getting ever so annoyed. She looked so funny. When she was doing this Mr Richards said that it wasn't too late for next year and they could still make the swimming pool now. This got me real worried, so much as I stopped crunching and nearly fell out of the tree. We had all this last year and I thought Mr Richards had forgot the idea. But now I suppose it will be up to me to do something again. I said to mum and dad about it when I got back to the house.

"What's up Rachel?" asked my dad. I reckon I must have looked annoyed straight away.

"I've been down the bottom of the garden," I said, and told him what I heard.

"You shouldn't listen in on people like that." This was my mum. She was getting the Sunday dinner ready and she didn't seem to care. "Anyway, what were you doing up an apple tree? You know you're not allowed to do that." I knew I should have left that part out. Then my dad joined in. "Don't go up there any more," he said looking real fierce, but then he smiled and said, "Look Rachel, you're a very special girl and we love you very much. We just don't want you to go hurting yourself falling out of trees, okay?"

I said yes, but I was wondering how trees could hurt you and how come he didn't care about what I'd said.

Sometimes stuff like that really makes me annoyed. When my dad said I am special he means because I go to a special school. They don't think I know what that means, but I do, a bit. Like I'm not so clever as other children. But sometimes I think I'm more clever than my dad, because I have to explain to him stuff like if Mr Richards wants to build a swimming pool again, then he'll want to cut down the big tree again, but my dad doesn't get that.

I suppose I will have to explain why the big tree is so important. It's at the end of our garden. It's really in Mr and Mrs Richards' garden but the branches come right over into our side because it's very old. There's only a bit of wire between our garden and theirs. The leaves fall on our side too. It's so old I reckon no one in the world can remember when it wasn't there. I'm fourteen and I'm only this tall and my dad's much older than me but he's not very tall, no one's as tall as the tree not even the house. Sometimes I try to remember when it wasn't there, but I'm not really remembering because I wasn't there, but I'm thinking about it anyway. I wonder what the tree had round it then. You never know if famous people ever saw it. Like Dick Turpin might have sat down under it to have his dinner, or maybe there was a battle all round it where our garden is now. That's what I think about sometimes, when I'm looking at the tree. Then when me and mum and dad are all old. Maybe there will be aliens and stuff all around and people will have robots and flying cars. But there should still be the tree I reckon. The garden is the tree's more than it's ours because it's been here longer. That's what happens at school. If you're playing with something and someone tries to take it off you, you can get them in trouble, because if you had it longer then it's yours till you've finished with it. So I suppose we're in the tree's garden really. But Mr Richards doesn't think that. Let me tell you about what I said to Mr Richards last year when this happened once before. I was talking to him and we were looking at the tree. He was telling me that the men had told him that if he wanted to build the swimming pool, he would have to chop the big tree down, because the roots of the tree were in the way. He said that when the swimming pool was done, I could go over in it all the time. But I told him I wished people would not think I'm stupid all the time and that I knew the tree is better than a swimming pool even if he didn't. This made him really surprised and he looked a bit funny. People never expect me to tell them what I think. I don't think Mr Richards expects anybody to tell him anything. He looked at the tree and he looked at me again. I can still remember all this real clear even though I forget loads of other stuff.

"What about all the things in the tree?" I asked him. He kept on looking at it but he couldn't seem to see anything. This is what I mean when I say that sometimes I think I am cleverer than people, because I could see all the stuff in the tree but Mr Richards couldn't and neither can my mum or dad. So I suppose I acted a bit rude then and I sort of sighed like my mum does when she's fed up and I started talking slow as if he couldn't understand me. That's one thing about grown-up people, they like to think they understand everything, even when they can't see the easiest stuff, like what's in the tree. They can't even see how beautiful the tree is, never mind what's in it.

"Up there's where birds build their nests," I said and pointed, "and inside there are squirrels. If you're sitting under the tree quiet enough they come right down and you can see them real close up." Mr Richards said he'd never even noticed any squirrels in the tree - see what I mean? Anyway, in the end he never chopped the tree down last year, but you can see my problem now he wants to do it again. It's lovely under that tree in the summer too. And there's moss and flowers at the bottom and things live on that too. Real small stuff. There are tiny little insects in the flowers and bees come to get honey. The closer you look, the more stuff there is living in the tree. I think there's an owl up there too. I've been right up the garden in the dark but no one knows that. I'd only get mum annoyed. So the problem is, why does Mr Richards want to kill so many things to make a swimming pool? All you'll get in that is dead flies.

My dad says there are loads of other trees, but that doesn't matter. When he said that I said, "there are loads of other children but what if someone wanted to chop *me* down?" He didn't get that though. He can't see that it doesn't matter to the tree how many others there are. Anyway, a few days after I heard Mr and Mrs Richards talking in their garden my dad came to see me while I was sitting under the big tree. He didn't even look up at it, he just sat down and started pulling at the grass, pulling bits off. I thought he might want to see what it was like and all the insects and birds and stuff and the different colours of the leaves. When the leaves are little they're real soft and bright green, but when they're old they're darker. That's before they change colour again and fall on the ground. At school the teacher said that in the Autumn the leaves go brown and fall off, but that's a load of rubbish. Some of them go brown okay, but some go yellow and some go orange and some go light brown. Some fall off when they're still a bit green. Then you find hedgehogs and stuff in the leaves making nests and that. I started showing him where there was a squirrel over our heads.

"Oh yes," he said, and looked back down at the grass again. I thought he was a bit stupid. So I asked him how old he thought the tree was. I was trying to make him talk because he looked so fed up. He didn't seem really interested in that either, he just kept on pulling on that poor old grass. "Listen Rachel," he said, really slow, "I want to talk to you about this tree." I rolled my eyes and tried to look fed up too. I knew what he was going to say. I'm not so stupid as they reckon.

"Now Rachel, don't be like that. Listen to me." So I listened. "You know that this tree isn't ours, don't you?"

"Yes." This is what I just said isn't it - about the tree not belonging to anybody - so I thought that was right.

"And that Mr and Mrs Richards own it, so they can do what they like with it."

I didn't think that was right, so I didn't say nothing. I just looked up at the squirrel. He was so high up I don't think he could hear my dad.

"Rachel?" He wanted me to say yes, but I didn't. I was watching the squirrel.

"Now Mr and Mrs Richards want a pool in their garden for the hot weather, and they've even said that you can learn to swim in it if you like."

I think my dad was getting fed up of me not talking. He gets fed up all the time if everybody doesn't agree with him. Even my mum says so.

"Look Rachel, the Richardses want to use their own land to

their own advantage and there's nothing wrong with that. Nobody expects you to understand the value of property and the mechanics of laying the foundations of whatever for a swimming pool, but I do expect you to stop being so silly and to stop this attachment to one stupid tree. Do you understand?" He was pretty annoyed now. I didn't know what he meant quite but I said yes because I know my dad and when he starts getting annoyed you better say yes even if you don't know why. Unless he wants you to say no. Then he got up.

"But dad, what will happen to all the birds and animals without the tree?"

"They'll find another one." I thought about that. I was glad they would, but didn't think I would ever find another tree. Somebody might try to chop that one down too.

The day came that the tree had to be chopped down so that Mr Richards could dig a great big hole in the ground to put a stupid pool in. Some men came. They all went down the garden and put ropes all round the tree even in our garden. We weren't supposed to go there I don't think but we all went down and we had to stay behind the ropes. No one was crying but me. The poor animals didn't know what was happening and I felt sorry for the great big tree. I wanted to make it feel better even though it was going to die. I thought of all the bad things that had happened to it in the hundreds of years it had been there but nothing had killed it till now.

They started cutting it down with these great big buzzing saws and I saw all the birds fly out. I was getting real worried about the squirrels. I felt so sad for the poor old tree and I was crying and holding on to the stupid rope.

I felt like I was its only friend in the whole wide world. So I quickly got under the rope and I ran up to it as fast as I could. As I was running I could hear the buzz and my mum screaming and I saw it start falling towards me. I could smell the wood. It was coming down real fast, and I opened my arms out wide, to hold it tight when it landed.

GIRL'S WORLD

Roger Williams

The stench was overpowering and the fumes were beginning to burn the inside of my throat. Throwing myself back into the high chair to try and escape the cloud of thick hair-spray that was filling the room, I pressed my head into the slippery cushion, braced the armrests tightly, and clenched my teeth like a condemned man trying his best not to inhale the lethal gas.

Glaring into the metal barrel of the hairdryer looming above me, I pinched my nostrils shut with my fingers, held my breath, and counted to ten. Bliss for a few seconds before involuntarily spluttering and choking my way back into the reality of the hair-spray polluted atmosphere.

"All right there, bach?" Jephna asked as she scuttled over to us. "Won't be long with your Mam, and then I'll give you the once over with the clippers if you fancy." She smiled, took my mother's coat, and led her away to the backwash.

I cemented my lips together and breathed through my nose. At least this way I didn't have to endure the sour taste of the metallic vapour on my tongue.

"Put your head right back then, love, and we'll give you a good scrub," Jephna told my mother as she turned on the water and rolled up her sleeves.

Squirting shampoo liberally into her hands, Jephna went to work, and launched into yet another 'How-are-you-today-then?' conversation. Her bangles clattered as she soaped my mother's scalp, and set the conversation rolling.

Jephna was chief stylist at the salon, and the undisputed queen bee. She was a short woman with tall black hair, and a face that was always heavily made up. Her lipstick-stained mouth was constantly talking to someone or other, and her mascara-bled eyes chased you around the room while she trimmed, curled, and blow dried.

Jephna's hands were large, almost like a man's, and had it not been for the ten red long nails which jutted out from her fingertips you could easily have mistaken them so. Jephna was the power house of the salon. Nobody dared argue with her because the salon was her territory, and her personality saturated it.

The salon, like Jephna, had hardly changed in all the time my mother and I had been going there. It still had the same orange and black carpet tiles on the floor, although one or two had been dislodged over the years, or had developed bubble gum blisters.

The actual hairdressing took place in a series of small plywood cubicles at the centre of the room.. Inside each little pen was a fitted dressing table filled with a selection of pots, potions, brushes, and other hairdressing necessities. Large heavy mirrors were bolted to the wall above each desk; making the tiny cubicles seem twice the size they actually were. These mirrors towered upwards, stretching for the ceiling, and made your face look fat and your neck look long. Giraffe-like.

This was where I'd been brought every Saturday morning at ten-thirty for as long as I could remember to keep my mother company and watch her hair being revamped, revitalised.

I loved coming to the salon. I enjoyed being around so many busy women, where the air was stodgy with laughter and gossip. The salon was a playground, and apart from the stink of hair-spray that was always heavily present, I enjoyed lounging around waiting for my mother, and overhearing the customers' animated conversations about anonymous next-door neighbours and scandalous second cousins.

Sometimes I would even get to sit in the hot-seat myself and watch one of the girls dig into my mop of hair with her scissors and comb, working away like a knife and fork in a bowl of spaghetti. I loved seeing the hair fall away, slide down my shoulders and land on the floor where it made a thick carpet around my heels.

While I waited patiently for my mother I entertained myself with the piles of women's magazines that were stacked around the room. These magazines were very probably the only dynamic element in the salon, and every week I would pick up a new one and read it greedily.

I flicked through the problem pages, devoured the real-life

stories, and studied the fashion make-overs that were contained inside. They provided a new education, and it was during these unsupervised Saturday lessons that I learnt six essential back-combing techniques, the perfect Swiss-roll recipe, and fifty proven ways to keep your man happy.

The stacks of magazines were reliable pillars of wisdom. I was amazed to hear how Linda of Weymouth had successfully raised seven beautiful children while holding down two part-time jobs and coping with an abusive husband. And I relished reading Margo's regular columns of wise words for readers who wrote to her problem pages.

Should Jane, 26, tell her loyal husband Brian, she caught crabs from an over-sexed co-worker? Should Anthony, 45, tell his wife he enjoys wearing her underwear when she goes out to the supermarket on Saturday mornings? Is it true you don't get pregnant if you have unprotected sex standing up in a doorway? What's the best way to get red wine out of shagpile? Margo had all the answers, and I remembered every sacred reply.

When I occasionally looked up from my magazines to catch my breath, or to make sure nobody was secretly watching me excitedly consume the stories I was sure a boy of eleven wasn't supposed to be reading, I would catch sight of two bold notices that were on permanent display.

The first was a reminder that the salon did not under any circumstances take responsibility for "dye jobs that go wrong", and forcefully asserted that customers were expected to pay the full price for all treatments given, regardless of results. An additional note had been made beneath it in thick black marker pen which read: "Non-payment may result in persecution".

The second was a more professionally made notice laid out in white writing on black card. It was held up by four drawing pins, three blue, one yellow, and read: "We have private rooms for wig fittings." On the shelf just below was a polystyrene head complete with skewiff jet black ladies' hairpiece. The head had obviously been spray-painted gold with an aerosol can, and the wig was resting on top of it at such an angle that it was in serious danger of slipping off. Every week I'd make myself comfortable in the chair and watch the wig inch itself down the mannequin's scalp. Nobody else seemed to notice. It was never straightened.

I had read these notices on so many previous visits to the salon that I was now able to remember every single word, and could even offer a thousand interpretations.

Did people really walk into the salon and ask about the private rooms for wig fittings? Did they have to book ahead? Why was it all so secretive and discreet? Perhaps there was a feature about wigs lurking in one of my magazines? Did Margo have an opinion on the issue? What did she have to say to women who were considering giving a nice warm wig a good home? I always returned to my magazines to find out.

Jephna and my mother reappeared from the backwash just as I was about to pick up my first magazine of the morning. My mother was now wearing a turban-like towel around her head, and was clutching a battered copy of *Hair Today*. She smiled tight-lipped, waved, and dipped into one of the cubicles at the centre of the room before I could respond.

"Hey, she's got it on her today," Jephna bellowed. "She's decided to have a colour dye. I told her it'd make her look ten years younger. What d'you reckon?"

Jephna rolled her tongue around her ruby red lips and tugged on her left earring, waiting for an answer.

"What sort of dye?" I asked.

"We haven't chosen a colour yet, but whether it's black, blue, red, or green, it'll be fab! Promise you! I love it when one of my ladies decides to take the plunge!" With which she popped her tongue back into her mouth and followed my mother into their coven.

I loved my mother's hair. I'd loved grappling with it when I was a baby, grabbing fistfuls while discovering the world, and playing with it when all my other toys had lost interest. I'd tugged it hard when I was angry and frustrated, and fallen happily asleep in its weight when I was tired out, and lost to the world.

What was going on? I couldn't let Jephna go in with all guns blazing and re-style my mother's hair on a whim. I had to say something. I had to find out exactly what was being planned before any damage was done.

But just as I was about to rise from my seat to find out, a sudden burst of laughter, led by Jephna's unmistakable cackle, erupted from my mother's stall. A warning shot? They sounded like two schoolgirls sharing a secret, and from the tone of their laughter I guessed it was too late to interfere; the decision had been made. I stayed in my chair, squirming as I imagined the terrible possibilities Jephna was plotting.

I picked up the first three magazines my hands found to try and forget about what was going on merely ten metres away inside my mother's cubicle. I looked over the covers, but was disappointed to see the familiar images of old editions I'd read before. So I knelt down and searched through the pile more carefully, inspecting the pages for articles I perhaps hadn't read, letters I'd overlooked, or cake recipes I might have skipped.

I glanced around the salon to see whether anyone else was perhaps reading the new magazines which should have been added to the pile, my pile. But no, the only other person in the waiting area was busily clicking away on a pair of knitting needles.

As the knitter rose her head and smiled at me, Jephna's voice boomed up from out of nowhere again. "Has anybody seen my reds?" she squealed, "I need my reds, girls. Who's got 'em? Own up!"

She appeared from behind the door a few seconds later, and looked around at everyone accusingly; an angry headmistress eager to find out who had giggled during the Lord's Prayer.

"Come on now. Look around. Who's moved my reds?"

A chilling silence ensued before a young apprentice stepped forward with a small brown box, and offered it to Jephna, the frustrated artist. Jephna scowled at her, and then cast her eyes around the room once more, a periscope looking for a foreign vessel, before finally settling them on me, where thankfully her usual smile developed.

"It's going to be lovely, honest to God it is! You've never seen the like! You're going to be so proud!"

I decided to reply. I had to.

"Jephna?"

"Yes, bach."

"Am I right in thinking you're dyeing Mam's hair?"

"Yep, that's right. We're going to paint it on!"

"Paint?"

"Yep!"

"Have you picked a colour then?" I asked.

"She's gone for autumnal colours love. Reds, oranges. Y'know?"

"Red! Will it wash out?"

"Wash out! God no! There's no half measures here, bach, it's permanent."

"Permanent!"

I dug deep to find the courage. I had to speak up now before she went any further. I had to make sure it wasn't going to be too terrible.

"You're not going to go over the top, are you, Jephna? You won't go too far with Mam's hair?" I asked innocently.

And as the words left my mouth the salon fell silent. The chatter ceased, and hair dryers stopped whirring.

Jephna's face jumped; surprised, offended.

"Too far? Don't be daft. Jephna never goes to far."

Silence still.

"Does she, girls?" Jephna demanded. "Jephna never goes too far, does she?"

There were half-hearted mutterings of "No, never," from some quarters, but I wasn't convinced. Her eyes roasted me for asking such a question.

"Can I see my Mam, Jephna? I'd like to hear what she's planning," I asked hoping to be invited inside the cubicle. I wanted to know what was going to be done.

"Don't be silly, mun! You enjoy yourself there a minute now. Trust Jephna, isn't it?" she assured me, quickly taking control of the conversation again.

"But I'd like a word," I repeated.

"Your mother's fine!" she asserted; shooting me into an embarrassed silence. "You are all right over there by yourself, aren't you, bach?" Her voice grated. "You are big enough to sit on your own?"

"Well, urm, the magazines..." I asked desperately trying not to show that I'd been bruised.

"Yes, bach?"

"There's usually new ones on a Saturday, but I can't seem to find them today."

"Magazines? Magazines? Oh, they're probably still upstairs, waiting to be brought down. Why don't you pop up and see if you can find them, eh?"

"Upstairs?" I asked.

"Aye, turn right at the landing. Help yourself. And don't worry about your Mam. Jephna's in charge now, okay?"

She turned on her heel, scowling at the trainee who had mislaid her pallet and returned to my mother.

I followed Jephna's tip and made my way through the yellow streamers which dangled down over the open doorway, and climbed the stairs.

Why was my mother having her hair dyed red anyway? What sort of red was it going to be? Were we talking Ginger Rogers red, or Ronald McDonald red?

I tried not to think about it. It was her doing, and if it looked terrible, then it would be my mother's fault for not consulting me. It would be her fault for not talking it over with me first as we usually did. She and Jephna would have to take responsibility.

Reaching the landing, I looked around for a small pile of neglected magazines. Nothing. The air was clearer up here though; the hair-spray obviously too dense to rise upwards.

There were two doors in front of me, and failing to find the weekly periodicals in the stairwell, I guessed they had to be hiding inside one of the rooms. One of the doors had a sign across it which read, 'Taff Only'. An 'S' must've fallen off along the line and hadn't been replaced. This was where Jephna held court at lunch times, and where the other girls came for a long cigarette and a quick coffee between clients. This was where the magazines had to be. The staff room.

The girls would almost certainly hijack them as soon as they arrived from the newsagent, and monopolise them until they had read all the best articles, entered the competitions, and cut out the coupons. It was only then, when they had been completely drained, and were no longer of interest to the girls who had laughed as they read Margo's problem page aloud to one another over their sandwiches, that the magazines would make their way down the stairs to the salon, to me.

Quickly looking over my shoulder again, I stepped inside to reclaim the treasure.

I was disappointed by the ordinariness of the room at first. Everything was plain and lifeless. Along one wall were a series of hostile looking lockers which I assumed were for the women to use during working hours to store their personal belongings.

There were four back-breakingly low armchairs lined up on either side, a fold-away kitchen table which was extended to snapping point by the sink, and a grubby green carpet which had shrunk away from the skirting boards, and was now trying to edge its way towards the centre of the room where I imagined it would eventually form a nice rug.

The room's only window was wide open and the two ragged curtains which hung on either side were being sucked outwards by the late summer wind. The only sounds around me were the buzzing engines of cars funnelled up from the street below, and the heavy ticking of a large clock which was no doubt there to remind the women they only had a short sixty-minutes to devour their packed lunches before heading back to work.

I spotted the magazines I was looking for sitting on the table, weighed down by a dirty coffee cup that had glued itself to one of the glossy covers. I prized it away gently, trying not to rip the paper or cause any further damage before gathering the bundle up in my arms and turning to leave the room.

As my hand met the handle though, I noticed that a row of Polaroids had been sellotaped to the back of the door. The pictures were of various members of staff at what appeared to be a restaurant. It was obviously some kind of birthday party. Everyone was smiling, and most had a glass of wine in their hands. Some of the girls in the pictures were kicking their legs up and blowing kisses, while others were trying to hide their faces from the lens, embarrassed at being caught enjoying themselves.

One of the younger girls had been photographed with a pair of knickers stretched over her head, her ears appearing through the leg holes, and another was shown dancing alongside a startled pianist on a table. My eyes moved along the collage.

Half way across was a picture of Jephna drinking from a large cocktail glass through two long bendy straws. She was wearing a fake red rose in her hair, and her eyebrows were raised high as though she had been caught-in-the-act. In the act of what I wasn't sure.

I looked at the picture and remembered what Jephna was doing downstairs with my mother. I remembered the way she'd ignored my worries and treated me like a baby. It was then that I had the sudden urge to make an addition to the photo. An excitement grew within me.

Taking a red ink pen from the table I pulled off its cap and gave the picture of Jephna a long bushy moustache, and drew a large pair of devil's horns above her head. Satisfied with my efforts, I admired Jephna's new make-over one last time, smiled, and pulled the door wide. Margo's latest advice was waiting to be read.

As I stepped back onto the landing, I noticed that the second door across the hallway was now slightly open. I looked through the gap and saw that one of the older hairdressers was in the centre of the room talking to a small elderly lady who was scrunched up in the bucket of a large revolving chair. The hairdresser was flicking through a series of smart catalogues, and waving her hands around frantically as though demonstrating an important scientific fact.

I crawled inside the doorway, sat up on top of the stash of magazines, and listened to their conversation. Trespassing again.

"You see, this new range is much more suitable for the mature lady, far more flattering. Do you see how the edge of the hair falls away from the ears and curls upwards? Beautiful. Beautiful craftsmanship." The hairdresser smiled. "Would you like to see one from this range, madam?"

The lady in the chair nodded politely and the hairdresser scurried over to a tall Welsh dresser in the corner of the room, tugged open a drawer, and looked inside.

"Won't be a moment," she said as she plunged her hand down into the drawer and brought out a small gold box which was later placed on a portable table that wobbled whenever it was moved.

Then, from her top pocket, the hairdresser fished out a nail file which she used to break the seal of the package. Smiling throughout, she lifted the lid and began to remove the sheets of tissue paper, folding each one neatly into quarters.

"So, as you can see from the pictures, the style you're looking for can be achieved very easily without any inconvenience to yourself, and they're very easy to use," the hairdresser explained. "Would you like to try it on?" And as she asked the question, she proudly lifted a silver grey hair piece from the box, and held it up for the lady's inspection.

The lady in the chair stretched her long neck forward to look at the wig, and nodded again, before removing the hair piece that was already sitting on her head. The hairdresser stepped forward on cue to help her, and after a brief struggle, the wig was lifted completely away from the lady's scalp, and she sat there, her head bare, bald.

"So what d'you think about the weather we've been having then? There's hardly been a summer, has there?" the hairdresser babbled as she laid the new wig out on a plastic mannequin's head, and brushed it attentively. She chatted casually, as she might have done with any of her other customers who were in for their usual perm, or cut and blow dry. The lady in the chair turned around to face her, and in doing so, spotted me, the intruder, crunched up inside the doorway.

Her wrinkled face caught mine, and I found myself staring at the strange creature. Her head, so old and worn, looked strange and alien without a layer of hair covering it. Her face seemed disjointed, unreal. Her sad eyes flickered as a small nervous grin grew over the thin, cracked lips that were smudged with a light coating of pink lipstick. Her cheeks were sagging, and the face powder she was wearing made them look even heavier and tired.

I watched her and she watched me while the hairdresser rambled on about her recent mini-break to Bournemouth and her husband's back-ache, oblivious that we were looking at one another.

When she had finished smiling, the lady in the chair asked the hairdresser to close the door. She could feel a chill. Terrified, I stood up quickly, ran down the stairs and back into the salon, clutching my magazines tightly to my chest.

My eyes winced as I landed back in the hair-spray polluted room. I squinted my way into normal vision, and as I did so, focused in on a huddle of women who were chatting excitedly, as they picked over something, someone, caught in the epicentre of their circle.

"Doesn't it look tremendous?" Jephna beamed. "We're so pleased! It's come off marvellously!"

As I walked towards the group I began to see what was causing such interest. It was my mother. I crept towards her, and gasped aloud when I saw the short wave of bright tomato red hair that was now proudly straddled across her head.

"Well, what d'you think?" Jephna wailed.

A timid smile wavered on my mother's face, looking for approval, reminding me of the way the elderly woman had winced when she caught me spying. Her eyes had also searched for acceptance in my face, and it was then that I realised the horror of it all. The horror of the elderly woman who was hiding away upstairs, and the horror of my mother who had ruined her appearance by cutting away her handsome long brown hair, and stained what was left the colour of blood.

My mother celebrated her transformation with the others, but I felt sick as I looked at her hair cut for a second time. I stepped back.

"Come on, speak up, bach!" Jephna appealed. "Tell your Mam how pretty she looks!"

But I couldn't. I couldn't give my usual answer. I couldn't flatter her by saying how lovely she looked because she didn't. Her hair was hacked, torn, red, ugly.

I lunged towards my mother and held her closely while the tears grew in my eyes. I tried to think of something clever to say. But as I flew towards her, the magazines I'd been carrying fell to the floor and scattered around our feet. I looked down and saw the front-cover photographs of pretty young models staring back up at me; puzzled, trying to work out what the problem was, confused, trying to work out why I'd let them go.

I squeezed my mother tightly as I remembered what I'd seen. Mourning a beautiful woman who had been destroyed.

CEZANNE AND THE PICKLED CUCUMBERS

Penny Simpson

Jacob should have been the first to know, but now I think he will be probably be the last. This is a mistake, as I can tell from Miriam's reaction.

– What if he finds out from someone else?

She pushes her thick arms out through the steam pouring from her cooking pots and grabs my shoulders.

– There will only be more arguments, Lily!

Miriam throws her arms into the air and then lets them drop down by her hips. She seems resigned to the course events will take without her further interference. If Jacob and I end up shouting, she will simply retreat into the kitchen and pickle cucumbers. It won't be her ears taking the brunt of my father's accusations. I stand over a dish of cooling peppers and tease the skins away from their flesh with the tip of my forefinger. Miriam is back at the stove, but she wags her fists at me in a playful gesture. She is only ever angry for a minute and then her bad mood evaporates. When you confess to Miriam it's like catching a piece of gristle in your food, a nasty taste, but in a moment it's replaced with something more palatable. Chewing the cud with my father is a more dangerous operation. I suppose that's why I'm still standing in the kitchen fiddling with these peppers. I'm looking for a way out.

– Just go and talk to your father, please, Lily.

– He'll be angry, won't he?

– Yes, but you can't keep avoiding him.

I stare at Miriam's face in the mirror that hangs above the kitchen table. Her reflection seems to dribble down its surface, because the steam has condensed on contact with the cold glass. She wears one of my old school pullovers over her blue dress. It has shrunk, but she has somehow managed to stretch it over her broad shoulders. Miriam has spent years rescuing unregarded treasures like these from out of our household rubbish.

– Waste not, and the pennies will always look after themselves, she says.

I've been watching everybody in mirrors ever since I can remember. The reflected surfaces of my home allow my world to unfold as if it were captured in one of my father's paintings. There are fifty mirrors in my father's house and in them I catch the secrets of our world, catch them like I do the summer moths flying in through the broken window shutters. I keep my back to the rooms where Jacob prowls and Esther, my mother, seems always to be asleep. You find constant movement only in the kitchen where Miriam circles the flagstones, preparing the food my father insists on and the rest of us eat in hostile silence: boiled fowl legs, pickled cucumbers, deep fried potato bread...

You must know that I have never really been able to talk to my father. He remains apart from the rest of us. When we eat together, his hands are always restless, sketching out his ideas on the table top between courses. Usually, you know within seconds of sitting down whether there will be an argument, because the atmosphere stings you. I sit silent, my skin prickling up and my fingers shaking. Miriam encourages me to eat, because no one else notices me.

My mother digs her fingers into her palms and watches Jacob's skating hands, which rarely seem to pause. A fork scrapes on a plate. Teeth catch at a bone. Water sluices in a glass and my father's hands pirouette up and down the tablecloth. I try to distract myself by timing my mouthfuls with those taken by my father. Oh, those endless meals filled with furious silence, broken only by Miriam's criticisms.

– You must eat up. You can't paint on an empty stomach, Jacob. You will rush things and end up with sloppy results.

Miriam was the only one who dared openly challenge my father at meal times.

Nor could she understand why we had so many mirrors hanging up throughout the house. We are all as untidy and as badly dressed as tramps. My mother tries to explain how the mirrors help Jacob paint his pictures. He paints self-portraits. Sometimes, but only sometimes, my mother and I are caught walking in to the edges of his canvas.

– Stand still, Lily. Is that the same shirt you had on yesterday? Sure it wasn't the red one? I want the red one. Go and change.

– But I'm going out, daddy..

My mother whispers that Jacob was not always this bad-tempered, that he has become worse since his gallery has fallen on hard times. He no longer exhibits with the owner Imogen Jeffries, an extraordinary woman who came and stayed with us last summer. I hid under her bed in the spare room so I could breath in her perfume. I decided that one day I was going to be as sophisticated and as beautiful as this gallery owner, but now I think I'm going to be a painter.

– But please, please, don't tell Jacob, Miriam.

– Silly. Having secrets.

– But everybody has secrets. What are yours?

– No time for secrets. I'm preparing for your father's birthday party!

Jacob is going to be fifty-five the day after tomorrow. He says he wants no presents, no fuss, no toasts, and definitely no cards, particularly ones with crude ageist jokes on them.

– And definitely no surprises, my mother warns us, her voice hostile with anxiety.

I keep watch in the mirrors as the arguments wax and wane throughout the house. My father has gone back to his studio in the attic and locked the door. He is threatening to stay there until his birthday is over. My mother, exhausted by dispute, has finally fallen asleep on the cracked leather sofa in our front room. She has had to wedge the room's broken shutters together with a mop handle. It's still wet from being used to clean the kitchen floor this morning. I can hear the slow drip of water from its head of string even though I'm standing out here in the hallway, but my mother remains sound asleep. Her mouth has fallen open and soon she will start to snore. I check the stairs. Nothing. I look back down the corridor towards the kitchen. Miriam is busy. The kitchen door with its distinctive stained glass panels is only half-ajar. I won't be seen. I take my place beside my mother's slumped body. I'm so close, I can see a little stream of phlegm fall from her bottom lip.

Slowly, I begin to draw. I never draw anything inside mirrors.

When did I first start drawing? Miriam has kept a few of my old school paintings, which I gave to her as presents each Christmas. They are full of bonfires and little people with no hands. Presumably, I couldn't draw fingers at that stage. When I decide to apply for the local art college where Jacob began his own career, Miriam suggests I practise by sketching her hands. They are stained purple with beetroot juice. I draw her at work in the kitchen amongst her pots and pans, her fingers always on the move, stripping down cauliflowers, slicing carrots, and peeling onions.

– Have you never thought what it must be like to grow old? she asks me.

I have finally persuaded her to sit still one evening as she waits for her pickles to cool in their big glass jars. Miriam has folded her hands on her lap and I have just commented on the dozens of brown freckles that decorate them.

– Jacob is jealous of you, because you have a future. He thinks his life is reduced to what he can see in a mirror.

My own hands fall still. Miriam is asking me to think about my father in a way I have never imagined possible before. She presents him as a man with an emotional life that does not necessarily include reflections on me, his only child.

– He's frightened, Lily.

– Of me? Oh, I don't think so, Miriam. I'm scared though. How am I going to explain to him?

After all, Jacob banned me from his studio when I was just seven years old.

I had knocked over one of the old white plates he used for his palettes and he no longer wanted me near him, or his paintings. I was seven years old and I was clumsy, but I appealed to my mother for the ban to be lifted. She had curled herself up in their bed and suggested I take long walk instead and enjoy the countryside. It was Miriam who had to rescue me again. She pinched my cheeks and lifted me up to the kitchen mirror so I could write my name across its steam-covered surface:

– LILEE LIVES HERE!

Jacob had roared with laughter.

438

– She can't even spell her own name. Can you credit it? She's stupid.

Miriam had turned her back on my father and busied herself beating a slab of steak with a small wooden hammer. I was disappointed by his response too, but I was accustomed by then to my father addressing the thin air above my head. At home, you see, I had learned to listen, but not to speak. Jacob spoke to thin air, my mother rambled in her dreams and my own sentences splintered like pieces of dry wood. It was Miriam who understood this best. She was always more than the cook in our household. When I couldn't sleep, I would crawl under the table in the kitchen and watch her shuffle and wheeze her way around her nightly cleaning routine. Miriam spoke all the time, accompanying everything she did with great volleys of sound. She knew I was down there, eavesdropping on her solitary conversations, but she did not mind, so I stayed tuned in and tried hard to ignore the reflections surrounding me.

I only saw my father cry once. This is what happened. I had taken up my usual position in the hallway, my back to the front room and my eyes glued to the mirror leaning against the wall . The open door was reflected inside the mirror and I could clearly see most of the room's interior. Jacob was sitting on the sofa, picking at one of the seat's big cracks. It looked more like an open wound than a distressed piece of stitching. Imogen was stretched out on the floor by his feet. I think she was older than my father. She dressed in vibrantly coloured clothes that were far too tight for her and her hair was stiff as wire. You breathed in her spicy smell and then you breathed in trouble. Imogen was trouble.

– The colours just don't work anymore...

My father held himself very still, his hands curled up into two big red patches on his denim knees. He looked old. His hair was threaded with silver and it looked just too long and too shabby set alongside Imogen's shiny jet black bob. Standing in front of the mirror, I watched my world shift a gear. Jacob was vulnerable. There were tears falling down his cheeks. A few minutes had passed and I had learned to hate the woman and the man sitting inside our front room. I hated Imogen for making my father cry, naturally enough, but unnaturally, I resented my father for his weakness. He was cruel and indifferent, but he cried and that made him like me, or possibly, it made me more like him.

The rush of emotion as I watched this scene being played out inside the mirror. Then Imogen took off my father's shoes and began stroking his long toes. I ran down the corridor at this point and into the kitchen where I could hide myself under the table. Miriam was chattering on to herself as usual and the world slowed up again. Her voice filled my head as it had always done, except there was always going to be this memory running alongside it: the memory of a strange woman's hands lying on my father's bare feet.

– **W**ho the bloody hell do you think you are anyway? Cezanne?

There. I had said it at last. Jacob stood shaking in front of me, his rage swelling up inside him, like an unruly sail. He threw down the rag and the brush he was cleaning and let his freed hands rise up above his head. I was convinced they were going to come down on top of me. Thump, thump. He had never brushed Imogen's hands away, but his clumsy daughter's words could be easily scattered. A blow to the right. A blow to the left. But he held them still in mid-air when he saw my face had crumbled into tears.

– I like seeing women cry, he said.

– What?

– Your mother never listens. Who else can I talk to?

Later, I told Miriam how I had ridiculed my father, even though I could see how it made her kind heart seal up with fear.

– Then why do you want to become a painter?

Why indeed? If you skim-read through the newspaper cuttings my father keeps in an old suitcase under his bed, you find yourself covering his life as quickly as you draw in breath:

'In his heyday...

..no longer in his prime..

..as a young man..

..precociously talented..'

I begin to understand his fear of failing as I unfold and read each one of these buried tributes. Then looking up, I catch sight of myself in the mirror that stands opposite my father's bed. My disembodied head floats above its patchwork quilt. For years, I have been staring at my face in mirrors hoping the reflections I see might turn into the answers I have sought for so long. I forget that the minute I turn my back, these pictures disappear and something else immediately takes their place: the room in front of me; the coils of oil paint laid out on a white plate; Miriam's dishes of pickled cucumbers. These are all tactile things and not just reflections. I can move my hands across them, turning and touching them, like the strange woman did my father's feet, until I know for sure they exist in the world outside the mirrors.

If I start painting at art college next year, I will cover up any mirrors that might be around me. I will stand so close to my subject, I will be able to see sunlight warming a pepper skin that is as red as a letter box. I will paint pickled cucumbers and I will know that my father is not Cezanne. I think only then will I be happy. Maybe tomorrow I shall tell Jacob this and nothing more?

THE DAY JOB

Elizabeth Ashworth

The toad was flattened into a cutout baby shape, black and crinkly, and left for people to notice or ignore on their way to the train. It was in the wall, a foot away from the noticeboard with the timetables pasted inside.

It was there for two weeks, and then it had gone. She wondered who'd moved it – or if anyone had thought what it might be doing there, and how it had got so squashed.

She had imagined it had been run over when she picked it up, and thought for a moment it was a frog. But it was too big, she decided, and was glad as she placed it in the cavity between the weathered stones, so it could be a toad in the hole.

Linton wouldn't touch it at first.

"They're unlucky."

She felt irritated. He was such a depressing little lad. What could he possibly know about what was lucky or unlucky? He could hardly read or write, for God's sake. She hadn't understood just how illiterate he was until he'd shown her his geography homework on the train one day. He'd insisted on it, even though she hadn't really wanted to see it. She'd been teaching kids like Linton all day, and was exhausted by special needs. But the work was earning her some good cash – even if it would only last for a few more weeks. Then, at least, she could have a break from teaching until the next call – she was a supply teacher – and get on with the writing and the painting.

The geography book was covered in wallpaper: thickly embossed in silver on grey. It oppressed her because the wallpaper was too important for the book. The wintry sun shone in through the carriage window, while Linton rooted about in his bag, and she felt tired and uncomfortable.

"I'm going to the library to get a book out for this project I'm doing on Mary, Queen of Scots," he boasted.

He spoke in such a light voice, though, that she couldn't

really hear him or understand everything he said, so she took to saying yes or no and looking out of the window, hoping evilly that she might give the wrong answer. He stared and talked and rummaged around in his bag, smelling like children who don't belong anywhere: the scent of neglect and Shroud of Turin underpants and unwashed hair.

He was a little runt, she decided, but out of perversity asked him his name and feigned a polite interest, on the first morning they walked to the train together.

"Linton."

And his sister was Donna, and his real dad lived in Manchester, but came to see him now and then, and took Linton sailing and climbing. He told her how good he was at Kung Fu and talked into the wind about Bruce Lee's funeral.

"I saw a ghost last night," he said, as they turned into the path for the station in a strong cold sea wind, which spotted them with rain.

"Did you tell anyone?"

"I told my mum. My mum said it was my grandpa."

She told him she had a ghost cat.

"That's unlucky."

Coming back that evening, she went into the station café. She'd made a litle progress at school, but had been appalled at how inadequate the children were. The petulance of boys of twelve who couldn't understand or be understood dismayed her: they were bursting with rage at the world, at themselves, and at her. But she was learning to coerce, to praise and disarm while they repeated a rhyme or copied a title from the board, then to colour it, and the date, in felt-tip pen. They looked at pictures of foxes and ducks in simple reading books in the library, where handsome sixth-form girls with smooth hair and stylish uniforms helped them with their reading. In unsupervised moments, they talked about the fights at home the previous night, or the sex scenes on a latest video. They switched from desultory repetitions of 'Mrs Daffy Duck goes to market', to subtle swearings at her through what could almost have been their milk teeth.

"Hiya."

She looked up from the hot chocolate she was gulping, in

the hope of increasing her blood sugar. She had a bag of crisps and offered Linton one. He felt showily in his pockets and said he'd lost his money. She gave him 20p for an orange juice and they walked out to the train, standing together in the bitter cold on the platform.

"I think it'll snow," she said.

"No, it won't," he answered, Manchester-wise, waving his arm towards the sea.

"You mean because of the salt air? It still snows here, you know."

She wished it would snow, just to show him.

On the train he was staring at her.

"Will you be on this train tomorrow?"

"Yes. Did you tell your teacher about the ghost?"

"Course not," impatiently. "We're having a geography test on Friday, and it's hard. I'm going to have to get a book out of the library again."

"A friend of mine might get on at the next stop," she said, hoping that the man she vaguely knew would be there and sit next to her. She didn't really like the man – a pipe-smoking civil servant – very much, and until now she'd avoided him.

But all that was on the platform was a bananaskin, and Linton stared triumphantly at her reflection, as she silently examined it.

Then they passed a field, where she saw a horse standing in a green cape which had blown over its haunches so it looked a bit like Pegasus. She glanced to the hillside, then back to Linton.

"There you are – there's snow on the mountains," she said, as they raced along.

He ignored her, instead demanding to know what she taught and where she had her dinner. She was angry, and moved to sit behind, saying she was too hot. Linton then placed himself in what had been her seat. From her new position, she could now see both their faces, reflected from the glass panel behind the driver, and she focused on her own eyes, looking at herself. Then she realised that Linton was staring hard at her again. She flicked her glance away to the hills, then back: he was still watching her. She was uneasy: It reminded her suddenly of her schooldays, when she was in the sixth form – insouciant and popular, with a brown ponytail. A second-former had fallen in love with her – a little fat boy, called Peter. He'd written her poems and letters which she'd laughed at. Then one day a letter came asking her to meet him by the boating pond in the park after school. She didn't go, of course, and afterwards joked about it with her friends and boyfriend. A letter came from Peter the next day: "I waited for you and when you didn't come it felt like a knife through my heart." This note had meant absolutely nothing to her then – but she remembered it now as Linton's eyes stared unblinkingly at her in the glass.

The ticket collector came up and Linton gave him his.

"Heyar. You can keep it." Then he looked at her. "I always have to tell him he can keep it."

They got off the train together and had started the walk home, when a local man drew up to offer her a lift. Thankfully, she ran across the road: "See you, Linton!" – not even caring if he wanted to come, too. She was a grown-up, and he was a kid, after all. Anyway, she'd seen through his little games: he'd tried to borrow another 20p from her to buy a bottle of pop, but she said she hadn't got anything this time.

He looked deflated as she turned to wave.

But, next morning, he was waiting to walk down.

"I've just seen that friend of yours who gave you a lift last night – he didn't speak to me."

Good, she thought.

On the platform, the sun broke through the mist over the quarry. Linton was glum, mumbling about volcanoes and the end of the world.

"You'll be dead by then," he said.

"You must think I'm old, then?"

He didn't reply as the train drew up, and he got on to sit opposite her, without speaking.

During their evening conversation he talked about Bruce Lee, the weights his mum had ordered for him, virgin birth and divorce. He pulled up his jumper to show her his belly – where the muscles would be when he got them. Then he asked about her boyfriend – if he'd ever been married. She wondered then why she bothered talking to him. There was nothing poignant or lovable about him – she didn't get the warm, maternal feeling she sometimes had with the kids at school. He'd insinuated himself into her field of attention, willy-nilly. She should have ignored him the first time they spoke, and, a long time ago, as a schoolgirl, she would have.

From that cruel, unsentimental, yet true young centre, she had known what was crucial – and what was irrelevant – to her development. But, somewhere in later adolescence, when she was at art school, her responses had become framed in shadows, and something in her hushed, and put on hold, to return to, later, when she was sure of things again.

And there was this dream: partying in a city, running from street to street, throwing money in the air, laughing with her companions, confident that lovers would always want her and wait for her. Later in the dream she had found a child, which she had mutilated, and, when it was dead, embalmed in pitch – but there'd been the sense that she'd meant to come back to it, when things were alright again, to breathe fresh life into it.

"Better for you, then," – when she said her boyfriend had stayed single.

"Why?"

Linton shrugged.

"I've been divorced a long time," she told him.

"I think divorce is terrible," he said.

She took the train to the day job which gained in importance as she focused more on the needs of the children and helped with the work which she corrected from above their spiky hairdos. Then one day with her boyfriend in the library she saw Linton on a chair, taking out a book on Kung Fu.

"There's that awful kid who follows you around," laughed the young man.

That Sunday night, after seeing her lover off on his train to the town where he worked, she turned for home. Waiting for her by the hole in the wall was Linton, and they walked together up the hill. The wind was blowing in their faces as he told her that the weights had come; he'd started the exercises.

She knew that next day the special needs' class would welcome her in their graceless way...they were really improving with their reading.

She felt sick, hearing Linton talking about his dad in Manchester.

She clutched at her coat, in reluctant politeness and despair at his self-important tones.

Just a few more weeks of school, then there would be all the time in the world for the writing and the painting, she reassured herself, watching the seagulls, as they wheeled and cried, back and forth, over the ocean.

FEEDING THE HOUSE CROWS

Lewis Davies

I shouted hard, trying to deflect the man's threat, but he just smiled, motioned with his arms over brown spindle legs and thin stretched ribs before extending his open palm to me once again. I closed my eyes, lay back against my heavy green rucksack and imagined myself on a beach in the South.

A thin, bearded Norwegian at a Rest House in Hardwar had told me it was bad karma to ignore the requests of a sadhu. We had been drinking tea on the terrace in the early morning, warm and comfortable before the real heat of the day. A man had appeared at our table. He was naked except for a deeply stained orange loin-cloth that was curled around his waist and draped over his right shoulder. The solitary waiter noticed his presence but refrained from approaching. He didn't say anything, just offered his hand, calloused and empty, which the Norwegian filled with a roll of brown notes. The hand moved in my direction, and I complied without thinking. His eyes registered no reaction as he spirited the money into a fold concealed within his cloth.

My companion seemed unconcerned by the transaction, but I couldn't shake the feeling I'd been rifled. The eyes had given nothing to me. Just a calm acceptance of my money. I was just drifting past. Someone not from his world. Empty.

The beggar, dressed in the same orange cloth of a holy man, must have followed me through the tight throng of travellers on the station platform. I had secured a square of empty floor space on the far side of the rest rooms. The train was delayed, and it was late into the long tense afternoons that stretch through the Winter on the Ganges plain. He appeared as I turned to check the clock.

A mass of black matted hair that merged with a thick, betel-stained beard. Faint smells of sandalwood and sweat. Three teeth surfaced from behind the hair as his first request for alms was refused.

Initially I tried to look beyond him, concentrate on the peopled platform that grew and surged in anticipation of the expected train still a hundred miles away. A single House Crow skipped down between the oily rails, searching for the scraps of dried paratha an old woman had thrown away from her meal. It dug quickly twice under a sleeper before lifting sharply upwards to a beam across the arched roof.

The sadhu didn't move, just waited. I looked directly at him, waved a hand firmly and shook my head.

His teeth slid away, but his eyes still held me, and a hand remained outstretched.

I shrugged before brushing the dust on the floor clear for a seat. The man squatted where he was. The hand still asking.

I gleaned a book from the side pocket of the rucksack and pretended to read, but my concentration held only in short bursts punctuated by the continued insistence of the man's presence that I should give him money.

'No, not today.'

The shout had no effect on him but succeeded in attracting the attention of a trio of suited businessmen who were playing a game of standing cards a short distance down the platform. I watched as they discussed the odd duo facing each other. The sadhu had marked me out. He had approached no one else and now squatted obstinately a yard away, palm outstretched, impassively open, waiting for my reaction.

Other heads turned as the continuous traffic of people coursed up and down the platform. A girl with big brown bug eyes pointed; her mother followed her gaze before sharply pulling her away.

'Why not ask somebody else,' I gestured. A few interested heads turned back but the sadhu was fixed. They were of his religion, I assumed, but I had money. It would only take a handful of rupees, but I couldn't force myself to open the money belt that stuck with sweat and dust to my waist.

The man pulled his cloth further from his body to

emphasise the fact that he had nothing. Desired nothing. Nothing permanent. The money would only buy him food.

One of his testicles hung forward from the side of his loin cloth, long black hairs pulling the skin to small nodules on his scrotum. It lolled in the open before he eased it back with a push of his finger.

I shifted uneasily against my rucksack. An announcement strained through the public address system. A baby cried before being pushed inside its mother's sari. Shyly the woman pulled a hood over her head to protect them.

The voice was consumed into the shimmering heat that festered under the ochre-shaded beams of the station roof. People stirred, shifted, checked possessions and children but there was no movement to the edge.

'Go away.' I emphasised each syllable.

One of the businessmen who had been playing a hand of cards tapped the squatting sadhu lightly on the shoulder. He didn't look up. The action was repeated with the same result.

There was an unease as the businessman touched the sadhu's shoulder. He was reluctant to directly confront him. It was a request for attention, and it was being denied.

He cautiously suggested a question. It was a polite petition, a reasoning that I sensed, even though I understood nothing of the rising flowing words. The sadhu waved his hand away brusquely. The man looked at me, shrugged his shoulders and returned to his friends. They waited for the next development.

I turned my head down. I could wait until the train arrived. Then it was sixteen hours on a sleeper. Tomorrow would be another city, another place, and this station would be a memory to store with the rush of people and places that was becoming India.

More time slithered by. Seconds moving on. Waiting.

The only thing the man carried was a leather pouch strung by hide around his neck to his waist. As he demanded with one hand, the other would gently ease up and touch the bag as if to ascertain that the charm was still there.

Now he clasped this bag tightly and began murmuring something low and unintelligible.

'English mate, speak English.' I shouted at him. I could sense a sap of anger rising but a public show of aggression would get me nowhere. This was a holy man. Everyone showed deference.

As his murmuring continued, deep guttural sounds uttered without moving his lips, he loosened the string that clasped the leather pouch together and pulled out what I first thought were white incense sticks. But as he opened his hand he revealed a necklace of small bones strung together on a string of gut. Three bones tangled together, they looked like femurs, but tiny, delicate femurs six inches long. He lifted them to his mouth, pursed his lips gently over their bleached surface before allowing two to fall from his hand, holding the gut between his forefinger and thumb. They bounced, then swayed as he drew small circular motions in the air.

I woke to a rush of steam, noise, and adrenaline that floods into a platform with a late train. Panic screamed through me as I reached for the rucksack but it was there, green and comforting with its bulk and promise of useful possessions. The moving crowd surged around, the beggar gone.

The scramble for the train continued unabated. The long wait had sharpened everyone's desire to be away from the city. Stations are designed to be passed through; quickly, without effort. When the flow is baffled, frustrations merge in eddies of stress twisting between the pillars, sharpening tempers, scattering the sparrows that scavenged at the margins.

But the train had arrived. A vast iron carriage in dull amber green, sprayed with the baked brown dust of the Ganges. Figures streamed into open doors pulling belongings and children through with them. I checked my ticket; it had a number and reservation. But then so did everyone else.

The inside of the carriage bulges and strains as the monster swallows its captives: women with children, men in suits carrying briefcases, an old man twisted with arthritis helped to his seat by a girl.

I secure my seat a third of the way along the carriage. The

enthusiasm of the first assault has faded to a determined securing of positions. The number I have drawn is a window berth running parallel to the length of the train and facing a cubicle of six berths at a right angle. The berths are already filled. Bright smiling faces nod in my direction.

I try a simple greeting in Hindi which produces a duplicate and smiles but no conversation. They probably guess I can't speak it.

The train waits another twenty minutes. The heat in the carriage begins to swarm upward, merging with a thick swell of sweat.

'Chi chi ?' The cry cuts through the carriage as a terracotta bowl of tea is thrust through the open window of my berth. I gladly hand two rupees out to the eager hand.

The tea is warm and sweet, but I feel a shiver of sweat ooze from my skin as I swallow a second time.

The berths opposite are all occupied by men. They seem to be related, as there is a perceptible deference to an older man who dominates the conversation.

I watch as they settle into the compartment. Suitcases are carefully placed on the top bunk; chains appear which are weaved to secure the handles to the steel supports of the sleepers. The middle bunks are folded back to allow the occupants to sit in two rows of three facing each other. They huddle together conspiratorially. I wait for the train to move again.

Then a shiver, a click and the first pull of the engine on the carriage as the machine fights for momentum. There is a subdued cheer as the fixed points on the platform begin to edge past the windows. A warm fetid breeze clamours down through the people; the stagnant air is brushed on.

After the still, listless afternoon the train appears to move at an incredible speed out of the city. Squat flats decorated with washing and aerials cut into the first thick slums of corrugated iron and plastic, festooned with wires and coloured red flags, sky quartered by dark Pariah Kites. Then a river, peopled and sluggish with a languorous scum that children splash through. Further out the dwellings thin to tight fields flushed with irrigation channels and watched by egrets: white and sentinel in the wider margins.

More track and a solitary ox whipped onwards into the evening.

The men opposite my berth produce a blanket which is spread out over their knees and the gap between the berth. Held taut at the corners, they flick playing cards inwards in a highly charged game of Trumps. The cards are worn at the edge; bright reds and dark blacks collide inwards before a sharp shuffle and a spinning deal.

After each round there is laughter and a mutual reckoning of the scores. One of the younger boys notices my interest and whispers something quickly to his father. The older man looks up, smiles and beckons me to join. I smile back but wave my refusal. He seems to understand.

The game fades into evening as the lights flicker on in the carriage. The pulse of the train moving forward and swinging sidewards maintains a constant rhythm of motion and noise. People begin to prepare for the night. Bunks are lowered. There is a steady stream to the toilet, which casts its own insistent mephitic odour along the corridor.

The card players play a last hand before unpacking an evening meal. Tiny parcels of rice and potato wrapped in thick chappatti are revealed and shared. Stubby fingers enthusiastically grasp the dhal-stained rice.

I unpack two dried parathas.

As the food settles I slide into a half sleep of moving stations that drift by in voices and a chorus of offers. Cockroaches scuttle across the dust: unpaid cleaners. A man sings, voice rising, then fading to an evening's lament. Stalls for no reason. People moving; leaving.

I wake to a flickering light in the bunk above the carriage door. I see a face; then it is gone. I turn to face inwards. A teasing of absence, then a slap of shock. The rucksack is only a space.

My hands draw desperately under the bunk scattering cups, dust and cockroaches but nothing else. Then the ease of movement, and I gasp for a belt that is no longer there.

The tighter, stronger gushing of panic begins to flood the adrenaline. My head spins without a stable thought. A rush of ideas and possibilities.

I burst into the compartment of the men and begin turning the cases that are stacked on the floor. Voices in anger and surprise surround me in a language I don't need to understand. I shout back.

Lights begin flickering to life in other sections of the carriage. I realise they haven't taken anything and edge out.

A guard arrives. Shouting in Hindi, arms waving, concerned but not conciliatory.

'My rucksack, it's been stolen.' I yell pointing at the empty space. 'Rucksack.' I strike my shoulders aggressively. The guard is three inches away and he shouts back. I catch nothing.

'He says calm down, he will report it at the station.' The translation is from the card player who had noticed my interest earlier. I wheel on him.

'It'll be too late then.'

The man smiles at me as my anger soars.

'Tell him it'll be too late.'

He reluctantly translates. There is another burst of Hindi. I swear viciously to myself.

'He says we will be at Gorkapur soon, then he will report it. There is nothing he can do now.'

'Search the carriage.'

'He cannot, he does not have the authority.'

'Shit.' I stare into the dark eyes of the guard. I know it's not him I hate. I feel the engine begin to ease as the first sporadic street lights of the new town fly past the window, then harder as the buildings thicken to a centre. The guard rushes to the carriage door as the platform appears. All the lights are now on in the carriage and all eyes are on me. I am the entertainment.

The door is thrown back and the first chi seller is barred by the guard. He beckons me forward. The train is surrounded by a horde of hawkers selling tea and peanuts. Hands are thrust through the windows seeking a sale. I reach the door at the same time as a soldier from the platform. He points a rifle at me. There is an absurd reaction to lift my hands which I can't resist. He smiles and shakes his head, beckoning me onwards with his rifle. I notice it has a wooden barrel and a bolt lock. I can't take my eyes from the darkness of the steel.

The platform is vast and empty after the cage of the carriage. Only hawkers, and they drift away from us as the soldier leads me along. I notice the details: the heavy fall of the man's boots, a cockroach flat and lifeless, a beggar curled and old, a sign in script, Gorkapur. The station clock. It is after four. Eyes stare out through the bars of the train. A man and a soldier.

He leads me to a guard's room at the far end of the station. A single room, a covered desk, timetables and directives on the walls. Other soldiers have appeared. One directs me to sit in the chair facing the desk. The fan on the ceiling turns sluggishly. I ask about the train. Is it going to leave ? Soldiers shake their heads. I can just see the last carriage through the door. They appear to be waiting for someone. Orders ? A door to an anteroom swings open and the soldiers stop talking. The officer is obviously tired; his shirt hangs loose and open over a brown vest. Trousers slack and unbuttoned. He barely looks at me as he straddles his chair. Then he gestures with a lazy hand.

'Stolen ?'

'Yes, a rucksack, from the train, I was sleeping, then..'

He waves a hand to stop my burst of words.

'That is a very bad train, many things stolen.' He appears about to elaborate but contents himself with a turn of his hands.

'You have to make a report. But perhaps not here. Tomorrow, at Agra Cant.'

'But it'll be too late then.'

He laughs to himself.

'Too late, too late for what?'

A tap on my shoulder spins me around. The last carriage has gone. I dive for the door. It's fifty yards down the platform but has yet to pick up speed. I am conscious of nothing but the need to reach the train. Boots hitting the platform hard and fast. The blur of night flying past. The green retreating back. No thought of breath as flight sucks me on. Urging my legs, sight fixed. Brushing through hawkers, past sleeping beggars, catching the train. There's a figure at the door. Arms waving me on, then grasping as I judge the speed before making the leap. I fall forward into the carriage.

Chest rising; forcing air back in. The breathing eases with the climb of the train pushing on. I look up; it is my translator. His eyes consider me, searching for something, an explanation perhaps? Then he smiles, a wide, easy, amused smile before proffering a cigarette. I take it without thought.

OUT OF REACH

Lloyd Rees

It was not until the third day that the lodger began to panic. Linda had told her husband that, though he was intensely quiet, there was something weird about him, but Robert had dismissed her fears with a lazy shrug.

"He hasn't missed a week's rent. He's as quiet as a mouse, and you think everybody who wears glasses has a shifty look about them. He's alright."

Linda had not been so easily reassured though. Once, when she knew the lodger would definitely be out, she had offered to go up to empty his gas meter.

"It doesn't need it," Robert had sighed, but she had taken a key and gone anyway. She came back within five minutes, but this was a couple of minutes too long. Robert looked up from his paper.

"You haven't been sniffing around in his room, have you?"

Linda blushed.

"Oh come on, that's not fair. He doesn't bother us."

She sat down next to him and put her hand on his leg. "That's the point," she said. "I just wanted to know what he does in there all the time. He hardly ever goes out."

"He's a single man in a bed-sitter – what do you think he does?"

Linda shrugged. "Well, it's clean enough. Nothing there really. A lot of papers on the table, that's all."

Robert fought with his newspaper in order to read the centre pages. He was not interested. After a while he said, "Well, he's a student, he says."

There was no further mention of the topic until the man in the shop downstairs went away and shut up for a week.

They had decided to let the top bedroom when Linda got pregnant and had to give up work. Arthur, the vacuum cleaner man, had let them put a card in his window and the silent lodger had turned up and moved in within a week.

On the Tuesday after Arthur had gone away, there was a sharp knock on the lounge door and Linda had been startled by the obviously distraught figure of their lodger. He was still in a dressing-gown although it was late morning. His hair looked like a child's drawing, or as if he had washed it and slept on it without drying it. He pushed at his glasses and gave a sort of snort before starting to speak.

"My letters!"

Linda stared in incomprehension.

"My letters!" he gasped again. "They're in the shop downstairs. I can't get at them."

She managed to get rid of him, though she could not remember what she had said when she had related this encounter to her husband that evening. Robert nodded. Yes – he had noticed an electricity bill for them through the glass door to the shop. There were a few letters, in fact.

"He's desperate!" Linda cried. "You'll have to get them out."

"How can I get them out? The door's locked and Arthur won't be back till Saturday or Sunday. They'll just have to stay there until he gets back, that's all."

Linda banged down his plate on the formica kitchen table. "*You* tell him that. Don't leave me to face him tomorrow."

Robert winced at this irksome task, but when Linda refused to talk throughout their meal, and then raised the matter again as he went to switch the television on, he snapped: "Alright, I'll do it!"

"I need a tobacco tin. I don't smoke, you see." The lodger had bustled Robert back down the narrow stairs that led to his attic room as soon as he had knocked on his door. "You must have a tobacco tin," he urged. He hovered outside the lounge as Robert went in there, shrugged at his wife and opened a drawer where there was an old tin he kept elastic bands in. He handed the tin to the lodger.

"Weights."

Robert misunderstood. He waited.

"I need weights," the lodger insisted, his voice sticky and dry. "Do you fish?"

Robert shook his head. He wanted to help, or rather, he didn't want not to help, but the young man's monosyllabic nature was not encouraging.

"Wait here," the man said. Robert obeyed. He was tired from work but he sensed that this was something he could not ignore. Within moments, his lodger had reappeared and he was shaking the tobacco tin, holding it to his ear, testing it with a thumb.

"Water's no good," he sighed. "The tin leaks. Is this the best you've got?"

Robert was not a smoker. He ignored this last question. "What on earth are you up to?" he asked.

The man tutted. "I need something heavy," he said. "To put in the tin."

Robert looked around, but they were standing in the hallway. There was nothing but an upright vacuum cleaner in the way of anything heavy.

"Plasticine. Or playdough," the lodger exclaimed.

"Blu-tak?"

"Yes – that might do."

Robert went to the back of the drawer where he had found the tin and brought out a new packet of adhesive gum. The lodger was bounding down the stairs, pulling with his fingers at the base of the tin. He seized the adhesive, rolled it into a sausage and pressed it into the tobacco tin. He then carefully rolled a thin strip around the edge of the tin and pressed on the ill-fitting lid.

"Not bad. Sellotape to make sure, though."

Robert felt like pointing out that he was not an office supplier, but he fetched the tape. The lodger wrapped a long strip around the tin and weighed it in his hand. "Fine!" he said. Then he took out a piece of string from his pocket and held it against the lid. "More tape," he demanded.

Robert held it out and the lodger bit off another long strip. He watched as the string was attached.

"Just need a rod now. Hold that."

Robert took the tin and felt the gummed sticky tabs on its

underside tacky against his palm. He realised the madness – late-night fishing for letters, through the letterbox of a locked shop door. He said nothing, though, when the man returned with a piece of plastic tubing that looked like part of the frame from a child's Wendyhouse. He watched as a knot was expertly and quickly tied and he followed obediently downstairs to the glass door where a small heap of letters lay temptingly in view.

Two men stood in a darkened shop doorway. Robert thought, if a policeman passes, I'll just say I found him inserting this tin through the letterbox and I stopped to see what he was doing. Much the same as you, Officer!

"That's yours on top," the lodger said.

Robert smiled. It was a bill. There would be a reminder in due course anyway, and this could take hours. He remembered playing a machine at a fairground where you tried to seize hold of a shiny metal cylinder with ten Weights perched in cotton-wool, using a metallic grab that invariably slipped off and deposited air into the 'win' chute. But the lodger had either never been to a fairground or was possessed of more patience. He lowered the sticky, heavy tin through the letterbox and waited as it spun, then he eased it onto the manilla envelope. He tried to drop it down heavily to make it stick, but the first three or four times he reeled up nothing more than a tin of blue-tack. Then – it worked.

He eased back his plastic tube, then seized the string and delicately reined in an electricity bill to within an inch of the letter-box. Agonisingly, the friction against the door caused the letter to dislodge and flutter back to the floor.

"Do you mind if I go back for that one after?" the fisherman said, desperation glinting in his otherwise darkened face.

Robert shrugged. He was hooked on the man's strength of purpose now; he was almost enjoying himself.

The lodger had not waited for an answer but had turned back to his task. The second time he was successful, slipping two fingers through the spring-loaded letter-box and working his rod-hand carefully, an operation which took several minutes. The third time, the tackiness of the adhesive labels on the base of the tin was no longer strong enough, and the tin had to be withdrawn and re-labelled.

Then, over a space of about forty minutes, six letters were retrieved. The electricity bill still lay almost within reach, but several casts failed to land it.

"Do you want that one?" the lodger asked. Then: "I've got one for you from the District Council here – must be rates. And there's one here for the shop." He pushed the letter back through the opening and flung it as far into the shop as he could.

Robert said: "Let me have a go." He twisted the tin and thrust the tube back and fore until he finally managed to land it on the cellophane window of the envelope. The lodger did not take his eyes off the operation, despite the fact that he had a small wad of envelopes of his own in his hand. Robert managed to raise the bill until one corner was resting on the frame of the letterbox.

"This is the awkward bit," advised his friend.

Robert got two fingertips to the envelope and pulled it, crumpled, through the slot. "Got it!"

"Well done!"

"That was a good idea." He paused. The lodger had mentioned his Christian name when they first met, but Robert had never had cause to use it and he was embarrassed for a moment as it eluded him.

"John."

"Yes, John. Sorry. I'm Robert."

"I know."

They stood for another few seconds, looking down at their haul of letters.

"Better go up then," Robert said at last.

The man nodded.

Linda was in bed, but still awake, when Robert re-entered the flat. She had moved her swollen body across to her side of the bed as if it was someone else's body, or an inanimate thing, and Robert slid between the rough winceyette sheets.

"It's cold," he said.

"You'll warm up," she murmured.

He did not reply.

"What was all that business with the Sellotape and the blu-tak? That man's weird!"

"I'll tell you in the morning – I'm tired."

She did not pursue the matter and presently her breathing slowed and her body lurched in a last spasm before deep sleep.

He listened to the traffic outside. The house was a hundred yards from a set of traffic lights, so there would be a lull for a while, and then a burst of cars, invariably changing into third as they roared past. He had got used to this pattern of noise, but he could not blot it out tonight as he lay wide-eyed staring at the ceiling. He was suddenly bitterly lonely.

Upstairs, John the lodger was at his table with four identical slim white envelopes before him. He would be smiling now, devouring words slowly like a beautiful meal. A floor below, in an unlovely bedroom with an unopened rates demand and an electricity bill on the bedside table, Robert lay stiff as a stained handkerchief. Out of reach.

DISORIENTEERING

Bryn Daniel

The handle of my suitcase was getting slippery and the two little wheels were jamming. I was staggering on to a moving floor to be ferried down a corridor of brightly coloured advertisements for fractured eye-sockets that mirrored themselves right the way to the end, to the strip lights, where I was once again asked to choose from a bewildering selection of arrows. Which way should I step? At last I found my way outside, and then I was aboard a double-decker, which was unusual, leaving the port. Through the window I looked over Salacacabia, the city I had come to join. People criss-crossed in the street, carrying takeaways, telephones, sometimes each other. I saw a child with false whiskers and rabbit ears rattling a can. Two men in boilersuits jumped the traffic with a pond mould. I saw people on rooftops, on ladders; others folding out of armoured cars with moneybags. One man was scrambling from a hole in the road, his yellow hat gleaming in the sunshine — a girl in a bikini side-stepping the luminous tape. When we reached the bus station the driver helped me with my suitcase and pointed me in the direction of Tourist Information. But I wasn't sure if that was what I needed, and hailed a taxi. After all, I had come to the city to stay.

For the first three days I stayed at a hotel, until I realised that I could get a cheaper room if I moved out of the city centre. Following a conversation with a disappointed pharmacist in a bank, I discovered B&Bs. I settled in. I got to know my bearings. I read the newspapers. It was extraordinary the things you could buy from them. Anything from a platinum bookcase to a second-hand sleeping bag. (I rather liked the sound of the former.) I familiarised myself with the bus routes. I went to a tennis semi-final. I bought an automobile. I even got involved in a drunken brawl at the zoo. Then I took the keys to a studio flat in Sulkside, and each morning I drew the blinds on flocks of screeching gulls.

'Be wary of them,' my neighbour whispered, 'they will scoop out your eyes.'

I didn't know what to make of such advice. After all, they were only gulls. I asked her about the central heating.

'I have a chill,' I said.

'Bah,' she said, straightening up, 'a young man like you?'

Eventually I found it. It was behind a sliding door that itself was inside a cupboard. After I thought I'd properly activated it I put on my boots and went for a six-hour walk up Salac mountain. The view of the city from up there! Boy, it was magnificent! I marched through the bracken shading my eyes from the sun, thrilled to hear the sound of crickets (or were they grasshoppers?), for I hadn't heard them since I'd arrived, and their chirr reminded me of... Now I was alive! I wanted to enjoy, to suck everything in, to wonder, to scan, to scrutinise...

But I suppose that is neither here nor there. What is, what I mean is, is that by the end of my first week I felt part of the city and ready to take employment with a suitable firm or company, should I so desire. One morning I awoke in such a fluster. I'd dreamt I was in a train crash. I'd survived, but I was surrounded by walls of flame and there was no way out. That was when I ripped open my eyes to find the VCR rewinding. It whined over six hours of tape and came to an abrupt and noisy halt. There was a moment of relative calm, silence in the night. Then I heard a train not so far away, shuffling in or out of the city. I concluded, lying there in my bed, that it was time to counter my relative inactivity and find myself a job. Light minds lead light thoughts, I suppose.

So in the morning I went to an employment agency, Fernseeds on Main St. It must have been the humidity, or an after-effect of the dream, but the people coming through the doors seemed curiously translucent. I felt that I could almost see through them, and when I looked on the wall at the photographs of the Temporaries of the Month I saw phantom bottles of wine and young women and men with their arms round no one at all.

A very pretty blonde saw to me. She had a badge on her lapel that said, 'Jackie'. Underneath her jacket Jackie was wearing a see-through blouse. When she sat on the couch I could see up her skirt, though I tried my best not to look, though I wanted to. I gave her my details and sat a brief test, which involved entering data into a PC, and Jackie was pleased with the results. She told me I could begin work tomorrow if I liked. There was an established insurance company that was always looking for people with my qualifications. It was such good news that I could not bring myself to tell her I was unfamiliar with insurance: I decided I should not be daunted. 'That's excellent!' I said. Afterall, I was a man of letters and a quick learner.

The training room at Koel Insurance was on the fifth floor, and I sat waiting with eight other temporaries. We partook in idle chat. Then a man in short sleeves entered 500 and introduced himself as 'the trainer'. He gave us 'temps' a general rundown on the company. He made us answer the simplest questions, marking our answers on a flip-chart. Afterwards we were invited to stand and individually present ourselves, something he called 'ice-breaking' (although it seemed a little topsy-turvy to me). A man in a blue shirt and yellow tie was first to speak, and his words were largely typical of those that were to follow — including my own. He was feeling enthusiastic about the position, was eager to learn, was fond of ten-pin bowling, public houses and the movies, and the person he'd most like to meet was a highly successful microchip entrepreneur who'd recently moved into smaller premises. The girls tended to go for movie stars. Seventh down a man all in black and sunglasses stood up and said, 'My name's Borris. I'm into *scissors*.' Wisps of grey, wisps of death flecked his black hair.

For the next three days we inputted fake data into PCs in Room 500. There was nothing arduous or complicated about it. Our trainer diligently answered the questions and re-booted the systems when something failed. We were soon six in number, for three temps quit after the first day (apparently 'fall-out' was expected), but the rest of us competed with one another in the speed in which we grasped the learning, and were self-congratulatory when we succeeded.

Friday night I saw Borris in Primaries. He was in conversation with a supermarket employee. 'I can do an NVQ in bakery?' he was quietly saying, scanning the leaflet in his hand.

I was waiting for my pie. The ones in front of me looked

just right, crispy but not too hot. They were on the lower shelf and the girl was creaking her knees to go down for them — but then from the corner of her eye she saw a tray of fresh pies coming from the oven. And so she straightened, and I had fast-food I couldn't eat for ten minutes. Ah well, mustn't grumble.

Tuning in I heard, 'Bun studies! What happens there then? Do I have to get up at four in the morning to take the exam, then run out of answers before I get to the end? When I go to hand in the paper do I ask the examiner if he wants it sliced? No, I don't think so, sunbeam,' Borris said and passed the leaflet back to the employee. He pushed his trolley towards the cakes. When I caught up with him and tried to be cheerful he told me to eff off.

Later, my neighbour accused me of talking about her behind her back. 'I've heard you calling me a...' and she used a filthy word. I assured her that I'd done no such thing but she was adamant, and in a flurry of profanities threatened the nastiest retribution if I did not put an end to it.

A good many people in Salacacabia use foul language. Personally I deplore it. It is such an asinine form of communication.

Claims was divided into six zones and on Monday I was placed before the team-leader of one of them. For a little while I sat at a PC trying to remember that two spaces were necessary after a full stop, but then a permanent member of staff flexed in and I had to leave his seat. 'Eventually you'll get your own desk,' the team-leader said. 'But for now... Can you vet?'

I was confused. I could not answer.

'Can you batch?'

I shrugged. She wasn't looking at me; she was innocently drawing single strands from her auburn hair, scanning my résumé.

'Can you photocopy?'

I said, 'Of course.'

She went to consult a man who was hanging his coat on a hat stand. She spoke while he opened his umbrella to dry at the foot of the stand. There were umbrellas is clumps all over the office. They made me think of toadstools or large mushrooms. Presently she returned.

'Before we go on,' she said, 'I want you to copy your CV.

Here's one I've already done. You can use it as a start. I've taken your original for Head Office.'

'How many copies?' I asked.

'As many as you can,' she answered.

I spent the morning photocopying my résumé. I believe I adapted to it well. Even if I say so myself, my copies were excellent. Maybe I was a natural. Then, at twelve-thirty, my work was taken away to be assessed. Returning with them after lunch my team-leader introduced me to the shredder, and I began to feed my copies to the machine. It was amazing. It transformed the sheets into thin, coiling strips. After a short while, and I must confess some instruction, I began to feed them two, three and then six or seven at a time into the shredder. It was superfast work, and when all but one of the copies were little strips my team-leader guided me back to the copier. There she lifted a small flap and said, 'See this?' I looked. Displayed on a small monochrome screen was: |||||

'Now see what happens when I press.'

She lifted her finger —

||||

'Er... There're only four lines?'

'Precisely,' she said, and passed me the last copy. '*Now* let's see how you get on...'

I thought it would be more efficient to copy then shred, copy then shred, copy then shred, but when the team-leader learnt what I was doing she took me into her office for a gentle reprimand. 'You copy, you copy, you copy...' she commanded, '... *then* you shred.'

On the way home I saw Borris standing in front of a shop window, crunching mints. The glass had said CLOSING DOWN SALE SATURDAY but now all the letters, save four, were scratched away; you can probably guess which ones remained. He seemed to have forgotten who I was. 'It used to be a binoculars shop,' he said.

'I'm sorry,' I said, 'are you talking to me?'

I went home hoping not to run into my neighbour. I ducked beneath the foliage and scampered up the path. I don't think she saw me. But one of my teeth had come loose and I pulled it out with my fingers during the TV news. I was confused. But I reasoned that I had so many teeth one less would scarcely make a difference. It wasn't as if it was one of my incisors, after all. To avoid infection I went drinking in the city centre. There were dozens of scissored girls in the public house I visited: they were red faced saying '*infrastructure*' time and time again, in the way only girls can. For a short while I chatted to a nurse named Katy. Katy was an all-day breakfast: she was huge. She asked me if I'd like to go back to her place; she shared a house by the hospital. I must say, even her friends seemed keen on me: 'Yeah, come along,' one of them said, 'we need someone to sit in the front seat of the taxi.' But Katy was not my type, I'm afraid. I prefer petite women. I had to decline. I took her number only so I wouldn't hurt her feelings.

Wednesday I was learning how to copy with three lines when the team-leader approached and said, 'Oi.' She led me to the fifth floor for 'the assessment'. What assessment? She said it was nothing to worry about and we took the elevator. Inside 550 a large table was ringed by temps. I took the vacant chair beside Borris.

'I'm thinking of joining the police force,' he said.

'Borris,' I said freely, 'I don't think you belong in the police force. The drunks'd be locking *you* up!'

I thought he was going to punch me in the face. I turned away gritting my teeth, expected it to come.

The team-leader was counting answer books. She was saying, 'Now this is easy-peasy. Just simple alpha-numerical, then one to see what your personality's like.'

'So how do you think they can determine your personality though a written test?' a fair-haired girl from a different zone whispered to Borris.

'Who cares?'

'I hope this won't be stressful. I'm stressed already.'

'Yeah,' said Borris.

'You look calm.'

'I just had a w — '

'And can I stress,' the team-leader said, 'the importance of accuracy. Avoid wild stabs in the dark. If you don't know the answer, leave the question blank.'

The first part of the test was easy: percentages. True, the more I did, the more difficult they became, but I burrowed on confidently with my calculator. After ten minutes we were told to stop writing. The next paper was identification and comparison, and that too was fine. The third was comprehension: twenty pages of boxed paragraphs, then four questions where you had to answer Yes, No, or Can't Be Sure. I was on question twenty when two people across the now unsupervised room started whispering. I read the paragraph again. It was about motorcycle accidents. 'Be quiet,' said Borris, flapping his shades. Now they were talking; in conversation. I deduced that they had completed the test and I read question twenty once more, and I would have read it a fourth time had not the man in black exploded and skied the chatterboxes off their chairs (their heads were together when it happened). Something of a scuffle ensued... and three temps left the building: two to the medical centre, one to the police station.

By the end of the second week I was down to two lines, and my shredding was 'top stuff'. Dutifully did I go to my position each day; loading the paper tray, replacing the toner, taking a steady stance before the square green button, index finger poised. I worked quickly and efficiently, without need for assistance. After a month I was producing (and shredding) essentially-faint one-line copies. Then, coming in for overtime one Saturday I managed to copy without a line at all! Yes, yes I clearly remember that moment. My copies were stark, white and — dare I say — beautiful creations. That day I copied more than a thousand brand new résumés. It was a wrench to have to shred them. When no one was looking I concealed one in a paper folder and sneaked it home with me, thinking of framing it, but in the end I got it laminated at a printers near Sulkside. My life was white ducks on the water.

You can imagine my surprise, then, when I was told, the following Monday, that I was no longer required at Koel. My team-leader gave me a bin liner to clear the desk I never had. She was very kind. She wanted to offer me alternative employment. 'My husband's car needs washing. If you like I could arrange...'

'Thank you,' I said, but then I remembered that my car was in need of a service and had to decline. There was something good to come from my sudden unemployment, after all: tomorrow I'd have the time to seek that necessary mechanic.

But as things went, the next day I was back at work — not at Koel, you understand, but for the city council. Fernseeds were good enough to find me a new job straightway. I painted yellow lines in a car park, marking boxes, helping to change the blank tarmac into an organised grid. My boss recognised my worth. 'Don't worry if you do it wrong. You won't be here long enough to face the consequences,' he said. The next day I laid carpet tiles in empty offices. But it was only a two-day placement and Friday morning I was back at Fernseeds.

Jackie came to sit by me. She was apologetic. 'I'm afraid I've got nothing for you today.'

'That's all right,' I said. Her thighs were nicely tanned.

When I took my car to the garage the mechanic seemed surprised when I inquired if he'd object to my watching him at work: he expanded an eye and slid beneath the engine on a wheeled tray. After a while I began to think, and then, over the clank of spanners, decided to volunteer my thoughts. 'You know, your job is just like a doctor's,' I said. The mechanic did not respond, so I decided to elucidate. 'When an automobile is faulty the mechanic examines it. And, by a process of elimination, he comes to identify the fault. Then, like the doctor, he uses reason and prescribes a cure or remedy...

'You see,' I said to the man beneath my car, 'an engine is much like a body. Think of it. The battery is like the brain. The heart is like the fuel pump. The veins are the fuel pipes. The air filter is the lung. Similarly, the oil filter is the liver. The high-tension leads are the neurons... from the spark plugs, which are the nervous system, and the exhaust is of course, the anus,' at which point the little tray slid into the light and a voice said, 'Why don't you fuck off?' I left the forecourt and went into the office to ask the secretary to call me when the car was ready. When that was done I tripped away, losing myself in the city hubbub. The mechanic's reaction had upset me, and I didn't know why.

When I got back I found that my clothes had been stolen. Someone had snatched them off the line. I peered through the window of my flat. 'Phew!' At least they hadn't forced their way inside.

I lit a cigar and had a think.

Some time passed — five minutes, an hour, I cannot recall — and then I was standing by the telephone with Katy's numbers in my hand and head. But I couldn't call her, and the receiver came down after three digits. I took the circular route down to the bay, to count the waves, and there, standing Y-shaped on one of the rocks a figure with field-glasses scanned upwards, outwards, maybe for wings or ships. Counting the waves I plucked another loose tooth from my gum and flicked it over the rail. In no time a gull was swooping for it.

I was lying in bed listening to the cricket, in the cold, thinking about Jackie's thigh, the way I saw it and had to turn my eyes away when she rocked back in her chair, now rolling my ear off the pillow so I could hear the cricket better. And her white top with the buttons undone and her bra showing, the skimpy one with the frills.

Then, half-closing my eyes and twitching my ears I realised I could no longer hear the cricket. I got out of bed and padded over the room to the tank. For some reason it had stopped chirring. Why? I wondered whether I should find it a new leaf. I slumped at the tank, dropped to my haunches to look at the insect through the glass. Suddenly I was overcome by a deeper philosophical supposition to the problem. My cricket was lonely: it had no-one to sing to, so there was no reason to carry on.

My door-snake was curled like a Cumberland sausage. I let it stay curled and went downstairs for breakfast: a sandwich, sliced banana with hundreds and thousands sprinkled on top. While my teeth tore at the bread I thought of the cricket and Jackie. Soon I was at the revolving doors of the government building, showing the security guard my pass, taking the stairs to Silenus on the fourth floor because I spent so much of the day in the lift I was starting to lose balance.

I removed my coat and folded it on top of my kit bag, which I'd snuk into the shadow of the build room's outer doors. It was the drill. Then, flapping my tie and backtracking one or two paces, I bashed through the doors and, without looking up, focused for a not so faraway keyboard and began to detach a mouse. Only when I was coiling its tail did I scan the room, and there was Klive, my boss...

Who was glancing at the inside of his wrist. But he couldn't be sure that I'd just made it in: after all, I looked busy. There was sufficient doubt in his mind to release a pang of apathy, and so he said nothing to me.

He was clicking a mouse, trying to be cool, though there was nobody in the room to impress. Now I was resting against a cabinet overstuffed with unwanted CD-Roms. I yawned. My boss snatched papers from a printer. He pointed to his nose (which he did whenever he was confused or about to make a statement). 'I've got lots of calls for you this morning...'

But at least I had new shoes, and they were sweet shoes. I discovered this as I took dinosaur kit down to the store. The trolleys were designed to be pulled rather than pushed and often, especially when I was forced to reduce speed as I approached fire doors that had to be pulled, the trolley, heavy with old kit, caught up with me and the top of the wheel nipped my heel, bit into the skin. I got depressed each time it happened. But now when the trolley bit me I didn't feel it, because my new shoes had reinforced ankle protectors. The next time I came to fire doors I allowed myself to be caught, just to make sure, but it was true: it didn't hurt — the trolley couldn't reach me any more.

I tried to get the store keys from the Dutchman. The Dutchman was in charge of stock and had a desk on the first floor.

'Why do you want the keys?'

He always asked.

'Are you putting things in or are you taking things away?'

He always suspected I was stealing.

With my trolley of dinosaur kit I went down to the basement, to the store.

Sometimes I caught people going my way and then they'd help me by holding a few doors — until it became too much, whereupon they would meticulously, and deliberately, slow down, or accelerate so they wouldn't have to do it anymore. The girls I passed looked through me when I looked at them. I was a trolley boy —

Fading like the dusk

Inevitably
Water me
Clear and useless — Oh no!
The trolley moves itself to TB1

Unlocking the store's outer door, I squeezed through the gap between the kit and the wall so I could draw the trolley in. I was in a dark, narrow corridor twenty feet long. Piled against one wall were old computer books, disks and junk, and some of them had toppled over so I had to flick them with my toe as I went to open the inner door. The key was bent so it wasn't easy. The Dutchman bent it to save people making copies and having stuff away. I opened the door and returned to the trolley, positioning it in such a way so that it would be a hazard to anyone coming to check on me, so that if the boss came wandering the outer door would clunk on the trolley and forewarn me of the pending disturbance.

The store was as big as my bedroom — in fact, I imagined I was in the exact dimensions. It was stuffed with dinosaur kit, on shelves, on tables, on the floor. Monitors, motherboards, printers, keyboards, mice, books, disks... I was meant to list the serial numbers of the kit and give them to the Dutchman (it was a security measure), but I went for a nap on the bubble wrap I had neatly stashed beside the few laptops I'd often thought of lifting. I unrolled the bubble wrap and lay down, resting my head on one of the softer, older boxes. I made myself comfortable. Nobody could see me down here. What's more, no one would think of me for hours. You could encounter all sorts of problems tackling the simplest of tasks. And with the trolley alarm I had seven seconds to sit up and pretend to scrutinise a serial number. Lying there then I wondered if there were sometimes advantages to being invisible.

One night I spent two hours making calculations in a notebook and realised that my car had to go and the cost of my accommodation needed to be reduced. But two negatives always make a positive. I'd scarcely miss my neighbour and the car was beginning to disappoint me anyway. Aside from the engine the mechanic had not fixed, the electric window on the driver's side was stuck, the door wouldn't close properly, I had a slow puncture that demanded air every third day, and the rubber had flapped off a wiper. With the money I got for it I paid three month's rent, in advance, for a room in a shared house in the city centre.

Fernseeds called. For two weeks I had a job in an office a short walk from the house. It was up two flights and dealt with mortgages. The manager, she was slightly odd. She willed her eyes when she spoke to me and whistled when I answered. The first day she asked me to empty the snacks machine and count the coins. She was friendly: she let me sit on the other side of her desk while she worked, while I counted and towered the coins in piles of ten. 'It's nice to have a normal temp,' she said. 'Most of the temps we get are either homeless, stinking to high heaven, on drugs or alcohol or ex-convicts.' Most of the time I toiled in the post room, zipping mail in wire baskets, weighing padded bags and ensuring the franking tape was running straight. It was hard work and at the end of the day I was quite tired. But, aside from the clear financial and career-climbing benefits, there were other perks to be had from the job. I confess, I was naughty and sneaked some of my up-to-date résumés through the franking machine, winging them off to prospective employers near and far. I told myself I was combining initiative with self-factory insight, and only felt guilty the first time I did it. As things transpired I wasn't successful with these furtive enquiries and I suppose it must have been my comeuppance for taking advantage of the company I was meant to be working for. Anyway, once that job was through it was time to retreat to Fernseeds. But the children were back in school and there was much competition for placements. Jackie warned me that I might have to wait a while till things settled down. I skushed through leaves into low-angled suns, the shortened days warmed by amber skies.

'Oi, why the long face?' the landlord inquired one morning. He had nudged me from my daydream. I was squatting on the floor by the telephone that never rang for me.

'I need a job.'

He crouched and cupped a hand round his ear. 'Eh?'

'I'm behind on the payments. No, not to you. On the tank. My cricket tank. They're already threatening to take it off me.'

'What about,' he said, 'what about social security?'

'Foreigners can't apply.'

'Hmmm.' He was picking at the wall. Suddenly he balanced his thought with a gesture that united head, mouth and shoulders. 'Can you paint?'

I started in the utility room. 'I want this house to be bright and colourful even in the middle of winter,' he said passing me two cans: matt orange for the walls, gloss turquoise for the window frames and skirting board. I didn't have a ladder, but I had a back-copy of *Easy-Ads* and made a call (it was my second purchase that week, for I'd been fortunate to find a man's suit for *one pound* on Tuesday — a giveaway). For the rest of the week I stooped over the ladder, dusting, scrubbing, pin-pulling, gum-scraping, painting. I was content. I was serene. Carefully I manoeuvred my brush around pipes, the backs of radiators, swiping the cobwebs with my free hand... then, tripping on dust sheets, I suddenly realised the room was finished. Even the people with whom I shared the house were moved to comment. 'All in a day's work, eh?' the vegetarian said. Trailing behind him, twisting her way round the pots, the girlfriend grunted, 'Someone's been sick.'

'It's much better,' the landlord said. 'Would you like to start on the lounge?'

This time the magnolia walls went white; the window frames rotten-bruise to blue. One time I was suddenly moved to hover my bristles above an earwig. An earwig had lost its way and was washing itself, presumably confused, on the curtain rail. I reasoned it would leave blue footprints down the wall, so I painted over it. Later I was standing in the kitchen admiring the miniature galaxies that had splash-formed on my black shoes, when a fly zummed through the open window. Fortunately I caught it before it had time to reach the lounge. It tickled my palm for a while, then its back clicked as it hit the table top.

The vegetarian took the expiring fly in his own hand. He placed it out the back door.

I said, 'What did you do that for? Now it can come back inside and get stuck to the walls.'

He was wiping the place down. I repeated myself. Finally he faced me.

'*How will you know it's the same fly?*'

That Sunday, opening the door of the washing machine, I discovered that all of my whites had turned grey. A stray black sock had tainted the wash. Immediately I went to my room... and there I stayed for two hours, sitting on the end of my bed munching koekies (I did rush back to the kitchen for the syrup, but someone had been in my drawer and the can was gone). The vegetarian had deliberately put the sock in the machine when I wasn't looking. You see, there is an acclaimed movie about a scientist whose experiment with teleportation goes awry, as at the crucial moment the telepod is contaminated by an insect. The teleported scientist eventually becomes more insect than man. The movie? *The Fly*.

On a whim I called Katy. She didn't want to come out as she was busy digging, but she was going to a party on Friday, if I was interested. I said I might be.

'It depends on my schedule,' I said.

'It's fancy dress,' she said.

I went back to Fernseeds. Jackie said she'd lost my number. She was wearing a different blouse. She seemed tired, and this time she kept to her desk. I was squinting at her blistered face when she slightly raised an eyebrow to a beeping screen and said, 'But wait a minute — a six-month placement's just come up.'

I rocked, 'What luck!'

Next day it was raining and I considered the dilemma of which shoes to wear. You see, the pair with soles had holes and let the rain in; the shinier ones had no grip at all and it was dangerous to wear them when it was wet. At last I chose the latter pair and skidded and slipped on every soaking leaf, taking an hour over a twenty minute walk. My boss at Corrupt & Vague was not fazed by my lateness. Indeed, it was as if he had expected it.

The job entailed entering numerical data into a terminal. There was no training, but each case was similar and my questions lessened with passing quarter hours. I sat at a desk all day punching numbers, playing with sheets of paper, mouse tails, *Yes-No* boxes, *Tab* arrows, *Num Lock* and *Ins* buttons. I was eager to work well and didn't talk to anyone. The other temp starting that day was a rich girl who kept telling people she didn't want to stay. She didn't fulfill the duties asked of her, rather she did the things she wanted. Perhaps she escaped reprisal because of her looks. Whatever. I was far from concerned. My progress would compare favourably against hers.

By noon I calculated that I'd already 'spent' more than £100,000 of other people's money. I slipped up Main St, heading a little further for the cheaper bakery, and afterwards sat on a wall juggling chunks of scalding meat-substitute round the inside of my skinless mouth. Oh the irony of it all. Here I was in soleless shoes, charity trousers, a belt I'd whisked from my foul-mouthed ex-neighbour (and snipped the spiked end with her mother's scissors so it wouldn't look so girlish), charity shirt, found tie, my gold watch insulating tape-strapped, my secret narcotism and my paranoia, and I had suddenly aspired to the status of financial whizz-kid! That afternoon I worked like a bee and 'spent' a further £150,000, which made it a quarter-of-a-million in one day. Leaving the office at dusk, however, I was at a loss to understand my melancholia. Shouldn't I have been happier? I was still brooding when, quite by chance, I bumped into Borris in a mini-market. For a moment he said nothing. But then, on the fifth time of asking, he wearily let slip he was on the late shift at the hospital.

'How did you get into that then?' I asked. I wanted someone to talk to; I needed to stretch the encounter for as long as I could. I followed him across the shop. 'What happened after Koel?'

Borris' mouth hinted at a smile. He fingered his shades. In a rush, as if he'd decided to speak first and think later, he said, 'I had an ongoing contract at the AA. After two weeks they asked me to train the typists to do my job so they could throw me out without a bean when I eventually succeeded.'

'What happened?'

'Then I almost went into retail. Fernseeds sent me to Cuckoos.'

'The superstore?'

'For two hours I sat in a basement being told how much better Cuckoos was than Magpie. Then they started showing these security videos. They had one on shoplifting.' He laughed. 'I was in it.'

'So what do you do now?'

Borris tutted and rapped a tube of mints on the counter. 'I pick up other people's sneezes.'

'Oh.' I looked at his mints. 'My teeth are falling out.'

'I don't give a shit.'

'I'm going to a party on Friday. Want to come?'

'Fuck off.'

'You needn't be so uncouth,' I said. 'You only had to say — ' But when I looked up he was gone.

In the morning the telephone rang. It was Jackie. Corrupt & Vague didn't want me back. They didn't give a reason.

'Oh well,' I said. 'Mustn't grumble.'

I tried to prepare my breakfast stooped over yesterday's paper. Well I never, there was going to be a solar eclipse over Salacacabia on Friday. But the banana was overripe and inadequate and I became a little flustered. What could I do? I looked in the fridge but I couldn't decide. Sausages or orange juice? I didn't know. The refrigerator clicked; I got confused. There was the sound of a cat miaowing and this time it wasn't the old door opening. On Wednesday I made peace with the vegetarian. I told him I was not a vindictive person: I'd been picking up all the spiders by hand and *putting* them out the back. On Thursday I developed a rash on my face. The dry air from the sun-lamp was making my skin peel. I found a metal plate behind the sink and ate pasta and mushrooms off it, believing it would help my complexion (the meal not the plate, though the latter was grand: it was that big you didn't have to be so accurate with your fork). I slept a lot too. On Friday I slept through the eclipse.

Friday was the night of the party, of course, and it began at the back of a reputable public house. The idea was to feast and play skittles, then head for a nightclub. I had decided that Katy was teasing me over the fancy dress and arrived at the inn in my suit. My mistake. A dozen girls in varying degrees of fantastical costume were camped sucking straws round three tables. Incompletely with them, standing, crooning on the periphery, were two boys, and I was at least pleased to find that it wasn't just me who had come ill-attired. I sipped a beaker (making a noise when I swallowed) and did my best to beam in. One girl was dressed as a French window, another as a skeleton. There was also a monkey, a witch, a werewolf, three Roman togas, a sheik, a sheep and Idi Amin. Katy was dressed as a honey bee. I made an attempt at complimenting her on the costume, but either she didn't hear or she elected to ignore me. I turned away, faced the skittle alley. A single wooden lane, three wooden balls, and nine time-chunked wooden pins...

But never mind the skittling, everyone was waiting for the buffet to be served. Then, when we all had our paper plates and chicken legs dripping from our lips, the girls took it in turns to remember how they'd bled once upon a time in showers and classrooms. Afterwards they talked epidurals and childbirth; the sheep, the one who referred endlessly to a life in New Zealand, saying, 'I said to him, I said, "You wanna know what it's like to give birth?" I said to him, "Just imagine having to squeeze a melon through your Jap's eye."' I looked across at Katy and saw that her yellow-and-black stripy chest was heaving. Her face was stuffed with chips. They were twirling from her mouth at all angles, like whiskers. I felt a little queasy and excused myself to take fresh air outside. And it was while I was righting myself, sucking the tang of the mulched leaves and monoxide, that Katy appeared and asked if I was all right.

'I'd like to go home,' I said.

'You only had to ask,' she said. 'I'll get my coat. Wait there.'

I didn't think I would, but I did, and we taxied to her place. I paid the driver and went into the house. Katy was upstairs. I had to try several rooms before I found her, and she feigned to look at an imaginary watch when I eventually located her bed. On the bed she smothered me. She smelled of potatoes. She pulled up her top and the cups of her bra were like small urinals. For a moment I felt a bit dippy: I liked the way her antennae bounced off my face and shoulders.

She said, 'Why are you shivering?'

'It's a natural reaction,' I gasped. 'I always run away from things that are good for me.'

'Why do you think I'm going to hurt you? Why do you keep flinching? Keep thinking I'm going to poke you in the eye?'

One time she froze and gravely whispered snackfoodingly in my ear: 'Don't get fond of me, will you?' Her antennae began to bounce again. 'I won't hurt you. Not physically anyway.' I went into a cataplectic fit and did not recover till dawn. I was on the carpet, then, and Katy was snoring up above. I sneaked out the back door and frittered time in McBitterness until Fernseeds opened.

Jackie said, 'D'you want to earn money and keep fit? This placement is being re-advertised due to excessive time-wasters.'

'I don't want to deliver telephone directories. I want a job indoors.'

She shrugged and pressed Return. Her blisters had cleared. 'Very well. How about... Large financial... Three duh-duh-duh-duh-duh an hour... D'you like filing?'

'Show me where to 'ang me fuckin coat!'

The office was similar to that at Koel: desks, plants, terminals, antiseptic drudgery in all directions. In my new suit I sat on the floor sorting files. I went into a dream. I was the little boy ('Ah, isn't he cute...') with the building bricks box in the bank. I wanted to dribble on the files. I wanted to put them in my mouth. I began to lose focus, the letters self-jumbling in a temporary dyslexia. I wanted a rusk... to go out on my bike... play with my friends...

Next morning... Well, next morning I didn't want to get up. I had to, because the telephone was ringing, but that didn't mean I had to leave the house. I shivered in the blankets, listening to Jackie. She said the office had been on to her. Why wasn't I there? 'It's too cold,' I told her. Later, when the sun came out, I went back to Fernseeds.

And that was when I went to work for Silenus in the government offices.

The big cheese was Osca, my boss was Klive, and then there was the Dutchman...

One lunchtime Klive asked if I'd dealt with all my calls, and I replied that I was still taking old kit away. The Dutchman nodded, almost regretfully. Klive told me to tuck my shirt in. Osca laughed. Obediently I lowered the knife and fork and wiped my hands on a serviette. I had bought extra chips because Klive always pinched a few after he'd finished his meal, his knife in the wrong hand, his knuckles scraping the table when he tore the meat with his fork. 'And put your tie straight. Haven't you got any better ties? Where'd you get that thing, a charity shop?' Klive said ruffling my rag.

Osca and the Dutchman laughed, I shrugged, Klive went into his wallet.

'See what I've got now? Look at these.' He was fanning cards in his hand. 'Barclaycard, credit limit £1000. Visa, £1000. Amex, £1000. Awesome. What've you got?' With a sigh I showed him my Library card, Primaries Reward Card... 'Pathetic,' said Klive.

But then I showed him my Fernseeds ID card. 'You haven't got one of these. This entitles me to snap car aerials and chuck McBitterness chicken boxes in the street.'

'Talking of which, what are you doing this weekend? Tell you what,' said Klive, taking another chip, 'a friend of mine is moving house on Saturday. Do you think you could help her with the boxes?'

I said no thank you, I had to sort my cricket out.

'Cricket?'

'Yes cricket.' No they weren't the same as grasshoppers. What's more, mine was a mole cricket, and that the only time I realised he might be lonely was when he stopped rubbing his wings together... or chirring. Mole cricket's were intelligent. Klive wanted to know how I'd come to this conclusion. 'I mean, aside from a tenuous sense of irony and a sensitivity to depression, how are you able to ascertain...?' So I told him about the special forelegs. They were larger than normal cricket forelegs; flatter too. 'He digs an underground nest with a twin entrance. Then he sits at the junction and chirrs through both entrances, left and right. He's got stereo. And he uses it to attract the girls.'

Klive took another chip. 'You know the best thing about you being a temp? I can get rid of you just like that,' he said clicking his fingers, and he, Osca and the Dutchman got up from the table, laughing.

That day I made a detour to the pet shop, but for some reason it was closed. I put my nose to the glass and looked at the empty cages. Perhaps I didn't fit. Afterall, I didn't have a deep blue shirt and a yellow tie. I didn't super-casually swerve the lunchtime shoppers, hold the look and feeling of worth chewing a tuna-salad baguette.

I sat head-bowed at the end of my bed in a chirrless, koeki-free room. I heard the vegetarian's girlfriend on the telephone say, 'No he isn't in,' and run back into the kitchen. It seemed that my every breath was corrupt. I switched on the radio and heard, '*admit admit you're shit you're shit you're shit...*' My eyes were all wet, and it had nothing to do with the rain.

It took Klive three days to notice that I'd stopped wearing a tie, and then when he complained I told him it was a conscious act, that its absence was in respect for a relative I never knew I had... until now.

Klive pointed to his nose and said, 'What *are* you on about?'

'He was hanged in 1944. Now I sweat when I wear a tie.'

'What was he hanged for?'

'Failing to wear a tie.'

It was fictitious of course, and I didn't think Klive would believe me for a moment, but when I came to work tieless next day he said nothing about it. He was on the telephone at the time, talking to Osca. I knew that because the latter's voice was coming through the speaker. 'What's the name of that bloke who works for you?' he was saying. 'Oh, I don't give a toss what his name is, just send him down here to take some old kit away.' So I took the stairs to the first floor. Again the Dutchman asked me why I wanted the store keys: 'Are you putting things in or taking things away?' I told him I needed to get software for the laptop I'd stolen last week. When he frowned I said, 'I removed the pages of a lever-arch file and smuggled it out.'

Later, Klive *asked* me to fetch a drink from the machine next door. It was odd, when he wanted something non-work related he tended to omit 'tosser' from the request. That time he seemed uncomfortable with his want until he'd added, 'And while you're at it, go and stand a minute in that shadow. You look like you could do with company.'

The following Monday I removed my shoes the moment I

reached the build room.

'Now what?' said Klive.

'It's winter.'

'So what?'

'Two years ago I broke both my feet. When the weather turns cold I suffer in the joints. This is only alleviated by the absence of footwear.'

'Look, see these labels? I want them stuck to every PC in this room. And when you've done that... er... er... pick up all the letters from those smashed keyboards on the floor.'

So I fell on my hands and knees to retrieve the scattered *A*s and *B*s, *Ctrl*s, *Alt*s, *Pause*s, *Tab*s, *Bk Sp*s, *Pg Dn*s, *Del*s, space bars and *Esc*s...

I sneaked into the house. There was no key in the vegetarian's door, so he was out. The girlfriend's mail hadn't been taken from the mat, so she was absent too. It was safe. Straightening, I went to my room and looked in the mirror. To my horror I saw my hair was turning grey. Was I seeing things? I needed someone to talk to, so I rang Katy. She was not at home. I called the hospital and eventually got through to her ward. She hummed while I told her my hair was falling out.

Then I said, 'I'm worried about my job, Kate. I think I need more training.'

She said, 'Have you had any feedback?'

'Not really.'

'Then you're probably doing better than you think you are.'

'You don't know how well I can tread water,' I said.

'Look,' she said, 'I have to go — they're wandering off...'

One night I dreamt of a future society where everyone was concerned with the elimination of white maggots. The maggots were put in a box then frozen in giant freezers, and I saw myself in face-mask and gloves, dressed head to toe in white plastic fulfilling this never-ending chore.

And now they were selling antlers for a pound in Main St. Silenus were having a Christmas function, an adventure weekend in the hills, and I started to wear my shoes and tie again.

Something else was distracting me. For once the

Dutchman wasn't quizzing me over the keys. You see, he was set to be disciplined. Aside from storage, he was also in charge of company stationery. Now he'd spent the money and forgotten to declare the bonus Primaries vouchers that accompanied each order, and when it had come to the attention of the ultimate superior he'd been able to account for just half of them. Were they taking him in or putting him out? 'Dutchy,' I said, 'if they ask me, I'll vouch for you.'

I didn't want to rock the boat: I was looking forward to going away. Indeed, I laughed when I heard Klive giving Fernseeds a telephone report on my progress with Silenus: 'Not really,' he said, and raised his voice and stared as he became aware of me, 'he needs twenty-four hour supervision and he slashes chairs.' I shrugged it off as a joke. Similarly, I hid my disappointment when my number came up in the Christmas raffle. 'No, I think the prize should go to a permanent member of staff,' Osca said taking the champagne from my hands, pushing me into the shades where I watched the Dutchman win the re-draw.

On Friday I was in the build room marking the week's time-sheet for Fernseeds, adding five minutes here and there, scratching my chin, being furtive, secretive. I went down to the first floor. Osca was talking to Klive about the adventure weekend. I waited till I saw him laughing and jumped in with my time-sheet. Osca said something; I had my chuckles ready and watched him lower his eyes to the sheet. Uttering trivia, praising him, I tried to distract him.

'Ah, but you may have to go some to outwit my orienteering skills. I'm an experienced trecker, and my familiarity with compass bearings is well renowned.'

Osca looked up, frowned at Klive.

'What do you mean,' said Klive, 'you're not coming.'

'Temps aren't invited,' said Osca. He flipped to the second page of my time-sheet with the nib of his pen, not touching the paper. 'Are we still short of printers? Someone on TB2's been waiting two weeks.'

Quietly I said, '... I know where there's a spare one.'

'Hmm.'

'I can get it if you like.'

He lost focus: in a rush scribbled his signature over the contaminated paper.

'Run along and fetch it then.'

And I'd skipped twenty yards down the corridor before I pulled up.

BARKING AT OWLS

Penny Anne Windsor

How was I to know that I would never sleep in my house again?

How was I to know that it was not to be an ordinary day?

It was raining, as it had yesterday and the day before. It was the same distance to the school, approximately a quarter of a mile.

I carried a gold bag left over from Christmas. It was a Lucky Dip. The children put their hands in and drew out a mountain, a burnt-out car, a pond, a tree. I could feel them rummaging in the corners of the golden bag.

Me, miss, they shouted. Me next, miss. I haven't got one.

One at once I called. There's plenty of time.

But there wasn't.

Before break we linked the pictures to the hill. The hill above the city. It had forests grown on soil poisoned with arsenic. Horses and jay birds. A ruined windmill and a TV mast.

I learnt some of their names – Jason, Lisa, Mandy, Daniel, Rhiannon.

At break the phone rang.

Mrs Trembath? Emma for you.

But I thought she was in school.

Her father phoned. She's ill.

Mamma?

Yes, lovely girl, it's me.

I don't want to go, Mamma. I don't want to go.

Where, lovely girl, where don't you want to go?

I don't want to go. Too long away from my Dad.

Emmi-Anne, we'll only be in Poland for ten days. You were three weeks away with your father in Ireland last August. We'll be in the Tatras Mountains. It's very beautiful there.

But Mamma, I don't want to go. I love you, Mamma. I want to live with my Dad but I want to see you and I love you, Mamma.

Where are you now, lovely? Where are you phoning from?

The phone clicked.

I phoned Colin.

She phoned me here, about half an hour ago. She said something about having a headache. She sounded strange. I'm driving down now.

The golden bag faded. We made an A to Z poem of the hill. A was for ... B was for .... C was for .... D was for .... The children shouted out ideas. ABCDEFG they shouted. And in my head they shouted, *I don't want to go. I want to live with my Dad. But I love you, Mamma. I love you, Mamma.*

And then click.

Where are you, lovely? *Click.*

Where are you? *Click.*

Where?

Mrs Trembath. Mrs Trembath. The Headmaster ran down the lane which led from the main school door past the garage-that-did-all-types-of-jobs. Rubbish skittered in the damp summer wind.

I stopped. The Headmaster took Gym Club. But he never ran.

I didn't want you to go home without knowing.

He puffed and blew gently.

To find the tape. I've had one but I haven't had time to listen to it. It's from Emma. And the letters. They're from her, too. Can I do anything? Do you want a cup of tea before you go?

I said, I'm fine, but thank you. I always do – say that.

The world tipped on its side. Swayed. Came nearer. Like wearing someone else's glasses.

Two empty cans of Special Brew glared, drab gold. Large dollops of dog shit in close-up. Weller Diamond, the old piss artist of a fisherman called over what passed as a green.

"Hi ya, Annie. Miserable day, darling, and more for tomorrow. Never mind, bach, the sun's round the corner so they say. Always just around the corner. See you then. Got to get on."

A number 32 bus drew up at the stop from the Trallwyn estate, hesitated in the drizzle and slid away into the city.

Rigid in Colin's arms, we said sensible things.

We must see what's at the house and decide from there.

I'm sure she's alright.

No jumping to conclusions.

No, absolutely no jumping to conclusions!

Chucklebug, the letters were signed, Emmi Bo-Bunnett, Beauty – all the silly names I call her. In her own writing. Oh yes, in her own writing.

I love you Mamma but .. .

But he had trained her. Trained her like a dog.

Stupid woman. Not fit to be a mother.

Held the child's hand. They stood together in the doorway, on the hill, on the bus, at the ferry port.

Stupid woman, they chanted.

Then she spat and her arms whipped the air like his, in one of his tantrums.

An injunction to try stopping you taking Em from the country.

My Solicitor on the phone. Can you come to the office straightaway? I've had a letter from Emma.

But he informed on me to the Legal Aid.

It's an emergency.

I'll get Legal Aid?

Almost certainly, yes.

It was Swansea. A car park at the end of Wind Street. There was no question where I was. Thirty years a Cornish exile though I was!

But where *was* Em?

Don't stop, don't stop, imagination. Not where, but what and how.

How was Em?

What was happening to Em?

Did she still know me?

Who *was* the child who could only repeat phrases like a recorded message machine?

488

Who? How? What? Where?
Em – *Em.*

She fastened in my old womb relentlessly. Got through potato picking on the Pembrokeshire coast and backpacking along the lakes of Finland. I liked her/him, him/her. Stubborn. Gasping for breath. Only just born alive, on a crisp February night, over 8 years ago now.

The car was parked. I was once again and quickly my sensible and professional self. I put up my umbrella.

So now it was a matter for the solicitors and barristers, the magistrates, the clerk of the court, the family court welfare officers, the police.

Is there any contact number?

The grandmother.

Phone her now, from the office.

I have. She has no address.

Phone her again.

Mabel?

Yes?

Where's Emma?

I've no more news. All I know is he said he was taking her somewhere on Gower.

But where? Steven wrote a letter to me which I only received an hour or two ago. He said you had a contact address.

Oh dear, well, if that's what he said, he'll probably phone later. I don't know any more. As soon as ...

I cut grandmother off.

And now?

There'll be a court hearing.

When, how soon?

Thursday.

This Thursday?

Yes. It's being treated as an emergency. I told you that.

My mind swivels, blinks, shrinks, retches.

Sorry, yes of course you did, says my sensible self.

Was the weather fine after that? Did the rain go on? Was it

warm? What was the news? Who did we meet? What did we say to each other? Did we sleep?

The trouble is, I can't remember. I can't describe these things for you. Set the scene. Build up the tension. Writer though I am, I am not willing to fill in the gaps with plausible events and thoughts. I prefer, though, to leave you with the gaps, the holes, the tears in the fabric, the cavities. And the high-pitched buzzing like a bee in a jar. You see, although I need to tell you about these events, it has to be in my own way... in my own time. It has to be true.

Em was not even Em. I didn't recall her, her jokes and puns, her repartee sharp as meadow grass.

I'm a seven pee aire, a seven pee aire. Dancing through the streets of Ammanford. Not a million aire, a seven pee aire. Do you get it, Mamma?

Mr Jones has a heavy burden on his shoulders because Mr Williams – you know he's the deputy head, don't you? – he's shut himself in the classroom with Year 4, doing chemistry. I think he's blowing them up. The lines are getting shorter in the playground. Do you get it, Mamma ... blowing them .... Mamma ... Mamma.

Lost tunes now. The third or fourth echo indistinct, drowned by the sound of the trapped creature in the jar.

Do you want to leave the room, Annie?

I jerked into the present. Word processors and fax machines. Barristers and secretaries.

Piles of paper. The rustling. The clicking.

The tape. Do you want to hear it?

Em's voice?

Yes.

Who else speaks?

Steven and his partner, Pauline. They interview her.

What's it like? You played it Colin. What's it like?

Like a police tape.

I picked up the Western Mail in the waiting area. It had the same format as usual. The same number of clouds over Swansea.

The temperatures in London, Spain, Africa. And Poland.

I'll have to jump a bit now. I can't remember. Except I remember a phone call from my older daughter, Rachel, from Cheltenham. She had a copy of the tape. She'd listened to it – and binned it.

He's evil, Mam. He'll stop at nothing.

And on Wednesday evening I do remember that it rained. Fiercely. Almost like a monsoon. The Black Mountain above Colin's house, Mynydd Du, was walled in mist.

There was a phone call from Steven.

You can fetch Emma by 6 o'clock.

We can't get into Swansea by then. You know that.

Half past six then. Here.

No, my house.

I can't get her there.

It's a five minute walk.

You want a young child to go out in this rain?

Pauline has a car.

She's drunk half a glass of cider. You never drink and drive.

The phone clicked.

I think I cried. I may not have done.

Em will think I don't care. He'll tell her I don't.

It's a trap.

I know.

We said a lot of clichéd lines like that at the time. And there were more to come.

She'll do what her father says. She has no choice. We'll stand at that back door and Steven will sit between her and the door and she'll chant, *I don't want to go.*

*Had I let it happen? Where was **my** blame, **my** responsibility?*
Had I condoned the kidnap of my own child? Colluded?
Or was it just one more game he was playing? This time with Em.

I remember some of his games.
Relax, it's my birthday. Have another drink.
And tomorrow?

*Tomorrow we'll make love all day. We don't **have** to do anything.*

And when tomorrow came –

My mother's coming at ten.

But you said ...

I forgot to mention it.

And the bath. The bathroom door flung open.

You're beautiful, aren't you – it's a pity you're so flawed. If people only knew. All those people who like and admire you. If they just knew the truth.

And the attack in the bedroom. Pushed back on the bed, his hand clawing between my legs deep in the red skirt.

All you want is sex. Tell the truth. That's all you want.

Beautiful but flawed.

Relax.

Unfit to be a mother.

You fell down the stairs. You punched your head on my knee.

Selfish bitch.

Beautiful wife.

Witch woman.

Bitch woman.

Lady.

Whore.

Sweetheart.

Traitor.

And after I evicted him – the devil's pact. He got out. In return for shared care of Em.

But always the voice on the phone, the voice on the answering machine, the letters through the door.

The sound of bracken and gorse breaking on the path above the house. My dog barking at the black backyard window. The tap of his stick along the terrace in the early hours. The clip of the letter box like the click of the phone.

I had still not touched her. I was still not sure where she was. Or how she was.

The morning of the hearing. Colin takes a shower. A voice

on the answering machine.

Mamma, why didn't you come to get me? Daddy said you would.

Games.

Shutting his mother in the coal shed and leaving her all day long. A game.

Hiding with Em in the forest. Whispering. A game.

Playing with the police and doctors and educational welfare officers. Of course she's not mad but her family, so she tells me, have a record of mental instability.

I'm not saying she doesn't care for the child but, well, the menopause may help to explain her erratic behaviour.

She was always a worrier and having a baby late in life has made things worse. I do my best but even her older daughter has noticed her strange behaviour.

And so on and so forth. Repeated. Rephrased in letters to my friends. Notes in block capitals – on the toilet seat, by the taps, above the bath, on my bookcase. The contents of the notes shouted as I ran down the street.

Away from him, Em. Not away from you, lovely. Never away from you.

And so it was. The Emergency Court Hearing on the day after the day after the snatch, in the summer of 1997.

The same car park at the end of Wind Street. The everyday battle for a space, for change for the ticket machine.

The Barrister was short and impeccably dressed. Scrubbed. I felt, he felt, another case.

Chit-chat outside the court.

Steven was representing himself. I didn't look at him. I smelt him.

Do you write and perform poetry?

Yes.

Would you call your poetry sexually explicit?

Some of it could be called that.

Has Emma ever been involved in your poetry performances?

Yes, at times.

You mean you perform sexually explicit poetry in front of Emma?

No, I don't mean that. I do my best to perform poetry appropriate to my audience.

A break. Like the adverts. I sat by Colin on a bench and smoked.

The Barrister said, He wants to produce a poem in evidence.

Which one?

I don't know yet. I'm inclined to let him.

The poem was passed from Steven to the Barrister to myself to the Clerk of the Court to the three magistrates.

Basic de Luxe. A Trilogy for Our Time.

I'm sorry, Steven said on submitting it, because I know how you suffered when we parted.

Basic de Luxe – the story of my hunt for a vibrator, my adventures with the frilly underwear catalogue, my feeling it was a poor substitute. My tragical-comical search for the Holy Grail of Love. Now in the court records.

The Barrister mellowed towards me in inverse proportion to his growing dislike of Steven.

And could you explain exactly why you took Emma for anti-rabies injections?

We travel a great deal. I thought it was a wise precaution.

You understood the risks to a child?

I took the doctor's advice.

But not the mother's ?

I discussed it with her.

She says not. Tell me, Mr Jones, had you any reason to think that Emma was in danger of being bitten?

She was bitten once on a visit to Warwickshire. By a hamster.

I see. And you thought she might be bitten by a hamster in Madrid or Athens?

Possibly.

Did you have these injections, Mr Jones, since you say you travel with Emma?

No.

Pauline came on the stand. Red face, permed hair, rolling eyes, flabby.

So Emma leaves school at what time?

About half past three.

And she's home by –?

About quarter to four.

And when exactly was this tape made?

That evening.

The chief magistrate sat up straight and stared at Pauline over his glasses.

And when did you say you left for this trip?

About half past four. I'm not sure. I was making notes for my work in another room.

So between a quarter to four and half past four you and Emma's father and Emma herself made this tape?

Well, yes, perhaps it was five o'clock when we left, now that I think of it.

Did Emma have anything to eat?

I was in another room as I said. I think her father gave her some tea. Yes, he gave her some pasta. I remember now.

So... The Chief Magistrate crammed his glasses firmly on his nose....When did she write these letters? There are three, to her mother, to her headmaster and to her mother's solicitor?

We stopped in a lay by.

Emma wrote letters in a lay by?

Yes.

Where was this?

On the Gower somewhere. I don't know exactly where. I don't know Wales very well.

And where were the tapes copied? Again there were three – to her mother, to Rachel, who I understand is Emma's sister, and to her headmaster.

I don't know.

The Chief Magistrate was, by now, unstoppable.

And where did you stay that night on Gower?

I don't know. As I said, I don't know the area well. I think it was a place called Rhossili.

Did you stay in a Bed and Breakfast or did you camp?

Bed and Breakfast.

Mm – Mr Jones said you camped. Never mind. Let's go on. The next day, where did you go?

We drove back to a place near Swansea, near Olchfa School. I had some work to do.

And then?

We drove – well – I don't know – maybe somewhere else on Gower. We passed some caves called Dan yr Ogof. I remember seeing the sign. I think it took about an hour. A place called Brecon.

The Chief Magistrate frowned. I take it you mean Brecon in Breconshire?

I suppose so.

Pauline rolled her eyes back into her head.

They let me leave the court while they listened to the tape. I sat in the narrow passageway and looked at my feet.

Finally there was the judgement. It was already eight o'clock. Six hours of it. I had an Interim Residency Order. Steven had limited contact and a Prohibited Steps Order forbidding him taking Em out of Swansea without my permission. Em was to be delivered to my home by 10 o'clock that evening.

But it wasn't to be as straightforward as that.

Steven rang almost as soon as we entered the house.

When are you coming to collect Emma?

You're to deliver her here.

The court said you were to have her with you by 10 o'clock, not that I should deliver her.

And so it went on.

We've got to try, Colin. Perhaps if she just sees me.

Then you've got to be prepared to walk away. It will be the hardest thing you ever do in your life.

I phoned my Solicitor.

You're right. Steven was to deliver her to you. Try collecting her before you go any further. Phone me back.

In the front of the house, a high privet hedge. A permanently locked side door. At the back, a scrappy garden. Dog shit on pocked grass. Tall fast-growing conifers.

Steven sat in the middle of the kitchen by the table preventing any entrance or exit.

Emma, your mother's here. The court says you've got to go with her.

Em appeared at the bottom of the stairs. No coat, only slippers on. She stood in the doorway. Flushed. Large feverish eyes.

Steven tapped the kitchen table. Get your shoes on Emma. You know what the court said. You've got to go.

I don't want to go. I don't want to go.

Her face became more flushed. Her eyes? Was she ill? Or drugged? Or hypnotised?

On Monday when I had taken her into school she had been a normal child. She had been Emma. On Thursday night of the same week she screamed. Chanted. Cried.

Em, I've brought Love Bear. I held out the large white bear with the red bow.

I don't want to go.

Colin, she can't see me. Can she see you?

Walk away Annie, walk away.

We left.

This part is one of the most difficult. I have made up my mind to tell you how it was. I should say that I became hysterical, cried my eyes out.

But I didn't.

We sat. In the back room of the terraced house below the steep garden. Waiting. We didn't know for what.

The call was from the police.

Family Support Unit, Skewen. We've been called by Steven Jones. He wants us to go round. He says the child is refusing to go with you and he doesn't want to force her.

I explained as I had never explained anything in my life before. I remember my passion, and the desperation, and the term I used – *psychological abuse.*

You've got to get her out of there.

Yet another cliché.

The problem is I can't do anything without authorisation.

I phoned the Solicitor, the Solicitor phoned the Barrister, the Solicitor phoned the Policeman. The Policeman phoned me.

Please, she's not my Em. She's like someone else. You must get her out.

Somewhere I knew I was raving.

You don't think we could wait until tomorrow?

No.

Anything could happen overnight.

Strange dreams. Ideas in her feverish brain. The last part of a vile game played out.

The buzzing in the jar grew louder.

Nothing.

The time?

I don't know.

The terrace slipped into silence.

The phone call was very late.

We're going in, I said to Colin. The cliché of them all.

We drove again to the house on the estate, on the side of the hill. Five minutes' walk away.

I said, I don't want to go in there with no protection. He's violent.

I remember that moment. Even then it was funny. The policeman broad as a barn.

He won't get past *me*, love.

I hesitated. Felt guilty of smiling.

Down the drive. Round the corner of the house. Through the kitchen door. Past Steven in his chair. Past Mabel and Pauline. Across the hall.

I love you Mamma. **I don't want to go.**

I **don't want to go**, *Mamma but I love you.*

Don't want to go.

Love you.

Mamma.

Like a faulty switch. Back and forth. Back and forth.

No end to the speeches of the reasonable mother. No end to the vacillation of the haunted child.

I picked her into my arms. She shrieked.

We're going, lovely girl.

And we did.

Steven laughed in the chair by the kitchen table.

Mabel and Pauline attacked me. Mabel meant it.

Strong old bird! the Policeman said later.

My child did not flutter against my breast! She fought me. But I knew. I tripped on the kitchen step, fighting Em and fighting the two women. Round the corner of the house. The hot house with the medicines, the demented, black-souled man – the smell of him – rich and intoxicating and foul.

Em's hand clutched the back gate.

I called into the night, Can somebody help me? And Colin ran and took her in his arms.

It's alright, darling. You're safe now.

What's happening, she said, *what's happening.* She sank against his shirt.

Em and me joked on the short journey back to the house. Then she sat on Colin's lap and they told each other stories while I asked the Policeman what details he needed for his report.

We drove back in the early hours to the house by the river just below the Black Mountain. Em slept until noon.

This, of course, is not the end of the story. Terrible things were done to us both.

Em still shouts in her sleep. *Help. No more. No more please.*

But now we are coming into the spring of the following year. Frogspawn in the pond by the goat shed. One or two celandines. Daffodils in the shops for St David's Day. A mellow Black Mountain, clear in the last winter frost.

Em is Em again and continues to be.

We never again slept at our terraced house in Swansea. It's sold now.

We never got to the Tatra Mountains in Poland. But we will one day.

Steven went there. Searching us out.

The courts decreed Em lived with me but that he should still have some contact with her. Because he is her father. They say it's in Em's best interest. I don't believe a word of it and each time she goes with him I pray for her return.

And I hope every day that he will stop his continual harassment.

The Policeman from the Family Support Unit said, in his report, that Steven had programmed Em. And when she wanted to leave he denied her her soft toys, which she still calls her cot friends.

But now she lives with Colin and myself within the safety of the River Aman just below the house and the Black Mountain just above it.

Now she deals in images. Calls our battered car, the Getaway Car. Makes me a house from brightly coloured lego with a propeller, so we can fly away if necessary. Dreams she throws her cot friends out of a high window, to safety.

In the night we sometimes wake and listen to her dreams and to the river. And sometimes to our dog barking at owls, in the trees beyond the kitchen window.

Anyway, thank you for listening – I had to talk to someone.

I haven't written anything since it happened, except this.

And, except for the nightmares, Em has never mentioned these events, to this day.

ROSIE MY CAT

Anne Louise Williams

I have a lovely black cat named Rosie.
I had her from the Cat Protection League.
She is all black and a little bit of white
and has yellow eyes and she's my friend
forever and I love her.

THE WRITERS

Elizabeth Ashworth has worked as a journalist and taught in Sicily and Greece. She now lives in North Wales, where she teaches, writes and paints. Her poetry, journalism, paintings and stories have all won prizes. Her first novel, *So I Kissed Her Little Sister*, was published by Parthian in 1999.

Jacinta Bell has been writing for many years, and her stories have appeared in several magazines and anthologies as well as having been broadcast on BBC Radio 4. Her first novel, *Exiles* was published by Parthian Books in 1998. She has led writing workshops for young people and adults, and lives in mid-Wales with her husband and three children.

Leonora Brito was born in Cardiff and grew up there. Her stories have been included in anthologies published by Penguin, Sheba and Seren. She won the Rhys Davies Short Story competition in 1991. Her collection of short stories, *Dat's Love*, was published by Seren in 1995.

Phil Carradice is the editor of *The South Wales Golfer*. He has had eighteen books published, including *The Last Invasion*, about the Last Invasion of Britain in 1797. His work as a poet, historian and story-writer has been featured in many magazines and papers, and broadcast on both Radio 4 and Radio Wales.

Boyd Clack is actor, singer, writer, and mystic. He has written widely for television, including the sitcom *High Hopes*, and co-written *Satellite City* and *The Celluloid World of Desmond Rezillo* for the BBC. *The Vanishing Lake* has been broadcast on Radio 4, and he says it is semi-autobiographical.

Sarah Cornelius lives in Caerphilly.

Bryn Daniel was born in 1965 and lives in Cardiff.

Lewis Davies lives in Cardiff. He set up the Parthian Collective with two friends in 1993 to publish *Work, Sex and Rugby*. Other work includes *Freeways* which won the John Morgan Award and two plays for Made in Wales. He won the Rhys Davies Short Story Competition in 1998 with *Mr Roopratna's Chocolate*.

Stevie Davies was born in Swansea and now lives in Manchester. Her novels include *The Web of Belonging* and *Impassioned Clay* both published by the Women's Press. She won the Fawcett Book Prize in 1989 with her first novel *Boy Blue*. She is a Fellow of the Royal Society of Literature.

T. J. Davies was born in Banbury, Oxford. He was educated lengthily, before trying his hand at various pursuits - teaching, engineering, sales, accountancy - and he is currently staff nurse at UHW. His writing has appeared in *Planet, New Welsh Review*, and *Cambrensis*, and broadcast on BBC Radio. He is currently holding a hostage in an attempt to have his first novel published.

Nigel Duke was born in Merthyr Tydfil, where he lived comfortably until moving to London in 1975 to study. He has since worked as Security Officer for the Canadian Government, Tour Manager for a holiday company, Life Model, and Clerical Officer for the Inland Revenue; and is currently employed as a Teacher of English as a Foreign Language in Swansea. Nigel divides his time equally between religiously filling out lottery slips twice a week, and advertising for a rich widow who owns a pub next to a golf course.

George Brinley Evans started work in the Banwen colliery aged 14, and after joining the army he was stationed in Burma. After returning to mining, he was invalided out in 1961. His first story was published in *The Anglo-Welsh Review* in 1978, but he didn't take up writing again until ten years later, when he was encouraged by Alun Richards and Neal Mason at classes in Banwen. One of his sculptures is now on display at the Swansea City Museum, and his stories have appeared in *Cambrensis*.

Elizabeth Griffiths was born in Carmarthen in 1959, brought up in Pembrokeshire, and studied at St. David's University College, Lampeter. After training as a journalist on the *Barry and District News*, she returned to Pembrokeshire, where she now lives and works with her artist husband.

Niall Griffiths was born in Liverpool in 1966, and since then has lived in many parts of the British Isles, doing many different jobs, all of varying degrees of dullness. He is now living in Aberystwyth, edits *Chasing the Dragon*, (http://www.aber.ac.uk/~hht.93.htm/), and has a novel, *Grits*, out from Jonathan Cape in early 2000.

Richard Griffiths was born in 1969. He was educated at Ysgol Gyfun Llanhari and University of Wales, Cardiff. The pivotal moment in his life was hearing 'Strawberry Fields Forever', aged ten. He teaches physics in Aberdare and is currently working on a novel.

Anna Hinds is nineteen and living in Swansea with her crazy mother (see below). She has had two books published, and a third - a collaboration with the afore-mentioned relative - *The Generation Gap* (Kevin Mayhew), is due out autumn 1999. She has been writing fiction for two years. She is currently making her living from thin air, and leaves the nest to study at Cardiff next year.

Liz Hinds qualified as an oceanographer before starting work as a computer programmer at the (then infamous) DVLC. It wasn't all bad though, because while working there she met and married her husband, and left, gratefully, to have babies. She took up writing about six years ago and has had several articles and two non-fiction books published. She is very good at building castles in the air but has not, yet, built a bunker in Sainsburys. When asked what she does, she still shrugs and says, 'nothing.'

Gail Hughes was born in Western Canada and has lived in Quebec, the Middle East and, for the last seventeen years, in Gwynedd.

Jo Hughes was born in Swansea in 1956 and has lived in Aberystwyth and London. She has published work in a number of magazines and anthologies, and broadcast on Radio 4. She was one of the winners of the Rhys Davies Short Story Competition in 1995 and 1999. She is a designer, illustrator and photographer and lives in Swansea with her daughter.

Siân James was brought up and educated in West Wales. Her ten novels and a short story collection have won awards including the Yorkshire Post Best Novel Award and the Welsh Arts Council Book of the Year (*Not Singing Exactly* - pub Honno). Her tenth novel, *Summer Storm*, was published in 1998 by Piatkus.

Anthony James was born in 1956 and studied at Swansea University. His fiction, poetry, essays, criticism and reviews have appeared in magazines in the UK and abroad. He has had poetry and fiction for younger readers published, and a short story collection *The Serpent in April*, under the name Antonia James, all published by Karhu.

Nigel Jarrett lives in Gwent. He is currently the music critic of the *South Wales Argus*. In 1995 he won the Rhys Davies Short Story Competition, and his poems and stories have appeared in many literary magazines. He is the co-editor of a book of fugitive pieces by the Gwent-born cult writer Arthur Machen.

Mike Jenkins lives in Merthyr.

Ray Jenkin is a native of Cardiff. He was aged 20 when his first published story appeared in the *South Wales Echo* and is a frequent contributor to *Cambrensis*. He had a story broadcast on Radio 4 last year; and has recently completed a novel.

Adam Thomas Jones was born in 1970, grew up in Blaengarw, and graduated in English at Bristol. He now lives in Pontyrhyl with his wife, Rebecca.

John Sam Jones travelled Wales and the US for his education. He now works as a sexual health promotor in North Wales, and contributes regularly to Welsh-language radio and television. His work is inspired by the lives of gay men in Wales. His first collection of short stories is due to be published by Parthian in 2000. He lives with Jupp, his German partner of fourteen years.

Alex Keegan has had published five crime novels and more than fifty short stories worldwide, in publications including Cambrensis and the New Welsh Review. He was a winner in the 1998 Rhys Davies Awards and the Bridport Prize.

Tim Lebbon lives in Goytre with his wife Tracey and young daughter Eleanor. His first novel *Mesmer* was published by Tanjen in 1997 and last year was shortlisted for a British Fantasy Award for Best Novel. His second book *Faith in the Flesh* is a volume of two novellas. He says *The Cutting* is based on a true story - his father was the prisoner of the Japanese who got the knock at the door.

Claire Lincoln, a former international assassin, now lives peacefully in Cardiff, with 12,000 cats and a stuffed canary. A fanatical vegan and primary alphabetologist, Claire will eat only artichokes and asparagus. Other hobbies include outrageous fibbing, quests for world domination and accepting huge amounts of cash for making stuff up.

Barrie Llewelyn was born in Los Angeles, but has found her true calling in the hills of South Wales. She has recently completed a long and laborious education in creative writing at the University of Glamorgan. She says that her greatest source of inspiration are her two children.

Catherine Merriman is the author of four novels and two collections of short stories. She won the Ruth Hadden Memorial Award for best first work with her novel 'Leaving the Light On' (1992, Gollancz/Pan) and has twice been a Rhys Davies Short Story Award prize winner. She lives near Abergavenny in Monmouthshire.

Robert Nisbet, after decades working as a secondary English teacher, is now a freelance creative writing tutor, press officer for Haverfordwest football club, and a museum assistant. His sixth short story collection, *Entertaining Sally Ann,* appeared recently from Alun Books. His stories have appeared regularly in *Planet, New Welsh Review,* and *Cambrensis,* as well as in the USA, Germany and Romania.

Kaite O'Reilly is an award-winning playwright and short story writer.

Fiona Owen was born in Cumberland, grew up in Arabia, and finally settled in Wales in 1974. She is an Associate Lecturer for the Open University, and teaches creative writing for the WEA. Her work has been published in various Welsh and international magazines, and is included in the anthologies *Needs Be* (Flarestack 1998) and *Anglesey Anthology* (Gwasg Carreg Gwalch 1999).

Siân Preece was born in Neath in 1965 and educated at Swansea University. After five years in Canada and France, she moved to Aberdeen, where she is currently working on a novel. Her work has been broadcast on BBC Radio, and she was the recipient of a Scottish Arts Council Bursary in 1998. Her first collection of short stories, *From the Life,* (Polygon) is due out in Spring 2000.

Lloyd Rees was born in London, brought up in Swansea and educated at Sussex and Swansea Universities. His first novel *Don't Stand So Close* (Seren) was shortlisted for BBC Wales' Book of the Year 1993. His second novel was *The Show-Me State (Seren, 1995).* He has published many stories in *Cambrensis, New Welsh Review, Bridport Prize Anthology* and also three volumes of poetry, the latest being *Mangoes on the Moon* (Alun Books, 1999).

Alun Richards was born in Pontypridd in 1929. His short story collections include *Dai Country* (Michael Joseph 1973), *The Former Miss Merthyr Tydfil* (Michael Joseph 1976), *Selected Stories* (Seren 1995). He is the Editor the *New Penguin Book of Welsh Short Stories* (1993). He has also written extensively for radio and television. His stage play, *The Horizontal Life,* dealing with the

Italian actress Eleanora Duse was performed in Italy in 1998.

Don Rodgers has had poems and stories published in a variety of magazines, newspapers and anthologies. He is a former winner of both the Drama Association of Wales Playwriting Competition and the One Voice Monologue Competition, and his radio play *Clown* was broadcast by the BBC on Radio 4. A collection of his poems *Moontan* was published by Seren in 1996. A second collection, *Multiverse*, is due out in 2000.

Sharon V. Rowe was educated in Cardiff and Bristol and has spent some time living in the U.S. When she returned home to her roots in 1995, she began to write short stories and poetry. She is employed as a bookseller in Cardiff and is currently working on her first novel.

Penny Simpson studied at Brighton Art College and Essex University. Her short stories have been published by Bloomsbury and Virago. She was the recipient of a 1999 Arts Council of Wales travel bursary, enabling her to visit Berlin to research a novel.

Brian Smith has had short stories and poems published at home and abroad. He has won the Independent/Orchard Books Picture Book Award. He lives and works in the Swansea Valley.

Othniel Smith was born in Newcastle-under-Lyme in 1962, and has lived in Cardiff since 1980. He has had a number of plays and short stories broadcast on BBC Radio. In late 1998, his stage play, *Giant Steps* was produced by the Made In Wales Stage Company in London and Cardiff. He is currently studying for an Open University M.A. in Humanities.

Robert M Smith hails from Ebbw Vale. He teaches Maths in Pontypool, and has been writing short stories for about 5 years. He was a Rhys Davies award winner in 1995 and in 1997 *Hast' al* won the Valleys' Literature Award. When not writing, ironing or marking schoolwork, he enjoys music, comedy, playing cricket and supporting his beloved Ebbw Vale RFC.

Meic Stephens was born in Trefforest, near Pontypridd, in 1938 and educated at the UCW, Aberystwyth. He founded *Poetry Wales* in 1965. He has edited a number of poetry and fiction collections, including the translation of new Welsh short fiction, *A White Afternoon* (Parthian, 1998), and he has translated novels. As well as being freelance journalist, translator, editor and literary agent, he teaches at the University of Glamorgan and the Centre for Journalism Studies at Cardiff University.

Kate Terrell is a bit of a mystery.

Rae Trezise is currently reading Media Studies and English at Glamorgan University and lives in the Rhondda valley. She intends to write for the popular press and continue to write both fiction and non-fiction.

Ron Unsworth was born in 1947. Now retired, and encouraged and inspired by local writing classes, he has begun to pursue his writing. He has completed a novel researched and set in Greece,which is as yet unpublished. His interests lie in historical fiction.

Barbara Walters was born near Port Talbot in 1926, where her father worked at the South Pit. When she left school, she ran a milk round with a horse and cart, and joined the Land Army during the war. She has had four stories broadcast on Radio 4, and her work has been published in many anthologies including Two Valleys, Cambrensis, Poetry Now and Black Harvest. She is presently working on an anthology of poetry which reflects on her life; from the valleys in the '30's to modern life in Glyncorrwg.

Caryl Ward has had stories published in several magazines and anthologies, and was a prizewinner in the 1998 Rhys Davies Competition. Her collection of poetry *Muddy Eyes* was published by Red Sharks Press. She lives in Llantwit Major.

Gee Williams was born in Flintshire and now lives on the Wirral Peninsula. As a poet and writer of short fiction over the last ten years she has had work in some very disparate places: from *The Pan Book of Horror* to *The Sunday Times*. Radio 4 has been a regular broadcaster of her short stories. Her first full-length play will be broadcast by Radio 4 in 2000.

Herbert Williams is a writer of poetry, fiction, drama, biography and popular history. He has had poetry and story collections published, including *The Stars in their Courses*; and has written for television and radio. He was one of the judges of the 1998 Rhys Davies Short Story Competition.

Nia Williams was born in Cardiff and educated at Rhydfelen, Exeter and Reading. After working as a journalist, she became a freelance editor and feature writer in 1987. Her work has appeared in a range of books (published by Parthian and Honno) and magazines - including *Cambrensis* - on subjects ranging from womens' history to finance and folklore. She has also written travel guides to Wales, Britain and France.

Roger Williams has written plays for BBC Radio, HTV, S4C, The Sherman Theatre and Made in Wales. During 1998-1999 he was writer-in-residence at Sydney Theatre Company and The Australian National Playwrights' Centre working on his latest play *Killing Kangaroos*. He is 25 years old and lives in West Wales.

Anne Louise Williams lives in Aberdesach with Rosie.

Penny Windsor has had work publshed in over fifty journals, numerous anthologies, broadcast on radio and television, set to music, especially jazz and modern classical, and performed in venues throughout the UK, Europe and USA. Her poetry collections include *Dangerous Women* and *Like Oranges* (both published by Honno).

Arthur Smith's interest in editing and publishing magazines dates back a long way. At ten he was hand-writing his own newspaper for his relatives; in college he edited the student magazine *Y Bont*, and for the next twenty-three years he continued publishing small magazines for the British Amateur Press Association. Since retiring from his work with the South Wales Electricity Board, Arthur founded and now dedicates his time to just one magazine: *Cambrensis – Short Story Wales*. He invited submissions by letter for the first issue in 1987, and from these humble beginnings he has received over 2,500 stories, and published 450 of them. Of *Cambrensis*, he says, 'I'm doing something I've always wanted to do. And even if you do have to chip in with your own money, it's better than throwing it away on drinking or fast cars.'

CAMBRENSIS
The National Short Story Magazine of Wales

'One of the bravest literary magazines around'
(Western Mail)

Founded in 1987 by Arthur Smith, the *Cambrensis* magazine is a quarterly rich in the up-and-coming literature of Wales. It has featured work by many leading Welsh writers, including Welsh Book of the Year winners Siân James and Mike Jenkins, alongside the best new talent.

Robert Smith from Pontypool is a writer, and one who speaks highly of the magazine. '*Cambrensis* has a kudos and a following and because he's [Arthur] very discerning, you know that if he accepts something it's OK.'

New submissions are welcome on any subject – the magazine contains a mix of reviews, writers' news and feature articles as well as short fiction – and payment is in copies of the magazine.

One year's subscription only £6-00 including P&P.

For submissions or subscription please write to:
Arthur Smith
41 Heol Fach
Cornelly
Bridgend
CF33 4LN

Short story submissions - one at a time please - with an SAE to same address.